D0399060

BON MARCHÉ

CHET HAGAN

TOR

This is a work of fiction. All the characters and events portrayed in this book are fictional, and any resemblance to real people or incidents is purely coincidental.

BON MARCHÉ

Copyright © 1988 by Chet Hagan

First printing: April 1988

A TOR Book

Published by Tom Doherty Associates, Inc.
49 West 24th Street
New York, NY 10010

ISBN: 0-312-93062-3

Library of Congress Catalog Card Number: 87-50870

Printed in the United States of America

0 9 8 7 6 5 4 3 2 1

· 1 ·

DEWEY GENEALOGY

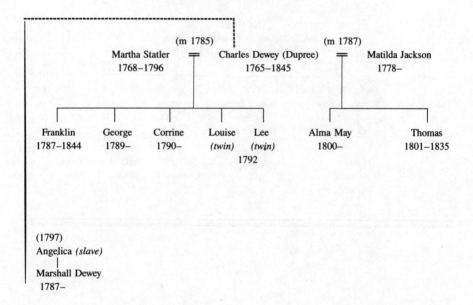

(m 1785)   (m 1787)
Martha Statler ══ Charles Dewey (Dupree) ══ Matilda Jackson
1768–1796   1765–1845   1778–

Franklin   George   Corrine   Louise   Lee   Alma May   Thomas
1787–1844   1789–   1790–   *(twin)* *(twin)*   1800–   1801–1835
                                           1792

(1797)
Angelica *(slave)*
|
Marshall Dewey
1787–

· **2** ·

DEWEY GENEALOGY

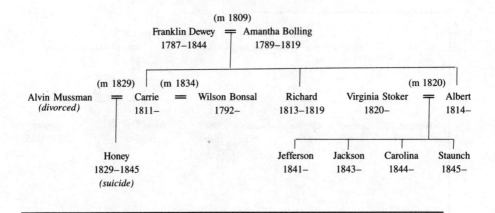

(m 1809)
Franklin Dewey ══ Amantha Bolling
1787–1844   1789–1819

(m 1829)   (m 1834)   (m 1820)
Alvin Mussman ══ Carrie ══ Wilson Bonsal   Richard   Virginia Stoker ══ Albert
(divorced)   1811–   1792–   1813–1819   1820–   1814–

Honey   Jefferson   Jackson   Carolina   Staunch
1829–1845   1841–   1843–   1844–   1845–
(suicide)

DEWEY GENEALOGY

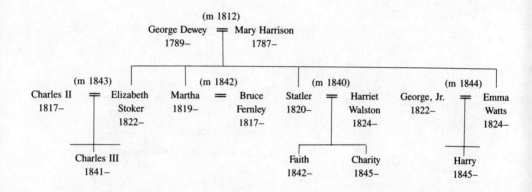

· 4 ·

DEWEY GENEALOGY

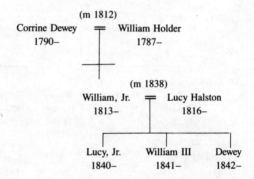

· 5 ·

DEWEY GENEALOGY

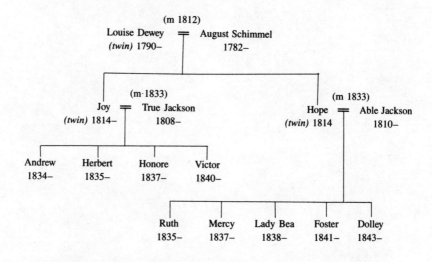

(m 1812)
Louise Dewey ══ August Schimmel
(twin) 1790–   1782–

(m·1833)
Joy ══ True Jackson
(twin) 1814–   1808–

(m 1833)
Hope ══ Able Jackson
(twin) 1814   1810–

Andrew 1834–   Herbert 1835–   Honore 1837–   Victor 1840–

Ruth 1835–   Mercy 1837–   Lady Bea 1838–   Foster 1841–   Dolley 1843–

· 6 ·

DEWEY GENEALOGY

(m 1817)
Alma May Dewey ══ Nathan Ludlum
1800–   1792–
divorced, 1822

Prologue

AMONG all the numerous varieties of domestic animals which a benevolent Providence has created for the use of man, the blood horse stands preeminent, without a compeer in the animal kingdom.

In beauty he is without a rival—a coat as fine as the finest satin; his eye, in repose, as mild and gentle as a lamb; under excitement as bright as the eagle and as bold as the lion, denoting the energy of his nature; his skin as thin and elastic as the fawn; his form as perfect and well placed as beautifully defined muscles can make it.

This is his exterior, or that which is visible to the human eye. But there is an interior, or invisible, structure which contributes more perhaps to his powers than even his perfect exterior formation. His large heart and capacious lungs give him the wind of a high-bred hound; his large blood vessels and soft, thin skin enable him to throw off the excess heat that must be generated by great and rapid exertion; his muscles firm and beautifully defined with bone of ivory texture—all combine to give him strength, endurance, action, and beauty far exceeding all of the equine race.

The uninstructed in horseology may ask, "What do you mean by a blood horse, or thoroughbred?" I mean the horse which traces back, with certainty, through a long line of distinguished ancestry to the beautiful and game little creatures which were imported into England from the deserts of Arabia about the middle of the sixteenth century. How they came there, or by what means they had been brought to the degree of perfection they possessed at that early period, I am not able to answer. From that time to the present, the best talent of intelligent breeders has been zealously and energetically employed throughout the world, aided, too, by all the leading governments, except our own, to develop and improve this noble animal. They have not failed.

By attention to his comfort, with a liberal supply of proper food from infancy to maturity, his size has been enlarged, consequently his strength and speed increased; though beautiful when brought from his native desert, he is now magnificent. He has been made so nearly perfect that breeders of the *present period are puzzled to know what further improvement can be anticipated.*

To form an idea of the wonderful power of the blood horse, we will suppose his weight to be nine hundred pounds, this being about the weight of the racehorse. By the strength of his muscle he carries this weight together with his rider, one hundred pounds more, making one thousand pounds, not on a downgrade, but on a horizontal line, a mile in one minute and forty-three seconds, almost equaling the power of what we know of steam. Of all animated nature the feathered tribe alone can equal his speed. If we imagine a feathered monster of equal weight, I doubt whether he could surpass him in his flight.

The uninformed may see him only as a beautiful creature, imagining that he is bred for a race alone and being fit for nothing else, believing he has no other value than occasionally to contribute to the amusement of the public on the racecourse.

This is an egregious error!

The racecourse is only the school to educate and prepare him to exhibit his wonderful powers in competition with the best of the royal family—a field the plebeian dare not enter, no scrub ever having won a prize with thoroughbred competitors. Ten drops of plebeian blood in one thousand would endanger his success.

The racecourse is, therefore, a necessity, for through its instrumentality the blood horse has been brought to his present high degree of perfection. Human judgment is often in error, but on no subject more frequently than in the opinions we form on the relative power and value of the horse. It is as easy to judge the powers and qualities of man by the eye, and all will admit the fallibility of such judgment.

No, my friends, we can only judge correctly the intellectual and moral worth of our great men when we view them on the world's stage in competition with distinguished competitors. Without a theater the world could never have known those distinguished delineators of human character whose names now fill many an honored page in history. The same is true of the blooded horse. The racecourse is his stage, his theater.

I am aware of the prejudices existing against the racecourse by religionists, generally on account of its immoral tendency. That these prejudices are not altogether groundless, I admit; but that the immoralities of a well-regulated racecourse are greatly magnified by those who know the least of their operations, I am perfectly satisfied; that it may be still further improved, I earnestly desire.

For more than sixty years I have been a breeder of the blood horse, and an active participator in his education and development, and can affirm that vice and immorality do not necessarily attach to racing and, as before remarked, the racecourse is a necessity, for without it the breeder could not know the superior horses and the best strains to propagate, and without this knowledge his improvement would cease and deterioration begin.

Here the question arises whether we will permit this noble and most useful creature, which has been brought to his present degree of perfection by the efforts of breeders for near two hundred years—and by the expenditure of as many millions of dollars—to retrograde into the coarse and clumsy brute he was prior to the introduction of the Arab, or to go on to improve and develop still higher and more useful qualities. For one, I advocate his preservation and at the same time call upon the moralist to unite with me in the effort to remove all objectionable features that may attach to the institution so necessary for his development.

Beauty, speed, action, durability, and the many admirable qualities I claim for this magnificent animal do not constitute his chief—nay, or his greatest— value. His mission is to improve his race. The pure and unadulterated blood which flows in his veins improves and gives additional value to ALL the horse family.

CHARLES DEWEY
Bon Marché, 1845

BOOK ONE

If there were no God there would be no blooded horse.
—Marshall Statler, 1781

BOOK ONE

1

SHIVERING in the early-morning chill, the cabin boy stood naked on the aft deck of the *Ville de Paris*, pouring buckets of water over his head. It was going to be a very special day for him, one warranting a bath.

The ship's log placed the date as October 19, 1781. "Standing off York-town, Virginia," it noted.

The night before, the lad had received the grudging permission of Comte François Joseph Paul de Grasse, Admiral of the Fleet, to be part of the flagship's contingent at the formal surrender ceremonies. But it wasn't the capitulation of Major General Sir Charles Cornwallis that occupied his thoughts now.

As he bathed, he contemplated the orders he had received from his guardian spirit.

Through all of his sixteen years the spirit had been with him, sustaining him. He had always been certain of that. There was a motto by which he lived: *Aide-toi, le ciel t'aidera*—"Help thyself, and heaven will help thee." He had never been hesitant about helping himself.

His name was Charles Dupree. Or so he believed.

He had been a *gamin*—a street boy—surviving alone on the inhospitable thoroughfares of Paris. He couldn't remember ever having been held to a mother's breast, although there were faint shadows in his memory of a woman who might have been his mother. A father was not someone he knew, not even as a shadow. And he had never really lived anywhere—not in a house or a flat or even a room. Just finding a place to sleep had been a challenge every single night of what he could recall of his life before the navy.

On this morning, as the sun rising in the east dried him after his bath, Charles remembered his past. Vividly. It was important to him that he did— that he never forget.

His memories were his incentive.

II

MARIE sat huddled in the middle of the disheveled bed, drawing her bare feet up under her, watching with frightened eyes as the lad poked into the corners of her room with a heavy club.

"Do you see him, *chéri?*"

"No, not yet," the boy answered, continuing his search.

The girl shuddered. "Oh, I hate them so!"

Suddenly the boy raised his club and brought it down with great force on something in the shadows. There was an animal squeak. When he turned to the girl, he was holding a huge rat by the tail, its ugly fangs clearly visible in its open mouth.

Marie screamed.

Grinning, the youngster went to the open fourth-floor window and tossed the dead rat into the street below.

The young woman giggled nervously. "My hero!" Her giggle turned into a full-throated laugh. "You should have seen Monsieur Farinet scoot when he saw that beast walking across the top of the commode." She shrugged. "Ah, but it cost me money."

"That's too bad."

The boy was only nine, but he knew of the trade of the prostitutes—*les filles de joie.* A host of them were quartered in the five-story brick pile of a tenement three or four twisted, dirt-strewn streets removed from the splendor of the Boulevard Saint-Germain. Tenements were jammed together in the narrow back streets, each one five to seven stories high, twenty-five rooms to a floor. Warrens for people. And rats, too. He had come to the woman's rescue when she screamed out of the window of one of them.

Marie got out of the bed, stretching her slim limbs, loosening her corset, dropping it to the floor with a contented sigh. She stood naked for a moment, languidly arching her back, thrusting out her small, firm breasts as the boy stared. Retrieving a thin *chemise de nuit* from the back of a chair, she wriggled into it, half covering her nakedness.

"Now—how can I reward you, *chéri?*"

"Some food maybe—" the boy said hesitantly.

"In the pantry." She pointed to a door. "Some bread and cheese."

He went into the pantry, cut a thick slice from a block of molding cheese, and tore a chunk of bread from a long, hard loaf. When he returned to the bedroom, he nodded to her. "*Merci, Marie.*"

"You know my name?"

"Yes."

"How's that?"

"I saw you on the street many times. And I asked someone."

She laughed, strangely flattered that he had made an effort to learn who she was. "Did you, now? And what's your name?"

"Charles."

"Well, Charles, why don't you sit down and eat your food?"

He perched tentatively on the edge of a chair opposite her, hungrily wolfing the bread and cheese, keeping his eyes on the attractive young woman.

"Where do you live, Charles?"

"Out there," inclining his head toward the open window.

"On the street?" Her face went sad. "Are you an orphan?"

The *gamin* thought for a moment. "I take care of myself," he replied firmly.

"*Chéri*," Marie said, smiling, "you might take care of yourself, but, dear God, you're dirty!" She wrinkled up her nose. "And smelly! I'm going to give you a bath."

Charles came quickly to his feet. "No, no!" He edged toward the door leading to the hallway.

Marie moved with alacrity to entrap the boy, dragging him to a corner where a large metal tub was propped against the wall. She stood it upright with one hand, keeping the other on his collar. Then she began to strip off his clothes. He struggled, but not hard enough to get away.

"Now, you stay right there," she ordered, "until I get the water."

Into the pantry she went, returning quickly with two buckets of water, pouring them into the tub.

"It's cold, but it'll get you clean. Get in."

When he hesitated, she picked him up bodily and plunked him into the water. He was surprised by the strength of the girl.

Kneeling by the tub, Marie began to rub soap on his body. Splashing water over him, laughing gaily. She made a game of it, and he enjoyed it, especially when she touched him where no one else had ever touched him before. The whore scrubbed him clean, and, although he objected vehemently, she poured a few drops of cheap perfume into the water, splashing it over him again.

When it was over and Marie was drying him with a piece of sheeting, she was nearly as wet as the boy. But the intimacy of the bath had made them friends.

She watched him as he pulled on his dirty clothes, wishing that she could wash them, too, but knowing she had done as much as he would allow.

"Isn't that better?"

"Yes," Charles admitted.

"Can I call on you when I need a ratter again?"

"Sure."

She kissed him on the lips. "*Mon chéri,*" she laughed. And Charles left her rooms.

The boy had another piece of information to file away in his mind. When he really needed food, he could always go back to Marie and kill another rat. It was bits of knowledge like that that kept him alive, that made him a survivor in the frantic hive that was the Paris of the mid-1770s.

He knew a lot of things: of the cafés that put out the best garbage, of the money-changers and goldsmiths at Pont au Change where he could run errands to earn a few coins, of the *maisons de confiance* where he could spend his money—when he had it—for food without getting cheated, of the alleyways and cellars where he could sleep without risking being murdered in the night for his shoes or his tattered coat.

And he kept one rule: he never begged. There were beggars everywhere on the streets. Charles thought them a pitiable lot. With no pride. Whatever else he might become, he promised himself, he wouldn't be a beggar. He was better than that.

Most times he could read the mood of the city. It was a live thing, with its street singers and jugglers, its pickpockets, its vagabonds, its thieves, its grand ladies being transported in sedan chairs, its effete gentlemen in their colored knee breeches and stockings of white silk and long coats of velvet, its mountebanks, its rich, and its rabble. And the moods of Paris were as varied as its people, gay at times, but often cruel as well.

A popular public amusement was the administration of the stern justice of the city. The sight of a dishonest merchant locked in the pillory was entertainment for many. As was the flogging of thieves as they were trundled through the streets in crude carts. On occasion, there was the capital punishment of a murderer, a sorcerer, or even a blasphemer. The criminal was bound to a wheel, his arms and legs broken with a heavy iron bar, after which he was left to die on the wheel, without concern for his pain. The real punishment was the slowness of the death. Even more gory, a *truly evil* person, perhaps one found guilty of incest, would sometimes be drawn and quartered in full view of the delighted crowd. Charles watched these events, but failed to understand the general glee.

The punishments made Charles wary of the efficient municipal police. He kept clear of them, his careful study of their methods making him aware of what they planned to do before they did it. It was in mid-September, some two months after he had killed the rat for the prostitute Marie, that he saw something beginning. Something familiar. He rushed to Marie's rooms.

Banging on her door: "Marie, it's Charles!"

"Go away." She wasn't angry, merely occupied.

"Come now!" he insisted. "There's a roundup!"

Most often the gendarmerie looked the other way at the activities of the whores, recognizing that they performed a necessary function in the teeming city. But on this day, following what must have been a highly placed complaint against a prostitute, the police were sweeping through the streets, gathering up as many of *les filles publiques* as they could find.

Marie opened the door.

"The police," Charles said breathlessly. "They're in the next street!"

Her customer, hurriedly getting into his clothes, brushed by them at the door and ran off down the hallway.

Marie was thoroughly frightened. Pulling on a gown, she permitted Charles to lead her out the rear door of the building into the alley and down into a filthy basement he believed to be safe. They huddled there in a dank corner, the sounds of the police roundup coming through to them from the street above.

Finally, Marie spoke quietly. "My hero again, eh?"

"I didn't want to see you caught."

Charles had seen prostitutes who had been swept up in other raids, released after a few days in prison, shorn of their hair. He couldn't imagine Marie without her flowing auburn hair.

"It's getting bad," she sighed. "The last time the police did this, my friend was sent to Louisiana."

"Where?"

"Louisiana—in the New World. To work on a sugar plantation, it was said." Another sigh. "I don't imagine I'll ever see her again."

Charles cocked his head, listening to the nuances of the noises of the street. "I think it's safe now."

"How can I pay you?"

"Don't think about it." He wasn't hungry then.

But as September lengthened into October, and October into winter—a bitter winter of unrelenting cold that froze over the Seine—all of Paris was hungry. There was competition now for the garbage from the cafés. Deadly competition as desperate fights broke out in the back streets and alleys.

There was no bread; the French wheat crop had failed. The rich always ate, of course, but now the middle class had difficulty getting bread; the poor got none at all.

A rumor ran through the alleys that a *boulangerie* on Boulevard Saint-Michel had bread. Charles was only one of hundreds who answered the rumor's siren call.

Police tried to cordon off the bakery, but there weren't enough of them. When the rioting started, Charles was caught in the middle of it. In the struggle he came face to face with a policeman. A club was raised and came crashing down on the side of his head just above the ear. There was sudden warmth in the cold, the warmth of the blood gushing over the right side of his face.

On his knees, the boy tried to crawl free of the mob. Someone stepped on his hand. And his back. There were minute flashes of unconsciousness, and consciousness again.

Somehow—*and it just had to be by the intercession of the spirit!*—he found himself clear of the main body of the angry mob.

Struggling to his feet, he stumbled away.

To Marie.

Alternately weeping and offering him consoling words, the whore washed the blood from him and bound up the cruel cut on his head. She made a nest of blankets for him in the pantry. And she poured hot tea down his throat. He vomited, but Marie cradled him to her accommodating breast, rocking him, cooing *"mon chéri, mon chéri"* over and over again.

A week went by. And two—before his fever and nausea and pain passed and he was strong enough to consider doing what his guardian spirit had told him to do.

It was on an afternoon when Marie was busy at her trade in the bedroom that Charles left, unable to find the words for a good-bye.

He presented himself to the French naval recruiting station on the Ile de la

Cité, where a scowling older man, with tattoos on the backs of his hands, showed his skepticism.

"Are you sure, boy?"

"Yes, sir."

"What about your parents?"

"I don't have any."

"An orphan, then?"

Once more the boy's lack of knowledge of his parentage caused him to pause. "Yes, I guess I am," he said finally.

"Your name?" The recruiter dipped his quill into an ink pot.

"Charles Dupree."

Someone had called him by that name once; he couldn't remember who that might have been or when it was, nor did he have any idea why his name might be Charles Dupree. But that was the name he said.

"How old are you?"

The boy hesitated.

"You have to be ten to sign on as an apprentice seaman."

"Oh, I'm ten—*older* than that, sir." Was he lying? He honestly didn't know.

The recruiter looked hard at him, then wrote the numeral 10 on the enlistment paper.

It was the first documentation of Charles's life.

III

WRINKLES smoothed from his buff uniform, his long hair pulled back into a queue and fastened with a light blue ribbon, Charles presented himself for inspection by Admiral de Grasse. The officer was abed in his cabin, afflicted with an intestinal ailment that was keeping him from the Cornwallis surrender ceremonies.

"Very neat, boy," de Grasse commented.

"Thank you, sir."

"You'll be witness to great history today, young Monsieur Dupree," the admiral mused. "More than you can fully appreciate, I'll wager."

Charles found himself resenting the remark, believing he understood the implications of the English capitulation as well as any man.

De Grasse sighed. "There's something sad about a surrender. Brave men on both sides have died. And one must wonder whether the bravery of the defeated was in vain. Were they any less brave because they fought under the wrong banner?"

Charles stood stiffly silent, knowing an answer wasn't expected.

"War is not kind to the losers." Another sigh. "Well, it's time that you leave."

"Yes, sir."

"And, son—"

"Sir?"

The admiral's words cut him. He was disappointed, annoyed, that on this most important day de Grasse would see fit to remind him of his lowly position. He felt he didn't deserve that kind of chastisement, no matter how fatherly it might have been meant to be, in light of the three years of loyal service he had given the nobleman. It made him even more determined to carry out his plan.

Without a word to anyone else, and seeking to be as inconspicuous as possible, Charles boarded the launch just as it was being pushed off in the direction of Yorktown.

For no apparent reason, his mind's eye showed him the rugged face of Captain de Boade.

IV

APPRENTICE Seaman Charles Dupree presented himself aboard the warship *Refleche* at the Atlantic port of Bordeaux. His first station. Captain de Boade scowled as he looked at the papers the boy had handed him.

"A bastard, eh?"

"No, sir."

De Boade's right hand lashed out, catching Charles high on the cheek, sending him sprawling on the deck. Sailors standing nearby laughed.

"On this ship, Dupree," the captain shouted, "the master is never wrong! Now let me ask you again—are you a bastard?"

Charles's answer came as he was still scrambling to his feet. "Yes, sir."

"I hope so, boy, because on this goddamn devil-infested vessel, every mother's son is a bastard as far as I'm concerned!" He was bellowing. "Does that please you?"

"Yes, sir."

"Good, good," the captain responded, laughing boisterously. "You should know, then, that the master is a bastard, too!"

The sailors joined in the laughter, Charles following suit, realizing that it was expected of him.

De Boade wasn't a nobleman, like many other French navy captains, but a career sailor who had been in the navy since his youth. To Charles, though, de Boade was an ageless man, giving the impression of *always* having been captain, of *always* having commanded men.

He had a wide purple scar on his left cheek, the trophy of earlier hand-to-hand combat while repulsing a British boarding party. De Boade hated the English because of that disfigurement. But as Charles got to know him, he realized that the captain's hate was more basic than a saber cut. He hated the English just because he was French.

For young Dupree, de Boade represented an opportunity. He could learn a great deal from the captain, and once having absorbed his lessons, he might use de Boade for his own advancement.

Charles ingratiated himself with the captain, being ever vigilant to his slightest needs. Eventually, he plumbed the master's weakness—his ego. De Boade loved to talk about himself, about his adventures, and Charles gave him slightest needs. Eventually, he plumbed the master's weakness—his ego. De Boade loved to talk about himself, about his adventures, and Charles gave him frequent opportunities to do just that, framing questions that opened the floodgates of self-aggrandizing storytelling.

In time, Charles made the ultimate breakthrough with the rough sailor. He was no longer just the captain's cabin boy; he was his friend.

De Boade was unmarried and fond of proclaiming, "*Aujourd'hui marié, demain marri*—today married, tomorrow sorry." But he had an all-consuming weakness for women, and Dupree's understanding that his association with de Boade had reached a new and more intimate plateau came when the *Refleche* put in at the Mediterranean port of Marseilles for refitting. Charles had been aboard the man-of-war for nearly two years.

"Tonight, my young rooster," the captain boomed, "we're going to sample the fleshpots of Marseilles. It's time you know the pleasures of the female body. Time to make the hens cackle, eh?"

"Yes, sir," the cabin boy answered with little enthusiasm.

De Boade grinned at him. "Lad, there are few enough pleasures in life. When you find one as accommodating as a soft, warm woman, only a fool would deny himself."

They started drinking before they left the ship, then visited several taverns on the quay along the way. By the time the captain guided Charles to the *maison de tolérance,* they were both quite drunk. But intoxication didn't seem to diminish de Boade's sexual appetite.

On his orders, the madam lined up her girls—perhaps a dozen of them—for the captain's close inspection. It was a naked international assemblage: blacks from Africa, women from Greece and Turkey and Italy and Tunisia, a few natives of France.

"In light of this special occasion, Dupree," the captain roared, "you shall have the first choice."

Charles stared at them, trying to focus his eyes and his mind on the task of selection. Finally, without a word, he pointed to a dark-haired, petite Frenchwoman. Perhaps she reminded him of Marie.

"No, no, no, *enfant*," de Boade interrupted. "Not for the first time! You need something more . . . eh . . . *passionnante.*"

He walked over to an earthy-looking Turkish woman and draped one arm over her bare shoulders. "*This* one, lad. With the broad hips, the full breasts. Yes, yes—this one!"

For himself the captain chose a long-legged Greek girl. As they went off toward their cribs, de Boade shouted to the Turkish whore: "You have a great honor, *mademoiselle*. My friend is a virgin! Perhaps *you* should pay *him*, no?"

His laughter could be heard even after he had disappeared from sight with his Greek.

To Charles, it was all confusion. His only clear perception, in his drunken state, was of a woman undressing him. After that it was an unreal mélange of sensations: soft flesh, sweat, musky odors, groping, kissing, sucking. If, in the midst of all that, there was consummated a full sexual act, he wasn't aware of it.

How long it went on, he didn't know. He fell asleep. Or passed out.

The next reality he knew was being carried back aboard the ship over Captain de Boade's shoulder like a sack of grain. He was set on his feet, and as he weaved unsteadily, de Boade bragged to the crew.

"You should have seen him," the captain exulted. "He had that whore at his mercy—a true Frenchman, our brave Dupree!"

The sailors' raucous laughter was the last thing Charles heard as he collapsed slowly in a dissipated heap.

There were other ports, other whores, other debaucheries. Master and cabin boy—they were partners in it all.

Dupree, his friendship with the captain secure, did not hesitate to approach de Boade with a request.

"The word is, sir, that the *Ville de Paris* will be commissioned soon."

"Aye, and a fine ship, too, it's said. The largest man-of-war ever built."

"Sir, I want to serve aboard her."

The request shocked de Boade. After a moment of reflection: "I'd miss you, my boy."

"And I you," Charles assured him. "But if I'm to make my way in the navy, if I'm to follow in your footsteps"—he knew the captain's ego would welcome the remark—"I'll need new opportunities."

"Aye, that's true."

De Boade made the recommendation to the master of the *Ville de Paris*, Comte de Grasse, the Marquis de Grassetilly. The nobleman, aware that the flamboyant Monsieur de Boade, although he was crude and hardly a gentleman, turned out good sailors, accepted a lad named Charles Dupree as his cabin boy.

The move—directed, Charles believed, by his guardian spirit—probably saved his life.

In the sea battle off Cape Henry, Virginia, that denied the British fleet entrance to the Chesapeake Bay, effectively trapping General Cornwallis at Yorktown, the *Refleche* took a direct hit from an English broadside.

Captain de Boade was killed instantly.

His cabin boy, except for the intervention of fate, might have been standing by his side.

V

THE *Ville de Paris* contingent, one midshipman carrying a flag displaying the de Grasse family coat of arms, marched smartly toward the Yorktown surrender grounds, the flagship's cabin boy at the end of the column.

In his station.

His insignificance a shield.

Charles marched more slowly than the others until some distance separated him from the main body. He watched for the best opportunity. It came when a farm cart, drawn by a lop-eared nag that had never known a brush or currycomb, crossed the road in front of him. He stopped marching, becoming just one of the people along the road.

"*Adieu, pour toujours*," he muttered aloud to himself. Then, in English: "Farewell forever."

He glanced at the morning sun, put his back to it, and walked westward into America.

His America!

2

SUNLIGHT filtered through the cracks between the logs and played on Charles Dupree's face, waking him finally. He groaned sleepily, stretching aching muscles, pushing back the old hay that had kept him warm during the night.

He knew only that he was in a small barn—little used, apparently—hard by a road some miles west of the village of Yorktown, Virginia. And that the month was October 1781. But he didn't know exactly where he was, or how far he had walked before darkness halted him, or what his next move ought to be.

However, there was one other important realization: he was now an American. His guardian spirit had willed that he be an American; that was why he had walked away at Yorktown, without concern for being a witness to the drama of the surrender ceremonies. He had missed it all, but he didn't care.

An American? How? With what skills? It was necessary, he reasoned, to assess his qualifications.

He had some education.

Admiral de Grasse had seen to it that he was tutored by Monsieur René Boulange, the ship's surgeon, who had been schooled in England. The doctor had been a somewhat uneven teacher, but Charles could cipher some; he could read and write, both in French and English. Those were advantages, certainly.

He could speak English.

Well enough, he was sure, to make his way. But his accent would tell everyone he was French. Would that matter? He thought not. The Marquis de Lafayette was a Frenchman, but perhaps more of a true American than some of those native to the land.

And what else?

He had his wit. His ambition. His determination. His *spirit*. In sum, all of those counted for something.

Charles lay in the hay, contemplating his first move as an American. His name, he thought, was *too* French for continuing use. He'd have to change it. There was no reason to keep the name Dupree; he wasn't even certain it was his name.

Charles was all right, though. He had always liked the sound of that; it was comfortably familiar. So—Charles what? He said "Charles Dupree" aloud, stretching it out, listening to the full sound of it for perhaps the first time. Again: "Charles Dupree."

He experimented with it, shortening it. "Charles Du . . ." Once more: "Charles Du . . . " He was onto something. "Charles Du . . . Charles Du . . . ee." *That was it!*

Again and again he pronounced it, louder and louder, until finally he was shouting it. "Charles Du . . . ee! Charles Du-ee!"

He couldn't just say it; he'd have to write it, too. More contemplation, trying to visualize how it would look on paper.

He brushed aside some hay, exposing the dirt floor of the barn. With his forefinger he laboriously traced out the letters: C-H-A-R-L-E-S D-U- *No! Not that way.* He erased the "U" in the dust, beginning again. Carefully and deliberately he spelled out his new name: D-E-W-E-Y. He didn't know why he did it that way; it was as if someone was guiding him. But, he liked it. D-E-W-E-Y. He grinned in satisfaction.

Pushing himself to his feet, Charles bowed formally, announcing: "Good afternoon, sir. My name is Charles Dewey."

He laughed heartily.

The new American swung open the door of the barn, to be instantly warmed by the bright sun of the October morning. He was glad for that. His thin uniform gave him little protection from the cold.

Once more he walked westward.

II

AHEAD of him he could see an approaching squad of Continental soldiers. An officer was mounted, but the others were afoot, pushing in front of them a group of Negroes, roped together.

Charles Dewey felt a sudden fear. For the first time it came clear to him that he was a *deserter!* If he was caught now and sent back to the French navy, Admiral de Grasse would have no choice but to hang him.

He saw himself, in a momentary mental flash, with the cruel rope knotted about his neck, his eyes bulging from their sockets, his face a ghastly purple. And hanging on his chest a crudely lettered sign: *Déserteur!*

Charles shook his head to dispel the vision.

These Continental soldiers wouldn't know he was a deserter. Nor were they likely to care, if they did.

Having reached that conclusion, Charles called to the officer, as the men came abreast of him: "Good morning, sir!"

"Good morning," the officer—a lieutenant—replied. He stopped the column. "A rare fine day, isn't it?"

"Indeed it is." Charles smiled.

"Where are you bound, sir?"

"Westward." Dewey had no better answer. "I'm just mustered out of the French navy. At Yorktown."

The lieutenant sighed. "We had hoped to get finished with this damned job"—he gestured toward the Negroes—"in time to get to see the surrender. But—"

"It was a magnificent sight!" A safe lie.

"I'll bet it was." Another sigh. "Well, we must be getting on."

Dewey's curiosity got the better of him. "Who are these men?" Meaning the Negroes.

"Runaway slaves," the officer told him. "They've been working for Cornwallis." He laughed. "The general's people told them they weren't slaves anymore."

Charles stared at the sad-faced black men. One of them was a boy of no more than twelve, terror written in his eyes.

"See that buck over there?" the American went on, pointing to a muscular young giant. "He belongs to General Washington. Ran away from Mount Vernon, if you can believe that." The officer obviously found such an act incomprehensible.

"What happens to them now?"

"They go back to their owners. If we can't find the owners, I guess they'll be sold again."

The company moved off. Charles watched them go, his emotions disquieted. He had never seen slaves before. He didn't like what he had just witnessed.

Hunger pangs assailed him, causing him to quicken his pace. Still westward.

III

THE broad main thoroughfare of the town surprised Charles. It was almost Paris-like in his eyes. Yet, what he saw wasn't really a city, but a substantial village with a great bustle of activity on the wide principal street. He was impressed by the number of fine brick buildings. Public buildings, he thought.

It was nearly noon, and he had walked some distance since he left the barn armed with his new name. He guessed that he had come the better part of eight or nine miles. He was somewhat light-headed from hunger; he had not eaten since he broke his fast aboard ship a day earlier.

The young Frenchman stood in front of a large steepled church, watching as a two-wheeled farm cart, drawn by a team of oxen, lumbered slowly along the boulevard. Two fine carriages, moving much faster, wheeled around the cart, making their way toward a handsome palace-like building, its entrance framed by ornate wrought-iron gates.

From the church came an elderly man, finely dressed in velvet coat and knee breeches, his powdered wig topped by a velvet tricorne. The gentleman nodded slightly to Charles as he started to pass him.

"My pardon, sir," Charles said boldly, "but what town is this?"

"What town . . . ?" The man laughed. "This, young sir, is Williamsburg."

"Williamsburg?"

"It is, sir. The capital of Virginia until just recently."

"I see. Is there a place where I might seek some honest work?"

The gentleman studied Dewey. "French?" he asked.

"Yes, sir. I've come from Yorktown, where I was mustered out of the French navy after an enlistment as an aide to the Comte de Grasse, Admiral of the Fleet."

He watched the man's face carefully, trying to gauge the reaction to his explanation. He was pleased that he saw no doubt registered there.

"The French have certainly been our dear and loyal friends. Papa Rochambeau spent some time here in Williamsburg, at Mr. Wythe's home, prior to the Yorktown engagement. A charming man. I understand he's expected to return soon. Are you acquainted with General Rochambeau?"

Charles decided that he had lied enough. "No, sir. I'm aware of his reputation, of course."

"The word is that he'll be wintering here with some of his troops."

The young man just nodded.

"Oh, I'm sorry—I seem to have forgotten my manners. I'm George Milton." He offered his hand.

Charles shook it. "Dewey," he said, "Charles Dewey." It sounded so correct!

"Well, Mr. Dewey," the gentleman said in a kindly manner, "how may I be of service to you?"

"If there is some work I could do, perhaps just for meals . . ." There was a sense of urgency in the words. He added a phrase: "And lodging."

"What kind of work do you seek?"

"I'm afraid I have few skills," Charles admitted with a grimace. "I've been a sailor, and —"

"And hungry, I'll wager." Milton spread his hands apologetically. "I've been standing here chattering away when it's obvious that you've a great desire to eat something."

"Yes, sir." He saw no need to deny his hunger.

"Come. We'll test the victuals at the Raleigh."

Putting his arm around the shoulders of the younger man, the gentleman guided him to the tavern. Inside, it was crowded, warm, comfortable. Milton found them a table. As they sat down, the wonderful smells of the place stirred the juices in Dewey's empty stomach, bringing on small, pinching pains.

What happened next astounded him. A large slab of roasted beef was put on the table, and a smoked sausage of some kind, apparently fried in its preparation, and a whole fowl, along with cheeses and a variety of steaming vegetables. A tureen of melted butter came forth, and another filled with dark gravy, nodules of fat floating on top. And there were pickles. And jams. And a plump, round loaf of freshly baked bread. And rich black coffee, already heavily sweetened. He scarcely knew where to start.

Charles ate carefully, trying not to wolf the food, but consuming a great deal.

Milton watched him with a satisfied smile, examining him. He was a strongly built lad, broad-shouldered, slim at the waist. In spite of Dewey's youth, the Virginian thought he carried himself maturely. In a manly manner.

He had light blond hair; his eyes were of a startlingly intense hazel. It couldn't be said that his face was classically handsome; it was too squarely cut, perhaps, with angles a sculptor wouldn't have chosen. But there was character in it. Strength in it. Self-assurance in it. Even, Milton concluded, a hint of arrogance in it.

"I trust our American repast is to your liking," the host said finally.

"Oh, yes, sir!"

"Plainer, perhaps, than French cuisine."

Charles struggled to keep himself from laughing. *French cuisine?* He thought of the garbage he had eaten in Paris alleys just to sustain life. And of the often inadequate fare of the French navy, the meat frequently alive with maggots.

"This is the finest meal I've ever had, sir." He was telling the truth.

"Perhaps on this important natal day as an American," Milton said, "we should offer a toast."

He ordered a bottle of Madeira. When the wine was brought, he poured for both of them, raising his glass.

"To Liberty!"

"To Liberty!" Charles repeated, draining the glass.

By the time they had finished the bottle, Dewey had told the older man of his dreams. He had even told him of the orders from his guardian spirit: to seek his fortune in the new country. He didn't tell him, quite naturally, that he had become a deserter to follow those spectral orders.

"This nation, for so it shall be now," Milton said, "offers great opportunities for young men such as yourself. I dearly wish that I could be thirty years younger."

In the course of their conversation, Charles learned that his effusive benefactor was an exporting agent for Virginia tobacco growers. He surmised, also, that the man had a number of other special interests. Clearly an important individual.

"Well, young sir," the Virginian said after a while, his words slurred by the wine, "perhaps we ought to take a stroll to clear our heads, eh?"

Charles followed him out of the tavern into the late-afternoon sunshine, walking somewhat unsteadily. As they moved along, Milton pointed out the numerous public buildings of the town.

Finally: "That's where we met, Mr. Dewey. The Bruton Parish Church."

"Yes, sir." He had the sinking feeling that his newfound friend was about to bid him farewell.

Milton turned into the walkway leading to a neat brick home across the street from the church. It was a small house, but well built. Charles hesitated.

"Come, come," Milton ordered.

Charles went with him to the house, and before the gentleman could turn the knob, the door was opened by a large black man in livery. "Good afternoon, Mr. Milton, sir," the Negro said with a trace of an English accent.

"We have a guest, Albert. Please make welcome Mr. Charles Dewey."

"Mr. Dewey, sir," the black man responded, bowing deeply.

Charles returned the bow. There was a startled look in the Negro's eyes. Evidently the young man had done the wrong thing.

Milton chuckled. "Mr. Dewey is new to America," he said by way of explanation. He handed his hat and his wig to the servant. He rubbed his nearly bald pate with a great deal of satisfaction.

"We'll have a bottle of Madeira, Albert."

"Yes, sir."

Milton led the way into a cozy sitting room where a fire had been set against the chill of the October afternoon. "Albert's a unique man. I picked him up in London—oh, some ten years ago. I have reason to believe he was the son of a tribal chieftain in Africa. That comes out in him every once in a while in a bit of arrogance. But I swear to you, I can't imagine being without him."

"Excuse me, sir . . . uh, is he a slave?"

"A slave?" Milton's eyebrows rose. "Yes, I suppose he is." It was as if he had never thought about the black man in that light before.

Albert returned with a bottle of wine and two superb crystal glasses on a silver tray. He filled the glasses, then backed off, standing in the shadows of the room.

There was no toast this time. They simply drank, chatting like old friends. Milton confided that he was a bachelor. "I never married," he laughed, "because I could never find a woman who deserved me." Charles's giggle made him realize that both he and his host were getting quite drunk. For him it was a marvelous feeling, one of complete well-being.

For more than an hour they sat that way in front of the fire. Suddenly Milton clapped his hands together and Albert was instantly at his side.

"Our young friend, Albert, will stay the night. Make a bed ready for him."

"Yes, sir."

Charles thought that he ought to protest the continuing gracious hospitality. He didn't, however. He was perfectly willing to accept the largess of the outgoing gentleman. And he was too drunk, he knew, to venture out.

Within a few minutes Albert was back. Without further orders, he hoisted Charles to his feet and guided him up a narrow flight of stairs to a bedroom. He helped him undress and manhandled him into the bed, gently but firmly.

The coolness of the fine linen sheets shocked Charles. So, too, the softness of the goose-down mattress. He had never known such luxury. Indeed, he had never slept in a real bed before.

Never.

IV

A muscular hand gripped his shoulder, shaking him with authority, spoiling a marvelous dream of silk-clad ladies and heroic gentlemen. The beautiful music that had accompanied the idyllic visions ended in discordant notes as Charles came awake.

"Mr. Milton requests your presence at breakfast, sir," Albert was saying to him. "He has instructed me to help you dress."

The words of the black man were proper enough, but the tone of them reflected Albert's annoyance at having Charles as an interloper in *his house*.

"Good morning, Albert," the young Frenchman said with a smile. He made no effort to rise.

"Mr. Milton is waiting, sir."

"Yes, of course." But when Charles sat up in the bed, his head throbbed from too much wine. He couldn't suppress an audible groan.

"You're ill, sir?" Albert asked with some sarcasm.

"No, no, I'm just fine." He swung his legs out of the bed and stood naked on the chilly floor. "Just fine." He thought it best not to show any sign of weakness in the presence of the no-nonsense Negro servant.

Albert had brought a basin of steaming hot water. He pointed to some clothes he had hung over the back of a chair. "After you've washed, sir, you are to dress in those clothes. Mr. Milton feels they will be more appropriate."

On the chair were a pair of buff-colored heavy-cord breeches, a plain white shirt, a substantial buff wool waistcoat, a coat of blue broadcloth, a service-able broad-brimmed wool hat, and a dark green cape, also of wool. Charles guessed that the cape would reach his knees. By the chair stood a pair of sturdy black knee-high boots.

"Those are for me?" Charles asked in surprise.

"Quite," Albert replied stiffly in his British manner.

"But my own clothes—?"

"Your underclothes have been washed and ironed, sir, and your other clothes have been put away in a saddlebag, ready for your trip."

"My trip?"

"Mr. Milton will explain, sir," Albert snapped. "Will you require my further assistance?"

"No, no. Thank you, Albert."

The Negro backed his way to the door, bowing slightly. Before he left the room he gave his final order: "Mr. Milton is anxious that you be prompt, sir."

"Thank you, Albert," Charles said again, feeling some resentment of the black man's imperiousness. Nevertheless, he washed and dressed quickly, draping the cape over his arm and making his way to the ground floor, where he found George Milton seated at breakfast in the small dining room.

"Well, good morning, Mr. Dewey," Milton said cheerfully.

"Good morning, sir." He bowed. "I must admit that it has been an eventful morning. These clothes—"

"You couldn't go traipsing around your new country in that rather flimsy French naval uniform, could you?"

"No, but—"

"Sit," Milton said with a gesture, "and have some breakfast. I'll explain."

Charles hung the cape over the back of a chair and joined Milton at the table. Albert was immediately at his side with a cup of hot chocolate and a plate of freshly toasted bread, heavily buttered.

"We Americans eat a modest breakfast," Milton told him. "I hope it's to your taste."

"Yes, it's fine." He bit into a piece of toast.

"Now, young Mr. Dewey, I want you to understand that I have my own reasons for providing the new clothes—sturdy enough, I trust, for the fall and winter." Milton smiled at him. "I need you to do a chore for me."

"Of course."

"I have a decently bred mare that has to be delivered to Elkwood, some sixty miles inland along the James. I intend to have her bred there in the spring, but I find it inconvenient to make the trip myself, now or later."

Charles nodded.

"And I'm asking you to make the delivery. Do you ride?"

"Unfortunately, Mr. Milton, I have never been on a horse in my life." Charles felt inadequate in making the admission.

"Ah! I suspected as much. But you shouldn't have a problem with Abigail; she's a gentle beast." Milton saw the apprehension on the young man's face. "We'll have some time to give you a rudimentary lesson in reining, and you should have no trouble. I daresay you'll probably just have to guide her."

Dewey laughed nervously. "I hope the mare will understand that."

"She will, she will," Milton assured him. "But because you are new to riding, I've plotted out a two-day journey. You're to ride from Williamsburg to an ordinary."

"An ordinary, sir?"

"An inn of sorts. We Virginians call them ordinaries because most of them *are*. Rather ordinary."

He laughed loudly at his little joke.

"In any event, I've written a letter you'll carry to Mr. Stannard, who owns the ordinary west of Richmond, and you'll stay the night there. Then, tomorrow, you should comfortably make the rest of the way to Mr. Marshall Statler's Elkwood plantation near Goochland Courthouse."

"Will I have a chart . . . uh, excuse me, a map?"

"Yes, although you'll follow the principal road west from here, having no difficulties, I'm sure. This isn't wilderness any longer, you'll discover, but in the current . . . uh . . . unsettled period, I suggest that you not attempt to ride at night. If you'd feel better about it, I could provide you with a pistol."

Charles hesitated. "No, I think not. I'd rather not be armed."

Milton nodded agreement. "Most wise. Guns have a way of inviting trouble."

V

ABIGAIL was, as Milton had promised, a gentle animal. Dewey had little difficulty getting used to reining her under his host's expert guidance. As they rode through the streets of Williamsburg during the brief training session, the older man spoke of the breeding he had planned for the mare.

"Statler is standing a son of Yorick," he explained, "a very good racing stallion campaigned by John Tayloe of Mount Airy. I swear to you that if I get a colt of the quality of Yorick, I'll be able to win some substantial wagers with him."

"Is there a lot of horse racing in Virginia?"

"A lot of racing—?" Milton seemed taken aback by the question. "Young sir, let me tell you this: a Virginian has two important considerations in his life—his racehorse and his woman." He grinned. "I suspect that he would place them in that order of priority."

He held forth for some time, without interruption from Charles, about the importance of horse racing in the Dominion. About the racetracks at Williamsburg and Richmond and Alexandria.

"The war—damn it!—disrupted all that. But now, I vow, it'll be back. Some of my associates and I are banding together to build a new track at Petersburg. We hope to interest Squire Washington in it."

"You mean *General* Washington?"

"The same. In earlier days he was involved in the race meetings at Alexandria and frequently subscribed to the purses at the Williamsburg Jockey Club. A fine racing gentleman he was. I hope he will find the time to be so again."

For nearly an hour they crisscrossed the streets of Williamsburg, until Charles announced that he was reasonably comfortable with the mechanics of guiding Abigail.

Upon returning to Milton's house, Charles was given a saddlebag containing his old clothes, some food for the trip, a map, and two sealed letters: one to Mr. Stannard at the ordinary, the second to Marshall Statler.

"You'll like Statler," Milton assured him. "He's a gentleman in the finest sense of that word. I've suggested to him that perhaps he might find a position for you at Elkwood. Of course I have no way of knowing what his exact situation is right now, but I've made the suggestion nevertheless."

"Thank you, sir."

"You may like Elkwood for other reasons—two of them." Milton grinned wickedly. "Statler has a brace of young, nubile daughters. Something a virile Frenchman can appreciate, eh?"

Charles just smiled.

"Now I think you should be off. Godspeed!"

The Virginia countryside was a revelation to a sixteen-year-old whose total experience had been in a crowded, noisy, demanding city and in the confining community of a ship at sea. The comparative vastness of it all nearly overwhelmed him, as did the immediate oneness he felt with the new environment.

Now that he was alone, Dewey was free to turn the horse in any direction he chose. He knew that if he wanted to—and the thought of it was a bit frightening—he could abandon the route George Milton had set for him. And the task. He could go to Elkwood plantation. Or not go.

Free to choose!

It was heady wine.

3

CHARLES Dewey's every muscle ached.

Two days of having his legs in an unaccustomed attitude—spread across the broad beam of a horse—had numbed them. When he shifted them to seek a more comfortable position, they rewarded him with spasms of pain.

His rump was sore, chafed raw by sixty miles of pounding against a saddle that was rock-hard, not leather-soft. His back hurt. His fingers were cramped around the reins. And, because everything else about him was suffering, his head throbbed.

He knew, from having stopped at Stannard's ordinary the night before, that getting off the horse brought him no relief from the misery. It meant only that he had to get back on the animal again—and that was more torment.

Charles wondered about George Milton's enthusiasm for horses, concluding that the Virginia gentleman and all his ilk were certainly mad!

Then, too, he was concerned whether he would ever reach Elkwood plantation. When he left the ordinary that morning, Mr. Stannard had told him that he ought to be at Elkwood by midafternoon. But midafternoon had passed; the sun was fast approaching the western horizon.

Just as those thoughts were running through his mind, he saw it. Off in the distance was the mansion Stannard had described to him, beautifully situated atop a small hill, its white columns gleaming against the dark red brick facade.

He dug a heel into Abigail's side, asking her for more speed, even though the faster pace brought new agony to his rear end.

The road led him directly to two ornate brick pillars, connecting scrolls of wrought iron forming an archway over the wide lane between them. He stopped the mare. From his vantage point Charles could look down the lane at the perfect symmetry of the huge trees that lined both sides. And at the end of the tunnel of trees, he could make out again the white columns of the big house. It was a magnificent sight.

As he sat there, a farm cart rumbled up behind him, driven by an elderly Negro man.

"Pardon me," he called to the black, "is this Elkwood?"

"Yas, suh, it is."

"The home of Mr. Marshall Statler?"

"Yas, suh."

Charles tipped his hat slightly, kicking the mare forward. Slowly. He had the feeling, as he moved between the trees, that he was riding into another world, one he couldn't begin to comprehend.

His progress was uphill. It was not something he realized at first, so gradual was the upward grade of the lane. But when he turned in the saddle to idly look back at the entrance arch, he found that he was gazing *down* at it.

Although he guessed that he still had half a mile to go in his ascent to the mansion, he was close enough to see that the house had three stories dominated by the massive columns across the front. Six of them. A balcony off the second floor was supported by those columns. The full third floor was under a slate roof, and featured six large windowed dormers. Double chimneys extended high above the roof on both ends, wispy smoke curling up from them in the near calm of the day.

Nearer now, and it came clear to him that there was a fourth floor; a basement level, really, with half-windows visible above the ground. Therefore, the entrance to the mansion—Charles reasoned that it must be the main floor—was up some dozen stone steps, guarded on both sides by carved marble balustrades.

In front of the house was a sweeping circular drive, in the center of which stood giant evergreen bushes—taller than a man, that had been trimmed into perfect spheres. Boxwoods, he was to learn later.

As he rode into the circle, the heavy mahogany double doors at the entrance opened and a liveried black man hurried down the steps to take hold of the horse's bridle, bowing at the same time.

"My name is Dewey," Charles announced formally, "and I bring a message for Mr. Statler."

At the top of the steps now stood another Negro, dressed in a somber black suit and a starched and ruffled white shirt. A Negro of some importance, apparently.

"Yes, sir, Mr. Dewey," he called out. "Won't you come in? William will take your horse." His speech suggested a good education.

Charles handed the reins to William and slid to the ground. He groaned audibly as his aching legs protested the sudden movement. Removing the saddlebag, he mounted the wide steps, noticing out of the corner of his eye that William was leading the mare away at a trot. To where, he didn't know.

"I'm Samuel, Mr. Statler's butler," the black man at the door explained, holding it open for Charles, gesturing him inside an entrance hall so large that Dewey imagined George Milton's compact Williamsburg home might fit inside it.

"If you'll be comfortable here, Mr. Dewey," the butler was saying, "I'll inform Mr. Statler of your arrival. May we know whose message you carry?"

"It's from Mr. Milton of Williamsburg."

Samuel nodded. "Just a moment, please." He hurried away.

Charles gazed around at the beautifully paneled entrance hall which was dominated by a handsomely carved walnut stairway that climbed a well three stories high. It was astounding, seeming to just hang there in midair without adequate support.

Numerous portraits hung on the walls. One, especially, caught his eye. It was of a young woman of exceptional beauty, her honey-colored hair framing a flawless face. And eyes of such blueness . . .

He wished that he could know her.

II

MARSHALL Statler came forward from behind a desk in his drawing room. In back of him, two large windows, which came almost to the floor, gave Charles a view of a sprawling valley behind the mansion.

"Mr. Dewey." Statler greeted him in an easy manner, bowing slightly. "Samuel tells me that you bring a message from my old friend, George Milton."

Charles returned the bow. "Yes, sir, I do." He reached into the saddlebag and brought out the letter.

Statler took it, leading the way to two chairs positioned in front of a white marble fireplace where a fire crackled invitingly. The visitor sat down with some care, his bottom still hurting from his many hours in the saddle.

"Tea, Mr. Dewey?"

"That would be most welcome."

The master of Elkwood nodded to the butler as he broke the wax seal and read Milton's letter:

My dear Marshall,

   This letter is being brought to you by a charming young Frenchman who calls himself Charles Dewey, although I suspect the name is an accommodation to his newly found status as a fledgling American. He is late of the French navy, having left it at the conclusion of the happy circumstances at Yorktown. His appearance before you has a twofold purpose: first, to deliver to your stud the mare Abigail, to complete the breeding we had previously arranged; second, to follow on a discussion we had several months ago regarding your desire to find a tutor of French for your lovely daughters.

As Statler read the letter, Charles had an opportunity to study him. He was tall, perhaps six feet, and most sturdy. Big-boned. The hands that held the letter were huge. His face was square and ruggedly handsome, unmarked by wrinkles. It was well tanned, making it clear that he spent a great deal of time out-of-doors. His black hair was cropped short; he wore no queue. Dewey thought him to be in his mid-forties. The clothes he wore were simple in style. Serviceable, not unlike those Milton had provided for Charles. In spite of his obvious gentleman's station there was nothing effete about him. There was no commonness, either. Marshall Statler carried himself in the manner of a leader. A master.

Statler was still reading the letter:

Young Dewey is well spoken, as you will be able to determine for yourself, although with almost no formal education. Correction: No formal education at all! He has told me of having a ship's surgeon as a tutor, apparently under the patronage of the Comte de Grasse, admiral of the French fleet. If this be true—and I have no reason to doubt it—it demonstrates the young man's ability to ingratiate himself with personages above his social rank; no mean talent, I'm sure you will agree.

Samuel came into the room with a large silver tray. He placed it on a table between the two men and poured tea into two dainty porcelain cups, adding a dollop of thick yellow cream to each. Charles took his cup and tasted the brew rather tentatively; he had never had cream in tea before. It was delicious.

The plantation owner paused in his reading to sip at the tea.

I cannot vouch for his morality, having known him for only a day. I know you must think me mad for sending him to you with such limited opportunity to gauge his qualifications for any kind of employ. Yet, as you are already aware, I pride myself on an ability to quickly judge the personalities of men (an ability that has served me well over the years), and I am much taken with this lad. I have told him only that I was going to suggest to you that you consider finding him a position. Nothing was mentioned about our earlier conversation regarding your search for a French tutor.

"If your evaluation of Mr. Dewey is in opposition to mine, so be it. Your saying yea or nay to him will in no way change our affectionate friendship. I pray that this finds you and your charming children in the bloom of health and contentment. I pray, too, that Abigail shall welcome the entreaties of your fine stallion, and that any issue therefrom might see fit to win a race or two.

Statler folded the letter slowly and put it aside. "May I show you around Elkwood?"

"Sir . . ." Charles began hesitantly. "I've ridden a long way—a long way for *me*, that is—and I'm extremely tired." He was embarrassed at having made the admission. "Might the inspection be postponed until—"

"Of course," Statler interrupted. "I should have been aware of the tedious ride you've had."

Charles forced a laugh, trying to make light of his predicament. "Tedious, sir, might not be the best descriptive word. My very bones ache, it seems."

"Oh?"

"Yes. You see, Mr. Statler, I was never aboard a horse before yesterday."

"What! Good Lord, it's a wonder you can walk at all! Sixty-odd miles in a couple of days is a test for an *experienced* horseman."

Dewey just grinned. He had made his point.

"Samuel will show you to your room and make you comfortable so that you can rest for a few hours." Statler chuckled. "Never on a horse before yesterday?"

"No, sir."

"Well, you'll be called in time for dinner, even though you may have to eat it standing at the mantel."

III

A massive crystal chandelier, lighted by as many as three dozen candles, hung high above the polished walnut surface of the oval dining table, which had been set with delicate rose-patterned china, gleaming silverware, and spotless linen napkins. In the center of the table stood a large cut-crystal bowl filled with water on which floated roses in a profusion of colors: red, pink, white, yellow. *Roses in October?* Charles had little knowledge of growing things, but he was certain that roses didn't bloom in October. Yet the blossoms were real; he wondered what magic had been performed at Elkwood to accomplish that.

There were five for dinner: Statler and Charles, a young man who was introduced as Andrew MacCallum without further immediate identification, and Statler's two daughters.

Katherine, the elder, was dark like the father, and her handsome face had his same squareness. Indeed, she was a feminine version of Marshall Statler. Her nut-brown eyes reflected the same self-assurance; there was even a hint of imperiousness. In command, as it were. Charles speculated that she was two, perhaps three, years older than he.

The younger Statler daughter, Martha, was the beauty he had seen in the portrait in the entrance hall. But the painting, Dewey thought, was only a weak approximation of her loveliness. The blue eyes were of such translucence as almost to disappear at times, depending on how she tilted her head in the light. She was of a shy nature; that was immediately apparent. And although she might have been four or five years younger than Katherine, Martha was more buxom. More of a woman, Charles decided.

He was immediately taken with her, even though it was Katherine who seemed more interested in, and more intrigued by, him.

It was during the serving of a hot creamed soup—Dewey couldn't identify the ingredients—that MacCallum's identity became known.

"Well, Mr. MacCallum," Statler said, "what have you to report on the progress of my daughters' studies?"

"Father," Katherine protested, "our guest certainly isn't interested in talk of ciphering and penmanship."

"Perhaps Mr. Dewey will excuse just a moment or two of family discussion," the father responded sternly. "Mr. MacCallum?"

"Latin continues to be . . . uh . . . vexatious for both young ladies. On the whole, though, I'm pleased with our progress."

The tutor was choosing his words carefully.

"Miss Katherine continues with her proficiency in mathematics, and Miss Martha remains more interested in literature. But as you've instructed, sir, I'm making every effort to balance their . . . uh . . . enthusiasms."

A slight smile came to Statler's face. "And with little success, eh?"

"With some, sir," MacCallum answered flatly.

Statler turned to his daughters. "Young ladies, we have had this discussion before, and we're going to have it again, I'm afraid. I must insist that you be more cooperative with Mr. MacCallum in those studies that you've decided are dull or boring. Well-roundedness is what I want in your schooling—and what I shall have!"

"Father, please!" Katherine protested once more, inclining her head toward Charles.

Statler laughed lightly. "Someday, Mr. Dewey, you may find yourself in a similar situation as the father of daughters who imagine themselves grown and capable, even though they've barely escaped puberty."

"Father!" This time Katherine squealed.

"Oh, very well," Statler shrugged, "the table is yours, Katie."

She turned to Charles, all brightness and enthusiasm. "Do tell us about Yorktown, Mr. Dewey."

Charles lied.

The truth of his lack of knowledge of the surrender of Cornwallis—an event he had used only as a vehicle for his desertion—was something he didn't want anyone to know. He had no choice but to lie.

Carefully, he kept the lies to colorful generalities.

"The flags and bands and thousands of troops—well, it was a magnificent sight."

And: "General Washington appeared in his full-dress uniform, of course, presenting a regal picture."

And: "The Comte de Barras represented the French naval forces in the absence of Admiral de Grasse, who was ill, I'm afraid."

That last, at least, was a fact.

As he spoke, a leg of lamb on a huge white platter, its exterior crisply roasted and its aroma delightful, was placed in front of Statler.

Martha spoke for the first time. "Did you see General Lafayette, Mr. Dewey?"

"Unfortunately, from my vantage point—"

Katherine interrupted with a giggle. "Martha is partial to Frenchmen—" A hand went to her mouth. "Oh, I'm sorry, Mr. Dewey. That must have sounded terrible! I didn't mean to—"

"That's all right, Miss Katherine. There's no offense. I'm rather proud of being French."

"Of course—as you should be."

"But I'm more proud of being what I am now—an American."

"Perhaps we should allow our guest to eat," Statler suggested.

Katherine ignored him. "And the redcoats? How did they appear?"

"Katie!" her father remonstrated. "Please permit our guest to enjoy his meal."

His daughter's face was sullen. "Yes, Father."

"I'm sure you'll have other opportunities to hear from Mr. Dewey." To

Charles: "I hope you'll excuse my daughters' demands for news from outside. We get precious few visitors here."

Dewey nodded his understanding. He was grateful that Statler had rescued him—now he could end the lying. And he was hungry, too.

With the lamb were served golden-bright yams smothered with butter and some kind of boiled greens, bitter to his taste, but he ate them anyway, fearing that he might insult his host if he didn't.

As dessert was being served—a sweet white cake swimming in a thick sauce laced with rum—the master of Elkwood made a family announcement: "I've had a communication from Mr. Lee, and he has kindly offered us the use of his coach and horses to get to church on Sunday. I've accepted."

He turned to MacCallum. "Lee tells me, too, that carriage horses might be available in Charlottesville. Perhaps we can make arrangements to go there within a week or so and look at them."

"Of course," the tutor replied.

"That damned Tarleton!" Charles saw anger in Statler's face. "Leaving us without even the horses to go to church!"

No one commented. Apparently the subject of the person named Tarleton was one that had been amply covered during other meals.

Statler rose from the table. "Well, I'm up early." He looked at Charles. "May I suggest, Mr. Dewey, that we conduct our postponed tour of the estate first thing in the morning?"

"As you wish."

"Good. I'll have Samuel wake you at five-thirty."

Charles groaned inwardly, but he welcomed the opportunity to escape any more questions about Yorktown.

IV

IN a large bedroom on the second floor of the mansion, Martha Statler prepared for bed, clearly annoyed. Her sister was perched on the arm of a chair, watching her intently.

"Why don't you go to your own room?" Martha snapped.

Katherine giggled. "I'm just looking for a sign."

"A sign of what?"

"Of how the charming Mr. Dewey's presence has affected my little sister."

"Katie, you're dreadful." Martha tried to make light of her sister's innuendo, forcing a smile. "What kind of sign could there possibly be?"

"Oh," Katherine answered, grinning impishly, "a slight shortness of breath, a rosy blush on the breast . . ." She dropped her voice into a conspiratorial whisper: "Perhaps even an erect nipple."

"Katie! Really!" Martha turned away from her. "There are times when you can be quite crude! Please go to your own room."

"Oh, dear, is my darling sister embarrassed by the truth: that the handsome Frenchman, with his fair blond hair, raises some desire in her?"

Martha didn't reply.

"That perhaps she imagines herself in her soft bed with him, intent upon—"

"Stop it!" Martha cried, rushing at her, a fist raised menacingly. "Stop it!"

Katherine, easily dodging the half-hearted assault, sauntered to the door. "So it is true, dear Martha," she teased. "Our young guest *does* stir the passion in you."

Martha, wanting to end the baiting, remained silent.

"Do you think he would be exciting in bed?"

No reply.

"Probably not," Katherine shrugged. "But then again, perhaps . . ." She opened the door to leave the room. "I'll tell you what, my virginal sibling . . ." She was smirking. ". . . I'll try him out for you and give you a report."

"Katie!" It was a shriek this time, Martha hurling herself at her sister, who skipped through the doorway, slamming the door shut in her face.

The younger girl rested her forehead on the door panel, struggling to restrain her anger: anger because of what had been said, and anger because she had allowed Katie to use her once more in one of her little games.

There were times when she *hated* Katherine.

4

Marshall Statler's tour of the Elkwood plantation was strange.

As promised, Dewey was awakened at five-thirty by the butler, who brought him a simple breakfast of coffee with heavy cream and buttered toast.

Fifteen minutes later, Statler led Charles out of the rear of the mansion into a great bustle of activity among the numerous outbuildings.

"The tobacco shed," Statler said as he pointed to a small barn. "Next to it is the shed where we do our wool carding. And that's the smokehouse. We're most proud of our hams."

He moved rapidly, not waiting for questions or seeming to invite them. "The icehouse there. Next to it the bakery, which also serves as our summer kitchen. We do our own hide tanning in that rather unattractive building there." Another pointed finger. "The greenhouse—"

"Excuse me." Charles risked an interruption. "The roses I saw at last night's dinner—were they raised in your greenhouse?"

"Yes, that's the place," Statler answered, offering no other detail.

His long strides, with Charles hurrying to keep up, quickly took them through the cluster of dependencies. The visitor marveled at the large number of Negroes he saw at work; how many he couldn't even guess.

He was led to a broad pasture next to a massive, handsomely appointed barn. Statler stopped at the fence to gaze out over a field partly shrouded in an early-morning mist, his attention on a dozen or so mares grazing there.

"And that's the heart of it," he said quietly, almost reverently. "The horses."

He pointed once more. "That's Abigail over there to the left, the mare you rode from Williamsburg."

Charles wondered how Statler could identify Abigail with such certainty. The horses all looked more or less alike to him.

"She's to be bred to Skullduggery, from the Yorick line. And that's a good one, indeed."

Statler sighed deeply. "In truth, Skullduggery and those few mares are all that remain of the Elkwood stud. The war has been most cruel to our breeding efforts. And that damnable Tarleton!"

His sudden anger was very real.

"That fine English gentleman, Colonel Ban Tarleton, and his vaunted mounted infantry! Lord, what an insufferable ass!"

Charles dared not speak. Now, at least, he knew who Tarleton was.

"He swept through here, seizing every serviceable mount we had. Even my own hunter. And, then . . . then he had the gall to question the *quality* of my horses! What arrogance!"

There was a pause as Statler sought to restrain his anger at the memory of what had happened.

"Skullduggery was spared only because of his crippled right hind." He shrugged. "The rest, though, are gone. Our hopes for the future rest in seven of those mares that are to foal in the spring. I'd prefer it if I didn't have to return them all to one stallion. Perhaps Mr. Washington might entertain an offer for his fine stud, Magnolio." A slight laugh. "Of course, that's only wishful thinking. Certainly the good squire is going to retain him at Mount Vernon."

Statler turned suddenly, making his way toward the barn. "Come," he called over his shoulder to Charles.

As they entered the barn, a combination of odors assailed the boy: of hay, of manure, of animal. Altogether not at all unpleasant. The barn was spacious, with many individual stalls, only one of which was occupied. As Statler went to it, Charles at his heels, a big bay horse inside the stall nickered softly, coming to the front of the enclosure to put his head over the half-door that kept him in.

"Good boy . . . good boy," Statler clucked to him, patting the animal's nose with genuine affection.

"This, Mr. Dewey, is Skullduggery. He's only five and should just now be coming into his own as a racehorse. Unfortunately, he never will." He pointed to the twisted right hind leg. "It was injured when he was just a foal. Ordinarily, he would have been destroyed. But I believed he might be carrying the abilities of his sire, Yorick, and I hoped that he'd be able to pass them on to his progeny. Hope, sir, is what motivates a horseman."

Statler smiled. "What is it the Psalm says? 'Happy is he whose hope is in the Lord thy God.' Well, at the risk of blasphemy, I can paraphrase that: Happy is the breeder whose hope is in the next foal crop."

Charles remained silent, instinctively understanding that Marshall Statler wasn't expecting a reply, nor would he have welcomed one at that moment.

"There are those, as you know, young sir, who profess not to believe in God. I suspect that they have never known the joy of association with a truly high-bred horse. Of all of the varieties of domestic animals which a benevolent Providence has created for the use of Man, the blood horse stands alone, without a rival in the animal kingdom. Who but God could create such beauty, such form, such stamina, such power, such courage, such speed, such . . .

heart in a single creature? If there were no God there would be no blooded horse."

The younger man felt tempted to shout "Praise God!" in response. But he restrained himself.

"Well, Mr. Dewey," Statler added, exhaling a long breath, "you've just heard what my daughters call my sermon. I must apologize for boring you with—"

"Oh, no, sir, I understand perfectly."

The master of Elkwood chuckled. "Do you, now?" He patted Charles on the shoulder. "I thank you for that indulgence."

A Negro groom approached, carrying the equipment needed to muck out the stallion's stall.

"Skullduggery looks mighty fit today, Malachi," Statler said to him.

"Yas, suh."

"He cleaned up all of his grain this morning, did he?"

"Yas, suh. Real slick like. He jest full o' hisself." The black man laughed heartily. "Seems like he cain't wait fer them ladies t' come in season."

II

THEY sat on the fence overlooking the pasture as Marshall Statler gave his young guest chapter and verse on the pedigrees of the mares in the field in front of them. Andrew MacCallum, the tutor, joined them.

Charles had the immediate impression that MacCallum's arrival had been prearranged.

After several minutes of pleasant inanities, Statler grew sober. "Mr. Dewey, for some time now I've been wanting to add the French language to my daughters' training," he began, "and although Mr. MacCallum is a graduate of the New Jersey College at Princeton, French was not in his curriculum. We've been discussing the possibility that you might undertake to teach them—"

Dewey was shocked by what he was hearing. "Sir, I don't think I have the ability—"

Statler's laugh interrupted him. "You do speak French?"

"Yes, but I don't have the training necessary to teach it to someone else."

"Under Mr. MacCallum's expert guidance, we believe that your lack of training can be compensated for."

Charles shook his head in doubt.

"Perhaps, Mr. Statler," MacCallum interjected, "we should hear something of Mr. Dewey's background."

Charles began to realize that if he wanted to stay at Elkwood—and he had made that decision during Statler's "sermon"—he had better seize this opportunity.

"My background, gentlemen," he said, "is most limited." He told them everything he could recall of his sixteen years: of his orphan status, of the terrible years he had spent on the Paris streets, of his enlistment in the French navy at ten, of the patronage of Admiral de Grasse, of his lessons with the ship's surgeon. He omitted only one fact: his desertion from the French navy.

"A difficult life," Statler commented.

"In one sense, a learning process." Charles was pleased with that phrase. "And one that has led me here, to this country, where I'm told opportunities are unlimited for one with ambition."

Statler nodded. "Well, other duties require my attention." He slid down from the fence. "Maybe it would be best if you discussed this matter further with Mr. MacCallum before giving me your decision." He left them quickly.

There followed a strained silence, during which Charles assessed the tutor. He was in his early twenties, slightly built, an inch or two smaller than Charles in stature, with brown hair and eyes, and a pleasant enough face, but one that Charles thought of as gaunt.

The young Frenchman spoke finally: "Mr. MacCallum, I appreciate that you might not want me here in these . . . uh . . . circumstances. Would you be happier if I moved on and didn't intrude?"

"No, no. Elkwood, as much as I enjoy it, isn't going to be my total life, Mr. Dewey. There'll come a time when a better opportunity arises, and I shall take it." A wan smile. "I'd like to correct one small detail of Mr. Statler's earlier narration: I *did* study French, however briefly, at Princeton. I had difficulty with the pronunciation, however, and in my Scottish stubbornness, I abandoned it for what I considered more worthwhile pursuits.

"No offense intended to the French language. Now, however, if Mr. Statler wishes that we"—he stressed the plural pronoun—"attempt to teach his daughters French, then I'm willing to try. And I'm certain that I shall benefit as well."

"That's very kind." Charles pondered his decision for just a moment. "I place myself in your hands."

"Fine, fine." MacCallum grinned. "Mr. Statler gave me the authority, in the event you agreed to his plan, to explain the terms of your employment at Elkwood. He proposes to offer you room and board and the amenities—clothing, a horse to ride, and the like—"

"But no money," Charles interrupted.

"No money," MacCallum confirmed. "Under the circumstances, however, I believe his offer to be generous."

"So do I." Charles extended his hand. MacCallum shook it warmly.

"In light of your acceptance," the tutor said, "perhaps we should continue our discussion a bit longer." He grimaced. "Are you wed to this fence?"

"Hardly," Dewey laughed. "My bottom is still sore from my two days on horseback."

"Then let's walk."

III

"I believe the first thing we should do," MacCallum said as they strolled across the vast lawn behind the mansion, "is to dispense with formalities. I'm Andrew. And you're Charles."

"Agreed."

"Uh . . . permit me a confession to start our cooperation. You were no sooner in the house, Charles—within an hour of your arrival—when Mr. Statler came to me with the idea of you teaching French to his daughters. Frankly, knowing nothing at all about you, I was skeptical. I expressed my doubts. Mr. Statler, however, persisted. He told me he believed you to be a young man of talent. I've been at Elkwood long enough to know that Mr. Statler has a weakness for snap judgments of that kind. And not always accurate judgments.

"Having now learned of your background, and having heard you speak last night at dinner and again here this morning, I'm inclined to agree with him. It's a talent, indeed, for you to have risen so far above your environment. I know that must sound condescending to you, but I mean it only in the most flattering way."

"You're most kind. I had a good tutor aboard the *Ville de Paris*."

"And he had a facile pupil."

Charles was embarrassed. "Again—you're most kind."

"Yes, well . . ." MacCallum smiled. "So much for that. Now, Charles, please bear with me as I outline certain realities of living here at Elkwood. I couldn't help noticing your almost instant fascination with Miss Martha. While I can appreciate that fascination, it mustn't be allowed to blossom into anything more. I understand the Frenchman's proclivity toward the opposite sex, but—"

"I don't understand that last remark," Charles cut in.

MacCallum stared at him for an instant. "It's well known that Frenchmen have a . . . well, an appetite for women."

"More than Scotsmen?"

The tutor laughed loudly. "So it's said. Am I to understand that you have no such appetite?"

"Appetite? You make it sound like a meal."

"I seem to be doing this rather badly," Andrew chortled. "But I'm going to muddle on and assume that you've had *some* experience with women."

He paused, waiting for a response from Charles, who remained silent.

"What I'm trying to say, Charles, is that with the Statler daughters you must be like Caesar's wife."

"Pardon?"

"Like Caesar's wife: above reproach." He quickly realized his error. "Of course, you haven't learned of such things. We'll rectify those . . . uh . . . shortcomings as we go along. The point is, Charles, that you *must not* in any way, make overtures to Miss Martha or Miss Katherine."

MacCallum sighed. "And let me tell you that won't be easy. Miss Katherine, especially, is at an age where she's feeling her womanliness. While I'll not go into details, I can tell you that Miss Katherine might give you cause to believe that her . . . uh . . . favors are available. Lord, this is difficult!"

"I understand, Andrew."

"Ah! You say you do, but could you resist if an opportunity presented itself?"

Charles was sober-faced. "I'd make it a point to do so."

"Fine. You'll not be alone in this. If I see something brewing, I hope you won't be offended if I bring it to your attention. Privately, of course."

"I'd be most appreciative."

Andrew laughed again. "Let's hope so."

"I would—honestly!"

"I don't wish to belabor this matter, but you should also know about Mr. Lee, of whom Mr. Statler spoke. He is Funston Lee, the son of a rather obnoxious man who lives some five miles removed from Elkwood—a Virginia gentleman, he insists, though I have my doubts about his credentials. In any event, the younger Lee, Funston, is paying court to Miss Katherine, and she's not above attempting to make him jealous by paying special attention to you. Be aware of that, and be especially meticulous in your conversations and actions when Lee is about.

"In this part of the country, Charles, it's not unique for one gentleman to challenge another to what you French call an *affaire d' honneur*—you see, I do know a little French—over the affections of a young lady. Nor is it unique for a young lady to try to precipitate a duel as an affirmation of the love, if we may call it that, the young gentleman professes for her."

"I'll be most careful," Charles assured him.

"Good! Someday it may be worth your life that you are."

MacCallum picked a spot under a leafless maple tree, dropping to the ground with a satisfied groan. He gestured for Charles to follow his example.

"Now, Charles"—the tutor leaned back against the trunk— "another reality of Elkwood. Mr. Statler, a widower of some seven years, has only daughters as his issue, as you're already aware. He doesn't enunciate this, but he's deeply distressed by the fact that he has no male heir. Therefore, there's a tendency on his part to . . . uh . . . overindulge a new male inhabitant of Elkwood, to look upon him as a son. It has happened to me, and I'll wager it'll happen to you. If you don't want to be a surrogate son, you'll have to resist his entreaties."

Andrew paused briefly. "Of course, perhaps you'll see such an opportunity differently than did I. I call this to your attention only to make you aware of it. It will make no difference to me, one way or another, how you choose to handle it."

Charles nodded. He saw no reason to comment. But he was intrigued by what the tutor had just told him.

"Finally, a third warning, if I may," MacCallum went on. "The institution of slavery is deeply ingrained here. As a northerner—I was brought to New Jersey from Scotland at an early age and raised there—that institution remains foreign to me. It would be wise for a newcomer such as yourself not to intrude into the matter of the treatment of the slaves—*not intrude in any manner!* Such intrusion, believe me, will be resented. With vehemence. If slavery offends you, keep your own counsel. Nothing will bring you more trouble, perhaps not even the dalliance with a daughter, than expressing your disapproval of slavery. It's a fact of life here. Accept it in silence."

"I appreciate your . . . uh . . ."

"*Candor* is the word you seek, Charles."

The young Frenchman laughed. "Thank you. I can see that I'm going to learn much from this association."

"And perhaps I'll learn to contend with French pronunciation," MacCallum countered. "If we had a bottle of wine here now, I'd propose a toast." He pantomimed pouring the wine, and lifting the glass high. "To a happy collaboration!"

"To a happy collaboration!" Charles repeated, duplicating the mime.

IV

DEWEY'S first few days as a French tutor went well enough, under the firm direction of Andrew MacCallum. Since Charles knew only conversational French and had no grounding in grammar, Andrew had him give the girls a list of often-used words at first. Correct spellings were gleaned from the appendix of a very old and very large British dictionary in MacCallum's possession.

Katherine and Martha wrote the words in their copybooks. It wasn't "lessons," really—it seemed like great fun.

And rudimentary. *Tête*, head. *Oeil*, eye, and the plural, *yeux. Bouche*, mouth. *Menton*, chin. *Goulot*, neck, and the feminine, *encolure. Corps*, body. *Poitrine*, breast. Charles noticed that Martha actually blushed when he included the word. *Bras*, arm. *Jambe*, leg. *Pied*, foot.

They counted: *Un, deux, trois, quatre, cinq, six, sept, huit, neuf, dix.*

Into the copybooks went the common greetings and social niceties: *Bonjour, bonsoir, au revoir, enchanté, merci, s'il vous plaît.*

At the end of the second day, Katherine interrupted the rote lessons. "Monsieur Dewey, you haven't mentioned the most important word of all."

"And that would be?"

"Love!"

"Ah, *mademoiselle*," Charles answered playfully, "that would be *amour*."

"You'll note," MacCallum interjected, ever the tutor, "that it has a Latin root: *amor*, which is the Latin word for *love*, you may recall."

Katherine ignored him. "*Amour*," she repeated in a husky whisper. "There's such a lovely sound to it."

Charles nodded. "And there are so many ways to use it. *Affaire d'amour*, a love affair; *s'amouracher*, to fall in love; *mal d'amour*, lovesickness; *amourette*, passing fancy; *amour-propre*, self-love."

"I think it's important," MacCallum insisted, "that you recognize the Latin base in so many languages—Italian, Spanish, French." He tried to make his point in the context of what Katherine had started. "The Romance languages, they're called. It was the ancient Romans who said, *Amor vincit omnia*—love conquers all."

"Does it, Monsieur Dewey?" Katherine asked.

Charles gave a Gallic shrug. "*Amour fait beaucoup, mais argent fait tout.*"

The young woman was perplexed. "What does that mean?"

"Love does much, but money does all." He laughed.

"Mr. Dewey, you're simply horrid!"

"*Monsieur* Dewey," MacCallum corrected her.

"Very well . . . *monsieur*," Katherine pouted. "But he's still horrid."

Then she smiled at Charles.

Invitingly.

5

CHARLES Dewey knew there was a God, even though he had never been inside a church.

He could recall having been witness to only a single religious ceremony, when the bodies of three seamen killed in a gunnery accident off the West Indies were consigned to the waters of the Caribbean.

What religion he knew had been assimilated into his consciousness as a result of what he had heard. But what told him there was a God, what made him a believer, was the sure knowledge that his life was directed by a guardian spirit. Who else but God could be responsible for such a spirit?

In that somewhat narrow sense, he was a *devout* believer.

The prospect, then, of going to church with the Statler family on his first Sunday at Elkwood was pleasing to him. Until he met Funston Lee.

As Statler had announced during dinner at the beginning of the week, Lee sent his coach to take Marshall Statler, his daughters, Andrew MacCallum, and Charles to the services. But Lee himself arrived with the coach, and there was limited room inside it.

Charles's trouble began early, when they were just leaving the mansion. Katherine suddenly took his arm as they went down the stone steps, holding it tightly, walking closer to him than was necessary. Hurrying ahead of the others, she guided him to the coach where Lee awaited the Statler party.

Lee was tall and slim, with smoldering, deep-set eyes. His thin lips were pressed together in disgust at that moment. He was grandly dressed; his lavishly embroidered cape was trimmed with rich fur.

"Funston dear," Katherine cooed, pressing so close to Charles that he could feel her thigh, "I wish to present Monsieur Dewey."

Lee glowered at him for an instant, then removed his black velvet tricorne and made a sweeping bow so exaggerated that it could only suggest contempt.

"Ah! The Frenchman," he said. "Your servant, sir."

Imprisoned by Katherine's determined hold, Dewey couldn't return the bow. The others were at the coach now, with MacCallum helping Martha inside. Lee extended his hand to Katherine. Before relinquishing Charles's arm, she patted it affectionately, a gesture that Lee was meant to see. Katherine boarded, then Statler and the tutor.

"Oh, dear," Funston said, glancing inside the coach, "I fear the ladies will be most uncomfortable if we attempt to crowd a half-dozen in there."

He paused in feigned thought, turning finally to Charles. "Perhaps Monsieur Dewey will play the gallant Frenchman and ride on top . . . with the coachman."

The insult was obvious. A half-bow and Lee sprang into the coach, shutting the door firmly.

Charles quickly climbed to his seat, smiling at the black driver. He was determined not to let his anger show.

A cold, light rain began to fall as the coach made its way toward the church. He pulled his cape tighter around him, glancing over at the Negro coachman. "Under these circumstances," he said, making an attempt at lightheartedness, "perhaps we shouldn't have ventured out."

"Yas, suh." The black man didn't look at him.

"May I ask your name?"

"Ah belongs to ole Mistah Lee."

"But, you *do* have a name?"

"Mistah Lee call me Driver."

It seemed to Charles that the Negro was having difficulty keeping his answers civil. "What does your family call you?"

The coachman looked over at him at last, surprise registered on his face. "Ain't got no family, suh. An' mah name's Driver."

Dewey kept silent after that.

The drizzle had ended by the time the half-hour drive to the church was completed, but it had done its damage. Charles's cape was wet, and he was shivering from the cold.

His spirit was dampened as well.

II

THE scene at the rural Virginia church was not at all what Dewey had anticipated.

Almost immediately after leaving their carriages, the women of the congregation disappeared inside the small white clapboard church while the men stood around in groups outside the building, not discussing matters of religion. The talk was of tobacco prices, the manner in which grain would be sown in the spring, trouble with slaves. And horses.

Marshall Statler got into a protracted conversation with a gentleman who had been introduced to Charles as Mr. Ransom.

"I swear to you, Ransom," Statler said, "that there's never been a finer stallion in Virginia than John Tayloe's Yorick. Why, after six seasons at stud, Tayloe was able to return him to training to accept a challenge from Dr. Flood's breed horse. Let's see—that was in seventy-three, as I recall it."

"Yes, I believe it was."

"Did you see that match?"

"No," Ransom admitted.

"Well, sir, I had that great good fortune," Statler continued enthusi-astically. "It was agreed that they run a single five-mile heat at five hundred pounds a side."

The master of Elkwood laughed. "I was able to find a hundred pounds as an added wager on Yorick. And it was devastating, sir, absolutely devastating! He covered the distance in"—a pause for thought—"in twelve minutes and twenty-seven, if my memory serves me, and Yorick was in hand the whole way. That was carrying one hundred and eighty! And Yorick, by that time, was thirteen. A truly amazing racing stallion, Mr. Ransom. It's why I'm so pleased to have his son, Skullduggery."

"Hmmm. I've always been partial to the *Fearnoughts.*"

"Oh, yes," Statler mused, "he was most prolific and his issue always had good size and stamina. But I always questioned his stud fee—ten pounds seemed exhorbitant."

"He *was* important," Ransom said defensively.

"True. And I hope that when the war is finally concluded we can look to England again for some new bloodstock. God knows, we can use it."

"Will your Skullduggery be open to service outside mares?"

"Of course," Statler answered. "I don't have enough mares left to keep him content. Does two pounds seem fair?"

"Eminently. We'll talk of this again in the spring."

"Fine, fine."

Another large coach drew up. Andrew MacCallum nudged Charles. "Here comes John Lee," he whispered. "Be most careful with this one."

"Funston's father?"

"The same."

The elder Lee, obsese and carelessly dressed, grunted his way out of the coach and walked slowly to the knot of men around Statler.

"Good day, Marshall," he said sullenly.

"John," Statler nodded. "May I present Mr. Charles Dewey?"

"I've heard that you had a Frenchman in your household now." He studied Charles as he would have examined a horse or maybe a slave. As a commodity. "Funston tells me that you're late of the French navy."

"That's correct, sir."

"Mr. Dewey," Statler explained, "had the good fortune to have been at Yorktown."

"Yorktown," Lee snarled, "was the ultimate victory of the rabble."

Statler laughed. "Don't let Squire Lee frighten you, Charles. He's inclined to pretend to be a Tory, although he's in the same boat as we . . . uh . . . rebels. He delights, however, in the role of devil's advocate."

"You may be content with the republican nonsense of Mr. Jefferson and his ilk, but I'm not!" Lee's fat face was flushed. He looked directly at Charles. "And I place that young upstart, the vaunted Marquis de Lafayette, in that same dangerous company."

Charles bridled.

"Careful," MacCallum warned under his breath.

Statler laughed even louder. "See—what did I tell you?" To Lee: "Young Mr. Dewey comes to us under the aegis of our mutual friend, George Milton."

"Milton!" Lee exploded. "That scoundrel is no friend of mine. He robbed me on my last consignment of tobacco to him."

"John, John," Statler chuckled, "entirely predictable."

Lee snorted in derision.

A young man came to the door of the church and called out, "Gentlemen, the services are about to begin."

III

As one body, the men trooped into the church and noisily took their seats on the side opposite the women.

To Charles, the service appeared hurried. Prayers were mumbled hastily. The minister—MacCallum said his name was Lawrence Smith—spoke for only a short period on what he called "being," with liberal mention of Aristotle and Plato, speculating on whether there was anything permanent in the changing phenomena of nature and whether God the Creator bore the same relationship to nature as to man.

It was confusing. And boring, made more so by the monotone in which Pastor Smith read his text. Fortunately, the sermon lasted just about a quarter of an hour. It was followed by the desultory singing of a hymn, *a cappella*, and a final rapid prayer. The entire service was concluded in half an hour.

As they left the church, Charles asked MacCallum: "What was that about?"

Andrew grinned at him. "Metaphysics."

"What?"

"Metaphysics," the tutor repeated. "The study of—let's see if I can recall my philosophy classes—of fundamental problems relating to the ultimate nature of reality. Of 'being,' as Mr. Smith put it, and of human knowledge. There," MacCallum added proudly, "I *did* remember!"

Dewey stared at him. "But that doesn't make any sense, Andrew."

"I admit it's abstruse. Old Aristotle could be that way at times."

"But as a sermon?" Charles was still confused.

"Oh, that. It's safe, you see. Also, a lot of ministers like to show off their scholarship. But, primarily, it's a safe subject."

MacCallum drew him aside. "What you have to understand is that the church in this country is as much involved in the Revolution as is the political structure. In somewhat of a nutshell, Charles, the Anglican church, or the state church, has been equated with British royalty. Wherever the Anglican church was established, the colonists had to pay taxes to support it. Many Americans were not inclined to do so.

"But they were, nevertheless, believers and didn't want to disassociate themselves from God. Catholicism was not an answer for them, so they split within the Anglican church. Again in the most simple terms, the conservative members, primarily the Tories who opposed the war against the Crown, remained Anglicans. Dissenters, those who were opposed to the tax-supported church, and mainly those who supported the war, became Presbyterians."

He gestured toward the building. "That's a Presbyterian church. So abhorrent is the idea of a state church—especially among these Virginia planters, it seems—that the ministers find it impossible to speak on anything that even remotely mirrors the real world: politics, the war, taxes, commerce. Even the Bible. So thay take the safe road. Metaphysics is safe because no one understands it—including, I'm inclined to believe, the ministers themselves."

Charles shook his head. "I don't know—I just expected something more . . . well, *religious.*"

"It will come," MacCallum said matter-of-factly. "It's just that the church is in transition right now. Like you, I think the transition is rather bland. Spiritually unrewarding."

IV

THERE was no move among the worshipers to leave the church grounds. Men and women gathered in clusters, and once more there was no talk of religious matters. Charles and Andrew made their way to a group surrounding Marshall Statler and John Lee, the Reverend Mr. Smith now among them. The subject under discussion was cockfighting, with Mr. Smith being lavish in his praise of a bird he had bred.

"Powerful across the breast," he was telling the others, "and with a most aggressive spirit."

"Tested, Lawrence?" Lee asked him.

"Only in hand, John." He smiled. "Kept in restraint with difficulty. He's a red, similar to that good one I had two years ago."

Lee nodded knowingly. "You'll have to bring him around some day, Parson. That is, if you're prepared to back your bird with a wager."

"It'll be done, John. Be assured of that."

Dewey turned away from the conversation, revolted by it. Cockfighting was a favorite diversion on French warships, and he had always hated it: the torn flesh, the lacerated eyes, the ignoble death. He remembered the glee exhibited by Captain de Boade at cockfights aboard ship. Now he was seeing the same enthusiasm, only a bit more restrained, in a minister of God. It made him ill.

He found himself looking around for Martha, finally spotting her among a small group composed primarily of women, in which Katherine and a laughing Funston Lee were the center of attention.

Katherine saw him approaching and called out to him: "Mr. Dewey, please come and let me present some of the ladies."

Quickly, she made introductions to some half-dozen women, one of whom was the Reverend Mr. Smith's wife. Charles couldn't help but wonder what she thought of her husband's preoccupation with cockfighting.

"Do tell the ladies about Yorktown, Mr. Dewey," Katherine insisted. That brought a scowl to young Lee's face.

"I don't wish to bore the ladies," Charles said, hoping to get out of his predicament.

"Bore them? Of course you won't."

He gave them an abbreviated version of what he had earlier told the Statler sisters.

The same lies.

Even so, his concocted stories of the unobserved surrender ceremonies drew appreciative oohs and aahs from the listeners.

"What role did you play in the festivities, Mr. Dewey?" an annoyed Funston asked.

"I was with the delegation from the *Ville de Paris*, flagship of the French navy."

"In what capacity, sir?"

"As a member of the staff of the Comte de Grasse, Admiral of the Fleet."

Charles found it strange that he didn't mind lying in response to Lee's goading questions.

Funston persisted. "A ranking member?"

"As Comte de Grasse's personal aide, Mr. Lee." The lying had become fun; he was making Lee very uncomfortable.

"Aren't you a bit young to hold such an exalted position?" Lee continued sarcastically.

"Age—young or old—was not a barrier in this war. Indeed, there were quite a few of *your* age who saw fit to serve at Yorktown."

Katherine giggled, and several of the other ladies tried to hide smiles.

Lee's rage was a sudden thing. His face went black with it. "You give me offense, sir!"

"Oh? In what way?"

"By innuendo, sir. There are good and valid reasons why I didn't serve in the army."

"I'm sure there are, Mr. Lee." Charles grinned at him. "And I see no reason why you should have to detail them in this . . . uh . . . innocent conversation."

"You, sir, are insufferable!"

"Funston, please," Katherine begged, having seen his uncontrolled anger before.

"Stay out of this!"

Mrs. Smith, the pastor's wife, spoke up. "I suggest, Mr. Lee, that perhaps this has gone far enough."

Her no-nonsense words brought him up short. He bowed to her. "Of course, Mrs. Smith, you're correct," he said unctuously. "I do hope that you can excuse my boorish behavior."

The matron patted Lee's arm, smiling at him reassuringly. "I like to think that I can still appreciate the spirt of the young."

A hand tugged at Charles's sleeve. He turned to find Martha by his side.

"Perhaps Mr. Dewey would like to meet some of the other ladies," she said softly.

He permitted her to lead him away.

"You made a mistake, you know," Martha said as they walked slowly toward another group of women. "Funston can be mean. He won't forget what just happened."

"And what *did* just happen?"

"You made him look the fool."

Charles laughed. "He does that fairly well on his own."

"Don't make light of this. Funston has a cruel side. He's already killed one man in a duel."

"Really? On what pretense?"

"Over the sale of a horse. He accused the other man of selling him a horse he knew to be permanently lame." She furrowed her brow. "He's dangerous when he believes he's been crossed."

Charles was warmed by her concern for him. "Miss Martha, I'm sorry if I brought you any distress." A pause. "Uh . . . are they going to be married—Lee and Miss Katherine?"

"I hope so," the young girl replied. "It would serve her right."

He grinned. "A little sisterly animosity?"

"No, truthfulness."

The word brought him up short. He stopped walking. "Uh . . . Miss Martha, I'd appreciate it, when I meet the other ladies, if there's no more talk of Yorktown."

She gazed up at him through those lovely blue eyes. Admiringly. "Your modesty becomes you, Mr. Dewey."

Charles swallowed hard. "Yes, well . . ."

Martha smiled at him. "Very well, Mr. Dewey, no more talk of Yorktown," she promised.

They arrived at a second group of women. Martha introduced him and then led him away to yet another knot of ladies. And another. And another, until Charles was certain that he had met every lady of the congregation.

Finally they stood alone under a large tree at the edge of the churchyard.

"Thank you, Miss Martha," he said, "for being so kind to me."

She didn't answer him, looking shyly at the ground.

He reached for her hand and held it tightly. "You're very beautiful." The words were tender.

Martha's reply was an almost imperceptible squeeze of the hand, but she kept her eyes downcast, not looking at him. Her shyness made her even more appealing to him.

"Well, there you are!" MacCallum's cheery voice broke the spell of the moment. "Miss Martha, your father has asked me to tell you that he's ready to leave. Would you inform Miss Katherine, please?"

Charles watched her leave, and turned to MacCallum with an embarrassed laugh. "Brewing?"

"Most definitely *yes!*" The tutor wasn't happy. "It seems that my warnings fell on deaf ears. Your little encounter with Funston has now made the rounds of the entire congregation." He was angry.

"I think *encounter* is too strong a word."

"To young Lee it was an encounter. Believe me!" Andrew sighed. "And then you top it off with a hand-holding *tête-à-tête* with an unchaperoned young lady—" He threw up his hands.

"You're exaggerating the whole thing," Charles insisted defensively. "We were just standing here. It was innocent."

MacCallum shrugged. "I'll accept your protestations of innocence, but others may not." Another sigh and the tutor clapped Charles on the back. "Come—we're all to dine at Marsh Run."

"Marsh Run?"

"The John Lee estate. Mr. Statler has accepted an invitation for Sunday dinner."

Charles blanched. "Oh, God!"

"Exactly." But Andrew was smiling again. "This time, my impetuous young Frenchman, stay by my side, speak discreetly only when spoken to, and keep your hands to yourself."

"Agreed."

V

DEWEY's forced semisilence at Marsh Run gave him an opportunity to observe a traditional Sabbath dinner on a Virginia plantation. There were other guests besides the Statler entourage: other planters and their wives and children, plus the Reverend and Mrs. Smith. Twenty-seven in all.

And there were surprises. John Lee, although a bit loud, was a gracious host, presiding over a truly sumptuous meal: beef, ham, wild turkey, goose, half a dozen different vegetables (including the bitter greens, identified this time as "collards"), a bewildering choice of wines, and a delicious frozen dessert that Lee called "ice cream."

(Charles didn't know—and Lee probably didn't, either—that ice cream had long been a delicacy in France; but not in the society of one Charles Dupree.)

Mrs. Lee, too, was a surprise. When he had been introduced to the ladies at the church, Charles had not met Mrs. Lee. He wondered why. Now, at dinner, he found that John's wife was a frail woman, her face drawn as if in constant pain, her hair nearly white, and she was confined to a chair to which wheels had been attached, a blanket covering her legs. Mrs. Lee was not introduced to Dewey, and she said not a word. Charles surmised that the woman was unable to speak.

She had been pushed to the table in her wheeled contraption by a light-skinned Negro serving girl—a tall, slim young woman of considerable beauty.

Later, when the men retired to Lee's drawing room for brandy, the light-skinned girl was there again, serving the liquor. It was in that circumstance that Charles learned her name: Melody. It fit her. The few words she had to speak in the course of her duties were delicate, almost musical. He found himself following her moves about the room. She was the kind of woman who captured the eyes, holding them prisoner.

The conversation—was it inevitable?—turned to racehorses.

"I'm led to believe, Marshall," the elder Lee was saying, "that this man

Shackelford, at Charlottesville, has several young blooded horses he may be willing to part with. If you're going there anyway, to look at those carriage horses, it might be worth your while to check out Shackelford's animals."

Statler's interest was obvious. "I'd hate to think there'll be racing again in the spring with Elkwood not represented. The way my situation is now, it'll be three or four years before I can develop my own runners once more."

"Tell me about Milton's plans at Petersburg."

"I know only that he's building a track—he and several partners—and the word is that it will be ready in the spring. June, I believe." Statler grinned, childlike. "Lord, won't it be good to get to racing again?"

Lee agreed, asking, "Any word about racing at the Charleston track?"

"No, there's still some fighting in the Carolinas."

"The damned war!" the elder Lee growled.

"The *necessary* war," Statler countered.

"I doubt that. The Congress might have made some reasonable accommodations with the Crown if it hadn't been for the likes of the Adamses, stirring up matters in their Boston hotbed until blood was spilled!"

"I seem to recall," Statler replied, "that our own representatives were reasonably vehement in calling for war."

"Yes, and I venture that that firebrand Henry will live to regret his words. That 'give me liberty, or give me death' nonsense! I know you accuse me of having latent Tory sentiments," Lee continued, "but I'm deeply concerned about our future. There was some stability under the Crown, even though we might not have liked all of the machinations of George the Third. But, as Englishmen—and let's not forget, Marshall, that's what we are!—we had the protection of English common law. Now what? Can we survive this squabbling confederation of states? What will hold it together?"

"Our faith in our own abilities to govern."

"Poppycock! You've been seduced by the honeyed words of the gentleman from Monticello. He's a dangerous man, I tell you! If what he proposes becomes reality, Statler, we'll have anarchy. Anarchy!

"The strength of this colony, of *our* Virginia, has always been its landholders. If we are shunted aside, if the government falls into the hands of the mechanics and the shopkeepers and the ne'er-do-wells who are without land and without substance of any kind, not only will *we* be destroyed but so will Virginia. Without Virginia a confederation of states is a straw house."

After a pause for reflection, Statler answered him. "We cannot forever maintain our . . . uh . . . artificial dominance, John. *All* the people must be involved in our government if it is to prosper. I happen to believe what Jefferson wrote about the equality of men."

"Equality! Good Christ! You may believe that a mechanic, who can't read or write, is your equal, but I don't. Such a man could never be my equal! I'm an aristocrat, and I make no apologies for it."

Several of the other men in the room were moved to respond: "Hear, hear!"

"Let me ask you this," Lee went on, "are your nigras equal to you?"

"No, but—"

"Well, Marshall, there are those—and some in this state, too—who will tell you that nigras *are* equal! How many blacks do you have?"

"One hundred and fifty three." The figure came out with no pause for thought. Statler was certain of his holdings.

"And how many whites at Elkwood?"

"Eleven, not counting my daughters."

"I have nearly two hundred nigras," Lee continued, "and there are fourteen white men here. Now, what's going to happen to us if the slaves get it into their heads that they're *equal*, for God sake? We'll be murdered in our beds!"

John Lee's face was flushed. "In Virginia, there are enough nigras to take over, if we let them. And in the Carolinas, too."

Statler groaned. "John, you're overwrought on this subject."

"Maybe. But I have enough intelligence to feel some honest fear. There's no more reckless man than one without fear. I'll not sit by for a single moment, Marshall, if I hear talk of nigra equality on this property. No black at Marsh Run is going to say those words more than once, because he'll be a dead nigra!"

"You're a harsh man, John."

"So should you be, my friend. So should you be."

VI

DEWEY was already in bed, after the return to Elkwood, when there was a knock on his door.

"It's Andrew."

"Come in."

The tutor entered, still fully dressed, carrying a bottle and two glasses. "I thought I'd better not arrive at this late hour without the solace of some good sherry." He held up the bottle. "This is an amenity of your employment. Good wine is one of the rewards of an ordered life."

Charles smiled. "So I'm to be rewarded. For my good behavior at Marsh Run?"

"I watched you staying on the other side of the room from Funston. Very carefully and very wisely, I thought."

Dewey continued grinning.

"That's not the reason for my visit, though. I've come with some interesting news," MacCallum announced. "Mr. Statler is arranging to travel to Charlottesville at the end of the week. The three of us, with an eye to buying some horses."

"He wants me to go along?"

"Yes," Andrew said soberly. "I suspect that he doesn't want his young Frenchman left alone with his daughters."

Charles showed concern. "You think that's the reason?"

"Of course not," MacCallum chortled. "That was just my attempt at humor. A poor attempt, apparently."

"I'm sorry, Andrew, if I seem humorless. It's just that I feel I might have behaved so badly today that—"

"Nonsense! Mr. Statler told me that he wants to begin to educate you about horses." A hesitation. "This may be the start of his Charles-as-a-son phase."

"More humor?"

"No, this time I'm serious.

"But, Andrew, I've been here less than a week—"

"And you've already made your mark. He heard, as everyone else did, of your incident with Funston. I believe he's proud of you for having stood up to that arrogant . . . uh . . . . fop."

Charles laughed. "You were going to say something else."

"Yes, but he isn't worth the effort of a good, strong obscenity."

"Then you don't think Mr. Statler is displeased with me?"

"Not at all. So rest easy." He poured the sherry into the glasses and handed one to Dewey.

"Something has just now occurred to me," Charles said. "We will be going to Charlottesville to buy horses to replace some of those stolen by Colonel Tarleton. Yet John Lee seems to have his horses intact?"

"Tarleton found something better at Marsh Run," MacCallum explained. "Beef cattle. He ran off with Lee's entire herd. More than two hundred head, I understand. Colonel Tarleton didn't leave any of the plantations in this area unscathed, believe me."

A brief silence as they sipped the wine. "Andrew," Charles said finally, "how seriously should I take that conversation tonight—I mean Mr. Lee's vehemence about his Negroes?"

"I'm sure he meant it. But you shouldn't be overly concerned. It's not something we'll have to deal with. Both of us are outside the establishment, so to speak."

The tutor poured them a second sherry. "Did you notice that mulatto girl, the one called Melody?"

"It would've been difficult not to notice her. She's a real beauty."

"That's John Lee's daughter."

"What?"

"Yes, and no one denies it. As I understand it, Mrs. Lee has been confined to her chair for some twenty years. She lost the use of her legs in an unfortunate fall from a horse. While fox hunting, as I hear it. After, when that happened, the elder Lee had to look elsewhere for his . . . uh . . . well, you understand."

"He took a black mistress?"

'He's not unique in that, you know."

"Does Mr. Statler—?"

MacCallum tilted his head. "To my knowledge, no. It's possible, of course, but I doubt it. I would think that he would consider the feelings of his daughters first. Suppose they should learn of such a thing . . . ." He shrugged. "But, I can't honestly tell you that he hasn't."

Charles Dewey slumped down on the edge of the bed. "Will I ever understand all this, Andrew?"

"In time, you will. You may not agree with it all, but you'll understand it."

6

It came swiftly.

Less than two weeks after his arrival at Elkwood, Dewey was in Charlottesville, beginning his understanding of horses.

On the two-day journey—which the three men made in a farm wagon drawn by a team of oxen in lieu of draft horses—conversation, between bumps and jolts, was all about horses. As MacCallum had predicted, Marshall Statler began to sound like a father when addressing the young Frenchman. He used the word *son* frequently.

"Son, the first thing you have to understand about horses," Statler was saying as they bounced along, "is that there are some who have the eye of a competitor. You can see it—*really see it*—in their eyes. A dull-eyed horse, believe me, will not be much good at the races. A clear, determined eye is the first thing I look for in a horse."

Their first move at Charlottesville was to visit a horse trader named Amos Darnell, a dour-faced man, a bit paunchy, who smelled of horses.

"Your letter, Squire Statler, spoke of the need for carriage horses." Darnell winced. "The war, sir, hasn't been kind to the horse trade. But"—he smiled slightly—"I *am* in possession of a matched pair of light draft horses— crossbred, actually—that might suit you."

He led the way into a large barn and signaled to his black servants, who led two well-muscled bay horses, with neat white blazes on their faces, out of their stalls. To Charles they were so nearly alike in appearance as to be twins.

"A gelding and a mare," Darnell explained, "the progeny of identical breeding, of course. The dam was a blooded horse."

Statler nodded, examining the animals closely, running his hands firmly down their legs and staring into their eyes. He made a gesture, and the Negro handler walked the horses down the barn aisle and back again as the master of Elkwood watched every move.

He silently studied the horses for several minutes. "Five . . . six years old?" he asked.

"You know your horses, Squire Statler," Darnell answered him. "The mare's seven, the gelding six."

"Hmmm." Statler scratched his chin.

Darnell knew it was time to talk money. "The owner, for whom I'm the agent, requests that I ask five hundred pounds."

A startled look came to Statler's face, followed by a hearty laugh. "Five hundred pounds! I'm aware of the inflated prices of these days, Mr. Darnell, but I suspect that your client has lost his senses."

Darnell shrugged. "These are difficult days, sir. Continental paper money, and the Virginia paper . . . well, it jumps around in value so much—"

"What if I were to pay for the horses in English pounds?"

Another shrug. "Perhaps, then—"

"In gold?"

Now it was the horse trader's turn to express surprise. "You have gold?"

"I might," Statler replied cautiously. "If we deal in gold, what then would you ask?"

"Oh, two hundred sovereigns."

Statler laughed once more. "One hundred, Mr. Darnell."

"Squire, there must be something in it for me. At one hundred, I see no profit."

"One-ten, then."

Darnell pondered the offer for a moment. "Done! One-ten the pair."

"What else have you, Mr. Darnell?"

"Very little, sir."

"A serviceable riding nag, perhaps? Not necessarily blooded, but . . . well made. And kind."

"Age?"

"Not doddering," Statler insisted.

"Bring out the gray," Darnell instructed his handlers.

This time a dark gray horse, smaller than the matched pair, was brought out of the stall. His ears came erect at the sight of the strangers, and he jigged at the end of the lead rope.

"Gelded," the horse trader reported. "Nine years old."

Again Statler made his study of the horse. As he ran his hands down the legs, he turned to Charles. "I'm looking for heat," he explained, "and for tenderness that might suggest some problems with the legs. There's an axiom, son: no leg, no horse."

When he straightened up from his inspection, Statler said to Darnell, "Fifteen pounds, sir."

"Oh, come now, Squire—"

"That's my offer, Mr. Darnell."

"Gold?"

"As before."

The trader sighed as if making a great sacrifice. "Very well, fifteen sovereigns."

Smiling, Statler asked: "What do you think of this fellow, Charles?" He pointed to the gray gelding.

"He's very handsome."

"You've noted his clearness of eye?"

"Yes, sir."

"You approve of him, then?"

Charles didn't know how to answer. "Well, I—"

Statler grinned. "I hope you do approve of him, son, because he's yours."

"Mine?" Charles gulped.

"As Mr. MacCallum told you, your employment at Elkwood would include the amenities, and a decent riding horse is one of them."

"Thank you, sir. He's grand."

Statler brushed aside the thanks, going to the small strongbox that had made the trip in the bed of the wagon, opening it, and counting out what he owed Darnell. That was as much a surprise, an *astonishment*, to Dewey as was the gift of the horse. The strongbox had been in the wagon the whole time, overnight in control of the slaves who had come along, and it had no padlock.

Darnell was instructed to keep the three horses in his barn until they were ready to return to the plantation, setting the scene for the next step in the horse-buying operation: a visit to the blooded horses—the racehorses—of a gentleman named Richard Shackelford, who had been recommended by John Lee.

Shackelford, when they made their way to his farm the next day, gave them no reason to believe that they were welcome. He was a tall, gaunt, pallid man. Irritable and humorless.

"Mr. Lee shouldn't have sent you to me," he insisted. "I'm not a horse trader, sir. Indeed, my racing stable has been much affected by the war."

Statler nodded sympathetically. "Colonel Tarleton made certain that mine was stripped of all its runners."

"Most regrettable." He spoke the words in such a manner that it was evident he didn't care at all what had happened to Statler's horses.

"I'm surprised, Mr. Shackelford, that Tarleton didn't pay you a visit."

"He did. I was here. My horses weren't." He volunteered no other information.

"And the animals of your neighbors?"

"My neighbors keep their own counsel, as I keep mine."

Statler cleared his throat. "Might we impose on your kindness, sir, and ask to see your horses? Or would you prefer that we leave?"

"They've only just returned from the Shenandoah within the last few days."

"Of course, if you feel that they can't be shown to their best advantage . . ."

Without giving Statler a reply, Shackelford led them to a barn, but he didn't invite them to go in. Instead, he had a whispered conversation with a black groom, who entered the barn and, one-by-one, brought the racehorses out and led them around a small paddock. In all, Shackelford showed them eleven horses in that manner. All were young—several yearlings were included, and none was over three.

"Impressive," Statler commented. "None of racing age?"

"A few."

"Any for sale?"

"No."

Charles wondered why Statler persisted. There seemed no doubt that the surly horseman didn't want to sell, that he would have preferred that they leave. Statler recognized something, however, that Charles's inexperience didn't allow him to know—that Shackelford *was* a horse trader, despite his denial.

"I mean no disrespect, Mr. Shackelford, but I'm electing not to accept your 'no.' I'm prepared to offer *hard* money for horses ready for the track."

Statler paused to allow that fact to sink in. "In light of the . . . uh . . . strained economy of these days, perhaps we can strike a mutually satisfactory relationship in this matter. May I see your older horses?"

It appeared to Charles that Shackelford actually snarled. Whatever it was he did, he also gestured to the black groom, and another parade of horses was started.

This time Shackelford provided some information on pedigrees: a six-year-old chestnut horse by a son of Janus, out of a good racing mare owned by the Byrds of Westover; a seven-year-old bay of the Fearnought line, noted for stamina; a light gray, nearly white, five years old, by "Mr. Williamson's Arab." In all, they were shown eight horses in training.

"Very nice, Mr. Shackelford," Statler said, "very nice, indeed. The Fearnought, sir—how much?"

"Were he for sale, I'd have to ask six hundred."

Statler smiled slightly. "And were he for sale, I'd offer four-fifty."

"In what currency?"

"Gold sovereigns, naturally. Hard money, as I said. Were we talking Continental paper, your expressed valuation would be—what?—three or four thousand pounds? Or should I say dollars?" He laughed. "I'm never quite sure just how to make the transition from English to American money, in light of the rapid fluctuations in the value of our paper. But, sir, be assured that we *are* talking gold!"

Charles noticed that Shackelford's eyebrows twitched. Nevertheless, he said, "It's unfortunate the Fearnought's not for sale."

"I couldn't agree with you more," Statler replied, climbing aboard the wagon, gesturing to the others to follow.

The wagon was already moving when Shackelford called out to them, "What would you say to four-sixty, sir?"

The wagon was stopped.

"I'd say that it would be ten more sovereigns than I was prepared to pay."

Shackelford scratched his head for a moment. "Gold immediately?"

"This very moment."

The Charlottesville horseman nodded assent to the sale, somewhat sullenly, and the gold coins were counted from the strongbox.

Before the strange bargaining was ended, Statler had also bought the Arab gray as well as a muscular, untried three-year-old chestnut colt. He had spent a total of eight hundred seventy-five sovereigns. Only a few gold coins remained in the box.

Once more Statler asked that the horses be kept in Shackelford's barn until they returned for them.

When the wagon was driven out of sight of Shackelford, Statler broke into a gay laugh. "Did you see Charles's face, Andrew, during the bargaining?"

"Yes, sir," the tutor answered, joining the laughter. "It was most expressive."

Statler clapped Charles on the back. "Son, if you're ever going to be a horse trader you're going to have to learn to control what you say with your expressions. It was marvelous! I could read you like a book." He continued to chuckle.

Feeling some embarrassment, Charles tried to mask it by also laughing. "I'll admit," he said, "that I was mystified by your persistence when it seemed certain that Shackelford didn't want to sell anything."

"Rule number one, son, is that there's not a horseman alive who's not in the business of selling when the price is right. Also, I did some reading of Shackelford's situation. For example, everyone has been a victim of the hard money distress brought on by the war. Could Shackelford have been an exception? Hardly."

Statler went on: "Further, I reasoned that his ability to keep his horses out of the clutches of the British, especially Tarleton, was unique—that there had to be some method behind that uniqueness. Had he, perhaps, kept his horses by bribing Colonel Tarleton or one of his officers? If he did, it was with hard money, gold or silver. The English aren't fools. A bribe with Continental paper money would have been no bribe at all. Therefore, he could be—how shall I put this?—he could be *seduced* by gold, because he had none left. And gold immediately available. Cash on the barrel head, as it's said."

"Do you really believe he bribed the redcoats?" Charles asked.

"With all my heart. If he did send his horses to the Shenandoah Valley, as he claimed, it was more for show with his neighbors than to keep them out of English hands. His gold had already done that job for him. Now he was faced with the necessity of replacing some of his hard money, and he had only one commodity with which to do that: horses." Statler grinned. "Believing that, my strategy was simple."

The master of Elkwood sobered. "It may be, of course, that Mr. Shackelford will have the final laugh in this matter. My own hard money reserve is now badly depleted. And the horses we just bought might not be worth a damn." He turned to the tutor. "What say you, Andrew?"

"I'm much taken with that Fearnought," MacCallum replied with enthusiasm. "He's well put together. I think you've chosen wisely, sir."

Statler laughed loudly again. "This Scotsman," he said to Dewey, nodding toward Andrew, "has a fine eye for horses, a natural talent of selection that is wasted because, like many of his clansmen, he's close with his money. He loses heart when it comes to risking a pound or two. With all of his education—and I admire him for that—he's not learned how to find joy in backing his judgment of horses with a wager."

"Mr. Statler's characterization of a wager as a pound or two," MacCallum said to Charles, "is a bit off the mark, I'm afraid. A *hundred* pounds or two would be more accurate." To Statler: "My joy, sir, is found in other pursuits."

There was no rancor in the comments. It was all said in lighthearted fun.

"Sad, sad." Statler shook his head in feigned distress. "Charles, my son, if you learn nothing else from our association, I shall make certain that you appreciate the challenge of matching horses with money. It may rank as a *noble* pursuit, and, believe me, it's most invigorating."

He put his arm around young Dewey's shoulders. "Indeed, it's not unlike the satisfaction of being with an accommodating woman. And that, too, I'll wager, you'll understand for yourself someday."

II

UNDERSTANDING?

It came unexpectedly.

Charles Dewey had had experience with women: the whores in the cribs along the waterfronts in the warships' ports-of-call. But he never had the enthusiasm for the sport that had been exhibited by the insatiable Captain de Boade. Certainly there was nothing tender about those recollections. And the sum of what might be called his emotional attachment to a female was his moment of innocent hand-holding with the lovely Martha Statler on that first Sunday at church.

Although he admired the beauty of her form, he didn't think of Martha in any erotic sense. Instead, it was Katherine Statler who stirred something illicit within him.

He was wary of her, knowing that she was capable of using him—her baiting of Funston Lee at his expense was reason enough for Charles's caution. But, that aside, he wondered about Katie's clearly evident desire, her seeming availability. Andrew had specifically warned him of that, but as time went on, he was asking questions of himself: Was the attention she showed him designed only to raise young Lee's hackles? Or was there something more to it?

If there was something more to it, Dewey thought, a liaison with Katherine would have distinct benefits at Elkwood. His ambition told him that. And as his ambition grew, his wariness of her diminished.

Perhaps the grand holiday dinner on his first Christmas at the plantation— the sumptuous wild game pie, the spicy jam cakes, the mouth-watering home-cured hams—had given him a false sense of well-being.

Or perhaps it was the almost hypnotic effect of the scented candles glowing among the boxwood sprigs that decorated the classical mantels of the mansion.

Or perhaps it was the sense of family he felt during the holiday entertainments provided by Statler's guitar playing and Katherine's clear soprano voice accompanied by Martha on the pianoforte.

Or perhaps it was the cheery heat of the yule log, decorated with holly, crackling on the hearth.

Or perhaps it was just because he had drunk too much wine.

Whatever it was—and it might well have been a combination of all of those things—he was totally at ease with Katherine that evening. No warning was conveyed to him by her numerous touches—on his arm, his hand, his cheek— or even by the lingering kiss she placed on his lips as she presented her gift to him: a rich wool muffler.

No warning. It all seemed so natural. So right.

The yule log consumed, the candles melted down in their pewter holders, the entertainment ended, Charles lay in his bed, more content than he had ever been. Hands linked behind his head, eyes staring at the ceiling, thoughts on his good fortune, he thanked his guardian spirit.

There was a tiny squeak as the door opened slowly. In the dim half-light a silhouette entered his room; he knew immediately that the shadow was Katherine. It was almost as if he had expected her. She came to him, her dainty perfume adding to the intoxication he already felt: from the wine, the food, the fire, the candles, the belonging.

"I came to wish you a proper merry Christmas," she said softly.

Charles laughed. "Katie, *proper* is hardly the word to use under these circumstances."

She sat on the edge of his bed; he could see that she wore only a cotton nightdress. "Are you really concerned with propriety?" she asked boldly.

"No," he admitted. He was glad she was there.

A hand went to his cheek, so delicately he wasn't certain it was touching him. She leaned over him, her lips replacing the hand, and she kissed his cheek, his eyes, his chin, his mouth. Her arms went around his neck, imprisoning him, the kisses becoming passionate. Her fingers moved down his bare back. Enticingly.

Charles returned her kisses, matching her passion, gathering her roughly into his arms, pulling her tightly against him, feeling her small, firm breasts against his chest. He reached for the nightdress and started to pull it over her head. She helped him. With a great tug she tore it from her, ripping the cloth, dropping it to the floor. And she entwined herself with him, her hands roaming his body. He found her breasts with his mouth, his tongue bringing her nipples erect. Katherine moaned slightly, and, while he continued to kiss her there, she took hold of his hard penis, stroking it.

He thrust a hand between her legs, but as soon as he touched her soft, warm wetness, she pulled away from him. And when he attempted to roll over on her and gain control of the lovemaking, a kind of madness came over her. Katie fought him, while still holding his penis, manipulating it, faster and faster, with her strong fingers. As she brought him near a climax, he stopped struggling with her and allowed himself to explode in an ejaculation.

During all of that, not a word was spoken.

Katherine put her head on his chest, sighing deeply. Contentedly.

"You're a bitch," he said with some heat.

"Hmmm." She seemed unconcerned about his anger.

"I don't know why in the hell you came here!"

Katie affected a sultry whisper. "To satisfy you, dear Charles." She was acting.

That made him more angry. "And what of allowing me to see to your satisfaction?"

"I've had my satisfaction, Charles."

He felt humiliated. "That's perverse!"

"No," she said quietly, "it's just that I don't have a great personal need. It's a matter of being in control of my passions."

"And in control of mine, too, I suppose?"

She didn't reply.

He thought of overpowering her and taking her. He thought, too, of beating her. Instead, he turned his anger, his violence, to striking out at her with words: "And what of Lee? Do you play these same games with him?"

Katie raised her head from his chest, grinning at him. "Funston takes his joy in what I am."

"Well, I can't!"

She shrugged, unperturbed. Leaving the bed, she picked up the torn night-dress and walked to the door, making no move to put the garment on. Her movements were arrogantly slow.

With her hand on the knob, she turned to him. "Anyway, merry Christmas, dear Charles. I'm sorry you didn't appreciate my gift."

And she was gone.

Dewey's anger, his humiliation, gradually turned to a kind of sadness and then to concern. Katherine could ruin his future at Elkwood; he vowed not to permit that to happen.

For nearly an hour he sat in his bed contemplating what harm Katie could cause, sorting out his thoughts of how he could prevent any damaging mischief from her.

He'd need an ally to make certain he'd stay at Elkwood.

Martha?

If not one daughter, then the other. But it had to be handled carefully. That much he now understood.

III

UNDERSTANDING?

It came with study.

Elkwood itself was an encyclopedia for Charles Dewey.

He found it a complex society, a microcosm of a city, but one that was almost wholly self-sufficient. It produced its own food: corn, wheat, oats, barley, vegetables in great variety, fruits, beef, mutton, lamb, and fowl, milk and cheeses, wild game, fish from the nearby James River. It made its own products: leather tanned from hides, cloth spun from cotton and wool, lumber cut from its trees, bricks shaped from its red clay, bread baked from its grains, wine pressed from its fruits. It had its own exports: tobacco and cotton chief among them but also including lumber and wheat and sweet hay and indigo plants, from which an excellent blue vat dye could be made. It provided its own entertainments: horse racing, fox hunting, cockfighting, wild game hunting. It reveled in the beauty of its plant life; wildflowers, apple and cherry blossoms, boxwood, yew, pine, tulip poplar, dogwood.

Indeed, except for the need to go outside for the simple commodity of salt, Elkwood might have stood completely alone in the world, secure on its nearly six thousand acres.

What made the community unique and, at the same time, commonplace in Virginia, was that most of its inhabitants were in bondage.

Marshall Statler was, Charles believed, a kind man. But he owned more than one hundred fifty slaves, and it was impossible that one man could superintend the day-to-day activities of them all. Thus, he employed five overseers: four white men and a black freeman—Dewey found it difficult to understand *that*—and the treatment of the slaves was as diverse as five different men could make it. Statler gave his overseers full rein with their charges, exercising his own authority only when a Negro appealed directly to the "big house" for some kind of justice in a dispute. That such an appeal was allowed at all was a measure of Statler's sense of fairness. But Dewey recognized that the master's justice was often single-minded. Myopic, perhaps.

Charles was on hand in Statler's drawing room one day when Abner Caldwell, the overseer of the field hands, brought in a black man named Cephas. The slave knelt in supplication in front of Statler and, hands clasped in a prayerful attitude, said that Caldwell had denied his weekly ration of a peck of corn.

Cephas, although he was old—a lot of gray showed in his hair—seemed in good health and was well clothed. There was no indication that he had been physically mistreated. But his corn—his food—had been taken from him.

Statler heard the simple complaint without interruption. At the end, he looked at the overseer. "Well, Mr. Caldwell?"

"He's lazy, sir. He shirks, and the others see it."

Statler nodded. "Are you lazy, Cephas?" It was asked in a kindly manner.

"Oh, no, suh!" he protested. "Ah does what Mistah Caldwell sez."

"But Mr. Caldwell says you don't do as he asks. He says you shirk."

The Negro's gaze was on the floor. "Yas, suh." He had carried his complaint as far as he dared.

"Is that all?" asked Statler.

There was no reply.

"Well, Cephas, I think you'd better be more diligent hereafter."

And the matter was closed. The slave bowed his way out of the room, probably wondering what *diligent* meant, the overseer following him, and the penalty of withholding the ration of corn was allowed to stand. Trying for understanding, Charles reasoned that Statler had to support his overseers in matters of discipline. Nevertheless, the denial of food to an old man who was supposed to work hard in the fields made no sense to him. The logic of it defied understanding.

Statler didn't permit gratuitous beating of his slaves by the overseers. Dewey was to discover, however, that such a firm prohibition didn't apply on all Virginia plantations. The overseers at John Lee's Marsh Run, he had heard, had well-earned reputations for what came close to bestiality. And even at Elkwood, when there was a serious breech of discipline, a slave was whipped. Fighting was a reason for whipping. So, too, were stealing and showing open hostility toward an overseer. And when a whipping was ordered, the master of Elkwood was always a witness, lending his authority to the punishment.

Charles had seen brutal cat-o'-nine-tails floggings aboard the French warships, and what happened on the plantation was mild by comparison. The offender was bound with leather thongs to a heavy post, and the blows were struck with a riding crop in the hand of the black overseer, Moses. Welts were raised, but blood was seldom drawn. Statler himself counted out the lashes— the number determined by the severity of the infraction—and when it was done, it was Statler who released the thongs and who offered a few words of comfort. At Elkwood, though, a white man never struck a black man. That was Statler's hard-and-fast rule.

Dewey, when his own association with Statler was secure, asked him one day when a whipping had been administered whether there was an act by a slave that would bring more drastic punishment.

"Of course," Statler replied immediately, "murder. Or if one of the nigras should . . . uh . . . do harm to my daughters."

"What would be the penalty then?"

"Execution." There was no emotion in the answer.

"Have you ever had to carry out such a sentence?"

"Yes. Once." Statler thought for a moment. "Eleven, twelve years ago. One of the blacks was killed in a fight over a woman. There was no choice but to punish his killer."

"How?"

"A single pistol shot through the head." Again, a response without emotion. "I did it myself."

"The civil authorities weren't called in?"

"No. In the first place, what civil authority there was wouldn't have been interested." Statler sighed. "Secondly, the reality is, Charles, that I am prosecutor, judge, jury, and, unhappily, executioner here."

He closed his eyes momentarily, as if trying to block out a disagreeable scene. "I would hope that someday we may see fit to give the nigras the benefit of public law, but such is not the situation now."

Charles kept silent and Statler continued: "This is an artificial society, you know. And imperfect. Hardly a day goes by that I don't recognize those imperfections. Should one man *own* another? Probably not. It's degrading to the owner as well as the owned. Strange things happen in such a society. Samuel, my butler, is a freeman—"

"Really?"

"I hired him in Philadelphia, where he was born and educated. He works here for wages. Yet after he had been here for some time, he began to take on the attitude of the slaves. He has become . . . how do I explain this? . . . more deferential than necessary. He's *free*, but in this artificial society he doesn't *act* free. Perhaps he can't. Perhaps it was inevitable that this way of life would change him. Sad, isn't it?

"Some days I think that if I had it to do over again, I wouldn't build Elkwood on the foundation of a need for slaves. Maybe I would use the hired labor of immigrants from other countries . . . European countries, perhaps . . . I don't know. But a vast amount of labor is necessary for any enterprise as large as this estate, and that labor is . . . well, best found among the Africans. Economically, that's so. Better men than I have wrestled with this problem and have not come up with a solution."

He rubbed a hand over his eyes.

"It may be that we shall have to depend on time to solve it in its own inexorable way."

7

ELKWOOD and Charles Dewey. They became synonymous.

Time set up a tempo that far outpaced any dreams Charles might have had. Dreams were becoming realities.

Except for one thing: Martha Statler.

As days turned to weeks and weeks to months, Martha became his symbol of how much permanence he would have at Elkwood. The younger daughter could be a buffer, Charles was certain, against whatever trouble Katherine might initiate. With Martha by his side his place at the plantation, already firm because of the affection Marshall Statler had for him, would become secure. And he wanted that!

In his mind, then, the young girl became even more beautiful and more desirable. But as his desire heated—and he didn't care that some might interpret desire as ambition—she became more cool.

Comprehending that was like trying to grasp smoke. It wasn't that she was uncordial; she seemed perfectly at ease with him in daily polite conversation. They even laughed together. But it became apparent, as time went on, that Martha would not allow herself to be alone with him. Charles knew that because he had tried to be alone with her. Numerous times. And each time she had somehow maneuvered the circumstances so that someone else was present: her father, MacCallum, her sister, a housemaid. But someone.

At first, he put it down to her natural shyness. And then to simple bad luck. As he studied it, however, he realized that her actions were deliberate. *She didn't want to be alone with him.* Upset and frustrated, Dewey turned to Andrew MacCallum with his problem.

The tutor laughed at his concern. "You've simply been the victim of coincidence. Perhaps a series of coincidences."

"No—be serious," Charles snapped, annoyed by the laughter. "Is there some reason you've been able to discern that would make Miss Martha . . . uh . . . want to shun my companionship?"

MacCallum was still smiling broadly. "That's a rather archaic way to phrase the question, but, no, I haven't seen anything that would cause the young lady to, as you put it, shun your companionship."

"God damn it!"

The outburst sobered MacCallum; he had never heard Charles curse before. "Well, well . . . I had no idea the situation was that serious. I thought you were concerned for purely social reasons. I see now that it's deeper than that."

"Yes, it is."

"You mean to court her?"

"Yes. But how can I under these circumstances?"

Andrew shook his head disapprovingly. "I counseled you once, Charles, about staying clear of involvement with the Statler daughters . . ."

"I know." He thought of Katherine in his bedroom. He thought, too, of what he wanted at Elkwood.

". . . but since you now seem so determined, perhaps I can do some discreet investigating for you."

Charles's face brightened. "Would you?"

"I believe I've just volunteered for what may be one of the most foolish acts of my young life. I may find myself in a 'damned if you do, damned if you don't' situation."

II

THE bay mare Elkwood Mistress paced the stall nervously, a look of panic in her eyes, her teats dripping milk. It was dark in the barn, and two Negro grooms held oil lamps to illuminate the scene.

"It won't be long now," Marshall Statler said softly.

Charles nodded. Statler had briefed him on what to expect, but still he felt concern for the distressed animal. She stopped her pacing and pawed at the small pile of straw, seeming to search for something. Not finding it, she resumed the pacing, her tail elevated. She kicked lightly at her abdomen and turned her head full around to touch her nose to her quivering flanks. Her dark coat was gleaming with sweat.

Suddenly the mare dropped down into the straw bedding, rolling on her side, her flanks heaving rapidly. A flood of mucouslike straw-colored water gushed out of her. Gallons, Charles thought. At that moment, he could see the two front feet of the foal—tiny, delicate, dark hooves. With a great heave the mare was on her feet again, walking in tight circles. Charles turned to Statler, worry showing on his face.

"It's all right, son," the master of Elkwood assured him quietly. "She's not quite ready yet."

A minute. Two minutes. Three. Pacing all the while. Then the mare went down again in the bedding.

"Now," said Statler.

More of the feet showed, then the lower legs and the knees. As the knees became visible, Charles saw the muzzle of the foal lying against the foreleg just above the knee. Perhaps for the first time, as the head came into the light, he realized that this was a tiny horse being born. It was real—a living thing.

The mare, in full labor, contracted her powerful muscles, and the foal's shoulders slipped out. Statler moved quickly, removing a bit of fetal sac membrane from the foal's nostrils, then stepping back again. Another mighty contraction as the broad hips came through the cervix. It was done.

Charles marveled at how quickly it had happened. Certainly no more than ten minutes, once started.

Again Statler went to the foal, gently pulling it away from behind the rear of the mother and placing it near her side. Dropping to his knees, he massaged the small body with a soft cloth, drying the curly coat.

"Come here," Statler ordered, gesturing to Charles. "Feel this." He placed Charles's hand on the coat.

It was of the texture of the finest velvet. "Good Lord, it's so soft."

"Hmmm. I'm firmly convinced that God gave us the sense of touch just to have the sheer enjoyment of feeling the coat of a newborn foal. And those who haven't done so have been deprived. I can't think of another sensation of touch that rivals it. None."

Statler got to his feet again, having completed his small chore. "So you see, son, the best thing, with a normal foaling, is simply to let the mare do her job. She knows what to do, believe me."

The mare turned her head to nuzzle her newborn baby, and it let out a little squeal.

"What is it?" Charles asked.

"A colt. Another son of Skullduggery, and a beauty, too. Solid bay except for the star on the forehead."

"It's almost like a miracle."

"Not *almost*, son," Statler responded soberly, "it *is* a miracle. It's a proof—every time—that God is in His heaven."

They waited in the stall until the foal, all legs and wobbling erratically, struggled to its feet and instinctively sought the mare's teats, where it nursed for the first time. Greedily, making surprisingly loud sucking noises. Charles laughed.

Statler sighed contentedly. "Well . . . it's time we were in bed. It must be well after midnight. The blacks will stay to make sure all goes well, and that the mare passes the afterbirth cleanly. In the morning we can put them out in the pasture and watch while she teaches her son to do what he was born to do—run!"

As they walked toward the mansion, Statler asked, "Would you like to name him?"

"I'd like that very much." He paused in thought. "Since this is my first foal, so to speak, and the colt is marked as he is, would Premier Etoile—First Star—be appropriate?"

"Just fine, son, just fine." He chuckled. "Let's hope he's also a premier runner."

III

"JUST when I think I understand that man," Andrew MacCallum was saying, "he does something that I believe to be out of character.

"You mean the Rebirth decision?" Dewey was grinning.

"Of course, the Rebirth decision," the tutor snapped. "Don't take Mr. Statler's decision lightly, Charles. It was a difficult one for him to make. I saw how much he admired that Fearnought when he bought it in Charlottesville. He likes nothing better than having a winning racehorse, and Rebirth has the potential to be a winner. And now—"

Charles sobered. "You're telling me that you think Mr. Statler made an error in turning the horse over to me."

"Of course I'm not," Andrew responded defensively. "I've observed how good you are with horses. You have a natural talent. And Mr. Statler sees that, too."

"Then, why do I have the feeling that you disapprove of my training Rebirth for the races?"

"Disapprove?" MacCallum pondered that. "No, Charles, it's just that . . . well, I have great admiration for you, as I do for our employer. I don't want to see either of you unhappy. But Marshall Statler, you should understand, is not a man who tolerates losers with grace. It's my guess that his heavy wagers on his horses make tolerance most difficult, and—"

Dewey cut him off. "You're making me very uneasy, Andrew."

"I'm sorry. I didn't mean to do that." He sighed. "Mr. Statler has placed a heavy burden on you, and I can only wish you well with it."

"Thank you." The words were sullen.

The tutor tried to change the heavy tone of the conversation. "Are you pleased with the horse's progress?"

"Very much so. He has good early speed, and he's well muscled, with a competitive edge, I think."

MacCallum laughed heartily.

Dewey bridled. "Did I say something humorous?"

"Charles, Charles . . ." Andrew chuckled. "Six months ago you came here with a raw rear end from your first experience on horseback. I daresay you didn't know one end of a nag from the other. Now look at you!"

The young Frenchman finally smiled. "There has been a change, hasn't there? I think I've found my niche, Andrew."

"It seems that way, doesn't it?"

"Hmmm." A hesitation. "Uh, Andrew, have you spoken to Martha?"

"I have."

"Well, what did she say?"

"Nothing."

"Nothing?"

"I asked her if she was displeased with you for any reason," Andrew explained, "and she looked at me rather strangely, as if she considered the question stupid, and shook her head negatively. That was it. To me, that meant nothing. Or next to nothing."

Charles groaned. "Now what?"

"Let's go back to coincidence. That's what it must be, Charles—just coincidence that has conspired against your being alone with her."

"I wish I could accept that explanation."

"Try." MacCallum laughed again. "It might keep you from doing something rash."

It had been a day of exhilarating highs and depressing lows for Dewey.

Statler had informed him that the seven-year-old bay horse of the Fearnought line, which had been named Rebirth, was his to train for the races. Statler would step out of the picture, he told the young man, and concentrate on the training of the five-year-old Arab, Elkwood's White, and on the preparation of the three-year-old chestnut colt, which hadn't yet been named because it was unlikely that it would be raced until the age of five or six.

Charles hadn't expected any such move by Statler, but he accepted it readily. He had made a conscious decision to accept all that Statler offered. Statler's passion for horses became his passion. Statler's knowledge of racing became his knowledge. And, if he was to be a surrogate son, he'd accept that, too.

But what of Martha? Andrew's report worried him. If what he had in mind concerning Martha came to naught, all that Statler was offering him might one day simply evaporate.

He *needed* Martha!

IV

CHARLES was grooming Rebirth following a workout when Martha came into the barn. She stood watching him at his chores without speaking. It was only when he started to fork some fresh hay into the horse's manger that he saw her standing in the shadows.

"Miss Martha! Have you been there long?"

"Only a moment or two."

He walked to her. "It's nice to see you here. With the attention this fellow requires"—he jerked a thumb toward the horse—"I'm afraid I see you only at studies these days."

The polite conversation ended there. Both young people stood silently. Martha gazed at the floor.

"Would you like me to bring Rebirth out for your inspection?" Charles asked, wanting to keep her there.

"No, I didn't come for that." She looked up at him. "Mr. MacCallum asked me the other day whether I was displeased with you for any reason, and I didn't answer him. Since then—this is so difficult—I've decided I owe you an explanation for my actions." She hesitated.

"Miss Martha, I—"

"No, Charles, please let me go on while I have the courage. It's true, as you've probably suspected, that I have been avoiding you. But I don't think I can go on that way in light of the fact that we are"—she permitted herself the hint of a smile—"uh . . . practically brother and sister. Father has made that clear. So you should know why I've been behaving as I have."

Dewey waited for her to continue.

"I must confess that I felt some attraction to you when you first came to Elkwood." Again her eyes were avoiding his. "But I'm afraid that attraction was destroyed, Charles, when I learned of your . . . your intimacies with my sister. There! I've said it."

Charles groaned, turning away from her. "She told you what happened Christmas night?"

"Yes." Martha began to sob.

He wanted to scream curses at Katherine's name. "In great detail, no doubt?"

"Yes."

Dewey turned, coming close to her. "Did she also tell you that I didn't initiate it—that she came to my room uninvited?"

"Yes, she did." Anger showed for the first time. "But that's a poor excuse for you to make, isn't it?"

Charles nodded.

Her anger goaded her. "Katie's actions were perfectly in keeping with her convenient morals. But that *you* would be party to her . . . vulgar—" Tears came, halting the words.

"I can only ask that you forgive me," he pleaded.

"Why should I?"

"Because I love you."

Martha struck out at him, stinging his cheek with her open hand. "How dare you!" She raised her hand to hit him again, but dropped it. "Oh, what's the use?"

"The use, dear Martha," Charles replied, taking what small opportunity was presented to him, "is that we've got this terrible thing out in the open. Maybe now, with the kindness I know is in you, you'll be able to find a way to forgive me."

"No, I can't!"

"Perhaps you could try."

There was no response. Turning quickly, she left the barn.

Charles started after her, then thought better of it. He stood there, devastated. It was worse than he had expected.

Yet he wasn't really surprised at what had happened. He was trying to fathom the depth of the cruelty of what Katherine had done. Not so much to him as to her sister.

8

DEWEY paced nervously, whacking his riding crop against his boots, his mouth dry with tension. All about him at the new Petersburg racecourse, built by George Milton and his monied associates, there was an atmosphere of gaiety. Of celebration.

For Charles, however, it was a day on which he had to prove himself, and the doubts he felt were beginning to crack his veneer of confidence.

Carriages and wagons of all descriptions began arriving early on the lovely mid-June day, discharging their passengers into the open wooden stands that had been erected at the finish line. Many made for the large pavilion built along the home stretch, where the track management offered what had been widely advertised as "sumptuous dinners and the choicest liquors."

It was to be the first major race meeting in Virginia since Cornwallis's surrender at Yorktown. Although there was still some scattered fighting in the Carolinas, of which less and less was heard every day, a new English cabinet had agreed in March to recognize the independence of the colonies. Thus, the races at Petersburg were in the way of a genuine occasion for public joy.

Marshall Statler and his party had been at Petersburg for several days. The two horses he intended to campaign over the new course—Elkwood's White and Rebirth—had been tried on the track, satisfying Statler that they were ready.

Partly because of his reputation as a horseman, and partly because of his close friendship with George Milton, Statler had been invited to compete for the inaugural Petersburg Cup, a best-of-three, four-mile-heat event, the winner to take a silver bowl and a cash purse of some two thousand dollars that had been subscribed by the merchants of Petersburg.

Statler had used his influence with Milton to select his opponent in the cup race: a good competitor named Falconry owned by John Lee of Marsh Run. As a young horse, Falconry had gained a reputation as a strong runner, although his career had been limited because of the war. At nine, the chestnut horse, a grandson of the noted Maryland imported sire, Othello, was thought to be at the peak of his form. Statler's newly acquired Rebirth, on the other hand, was untested.

Nevertheless, Milton knew that a match race between horses owned by gentlemen of the stripe of Marshall Statler and John Lee would capture the public imagination. And the match was made.

Perhaps as many as five thousand—some would report that the crowd was larger—were on hand for the opening of the Petersburg course. All of them were anxious to wager not only on the longer heat races but also on the dashes—single-heat races of three miles.

Andrew MacCallum had been pressed into service as Statler's accountant. He followed the master of Elkwood around the course, making notes of his numerous wagers; the largest was a bet of "five hundred pounds English," which he made with John Lee on the outcome of the Petersburg Cup. Before the racing got under way, the tutor had written down wagers in excess of fifteen hundred pounds, plus even a few bets in Continental dollars. Included was a sum exceeding three hundred pounds on Elkwood's White, scheduled to go in the first dash of the day.

MacCallum, had he thought it worthwhile, would have protested his employer's heavy wagering. How ineffective such a protest would have been was indicated by Statler himself: "I'd like to recover the investment in these horses right off, Andrew, and by God, I think we have the opportunity here today to do that."

"Yes, sir."

"You don't approve, do you?"

"It's not in my place to approve or disapprove." The reply was stony.

Statler laughed. "You Scotsmen have the ability to disapprove just by your tone of voice."

"Am I that transparent?"

"Absolutely. But it doesn't matter, Andrew; it doesn't matter at all. We're going to win today."

MacCallum waved the copybook into which he had written the wagers. "I certainly hope so, sir."

"Guaranteed, Mr. MacCallum! I'd like to make a recommendation that you act on that guarantee." He was smiling broadly.

"Thank you. I'll give that some consideration."

Statler, laughing again at the tutor's aversion to gambling, strolled away.

In the first dash, in which Elkwood's White was ridden by one of the plantation's Negroes, a lad named Horace, the Statler horse won in a close finish, beating a Richmond entry by only a head. Statler's delighted whoops could he heard across the entire course as he dispatched MacCallum to collect his winnings. Andrew, still disapproving, hoped that he wouldn't be sent to pay off on the much larger wagers on the Petersburg Cup.

Statler, MacCallum, and Dewey had spent days discussing the strategy for the race against Lee's Falconry. While the slave, Horace, was an experienced jockey—he weighed only one hundred five pounds—it was decided that

Charles would ride Rebirth for the cup event. Statler reasoned, and Mac-
Callum agreed, that Charles was more familiar with the horse, having ridden
him during the entire training period.

"You can best judge the stamina of Rebirth," Statler told the young
Frenchman. "Ask for speed when you can; save him when you should—and
I'm not concerned about the added weight." Charles would ride at one hun-
dred sixty pounds.

The Elkwood strategists guessed that Falconry would be handled by Lee's
black rider, Cassius, who would be at about one hundred thirty. He was a
strong jockey, much experienced, but Statler was able to discount what might
have seemed an advantage for the Lee runner: "Cassius is a straightaway rider,
able to handle a powerful animal, but unable—or unwilling—to be adven-
turous. He follows instructions meticulously, and that makes him totally predictable. In a tight squeeze, Lee's boy cannot think for himself."

Dewey's nervousness as the race approached left him scarcely able to say a
civil word to anyone. When his first friend in Virginia, George Milton, came
up to him to wish him well, Charles could only mumble an acknowledgment.

"Saddle up!" came the command from the steward.

A Negro groom led Rebirth forward. Statler supervised the saddling as
Charles stood by, tense and tight-lipped.

"Remember now, Charles," Statler said when he was satisfied with the
saddle, "get an immediate lead. Not too far out, mind you, but a decisive
lead. And ride steadily after that, well in hand. We want Falconry to have to
catch us at the end."

"Yes, sir."

The steward called for Statler and Lee to draw lots for starting positions, and
Lee drew the inside spot. Statler shrugged; it meant little in a four-mile race.

As Charles stood waiting, trying to concentrate on what he had to do, Martha came up to him quietly, touching his arm.

"I thought perhaps you might want to carry this," she said, pressing a
delicate lace handkerchief into his hand. "For luck, you know."

He was flustered. "Miss Martha, I—"

"Later." She touched his lips with her fingers. "We can talk later. When
we're alone."

She smiled at him, brushed a kiss against his cheek, and skipped away.

II

"To mount!" the steward cried.

Statler boosted Charles into the saddle, making certain he was comfortable
with the stirrups. He patted his leg.

"Patience, son, patience. Remember that you've got another heat after this
one, maybe two."

"Yes, sir."

Charles wheeled the horse and trotted him slowly to the start line. Falconry
was already there, held firmly in hand by the strong Negro jockey. Charles

took his position to the outside, some twenty feet to the left of his rival. He wanted to be well in the clear at the start.

There was no noise from the crowd now; it had been replaced by the silence of anticipation. Both Falconry and Rebirth walked up to the start evenly, and the starter's drum tapped.

They were away!

Dewey rapped his mount smartly with the whip, asking him for speed. By the time they had gone two hundred yards, and were into the first turn, Rebirth was in the lead with an advantage of three lengths. Charles took a steady hold on the reins and had his horse under control, running easily.

And that's the way it went for more than three clockwise miles, with Rebirth maintaining his three-length lead under a stout hold.

As they came into the final half-mile, Charles glanced over his shoulder to see his rival, Cassius, going to the whip. The Negro jockey had been patient, saving his horse for one final challenge at the end.

Rebirth felt a slight prod of the spur, and Charles gave him his head without further urging.

Into the stretch they came, with Falconry gaining ground. Dewey, however, sat coolly. Unconcerned. He could feel that the horse under him had a lot in reserve. And he knew that Falconry's bid had been started too late.

As they neared the finish line, Charles could hear Funston Lee screaming at the Marsh Run jockey: "Whip him, damn you, whip him!"

They went across the finish line with Rebirth the winner by a single length, but the race wasn't really that close. Charles had done what he had wanted to do, what Statler had wanted him to do: he had won the race while saving the horse. Rebirth had not been extended at all; the blooded horse was barely drawing a deep breath as Charles dismounted to accept congratulations from the beaming master of Elkwood plantation.

Several yards away, Cassius, the Negro rider, had dismounted from Falconry to face the fury of Funston Lee.

"Damn you, boy, you let him steal the race from you! You could've won that heat, you ignorant bastard!"

Lee lashed out with his riding crop, striking the boy wickedly across the face. He was restrained by his father from doing more.

Charles turned away from the scene. It sickened him.

The time for the first heat was announced at 7:41½.

"My, my," Statler commented, "I didn't realize the pace was that fast." He grinned. "We seem to have got something really good from Shackelford for our gold."

In the period between the Petersburg Cup heats, when the racing managers had scheduled another dash, it was announced that the Marsh Run horse would have a rider change for the second heat.

"Mr. Funston Lee will be up on Falconry," the steward bellowed.

Statler was unperturbed by the news. "It doesn't change our plan," he said. "We ought to be able to get our initial lead again, because Rebirth simply has more quickness away from the start. But I'm certain that young Lee is going to keep him closer to the pace this time."

MacCallum added a caution: "Be careful of Funston, Charles. He's capable of doing almost anything to win."

III

THE second heat was called.

As Charles was boosted into the saddle again, Statler added his warning to MacCallum's.

"Andrew is right, son, you've got to be careful of Funston. Stay clear of him. Do you hear me, son? Stay clear of him!"

"Yes, sir, I understand."

Once more Rebirth was positioned some twenty feet to the left of Falconry, once more the starting drum tapped, and once more Charles shot his horse into the lead with a solid whack from his whip.

Into the first turn, however, Lee had Falconry up closer. Only one length separated them.

There was no relaxing in the ride this time. Rebirth maintained his slight lead, with Charles keeping his stout hold. But Falconry was right there, pressing the pace. Charles began to worry that perhaps the pace was too fast now, but he was determined to follow Statler's strategy to keep the lead as long as he could.

At the starting line, Statler was also worried. "Too swift! Too swift!" he complained to MacCallum.

They completed three rounds that way. Just a length apart.

As they swept by the stands to begin the final mile, Lee went to the whip. By the time they were into the turn, Falconry was breathing on Rebirth's flank.

In the run down the backstretch they were lapped on each other, Lee whipping all the way. Charles tried to sit quietly on his horse, knowing it wasn't time yet to make his move.

Falconry and Rebirth went into the last turn that way, stride for stride, running as a team. Lee was simultaneously spurring and whipping, before and behind the girth, raising his arm high in the air, his body thrown forward with every whipping exertion, punishing the horse.

Falconry threw his rail in the air, flagging it up and down in the manner of a tired runner. Or one in pain.

Into the homestretch now—still as one.

Suddenly, just as Charles raised his whip to ask Rebirth for his final effort, Falconry came over sharply.

They bumped heavily!

Rebirth bobbled momentarily in his stride, and Falconry shot into the lead, Lee whipping and driving almost insanely, screaming at the top of his lungs.

They crossed the finish line that way, Falconry the winner by half a length.

This time Rebirth was breathing heavily when Charles pulled him up, a white foam of sweat dripping from him. Statler ran to them, quickly examining the horse to see whether he had been injured in the collision. When he was satisfied that he hadn't been, Charles slid out of the saddle, and a Negro groom led Rebirth away, to walk him cool and prepare him for the final heat.

"He came over on me suddenly," Charles tried to explain. "It happened so quickly I couldn't avoid him."

"Of course you couldn't, son." Statler patted him on the shoulder. "I'm just thankful you didn't fall."

"I thought for a moment we would."

"Now you know why Andrew and I cautioned you about Funston."

MacCallum, who had gone to check on the conditon of Falconry, joined them.

"Lee's horse is badly distressed," the tutor reported. "He's been scoured at the girth—several spur cuts, I'd say—and in that wild whipping, Lee struck him too far back and has not only cut him on the sheath but has made a deep incision on the testicles." The Scotsman shook his head sadly. "The blood's flowing rather profusely from those cuts."

"Will he be able to start for the third heat?" Statler wanted to know.

"Were he my horse he wouldn't. But—" MacCallum shrugged.

The time for the second heat was announced at 7:44 flat. Statler groaned. "Oh, my, too fast! I hope Rebirth has something left."

IV

FALCONRY appeared at the starting line when the third heat was called. Statler shook his head sadly. "The damned fools!"

To Charles: "We have a fine horse here," he said soberly, "and I see no need to damage him to win this single race. You have only one duty, Charles, and that's to bring him back in one piece."

The master of Elkwood put his hands on Dewey's shoulders, holding him firmly, looking into his eyes. "One duty only, son. If you can win this race cleanly, I would prefer that. But if the horse becomes distressed, if there is *any danger at all* to his well-being, stop him and pull him up. No one race, no wager, is worth the life of a horse this gallant! Is that clear?"

"Yes, sir."

"One other thing: Whatever the conclusion today, I want you to know that I'm proud of how you prepared Rebirth for this race and of how you've ridden this afternoon. You have the makings of a fine horseman, son."

Charles thought he saw tears glistening in Statler's eyes. He had a lump of emotion in his own throat. He decided it was best if he didn't try to speak.

As the call of "To mount!" came again, MacCallum said, "Caution, Mr. Dewey, caution."

Charles smiled at him.

At drum tap for the third heat it was Falconry, with Funston Lee whipping and spurring, going into the lead. A mighty roar went up from the crowd.

Dewey was content to be two lengths off the pace, saving his horse as best he could. He could feel Rebirth's weariness under him, and he let him run without special urging. The pace was slow, but reasonably steady.

Falconry labored in front, his tail flagging all the while. Even the impetuous

Lee realized the distress of his animal, merely holding the reins, satisfied to be in the lead.

They covered three torturous miles in that manner, Rebirth two lengths back, seeming to be running easily.

As they went into the first turn of the final mile, Dewey needed to know whether his horse had anything left. He reached back to tap Rebirth with the whip to test his response. It was instantaneous, surprising Charles a bit. The competitive courage of the bay horse carried him abreast of Falconry as screams came up from the spectators.

On the backstretch, they were running as a team again, both riders sitting still.

Into the final turn now in that same manner. Lee looked over at Dewey momentarily, his face showing his anxiety.

Through the turn they went, matching strides, and the homestretch loomed in front of them.

Funston cracked Falconry hard with his whip. It seemed that the sound of it echoed. And he dug a spur deep into his horse's flank. There was an instinctive forward burst, and then Falconry bobbled, weaving erratically, drunkenly, as his legs failed to do what his heart instructed.

Charles guided Rebirth around the stricken rival, not needing the whip to do it, simply trotting to the finish line the winner.

Somehow Charles felt none of the exhilaration he had anticipated. He looked back to see Funston coming out of the saddle as Falconry went to his knees, his great body heaving convulsively.

Once across the finish line, and ignoring the cheers of the crowd, Charles dismounted, tossed the reins to an Elkwood groom, and ran back to where Falconry was down on the track.

"Is there anything I can do?" he asked Lee.

"Do? What the hell can you do?" Funston growled. "It seems to me you've done enough already."

John Lee came up to the distressed horse with two of his grooms, giving the blacks instructions on what to do for the animal, completely ignoring his son.

Charles watched the ministrations to Falconry for a moment or two. Then he addressed Funston again. "Don't we have some unfinished business?"

Scowling, Funston reached into his pocket, coming out with some money, counting bills into Charles's outstretched hand. He said not a word.

Dewey turned on his heel, moving quickly to where Rebirth was being unsaddled. "Is he well?"

"Exhausted," Statler answered, "but he doesn't appear to be in any distress."

"Thank God."

MacCallum tapped Charles on the arm. "What was all that about?" he asked, pointing to the Lee group.

"Oh, that? I was just collecting my wager. A hundred pounds."

"A hundred pounds!" Andrew was aghast. "Where did you get a hundred pounds to bet?"

"I didn't have a hundred pounds."

"But if you had lost—"

Dewey shrugged. "I would have thought of something."

Statler, laughing uproariously, gathered Charles into his arms, hugging him tightly. "Son, you've learned more than one lesson today." He looked at the tutor. "What say you now, Mr. MacCallum?"

"I'd say the both of you have lost your minds." But Andrew was smiling.

Katherine rushed onto the scene, trailed by Martha. "Oh, Charles," the elder sister gushed, "it was such a masterful ride!" She tried to put her arms around him, but Charles evaded her and walked to Martha. Very deliberately.

"This, I believe, belongs to you," he said, taking her handkerchief from his sleeve, returning it to her. "Perhaps you will lend it to me again, on another day, when I need the blessings of your luck."

"It will always be available to you," she answered shyly.

He bent and kissed her softly on the lips. "I'll count on it."

Katherine's face darkened. She turned angrily toward the Lee party, where Falconry was now on his feet, the grooms rubbing him with wet cloths. But before she had taken half a dozen steps in the direction of Funston, he was otherwise engaged. Two young women had come up to him, giggling coyly. And Lee walked off, one admirer on each arm, toward the refreshments pavilion.

"It's the defeated warrior who needs the solace," he said loudly. "You *are* offering solace, aren't you?"

The Petersburg ladies giggled again.

9

REBIRTH is what happened at Elkwood in Goochland County, Virginia. Part of it on the racing prowess of a bay horse by that name, and part of it on the unstinting endeavors of the human participants in the drama of making the plantation what it was before the war. And even more than it had been.

Marshall Statler spared neither personal effort nor money in his determination to bring renewed greatness to Elkwood. And side by side with him worked a young orphan of uncertain parentage, a deserter from the French navy, who called himself Charles Dewey.

A total stranger coming to the plantation in 1783 or 1784 would have immediately concluded that Charles was the natural son of the master of Elkwood. Their affection for each other was readily apparent. Charles had taken on the mannerisms of Statler—the way he talked, the way he gave orders, the way he smiled and frowned. His speech patterns were also Statler's, and little by little, the French accent was being buried in the soft drawl of Virginia.

In his second year at the plantation, Charles was given the position of horse manager, and all of his energies were channeled in that direction. He no longer had the time, nor the patience, for that matter, to teach French to the Statler sisters, but he made certain that his own education went forward—not in a classroom but through books Andrew MacCallum ordered for him from Philadelphia and New York and London.

And he had money of his own now, his purse starting with the winning of the audacious wager with Funston Lee in the spring of 1782 and fattened with a share of all the winnings of the Elkwood racehorses after that. In clear reality, Statler had made Charles his partner in the horse business.

Dewey didn't squirrel his money away. He purchased several blooded broodmares in his own name. In 1784, he helped to finance a syndicate of Virginia horsemen who imported the English sire, Medley. That stallion, moved to a different farm each year for breeding purposes, would stand his third season at Elkwood. Medley's predominantly gray get were most impressive.

Charles would further the horse business more than Statler had dared hope. He persuaded his patron to let him have three black lads as full-time jockeys so that he would not have to rely on the part-time riders they had been using from among the field hands. The experiment was a twofold success. Negro boys on the plantation could now look forward to some hope, to some goal in life, even though still slaves. That hope permeated the entire plantation, resulting in fewer conflicts with the overseers and fewer appeals by slaves to Statler's informal court of last resort.

Charles trained the young jockeys carefully, even supervising their diets. In sum, Elkwood had the best race riders in Virginia—making Elkwood the biggest winner at the Virginia tracks. And bringing more money to Charles Dewey.

Money, while he didn't hesitate to risk it on wagers or the purchase of horses, represented an important goal for him.

He wanted to marry.

II

"WHY?" Charles asked her.

"Pure selfishness," Martha replied, smiling sweetly at him. "I decided that Katherine had controlled my life long enough. That I deserved to have what I wanted for a change. And"—she hesitated—"I wanted you. Katherine's Christmas night affair, I decided selfishly, wasn't going to deprive me."

"I'm glad," Dewey said, surprised by her candor.

It was the weekend following the Petersburg Cup race, a hot late-June Saturday, and they were going on a picnic. By themselves. Where, they didn't know, but they followed the meandering course of the James.

It was the small grove of wild cherry trees that welcomed them finally, the land sloping off gradually down to the river. The trees formed an arbor of sorts, a natural retreat for them.

They watered the horses when they got there, tethering them where they could graze without the need for further care. Martha spread a tablecloth on the grass and set out a feast from the basket they had carried with them: fresh bread, cheese, jam, cured ham, cold chicken, wine. It was an idyllic setting, and they ate with hardly a word being spoken. It seemed not a moment for words.

The sun was directly above them as they ate, and when they had finished, they stretched out on the grass, looking up through the branches at the cloudless blue sky, their fingers touching. Content. They might even have dozed for a moment or two. Then Charles rolled over, his face above Martha's, and kissed her gently.

"You're the loveliest thing I've ever seen," he whispered.

She smiled at him. "There are a lot of things, dear Charles, that you haven't seen."

"Maybe. But I can't even imagine that anything lovelier could exist."

"Not even a blooded horse," she teased.

He thought for a moment. "Which one?"

Their laughter echoed through the glade.

Martha pulled his head down on her breast. He could feel the steady rhythm of her heartbeat, and he began to hum to its cadence.

"What *are* you doing?" she giggled.

"I'm singing the song of your heartbeats."

"Are there any words to the song?"

A hesitation. "Yes."

"What are they?"

"I love you."

"Only that?"

"No other words matter."

More silence passed between them—lovely, contented, happy silence. And they dozed again in the heat of the afternoon.

When Charles awoke he was thirsty. Coming to his feet, he stretched languidly. "Do you want to walk to the river?" He reached out for her, pulling her up to him, kissing her, holding her tightly.

Hand in hand they strolled down to the water. Charles dropped to his knees, made a cup of his hands, and drank from the clear river. "Come on," he said, inviting her to join him.

"You drink like an animal, and I'm not an animal."

"Oh, but you are!" He laughed at her. "You're my favorite animal. *Homo sapiens*, the wise and intelligent animal. Female branch, of course."

"Of course." She laughed, too—it was so easy to laugh—as she got down beside him and also drank.

"The water's pleasant," he said.

"Hmmm."

"Warm enough to swim." He began to take off his boots.

"Charles—"

"I've decided to go swimming."

She affected a pout. "And leave me sitting here on the bank?"

"No, I think you ought to join me."

Martha just watched him as he quickly stripped off his clothing and stood naked by the side of the river. With no embarrassment. Lithe and muscular and proud.

"I'll wait for you," he said as he dived into the slowly moving current and, with easy strokes, swam to the middle of the stream. He waved to her. "Come on!"

With less assurance, Martha also removed her clothes. Charles watched her from the river. And he gasped at the beauty of her—the perfect symmetry of her form, the firm, full, high breasts, the creamy smooth skin—as she stood momentarily in the bright sunlight and then walked into the water to be with him.

They frolicked like young otters, diving and surfacing and splashing and touching and kissing and laughing. For more than a half-hour they were aquatic beings—the only aquatic beings in the world. Finally, they made for the bank, Charles offering her a hand to bring her out of the water into his arms. He kissed her passionately.

Slowly they sank to the grass, not letting go of each other, and made love so naturally, so effortlessly, that it seemed the act had been created for that moment. They stretched out, in time, to let the sun dry them.

"Charles?"

"Hmmm."

"Ought we think about getting back?"

"To where?" he asked

Martha's tinkling laughter filled the grove. "To home, of course."

"I *am* home."

"Charles, dear, be serious." She glanced at the sun's westward course. "If we're not back by nightfall, Father will be concerned."

He groaned. "I suppose we ought to be practical, but I don't want to be. The way I feel now I don't ever want to be practical again."

"It *is* lovely here." She traced little designs on his chest with her fingers, kissing him as she did.

"What do you think your father will say?"

"About what?" she asked.

"When I tell him I want to marry his daughter."

"Don't you think you ought to ask the daughter first?"

Charles grinned at her. "A detail."

"Charles Dewey!" She punched him playfully.

He sobered. "Miss Martha Statler, will you be my wife?"

"Yes."

"And have my babies?"

"Dozens."

"And be my lover for life?"

"Your lover for life," Martha pledged.

III

"I MUST admit that the prospect is pleasing to me," Marshall Statler said, "but I cannot agree to it."

Dewey was shocked. "Why not, sir?"

"Because the two of you are too young for marriage. You're . . . uh . . . what?"

"Nineteen."

Statler smiled tolerantly. "But not quite, eh?"

"I may be older. I just don't know."

"Let me be charitable," the master of Elkwood went on, "and agree that you are nineteen. It's a fact that Martha is just turned sixteen. I'd be a poor father if I agreed to her marriage at that age."

Charles's face was sullen.

"There's another problem: My elder daughter is not yet married. It's my belief that she deserves the first opportunity to be married."

"Is that fair?"

The question rankled Statler. "Whether you believe it fair or not, that's the way it shall be!"

"I'm sorry, sir." Charles wanted no break with his benefactor. "I didn't mean to be disrespectful."

"Of course you didn't, son." Statler came close to where Charles was sitting and laid a reassuring hand on his shoulder. "There are times, Charles, when it's difficult to be a parent. I only wish their mother were here now." A pause. "But I must run this family as best I know how, and I believe strongly that my elder child must have some preference."

"Yes, sir." Charles carefully pondered his next words. "Isn't it possible, though, that Miss Katherine might . . . uh . . . delay marriage? Or not marry at all?"

Statler laughed. "Katherine? I would think that highly unlikely. Young Lee, after all, is paying court to her now."

"Yes, sir."

There was a strained break in the conversation.

"I don't want you to take offense, Charles," Statler began again, "but I must ask that you not force my hand in this matter. I would be most distressed—most distressed!—if I were presented with a *fait accompli.*"

"Sir?"

"If Martha became pregnant, to put a candid face on it."

Dewey said nothing.

"Ought I be distressed now?"

"Oh, no, sir. It's just that—"

"Son, don't imagine that you're the first young buck who's been in love and felt the . . . urgings of that love. I had those same feelings—God, it seems so long ago—and I understand how you feel now. But the fact remains: I can't agree to your marriage to Martha at this time. I must insist that Katherine marry first."

IV

THE stresses of Marshall Statler's decision were felt by all.

By Martha: "We'd be married now if it weren't for *you*," she blurted one day when Katie teased her about Charles. "It's the fault of your on-again-off-again affair with that ass Funston!"

"Ass!" Katherine responded angrily. "He's certainly a better catch than your bastard Frenchman, who saw nothing wrong in being intimate with your sister. Or have you conveniently forgotten *that* in your euphoric state of puppy love?"

"You bitch!" Martha screamed at her. "You horrid bitch!"

By Charles: "Why should *I* have to wait?" he complained to Andrew Mac-Callum, after several months had passed without news of any marriage plans of Katherine and Funston.

"Mr. Statler obviously feels that he's doing the right thing," the tutor commented.

"The right thing!" Dewey shook his head sadly. "What I can't understand, Andrew, is how Mr. Statler sees Funston as an acceptable son-in-law. He's such a—"

MacCallum grinned. "You don't have to say it. But look at it this way: the Lees are an important family in Virginia. And in this society, family—breeding, if you will—is paramount. Marshall probably isn't too happy with Funston. But he's a Lee! And there's value in the coupling of the Lee and Statler families."

"It sounds too much like horse breeding to suit me."

"In a sense, the same value judgments are in play," Andrew admitted. "Good blood with good blood."

By Katherine: "Ah 'clare," Katherine overheard one of the housemaids saying one day, "Ah caint unnerstan' why Miss Katherine don' grab thet stud by th' ears an' drag 'im to th' preacher."

"Mebbe the ears ain't where she ought to grab 'im," another suggested. The women roared with laughter.

As Katherine seethed.

Passage of time added to the stress, the pressure finally going back to Marshall Statler.

Early in January 1785, Charles sat down with Statler to review the racing season and to look ahead to the foaling schedule for the spring. Elkwood's record at the track had been an impressive one: its horses had started in sixty-seven races, winning fifty, a mark probably unequaled among Virginia horsemen. That Statler was more than a little pleased with the work of his protégé was obvious.

Charles sought the words to take advantage of that pleasurable feeling. "Sir, there's another matter—"

"Oh, by the way," Statler interrupted, "I've had a communication from Mr. Hyde at Fredericksburg about the possibility of importing an English stallion named Shark. A good one at the track, apparently. Winner of some sixteen thousand pounds and presented with 'The Whip' at Newmarket. That's the emblem of the British championship. Mr. Hyde believes he might become available."

"I think we ought to look into it."

"So do I. Now, you were saying, another matter?"

"Yes, sir," Charles started cautiously. "Martha's soon to be seventeen, and I'll be twenty, and there's been no move by Miss Katherine to—"

Statler smiled at him. "All right, Charles, I'll speak to Katherine. I can appreciate that you feel you've waited long enough."

It all came to a head on a cold February evening. Lee had come to Elkwood for dinner, and, as darkness fell, Katherine and Funston strolled away from the mansion, making their way to the breeding barn. As they had done on other occasions, they climbed the ladder to the loft on the second floor and settled down in the fragrant hay.

Funston fumbled to undo Katherine's bodice in a clumsy and rough manner. She pushed him away.

He laughed crudely. "I'm just trying to offer some warming exercise on this otherwise cold evening."

"Is that *all* you think about?"

"Occasionally other thoughts do manage to force their way in." He fondled her breasts through the clothing.

She heard a mental echo of the housemaids' raucous laughter. "Stop it! I'm not one of your Petersburg whores!"

Funston sank back in the hay, smirking at her. "You're right, Katie, you're not. You're much more talented than they."

Katherine fought to control her anger, determined to get the upper hand on the arrogant Lee. She smiled sweetly at him. "My superior talents, Funston, are more apparent than you think."

"Oh? How's that?" He was still smirking.

"I'm pregnant," she lied.

The smirk was gone. He stared at her. "Pregnant?"

"With child," she insisted, with as much pride as she could feign.

"Well, well," Funston sighed. He paused in thought. "Somehow what comes to mind, Katie, is a scrap from Mr. Shakespeare: 'she that makes me sin awards me pain.'"

"Funston!"

"Just seeking to bring some levity to this otherwise tense situation." His demeanor sobered. "What now?"

"I think we should go to Father and set a wedding date, don't you?"

Lee shrugged in agreement. And resignation.

10

INVITATIONS went out to some three hundred of Virginia's elite—the first families of the Old Dominion—to attend the weddings of the daughters of Marshall Statler.

Plural. Weddings. Daughters.

There was to be a double wedding ceremony at Elkwood on the first Saturday in April, a date selected because the weather could be expected to be cooperative then and the guests would be able to travel comfortably.

Unused to asking others to take a role in his decisions, the master of the plantation had decided on the double wedding arbitrarily but with the best of intentions. A double wedding, he thought, would be a happy compromise: Katherine would be married first, and Charles and Martha wouldn't have to wait any longer.

It was a compromise that pleased only himself.

Charles and Martha had wanted their wedding to be something intensely personal, not a show at Elkwood. Both realized they would offend Statler if they complained, so they kept silent. Except in those moments when they were alone.

"I hope I have the even temper," Charles said, "to share my most important day with that arrogant fool, Funston."

Martha tried to placate him. "You won't be sharing it with Funston, you'll be sharing it with me." She kissed him. "Funston will be merely a witness. One of many."

Her sister had to listen to a tirade.

"What an insult!" Lee stormed. "To be asked to be associated on my own wedding day with a . . . a *foreigner* of no known background! Good God! I have half a mind to refuse."

Katherine, who was also displeased with the turn of events, nevertheless sounded more practical. "Very well, then, refuse! And leave me with a bastard child."

She was comfortable with the lie. It had given her what she wanted.

II

"YOUNG ladies and gentlemen," Statler said with deliberate formality, "I wish to offer a toast to you all."

It was the third Sunday in March. Statler had planned a dinner that he meant to be sumptuous and special. He had gone into his wine cellar for his finest brandy.

They raised their glasses.

"To love, and its future at Elkwood," he intoned. "To health, and its continuation at Elkwood. To happiness, and its proliferation at Elkwood. And to Elkwood itself, which is about to embark on its most momentous era!"

Glasses were clinked together.

"Now," Statler continued, "there are some realities we must discuss—happy realities, really, because we are about to become one family, united in Elkwood. I need not tell you that I'm already proud of this plantation. But with the addition of these two young men"—a nod to Charles, then to Funston—"Elkwood will become even greater."

There was not another sound in the dining room.

"After a proper time for a honeymoon"—he smiled broadly—"Katherine and Funston will live here in this mansion. And Funston, as the husband of my elder daughter, will be placed in charge of the day-to-day operations of this estate."

Lee came half out of his chair. "Excuse me, sir, but—"

Statler raised a hand to stop him.

"One moment, please, Funston. Charles, as the husband of my younger daughter—and in recognition of the substantial role he has already played in this aspect of Elkwood—will be in complete charge of the horse breeding and racing. Because I realize that both of you young couples will want, in your married states, a measure of privacy, Martha and Charles will be deeded some six hundred acres, that portion of Elkwood adjacent to the river, where a new home will be built for them. Work will start immediately."

Statler clapped his hands together like a delighted child. "Now, what think you of that?"

Lee coughed nervously. "Sir, I'm appreciative of the offer, but my responsibilities, now and in the future, lie at Marsh Run, and I don't see how—"

"Your father and I have fully discussed this matter," Statler cut in, "and we're in agreement that, at this time, he is perfectly capable in his role as master of Marsh Run, and that my plan to have you manage Elkwood is valid now and for quite a few years into the future."

Funston was in shock. "But, sir . . . you will still be master here."

"That's just it, Funston, I won't be. I intend to retire. To be—how shall I put this?—Elkwood's elder statesman, available to both you and Charles for whatever guidance you may desire of me. But you young men will be in charge. Yes, young sirs, in charge!"

Lee's face was drained of its color. "I'm sorry, sir, I simply don't understand this. My ties with Marsh Run—"

"Will continue as before," Statler interrupted again. "There will eventually, it seems clear to me, come a time when the assets of Elkwood and Marsh Run will become one—a time when you and Charles will see fit to meld the two estates together."

He laughed gaily. "I can foresee the day when the joint racing stable of Elkwood and Marsh Run will be the greatest in this whole wonderful country!"

Charles was left almost speechless. Like Funston, he was appalled by the prospect of what Statler intended to put into being, with the acquiescence of John Lee.

He tried to put on a brave face. "I'm overwhelmed, sir, by your generosity. I'll make every effort to justify your trust in me."

They were empty words; the blow to the young man went deep. *Elkwood would not be his! Could never be his!* The thoughts that coursed through his mind made him feel guilty. But he couldn't dismiss them. It was an immutable fact that he was marrying the wrong daughter. Katherine, as the elder, could have given him Elkwood; Martha could not. He loved Martha, he told himself, but perhaps it was true that he loved the plantation, and the power it represented, more.

Young Dewey understood, if Statler did not, that the division of responsibilities gave Funston Lee control. No matter what Charles did, he would always be subservient to Lee. He would always be "that Frenchman."

That wasn't good enough for him. It wasn't what his guardian spirit had told him he would have. And he meant to have it—if not at Elkwood, then elsewhere!

The dinner ended, Statler sat in his drawing room with the Scottish tutor. "I wish I had the words, Andrew, to express to you how full my heart is tonight. I know there might be some . . . uh . . . growing pains in this arrangement, but I see a new day for Elkwood. A glorious new day."

"Yes, sir, I'm sure it will be." MacCallum didn't want to say anything to dampen Statler's enthusiasm.

However, the Scotsman was fully aware of the animosity between Charles and Funston. And he marveled at Statler's ability to submerge that reality. Statler, he was certain, recognized the hostility between the two men, and it was only the gambler in him that allowed him to risk the future of Elkwood.

It would be a wager this time with long odds.

III

FOR some months an idea had been bouncing around in Dewey's consciousness, although he had managed to dismiss it many times as either impractical or, worse, stupid. But on the night before his wedding, when sleep deserted him, Charles lit a candle and started a letter to the Comte de Grasse, Admiral of the French Fleet.

"Honorable Sir," he wrote, "I begin this communication with great misgivings, fully aware that my unexplained departure"—he couldn't bring himself to use the word *desertion*—"from the *Ville de Paris* might have brought you anger and revulsion. At long last I find the courage to offer an apology, knowing the inadequacies of such an act. There cannot, of course, be an apology for the naval regulations violated; therefore, the apology is to yourself, sir, for the violations of your kindness and trust.

"I am in Virginia, having changed my name to Charles Dewey. On the morrow, I am to be married . . ."

Charles wrote swiftly now, describing to the admiral his good fortune at Elkwood, explaining his work with the horses, making some laudatory comparisons of his patrons, de Grasse and Statler, telling of his schooling with Andrew, and adding a lavish, loving description of Martha.

"So you can see that I am the most fortunate of men, and could only be more fortunate if there was some assurance that I had, in small measure, your blessing on this happiest of days for me. I did not take leave of the *Ville de Paris* for reasons of dissatisfaction. Instead, I honestly believed that I had a calling to leave—to be an American! Time and circumstances have conspired to prove me right. Your kindnesses will always be in my heart."

Charles signed the letter, "Your grateful servant, Charles Dupree." He would address it later to the Naval Department in Paris, certain that it would be forwarded to a man as important as Admiral de Grasse.

He blew out the candle, lay back on his bed, and saw the image of Martha walking into the waters of the James, her hand outstretched to him, her beauty filling him with awe. The waking recollection melded into seeing her in his dreams as sleep finally came.

IV

CHARLES never would have admitted it, but the wedding day was a disappointment. So much effort had gone into the planning that the day itself seemed an anticlimax.

True, it was a day of beauty. The weather was superb. A Philadelphia decorator had turned the huge entrance hall into an exquisite wedding chapel filled with a wide variety of flowers and plants. And Martha, in her white Paris wedding gown of lace and silk and velvet, couldn't have been lovelier. Somehow, though, Dewey just walked through the ceremony, almost disinterested.

He would confess later to Andrew that he could remember clearly only one thing about the day: Martha's glowing face as they exchanged vows in front of the Reverend Mr. Smith. Andrew would reassure him, "Had I been in your circumstance, old friend, that's the one thing I'd want to remember. She was *so* beautiful."

Perhaps it was the crush of the wedding guests that disconcerted him, or the overexuberance displayed by Statler all day long, or the nervous wait he had while Katherine and Funston were married. Whatever it was, he had expected something else that he couldn't enunciate. And didn't find.

It turned into a long day, with too lavish a buffet dinner, too many toasts with French champagne, and too many gifts to be opened and fussed over.

Darkness had come before Charles and Martha could leave the Elkwood mansion to go to their unfinished cottage on the edge of the plantation, sitting on a knoll overlooking the James River. The blacks had worked hard to finish enough of their new home so that they could spend their wedding night there. In the morning, they were to leave for a honeymoon trip to Philadelphia, and the rest of the house would be completed by the time they returned.

They drove along a new road leading to the cottage in a small open cart, Martha nestled against him, and Charles holding the reins lightly.

"I thought of you last night," he said softly, "or perhaps I dreamed it, of you walking into the river to come to me."

"I remembered that, too, last night."

"Did you, really?"

"Uh-huh. And I remembered making love to you that first time. And I wished, right then, that I would be transported to *this* moment—going to my new home with my darling Charles." She giggled. "I was also wishing that you'd come to my room right then." Her arms went around his neck, and she kissed him again and again..

"You have a naughty streak in you." He laughed.

"I do. I admit I do." She kissed him once more.

"Was the day all you expected?" he asked.

"Oh, Charles dear, it was lovely!"

He sighed. "And a bit tiring."

"That, too. But the best part of the day is still to come—when I can go to bed with Mr. Charles Dewey, my husband. And love him and love him and love him." Martha snuggled even closer to him.

He clucked to the horse for more speed.

11

ADVERSITY was not a stranger to Dewey. Having been born to it, he had learned to anticipate it, to ready himself for it, to turn it aside, even to bend it to his advantage. That was a strength of his character. Yet he wanted to believe that adversity was not a necessity of living; that, given reason and rationality, the seeds of adversity need not be sown. And that desire to believe was a weakness.

Within twenty-four hours of his return to Elkwood after the honeymoon, and after the return of Funston and Katherine from a similar trip to Charleston, Charles learned that reason was not a weapon he could use with Lee. The young Virginia gentleman who was now his brother-in-law had no desire to be rational. He proved it with one impetuous act.

Charles's three young Negro jockeys, who had been under his guidance for nearly two years, were suddenly reassigned to the ranks of the field hands.

"It's my clear duty," Lee told him coldly, "to manage this estate. And I've decided that the special treatment allowed for those three can only cause feelings of resentment among the other nigras. Resentment can boil over into other trouble, and I'll not have any trouble among the blacks on this plantation."

Charles tried to remain calm. "That has not been the case here, Funston. The other slaves find some joy, some hope, in the good things that have happened to the jockeys."

"You're naive." Funston turned to leave. "My decision will stand."

Charles reached out, grabbing Lee's arm. "One moment! You speak of duty. Well, I have a duty, too. I'm responsible for the breeding and racing interests of Elkwood. Those jockeys are necessary to those interests."

Lee glared at Dewey, shaking his arm to loosen Charles's tight grip. "When they are needed at the races you will ask me to assign them to you."

"And the grooms and handlers?"

"The same."

"In other words, you're denying me the regular use of any of the Negroes in operating the horse business."

"I'm simply controlling the use of the nigras as I see fit." This time Lee managed to turn and walk away.

Charles had no choice but to go to Marshall Statler—with Lee—and ask him to mediate the dispute. In doing so he received his second shock of the day.

"I can understand that Funston must control the hands if he is to be manager of Elkwood," Statler said.

"But, sir—"

"Hear me out," Statler interrupted. "I can also understand that you, Charles, need the regular use of the experienced grooms and handlers and jockeys." He turned to Lee. "I propose that those blacks be assigned permanently to Charles—that, to preserve the integrity of the racing operation, we sell to Charles what nigras he needs, for the token sum of one dollar each. Now, won't that solve this little impasse?"

"Hardly, sir," Lee snapped. "You know as well as I do that selling those slaves for a token will merely put my accounts in arrears at the end of the year. If Dewey is to purchase those boys, I submit that he ought to pay full value for them."

Charles was disgusted. "I was under the mistaken impression that Elkwood was to be a cooperative venture—"

"Now wait, Charles," Statler interrupted once more. "Funston has a valid point. Are you able to make such a purchase?"

"Probably."

"Well, then, isn't that the best way to proceed? You simply reach an agreement with Funston on the value of the hands you need, and that will settle it."

"Will it?" Charles asked bitterly. "Am I to understand that all breeding and racing interests are no longer a part of Elkwood?"

"Of course they are," Statler insisted. "But I think you'd be happy with a bit of autonomy in this matter."

"If that's what you wish."

Charles and Funston wrangled over the prices, with Statler only a spectator. Funston wanted more than Charles thought reasonable, but Dewey finally agreed to two hundred fifty English pounds for each of the three jockeys, and two hundred pounds each for six grooms and handlers. It would deplete his reserves rather drastically, but he had no choice in light of Statler's failure to back him.

In the next several days, he found himself paying for other necessities. Hay grown on Elkwood acres was sold to Charles; so, too, were oats. Dewey realized that he'd have to be totally self-sufficient on his six hundred acres, and he moved to acquire ten other Negroes—from an agent, not from Lee—as field hands to clear the acreage and put in crops of hay and oats for his horses.

In the midst of all of that there was the traumatic recognition that he was now a slaveholder! A thief of another man's labor. That phrase, coined by Mr. Jefferson, tumbled around in his mind, and gave him more than one sleepless night. So did the certain knowledge that Funston Lee had managed to cut him off from the day-to-day activities of Elkwood.

It wasn't the last of the adversities he was to face.

II

LESS than a month after the weddings, Andrew MacCallum wound up his business at Elkwood and prepared to leave. Short of losing Martha, Charles could think of no worse loss. MacCallum, his tutoring no longer needed at the plantation, had made arrangements to return to New Jersey to teach at the college at Princeton.

Statler planned a lavish dinner to bid farewell to the young teacher, and many toasts were drunk, many kind words were said. They didn't change the reality of MacCallum's leaving.

After the dinner, Charles and Andrew strolled together across the broad lawn overlooking the valley behind the mansion.

"I don't know how I shall get along without your guidance, Andrew."

"Nonsense," the Scotsman said quietly, "you'll get along just fine." He paused. "There'll come a time, though, when you'll find a need to leave, just as I have. When that time comes, Charles, I hope you won't hesitate. Elkwood and Mr. Statler have been good to you. But there's more to this world than Elkwood. And Marshall Statler."

Charles laughed uneasily. "I think I've already discovered that."

"Hmmm. I know it's a tutor's failing, but tonight, as I watched you and Statler at dinner, I was reminded of some words of Mr. Shakespeare:

> " 'Men at some time are masters of their fates;
> the fault, dear Brutus, is not in our stars,
> but in ourselves, that we are underlings.
> Brutus and Caesar: what should be in that Caesar?
> Why should that name be sounded more than yours?
> Write them together, yours is as fair a name;
> sound them, it doth become the mouth as well;
> weigh them, it is as heavy; conjure with 'em,
> Brutus will start a spirit as soon as Caesar.' "

"You put me in important company," Dewey commented soberly.

"Perhaps. But I want you to understand, my old friend, that your future doesn't lie in Caesar—in Statler. It lies in yourself. I'm convinced you have it in you to be an important man in this country, and that your future won't hinge on being here at Elkwood. With Caesar, so to speak."

"I only hope I don't disappoint you, Andrew."

"You won't, Charles, you won't."

They embraced as brothers would embrace. And tears flowed unashamedly.

III

MACCALLUM had been gone only a few days when Dewey found himself wishing for his guidance. He had come into the little cottage after a long morning with the horses to find Katherine sitting at a table with Martha. The elder sister had been weeping; her clothes were disheveled, and there was an ugly purple bruise on her cheek.

"What—?"

"Funston has beaten her," Martha started to explain, near tears herself.

Charles was annoyed. "Ought we be involved in this?"

"She's my sister, Charles."

"Very well . . . what happened?"

"Funston went into a rage," Katherine sobbed, "when he learned I wasn't pregnant."

"That seems a poor excuse—"

"Oh, Charles," his sister-in-law wailed, "it's more than that." Her sobbing prevented her from continuing for several moments. "You see, he thought I was pregnant when we were married."

Dewey groaned. "My relationship with your husband, Katie, is already strained. I think that whatever problems you have with him ought not to be brought into this house."

"Charles, dear," Martha pleaded, "hear her out."

He shrugged.

Katherine drew a deep breath. "When you and Martha wanted to be married, and Father came to me asking about my marriage plans . . . well, I told Funston I was going to have a baby."

"You lied to him?"

"Yes."

"And when he found out the lie, he did that?" Charles pointed to her bruised face.

"Yes."

"What would you have me do?" His disgust was evident in the tone of the question.

"Come back to Elkwood with me, and —"

Dewey cut her off. "No."

"But I'm afraid of him!"

"Then go to your father," Charles suggested. "He lives in the same household. This has nothing to do with Martha and me. I'll not have you loading your personal problems on us."

Martha, in a quiet voice, spoke to him beggingly. "Isn't there *something* we can do, Charles?"

"Nothing! I'm not so sure, if you want my true feelings, that Funston wasn't within his rights. What you did, Katie, was despicable. I want no part of this! Now or in the future."

Katherine sighed, got to her feet, and left the cottage. Through the window they could see her slowly walking along the road toward the mansion.

"Weren't you too hard with her?" Martha asked.

"Do you really think so?"

His wife thought for a moment. "Perhaps not. It's just that—"

Charles went to her and gathered her in his arms. "I don't want this to come between us, Martha. But the cold fact is that you're too forgiving. Have you forgotten what she tried to do to us?"

"No." The reply was only a whisper.

"We'll not talk about this again." He kissed her. "Do you agree?"

"Yes." Again, very softly.

"Dear, sweet Martha, I love you so."

"And I love you, Charles."

"Then let's not risk that love by becoming involved in the insanities of those two."

IV

A SON was born to Charles and Martha in the latter part of May 1787. In the first week of June, the Reverend Mr. Lawrence Smith officiated at a simple christening ceremony at Elkwood.

"What shall be the name of this child of Christ?" Mr. Smith asked.

"Franklin Dewey," Charles answered proudly.

The minister dipped several fingers into a chalice of holy water and sprinkled it liberally on the baby's head, drawing a loud squall from the infant.

"I baptize you Franklin Dewey," he intoned, "in the name of God the Father, the Son, and the Holy Ghost. Let the word of Christ dwell in you richly in all wisdom. And whatsoever you do in word or deed, do all in the name of the Lord Jesus, giving thanks to God and the Father by him."

The Reverend Mr. Smith looked up at the small group of family friends who had been invited to the ceremony. "Ladies and gentlemen, may I introduce to you Master Franklin Dewey."

Later, in the drawing room, where Statler was serving his best wine in honor of the occasion, one of the women guests asked Charles, "Is Franklin a family name?"

"Oh, no, ma'am. He's named for Dr. Benjamin Franklin, for his vital life as an American, and for the role he's playing right now in the Federal Convention in Philadelphia."

Funston, standing nearby, laughed. "It seems a shame to name a defenseless baby after a profligate old bastard like Franklin."

Katherine tugged at his arm, trying to silence him. Shrugging her off roughly, he went to Charles. "Not being a native of this country," Lee said sarcastically, "you may not be aware of Dr. Franklin's reputation as a roué."

"I'm aware of that and much more," Charles answered, trying to control his temper. "He's been a great man in this country for many years. And he's served his country abroad—"

"Dallying with the ladies of the English and French courts all the while."

Dewey ignored the remark. "And now, in Philadelphia, he's a leader in the work to make this country even stronger—to preserve it for all time. I have no qualms about naming my son Franklin for him."

Funston screwed up his face as if smelling something rancid. "Well, Dewey, to me Franklin has the mark of a traitor. Senile, perhaps, but a traitor, nevertheless. The reports coming out of Philadelphia are that Franklin is a leader of that band of radicals who want a so-called constitution. That's not why the delegates were sent there —they were to amend the Articles of Confederation and nothing more!"

"Perhaps these times call for a greater experiment."

"Experiment!" Lee's voice rose, causing all heads to turn toward him. "Before those devils are through with that convention, we'll have more than an experiment, believe me. I hear there's even talk of freeing the slaves. Dangerous talk, Dewey, and dangerous men! And your precious *Doctor* Franklin is in the vanguard."

"Virginians should have no reason for concern. We are well represented."

"Well represented! Good God, man, Virginia is represented by republicans only. Our good governor, Edmund Randolph—a young radical! His past tells you that. And that Madison; he's nothing but a letter-writing politician. And George Mason . . ." Lee shook his head in disgust. "He's the owner of five thousand acres, yet he prattles about the rights of the common man. And Washington—he'd be king if we let him. And the others are just as bad."

Charles laughed at him. "I'm glad to see that you're consistent. Everyone's out of step but you."

"The greatest patriot in this state refused to attend that convention! Did you know that?"

"You mean Henry?"

"Patrick Henry! Right! He wouldn't go to Philadelphia because he smelled a rat." Funston drew himself up proudly. "I side with Patrick Henry. The only trouble is—in Philadelphia today there's more than one rat!"

Dewey was tiring of the game. "Lee, I believe I understand you for the first time. You see madness in everyone because you're just a little mad yourself."

"Be careful, sir—"

Marshall Statler came between them. "Gentlemen, this is hardly the occasion for such a heated political argument." He looked around at the others, smiling. "I must confess that I envy them their youthful exuberance."

Statler raised his glass high. "Come! A toast to my first grandson. To Franklin Dewey!"

"To Franklin Dewey!" the others echoed.

But not Funston Lee.

V

EACH day, each week, each month saw the steady erosion of hope that the brothers-in-law could be reconciled. Charles didn't want reconciliation, and Funston wouldn't have it. All stratagems employed by Statler to bring them together failed. One ploy was left to him: the Wednesday night dinners at the Elkwood mansion, Statler insisting that the two families dine together once a week. But the Wednesday nights only created an illusion of unity; the dinners were either sullen affairs where no one spoke, or shouting matches over any subject imaginable.

Perhaps Statler tried too hard to make the obligatory Wednesdays work. Often, in trying, he provided the spark for yet another argument.

Late in June 1788, the master of Elkwood said with too much enthusiasm, "It would be grand to be in Richmond these days to hear the verbal fireworks over the ratification of the Constitution." He laughed gaily. "The reports indicate that it's great entertainment."

"Let's hope that the Henryites prevail," Funston growled, "so that we can be done with this nonsense about consolidated centralized government and get the states back to the business of governing themselves."

"And bring what?" Charles challenged. "Chaos and disunity and weakness, leaving ourselves open to every foreign adventurer who would see the states as a prize ripe for picking?"

"That kind of talk is idiocy!" Lee waved a copy of the *Virginia Gazette*. "Patrick Henry, would they only listen to him, sees the truth in all this." He began to read a marked passage in the newspaper: " 'Whither is the spirit of America gone? Whither is the genius of America fled? We draw the spirit of liberty from our British ancestors. But now, Sir, the American spirit, assisted by the ropes and chains of consolidation, is about to convert this country into a powerful and mighty empire. There will be no checks, no real balances, in this government. What can avail your specious, imaginary balances, your rope-dancing, chain-rattling, ridiculous idea of checks and contrivances?' "

Funston slammed down the newspaper for emphasis.

Charles grinned wickedly. "I'll admit, Lee, that Henry is an orator of note. Why, it's said that he spoke for seven hours straight the other day. But to what avail? In his dotage he merely spouts words, Lee, thousands of empty words. But I must say that he's right about one thing: the Constitution will bring about a powerful and mighty empire. The great Patrick deplores that possibility, but it's exactly what we need!"

"If this constitution is so great, so necessary, why is it that only two of the eight Virginia delegates to the convention signed it?"

"Three," Charles countered. "Mr. Washington also signed it."

"Washington! Washington!" Funston spat the name. "I'm sick of hearing of him! This President the Constitution speaks of—would that be Washington?"

"One would hope so."

"And we'd have another King George. God help us, an American King George!"

"Preferable to the return of a British king, or a French one, or even a Spanish one. Or perhaps you believe the American people would want that instead of Washington?"

Lee laughed sarcastically, picked up the newspaper again, and searched it for another paragraph. "The people, you say. Well, Mr. Henry had the answer to that: 'Who authorizes gentlemen to speak the language of We, the people, instead of We, the states? The people gave them no power to use their name.' "

"It's refreshing to know that you can read, Lee." Charles got to his feet. "Perhaps, when you learn to *think*, we can resume this discussion." He stalked from the room, Martha dutifully following him, muttering apologies to her father.

A week later, when Virginia had ratified the Constitution by the slim margin of ten votes, the Wednesday dinner at Elkwood was devoid of conversation. Statler knew it was dangerous to bring up the subject of the ratification.

VI

IN July, William Greene, Esquire, a lawyer from Richmond, came to see Dewey on an important mission, carrying with him a sheaf of legal papers. He sat with Charles and Martha in the modest sitting room of their cottage, of the Elkwood "under farm," explaining that he had some news for the young Frenchman.

"Do you know a gentleman named de Grasse?" he asked. "The Comte François Joseph Paul de Grasse of Auvergne, France?"

"Of course. He's the Admiral of the French Fleet. I served under him."

"*Was* the Admiral of the French Fleet, Mr. Dewey," the lawyer said sadly. "I'm afraid I have the distressing duty to tell you that Count de Grasse died in Paris this past January eleventh."

"Good Lord!" Charles felt a genuine loss.

"There's more to my news," Greene went on. "Admiral de Grasse's lawyers in Paris have instructed me to inform you that the count bequeathed to you a sum of money in his will."

"To me!"

"Yes, sir. A rather handsome sum of money, as a matter of fact—ten thousand British pounds."

Charles gasped, and Martha let out a little squeal: "Oh, Charles!"

"Ten thousand . . ." Dewey was having trouble speaking. "Ten thousand pounds? But . . . why?"

Greene looked at his papers. "No specific reason is given. The entry in the will is very simple: 'To Charles Dupree, now known as Charles Dewey, Elkwood, Goochland County, Virginia: ten thousand English pounds.' That's all it says."

"You'll have to excuse me, Mr. Greene," Charles said with a nervous laugh, "but I'm having difficulty believing this."

"That's understandable, sir, but it is true. My information is that de Grasse had some financial interests in London—with wealthy men, money knows no nationalities—and that, upon getting your signature on this document"—he handed Charles a legal paper—"I'm instructed to send it to his solicitors in London. Following receipt there of the signed document, arrangements will be made to transfer to you the sum of ten thousand pounds sterling. If you will sign that, please, both as Charles Dupree and as Charles Dewey."

Dewey's hands shook as he signed the paper. "Ten thousand pounds," he said again. "My God, that's a fortune!"

"It is, indeed, sir." Greene smiled. "And you have my congratulations."

Charles and Martha talked for several hours about their windfall after the lawyer left, alternately laughing and crying.

"Admiral de Grasse must have loved you a great deal," Martha suggested.

"Hmmm." He had given in to his private thoughts. Once again, he realized, he had been given a vivid demonstration of the power of his guardian spirit. It wasn't any intimate association with de Grasse that had brought him the fortune; the spirit had simply used the proud admiral as a vehicle. Perhaps de Grasse himself would have been hard-pressed to give a reason for having made the bequest to his cabin boy. His *deserting* cabin boy.

A doubt struck Dewey. Could there be another explanation, he wondered, one not involving the spirit? Was de Grasse more to him than just the Admiral of the Fleet? Had de Grasse, by chance, known Charles's mother? Or his father? Then the most audacious of thoughts: Was it possible that de Grasse was his father? Could his mother have been a mistress to the admiral? No! All of that was impossible nonsense. Absolutely impossible! It was the spirit. It had to be the spirit!

At least the inheritance provided a new topic of conversation at the Wednesday night dinner. Only Funston Lee sat sullenly, saying nothing. The dinner lasted longer than usual, and when it finally ended, and Charles and Martha made ready to take their leave in the entrance hall at Elkwood, Katherine gathered her sister into her arms.

"I'm so happy for you, Martha," she said with a sincerity that surprised Charles. Then she looked at Lee. "Isn't it marvelous, Funston? Such good fortune."

"Marvelous? I suppose it is," he replied, bitterness in his words. "Astounding, really. Ten thousand pounds for the bastard son of a promiscuous French sailor—and this one dressed in silks and bearing a title!"

A little cry came from Martha's throat, and then, for just an instant, a dead silence.

Charles turned slowly to Funston. He was smiling. "Bastard? Ah! A subject well known to the Lee family, in light of your half-breed half sister. What's her name again? Melody, isn't it?"

Funston rushed at him, but Charles met him with a balled fist that smashed into Funston's surly face, knocking him sprawling on the floor of the entrance hall, blood spurting freely from his nose.

Wiping a hand across his face, Lee looked at the blood on his fingers for a stunned moment. "Sir, I will, of course, demand satisfaction!" He spaced out the words, leaving no doubt as to their meaning.

Statler was quickly between them. "I'll have no talk of dueling in this house! My God, brothers-in-law brawling like common field hands! I'll have no more of this! Is that clear?"

Charles answered first. Forcefully. "Yes, sir. I regret that this has taken place in your home. And I apologize for that."

The master of Elkwood reached out a hand to help Lee to his feet, but Funston refused his aid. "You have, sir," he said churlishly, "my apologies to you."

"I would much rather have the two of you exchange apologies," Statler answered.

Lee merely scowled.

After a moment, Charles spoke again: "I'm sorry, Marshall, but that's no longer possible."

Statler sighed deeply, suddenly looking much older.

At that moment, Dewey was seized with a desire to laugh, but he stifled it. Nevertheless he was struck by the humor of the situation. He had knocked Funston sprawling because he had said what Charles himself had thought earlier; that he might be the son of de Grasse. The bastard son.

VII

DEWEY moved quickly to take advantage of the money Admiral de Grasse had left him—for whatever reason.

A property on the James River adjacent to his "under farm," and, therefore, adjacent to Elkwood, was purchased from an absentee owner in Williamsburg, increasing Charles's land holdings to some fifteen hundred acres.

He began to cut a new road from the cottage to the public road so that he could get to his property without having to go through Statler's estate.

Although he was still in charge of Elkwood's racing interests, there were several race meetings at which he also ran a few horses in his own name. Statler allowed it because he needed Charles. More importantly, he wanted no final break with Martha's husband—with the determined young man he thought of as a son and in whom he saw a strange new restlessness.

Charles brought an architect from New York City to design and supervise the building of his new house. It was to be a grand place, with wide spacious verandas, large airy rooms, and plenty of space for a growing family.

Joyously, Charles and Martha planned their home, talked of the furnishings they would buy, and spoke of the children they would have to populate it. The foundations of the mansion were already laid when they finally selected a name for it.

It seemed most appropriate that they should call it *Fortunata*.

12

THE name of George Washington Dewey, second son of Charles and Martha, was added to the family Bible on April 30, 1789, the day of the inauguration of the first President of the United States in New York City. A year later the birth of a daughter, Corrine, was noted. And as January 1792 came to a close, two more names went into the biblical record: Louise and Lee Dewey.

Naming of the twins—it was Martha's idea—precipitated the first real quarrel in the Dewey household.

"I can't stand the constant grief of this alienation from my sister's family," Martha said, tears in her eyes. "I *must* do something to end it."

"That alienation is no fault of yours. Or mine," Charles insisted.

"I know that. But it seems that every time we have a baby I grow apart just a little bit more from Katie." She spoke softly, but there was determination in her voice. "It's as if I've insulted her somehow by bearing another child, since it seems she can't."

Martha sighed. "Oh, Charles, there's been too much hate. I want to demonstrate that I really love her—that I don't hate Katie"—a slight hesitation—"or Funston. Naming the boy Lee would be that demonstration."

"No, I won't allow it!"

"Charles!" She wasn't used to him speaking sharply to her.

His face was livid. "You speak of a demonstration. Well, Funston Lee has demonstrated nothing but contempt for me since we first met. And I can't recall that he ever showed any real affection for you, either. There'll be no naming a son for him!"

Nevertheless, Dewey finally gave in to Martha's constant pleadings. He found it impossible to deny her anything she really wanted. He forced himself to submerge his own doubts, his own hate, and convinced himself that Martha was right: that naming his third son Lee would help to repair the shattered relationship with his brother-in-law.

They went to Elkwood—the first time they had been in the mansion for months—with the news. Katherine was delighted. Even Funston managed a smile. No one was happier, though, than Marshall Statler.

He set about making the christening an important social event at Elkwood. Friends were invited from as far away as Charlottesville to the west and Alexandria to the east and north. As it had been for the double wedding, the entrance hall was turned into a lovely bower of flowers.

It was Katherine and Funston who held the babies—Katie carrying Louise, Funston gingerly balancing Lee—as the Reverend Mr. Smith officiated again.

"What shall be the name of this female child of Christ?" the minister asked.

Katherine, beaming, answered, "Louise Dewey."

"And what shall be the name of this male child of Christ?"

Funston, his face sober, replied, "Lee Dewey."

The guests, understanding the significance of that moment, applauded. Baby Lee, startled by the noise, howled.

Everyone laughed, Funston more gaily than all the rest.

II

TIRED but happy after the reception that had followed the christenings, Katie was pulling on her nightdress. She let out a long sigh. "Wasn't it lovely?"

"It was a damned disaster!" Funston shouted at her. "I've never been so humiliated in my life!"

His wife's mouth fell open in disbelief. "Funston, what are you saying? You were so exuberant about it."

"Good Christ, woman, you're stupid!"

Lee stumbled drunkenly to the bed; there had been a great many toasts at the reception. "Don't you realize what all those people—those smiling, smug hypocrites—were saying behind their hands? That Funston Lee had to stand up with Dewey's son because he hasn't any of his own!"

"Funston, don't be silly—"

He pushed himself to his feet and began to pace unsteadily about the bedroom. "Silly, am I? I saw through Dewey's plot to embarrass me in front of those I thought were my friends. That bastard will go to any length to belittle me—any length at all—including this charade of naming a son for me. And why shouldn't he? That sainted sister of yours can spit out babies like a stray bitch!"

Katherine went to him, laying a hand tenderly on his cheek. "Dear, don't spoil such a lovely day just because you've had too much wine."

He struck her in the face with his fist, sending her sprawling. A small rivulet of blood trickled out of the corner of her mouth.

"I wouldn't be a victim of this humiliation if my wife was half a woman instead of a cold, barren . . ." The sentence trailed off.

Katie, still on the floor, looked up at him, disgust evident in her eyes. "Perhaps I'm not the one who's at fault."

"Is that what you think?" he screamed at her. "You think I'm not man enough? I'll show you!"

He rushed at her, grasping her roughly by the wrists, pulling her to her feet, dragging her through the doorway and out of the room. "I'll show you!" He propelled her along the hallway and down the wide staircase.

"Funston, let go of me!"

"Shut up!" He cuffed her across the mouth with an open hand.

Katherine was whimpering as they left the mansion, with Funston half pushing and half pulling her in his uncontrolled rage. "I'll show you," he kept muttering. When she lost her footing and fell, he dragged her over the ground until she regained her feet and stumbled along.

Funston made for the cluster of slave cabins some two hundred yards from the main house. At the third cabin in the long row, he kicked open the door and pulled her inside. A black woman screamed.

"Shut up, Sarah, and make a light!" he ordered.

Trembling, Sarah lit a candle.

"Where's your son?"

The woman pointed to a box in the corner of the crude shack.

"Bring him here!"

Sarah obeyed, holding a nearly naked baby up to the light so that Funston and Katherine could see it.

"Is that your baby?"

"Yas, suh."

"Who's the father?" Funston demanded.

Sarah, her eyes wide with fright, just stared at him.

"Answer me, you nigger bitch! Who made that baby with you?"

The reply was almost inaudible: "Yawl did, mastah."

Katherine gasped.

"There!" Funston sneered, putting his face close to Katie's. "You think I'm not man enough, do you?"

His wife shuddered.

"You want to see how it's done? You want a lesson?"

Katie said nothing.

"Lie down there!" he screamed at the slave.

Sarah, in panic, returned the baby to the makeshift crib and hurried to her small cot where she lay down and pulled her dress up to her hips. Katherine turned her face away.

Lee, still holding his wife's wrist in a viselike grip, struggled to undo his belt with his other hand.

"Funston, stop it," Katie pleaded, weeping. "Oh, dear God, please make him stop!"

Unable to loosen his belt with one hand, he let go of Katherine and in one quick move loosened the belt and dropped his breeches. Katherine bolted from the shack, running madly along the road toward Fortunata.

For just an instant Lee seemed unsure what he should do. Then he pulled up his breeches and raced after his wife, catching her easily and knocking her to the ground face down. He jerked her around so that she faced him, then struck her with his fist. Once more. And again, knocking her unconscious. Blood flowed from her lips and nose and from an ugly cut above her eye.

Lee stared at her, smiled, and stood up. "So you thought I wasn't man enough," he mumbled. "Well, now you know."

He stumbled off in the direction of the mansion, stopped momentarily at the door of Sarah's cabin, laughed loudly, and continued on. Leaving Katherine in the dirt of the road.

Fifteen minutes later, two black men carried Katie to the door of Fortunata, pounded on it, then left her there and ran away, not wanting Lee—or any white person—to know who had come to the aid of the mistress of the main house.

Martha cried as she bathed her sister's battered face and heard the horrible story told through swollen lips.

Charles's concern was not for Katherine, but for Martha. She had lost much. Her loving, good-hearted, efforts to bring the two families together had been cruelly destroyed.

Her tears, he thought, were washing away the last of her innocence.

Elkwood, too, had lost. If not innocence, honor.

III

DEWEY'S problems weren't confined to Elkwood or Fortunata. Family concerns were not what worried him most.

To him, a greater concern was what was happening to racing.

An insidious reform movement was growing in the Virginia Assembly, fueled by ministers of the new evangelical sects that were replacing the toppled Church of England in the state. Those churchmen were quick to view all sports as frivolous, and they forced through the Assembly a bill prohibiting all wagers of more than seven dollars on "any horse race, cockfighting, or any other sport or pastime."

It was a law almost impossible to enforce, and, in truth there was only token enforcement. Charles and his racing fellows still made their large side bets, although they had to be kept secret now. And Dewey, thinking himself a proper American, felt some guilt about breaking the law, even one he viewed as nonsensical.

One contention of the reformers concerned him deeply: the charge that racing itself was somehow sinful.

In the latter part of March 1792 he rode to Richmond to appear at a church "trial" in behalf of a horse breeder named John Broaddus, a decent and honest man from whom he had bought several horses in the past. The last one—in November—had been a filly, which Charles had named Broad Hope. She was a three-year-old, and Dewey planned to campaign her for the first time—lightly, because of her age—in the summer meetings.

Broaddus and his wife had affiliated themselves with one of the new fundamentalist sects, and now the congregation was calling him to task for selling a horse he knew would be used for racing. *Sinful racing!* The breeder had written to Charles, begging him to appear before the congregation to attest to his good character.

It was a hostile audience of perhaps sixty of the faithful who greeted the master of Fortunata in the tiny wooden church just outside the capital city. An unrelentingly sober group, led by a citizen preacher who called himself Brother Mason.

Charles was ushered to a bench in the front of the church, where he sat through a series of interminable prayers, all promising the damnation of hell for those who wavered in their journey through life. Then Broaddus was called to stand before the congregation as Brother Mason castigated him for his "sin."

"Were you not aware, Brother Broaddus," the preacher shouted at him, "that a tenet of our faith is that gambling is a sin?"

"Yes," Broaddus said weakly, hanging his head.

"And were you not aware that gambling is the foundation of the sporting fraternity of horse racers?"

"Well, you see, Brother Mason," Broaddus tried to explain, "I don't gamble myself, and—"

"Then you don't know that certain horses are used for gambling?" the preacher asked sarcastically.

"Yes, I did. But not being a gambler myself—"

Again he wasn't permitted to finish his explanation. "Yet, Brother Broaddus, you sell horses to those who do gamble, those who do sin in that manner! You abet them!" The accusation was boomed out.

"I'm in the business of breeding and selling horses." Somehow that innocent admission seemed a weak defense.

"If you sold women to bawdy houses, would you not consider *that* a sin?"

"Yes."

"Yet you'd have us believe that the sale of horses to gamblers who violate the Sabbath with their races is not a similar sin!" Brother Mason swept his arm to encompass the whole congregation. "Is that what you'd like these good people to believe?"

"I don't believe selling a horse is a sin, no."

"Ah, Brother, but for what purpose? That's the question." The preacher looked down at Charles. "Brother Broaddus, did you sell a female horse to that man sitting there on the first bench?" He pointed an accusing finger at Charles.

"Yes."

"For racing?"

"I sold him a filly," Broaddus responded defiantly.

"A blooded animal?"

"Yes."

"With pedigree?"

"Yes."

"Are such horses normally used to pull carriages? Or for farm work, perhaps, Brother?"

"Not usually." Broaddus sighed deeply.

Brother Mason smiled for the first time. "In keeping with fairness," he said to the congregation, "Brother Broaddus has been permitted to have one witness to speak to his character. Do you wish to introduce your witness?"

"Squire Charles Dewey of the Fortunata plantation has kindly ridden in from Goochland County to be here," Broaddus said.

"Would you join us here, Squire?" the preacher asked, gesturing to Charles, who rose and went to stand beside Broaddus. "Now, sir, you are acquainted with Brother Broaddus?"

"Yes, I've known him for several years," Charles said forcefully, "as a gentleman of integrity."

"You've done business with him?"

"Yes."

"Bought horses from him, in other words?"

"That's correct."

Brother Mason's words got harder. "Specifically, did you buy a blooded filly from him in November last?"

"Yes."

"A racing animal?"

"I would hope so," Charles answered. "But I want to say something now, Brother Mason."

"Of course."

"My affection for Mr. Broaddus, my respect for him, is such that I want to offer to return the filly to him—at a loss to me, if necessary—so that whatever *crime* may be imagined in his sale of the horse to me is . . . well, doesn't exist any longer."

"You have a generous nature, Mr. Dewey." Brother Mason glared at him. "But I detect an attitude of disapproval concerning these proceedings."

"Yes, I disapprove. Mr. Broaddus is a good man. I hate to see him humiliated in this way."

"I see. God help you, Mr. Dewey, if you imagine this as just a *humiliation*. We are in a battle, sir! As soldiers of God, we must fight sin wherever we find it!"

"And it's viewed as a sin to sell a horse?"

"To sell a horse for evil racing, yes! Yes! Yes!"

The congregation took up the chant: "Yes! Yes! Yes!"

Charles knew that he wasn't helping Broaddus's cause, but he meant to speak out. "Brother Mason, I know of no place in the Bible where horse racing is in the catalogue of sins."

"But gambling is!" the preacher roared. "A terrible sin! When Jesus hung dying on the cross, the soldiers parted his raiment, Saint Luke tells us, and cast lots for it! Imagine! They *gambled* for the robe of Jesus! And if a horse is sold to promote the sin of gambling, then the sale of the horse is a sin as well!"

"Yes! Yes! Yes!" came the chant again.

As the chanting died away, Dewey shrugged. "So even if I return the filly to Mr. Broaddus, unraced, it won't make any difference."

"The deed is done, Squire Dewey, the deed is done!"

Charles returned to his seat, dejected.

"Brothers and sisters," Brother Mason intoned, "let us pray for the soul of our fallen brother."

There was a pause as he gathered himself for the task.

"Oh, God, Brother Broaddus stands before you, the instrument of sin. He willingly defied you, O Lord, and he deserves your punishment! He faces the burning fires of hell, and yet we pray for your mercy. Brother Broaddus, though he has sinned, wishes to atone. He begs you, O Lord, *we* beg you, O Lord, to allow us to remember the Holy words of the sacred Bible: 'Go ye, and sin no more!' "

He turned to Broaddus. "God, in His infinite mercy, says to you, 'Go ye, and sin no more!' Will you accept His mercy? Will you accept it now?"

A stillness fell over the congregation.

Broaddus, his head bowed again, said quietly, "I will accept it."

There were shouts of joy from the congregation. And Mrs. Broaddus, seated next to Charles, wept profusely.

When it was over and all had filed out of the church, Broaddus came up to Charles. "I want to thank you for your help."

Dewey smiled wanly. "I'm afraid I wasn't much help."

"No one else would have put himself on the line as you did. I thank you again."

"I guess I really came," Charles admitted, "because I wanted to see what this fundamentalism is all about . . . and because I'm concerned for the future of racing in Virginia. So perhaps I had a selfish motive."

Broaddus didn't say anything.

"May I ask a question?"

Now it was Broaddus who smiled. "You want to know *why*?"

"Yes."

"Because I *believe*. Because I think, as do all of these people, that gambling is a sin."

Charles stared at him incredulously. "You do?"

"Yes."

"But what of your business?"

"I'll still breed horses, but for other purposes. I made a mistake in selling you that filly. I've now accepted public chastisement for that mistake, and there'll be no more racehorses for me."

They shook hands warmly, and Charles began the long ride back to Fortunata. He admired Broaddus's courage, but he didn't really understand the reason for it. And he totally rejected the idea that horse racing, and the attendant gambling, was sinful. Surely God had more important matters with which to concern himself.

IV

THE *Virginia Gazette* continued to bring Dewey news of repressive acts being taken against racing in North Carolina, New York, Pennsylvania, and New Jersey. Reformers, political and clerical, were making their mark.

Only in the new land to the west was racing flourishing. When, on June 1, 1792, Kentucky was carved out of the western reaches of Virginia's original territory and admitted to the Union as the fifteenth state, Charles began to think that the West held his future. Remaining forever in Virginia didn't seem possible. Not when racing was thought a sin. And not when he contemplated raising his children in a society that permitted the likes of Funston Lee to prosper.

Andrew MacCallum had counseled him not to hesitate when the time came to leave. Still, he hesitated. It would be a difficult journey to Kentucky. No roads. Or poor ones. Savages. Uncounted other dangers. He told himself that he couldn't ask Martha to undertake such rigorous travel with two small babies; the older children—Franklin, George, and Corrine—were little more than babies themselves.

With his family's welfare in mind, he put aside any idea of Kentucky.

But not of the West.

In his private thoughts he had no doubt that he would make the move. Someday.

13

CHARLES had never been more shocked.

Marshall Statler stood before him, before the stud barn at Fortunata, and said: "What place is this, young man? Are you in charge here?"

Dewey stared at him, thinking Statler might be pulling his leg. But something about his eyes—a vacant look he saw in them—convinced Charles that something was dreadfully wrong.

For some months he and Martha had been concerned about the gradually deteriorating health of her father. He had been losing weight, and he complained of not being able to sleep properly.

But this?

"This is Fortunata, sir," Charles answered him, not knowing what to do except to humor him.

"A pleasant place."

"We think so."

"I noticed quite a few horses in the field as I came down the lane," Statler said. "Are you engaged in racing?"

"Yes." Dewey was disquieted.

"Hmmm. I had horses once. Not anything as fine as this, of course." He swept an arm in a gesture encompassing the estate.

Charles stood dumbly.

"Yes, well . . ." Statler sighed, turned, and started to walk away.

His son-in-law took his arm. "May I offer you some tea, sir."

"You're most kind."

Statler permitted himself to be led into the mansion, where Martha, struggling to keep back the tears, served tea to the stranger who had come to visit them.

"You have children?" Statler asked.

Martha swallowed hard. "Yes, five children."

"They must be a joy to you." A pause. "When you get old, young lady, you'll appreciate them even more. I have none, and it's a most lonely . . ." He didn't finish the thought.

His daughter turned away from him. She didn't want him to see her crying.

Statler turned to Charles. "I thank you for the tea, young man. I must be going."

"Perhaps you'd like to stay for dinner?" Charles suggested.

"No, no. I can't. I have much to do."

"May I ask what that is, sir—what you have to do?"

"Much," Statler mumbled. "Much indeed. Uh . . . much . . . yes, much, young sir—"

He slumped in the chair, seeming very tired, staring blankly at nothing at all.

They put him to bed, and Martha sat with him all night.

In the morning, when he awoke, he seemed normal. And he spent most of the day playing with his grandchildren, reveling in them.

II

IN July 1792, Dewey and Statler went together to Richmond for the race meeting there. The master of Elkwood was anxious to see Born Again, the first son of Rebirth, make his competitive debut in the Virginia Stallion Stakes.

He was a five-year-old, in appearance the exact image of his sire. Charles had told Statler that he had the distinct feeling that the young horse would be Rebirth all over again. "I haven't had a horse in years that I feel more sure about," he'd said.

When it came time for the feature event, Dewey instructed one of the Negro handlers: "Find Mr. Marshall. I want him to saddle our entry." It would be purely an honorary function for the older man, but Charles was trying to keep him interested in the horses.

After a few minutes, the Negro returned. "Ah caint fin' 'im, Mistah Charles. He ain't nowhere 'round."

Charles shrugged. Statler was probably in the refreshments pavilion, swapping stories with old cronies. The black man wouldn't have looked in that all-white sanctuary.

When the race was over and Born Again had finished a disappointing third in the three-mile dash, Dewey himself went to look for Statler. He hoped his father-in-law hadn't put a large wager on the Elkwood horse.

No one had seen Statler in the refreshments pavilion. Nor did any of Statler's friends recall having talked to him. Dewey panicked. Leaving only one handler with the horses, Charles and the plantation's Negroes spread out across the town in full search.

It was Charles who found him sitting contentedly on the grass under a tree near the capitol building.

Statler smiled at him. "Well, son, what are you doing in Richmond?"

It had happened again!

Dewey tried to keep the look of shock off his face. "Running a few horses," he said as nonchalantly as he could.

"Any luck?"

"Some." He reached down a hand. "Come, I'd be honored to escort you home."

"Home?"

"Yes, Elkwood."

"That would be most pleasant," Statler said, taking Charles's hand and getting to his feet. "I haven't been to Elkwood for some time, and I know it's beautiful at this time of the year."

"It is," his son-in-law agreed. "Very beautiful."

On that occasion it was two days before Statler's mental capacity returned.

For weeks at a time there were no problems and then he would just drift away, having no concept of time or place. For an hour, for several hours, once for a period of five days.

Even Funston Lee was solicitous of his father-in-law, assigning the old slave named Malachi to stay within sight of Statler at all times when he was out of the mansion.

September was a particularly bad month. On one cold night, Statler rose from his bed and just walked away. In the morning, a field hand found him, his back resting against one of the stone fences, shivering in his nightclothes. A doctor was called, but he reported that Statler was not physically harmed by his ordeal.

The diagnosis? "It's probably a condition known as early senility," the physician said. "It's rare, but not unknown. Unhappily, there's little or nothing we can do about it."

It was then that the butler, Samuel, began to sleep in Statler's room, following an explanation that it was because Samuel was "getting a bit old" and finding it difficult to climb the stairs to care for his employer. There was no argument from Statler about the move.

In the early days of November, Statler began to talk enthusiastically about Christmas, in rational, normal terms: what he wanted to buy for his grandchildren, what he planned for the Christmas entertainment—he began to practice his guitar again—when he would go turkey shooting for the holiday dinner.

The closer Christmas came the more he seemed to improve. A vitality returned to his stride, he began to give orders to the field hands and house servants, he consulted with Charles about the breeding assignments for the spring. His family began to hope that his affliction had passed.

III

FIVE days before Christmas, Marshall Statler strode along the row of slave cabins, happily calling out the names of half a dozen of the older black men.

"Boys," he shouted, "we're going into the woods to find a yule log—the finest we've ever had at Elkwood!"

Off they tramped, Statler leading the way, joshing with the blacks as they walked along.

Less than an hour later, the Negroes came back down the road, tears coursing down their ebony faces, carrying the body of their master.

"Ah don' know wha' happen, Mistah Funston," Malachi reported. "We dun fin' the tree Mistah Marshall wanna cut down fer the yule log, an' us niggers start a 'hackin' at it. An' Mistah Marshall jest happy laik he kin be, a' singin' an' all. An' . . . Lawd, Mistah Funston . . . he jest kinda fell over. An' Ah talks t' 'im—Ah say, 'Mistah Marshall, talk t' me.' An' he don' say nothin'."

The elderly slave wailed. "Oh, Lawd, Mistah Funston, Ah fears he daid!"

"Yes, Malachi," Funston said quietly, "he's dead. Send someone to fetch Mister Charles and Miss Martha."

When night came and the body of Marshall Statler was laid out on his bed, the dirgelike songs of the Negroes could be heard for many hours echoing over the acres of Elkwood. There was love reflected in the hymns. And respect. Charles Dewey pondered the irony of the situation—the man who had held them in bondage would be genuinely missed by the slaves.

The next morning, they buried him within the circle of giant boxwoods at the entrance to his beloved Elkwood in a rough wooden coffin cut from his own trees. He was only fifty years old.

Christmas would not be celebrated that year.

14

His monotonous tone belied the importance of what he was reading. Richmond lawyer Millard Exner, a self-important, pompous man who had trouble keeping his false teeth in place when he spoke, droned his way through the last will and testament of Marshall Statler. His audience in the Elkwood drawing room consisted of Statler's daughters and their husbands. The date was January 2, 1793.

" 'To my eldest daughter, Katherine, and her husband, Funston Lee,' " Exner intoned, " 'I jointly leave all of the property known as Elkwood, with the exceptions noted below.' "

A startled expression came to Lee's face when he heard the word "exceptions." He was disturbed, too, by the fact that the inheritance carried the joint provision. It was not normal procedure for a woman to be given a role in the control of property. But he said nothing.

There followed a detailed description of the assets of the plantation: acreage—a surveyor's report was noted—buildings, a full list of the slaves held, and inventory of the furnishings in the main house, a catalog of the livestock holdings. But no mention was made of horses. It was most thorough.

" 'To my younger daughter, Martha, and her husband, Charles Dewey, also known as Charles Dupree, I jointly leave the approximate six hundred acres originally deeded to them as a gift on their wedding day . . .' " It was plain that Statler had wanted no misunderstanding about the ownership of the underfarm property; the document was augmented with another surveyor's report.

" 'To the aforementioned Charles Dewey,' " the lawyer went on, " 'in recognition of his loyalty and his exemplary work in behalf of the Elkwood equine interests, I leave the following horses . . .' "

There was a roster of eleven stallions and twenty-three brood mares, a precise list including the dam and sire, and granddam and grandsire, of each animal. As Exner's monotone detailed the names of the blooded horses, Lee's face flushed angrily. " 'All other equines not specifically listed here remain the property of the Elkwood estate.' "

Then, at the end: " 'Being of sound mind and in full control of my faculties,

I do set my hand to this last will and testament, trusting in God and the laws of Virginia.' It's signed 'Marshall Statler,'" the lawyer explained, "and witnessed by myself and by the Virginia clerk of courts in Richmond."

Lee, in obvious annoyance, spoke immediately: "May I ask, sir, the date of that signing?"

"May 31, 1786. That was a little more than a year after your weddings, as you may recall."

"There's no doubt about that date?"

The lawyer frowned. "Of course not. Is there some reason you would question the date?"

Funston coughed nervously. "As you may be aware, Mr. Statler was, at times, mentally indisposed in his last years, and—"

"I can assure you," Exner interrupted sharply, "that Mr. Statler was, as the will says, of sound mind and in full control of his faculties when this document was drawn, which was long before his difficulties began." There was a pause. "Is there something that disturbs you about the terms?"

"Frankly, there is—the list of horses to go to Dewey. You may not be aware, sir, but that list represents *all* of the stallions—all of them!—and fully half of the broodmares."

"Yes. That was my understanding when I drew the will for him."

Lee grunted disconsolately. "A rather generous bequest, don't you think, to a man of . . . specious background?"

Katherine glared at her husband. Dewey's face was an impassive mask.

Exner struggled to maintain his professional demeanor. "The *background* of concern to Mr. Statler"—he searched the papers for the exact phrase — "was Mr. Dewey's 'loyalty and exemplary work.' It was for that reason that he made the bequest. I doubt that he thought it overgenerous."

"I find it hard to believe that he intended to give the Frenchman *all* of the stallions, leaving Elkwood without any." Lee continued to speak of Charles as if he weren't in the room.

"There's no doubt in my mind that such was Mr. Statler's exact intent," the lawyer said firmly.

"I fail to understand how he—"

Exner cut him off angrily. "Were I you, Mr. Lee, I would recognize the other side of the coin, sir! His bequest to you—and to your wife, of course— is quite substantial. Quite substantial, indeed. In the matter of horses, you retain all those in training and all of the younger animals born since the drawing of the will. So I question that you've been duly inconvenienced in your equine business. I might have expected, sir, that there would be a show of gratitude on your part!"

Lee was silenced by the chastisement.

"Are there any other questions?" the lawyer asked.

Katherine got to her feet. "No more questions, Mr. Exner. I appreciate the service you gave our father and this family. And I thank you for it."

When the lawyer had said his good-byes and had left the mansion, Funston snarled at Charles, "When can you remove the stallions from Elkwood property?"

Charles smiled. "The Frenchman," he said, "will do that within the hour."

"One other thing, Dewey—from this day I shall take over the running of the Elkwood horses. If there are any in training in your barns they should be returned immediately."

"As you wish." Charles made a mocking formal bow to his brother-in-law. "Your servant, sir."

II

DEWEY had not yet completed his breakfast the next morning when Marshall Statler's old butler, Samuel, was at his door.

"I believe that Mr. Statler told you," Samuel said to him, "that I'm a freeman."

"Yes, he did."

"But you may not know that my full name is Samuel Wilkins." There was a hint of accusation in the statement.

"No," Charles admitted, "I didn't know that."

"Well, it is," Samuel said forcefully, "and this morning I'm reclaiming that name! I'm free again."

Dewey nodded. He didn't know what he was expected to contribute to the conversation.

"I've left Elkwood for good," the black man told him, "although Mr. Lee has said that I couldn't."

Hate burned in his eyes.

"Last night I told Mr. Lee that I intended to return to Philadelphia, and we had a . . . well, a bitter argument. He told me, in no uncertain terms, that no nigger at Elkwood is a freeman, and that if I wanted to keep my position at the main house, I'd have to understand that from now on. He threatened to turn me over to Mr. Caldwell, the overseer of the field hands." Samuel shuddered at the thought.

"So you're running away?"

"No, sir, not running away. *Slaves* run away. I'm just leaving, as any free man would leave a position he no longer wanted to hold."

"I understand. You're right, of course."

"I was sure you'd understand," Samuel said. "And that's why I've come to you for help. I need a horse, sir."

"You have it."

"Thank you."

"Is there any other way I can help you?" Charles asked.

"No, sir. When Mr. Exner was here yesterday for the reading of the will, he told me in confidence that Mr. Statler had left me a personal bequest of a hundred pounds in cash. And he told me I could have it any time I wanted to claim it at his office. I intend to ride to Richmond now, get the money, and then proceed on to Philadelphia."

"Does Lee know you've left?"

Samuel shook his head. "I don't imagine he knows it at this moment—I left the mansion before first light—but certainly he'll know soon enough."

"Perhaps you ought to make haste, then."

"Yes, sir, I believe I should."

A good riding horse was quickly saddled. Charles boosted the black man into the saddle and bade him farewell.

"I'll send you money for the horse when I get to Philadelphia," Samuel said.

"No need. Think of it as payment for the kindnesses you have shown me over the years."

Samuel grinned. "I'll accept that, sir, and thank you again."

"God speed, Samuel . . . uh . . . Mr. Wilkins."

The black man nodded to him, spurred the horse, and was gone.

Charles expected that Funston would come calling later in the day, inquiring about the butler. But the day sped by without his hearing anything more about Samuel Wilkins. He felt good about that. One Negro, at least, would not know Funston Lee's boot again.

III

It was noon when Samuel reached the Richmond law office, collected his money, and rode north toward Fredericksburg. He rode easily, not wanting to use up the horse. By nightfall, he had passed Fredericksburg and had reached Accotink, south of Alexandria.

Dismounting in a small wooded glade, he unsaddled the horse, tethering it where it could graze. He lit a small fire. As he began to prepare a place where he might sleep, his horse nickered nervously. Samuel heard the snap of twigs.

"Who's there?" he called out into the darkness.

Two white men, leading their horses, came into the circle of light made by the fire.

"Well, well," the taller of the two said, "what's this? A runaway nigger?"

"No, sir," Samuel answered firmly but politely. "My name is Wilkins. I'm a freeman."

"Wilkins, eh?" The tall man laughed. "Would that be Samuel Wilkins?"

"Yes." He fought against showing his sudden fright.

"Mr. Funston Lee's Samuel?"

Now his fright was genuine. This white man knew who he was. "No, sir," he said, trying to be calm. "As I told you, sir, I'm a freeman."

The two men tied their horses to a tree and squatted down by the fire next to Samuel. Their actions were unhurried.

"Now, Samuel," the taller man said quietly, "we been ridin' after you all day an' our asses is sore. So don't give us no trouble. We know you're runnin' away from Mr. Lee. But, Mr. Lee, he's a generous man. He told us just to find you an' bring you back. An' no more'll be said 'bout this."

"I'm not going back. I'm a freeman!"

"That ain't the way Mr. Lee tells it."

"Mr. Lee is mistaken," Samuel insisted.

"You callin' him a liar, boy?"

"No, certainly not," the Negro said cautiously. "But Mr. Statler employed me some years ago in Philadelphia, and Mr. Lee may not have known the details of that employment."

The shorter man spoke for the first time. "My, don't this nigger talk nice? I declare, I think this boy's been to school."

"I have been," Samuel said quickly, seeing an opening that might convince the men that he wasn't a slave. "I was educated in Philadelphia, where Mr. Statler hired me."

"That sure is a nice story, boy. But it don't make no difference. Mr. Lee says you're his nigger, an' we was to bring you back. And that's what we plan to do."

"No!"

"You got a smart mouth, nigger!"

"Come on," the tall man said, "let's stop this nonsense an' get on with it. Saddle up your horse, boy, an' let's get goin'."

"I'll not go back to Elkwood. I'm a freeman, I tell you!"

The tall man slapped Samuel hard across the face. "I heard enough, boy! Saddle up that damned horse!"

"No."

Samuel came to his feet, backing away from them.

"Boy, don't give me no trouble!"

The tall man advanced on him, smashing a fist into his mouth. Samuel staggered but managed to keep his feet. He lunged forward, grappling with the younger and stronger man, managing to get in several blows before they overpowered him. They struck him repeatedly until he was unconscious.

"Sonofabitch!" the shorter man snarled. He spat in the Negro's face.

The tall man dropped to his knees, searching through Samuel's pockets.

"Hey, look at here!" he said, holding up the money he found. "This nigger is rich!"

"Lee didn't mention no money," the companion said.

"He didn't, did he?" Grinning, the tall man counted the money. "Goddamn! A hundred pounds! Now, ain't this fortunate? Kind of a windfall, you might say."

He divided the money equally, handing fifty pounds to the shorter one, who agreed, "Yep, a real nice windfall."

He raised a hand then, in warning. "Maybe this nigger'll shoot off his smart mouth 'bout the money when we get back to Elkwood."

"The way I see it, a hundred pounds is better'n the ten pounds Lee was gonna pay us for bringin' this nigger back."

"Uh-huh."

"Suppose we don't bring him back? We ain't gonna get the ten pounds from Lee, but we get to keep this hundred. Now, whatta you suppose we oughta do?"

"Ain't but one thing we *can* do," the shorter man said.

He drew a pistol and shot Samuel in the face. The impact of the point-blank shot blew the black man's features away.

"That oughta solve our problem, it seems to me."

"Yep, solves it real nice. 'Course Lee ain't gonna get his nigger back."

The murderer laughed. "Ain't it too damned bad we couldn't find him?"

"What are we gonna do with the horse?"

"Well, we don't want him wanderin' back to wherever the nigger got him. Somebody might start askin' questions."

The animal was dispatched with a pistol shot in the ear.

The white men mounted their horses, wheeled them about, and rode into the shadows.

In time, the small fire flickered out, the darkness of the Virginia night drawing a blanket over the horror of the scene.

Over Samuel Wilkins.

Freeman.

15

"THE soil here," the letter said, "exceeds any expectation. Oats and barley flourish—flax, hemp, cotton, and tobacco grow luxuriantly. And no part of the nation can exceed this country for grazing grass for livestock. Indeed, livestock turned out for the winter can support themselves in the woods and fields and keep in fine order. The Cumberland is navigable for 500 miles for large boats, and I daresay that some seasons it has enough water to float a forty-gun ship."

Dewey put the letter down on his desk, turning to gaze out of the window at a group of mares and their new foals grazing in the pasture. But his thoughts weren't on the horses. He was thinking of the West.

The letter had just arrived from a gentleman named Patton Anderson. He had sent it from a frontier town called Nashville, hard by the Cumberland River. Anderson was an enthusiast for the area. He had written to Charles several times about the horse racing in the West, frequently mentioning a horseman-gambler-politician named Andrew Jackson.

Charles's appetite for news of the western frontier was insatiable. He went to great lengths to learn everything he could about the far reaches of the nation, which now encompassed a vast area from the Atlantic to the Mississippi, from the Great Lakes to the borders of Spanish Florida.

In size, as great as all of Europe.

Four million people, unhappily including seven hundred thousand slaves, spread out over a domain of a million square miles. Room to grow. To prosper.

And the population was swelling every day as Europeans heeded the siren call of a country that promised fair wages, a long life, independence of action, and even wealth—untold wealth, perhaps—for anyone who was ambitious and industrious. All without concern for birthright or station.

Why, even the savages were being controlled. Hadn't General Anthony Wayne signed a peace treaty with the Ottawas and the Shawnees and the Miamis and the Iroquois in 1795?

There was a dreamlike image in Charles's mind of the forests and rivers and farmlands—the opportunity—that lay west of the Old Dominion.

He had followed, in his reading, the efforts of settlers in the western lands of North Carolina to establish the new state of Franklin. They had gone so far as to seek admission to the Union. That there were problems, that Franklin itself had come to naught, did not change the reality that there would be, someday, a new state in that region south of Kentucky.

Patton Anderson said that in his enthusiastic letters. And Dewey was certain that the West called to him. He had made himself an important man in Virginia. He was grateful for that. But he wanted more.

The West offered him more.

One question remained: When?

II

THE gray filly foal struggled to stand.

Charles watched her with half of his mind. That half told him the filly was big, healthy, energetic; the first daughter of Elkwood's White she was. The other half was still contemplating the letter he had received that day from Nashville.

"She's a special lady," Horace said to him.

"What?" He pulled his mind back together. "Oh, yes, she is indeed. Very special."

The two of them—the master of Fortunata plantation and the black jockey—watched as the foal finally got its footing and sought out the mare's teats.

"Let's get one of those small halters on her," Dewey said.

"Ain't none 'round, Mistah Charles. Had so many babies in this crop so far thet—"

"No mind. Get the housemaids to stitch up a few more in the morning, will you? The leather's in the tannery, all cut and ready."

"Yas, suh."

Charles yawned. It was very late.

"It just occurred to me," he said offhandedly, "that I left a couple of those small halters in a box in the loft at Elkwood." He shrugged. "Oh, well . . ."

III

HORACE was coming down the ladder from the Elkwood barn loft, two foal-size halters in his hand, when Funston walked into the barn, lighting his way with an oil lamp.

"Here, boy!" Funston shouted. "What are you doing there?"

"Ah come fer halters . . ." He held them up for Funston to see. ". . . thet Mistah Charles lef' heah."

"So you just came here to steal them!"

"Ah ain't stealin' 'em, Mistah Funston. Ah'm jest takin' 'em back 'cause Mistah Charles forgit 'em."

"Put them down!" Funston ordered.

Horace dropped the halters to the barn floor.

Lee came up to the young black and slapped him in the face. "Do you know what we do here with thieves?"

The boy was frightened now. "Ah ain't no thief, Mistah Funston, hones' Ah ain't!"

"Do these belong to you?" Lee asked, kicking at the halters.

"No, suh, but—"

"Then you're a thief." He bellowed: "Cephas! Jonas!"

Two black men came running to his side.

"Take this thief and tie him to the post!"

The slaves followed his orders without question.

"Rout everyone out," Lee shouted to anyone who could hear him. "And build a couple of fires. I want everyone to see what we do with thieves!"

Rapidly, two bonfires were built near the whipping post, and in what seemed only a few minutes more than a hundred slaves ringed it. The fires cast weird shadows on the trembling Horace, who was lashed tightly to the post.

"This boy," Funston announced to his audience, "is a thief! He came to my farm, climbed into the loft of my barn, and stole these halters." He displayed them to the sullen crowd of Negroes. "*My* halters!"

He was screaming. "Now he's to be punished for what he clearly is—a common thief!"

Slowly, with great deliberation, Lee walked to a pile of firewood nearby and picked up an axe. Returning to the center of the lighted circle, he gave an order: "Hold his hand firmly against the post!"

No one moved.

"Jonas! You!"

The elderly black man shuffled forward, grasping Horace's left arm several inches above the wrist and pinioning the arm against the post.

"Firmly, now," Lee instructed, suddenly appearing very calm.

The axe was swung in a giant arc, thudding into the post, sticking there.

Horace's agonizing scream echoed.

His severed hand dropped into the dust, soon to be made red mud by the bleeding stump.

There was silence, terrifying in its totality, broken only by the crackling of the bonfires.

Nonchalantly, Funston returned the bloody axe to the woodpile. He smiled. "Tie a rag around that mess and put him on his horse."

The smile grew broader. "Point him toward Fortunata."

IV

SOMEHOW, despite his pain and the loss of blood, Horace managed to guide his horse to the entrance of his master's house, where another slave saw him and ran to take the news to Charles.

Weakly, the jockey mumbled his story.

"Tell the smith to heat up an iron," Charles ordered, picking up the Negro in his arms and carrying him toward the blacksmith shop.

"I don't want to have to do this," he gently told the young man, "but you'll die unless we stop the bleeding. And quickly."

"Yas, suh."

At the smithy's Charles laid Horace on the ground. "Any whiskey around here?" An illicit jug was swiftly produced from under a pile of straw. Charles put the jug to the boy's lips. "Drink, lad, as much as you can."

Horace took several large gulps. He began to choke.

"Hold him down," Charles said. He undid the bloody rag, nearly retching when he saw the ugly wound. Dewey gestured for the white-hot iron, and the smithy brought it to him. "Hold the arm as steady as you can. Courage, boy." He didn't hesitate; the stump had to be cauterized.

Horace's screams chilled Dewey's blood, but he finished the job. The jockey was unconscious. "Put him in his bed and someone go for the doctor. Hurry! Hurry!"

By the time Charles got back to the mansion, his clothes smeared with blood, Martha had been told what had happened by one of the housemaids.

"Oh, Charles, it's just horrible!"

He didn't answer her, but went to his desk, and took a pistol out of a drawer. He checked the priming.

"Charles! What are you going to do?"

"I'm going to kill him," he answered with little apparent emotion. "I'm going to rid the world of that vermin."

Martha threw her arms around him, unmindful of the blood. "No, Charles, you can't! Don't do this! Please, darling—have someone go for the sheriff."

"There are times when there's only one way—"

"No! No! If you go up there with a gun, if you kill Funston, you'll be no better than he is! An animal!"

Charles stared at her for a moment, then dropped the gun on the desk. "Very well. Send for the sheriff." He dropped into a chair. Weeping.

V

HIS name was Caleb Mercer. He was a slovenly man with big hands and feet and a fat, puffy face. He was the sheriff of Goochland County, and he was unhappy that he had been rousted out of his home that late at night.

Charles told him the story.

"There ain't nothin' Ah kin do," the sheriff drawled.

"For God's sake, Mercer, Lee assaulted that boy—he cut off his hand! Don't you understand that?"

"Yas, suh, Ah understan' thet." He shrugged. "But after all, Squire Dewey, it were a nigger. An' he stole somethin' from Mistah Lee."

"Do you mean to tell me—" Charles couldn't find words in his angry frustration.

"He's only a nigger, squire."

Charles swept up the gun from the desk, pointing it at the sheriff. "Get out of here, you bastard, before I pull the trigger!"

The big man was unconcerned, perhaps because Charles had neglected to cock the pistol. He shrugged again, nodded to Martha, and left Fortunata, content in the knowledge that he had done his duty.

VI

HORACE survived the ordeal.

Charles Dewey's association with Goochland County, Virginia, did not.

Before that terrible night had ended, Charles had decided to leave Fortunata. He was going west. Now.

Uncharacteristically, he didn't discuss the decision with Martha. He simply told her they'd be leaving. His wife accepted the decision calmly, recognizing that there was no other way for him.

Martha wanted to ask him about the nagging feeling she had that Funston Lee was driving them away. But she thought it out, as she knew Charles must have thought it out, and concluded that there would be no happiness any longer at Fortunata.

For Charles. For herself. For her children.

16

LEAVING Fortunata was not something that could be done quickly.

Within the week, Charles rode to Richmond to consult with the lawyer, Millard Exner. He gave him power of attorney, asking him to begin to seek a buyer for the estate. The two men spent most of the day cataloging Dewey's assets, determining what would be sold and what would be taken along.

"Lee might be a prospective buyer," Exner suggested.

"Never! I'd put Fortunata to the torch before I'd sell it to him!"

The lawyer wisely changed the subject, asking about Charles's specific destination.

"Nashville, I think," he replied. "I have a friend there—a friend in correspondence, at least—and I've written to him asking about the availability of good property in that area."

"I know nothing about Nashville, but there's talk that our next state will come from that region."

"Most likely. And from what I've learned, it's an ideal place to raise horses." Charles smiled for the first time that day. "The racing there, according to my correspondent, is rather spirited."

"Well, wherever you go," Exner said, "you'll arrive as a rich man, I can assure you of that. Your assets add up to a rather impressive total. In one sense, you'll probably be more wealthy in the West than you are here in Virginia. Land values are cheaper there. So, too, should be the general cost of day-to-day living. More Spartan, too, I would imagine."

Charles made several major decisions that day: that he would carefully review his equine holdings and empower Exner to act as his agent for the dispersal of those horses he didn't want to take with him; that the lawyer would find him a competent and honest manager-in-residence for Fortunata for the transition period.

"What of the nigras?" Exner asked. "Are you going to take them with you?"

"I wish I could free them now, so that I could make my way to a new life without them."

Dewey grimaced. "But there's a strange reality about slavery, Squire Exner: it's difficult to let go of. If I freed them, what would they do? Most, I'll wager, would be back in slavery with someone else. Within days, probably; certainly within weeks. There are too many Funston Lees in Virginia to risk that. If I take them with me—as I must do, it seems—I perpetuate myself as a slaveholder. Maybe in the West I'll find a solution to the problem."

II

MARTHA began preparing the children for the move. Franklin, the eldest at nine, and George, at age seven, were the most enthusiastic. It was going to be a great adventure.

"Will we see any Indians, Mother?" Franklin asked, his eyes wide with the wonder of the thought.

"I imagine we might."

"Will they kill us?"

"Don't be silly, Franklin. Your father will be with us."

"Oh, sure." That was enough guarantee for the lad.

Corrine, at age six a very sober young lady, was concerned about one thing. "Will I take my pony along, Mother?"

"I would think so."

"Good, because I won't go if my pony can't go!"

Martha laughed at her, hugging her tightly. "We'll keep that in mind, darling."

The twins, Lee and Louise, less aware of what was really happening—they were only four—nevertheless danced about the mansion, singing a nonsense ditty taught to them by their black nanny: "We're going west, you hear, for to be a pioneer." Over and over again.

III

IN the first week of June 1796, Dewey heard the news that Tennessee had been admitted to the Union as the sixteenth state, with Knoxville as its capital. He had hoped to be well along on the road by that time, but dreaming of the West, and getting there, were two different things.

Charles was learning that there was a lot about preparing for travel in the wilderness that he didn't know. He had confidently designed a large, deep-bodied wagon, meant to carry the household furnishings both he and Martha wanted to take along. The body would be boatlike, so that it would float, if necessary, in fording the deep rivers.

There were to be two of the large wagons, and the slaves were set to the task of building them. When the first was finished, it was floated on the James River as a test. So cumbersome was it, and so unstable, that it listed to one side, shipped water, and sank.

A week, then, was wasted in trying to refloat the sunken wagon and salvage it. Only the wheels were brought out of the James.

After that experience, he re-adapted his design to widen the beam and to fasten pontoon-like devices on each side to keep the second wagon level in the water. But, that made it so heavy a team of oxen had difficulty pulling it, even before it was loaded.

Angry with himself because of his ignorance of wagon design, Charles abandoned what he had once proudly dubbed the "Fortunata wagons" sending a fast rider to Pennsylvania to order four of the tried Conestoga wagons from the craftsmen there. Three weeks passed before they could be delivered.

Yet another problem, and another delay, grew out of the difficulty of finding a manager-in-residence to look after Fortunata until it could be sold and until what he would be leaving behind could be brought to Tennessee at a later date. Lawyer Exner had made two recommendations to him, but Charles, after interviewing the men, had turned them down.

"Perhaps I seek a paragon," Dewey admitted, "but I must, initially, leave behind all of the blooded horses and a majority of the Negroes, and I need someone I can trust implicitly."

"I have such a man in mind," Exner assured him, "but he hasn't yet replied to my letter."

"Please do what you can to expedite this matter. I hope to leave by the end of June."

His first target date for departure had been the end of April.

By the third week in June, the Conestoga wagons had been delivered and were being loaded. Exner sent word that the man he was recommending "most highly" for the managerial position would arrive within two days.

On the morning of the second day, Charles paced the drawing room nervously, hoping that the lawyer had finally found the right man. When he heard horses on the road, he strode out onto the veranda and looked down the long lane. As the riders came closer, Charles gasped.

"Come quickly, Martha," he shouted into the house. "My God, it's Andrew!"

MacCallum raced his horse to the entrance of Fortunata, ahead of Exner, vaulted off it, and embraced his old friend. Martha, laughing and crying, joined in the welcome, kissing her former tutor in a most unladylike manner.

"You're to be my manager?" Charles asked, finding it hard to believe his good fortune. He hugged the Scotsman once more.

"I came, Charles," MacCallum said soberly, "because I'm so delighted that you're putting this . . . uh . . . stultifying life behind you. You'll remember I told you once that the time would come when you'd leave Elkwood—"

"I remember."

"—and that you shouldn't hesitate when that time came."

"Perhaps the time did come earlier, Andrew, but I couldn't leave while Statler still lived. His last days were very unhappy."

"So your letters told me. But now you'll leave, and I'm very pleased to be even a minor instrument in the beginning of your new life."

"I have a grand idea!" Charles exclaimed enthusiastically. "When we're established in Tennessee, and it comes time to bring the horses and the rest of the household there, you can join us!"

MacCallum grinned. "No, no, I'm not a frontiersman. I'm very happy in my post at Princeton. When this is finished, I'll be content to go back there. I'll leave the adventuring to you."

IV

WITH MacCallum at Fortunata, Charles pressed his plans to leave Virginia by the end of June.

It was an impressive caravan he put together: the four Conestoga wagons, each drawn by four light draft horses; two open-body farm wagons, with two horses each; riding horses for himself, Martha, the two older boys, plus the pony for Corrine; a half-dozen extra mounts, two milk cows, and seven slaves, including Martha's young housemaid, Angelica, brought along to help care for the children.

One of the six black men was Horace, who had pleaded with Charles not to leave him behind. "Ah'll work hard, Mistah Charles. This"—he held up his handless arm—"ain't gonna stop no hard work, Ah kin tell ya."

"I don't know, Horace. It's going to be a very difficult journey, and I'll need—"

"Please, Mistah Charles! Ah'm 'fraid when ya leaves thet Mistah Funston he gonna kill me!"

Dewey thought, at first, that the slave might be exaggerating the danger he faced, but the more he thought of it, the more he remembered about Funston Lee. Horace was added to the travel party.

Finally, June 28 was selected as the departure day.

On the preceding afternoon, after Martha had arranged with Katherine to have Funston Lee away from Elkwood, the Dewey family knelt at Marshall Statler's grave for a moment of silent prayer.

When they got to their feet, Charles said, "I hope that you older children will remember your grandfather. He was a great and kind man, and he loved you very much."

The sun was only a rosy presence in the east the next morning as the wagons lumbered away from Fortunata. Looking back at the mansion, Charles could see Andrew MacCallum standing on the veranda, waving. The Scotsman cupped his hands around his mouth and shouted: "God keep you all!"

The slaves of both Fortunata and Elkwood lined the road leading out of the plantation, many of them weeping.

Martha wept, too.

But Charles Dewey shed no tears.

It was too joyful a moment for that.

17

IT was three days to Charlottesville. By the end of the first week they had made the torturous climb to the summit of the Blue Ridge Mountains and had started down again.

Charles had decided to keep a journal on the trip. In it he wrote, "July 5: Slow going, but the weather has been most favorable. The children are delighted by seeing the countryside and all manner of wild creatures—none of a dangerous nature as yet. We hope for Staunton in two more days."

However, a wheel on one of the Conestogas was damaged when it bounced over a large rock, and it was four days, not two, before the travelers saw the village of Staunton. There they were to turn south to Lexington, cross the western reaches of the James and the Roanoke rivers and journey on to what was called the Wilderness Road, heading for Bristol on the mountainous border with Tennessee.

"July 10: Left Staunton at first light this morning, after having purchased a crude map of the wilderness area south of here. Much concerned about our slow progress."

Three days later they reached Lexington, the last substantial community they would see for some time. Charles and the family stayed overnight in comfortable accommodations at the Old Blue Travern, which was filled with travelers.

The children were fed and put to bed. Charles and Martha had the small luxury of eating together in the dining area of the tavern. The innkeeper, one Mr. Willingford, was an extrovert who chatted amiably with them.

"Where you headed, folks?" he asked.

"To Tennessee."

"A long journey—a long journey, indeed." He looked at them quizzically. "I gather that you're new to wilderness travel?"

"Yes, we are," Charles acknowledged, feeling inadequate at having made the admission.

When they finished their meal and had ordered ale, Willingford brought to their table a buckskin-clad young man named Abner Lower, identified to them as a long-hunter. His face was leathery; there was a greasy odor about him. Lower sat down with them.

"What is a long-hunter, Mr. Lower?" Martha asked.

"Some say a fool, ma'am." The young man grinned. "Some of us hunters go into the western wilderness for furs and stay several years at a time. A long time—so long-hunters." He pondered for a moment. "It's been three years since I've seen my home at New Market. I hope to be there in three or four days."

"Are you married?" Martha wanted to know.

The hunter laughed heartily. "I was when I last left. I'll just have to see if I still am when I get back to New Market."

Charles got out the map he had bought in Staunton spreading it out in front of Lower. "Is this accurate?"

Abner studied it. "Aye. Accurate enough, it seems." He looked up at Charles. "Those wagons outside, the ones with the nigras, are they yours?"

"Yes."

Lower shook his head doubtfully. "I'm afraid, sir, you might have a misconception of what the Wilderness Road is like." He nodded toward the map. "You see, it's more like a trace—a buffalo trace, really—pounded hard by God knows how many of those beasts over God knows how many years. It's clear enough to follow, that's true. But a road? Well, sir—"

"We didn't anticipate that the travel would be easy," Charles commented. There was a certain defensiveness in his tone.

The long-hunter sighed. "My daddy used to say that unasked-for advice is no advice at all because it won't be followed." A hesitation. "But I wouldn't be honest, Mr. Dewey, if I didn't tell you that you'll not make it over the Wilderness Road with those wagons."

Charles's shock showed on his face.

"Aye, that's right," Lower insisted. "The best thing I can tell you is to sell the wagons and most of what they carry, right here in Lexington, and make your way on horseback."

"But we can't," Martha cried. "All of our household furnishings are in the wagons."

The long-hunter grunted, sorry now that he had given the unsolicited advice. "Well, ma'am," he said pleasantly, "it's true that I never tried it with wagons myself, and maybe . . . " He drained his tankard, bowed to Martha, and left the table.

"Charles, we can't just abandon everything here," Martha insisted, tears coming to her eyes.

Dewey patted her hand. "Calmly, dear. We'll proceed as planned."

II

"JULY 15: Our first bad weather," Charles wrote in his journal. "Heavy rain, with severe thunder and lightning, swelled the Roanoke, turning the banks of the river into the stickiest mud ever seen. Waiting here on the north bank till waters recede for safe crossing."

It was the seventeenth before they could cross the Roanoke and continue their journey. Charles began to fume more and more about the slowness: "July 19: That long-hunter was right. 'Road' is a misnomer in this wilderness. At times it is but a footpath, and it becomes difficult to move the wagons through. I know now that I have made a basic error with the wagons, but we must persist, error or no. Becoming concerned that we may not reach our destination before winter. Damn the slowness!"

Three days later they faced another delay. The trace bar on a Conestoga was split when the wagon jolted over a deep rut, unseen because it was filled with leaves. Dewey had no choice but to pitch camp while the repairs were being made: "July 22: Probably couldn't have picked a more beautiful place to be halted. If there is more natural beauty on the face of the earth than this wilderness, I cannot imagine it. Shot a white-tail in the afternoon and all enjoyed its meat roasted over a large gay fire. All are well, in good spirits. All are working hard, including the older children and dear, uncomplaining Martha."

That night, as they slept under the stars on blankets spread on beds of fragrant pine needles, Charles was awakened by a slight moan. He listened for a moment or two. Then—a muffled cry. It was his wife. He could barely make out her form in the dark; her face was hidden from him.

Charles touched her. "Dear, are you ill?"

"No, no," she answered softly. "Just a twinge or two in my muscles. I'm a bit sore, I guess."

He leaned over, kissing her cheek. "I've been working you too hard."

"Don't be concerned, darling."

Charles relaxed again, trying to go back to sleep. Minutes passed, perhaps a quarter of an hour.

Suddenly, Martha screamed in pain.

Dewey shot to his knees, leaning over her. "What is it?"

She began to weep—hard, sobbing weeping.

"Get some light here!" Charles shouted.

Angelica brought an oil lamp, and one of the Negro men began to stir the embers of the fire to bring it to flame again. Charles was shocked by what the light showed him. Martha's face, running with sweat, was twisted in pain.

"My God, what is it? Tell me!"

"Oh, Charles—" She was biting her lip, drawing blood. "I didn't want you to know, to worry. I've been pregnant since mid-May."

"What?"

"I didn't want to delay your plans, so I didn't tell—"

"Are you aborting?"

"Yes . . . yes!" Her crying turned to a wail. "Oh, Charles, I'm so sorry."

By now all of the children were awake, and Charles tried to reassure them. "Your mother's ill," he told them, "but she's going to be fine. You can help by going back to your beds and by being quiet."

They obeyed him, but the older ones sensed that something was very wrong.

The black housemaid tried to help her mistress, but she couldn't stop the hemorrhaging. An hour went by. And two. Martha slipped into unconsciousness.

"Mistah Charles," Angelica whispered to him, "it ain't good, ain't good a'tall. Ah jest donna wha' to do 'bout these kinda things. Some ladies, they slip babies real easy like. But, other ladies—" There was no need for her to finish the thought.

Dawn came.

Martha's breathing was labored. Her face was a ghostly white. Charles sat holding her hand. Angelica was applying cool, wet cloths to her mistress's brow, knowing it would do no good, but needing to do something. The children stood a few yards off with the slaves. All were frightened.

It was only a twitch. Under other circumstances it would have gone unnoticed. But Martha's hand twitched briefly in Dewey's and then went limp.

He felt for her pulse.

There wasn't any.

Stunned, he sat for a moment or two looking into her face. Then he laid her hand on her breast and went to his children.

"God has taken your mother," he said to them, "to be with Him. She's in heaven now, and we must believe that she's happy."

They stared at him dumbly. Only Corrine cried, and she kept stabbing at her eyes with her fists, as if to push back the tears.

"Are we going home now?" Franklin asked.

"Home?" The question startled Dewey. "Our home, son, is still ahead of us. Your mother would want us to go on."

The boy drew himself up tall. "Then we shall."

"Yes, son, we shall." Charles dropped to his knees, gathering the children into his arms. They wept together.

Horace insisted on digging the grave. It tore at Charles's heart to watch the Negro struggling to do the job with only one hand. Several times one of the other men tried to help him, but Horace swung the shovel menacingly.

"Ah'm doin' it, nigger, Ah'm doin' it! So stay the hell 'way!"

They buried Martha beside the wilderness trail with only a mound of stones to mark the place, and some wildflowers that Angelica had helped the children gather.

On the largest of the stones Charles laboriously scratched a legend with a nail:

MARTHA STATLER DEWEY
1768–1796

III

Two more days on the Wilderness Road forced Charles Dewey to accept reality.

He guessed that his party had moved ahead no more than five or six miles in that time. The slaves were near exhaustion from their efforts to muscle the heavy wagons forward along the nearly impenetrable trail which was thickly lined on both sides by sycamores and oaks and chestnuts, some of them six to eight feet in diameter.

Charles stopped the wagons at a point where the buffalo trace narrowed even more and the giant trees crowded in to form a natural roof over them that blotted out the sun. The Conestogas were simply too wide to pass through. There was no way around the impasse. Virgin forest was everywhere.

The left front wheel of the lead Conestoga had struck against an oak, smashing it. They carried extra wheels, but it was useless to try to put on a new one.

What folly the wagons were, Charles thought. He wished he had listened to the long-hunter.

He sat down at the edge of the trail, listening to the cacophony of the hundreds of birds crowding the treetops, gazing at the profusion of wild-flowers. He marveled at the beauty of the wilderness. He cursed it, too.

Dewey let the slaves rest while the children ran in little circles, gaily playing a game of tag with Angelica among the flowers. Charles thought of their mother. It had been only forty-eight hours since they had placed that mound of stones over Martha's grave.

Forty-eight hours—an eternity!

After half an hour, he pulled himself to his feet, clapping his hands together. "Well—now we know!" he shouted. "Come, we have much work to do!"

He directed the unloading of the wagons—the four Conestogas and the two open farm wagons—making two piles of the items removed from them.

On the larger pile were chairs and beds and wardrobes and dressers: the household furniture that Martha had taken so much care in loading at Fortunata less than a month earlier. Charles would leave that pile behind, leave it to the demanding wilderness.

On the second pile were the things necessary for their survival: food, cloth-ing, blankets, tools, guns, ammunition. It seemed a pitiably small pile.

Darkness was already overtaking them when they started dismantling the wagons, taking them apart carefully because Charles had other plans for the wood in them.

They built a large fire in the middle of the rock-hard trace so that they might continue working into the night. Only when Charles realized that all—himself included—had reached utter exhaustion did he call a halt, dropping where he stood, falling asleep within minutes. Angelica had already bedded down the children in blankets.

Only the sounds of the night birds accompanied their slumber.

IV

"July 26: Finally got under way again at noon today," Charles wrote. "We have built a half-dozen sturdy sledges of the wood salvaged from the wagons. We loaded them with the necessary supplies and hitched them to the light draft horses—two horses to a sledge. In a very real sense, when we left the place where we abandoned the furniture we finally left Fortunata behind. But at least we move more quickly now. The party now includes myself, the five children, seven blacks, thirty horses (too many horses), one pony, and two milk cows. When—and if—we reach Bristol on the Tennessee border, I'll lighten this caravan even more. I'm determined to reach Nashville before winter."

It was sixteen more days to Bristol, situated some five miles off the Wilderness Road.

The little frontier community—just a collection of log buildings, really— was the northern gateway to the Tennessee Valley and to the rugged mountains that could have only one name: the Great Smokies. But, to Dewey, it was just a stopping point where they could regroup. He wanted to get back on the Wilderness Road as soon as possible, heading toward the Cumberland Gap, which would take him into the northeast corner of Tennessee, on the border with Kentucky.

At Bristol, Charles made the difficult decision to trim the size of his company. Two of the drags would be eliminated by repacking the supplies. He had determined that it wasn't necessary to have two horses on each sledge; one would be enough.

The entire entourage would be mounted: four of the slaves would ride the backs of the light draft horses retained to pull the sledges. Riding horses would be used for him, the two older boys, Franklin and George, the two other male Negroes, and Angelica, who would ride "double" with the twins. Little Corrine, of course, would have her pony.

That meant Charles could sell twenty horses. After hearing of the rigors they would face in the Cumberland Gap, he also sold the milk cows at Bristol. He didn't get full value for any of the animals; indeed, what he did was trade them for extra provisions—food stuffs, mainly, but also including four additional muskets and more ammunition.

While he was there he wrote two letters, after being assured that they would be taken to a drop on the federal mail route by other travelers coming through.

One letter was to Katherine at Elkwood, telling her of Martha's death but giving only the barest of details. He told her that the children were well but gave her no information about the problems they had encountered on the road. The letter was coldly factual, with no hint of affection in the words.

The second letter was to Andrew. It was a long, rambling, one-way conversation. A catharsis.

"Andrew," he wrote, "should I feel guilt for Martha's death? I tell myself I should; that, but for me, she would be comfortable now at Fortunata, happily awaiting the birth of her sixth child. Yet I feel no guilt. I think, as I look ahead at what still faces us, that she might be the most fortunate of us all."

Charles paused in his writing, to run a hand across his tired eyes. "My friend, I wish you could be here at this moment to talk to me, to counsel me, to explain for me the little madness that afflicts me now when I think of Martha. I have discovered—and I worry about my discovery—that I miss her not so much as a companion in my life, but because of the satisfaction she gave me as a loving bed partner. I realize that of all of the dreaming I've done about a new life in the West, Martha was not in those dreams. A woman was. But a strong woman. One of ambition. Another woman—not Martha.

"She was so sweet, Andrew, so eager to please me. And that I miss. But it comes running through my troubled mind that the Martha of Fortunata would not have been the companion I'll need on the frontier. Martha was pliant, not strong. And then I think that I'm the worst kind of cad to allow myself to make that kind of an evaluation of a wonderful woman—the mother of my children. It troubles me greatly, my friend."

He added a final thought: "I force myself to think of her. I want for me to cry for her. But I don't weep. Am I rational, Andrew? Or is this really madness?"

18

"August 16: Forded the upper reaches of the Tennessee River today," Charles wrote in his journal. "My map shows that we might reach Nashville by following the Tennessee, but there is a much more direct route by going through the Cumberland Gap and eventually linking up with the Cumberland River. That's my preference."

Five days later they reached the Cumberland Gap, through which the storied Boone had guided so many travelers.

Like the Wilderness Road, the Cumberland Gap was misnamed. It was a natural path cutting through the mountains, but no more than that. Less than that, in truth. Charles stopped his party to study the huge rocks they'd have to climb over, just as Boone's people must have done.

Dewey groaned. "We're never going to get the sledges over those rocks," he said to the slaves. "We'll have to make some slings from the linen covers we salvaged from the Conestogas, and load up the horses with supplies that way."

Three hours were spent in making the transition from the sledges to the slings, but there was still enough daylight to make it through the gap. He directed Angelica and Horace to lead the children through the rocks on foot.

"Take the easiest way," he said. "And carefully—make sure no one falls."

"I'm going to lead my pony," Corrine told him confidently.

"That's fine, dear." He gave his daughter a hug. "But keep a long lead on him. Don't pull at him. Let him find his own footing."

Angelica, Horace, and the children started through the gigantic rocks first. Charles and the five other slaves, each leading a pack horse, followed some hundred yards behind.

They were nearly halfway through the rocks when a scream echoed off the sides of the mountains. *Corrine!* Dewey tossed his lead rope to one of the blacks. Half scrambling, half falling, he made his way to his children. He was able to breathe again when he saw all five of them standing with Angelica and Horace.

Corrine, though, was shrieking. "Daddy! Daddy! My pony!"

The animal had slipped on the rocks, tumbling some thirty feet into a crevasse. When Charles got there he found the pony on his back, wedged tightly between two boulders, its legs thrashing in panic, its pained cries assaulting the ears. It took no knowledge of horses to make out that both forelegs had been broken in the fall.

Dewey went to his knees, cradling his tiny, distraught daughter in his arms.

"Baby, baby," he cooed to her, rocking her gently back and forth. "Corrine, darling, we don't always know why bad things happen. But they do sometimes, and we must be brave."

His words sounded so empty to him.

"The pony, baby, is badly hurt. He's in terrible pain." He paused, sighing deeply. "I'm going to have to end that pain for him."

He gestured to Angelica, who took the girl from him and led her away. Horace herded the other children after them.

Charles called for one of the Negroes to bring him a musket. The sound of the shot reverberated through the virgin mountains, bouncing back and forth, seeming never to stop.

"August 21: Poor Corrine," Dewey wrote. "How can I expect her to understand the sacrifices she has been asked to endure? First her mother. And now her beloved pony. I can only hope that a Benevolent Being gives her courage to go on. My God, she's only six years old! Did I do wrong in bringing the children on this sad adventure?"

That night Dewey took a blanket and bedded down away from the rest of the party. He had a need to be alone. The embers of the campfire were mere red dots in the wilderness as he lay on his back, his hands behind his head, gazing up through the openings in the branches to catch glimpses of the nearly full moon.

He must have dozed for a time, because he came awake with someone whispering to him.

"Mistah Charles—"

It was Angelica's voice.

He sat up quickly. "The children? Is something wrong?"

"No, suh. They's sleepin'. Ah'm sorry if Ah scared ya." Uninvited, she sat down beside him. "Ah jest thought mebbe ya was lonely."

"Lonely? Yes, I suppose I am."

The black woman reached out and took his hand. "Miss Martha, she love ya very much."

He didn't say anything. He didn't pull his hand away, either. Her touch was comforting.

"Sometimes a man he gits so lonesome it pains 'im."

"Yes."

Angelica gathered him into her arms, cradling him against her ample breasts as she would a child, as she had done with his children.

"We all loves ya, Mistah Charles," she told him. "We don't wanna see ya hurt this way."

He fell asleep again that way. For a long time Angelica held him. Finally, she eased him down onto the blanket.

"If ya ever needs me . . ." she whispered. And she returned to the children.

II

"AUGUST 25: Left the Wilderness Road this morning," Dewey wrote, "to head west. I never felt more alone than I do now. We have not seen any other person since leaving Bristol. The vastness of this wild country continues to astound me. I daily beseech my guardian spirit to bring my children through this safely. How foolhardy I was to undertake this journey without a competent guide!"

They continued to push forward through deep woods, with Dewey insisting that they not try to move too fast. He was afraid they would miss the connection with the Cumberland River. If they did, he knew they'd be lost in the wilderness, with not even the friendly buffalo trace to follow. Each morning he rode ahead of the caravan a mile or two to scout the area. He wanted to make no mistakes. His caution caused them to move only a few miles a day.

A week went by as Dewey's spirits dropped lower and lower. Then, just when he was debating with himself about whether they ought to retrace their steps to the Wilderness Road to seek a guide in one of the Kentucky settlements, he was able to write in his journal, "September 1: Reached what I believe is the Cumberland River in the midafternoon! Will scout a bit to determine whether there are other streams in this area. But once I convince myself this is really the Cumberland, we will finally be able to make speed to Nashville. Likely will be here several days to build rafts for the river. But tomorrow will just rest. Everyone extremely weary." He paused in his writing. Then he added just one word: "Angelica."

It flashed through his mind what he had thought when he heard of white masters who had taken Negro mistresses in Virginia. How abhorrent that had seemed to him. Now, however, he wasn't so sure anymore. He only knew that he wanted her. He knew, too, that she would come to him eagerly.

They were alone that night. They were one that night.

As they moved together, rhythmically, it was all so unaffected. So correct. For a few moments.

"My God!" he breathed as he reached a climax. He rolled off of her, suddenly struck with guilt. "Oh, Lord, I'm sorry, Angelica."

"Fer what?" she asked quietly. "Fer bein' a man what's hurtin' an' needin'?"

"I don't know," he admitted. "It's just that—"

"Is it 'cause Ah'm a nigger?"

The question was so direct that he had no ready reply for it. It shamed him.

"You're a warm, desirable woman," he assured her.

"Ain't thet 'nuff?"

She was wise, he decided. And they held each other. Content.

III

On September 3, the Dewey party began to fell trees to lash together into rafts. Charles had hoped to transport everything on the rafts—the supplies, the humans, the horses. But two days later, when the rafts were finished and floated, he had to change his plans again.

One of the larger rafts, built to carry animals, was pushed into the water and lashed to trees lining the shore to give it stability. A light draft horse, blindfolded to keep it from shying when it saw the unfamiliar craft, was carefully led on to the raft.

As soon as the hooves touched the raft it rocked in the water. The horse reared in fright, tossing one of the handlers into the river. The animal went down on its back on the roped-together logs, screaming and kicking insanely.

There was a sickening snap as the stricken horse's neck broke.

While the slaves dragged the heavy body of the dead horse off into the woods, Charles sat on his haunches on the riverbank, despondent, cursing himself for having tried an experiment he should have known was sure to fail. He contemplated his next move. *My next stupidity!* he thought.

"All right," he said after a few minutes, "we'll load all of the supplies on the rafts, with one man on the tiller of each of them." There were five of the log rafts. "The rest of us will be mounted. We'll try to stay together—the rafts in the river, the horses following along on the shore."

On September 6, he wrote in his journal: "We finally began the Cumberland River phase of our journey today. It seems to go smoothly enough, although at times the horses must be guided away from the river when the wild growth becomes impenetrable along the shore line. But we make good time. Estimate we covered better than ten miles today. Horace, who has to herd the extra horses, works especially hard to compensate for his missing hand. He's a brave man—he deserves something better than his sad lot in life."

Dewey learned soon enough that the Cumberland was a meandering river. What he had anticipated as a fairly straight course to Nashville was anything but. Nevertheless, they continued to move forward each day, and their steady progress made Charles believe they might reach their destination by the end of the month.

IV

"September 15: Saw our first savages today . . ."

"Father, look!"

Franklin was pointing off to his right, standing excitedly in his stirrups.

Some eighty yards removed from the Dewey party, Charles saw three faces in the brush. Painted faces. Stern faces.

Charles stopped his horse; the others did, too.

"Everyone sit very quietly," he instructed. "Don't make any sudden moves."

Slowly, his eyes fixed on the Indians, Dewey raised his musket over his head. He wanted them to see that he had a gun, but he wondered if it meant anything to them. Had they ever seen a gun before?

Once more Charles felt his lack of wilderness experience. For minutes—it seemed an interminable time—the white man and the Indians stared at each other. Dewey felt his right hand starting to quiver.

Just as slowly as he had raised the gun he lowered it to his shoulder, aiming it several feet above the Indians' heads, squeezing the trigger. The shot tore several branches from the trees.

The Indians were gone. Not that Dewey had seen them running away. The impression he had was that they simply . . . evaporated.

He let out a deep breath. The hand holding the gun was still shaking. His heart was beating much faster than usual.

"Will they come back, Father?" Franklin asked.

"I don't know, son."

"Do you think there were more than three?"

"I don't know."

Corrine piped up: "I wasn't scared, Daddy," she said forcefully. "I knew you'd take care of us."

Charles wanted to weep. Terrible questions coursed through his brain:

What if my shot had caused them to attack?

Were there three out there? Or thirty? Or three hundred?

Are they still there? Stalking us?

Corrine might not have been frightened, but Dewey was. Desperately frightened, because he had no answers to his questions.

He ordered the party forward again, at a faster pace, trying to put as much ground as possible between them and where they had last seen the Indians.

After a half-hour of what approximated a forced march, Charles stopped again, ordering the rafts brought to the riverbank.

Immediately, he distributed muskets to the Negro men, along with an adequate ammunition supply. He gave Angelica a pistol to carry. And to one-handed Horace, too.

He issued a stern order: "If we see savages again, we must shoot to kill. We must protect the children at all costs."

The blacks nodded solemnly.

As they made camp for the night, Dewey wondered what Funston Lee and his ilk would think about his arming of the slaves. It was the first time in several weeks that he had thought of the people back in Virginia.

And what of Andrew? Had Fortunata been sold yet?

V

"September 30: Exhaustion again," Charles wrote, "although we make progress. Have set up camp for two days. All need a rest. Angelica."

The first week in October brought heavy rains, flooding the Cumberland.

Dewey tried to push forward, but one of the rafts got sideways in the roaring waters, struck a large rock, and capsized. The slave manning the raft was pulled from the river, but the provisions were lost. One of the things claimed by the angry stream was their bag of salt. It was strange, but the lack of salt for the game they shot seemed a great hardship.

The flood halted them for two more days.

During the necessary idleness, Charles had an opportunity to marvel at the good spirits of the children. They were wet and dirty, probably bone-weary, but they didn't show it. The twins, especially, were gay youngsters under the guidance of Angelica, beginning again the silly little song they had chanted for so many days at Fortunata:

"We're going west, you hear.
For to be a pioneer."

Sober-faced Franklin, the eldest, insisted that Charles teach him to use the musket while they waited out the flood. They went into the woods for the lessons. The recoil of the first shot knocked the youngster to the ground, but he was up immediately, demanding to fire the gun again.

"We may need another gun, Father," the lad said, "if we see any more savages."

Dewey tousled his hair, continuing the instruction until Franklin's badly bruised shoulder brought it to an end.

Charles was proud of his determined son. Very proud.

By October 10, they were under way again, making good progress each day.

VI

ON October 15, Charles wrote, "Saw our first sign of Tennessee civilization today . . ."

They glimpsed a farm on the opposite side of the river. Dewey saw a man in one of the cultivated fields, and shouted over to him: "Hello, there!"

The farmer waved at him.

"Are we nearing Nashville?"

"Two days down river!" the man yelled back.

Everyone cheered.

On the night of the sixteenth, when the rafts were dragged ashore once more, Charles gave orders for everyone to bathe and prepare for their arrival in Nashville. Angelica went into one of the trunks lashed to the raft and brought out clean clothing for the children.

"What would I have done without you?" Charles asked the Negro woman as they sat before the fire that evening.

She smiled at him.

He returned the smile. No other words had to pass between them.

Three months and twenty days after leaving Goochland County, Virginia, late in the afternoon of October 17, 1796, Charles Dewey first saw Nashville, Tennessee.

Strangely, he wasn't exhilarated. His thoughts were on Martha as the rafts drifted up to the landing at Nashville and he slid wearily off his horse.

The rafts were unloaded quickly; what provisions remained were put on the backs of the horses.

Darkness was falling as they made their way afoot through the dusty streets of the frontier village to Mr. Parker's Nashville Inn, a rather handsome two-story frame building with broad porches across the front.

The horses and the slaves were bedded down in the stables behind the inn, and Charles sought two rooms for his family. He and the older boys, Franklin and George, would occupy one room. The younger children—Corrine and the twins, Lee and Louise—would have the other with Angelica.

"Uh . . . sir," the proprietor said hesitantly, "it's a rule of the house . . . well, coloreds aren't permitted in our beds."

"She's a nursemaid to my small children," Dewey explained.

"Nevertheless, I can't—"

Charles battled with his rising temper.

"My wife, Mr. Parker, died on the trip from Virginia." He was speaking softly, but the words were being forced through his teeth. "The children saw her die. Angelica is as much a mother as they have now. She's . . . going to stay . . . with . . . them!"

The innkeeper coughed nervously. "Yes, well, I suppose under those circumstances . . ."

Before retiring for the evening, Charles wrote a message to be delivered to Patton Anderson, his correspondent friend, informing him of his arrival.

As he put his tired body between the sheets of the first real bed he had known in nearly four months, he gave thanks to his guardian spirit.

It had sustained him again.

19

"YOU mean to tell me that you made that journey without a professional guide?"

Patton Anderson's tone was one of disbelief. The Nashville gentleman with whom Charles Dewey had been corresponding sat with him now at breakfast in the Nashville Inn.

"Yes, we did," Charles said, unable to hide the defiant pride in his reply. He was, however, unwilling to tell Anderson that he felt a fool for not realizing in the first place that he would need a guide.

"Astounding! That's what it is—astounding! And you had no brushes with the Indians?"

"Just one. I fired a shot in their direction and they disappeared into the wilderness."

Charles's new friend laughed loudly. "With that kind of luck, Dewey, I suspect that I ought to stay close to you. Does that good fortune follow you to the racetrack?"

"I've always believed that luck had very little to do with my success at the races," Charles answered soberly. "I'm very good with horses."

Another hearty laugh. "My God—luck and self-assurance, too! You're too good to be true, Mr. Dewey."

Anderson was only half of what Charles imagined he would be. His enthusiastic demeanor had been reflected in his letters, but Dewey had not expected a man who was such a dandy in dress. His mind's eye had seen Anderson as a rugged frontiersman; what he saw before him was a handsome, somewhat effete "gentleman"—not at all unlike many of the plantation owners he had known in Virginia. In a vague sense (Charles didn't really understand why), Anderson reminded him of Funston Lee. Perhaps that was why he saw in Anderson something faintly illicit. The word "shady" came to his mind, but he hesitated to accept it until he knew the man better.

Charles was anxious to catch up on the news. "I've been out of touch for a long time, Mr. Anderson. Tell me what's been happening."

"Happening? Well, Mr. Dewey— May I call you Charles?" Using 'mister' all the time is going to get tiresome."

"Of course. I'd prefer that."

"Well, Charles, the talk around here these days is of the presidential election. It's generally assumed that Adams will succeed Washington, although the preference here in the West is for Jefferson."

"I'd certainly like Jefferson better."

"Grand!" Anderson enthused. "It's good to know that we have another democrat among us."

Dewey grinned. "Democrat, eh? I'm not so sure that my political feelings are that much party oriented. Coming from Virginia, though, I'm familiar with Mr. Jefferson's views and agree with most of them."

"Good! Our own Andrew Jackson, as you'll discover, has views similar to those of Jefferson. They may be out of the same mold—politically, if not in life style. Certainly, they both believe in the rights of the people. It's expected that Jackson will be our first member of the House of Representatives come November."

"I look forward to meeting him."

"And you shall, very shortly. But, to continue with the news: While you were in the wilderness, Washington said his farewell to the country." He laughed lightly. "He warned against the growth of party spirit. 'Baneful,' I think he called it."

Dewey nodded.

"The other principal point he made," Anderson went on, "was that we should have peaceful commercial relations with all nations but no permanent alliances with any of them. If you'll pardon me, Charles, I think he was concerned about the French on that score. It seems that the French minister to our country publicly expressed his preference for Jefferson—which many considered undiplomatic." He laughed again.

Charles shrugged. "You give me no offense. I'm not French, you see; I'm American." A slight pause. "At least, I think I am."

"Oh, how's that?"

"Well, it has occurred to me that I ought to do something to legalize my citizenship. But I'm not sure what that something is."

"It's mighty simple here in Tennessee," Anderson assured him. "Six months' residence in any county constitutes citizenship. You, however, won't even have to wait the six months. Once you're a freeholder, as I believe you intend to be, Tennessee citizenship will come with only one day's residence. Obviously, Tennessee citizenship is tantamount to U.S. citizenship."

Dewey was pleased with that, and pleased, too, that the conversation had come around to the subject of land. "You mentioned in your last letter, Patton, a plot of land you thought might be to my liking."

"Right. Some two hundred and fifty acres along the east bank of the Richland Creek. Hard by what we call the Natchez Trace—the main road, if you can call it that, leading northward from the river port of Natchez. That's the Mississippi River, of course."

"Hmmm. Any buildings on it?"

"Only a log building. But rather substantial, Charles. Two rooms, both of good size. Its last use was as a trading post."

"And available?"

"Immediately so."

II

"WELL, sir, that's it!"

Patton Anderson swept an arm to encompass a small clearing in the woods dominated by a log building. Not a two-room cabin, as Anderson had suggested at breakfast, but two separate cabins connected by a roofed walkway.

Charles groaned inwardly. He tried hard not to compare what he was inspecting to what he had left behind at Fortunata. But it was difficult. He might dream of what he could make of it—he was long experienced at dreaming—but this was just a crude scene to him. He felt disappointment.

With Anderson, he had ridden in bright sunshine and with good spirit some ten miles from the center of Nashville to see the property his newfound friend was recommending.

"How many acres?" Dewey asked, although he already knew the answer. He had to say something to relieve his depression.

"Two hundred and fifty. Approximately. I suggest you have a survey done immediately."

"Hmmm. And no cleared land?"

"No, but it offers plenty of opportunities to open up some substantial meadows for grazing. The land here is very rich. Very rich, indeed!"

Charles slid out of the saddle, walking toward the cabins. Anderson followed.

"There's good water here," Patton said. "From the Richland Creek and from numerous springs as well. There's a spring serving the building." He pointed.

When they went inside the larger of the two cabins, Charles saw that it was incredibly dirty. Debris of the former trading-post business was scattered all about. Rats scampered away as they entered. Cobwebs covered everything. There was no glass in the few windows, and where the rain had come in on the wooden floor, the boards were warped.

"Of course," Anderson said, "it'll need some cleaning up."

Dewey laughed. "Indeed it will!" Somehow, his friend's inane remark had broken his depression.

They inspected the second cabin. It was no better than the first.

Outside again, Charles took a drink from the spring near the door. The water was sweet, cold, refreshing.

"Other parcels?" he asked. "Is it likely that land adjacent to this might also be available?"

"More than likely. Not too much of the land hereabouts has been improved by the owners. They're short of money, I guess."

"And that brings us to a key point, doesn't it? How much for these two hundred and fifty acres?"

"Twelve hundred and fifty," Patton answered.

Open-mouthed, Dewey stared at him. "Oh, come now, Patton, twelve hundred and fifty pounds . . . for this?"

Anderson laughed at him. "Not pounds, Charles—dollars! American dollars. You're not in Virginia any longer."

"Hmmm. Five dollars an acre? That seems fair."

"It's a damned good bargain, Charles, a damned good bargain!"

As they talked, a lone figure rode out of the woods on a large, decrepit mule. A white man. Tall and skinny. Dressed in somber black. A specter, it seemed.

"Good afternoon, sirs," he called out to them cheerfully.

"Good afternoon," Anderson answered.

The man stopped his mule in front of the larger cabin and sat staring at it. "Mr. Duncan? He's not in business any longer?

"Duncan's been dead for two years," Anderson told him. "Indians killed him."

"Is that a fact? Well, it's true that I haven't been through here for nearly three years. Duncan was a good friend—may God rest his soul."

"Have you just come off the Trace?"

"That I have. I've been preaching the word of God to those wayward denizens of the Natchez Trace from before the days it was called the Natchez . . . when it was still known as the Chickasaw Trail. For what lasting good, I don't know. Two nights ago, three of those blackguards jumped me. Took every cent I owned." He laughed. "Two whole dollars!"

He held up a well-worn Bible. "But they didn't get my sword!"

"It's lucky you weren't killed," Anderson commented.

"The Lord, sir, was my Protector. I'm sorry, I haven't introduced myself. I'm Brother John . . . Brother John Farnsler." Once more he laughed. "Well, if the truth be known, the name is Homer Farnsler, but Brother John has a better ring to it."

Anderson and Dewey completed the introductions.

"We're about to return to Nashville . . ." Anderson looked to Dewey for confirmation; Charles nodded. "We'd be pleased to have you ride with us, Brother John. In light of your financial straits, perhaps I can stand you to a meal at Mr. Parker's."

"I accept your kind offer"—the preacher grinned—"content in the knowledge that, once more, the good Lord has provided for His servant."

III

"YES, from my earliest days, Mr. Dewey, I've appreciated a good racehorse." He smiled. "And a good wager. My fondest hope is to build a track at Poplar Grove someday soon." A slight groan. "If I can ever find the time."

The speaker was a young man named Andrew Jackson.

Charles had been surprised when Jackson strode into the dining room of the

Nashville Inn for the dinner arranged by Patton Anderson. From Anderson's tales of Jackson's exploits—service in the Revolutionary War, attorney general of the Western District of North Carolina, proposer of the name of "Tennessee" for the new state, Indian fighter with the state militia, soon to become a member of the U.S. House of Representatives—Dewey had expected an older man. But Jackson appeared to be about Charles's age, maybe even a year or two younger.

He was tall—six feet or so—and slender with intense blue eyes and dark red hair. His pleasant face was pockmarked. There was a white scar on his forehead suggesting a wound from . . . what? There was a special presence about the man.

"I recall that quite a few officers in my company rode blooded horses from Virginia when we were fighting Cornwallis in the Waxhaws," Jackson was saying. "Those good horses gave them an advantage—they really did. Of course, that was some time before Yorktown. Patton tells me you were at Yorktown."

Charles was embarrassed. "I was in the French navy then, which was blockading the town. I can't honestly say I fought there, in the sense of seeing dangerous action."

"Well, it was rough in the Carolinas in those days, let me tell you." The good dinner, with several glasses of wine, had put Jackson in an expansive mood.

"Excuse me, sir, how old were you then?" Charles asked.

"Thirteen . . . fourteen." A hand went to the scar on his head. "I got this from the sword of an English dragoon officer who demanded that I clean his boots. I refused, and he did this."

Charles wondered how a man could tell that story without seeming to brag. But Jackson carried it off.

"But . . . I'd rather talk about horses, wouldn't you?"

Dewey nodded.

"I remember vividly the races at Charleston after the war. Charleston was a gay town then—I believe it still offers the best racing in America—and the courts and schools and businesses were all closed during the race meeting. I was fifteen and had just had the good fortune to inherit three or four hundred pounds sterling from an Irish uncle. A considerable fortune, as you can appreciate. But my selections at the track were faulty. Damned if I didn't lose it all!"

His laughter filled the dining room.

"I had an unhappy landlord in Charleston at that time," Jackson went on, "who wanted to know when I was going to pay my rent. Well, the money was gone. So I went to a tavern where I knew there was a high-stakes rattle-and-snap game. I put up my horse against two hundred dollars and rolled the dice. I won, too! And the landlord got paid."

There was more laughter.

"Mr. Dewey plans to establish a breeding farm here," Anderson interjected, "with blooded horses. Just today he made arrangements to purchase the old Duncan trading-post property on the Richland."

"Nice piece of land," Jackson commented. "May I ask what you paid for it?"

"Five dollars an acre," Charles answered.

Jackson cocked his head, looking hard at Anderson.

"That includes your commission, I imagine?"

"Including my commission," Patton said, grinning.

"In that case, a fair price." Jackson jerked a thumb toward Anderson. "You've got to watch this fellow, you know." He smiled broadly. "Last year at the Gallatin races, our friend here got . . . well, overextended a bit in his wagering—"

"That's an accurate description," Patton agreed lightheartedly.

"And his creditors got a bit obstreperous. They wanted to take it out of his hide, I imagine."

"They did! They did!" Anderson was already laughing so hard that tears were running down his cheeks.

"Well, Patton came running toward me, as the last friend he had in the world, with three or four of those fellows on his heels. It was dusk, you see, and while they recognized me, they had no way to know whether I was armed or not. I wasn't. But I had a tin tobacco box in my pocket, and I took it out and clicked the lid. In truth, it sounded for all the world like a pistol being cocked. The unhappy creditors scattered like sheep!"

Now there was general laughter at the table, turning the heads of all the other diners.

"Were the wagers every paid?" Dewey wanted to know.

"What? And ruin yet another tale of Andy Jackson coming to the aid of the oppressed?" Patton started to roar all over again.

Jackson sobered. "Mr. Dewey, I was bound to make common cause with Patton in that incident. He's my friend."

The conversation turned to the horses Charles planned to bring to Tennessee. He described the stallions he was going to move from Virginia in the spring, with full pedigree particulars.

Jackson seemed impressed. "You're making a wise move, Mr. Dewey. The opportunities for a horseman of your stripe will be boundless here in Tennessee. I look forward to competing against you."

IV

LATER, in his room, Charles started a letter to Andrew MacCallum, telling him of the land he had bought and of the dinner with Andy Jackson.

"I don't believe I would want to be counted among his enemies," he wrote. "He's obviously an important man here in Tennessee. Also a very knowledgeable horseman. Jackson is talking of soon building a track in Nashville; one already exists in nearby Gallatin. So there will be plenty of opportunities for racing next year.

"Patton Anderson, my correspondent, turns out to be something of a scoundrel, although a likable one. Inadvertently, he has given me the name for the new estate. He said the land I acquired was a good bargain, and so I shall call the farm Bon Marché—good bargain.

"How does that strike you?"

BOOK TWO

This would be an impossible world in which to
live if some of us were infallible.
—Andrew MacCallum, 1808

20

"Ya sonofabitch! The goddamned bet were twenty dollars!"

"Yer a pig-faced, lyin' bastard! It warn't but ten!"

Lunging drunkenly at each other, the two buckskin-clad young men grappled, tumbling heavily into the dust of the street, kicking and punching and gouging and biting.

Their fight was largely ignored by perhaps a dozen other men whose attention was on another battle: two fighting cocks slashing at each other with razor-sharp metal spurs, doing horrible damage. The birds were evenly matched in weight and frenzy, and the gamblers gathered around the cockpit at the Nashville Inn rent the late-afternoon air with obscene shouts.

Dewey watched them for a minute or two, shook his head in disgust, and entered the inn to have dinner with his children.

Nashville wasn't much.

Charles found it dishearteningly crude.

The hard-drinking nature of the frontiersmen who peopled the village was evident in the fact that there were three taverns plus a convenient distillery among the fewer than fifty buildings that made up the community. One of the taverns was operated by Captain Timothée de Monbreun, a French adventurer and Indian trader from Quebec who had been the first white man to settle on the Nashville site. His place of business was built of stone, suggesting the permanency of the liquor trade.

The town was an odd mixture of what Nashville had been and what it might become. Most of the buildings were of simple log construction. But the courthouse was of stone, the jail was surrounded by an attractive, if incongruous, white picket fence, and Mr. Parker's Nashville Inn offered amenities not expected on the frontier.

Then, too, there were signs of increasing commerce: J. B. Craighead's merchandise store was a two-story brick affair; one James Jackson also ran a store in a new two-story frame building, offering items from as far away as Philadelphia and St. Louis.

There was even a doctor, a man named Hennings, in residence.

In contrast to those minimal suggestions of civilization, Nashville also boasted a set of stocks in the public square, where law-breakers—most often just roistering drunks—were frequently on display. There was a whipping post, too. And that cockpit by Mr. Parker's inn.

The proximity of cockfighting to the inn was reason enough for Charles to move immediately to make the log buildings on the Richland Creek habitable. He didn't want his children exposed to the cockfights, and to the rough men who conducted them, for any longer than was necessary.

At Jackson's store he ordered glass to replace the missing windows at the former trading post. He bought beds and chairs and other furnishings as well—thinking then of the pile of fine furniture he had abandoned on the Wilderness Road. And he dispatched the six male slaves to his new property to clean and repair the buildings.

Within a week, although all of the furniture wasn't in place, the Dewey family left the comfortable accommodations of the Nashville Inn to begin a new life at Bon Marché.

II

ANDREW MacCallum's letter, addressed to Dewey in care of Patton Anderson, brought some solace to Charles, and some bad news, too.

"You should feel no guilt, my friend," Andrew wrote, "about dear Martha's death. I suggest to you that it was God's will and that you take heart in that. I suggest, too, that you not read too much into your dreaming, your subconscious contemplations, about seeing another woman by your side on the frontier. Do not allow the fact of Martha's death to twist your reasoning. It has happened. It's a tragedy, but it has happened. You need only remember her loving nature, the joys she brought to you as your wife, and then move on—looking ahead to what your young life still offers you. Be not melancholy, my friend. But revel in the enjoyment you find in the children Martha gave you. They are your future, not recriminations about what might have been."

Andrew's words brought some peace to Dewey. But not his other news: "Fortunata is not yet sold at this writing. Lee has made two offers for the property through agents, both below the announced price. I suspect he believes that if the estate remains unsold for a time, you will lose your resolve not to sell it to him. Be assured, however, that Lee will not get it—under any circumstances! Hard money is scarce, though, and a proper sale may be long in coming . . ."

Charles tried to put that out of his mind; he did so successfully for many hours at a time as he and the slaves readied Bon Marché for the winter. A third log building was erected as a sleeping quarters for the slaves. Charles purchased two sturdy mules to help pull stumps from the ground as work began on clearing the first of the pastures designed to keep horses.

It was hard work, but spirits were high.

III

"MISTAH Charles," Angelica said quietly, "Ah needs t' talk t' ya."

It was a bitter cold day in early December, and Charles was sitting alone on a pile of rocks that had been cleared from the number one pasture, surveying the work accomplished.

"Yes?"

The slave woman's eyes were downcast. "Ah'm gonna have a baby, Mistah Charles."

Dewey seemed unperturbed. Outwardly. "Mine?" he asked.

Sudden hurt showed in Angelica's face. She waited for a moment before she answered calmly, "Yas, suh."

"I see."

The nerves in Dewey's stomach were knotting, but he tried not to show his anxiety. "Yes, I see," he repeated, sucking in a long breath. "You're sure?"

"Yas, Mistah Charles."

His words came slowly. "Angelica, I'm certain you can appreciate that this news comes at a most inopportune time. I mean, just when I'm beginning to play a role in this community—"

She stared at him.

"Of course, I intend to have you receive the best of care, and for the baby to be supported—" He swallowed hard. "But I cannot acknowledge this child. It would be . . . well, most awkward. You understand that, don't you?"

"Yas, suh."

"What do you suppose would be the best way to handle this?"

Angelica had no words.

"I don't want you to have a bastard child. You're too dear to me to allow that."

Silence.

He had made his decision. "You must marry, of course."

The black woman's eyes opened wide.

"Yes, yes, that's the answer," Dewey went on. "You'll marry. I know that you're partial to Horace—"

"Oh, no, Mistah Charles!"

"I thought you admired Horace?"

"Oh, he a nice man, Mistah Charles, but he only got one han'!" She shuddered.

"That's hardly a reason to reject him," Dewey insisted coldly. "He's a hard worker, and he's kind. He'd look after you and your child."

Angelica was bold now. "It *yer* baby, Mistah Charles."

The knot in his stomach tightened. This wasn't going well at all. "Yes, I understand that, but I've already explained to you, Angelica, that my position in this new community—"

With defiance: "Ah'll have mah baby alone!"

"No, I can't permit that." He made his voice hard. "You'll marry Horace and that will settle it!"

"Yas, suh." She was still a slave. She recognized that fact.

Charles nodded. "I'll arrange it with Horace."

"Yas, suh." Tears began.

"Angelica, don't carry on so. You'll have a fine baby and a fine husband, and all of you will be taken care of."

She began to walk away.

"I'll see if I can find that itinerant preachers. Brother John, and we'll take care of this as soon as possible."

Angelica left him.

Dewey felt nauseated.

He knew that what he was doing was hurting Angelica deeply: a woman who had been kind to him, who had probably saved his sanity during the difficult wilderness journey. But she *was* a black woman!

Horace would do as he asked; the one-handed slave, he reasoned, would do anything he asked. The nausea grew. Those two gentle black people, Angelica and Horace, loved him. And, he was—

Charles shook his head to clear it. He needed a clear head now. Brother John would be a good choice to perform the wedding ceremony, because he probably wouldn't be around too much to serve as a reminder to Charles of what he had done. Was he really a minister? Did it matter?

His decision was firmly made. His plans for Bon Marché and for himself were too important to toss aside because of a half-breed baby.

He was, after all, the master of Bon Marché!

IV

THE slim young man with the aquiline nose and the thin lips wore a white satin ruffled suit. It was in the highest style, but badly wrinkled, suggesting that it had been packed away in a saddlebag for many days.

"Your Royal Highness," Charles said, bowing formally, not sure that he had used the proper form of address. *"Enchanté de faire votre connaissance."*

"Please, please," the Duke of Orleans said, "speak English. I'm quite proud of my English." He smiled broadly. "You must be the Monsieur Dewey whom Captain Maxwell told me about. Of the French navy, eh?"

"A very minor cog. It was a long time ago."

"Hmm. And what are you doing in this wilderness?"

"Breeding horses, Your Excellency—racehorses."

The duke's eyebrows rose expressively. "Ah! *C'est trop cher!*"

"Expensive? Yes, at times. But I've been most fortunate."

"You don't miss France, then?"

"I have few fond memories of France," Charles said quickly. "Oh, I'm sorry if I've offended—"

The French nobleman laughed. "Don't apologize to me for that. I don't look fondly upon the France of today, either."

Dewey was aware that Louis Philippe, Duc d'Orléans, had, as a Bourbon prince, been imprisoned by the French Revolutionary Directory and then exiled to the United States. He was taking advantage of that exile by touring the new nation with his two younger brothers, the Duc de Montpensier and the Duc de Beaujolais, also exiles.

It was mid-May of 1797, and the entire white population of Nashville had been invited by Captain Jesse Maxwell, at whose new hostelry the Frenchmen were staying, to a reception in honor of the royal trio.

Charles had thought about not accepting the invitation; he wasn't much interested in Bourbon princes. But it had been a long, hard winter at Bon Marché. And two days earlier a letter from MacCallum had put him in a celebrating mood.

"Good news finally!" his friend had written. "A Cornell Monkton of Richmond has met your price for Fortunata. I delayed giving him an answer until Lawyer Exner could prove to me that Mr. Monkton was not acting as an agent for Funston. Once I was convinced that he was not, the legal papers were drawn up. I expect him to sign them within the week."

MacCallum added a second bit of welcome news:

"That long-hunter, Abner Lower, whom you recommended as a guide to bring the horses to Tennessee, has accepted the assignment. As a matter of fact, he left two days ago with the horses you want and eight of the blacks. Lower has agreed to guide the remainder of the household on another trip as soon as I can wind up the business here. He seems a competent man. I like him. He says that he ought to be seeing you at the beginning of August, with luck, perhaps as early as late July."

Dewey tore his mind away from the memory of Andrew's letter and directed his attention once again to the royal guest. "How are you finding America?" Dewey asked the Duke of Orleans.

"Rugged! Most rugged, indeed. But invigorating, for the most part." He smiled. "We seem to have come to Nashville at the wrong time, though. What with the court being in session, the accommodations here are extremely limited. Captain Maxwell is a gracious host, but my brothers and I are forced to sleep three to a bed."

Charles laughed. "You're fortunate, Your Excellency, that your bedfellows are related. You might have been quartered with two strangers."

Orleans joined in the laughter. After another moment or two of polite conversation, Charles drifted away to Maxwell's well-stocked bar and asked for a bourbon. He was becoming quite fond of the local whiskey.

He stood nearly alone at the end of the bar, watching the gentry of Nashville being introduced to the Duke of Orleans, enjoying the scene.

Tim de Monbreun came in, the Quebec Frenchman all flustered at the thought of meeting French royalty. He shook visibly when he was introduced and let loose with a string of frontier Pidgin French expletives that brought a guffaw from the duke.

As Charles continued to look on, a petite young lady was presented. She had flowing auburn hair—Charles suddenly recalled his Parisian friend, Marie—wide, knowing eyes, and full rouged lips. Despite her small stature, she was full breasted, and her self-assurance was immediately evident; she seemed not awed at all at meeting a Bourbon prince of France. She curtsied politely, exchanged a few words with the duke, and joined the other guests in the crowded room.

"Who is that young lady?" Charles asked another man at the bar.

"The redhead?"

"Yes."

"James Jackson's daughter. The storekeeper, you know."

Nodding his thanks for the information, Dewey drained his glass, and made straight for her.

"Excuse me, ma'am," he said, "my name is Dewey—Charles Dewey. I'm told that you're James Jackson's daughter."

"Yes, I am." She studied him frankly.

"I trade at your father's store, but I've never seen you there."

"I've been away at school. In Boston." Before he could comment, she asked: "And what do you do, Mr. Dewey?"

"I'm a horse breeder. I'm building an estate out by Richland Creek, on the former Duncan trading-post property."

She smiled beautifully at him. "Oh, an estate! Not just a farm, but an *estate.*"

"Yes," he said defensively, annoyed by her sarcastic tone, "that's what I intend it to be. The finest estate in western Tennessee."

"I'm pleased for you, Mr. Dewey." She turned to leave him.

Charles placed a restraining hand on her arm. "Perhaps I can show it to you some day?"

"Perhaps." Once more she tried to move away, but his hand stayed on her arm.

"Perhaps tomorrow," he said insistently.

She stared at him for a moment, as she shook loose his light hold. "It must be a *grand* estate, sir."

"Well, not right now, but—"

"I mean, if I must see it immediately," she teased, "I imagine there is a marvelous house, with the most modern of appointments, and—"

"No," he admitted disconsolately, "I live in a log house."

"Log houses, Mr. Dewey, are easily seen here in Nashville, without riding way out to Richland Creek."

He knew she was making fun of him, but he persisted. "Miss Jackson, what you'll see there now—and what you'll see there in two, three years—will astound you."

"But, right now—not much?"

"Not much," Charles admitted.

"Two years, or three, would be soon enough to see the *magnificence* of your estate, wouldn't it?" Her eyes—they were what Charles thought of as spring green—sparkled. "Explain to me, Mr. Dewey, why I must see it now."

His mouth was suddenly dry. The words he was about to speak seemed not to be his; he felt they were being forced out of him.

"Because I intend that you, Miss Jackson, shall be the mistress there."

The girl laughed loudly, all heads turning toward them. Charles flushed.

"You are entertaining, Mr. Dewey." She paused, looking into his eyes. "I take it that you're serious."

"I am."

She stepped back away from him, running her eyes over him from head to foot and back again.

"Attractive enough," she said quietly. Not to him. To herself.

Her candor left him without words.

"Now, Mr. Dewey," she went on, "do you have a staff on this grand estate?"

"I have blacks, yes."

"And you live there alone with your slaves?"

"No," he replied hesitantly, "I . . . uh . . . have five children."

She gasped. *"Five children!"*

"Yes."

"And your wife?"

"She died."

The auburn-haired girl offered him no false words of sympathy. "And so you see me as a nursemaid."

"Good Lord, no!"

"What *do* you see me as?"

"As the beautiful mistress of Bon Marché."

"Hmmm . . . Good bargain?"

"Yes, that's what it means."

"I'm to be a good bargain, too, I imagine?"

He was suddenly angry. Her continual sarcasm did that. He wanted to end the conversation.

"Miss Jackson," Charles said in formal tones, "perhaps I spoke too hastily, too boldly."

She pouted. "Oh, you're withdrawing your kind offer?"

"It seems you wish me to."

Another beautiful smile. "Very well, Mr. Dewey, you've won me over. I'll see your *estate*. You may call for me at my father's store at noon tomorrow. You *do* have a carriage?"

"Of course."

"Noon, then."

She started to turn away from him. "Oh, by the way, my name is Matilda. Mattie, to my friends. You may call me Mattie, if you wish."

V

CHARLES was nearly an hour late in arriving at the store for Mattie Jackson the next day.

"I'm terribly sorry," he explained to the annoyed young woman, "but our servant girl picked this morning to have a baby. I simply had to be there."

"You must have a strong paternal feeling for your blacks."

"Yes, I do." He drew a deep breath. "You see, Angelica was my late wife's housemaid, and—"

Mattie interrupted his explanation: "I like that about you, Charles Dewey—your concern for your blacks."

While she still spoke candidly, the sarcasm of the night before had disappeared. They chatted incessantly during the carriage ride to Bon Marché, with Mattie telling him that she was a second cousin to Andrew Jackson.

"At least," she laughed, "that's what Daddy claims. It seems that he had a cousin in North Carolina who may have been a cousin to Andrew Jackson's father. It's all pretty vague, really. But we have fun with it. I call him Cousin Andy and he calls me Cousin Mattie, and everyone is comfortable with that. It really doesn't matter to me, one way or another. Cousin or not, I admire him immensely."

"He seems a unique man," Dewey commented.

"A *great* man!" she corrected him.

Charles was at ease with her. He told her of Paris, of the days in the navy, of his guardian spirit, and of the decision it made for him to become an American. Of Elkwood and of Fortunata. Of the trip west and of Martha's death.

Once again he omitted the fact of his desertion; he hadn't told Marshall Statler about it, or Martha, or even Andrew MacCallum. He saw no need to tell Mattie about it. That secret, he was determined, would die with him.

At the Richland Creek property, he guided her around, proudly showing her what had been done.

"My horses will be here in late July or early August, and then you'll see the beginning of what this"—he swept an arm—"is meant to be."

The afternoon passed swiftly. Looking at the sun moving westward, Charles said to her: "We ought to leave in a few minutes if I'm to get you home before darkness sets in."

"I haven't seen the new baby yet."

"Oh, that won't be necessary."

"I *want to,* Charles."

Reluctantly, Dewey led her to the cabin built for Horace and Angelica. Horace bustled about importantly as he greeted the visitor. Angelica, her face impassive, was sitting up in her small bed, nursing the light-skinned baby.

"Oh, it's darling," Mattie cooed. "A boy or a girl?"

"A son," Horace replied proudly. "His name's Marshall."

Charles explained: "Marshall Statler was the master of Elkwood plantation, back in Virginia." He tried to prod Mattie. "We really ought to be leaving—"

"May I hold him?" Mattie asked of Angelica as she finished the nursing.

The black mother extended the tiny bundle to her without comment.

Mattie took the baby in her arms, rocking it gently, cooing, thoroughly enjoying herself.

After another few minutes: "Mattie, if we're to be back before darkness—"

"Oh, very well." She surrendered the baby to Angelica. "Thank you."

Angelica nodded. She didn't smile.

On the drive back to Nashville, Mattie was exuberant about the children. "Corrine and I could be good friends. She's a very self-assured young lady."

"Like you, I think."

Mattie looked over at him. "Yes, isn't she? If I ever have any children of my own, I hope I'll have a daughter like Corrine." Grinning, "Franklin, though, is not so sure about me. I suspect that he sees me as a potential intruder."

"Franklin will love you," Charles interrupted. "He above all the others would accept you as a mother. He's a very realistic, sensible young fellow."

"Aren't you getting a little ahead of yourself?"

"What?"

"Talking of me as a mother of those children. I love children; you could see that, I'm sure. But a ready-made family is *not* what every young girl dreams of."

"But—"

"Charles, I went along with your suggestion that I might be the mistress of Bon Marché only because I thought it was a ploy, a way to meet me, to—"

"I was totally serious!"

"And ridiculous," she said forcefully. "I discovered today that I enjoy your company. That I like your children. That your dreams of an estate in this wilderness are challenging. But you've read too much into my acceptance of your offer to take this carriage ride with you. Much too much!"

"I apologize for that." Mattie had made him angry again.

They rode along in silence for a time, Charles getting into the horse for more speed. He wanted to get her home.

It was she who broke the silence. "That baby—you're the father, aren't you?"

Not looking at her, a scowling Dewey whacked the reins down on the back of the horse. He didn't give her an answer, but he had the horse at full trot now.

"I'd be thankful," the young woman said stonily, "if you'd slow the carriage a bit."

He obeyed her, but without comment.

"You *are* the father, aren't you?"

"Yes." It was a mumble, barely audible.

They were within sight of Nashville before Mattie spoke again. "Do you want to court me, Charles Dewey?"

Indeed, that was what he wanted. Yet the anger she had generated in him— brought on by her unrelenting candor and the admission she had wrung from him about Angelica's baby—would not abate quickly.

She waited a few moments for his answer. "Well . . .?"

"Yes, I do want to court you."

It was a factual statement, devoid of enthusiasm. She recognized that.

"Very well, let's give it a try," Mattie said. "But no promises. Not yet. I suggest that no promises be made on either side."

"I agree." He swallowed hard. "I was desperately afraid that when you learned about Angelica's baby—"

"Who am I to make moral judgments? The only thing I wanted, Charles, was the truth. If you had lied to me, there would have been no talk of courtship, believe me."

He exhaled a loud breath.

"Relieved?"

A smile came. "Yes—much relieved."

She was laughing as he drew the carriage up in front of the Jackson store.

"Could you come for dinner Saturday night?"

"I'd be pleased to."

"Don't be too pleased," Mattie giggled. "The dinner means that you'll have to make some kind of announcement to my parents about your intentions."

"Oh, God—"

"I know . . ." She patted his hand. "But Mother is one of those ladies who put a lot of store in such formalities."

Dewey grimaced. "Suppose she doesn't approve of me?"

"Oh, she won't. Without a doubt, she won't. You won't measure up to her standards. She sent me to school in Boston hoping that I'd meet a young, wealthy New England merchant from an impressive family."

Mattie edged closer to him, dropping her voice conspiratorially. "And I did meet such a young man. Mother doesn't know it, but I did. There was one little problem: he . . . uh . . . well, he had a rather serious quirk—he wasn't attracted to women." She laughed loudly.

Charles joined her laughter. "I don't have such a problem." He leaned over, trying to kiss her.

She avoided him. "You don't have to prove that to me, you know. Remember—I saw the baby today."

Dewey groaned.

"That wasn't kind, was it?" She kissed him lightly on the cheek. "Saturday, then. Seven o'clock. And please don't be late. You may not have as convenient an excuse as you had today."

21

THE mare writhed on the ground, sweating profusely, emitting sharp cries of pain, her legs thrashing.

"Don't nobody know what to do for her?" Abner Lower asked of the slaves who circled the stricken animal.

"It da colic," Malachi, one of the older blacks, answered with a certainty born of experience. "Her gut done git twisted, Ah guess."

"And what do we do?" Lower demanded. He disliked being in a situation where the Negroes knew more than he did, but he had never been involved in breeding horses and he had to rely on the slaves.

"Ain't nothin' to do, Mistah Abner. Da colic, it bad. She gonna die."

The long-hunter looked at the position of the sun. It wasn't yet directly overhead, although nearly so.

"Shit, we could make another six to eight miles today if it warn't for this!"

"Yas, suh," Malachi replied dutifully.

The mare's foal came up to her, nickering, trying to nuzzle one of her teats. He was kicked away by the pained mother.

"What happens to that foal if she dies?" the guide of the Fortunata party wanted to know.

" 'Nother mare might take 'im, but it ain't likely."

Lower frowned, walking away from the group, pondering. He glanced again at the sun. Moving quickly now, he went to one of the pack horses, and brought down a musket, and loaded it. The slaves melted away from the mare as the long-hunter approached.

"Ain't no point in standin' around here just waitin' for her to die," Lower muttered. No one disagreed with him.

He put the muzzle of the gun to her ear and pulled the trigger. The once-proud head of the blooded mare jerked convulsively as the noise of the explosion reverberated through the wilderness.

"Now, the foal—"

Malachi became bold. "Suh, he got ole Skull's blood runnin' in him. Mistah Charles, he partial to thet."

Lower hesitated, lowering the musket. "You think another mare might take him?"

"Ah try, Mistah Abner."

"How long?"

"It take time."

Their guide sighed. "Well, try, then. We'll make camp here tonight."

He spat in the dust, angry at the delay. "Shit!"

II

MATTIE Jackson hadn't been wrong. Her mother didn't approve of Charles.

"Frankly, Mr. Dewey, I had hoped for more for my only child than a debilitating life in this ungodly wilderness!"

Sarah Jackson was a humorless woman: sullen, argumentative, imperious, snobbish. And sarcastic. It was easy to see where Mattie got her casual sarcastic repartee. She got her looks from her mother, as well. Mrs. Jackson was a strikingly handsome woman, but her beauty was ruined by the perpetually stony expression.

Mattie's parents were a study in contrasts. Storekeeper James, whom Charles already knew, was extroverted, talkative, inclined to tell bawdy stories. He was cowed by his wife, however; she was clearly the dominant figure.

Thus the Saturday night dinner evolved into a competition between Dewey and Sarah Jackson.

"The wilderness can be difficult at times, ma'am," Charles countered, "but I've never thought of it as debilitating. *Challenging* and *invigorating* are more appropriate words, I believe."

Mrs. Jackson answered with a snort of derision. "I've seen women crushed by this frontier life—made old before their time." Looking directly at her husband: "I myself have suffered. There are simply no graces here, Mr. Dewey. None at all!"

"Those will come, Mrs. Jackson."

"So James has been telling me—for a decade now."

Mattie tried to placate her mother. A courtship, she told her, didn't mean automatic acceptance of a marriage proposal. "I'm not certain I want to marry Mr. Dewey. Or anyone else, for that matter. It's simply a period of time to get to know him."

"Hmmm." Mrs. Jackson was unconvinced. And the longer the dinner went on, the more hostile she became.

"Your family, Mr. Dewey—may we know about them?"

"I'm an orphan, ma'am," he said quietly. "From a very early age."

"My daughter tells me you served in the French navy."

"Yes."

"A rough upbringing, wouldn't you say?"

"Yes, it was. But a man can rise above his background."

"As the twig is bent!" she snapped.

James Jackson tried to interject one of his off-color stories; Mrs. Jackson would have none of it. She silenced her husband with a glare and continued her cross-examination.

"Are you wealthy, Mr. Dewey?"

Charles laughed lightly. "So my lawyer in Virginia tells me. I know for certain that I'm not poor, Mrs. Jackson. I really don't know how to compare my holdings with those of others, but I believe I have enough assets to be comfortable."

"And you're a horse breeder?" She made it sound like an accusation.

"Yes."

"A gambler, too, I imagine."

Charles hesitated. He decided not to deny it. "I wager on horse races, yes."

Sarah snorted again. "I must be frank with you, Mr. Dewey. I don't approve of your courtship of my daughter. I would much prefer it if she would find a young man in a more civilized section of the country. A professional man."

"I appreciate your concern for your daughter's well-being"—she was beginning to annoy him greatly—"but I suggest, Mrs. Jackson, that the opportunities in this area for a man of ambition are much greater than those in Boston or Philadelphia or—"

She cut him off. "So James has been insisting." She paused. "How old are you, Mr. Dewey?"

"Thirty-two."

"And you have five children?"

"Yes."

"My daughter," she intoned, stretching out the words for emphasis, "is but eighteen. I would think she has enough sense to see the dangers of a ready-made family."

"Miss Matilda has already expressed her reservations on that score."

Mrs. Jackson's eyebrows shot up. "Oh, she has? It seems that the two of you, in a rather brief time, have discussed a great deal!"

"We've been candid with each other."

"I'll be equally candid." Her voice rose. "I don't believe you are the right man for Matilda. You are much too worldly for her, Mr. Dewey." She sighed. "But Mattie is headstrong. I don't imagine she will listen to my objections."

"Mother," her daughter pleaded, "we're speaking only of a trial period—"

"Which could very well end with a pregnancy!"

"Mother!"

James Jackson interjected: "I think, Sarah, that you're being unfair to—"

"Unfair!" The woman's anger took over. "Was it fair of you to drag me into this godforsaken wilderness to . . . to serve drunks and illiterates and white men who are more savage than the Indians they trade with?"

Her husband had heard it all before; he had reached the limits of his forbearance. "Our daughter," he said forcefully, "is intelligent enough to make her own decision in this matter. I know Mr. Dewey as a gentleman. If they wish to consider marriage, I'm for it."

Sarah glared at him. But she had made her argument; she said nothing more, retreating into sullenness.

The dinner ended, Charles and Mattie sat on the porch of the store overlooking the village square, hearing the raucous noise from the Nashville Inn cockpit.

"I warned you," Matilda giggled.

"She is formidable."

"Uh-huh. And very unhappy. She really hates it here. I feel sorry for her."

Charles frowned. "Your father, it seems to me, deserves your sympathy more. He has built a good business here, becoming one of the most respected men of this community. Yet he gets no credit for it—only vilification."

"But, Charles, this is *Nashville,* not Philadelphia or Boston. Mother wants desperately to go back east." Her voice dropped. "I'm afraid I was her last hope for that. If I had married a Bostonian, she would have had an excuse to leave Nashville. To get back to civilization."

Dewey just nodded. He didn't want another argument.

"And I *am* her daughter. There's some truth, you know, in what she says. I'm not sure, myself, that I want to stay here."

He took her hand. "Then I'll just have to convince you, won't I?"

"You have a difficult task, Charles Dewey."

III

ABNER Lower groaned as he came awake. He had slept fitfully as, all through the night, the blacks had been trying to match the orphaned foal colt with a nurse mare. There had been much squealing and kicking and frustration.

The long-hunter got to his feet. "Well, Malachi," he said to the patriarch black, "what luck?"

"Ain't had none, Mistah Abner," the slave admitted. "Thet baby jest ain't wanted."

"And what now?"

"He die if he cain't nurse."

Lower shook his head sadly. "We can't let him die that way, can we?"

"No, suh."

Once more the guide went for his musket, once more the sound of a shot echoed through the woods.

"Come!" Lower called to the blacks. "We're movin' on! We have a long way to go yet."

He felt sad about what he had had to do. He was a hunter, but he never thought of himself as a killer. He hunted as a business; shooting the two horses seemed somehow wanton to him. But he had no other choice.

Opening the log book Andrew MacCallum had given him, he crossed off two entries: Estella, bay mare, by Messenger; unnamed bay foal colt by Premier Etoile, by Skullduggery, out of Estella. Lower wondered how much money was involved in the deaths of those two blooded horses. A great deal, he imagined.

IV

IN late June, Charles Dewey more than doubled the original acreage of Bon Marché. Patton Anderson offered him two parcels: one amounted to one hundred seventy-five acres at six and a half dollars an acre; for another oddly shaped piece of land encompassing two hundred sixty-three acres, Anderson was asking seven dollars an acre.

Charles demurred. The prices, he thought, were too high. Anderson, as agent for the sellers, was demanding too high a fee. After much haggling, they arrived at a compromise price of six dollars and twenty-five cents an acre for both plots. Yet Dewey felt that Anderson had taken advantage of him.

"But I want the land," Charles told Mattie. "The land is *everything* to what I want to do here."

"I don't like that man Anderson," she said.

"He's a good friend of your Cousin Andy."

"I know," Mattie said, frowning, "and I can't understand that. Sometimes Cousin Andy is loyal to the most unlikely people."

"Loyalty is an admirable trait."

"If it's not misplaced," she insisted. "Aren't there other land agents with whom you can deal?"

"Anderson has his fingers in a lot of pies in this area."

She was silent for several moments. Then: "Suppose I acted as your agent?"

"Oh, I don't know . . ."

"I'm intelligent," she said. "I meet a lot of people at Father's store. I hear a lot of things." A hesitation. "Or don't you want to be represented by a mere woman?"

He laughed. "My dear, I know you well enough to know that there's nothing mere about you. If you want to try . . ."

Three days later, Mattie took Charles to see the young widow of a frontiersman who had been killed in a brawl at de Monbreun's tavern. She lived in a mean little cabin on the edge of Nashville; her only asset in her widowhood was a parcel of two hundred fifty acres of uncleared land near the Richland Creek—not contiguous with Bon Marché, but close enough to be a desirable acquisition.

"Mr. Dewey is prepared to offer cash for your land," Mattie explained to her.

Doubt showed on the widow's face.

"Has someone else made you an offer?"

"Well . . . Mr. Anderson has said he might be able to get three dollars—"

"Mr. Dewey will pay you three-fifty an acre," Mattie said immediately.

Still the widow hesitated.

"Have you promised Mr. Anderson? Signed over the land to him, perhaps?"

"No."

"Then I suggest that you accept Mr. Dewey's generous offer."

The widow began to weep. "I don't . . . know what to do," she said between sobs. "I just want to go home . . . to Vermont."

Mattie went to her and cradled her in her arms. "Mr. Dewey," she said, looking at Charles, "will give you cash immediately—"

"By tomorrow morning," Charles agreed.

The deal was made.

As he and Mattie walked back toward the Jackson store, Charles chuckled. "I seem to have taken on a new land agent."

"And you can see what kind of profits Anderson has been making at your expense. Grabbing up land that he can sell to you for twice what he offered the owners."

"Probably." He sighed.

"Hereafter," she said coldly, "there'll be no more deals with Patton Anderson."

Dewey laughed. "That poor fellow. He has no idea what a fighter he has for his competition."

V

A week later, over Mrs. Jackson's vehement opposition, Charles and Mattie rode away from Nashville, heading north and east toward Lexington, Kentucky, some two hundred ten miles distant. Charles wanted to attend the races at the new Lexington Jockey Club track. He also wanted to arrange to breed several of his mares—still en route from Virginia—to a newly imported English stallion, Blaze.

They would be gone for nearly two weeks, and Mrs. Jackson railed about the impropriety of such a trip.

"Impropriety, Mother," Mattie had said, "has nothing to do with travel. We could just as easily behave improperly right here in Nashville."

The trip was a joy to Charles. The more time he spent with the self-assured young woman, the more he admired her. As they rode in perfect weather toward Lexington, the admiration turned, he believed, to love. At least for Charles. It was not something they discussed.

It was five days to Lexington, and when they got there, Postlethwait's Tavern, where the new track was located, was crowded.

"You're in luck," the tavern owner told them. "I have one room still available. It's in the loft, but it's comfortable."

"I was hoping for two rooms," Charles said.

"If my life depended on it, there would be nothing else available."

"Perhaps elsewhere, then?"

"Not within easy riding distance of Lexington. If you're here for the races, I suggest you take this one room now." He grinned lecherously. "Your wife and you will be comfortable, I guarantee that."

Mattie spoke: "Thank you, Mr. Postlethwait. We'll take what you have."

It was a tiny room, with space enough for just the one bed. But as the innkeeper had promised, it was comfortable. And clean.

"You take the bed," Charles said, "and I'll make do on the floor."

"Why?" Mattie asked boldly.

"Well, I . . . uh . . ."

"Don't you want to share a bed with me?" She showed him a pout.

"Your mother's concern with impropriety—"

"I'm not asking you to go to bed with my mother." She looked at him with wide eyes. "Of course, if *you're* concerned with what is proper . . ." She let the sentence trail off.

Charles had a sudden vision of a similar conversation with Katherine on a Christmas night at Elkwood many years earlier. And he thought now, in retrospect, how much that had changed his life.

"Charles!" She was annoyed by his silence.

"Oh, I'm sorry. A momentary reverie . . ." He grinned sheepishly. Boyishly.

"You were thinking of another woman?"

"Yes," he confessed.

"And you're not going to tell me about her?"

"No," he laughed. "It was many years ago, and it has nothing to do with us."

Mattie feigned anger. "I ought to insist that you sleep on the floor!"

"But you're not going to."

"No, damn you!" She kissed him. Meaningfully.

There was no more talk. They undressed quickly, sinking into the thick feather-filled mattress, making love feverishly at first. And then slowly and comfortably. They fell asleep in each other's arms.

With first light, Charles woke to her touch. She was running her fingers down his chest. Teasing him.

"Good morning," she said sleepily.

He kissed her tenderly.

"I enjoy making love to you, Mr. Dewey."

He smiled at her. "You know, I had that impression."

"Is there a reason to get an early start this morning?"

"The racing won't begin until the afternoon."

"Isn't that convenient?" She giggled, entwining herself with him.

VI

LEXINGTON, while it was still a frontier town, was a good deal more civilized than Nashville. It offered several good inns; there were numerous substantial homes in the community. It had a government, having been incorporated some fifteen years earlier. And there was a newspaper, the *Kentucky Gazette*, which Dewey found devoted a considerable portion of its columns to horse racing.

It was well past noon, the first heat of the first race already having been run, when Charles and Mattie made their appearance at the new Lexington Jockey Club racecourse. Charles made inquiries about a John Fowler, one of the owners of the imported English stallion, Blaze. When he was directed to the gentleman, Fowler greeted him effusively.

"I've been hearing a good deal about the racing around Nashville," Fowler said.

"Not so far advanced as it is here," Charles admitted, glancing around at the large crowd.

"Ah, but I believe we had a head start on you. There's been racing here, on a more or less formal basis, since 'eighty-nine. Here and in Georgetown and Danville and Equiria and Shelbyville and Bardstown."

"Hmmm."

"Kentucky, Mr. Dewey, is leading the way for racing in the West."

Dewey told him that he was interested in breeding some mares to Blaze.

"Do you want to see him?" Fowler asked.

"You have him here?"

"Yes, he's standing at a farm just down the road. I figured there'd be a lot of breeders here who might want to inspect him. He's the first true English horse to be brought to this state, you know."

Fowler led the way to a temporary paddock near the racetrack, where the big bay stallion pranced and postured. A large white blaze marked his face, obviously giving the horse his name.

"Impressive," Charles said.

"He had a decent race record in England," Fowler volunteered. "Of course, not as great as some others, but . . ."

Dewey decided to book three of his mares to the stallion, and an agreement was made for ten dollars a mating.

"Are you a wagering man?" the Kentuckian inquired.

Charles's hearty laugh was his answer.

"Might I suggest that you place a bet on a gelding named Boone in the three-mile dash coming up?"

"Well, I don't know your horses—"

"Believe me, Mr. Dewey, Boone is most solid in that race."

Dewey followed his advice, betting a hundred dollars on Boone in a public selling pool being operated by the jockey club. The gelding was distanced.

The visitor shrugged off the loss, but as he and Mattie walked away, Charles whispered to her, "Rule number one: *never* bet blind."

"Why did you, then?"

"Because . . ." He thought for a moment. "Hell, I don't know!"

VII

As they were eating dinner at Postlethwait's Tavern that evening, Charles said, "We ought to get an early start in the morning to return to Nashville."

"Hmmm."

He chuckled. "What I'm trying to say is that we ought to consider an early retirement."

"Because we have to rise at an early hour?"

"No," he admitted, "because I want to be in bed with you."

"That's a sensible reason."

He reached across the table, taking her hand. "Mattie, when are we going to be married?"

"I didn't know we were going to be."

Dewey's face mirrored his shock. "But I thought—"

"I like you very much, Charles Dewey," she said softly. "I like your love-making. But I'm not sure I want to be married to you. I need more time to decide that."

He sat silently, unable to find words.

"You see, I don't believe that going to bed with a man is reason enough to marry him. If I had believed that, I would have been married in Boston."

There were times when he hated her candor.

"You love the whole idea of Bon Marché," she went on, "of building it, nurturing it, making it the finest estate in Tennessee. That's admirable. But is it for me? I don't know. Not yet."

"So I must wait?" He couldn't hide his annoyance.

She nodded. "If you want me."

"I want you."

"You're a terrible romantic, Charles," she said soberly. "I'm much more practical than you."

"So I'm beginning to understand."

"Good!" She rose from the table. "Then let's be practical. It's time to go to bed."

22

"CHARLES! Charles! The horses are here!"

Mattie rode wildly into the clearing at Bon Marché, her horse heavily lathered.

"The horses," she reportedly breathlessly. "That fellow Lower arrived in Nashville with them this morning. I've led them out here. They're just a few minutes behind me."

She turned in the saddle, pointing down the wooded road leading into Bon Marché. She was beaming, proud of the service she had performed.

Charles helped her to dismount. "Didn't anyone ever teach you not to run a horse like that?" The remonstrance was mild, however, and was followed by a kiss.

"I think I'm as excited as you must be! Your horses are here!"

"How do they look?"

A frown. "I don't know, Charles. I'm not an expert on horses."

They stood together looking down the broad lane. A minute. Two minutes. Three. Charles shifted nervously from one foot to another.

Then, when he saw the Fortunata party coming out of the woods, Charles ran forward to embrace Malachi, the loyal old black man. "Thank God you've made it!"

"Yas, suh. We all mighty glad to be here, Mistah Charles."

Dewey stood silently as the horses were herded past him, counting them and clapping the other blacks on the back as they came by him.

Abner Lower, mounted and looking very weary, brought up the rear. When he came abreast of Charles, he slid to the ground and gave him a clumsy salute.

"Mr. Dewey—your horses."

"My God, Lower, they look . . . well, all wrung out!"

"Yes, sir. It was a difficult trip."

"I counted only twenty-five."

"Yes, sir. We lost three." He told him of the episode with the mare Estella and her foal. "And just two days ago, that two-year-old, Virginia Song, stepped in a chuckhole and broke his right fore. I'm sorry, Mr. Dewey, but I had to destroy him."

Charles groaned. He really wanted to weep. "Virginia Song? I had great hopes for him."

The hunter-guide nodded.

A forced smile. "Well, Lower, it's good to see you, nevertheless. I imagine it could have been worse."

"It could have been," Lower agreed. "To be truthful, I didn't realize how slow it would be, driving that many horses."

"Hmmm. I can appreciate the difficulties, believe me."

Dewey shouted to Malachi. "Put the mares and foals in that pasture to your left. The horses in training on your right. And take the stallions directly to the barn. Horace will show you the way."

Lower went to his saddlebag and took out the log book listing the horses. He handed it and another package to Charles.

"MacCallum sent these along. The larger package, he said, is the latest English Stud Book."

"Thank you, Mr. Lower." Charles shook his hand. "I know you must be tired and hungry. We have food prepared—"

"I just want to sleep."

"Of course."

As they walked toward the log houses, Dewey asked: "The slaves? They gave you no trouble?"

"No, sir." He hesitated, choosing his words carefully. "They . . . uh . . . well, dammit, Mr. Dewey, they love you."

II

LATE that night Charles sat in the light of an oil lamp, studying the log book of the horses. Mattie was quietly by his side.

He wrote a note in the book. "Note this date," he said to her. "August 10, 1797—the real beginning of Bon Marché."

"It's noted."

Charles repeated the date. "A beginning with twenty-five horses. Five stallions, seven horses in training, and ten mares, three with foals by their sides."

"You're pleased, aren't you?"

"Yes. I believe them to be the finest blooded horses in western Tennessee." He paused. "Or, I guess I should say *thoroughbreds*. I noted in the English Stud Book that Andrew sent along that that's the universally accepted term now—thoroughbred."

Mattie made no comment.

Charles smiled. "Thoroughbred? Andrew had an old English dictionary at Elkwood, when he was tutoring me, in which thoroughbred meant a well-bred or thoroughly trained person. But I think the term is well applied to our blooded horses. *Thoroughbred*. I like that—it has a good ring to it."

"I have five of the best stallions in this area," Charles went on. "Premier Etoile, a son of Skullduggery, by Yorick. Lord, Marshall Statler was proud of old Skull. And he allowed me to name Premier Etoile, you know." He laughed. "But of course, you *don't* know. I have so much still to tell you." Dewey leaned over and kissed her. "So much to tell you."

She smiled at him.

"Then there's Predator, by Shark, and Arrangement, by Medley—I had a role in importing both Medley and Shark." He paused in thought. "In '84 and '86, if my memory serves me.

"And New York, by Messenger." A grin. "Mattie, I actually sent mares all the way to New York to breed to that stallion. He's a bit small, but sturdy. The Messenger blood lines may yet be important. And, finally, Cranium, also by Skullduggery."

He sighed. "Skull's last foal colt. Not much at the track, but Martha was particularly fond of that one. I guess it's the reason I kept him. Oh, hell, Mattie, I must be boring you to death."

"You're not," she told him.

"It's late, isn't it?"

"Hmmm."

"I wonder what your mother is going to say about you staying out here tonight?"

"Do you care?"

"Yes, I care. She's bound to be unhappy with both of us."

Mattie shrugged. "I don't care." A deep breath. "It is late, Charles, but could we talk?"

"Certainly."

"I watched you carefully today with the horses, and for the first time, I realized what Bon Marché means to you. Angelica was with me, and she said something I haven't been able to dismiss. She said, 'He needs you, Miss Mattie. He can't do it without you.' Do you think that's true?"

"Angelica is a wise woman."

"And she loves you deeply. She makes me feel inadequate in that department. I'm not sure, Charles, that I love you as she does."

"Don't be silly."

"No, it's true. I admire you; you know that. But love is something else again. Yet when she said, 'He can't do it without you,' I knew she was speaking the truth. You need me, Charles, for my strength—"

"I do. And—"

She silenced him by putting her fingers to his lips. "Bon Marché needs more than a horseman. It needs someone to manage it, to make it grow, while you care for the horse business. If you'll take me on those terms, Charles, I'll marry you."

Delighted, he tried to kiss her, but she moved away from him.

"Will you take me on those terms?"

"Yes."

"Knowing that love is not yet there?"

"On any terms."

She kissed him, sealing the bargain. And she laughed. "After a good night's sleep—if that's possible with us—I'll ride to Nashville and tell Mother."

"You want me to go with you?"

"No, you have work here. I'll take care of Mother. I'll also have Father put in an order for sawmill equipment."

"Sawmill?"

"To cut the lumber to build the Bon Marché mansion. The best damned house this wilderness has ever seen!"

III

MATTIE'S news of her decision to marry Charles Dewey did not produce the anticipated rage in her mother. Instead, Mrs. Jackson accepted it calmly, with even a small measure of cheer, immediately setting about making plans for the ceremony.

Sarah ordered her own wedding gown of lace and silk removed from the huge trunk and altered to fit Mattie. She rented Mr. Parker's large parlor in the Nashville Inn for the occasion. And she ordered her husband to find champagne somewhere and have it brought to Nashville. It turned out that St. Louis was the nearest source of champagne—of whatever quality—and two riders were dispatched to fetch it.

A date was set—August 30.

Most troublesome in the planning was finding someone to perform the ceremony. Nashville was devoid of churches and ministers. Itinerant preacher Brother John wasn't considered by Sarah to be proper, but he wasn't in evidence anyway, busy wih his own saving of souls somewhere on the Natchez Trace. In the end, Superior Court Judge John McNairy—who was due to be in the community for a court session—made his services available.

Sarah had several disappointments. She sought a decorator to turn Mr. Parker's parlor into a wedding chapel. The closest such gentleman was found to be in distant Philadelphia; Mrs. Jackson decided to do the decorating herself. A professsional chef was not available either, but Sarah finally accepted Mr. Parker's assurances that the Nashville Inn cooks were equal to the important task of providing a sumptuous wedding dinner.

If Mattie was happy about her mother's sudden change of attitude, James Jackson was ecstatic. With tears in his eyes, he said to his daughter: "Your mother is a fine woman. I knew that when you decided to marry, she'd come around." He swallowed hard. "I've always loved her, Mattie, but now I can't express to you how deep that love has become."

IV

EVERYONE in the Nashville environs was invited to the wedding: the merchants, the tavern owners, the buckskin-clad hunters, the Indian traders, the gamblers, the rough denizens of the cockpit, the frontier entrepreneurs. Not the blacks, of course.

And everyone came.

Guest of honor was the Honorable Andrew Jackson, Senator of the United

States of America, properly dignified in breeches and a somber black coat with a velvet collar. Accompanied by his shy, quiet-spoken wife, Rachel, Mattie's "Cousin Andy" signed the marraige document as an "official witness."

It was a gay scene in the Nashville Inn parlor, made more so after the dinner—Sarah deemed it adequate fare, still wishing she had been able to find a proper chef—by two frontiersmen who broke out fiddles, leading to impromptu dancing.

The champagne disappeared quickly, but other spirits provided lavishly by Mr. Parker kept the wedding party alive. More than a few were taken drunk.

Mattie and Charles stood in a corner of the room, accepting the congratulations of the guests.

Senator Jackson came up to them. "Are you two planning a honeymoon?"

"A few days alone," Charles answered, "not a formal honeymoon. We're just going to ride out and lose ourselves for a time."

Andy nodded soberly. "A wise move. Being alone with the one you love, you will find, is often difficult. I myself find that a great luxury, what with my many responsibilities." He sighed. "Too many responsibilities, perhaps."

"Do you have to accept them all?" Charles asked.

"Someone must, sir, someone must."

Jackson drifted away to talk to others and, in a short time, left the inn. No one else seemed to. The revelry went on unabated.

Mattie nudged Dewey, inclining her head toward her mother, who could be seen in earnest conversation with the long-hunter, Abner Lower.

"That's an unlikely pairing," she said.

"Hmmm. Perhaps your mother has decided to make her peace with this ungodly wilderness." He laughed.

"For Father's sake," his wife replied, "I hope so."

V

JAMES Jackson awoke, squinting in the sunshine streaming through the window, his head aching mightily from the combination of too much champagne and too much bourbon. He groaned with the pain, but he was happy. Content. The wedding had been everything he had hoped for and more.

His wife wasn't in the bed, but he heard noises in the attic above him.

"Sarah!" he called out. "Is that you up there?"

"It is."

"What in God's name are you doing in the attic?"

"I'm packing, James."

Perplexed, he sat up in bed. "Packing what?"

"My clothing, my belongings." She sounded perfectly calm.

James swung his feet out of the bed, wincing at the shooting pains in his head. Pulling on his boots, he made his way up the narrow stairway to the attic.

"Sarah, what the devil—"

She stopped in her work, turning toward him. She was smiling. "I'm packing to leave, James," Sarah said calmly.

He just stared at her.

Only after she went back to stuffing her clothing in several large carpetbags did he find words.

"Leave? What does that mean?"

"It means what it has always meant. I'm going east, within the hour."

"Are you mad?"

"No, I'm perfectly sane, James. I've done everything I can do here. I stayed by your side until you established your business. I married off your daughter. Now I'm going to do what I want to do."

"But . . . where will you go?" he sputtered.

"To Philadelphia. To civilization. I plan to live with my sister."

"Philadelphia! How do you expect to make that trip alone?"

"Charles's guide, Mr. Lower, is returning to Virginia. he's agreed to allow me to accompany him to Charlottesville, where I'll be able to find a coach to Philadelphia."

James found comprehension difficult. "I don't . . . understand this sudden desire to—"

"Sudden?" Her calmness evaporated. "Sudden, you say! I've been pleading with you for years to take me out of this hellhole! Years! You never have. You never *will*. And now that Mattie has also made her decision to stay—"

"I won't allow it!"

Her face grew hard. "And I won't allow you to keep me here another minute longer!"

"But you're my wife."

"I'll remedy that when I get to Philadelphia." She grinned at him wickedly. "I'm sure you'll be able to find an accommodating woman—"

"But I love you!" he protested.

Her sarcastic laughter cut through him like a knife, bringing new pain to his head. James Jackson sank to the floor, defeated.

As she hefted the two large carpetbags, moving toward the door with them, he asked: "If you have no love for me, think of your daughter. What of Mattie?"

"What of Mattie?" she repeated, pondering the question. Sarah struggled through the door with the bags.

"Like you, James," she said over her shoulder, "Mattie can go to hell!"

23

It was a hot evening, as only a late summer evening can be when the moon seems to reflect the heat of the departed sun. They lay contentedly on their backs under a canopy of red cedar. Alone, even though they were less than fifteen miles removed from Bon Marché.

"Charles?" Mattie whispered.

"Hmmm."

"How long will this last?"

"As long as that moon persists." He pointed upward.

"No, be serious," she said with mild annoyance. "This is all new to me, but you've been married before. Do the pleasures of being together . . . well, do they last?"

"If we permit them to last."

"It's as simple as that?"

"Yes, it is."

"Lord, I hope so." Mattie giggled. "I do enjoy it so—making love to you!"

Charles laughed.

"That's humorous to you?"

"No, no." He turned on his side, leaning on an elbow, looking down into her face. "When I was being tutored by Andrew MacCallum, one of the things he insisted on was the memorization of passages from certain classical writings. Shakespeare was a particular favorite of his. And, I just remembered one of those passages—"

"Are you going to tell me what it is?"

"Perhaps I shouldn't."

"Charles!"

"Oh, very well. Mr. Shakespeare, in writing about love, said, 'Love is merely madness; and I tell you, deserves as well a dark horse and a whip, as madmen do; and the reason why they are not so punished and cured, is that the lunacy is so ordinary, that the whippers are in love too.'"

Mattie joined in his laughter. "Well, if I'm to be thought mad," she said, "I might as well prove it." She kissed him passionately, leading to them making love once more.

That's the way it had been in their four days alone in the wilderness. And, as before, the act of love led to quiet words about what they visualized for Bon Marché. In that sense, it had been a strange honeymoon: periods of intense passion followed by serious businesslike talk.

"Your mention of Mr. MacCallum," Mattie said, "brings to mind, Charles, that the children need a tutor."

"I'll write to Andrew and see if he has a young student he might recommend."

"Perhaps there's someone closer. Father has a friend in Charleston, a young man who's trained in architecture. It occurs to me that he might be willing to come here to design our home and at the same time tutor the children."

"I'll leave it to you."

"You'd be willing to do that?"

"Isn't that what you want?"

She laughed again. "Yes."

"And perhaps he'll stay around to also tutor the children we're going to have."

She was silent.

"You don't want children of your own?"

It was a long time before she answered. "I have five now. Six, if we count Marshall."

"Marshall is adequately cared for," he snapped. "He has his own parents in Angelica and Horace."

"But he's your child."

"Am I to be constantly reminded of that?" His anger was real.

She kissed him lightly, but made no apologies for having brought up the subject of Charles's half-breed baby. There were no more words. They just clung to each other in their need to be together. And they fell asleep that way on their last night in the wilderness.

II

Bon Marché was a demanding mistress.

It was just as well that she was. On their return to the plantation, they were greeted with the report that Mattie's mother had left. James Jackson told the story exactly as it had unfolded.

"She really said that?" Mattie asked incredulously. "She said I could go to hell?"

"Yes," her father answered sadly.

There was a moment of silence; then Mattie just shrugged. "Father, what's the name of that young architect in Charleston? You've mentioned him several times."

"That would be Wilbur Hopkins."

"Do you think he'd be willing to come here to design our home and to act as a tutor for the children?"

"I imagine he might welcome such an opportunity."

No more was said of Sarah Jackson, as Mattie plunged into the work of building Bon Marché, sometimes consulting Charles on projects, and sometimes not. And sometimes raising minor conflicts.

She put six of the strongest Negro men to work building a stone wall around the original clearing. Half of them had been working with Charles, clearing an area for a mile-long training track.

Gently, he chided her: "Dear, you've taken three of my best men to work on that wall. I want to finish the track before the winter sets in."

She laughed, kissing him. "Your horses, of course, have first priority."

Within the week, however, she acquired ten more male slaves, again without consulting her husband. It bothered him that they were adding slaves, but there was so much work to be done . . .

In the first week of November, the architect-tutor Wilbur Hopkins arrived from Charleston. He was a handsome young man with sandy hair, hazel eyes, and slightly built. A man of perhaps thirty, and a dandy in his dress. The children liked him immediately—except for Franklin.

At ten, Franklin was becoming a problem. He was sullen and uncooperative in Hopkins's classes, and Mattie finally spoke to Charles, asking that he intercede.

"Franklin," Charles had said to him, "I must insist that you be diligent in your studies. It's very important to your future."

"Did your wife complain about me?" the youngster asked in a surly manner.

"My wife? Young man, she's also your mother!"

"No, sir, she's not! My mother's dead."

"And she'd be most distressed at the way you're behaving."

Franklin glared at him. "I mean to be a horseman, not a . . . a prig like that fellow Wilbur."

Charles slapped him hard across the cheek.

"That fellow is *Mister* Hopkins, young man! If you continue in this attitude, I'll be forced to find further punishment for you."

The boy didn't cry, nor did he put a hand to his stinging cheek. He just glared defiantly.

His father wanted to smile—the lad was tough—but he resisted the temptation.

Franklin wasn't Dewey's only problem, however. He was becoming concerned with the inordinate amount of time Mattie was spending on planning the Bon Marché mansion.

In bed one night, he asked her, "How go the plans for the house?"

"It's going to be just grand, Charles!"

"I would hope so. I see you only at bedtime anymore."

"I have a lot of work to do," she answered defensively.

"Must you do it all with that Hopkins fellow?" He was sounding just like his son, but he didn't care.

Mattie let a moment go by before she answered. "Are you accusing me of something?"

"It does seem that Hopkins holds a great deal of charm for you."

"Charles Dewey, you're a damned fool! And insulting, too!"

He sighed. "I guess I am, and I apologize for that. It's just that I love you so."

She made no comment.

"I do love you, you know?"

"Yes, I know."

He waited for something more, wanting desperately to hear her say she loved him, too.

"Well," he said when she remained silent, "I hope you can forgive my boorishness."

"You're forgiven, of course."

She kissed him lightly, then turned away from him, feigning sleep.

III

IN the last week in February 1798, Abner Lower returned from Virginia with the rest of the Fortunata slaves.

Dewey immediately drew the long-hunter aside. "Tell me the circumstances of Mrs. Jackson accompanying you to Virginia."

"At the wedding," Lower replied, "Mrs. Jackson said she wanted to go to Philadelphia to visit her sister. I agreed to take her. I left her in Charlottesville to catch the stage." He shrugged. "That's all there was to it. She was a good traveler."

"It wasn't a visit she planned, Abner. She was leaving Mr. Jackson for good."

"Oh, Christ! I never would have taken her if I'd known that."

"I know," Charles said, "so don't concern yourself about it. One word of caution, though. Please don't say anything about Mrs. Jackson to my wife. It's a sore subject."

"What if she asks me about her?"

"She won't. Mattie hasn't mentioned her mother since she left."

Lower had guided twenty-two slaves from Fortunata, seventeen of them adults. Dewey's ledger book on the blacks, now kept up to date by Mattie, listed forty-eight slaves in all. Seven of them were women, six were children, including baby Marshall, leaving thirty-five males for the heavy work.

At dinner that night, Charles asked Lower: "What are your plans now, Abner? Back to hunting?"

"No, I don't think so. I've had my fill of it." He grinned. "It's already cost me a wife. Maybe I'll find something better to do."

Dewey glanced at Mattie. Then, to Abner: "Would you consider staying here? As overseer?"

Mattie nodded quick agreement.

"Well, I sure do like it here . . ." A pause for thought. "Sure, why not?"

Mattie reinforced the decision. "It could be an important job, Abner. We've only forty-eight blacks now, but we're going to need more as we grow."

Charles frowned. "A subject for later discussion, perhaps."

"Oh, Christ, I almost forgot," Lower said. "MacCallum sent a letter." He took a crumpled envelope from his pocket.

Charles eagerly tore it open:

> I can't tell you how delighted I was to hear Lower's news of your marriage. I believe you've done exactly the right thing. From Lower's description of her she must be a beauty. But—only eighteen? Are you capable of handling that? (You know, old friend, that that last was meant to be humorous.)
>
> Last night, just before Lower left, I took my leave of Elkwood, screwing up my courage to say good-bye to the Lees. Funston was his usual surly self, but Miss Katherine—I still persist in that mode of address for her—was genuinely charming. She sends her love to you and wishes you well in your marriage. And she asks to be remembered to the children.
>
> Now I go back to New Jersey. Frankly, I'm most happy to be leaving Virginia, although I have some fond memories of it. A final plea: Let's not let our friendship die because of the miles that separate us. Affectionately, Andrew.

Charles folded the letter, smiling.

"Good news?" Mattie asked.

"He says I've done the right thing in marrying you."

"A perceptive man, your Mr. MacCallum."

Charles laughed. "You don't realize how perceptive."

"What does that mean?"

"Later, dear."

"Charles Dewey!"

"If you insist." He grinned impishly at both Lower and the tutor Hopkins. "He wonders whether I'm capable of handling . . . yes, that's the word he used . . . *handling* an eighteen-year-old."

Mattie joined the general laughter. "How do you plan to answer that?" she wanted to know.

"I'm going to leave the answer to you."

"Do you need written confirmation?"

Charles coughed nervously, embarrassed now.

She laughed. "Well, you started it."

"Gentlemen," Dewey said, "let this serve as a warning to you: Don't marry a woman of candor."

IV

NASHVILLE and Bon Marché grew with equal vigor.

Religion came to Nashville when the Presbyterians built a stone church, suggesting permanency. No regular pastor was available, however, and a circuit rider conducted services only one Sunday in four. It seemed enough for the village. New homes were going up quickly, many of them built of sturdy brick on full acre lots. Population soared over one thousand. Farmers from the area built a long, rambling market building on the square, naming the thoroughfare in front of it Market Street. Trade on the Cumberland River increased dramatically, the wide river seeming safer for large boats of ten to twelve tons than either the Mississippi or the Ohio.

A pair of Moravian churchmen, in the area as missionaries to the heathen Cherokees, described the town as "the most attractive place on the Cumberland."

To Charles, however, the most important development was the establishment of the first newspaper. A printer named John McLaughlin had begun publishing a weekly called the *Nashville Intelligencer,* with a grand subtitle: *The Rights of Man.*

Along the Richland Creek, Bon Marché blossomed like a hothouse flower. Mattie's assiduous search for land made the plantation grow to nearly two thousand acres. The first bridge was built across the creek, and a stone dam was thrown up below it to provide power to run the new sawmill, an enterprise that was busy almost every hour of the day. Its products enabled Charles to put up a large circular stud barn with a handsome exercise yard in the middle. It was a barn he had visualized for many years.

The lumber available from the sawmill let Mattie begin, in the summer of 1799, the Bon Marché mansion, patterned after the Barker house in Edenton, North Carolina, which Wilbur Hopkins particularly admired. It was to be a two-and-a-half-story frame house with double brick chimneys at either end, a long sloping roof, and six slim columns across the front supporting a wide porch off the second floor. It was a spacious home, designed to provide separate bedrooms for all of the children, a handsome suite for Charles and Mattie, and accommodations for tutor-architect Hopkins and chief overseer Lower. There were quarters for the house servants—including Horace, Angelica, and little Marshall—in the basement level.

Mattie had wanted a broad circular stairway leading up from an impressive entranceway, but she sacrificed that idea to expediency in her desire to get the home built quickly. Even without the stairway, it was going to be the most impressive house in Davidson County.

How fast the West was growing was evident in what was happening to Davidson County itself. The Tennessee legislature, as the eighteenth century came to a close, carved yet another county from the southern reaches of Davidson, naming it Williamson County and fixing the town of Franklin as its seat.

Charles joked with young Franklin. "You see, son, how famous you've become. They've named a county seat for you."

The youngster was sober-faced. "Oh, Father, don't be silly. The town is named after Benjamin Franklin."

"As you are, son."

"Did you know Dr. Franklin, Father?"

"No, I didn't have that honor. But you can still take pride in the fact that you carry his name."

Franklin thought for a moment. "Mr. Hopkins tells us that Dr. Franklin might have been as great as Washington or Jefferson."

"In his way, son."

"Am I expected to be great, too?"

"You will find, my boy, that greatness comes only to those who are willing to seek it. It's something that has to be earned."

Another moment of pondering. "I don't think I want to be great, Father. I just want to be like you."

Dewey's laugh, it seemed, could be heard over all of Bon Marché.

Those were happy times. Christmas that year was particularly joyous. The mansion was beginning to take form, mirroring the rapid growth of the plantation. Everything seemed so right.

As the fire in their log cabin bedroom died to embers on Christmas night, Mattie asked, "Charles, could you be happier?"

"I doubt it."

"Even if I told you I was going to have a baby?"

"A baby!" a delighted Dewey exclaimed.

"Hush, dear, you'll wake the children."

"I don't give a damn if I wake the entire world!"

Mattie chuckled. "I doubt that my news merits that."

"When?"

"August, perhaps."

"It'll be a fitting start for a new century."

V

MATTIE's pregnancy didn't diminish her hard work. There were times when Charles worried about her, but he didn't chide her. She was young and strong and determined, making plans for Bon Marché's first real crop year. Wheat had been planted, and corn, tobacco, indigo. Hay, of course. And a cattle herd had been acquired.

She added more slaves as the work increased.

By March 1800, the list of blacks in the ledger had grown to seventy-five.

"Dear," he said one night, "I'm concerned about the number of blacks we're taking on."

"They're needed." It was a matter-of-fact statement.

"The idea of slavery doesn't bother you?"

His wife shrugged. "I didn't make the system. And the blacks here are well treated. Abner is very good with them."

"I know, but where does it end?"

Another shrug. "It ends where it ends. We may need a hundred or a hundred and fifty hands to run this estate properly."

He winced. "So many?"

"Unless you order me to desist." She was challenging him.

Charles was silent.

"Abner has suggested that he needs help, and I've given him the authority to find two more overseers."

Charles groaned, but he had no alternatives. And he went back to concentrating his attention on his horses. The horse business needed his full attention; it wasn't going well. Plans for a major track at Nashville, talked of in such glowing terms by Andy Jackson, failed to materialize. To race, Charles was forced to travel—to Gallatin, to Lexington, to Memphis. The travel had a debilitating effect on his horses, it seemed. He won little; his gambling was not much more successful. Availability of cash money was beginning to be a problem.

With the house nearly completed, Mattie began making major purchases of furniture through her father's store—furniture that had to be brought in, at premium prices, from Richmond and St. Louis and even Philadelphia. When she ordered two large mirrors to be placed above the main fireplaces on the first floor, at fifteen hundred dollars each, Charles tried to call a halt.

"Perhaps we should wait on some of this stuff," he suggested, "until the horse business becomes more stable."

"And perhaps," she snapped at him, "you should be more judicious in your gambling."

"Dear, it's just that—"

Mattie smiled at him, kissing him. "The house is nearly finished, and I *do* want it to be perfect. I thought, Charles, that maybe we'd hold a housewarming on July Fourth to introduce our friends to Bon Marché and to celebrate Independence Day."

He frowned, seeing more money being spent.

"It will be the greatest social event this area has ever seen," she continued enthusiastically. "Champagne and music and gaiety—"

"Where's the money to come from?"

"You said yourself, dear, that you ought to consider selling off a few of your young horses. Mr. Fowler has been after you to let him have several runners from the Medley line, hasn't he?"

"Yes, but—"

"Of course it's only a suggestion." Mattie smiled sweetly. "You must do what you think is best with the horses."

What was best, Charles decided, was to sell four good two-year-olds to the Kentucky horseman for seventy-five hundred dollars. He would have preferred to keep them to race under his own solid purple colors, but he needed the money.

VI

IT was only three weeks after the Independence Day housewarming, on which nearly ten thousand dollars had been lavished, that Mattie awakened him in the middle of the night.

"I think you ought to call Angelica, dear."

"You're in labor?"

"It's beginning," Mattie said quietly.

"I'll ride for Dr. Hennings," Charles said, quickly getting out of bed.

"No, no, that won't be necessary," she assured him. "Angelica and I can handle this."

Just before six o'clock on the morning of July 25, 1800, a daughter was born to Charles and Matilda Dewey, exhibiting a lusty voice and displaying a shock of auburn hair.

"She's beautiful," Charles said to his wife when the baby was wrapped in soft blankets and put in a delicate crib that Mattie had ordered from St. Louis. "Of course, that's no surprise, considering the beauty of her mother."

"You're an unconscionable flatterer." Mattie chuckled.

"Are you well, dear?"

"Perfect." She reached up her arms to her husband. "Ready to do it again."

He kissed her. There was a long tender silence.

"Charles?"

"Hmmm."

"I'd like to name her Alma May, after Father's grandmother. I never knew her, of course, but from Father's stories she was an able, strong-willed woman."

"I like the name. Alma May Dewey it is."

"You're very dear, Charles."

He laughed. "I'm aware of that."

"And I want you to know something."

"What's that?"

"Charles Dewey," she said slowly, "I want you to know that I am very much in love with you. As much as any woman could be in love with a man."

Mattie had said it. Finally. Dewey's world was complete.

24

Can you believe the swift passage of time? Charles wrote to Andrew MacCallum. Yesterday we observed the third birthday anniversary of our son, Thomas Jefferson Dewey; just two weeks earlier it was the fourth birthday celebration for little Alma May. I know I expounded on it earlier, but I continue to be convinced, as improbable as it may seem, that her birth signaled a turnaround in the fortunes of Bon Marché—as if she was a good luck omen given to all of us. But, then, what can you expect from a man who also believes his life is in control of a guardian spirit?

Even Franklin, who was having trouble accepting Mattie as a mother, has come around under the influence of the brilliant light that is Alma May. He adores his half sister, as do all the children. They, and we adults, spoil her outrageously, I'm afraid. Indeed, a competition has developed among the older children for the privilege of caring for her during the day. I've had to institute a schedule, if you can believe that, setting specific days for Franklin to be in charge of Alma May, and George, and Corrine, and the twins. We post the schedule every week on the back of the nursery door.

He neglected to mention to MacCallum that Marshall was also included in the schedule, something Charles had not wanted to happen, but Mattie had insisted upon.

"You can't exclude him from our lives," she had told Charles, "just because you find his existence embarrassing. He's a reality: he lives in this house. He has as much right to be here as the other children."

"It's not that," Charles answered weakly. "It's just that—"

"I don't know why you can't recognize that Marshall is a fine little fellow. He loves Alma May."

"I question the wisdom of allowing a black—"

"Charles!" The subject had angered Mattie. Again. "When are you going to stop this nonsense about your own son?!"

Dewey went on in his letter to MacCallum:

Alma May is treated like a princess. And we have all taken to calling her that: 'Princess.' I admit to you that I'm a bit concerned that we are overindulgent with her, but she is such a darling.

Little Tom is so different from Alma May. Shy. Reticent most of the time, but a fine boy. And we love him equally.

Dewey wondered whether the words he had just written were true.

You may remember that I wrote you about losing four horses to thieves coming off the Natchez Trace. Within the week they were caught. Justice was swift. . . .

II

A crowd had gathered around a temporary scaffold erected in the square in front of the Nashville jail. Charles, who stood there with his father-in-law, James Jackson, was moved to draw a comparison between what he had seen in Paris and the sullen frontiersmen brought out now for a public execution.

"As a youngster, James, I saw a great deal of public punishment of criminals on the streets of Paris. There always seemed to be a kind of carnival atmosphere in the French crowd—a joy of sorts. Here, though, it's all pretty somber."

"There's nothing pleasant about a hanging," Jackson commented.

"It's harsh punishment, that's true."

A grizzled old man standing next to them, clad in smelly buckskins, spoke up: "Ya'll pardon me, gentlemen, but hangin' ain't strong at all when ya think what they usta do to horse thieves hereabouts." He spat in the dust. "I recollect back in '93—thet a horse thief was fetched right here to this same spot. 'Course, the town warn't so grand in them days. An' he was tied to thet whippin' post to have more'n thirty lashes laid on his bare back. It warn't a pretty sight. An' then they branded him on both cheeks with the letters 'HT'— fer horse thief."

He laughed raucously. "Now, seems to me thet sech a punishment is a damned sight more sensible than just a plain hangin'."

Charles grimaced.

A young man, perhaps not more than twenty-five, with long blond hair and staring dark eyes, was led from the jail, the sheriff prodding him up the steps to the scaffold. The knotted rope was tightened about his neck, but he was not hooded.

"This man," the sheriff announced to the crowd, "was tried an' found guilty of horse thieving. The proper authorities of Davidson County has sentenced him to hang."

Without further preliminaries, the trap was sprung and the body hurtled toward the ground, stopped cruelly short by the stout rope. The sound of the thief's neck breaking could be plainly heard.

Charles turned away, sickened.

"'Scuse me agin," the old man next to them said, "but ain't ya Mr. Dewey?"

"I am."

"Seems to me ya be mighty pleased, it bein' yer horses an' all what was taken."

"The horses, however, were lost," Charles explained.

"But not the thieves, eh?" The man laughed loudly again.

The crowd started to melt away toward the taverns and the cockpit outside the Nashville Inn.

"I thought there were three of them," Charles said to James Jackson.

"There are. They'll be hanged an hour apart." Jackson frowned. "The entertainment is to be stretched out over the entire afternoon."

Dewey wanted to leave, but he felt he had to stay. He was the one, after all, who had complained to the authorities about his horses being stolen. Somehow it seemed his citizen's duty to be present at the punishment of the thieves.

Like the first, the other two men who were hanged that afternoon were not dignified with names when they were brought up to the scaffold. They had faces, though, and Charles saw them. He would continue to see them in his nightmares for weeks.

When it was all over, he and his father-in-law retired to Mr. Parker's inn, where Charles drank too much. As he was riding slowly back to Bon Marché, weaving unsteadily in the saddle, he wondered whether he would ever again be able to report the theft of a horse.

He hoped he would not have to. The Natchez Trace, after all, was becoming civilized. The federal government had taken over the trace now that the U.S. Army engineers were building a full-scale road from Natchez to Nashville. Treaties had been signed with the Choctaws and the Chickasaws for the land. In all, the Indians were paid some three thousand dollars in miscellaneous merchandise for the five-hundred-mile stretch of the trace. Six dollars a mile! He was saddened by the cheating on the natives.

Dewey drunkenly pondered the developments being made in the West. Why, hell, mail traveled from Natchez to the post office just adjacent to Bon Marché *in only eight days!*

But his thoughts were muddled. He saw again the bulging eyes and swollen tongues of the three men hanged that day for stealing his horses.

He shuddered.

III

FRANKLIN Dewey, displaying his customary solemnity, told his father, "I'm confident enough to bet a hundred dollars on Bon Star."

Charles looked at him in surprise. "Do you have a hundred dollars, son?"

"Yes." Franklin hesitated. "Well, Mattie . . . uh, Mother advanced me that much for the meeting."

Grinning, Charles clapped the young man on the back. His pride showed.

At eighteen, Franklin Dewey was training his first runner for the 1805 Hartsville spring meet: a six-year-old gelding named Bon Star, in appearance almost a twin of his sire, Premier Etoile, by Skullduggery. And the boy's horse would be, in the opening-day feature, matched against another gelding of note, Greyhound, owned by the prominent Tennessee breeder, Lazarus Cotton. It was to be the best of three two-mile heats.

"Don't expect too much," Charles cautioned. "You might well be overmatched with Greyhound. Don't you think you ought to spread your wagering over a few other races?"

"No, sir. Bon Star will win."

The master of Bon Marché shrugged. Greyhound was a heavy favorite; he had been brought to Hartsville as the horse to beat. Only a few thought he could be beaten, among them Andrew Jackson, who had entered Indian Queen in the event. Indeed, Indian Queen was the horse Charles would have chosen, but he had to place a token bet on his son's animal, while making no further effort to stop Franklin from posting the hundred dollar wager in the public pool. There was no other way, Dewey knew, to teach the young man about the intricacies of betting.

Bon Marché had brought six runners to the Hartsville meeting. Four of them were trained by Charles. Yet another thoroughbred, Hardhead, by Cranium, another product of Skullduggery, was being handled by George Washington Dewey, Charles's sixteen-year-old son.

On opening day, however, the emphasis was all on Franklin and his Bon Star.

Seven horses were led to the starting line and, when the drum tapped, Bon Star's black jockey shot him into the lead. When they straightened out in the backstretch for the first time, the Bon Marché horse was six full lengths in the lead.

"Your instructions, son?" Dewey asked quietly.

Franklin was intent on watching the race through his glasses. "Yes, sir, I told Hannibal to take him well out. They're going to have to catch us now!"

Charles simply nodded. He knew the pace was too swift, but, again, he had to allow his son to learn through his own errors.

By the time the field had gone a mile, the favored Greyhound was abreast of Bon Star, followed closely by Indian Queen. A hundred yards more and both Greyhound and Indian Queen had passed Franklin's horse. On the final turn leading to the homestretch, all the others had also caught the tired Bon Star.

At the finish line, Greyhound held off Indian Queen for a comparatively easy triumph, with Bon Star dead last, fourteen lengths off the winner.

Dewey put a consoling arm across Franklin's shoulders. "There'll be other days, lad."

His son stared off into the distance for a moment or two. "What went wrong?" he asked finally.

"Two things," Charles said, ready with advice now that it was asked for. "First, you put him in over his head with Greyhound. Second, you sent him out for much too fast a pace. Even if he had won, son, he'd have nothing left for the other heats."

Hannibal trotted the badly lathered Bon Star up to where they stood. "Ah'm sorry, Mistah Franklin. We sure was tryin'."

"I know," Franklin mumbled. To a handler: "Walk him cool and get him ready for the second heat."

The Negro jockey's eyes opened wide in surprise.

"Uh . . son," Dewey interrupted. "I don't think it's wise to put him in the second heat. He's given you everything he had."

"But, the wager—"

"Is lost, Franklin." Charles's words were firm. "One thing you have got to learn—right now. Never sacrifice a horse for a bet."

Franklin's head was bowed in disappointment.

"Bon Star is a useful horse. He'll win some, perhaps before this meet is ended. But not today, and not in this kind of company."

"Yes, sir." He didn't sound convinced.

In the second heat, when only four of the original field answered the starter's call, Andy Jackson's Indian Queen pressed Greyhound's pace for a mile and a half. But the big gray horse was just toying with his rivals. He easily pulled away in the last half-mile, winning by six convincing lengths.

Later in the afternoon, Charles came upon Jackson. "A difficult day, eh, Cousin Andy?" he said lightly.

Jackson frowned, annoyed by Dewey's flippant tone. "Greyhound will meet his match later, believe me. Major John Verell is coming with Truxton."

"The Virginia horse?"

"The same. A damned good son of the imported Diomed, out of the fine mare, Nancy Coleman. Bred by Tom Goode in Chesterfield County."

"I know Mr. Goode," Charles commented. "He has an outstanding reputation as a breeder."

"Well, he turned out an excellent one in Truxton, let me tell you. When he meets Greyhound, Charles, Truxton will take him. If you need a wager, that's my recommendation."

"I'll keep that in mind."

IV

A Greyhound-Truxton match, however, was not what occupied the thoughts of the Bon Marché family. On the third day of the meet, George Dewey sent out his Hardhead in a three-mile dash against eight others, winning in a drive by half a length.

Charles was more delighted than his younger son. "How much did you win in the pool, George?"

"Pool?" The boy shrugged nonchalantly, a smile lighting his handsome face. "I guess I forgot to bet."

George and Franklin were so different. Both had Dewey's good looks: blond hair, hazel eyes, rugged square faces. There was no doubt that they were brothers, or that they were Charles Dewey's sons. But where Franklin was sober and intense, George was easygoing and quick to laugh.

The sixteen-year-old had allowed Charles to pick the race for Hardhead and had followed his instructions to the letter, not concerned whether his father's advice was right or wrong. Franklin wanted to do everything himself, jealously guarding the permission Dewey had given him to make his own decisions.

On the fifth day, without telling Charles beforehand, Franklin entered Bon Star in another heat event, this time at three miles, but against maidens. At least, Charles thought, he hadn't overmatched the gelding this time. Franklin had the jockey keep Bon Star off the pace but within striking distance. They won the first heat by two lengths without pressure at the end. The boy had learned something; it was indelibly stamped on his mind. The victory was duplicated, almost stride for stride, in the second heat.

"Congratulations, son," Dewey said exuberantly. "You handled him marvelously."

Franklin nodded, his face a stern mask.

"Winning is supposed to be enjoyed," Charles laughed.

"I had no bet."

"Well, now you have a purse for wagering the next time."

"A hundred dollars only. I owe that to Mother."

"I'm sure she wouldn't mind if you risked it. After all, she expected it would be wagered when she allowed you to have the original hundred."

"She didn't expect I'd be a fool about it."

Dewey offered nothing more. He understood that his eldest son was going to make his own decisions, no matter what his father said.

It was at the end of the first week, on a Sunday, that the Greyhound-Truxton match was made. It hadn't been intended to be a match race, but no other horse on the grounds was entered in the three-heat four-mile event to challenge them.

The match drew a large crowd. Wagering was heavy. Major John Verell, the owner of Truxton, took every side bet offered him. Dewey had heard that Verell had wagered over ten thousand dollars, and he wondered whether the major had those kinds of assets. Obviously, he thought he was going to make a killing in the backwoods.

Charles went to study both horses. Greyhound, after his win on opening day, had won again under Lazarus Cotton's careful handling and seemed in the peak of condition. But Truxton was a big, strong horse, fifteen hands three, a handsome bay with white hind feet. Dewey decided to wager a thousand dollars in the public pool—on the underdog, Greyhound.

He had been invited to join the Jackson party for the race, and when he got to Jackson's carriage, where much drinking was under way, Andy asked him, "Did you take my advice on Truxton, Dewey?"

Charles smiled broadly. "I gave it my fullest consideration."

"Good, good," Jackson said, reading into the answer what he wanted to hear. "You won't be sorry."

It was a no-contest race. Greyhound humiliated Truxton, winning in straight heats.

Andrew Jackson was furious. "That damned fool! Verell had the best horse, and he let him get beat. Some men just don't know how to condition horses!"

Dewey said nothing, slipping away to collect his winning bet. He certainly didn't want Jackson to know that he had wagered on Greyhound.

When he returned to the Jackson party, Patton Anderson, Andy's sycophant, was just arriving at the carriage with Major Verell in tow.

"Major," Jackson said sternly, "news of adversity seems to travel more swiftly than news of a happy nature."

"So I understand."

"It has become common knowledge around the course since the race that you're in serious financial trouble."

"Picked clean," Verell admitted, with some grace.

"I'm prepared to offer you fifteen hundred dollars in cash for Truxton."

"I'd take it, but it wouldn't get me out of difficulty."

"What would?"

The Virginian sighed. "Well, let's see . . ." He consulted a slip of paper he withdrew from his pocket. "Over and above the fifteen hundred, I'd still be left with eleven hundred and . . . uh . . . seventy dollars to meet."

"I'll pay those debts as well," Jackson said immediately.

"But, sir," Verell said smoothly, "if I sold you Truxton I'd have nothing left to race."

"I have three geldings here of racing age, worth, oh"—he turned to Anderson—"what would you say, Patton?"

"Three-fifty, probably."

"The geldings go into the pot, Major."

In spite of his seemingly untenable position, Verell prolonged the bargaining. "Truxton, unless he suddenly falls dead, is certain to win some purses before the year is out. It seems that it might be valid that I share in those. Perhaps, sir, a percentage . . .?"

Jackson glared at him. When he spoke again, the words were delivered slowly and deliberately, making it clear that he would go no further. *"Should* we win a purse before the end of the fall season, Major, I'd consider a bonus of two other geldings of racing age, to be chosen by gentlemen's agreement."

Verell stuck out a hand. "Judge Jackson, you are now the owner of Truxton."

Andy pumped the hand vigorously. Turning quickly, he grasped Dewey by the arm. "Come with me. I have another chore to do."

Jackson sought out the owner of Greyhound.

"Lazarus," he said, "I've just acquired Truxton. I'm here to offer you a match race, on this same course in the fall meeting. Five thousand dollars a side."

Cotton studied Jackson for a moment. "This is not a jest?"

"I'm deadly serious."

"In that case, I must accept, mustn't I?"

As they walked away from Cotton, Jackson said sotto voce: "Indian Queen is going to be revenged." He laughed. "It's said that revenge is sweet, but that's only true when the revenge promises to be profitable."

V

BACK at Bon Marché at the end of the spring racing meeting at Hartsville, Charles found time to write to MacCallum:

> My two eldest sons are no longer maidens at the races! Both won at Hartsville with horses they trained, and I couldn't be more proud. I managed three wins myself, to prove to you that I haven't lost the touch. Racing in the West is most vigorous, although I must confess that, at times, the wagering patterns seem strange. You would be appalled at the betting that goes on here. To show disdain for money seems to be in fashion.
>
> Everyone is talking now of the fall meetings, both at Hartsville and at the Nashville Clover Bottom track. And most of the talk is of a rematch of the Virginia-bred Truxton and the Tennessee horse, Greyhound. There's no telling how much money and other things of value will change hands on that one. . . .

He turned eventually to political matters.

> Aaron Burr came to Nashville recently, the guest of Andy Jackson. I went to the reception in his honor only to please Mattie. As far as I'm concerned, he's no better than a murderer (he certainly shows no remorse for having killed Hamilton), and yet, Jackson embraces him. I guess it's the case of one duelist finding reason to applaud another. I don't know who's a worse renegade—Burr or Jackson!

25

CHARLES Dewey had not seen so many people at a race meeting since he left Virginia. Thousands jammed the Hartsville course, drawn by the appeal of the match race between Andrew Jackson's Truxton and Lazarus Cotton's Greyhound.

On the one hand, the master of Bon Marché was grateful for the crowds on hand for the rematch. It enabled him, in the days preceding the last big after-noon of the fall meeting, to meet a host of Tennessee and Kentucky breeders he had not known before and to arrange numerous matings for the Bon Marché stallions. He filled the books of three of them for the following season. But on the other hand, so many horsemen being at the course had made for greater competition than he had counted on.

Bon Marché horses won only three races. His sons, Franklin and George, did not win at all. Nevertheless, with judicious wagering, the Dewey coffers had benefited.

On the final day, Franklin said to his father, "I think all of Tennessee must be here."

"And half of Kentucky as well."

"How are you going to wager, Father?"

Charles challenged him. "What would you suggest?"

"Greyhound must be the favorite based on his past performances," the young man replied seriously. "Yet, Truxton's new owner will certainly have him in better condition than he was during the spring meeting."

"You're sure of that last point?"

Franklin's doubt showed. "No, sir, I'm not. Mother's Cousin Andy seems to have trained him . . . well, too harshly. Maybe he's worn him out."

Charles agreed with his son's evaluation. "So what's your conclusion?"

"I don't know. Maybe this is one to sit out."

"I'm beginning to think the same thing." Dewey looked around him. "Have you seen your brother lately?"

"George is occupied with the girls." The tone of his answer implied disapproval.

"He is, is he?" Charles smiled. "And you think there are better ways in which to occupy yourself?"

"Yes, sir, I do. Anyway, George isn't very choosy. Anything in skirts suits him."

Charles patted his sober son on the back. "The day will come for you, too, my lad. So don't be too critical."

"When it does, I'll be more careful."

"Yes, I'm sure you will be."

The ubiquitous Patton Anderson came up to them, grinning broadly and not too soberly. "Dewey! I've been looking all over for you. This is the race to bet the plantation on."

"It looks too close to call for me."

"That's absolute nonsense, Charles! Andy has this horse in top condition. Lean and hungry, as it were. Every penny I could get together is going on Truxton."

"I admire your loyalty."

"It's not a matter of loyalty," Anderson insisted, slurring his words. "Truxton is simply the better of the two. And since Greyhound is favored, you can get a price on Truxton. Why, I'm even betting fifteen horses on him."

"I didn't know you *had* fifteen horses, Patton."

Jackson's friend laughed uproariously. "I don't, old friend, I don't." The laugh turned to a drunken giggle. "Some of the horses I've put up might have ladies' saddles on them. I'm wagering them as an agent, so to speak."

"An unknown agent, I'd imagine."

Anderson grinned devilishly. "What difference does it make? Truxton will win easily, and I'll have fifteen horses!"

As he stumbled away, Franklin frowned. "He's really a reprehensible man, Father."

"Hmmm. Patton's a free spirit, son. Not my dish of tea, but a free spirit nevertheless. Come—let's take a look at Truxton."

The apparent condition of the horse shocked Dewey. Jackson's rigorous training had taken weight off of him; ribs protruded prominently.

"I don't imagine I have to give you advice on betting," Andy said to him.

"No."

"Good! You're a wise man." Once again, Jackson persisted in reading into Charles's simple answer what he wanted to hear. It was one of the little things about Mattie's cousin that sometimes annoyed him. This was one of those times.

They looked, too, at Greyhound, finding him fit, as usual. But the two Deweys stayed with their initial reaction. Father and son decided not to bet on the match.

Any type of wager was available on the course. In addition to the public pool, numerous side bets were being made. As Charles and Franklin strolled about, they overheard a conversation in which a six-hundred-forty-acre tract of land was being offered on Truxton. There was a ready taker; numerous land papers would change hands before the day was concluded.

At one point in their meandering, another of Jackson's friends approached them. "Have you heard of Andy's latest wager?"

"What's that?"

"He's bet fifteen hundred dollars against a like amount of clothing. With some tailor from Gallatin."

They all laughed about that.

Ahead of them they spotted George, with a young lady on each arm.

Dewey went up behind him and playfully tapped his shoulder. His son whirled around. His face was flushed, but not with embarrassment.

"Father! I want you to meet Dolly." She was a buxom girl on his left. "And this is . . . uh . . . ."

"Emily," the dark-haired girl on his right volunteered.

"Of course," George said easily, "Emily."

"Would you young ladies excuse us for a moment?" Charles asked. "A family matter."

He drew George out of earshot of the girls. "Have you been drinking, George?"

"Just a bit of hard cider, Father. Nothing to worry about."

"I do worry about it. I don't like to see my son drunk, especially when he's only sixteen years old."

"Not drunk, sir, just a tad happy." He grinned.

Charles sighed deeply, deciding to change the subject. "I've looked over the horses, George, and have decided to pass on the match. I suggest that you do the same. That is, if you've had time to think about betting in the midst of your . . . uh . . . female distractions."

"Too late, Father," George answered airily. "One of those mad Greyhound backers insisted on offering me odds of three to one. I took it for a hundred."

The master of Bon Marché groaned.

"But at three-to-one, sir!"

"I guess it's too late to say anything but good luck. One final thing before you rejoin the ladies—everything is packed and ready to go. We leave for Bon Marché immediately after the race."

"Yes, sir." George sauntered back to the girls, kissing both of them to signal his return.

Dewey couldn't help smiling at the self-assured young man.

In the race itself, Jackson's rigorous training of Truxton proved out. Greyhound was beaten soundly in straight heats. Routed actually, to a great roar of approval from the Jackson supporters.

As Charles and Franklin walked toward their carriage, they came upon Patton Anderson doling out cups of hard cider from a large cask. The agent was even drunker than he had been earlier.

"Dewey!" he called, holding out a cup.

"I'll pass, Patton."

Anderson pointed to a large basket of baked goods on the ground in front of him. "Some ginger cakes, then. Won them from a nice old lady from Kentucky."

"No, thank you."

"Have you heard the latest news, Dewey?"

"I'm almost afraid to ask what it is."

"Andy has bought Greyhound. He goes to Clover Bottom now."

At his carriage, Charles gave the final orders to the Negroes for the return of the racehorses to Bon Marché.

When they were ready to leave, George was absent.

"Go find your brother," Dewey told Franklin.

Harboring a resentment, which he hid from his father, Franklin began his search, without immediate success. Only when he happened to come across one of George's former companions did it end.

"Emily, do you have an idea where George is?"

The girl, smiling knowingly, pointed to a large barn where the managers of the Hartsville racecourse stored hay.

Outside the barn, Franklin shouted: "George, are you in there?!"

There was no answer.

He entered the barn. The interior was nearly dark now in the late afternoon. "George!"

Again no answer.

"George!"

This time there was a feminine giggle from behind some bales of hay. Franklin followed the sound. When he poked his head over the bales, he saw in the half light that the girl called Dolly had her bodice open, her breasts bared. George's trousers were down around his ankles.

"George, for God's sake!"

Slowly, his brother turned his head to look up at Franklin. "Well, if it isn't my older sibling. Say hello to Franklin, Dolly."

"Hello." The girl giggled, as unconcerned as George at being discovered in that delicate situation.

"We're ready to leave," Franklin told his brother. "Father's waiting!"

George shrugged. To the girl: "Family duty calls me, Dolly, sweet. This will have to wait until next time."

Dolly giggled again.

Nonchalantly, he got to his feet, pulled up his pants, fastened his belt, and left Dolly alone in the hay.

As the brothers walked to the carriage, Franklin asked in disgust, *"Where do you find them?"*

"They're everywhere, Franklin. You ought to look sometime."

Franklin didn't reply.

"I suppose you're going to report all this to Father."

Silence.

At the carriage again, the eldest son told Dewey, "He was collecting his bet. At least George had the right idea on the race."

George Washington Dewey flashed him a big grin.

II

CHARLES was in a mood to talk. About anything. Mattie had other inclinations.

Propped up in bed, he said, "Your Cousin Andy's Clover Bottom track promises to offer the best race meeting the West has ever seen."

"Yes, dear." She leaned over and kissed him.

"Captain Joseph Erwin has posted a challenge against all comers for his Tanner at five thousand a side. I wonder whether I have anything good enough to risk that?"

Another kiss. "You'd be the best judge of that, dear."

"I imagine that Jackson will take him up on it, now that he has Greyhound as well as Truxton."

"He probably will." She began to run a hand lightly down his bare chest. Slowly. Lower and lower.

"Oh," Charles went on, "I want to talk to you about George. It seems that young man is turning into quite a roue. Would it be possible, perhaps, for you to . . . discuss those things with him?"

"What things, dear?" The hand had reached his belly.

"Well, about women and the dangers of . . . uh . . . pregnancies and the like. Sometimes a mother can—"

"You think he's not a virgin, then?"

Charles laughed. "I'd bet on it."

Mattie's hand now rested on his penis, the fingers tickling him. "I was going to suggest," she said with some sarcasm, "that it's best for the father to have those talks with young men. But maybe you're right—I'd be the best one for such a discussion. At least I'm still alive."

"What?"

"Charles! What are we talking about?"

"George and his . . . dalliances."

Mattie sighed in exasperation. "Mr. Dewey, that's sex, isn't it?"

"It may be, but—"

"You've been in Hartsville with your damned horses for two whole weeks while I've been here alone. I'm beginning to wonder whether you found something there other than racing!"

"Don't be silly. It's just that—"

She took her hand away. "All right, let's settle this. One—I'll speak to George. Two—yes, I think Cousin Andy will have a simply marvelous race meeting at Clover Bottom. Three—no, I don't think you have a horse that's worth risking five thousand dollars against Tanner. Now, is there anything else on your mind?"

He thought for a moment. "No, I don't think so."

"Then, for God's sake, Charles, make love to me!"

"Oh . . . is that what you've been hinting at?"

"Charles! Damn you!"

He laughed loudly. "I wondered what all that hand manipulation was about."

Mattie struck out at him. But playfully. He caught her hand, pulling her to him. They made love as they had when they were under a canopy of red cedars on their wilderness honeymoon.

Both were half dozing when Charles whispered, "Mattie?"

"Hmmm?"

"You really don't think I have anything to challenge Tanner?"

"One of these days, Charles Dewey," she murmured, "I'm going to murder you right here in this bed."

III

CLOVER Bottom was the largest commercial establishment in western Tennessee. The one-mile race track, set on a beautiful oval meadow, dominated it, but Andrew Jackson and his partners had also built a vast mercantile complex on the banks of the Stones River, some eight miles from Nashville.

A huge store offered firearms and skillets and grindstones and calico. And broadcloth from Philadelphia, which sold at fifteen dollars a yard; Jackson had bought it for five. The store also sold coffee and salt and allspice. Anything that was needed. Because cash money was scarce in the West, much of the merchandise was traded for cotton, tobacco, pelts, and slaves—all of which were taken to New Orleans on flatboats for resale.

Clover Bottom also boasted a comfortable tavern, booths for hucksters, and a keelboat yard on the Stones. It was highly profitable. At times. But Jackson had a propensity for overextending himself, and the enterprise often lost money.

Whatever the state of his purse, however, Andy always seemed to have money for horse racing. As Dewey had anticipated, Jackson posted the five thousand dollars to have his Greyhound meet Captain Erwin's Tanner in the fall meeting of 1805.

Thousands were on hand on opening day for the match race, which Greyhound won in three difficult heats.

In the crowded and noisy tavern afterward, Erwin wasn't satisfied.

"Sir," the captain said loudly to Jackson, "perhaps we ought to match our stallions—your Truxton against my Ploughboy. I believe Ploughboy to be the best stud horse in these parts."

Jackson laughed. "It has always been the rule, hasn't it, that differences of opinions make horse races. Truxton is ready, of course. What say you to the best of three two-mile heats?"

"It's to be a speed race, then?" Erwin commented.

"Two thousand a side?"

"Agreed. And the forfeit?"

"Shall we make it eight hundred?" Jackson countered.

"Agreed, sir."

They shook hands. It was a contract.

Andy sat down at Dewey's table, where Charles was drinking with Patton Anderson, who was talking animatedly about the impending match race. "I swear to you, Charles, that there's nothing more invigorating than match racing."

"My father-in-law in Virginia," Dewey observed, "used to say that matching horses with money was as satisfying as being with an accommodating woman."

"By God, the man was right!" Jackson roared. "Absolutely right!"

Patton spoke. "Andy, have you talked to Captain Erwin about that matter with his son-in-law?"

A dark cloud came over Jackson's face. He turned in his chair, his eyes searching the room. When he saw Erwin in the crowd, he gestured to him. Erwin came to the table and sat down with them.

"Captain, it has come to my ears," Jackson said, "that your son-in-law, Charles Dickinson, has made some injudicious remarks about my wife's first marriage."

"Indeed?" Erwin seemed surprised.

"Yes, sir, and I respectfully suggest that you caution him against such indiscretions. He's a young man, not blessed yet with maturity, and I wish no quarrel with him. In truth, I suspect that he's being used by my enemies—that damned Governor Sevier and his cronies!"

The captain was apologetic. He understood how sensitive Jackson was about the controversy that surrounded his marriage to the former Rachel Donelson. There had been charges that Andy had wed her when he knew that she was still the wife of her first husband, charges using the ugly word *adultery*.

"I'll speak to Dickinson about it."

"I wish you would," Jackson said coldly. "In time, I would hope, to avoid further unpleasantries."

Captain Erwin got to his feet, bowed formally, and left the table.

Within minutes, Charles Dickinson presented himself to Jackson. He was not yet thirty, Dewey guessed, and he was dressed in the highest fashion. A dandy, with a ready arrogance. Andy didn't suggest that he sit down.

"Judge Jackson," the young man said, obviously choosing his words with care, "I understand that certain remarks attributed to me have brought you offense. I never intended that, of course. If I said anything at all that may have pained you, it might have come in moments when I was . . . well, to be candid, when I was drunk. Nevertheless, I offer my apologies."

Jackson scowled at him, nodded once to acknowledge the apology, and turned away. Dickinson stood there uneasily for a moment, then left.

"Damned puppy!" Andy growled.

26

CHARLES slammed a copy of the newspaper down on the table.

"I tell you, Mattie, there's grave mischief afoot with Andy!"

He picked up the *Impartial Review and Cumberland Repository* again, glaring at the front page.

"Your cousin has written a two-column letter in which he castigates that young lawyer, Tom Swann, calling him 'the puppet and lying valet for a worthless drunken blackguard scoundrel, Charles Dickinson.' My God, Mattie, everyone in Nashville expects a duel. Andy wants it, it seems!"

His wife shook her head sadly. "I know. When I went to see Rachel yesterday, she was deeply worried."

"Then why doesn't she talk to Andy?"

"No one can talk to Andrew Jackson when he thinks he's been offended."

Charles shrugged. "It's all so stupid! That damned Patton Anderson, continually goading Andy under the guise of being his friend. And young Swann, apparently enjoying his sudden notoriety as Dickinson's champion, unable to keep his mouth shut. Good Lord, Andy has already given Swann a severe caning. Isn't that enough!"

"Andy feels that Dickinson has insulted Rachel."

"But the young man apologized for that last fall at the race meeting. I was there in the Clover Bottom tavern when he came to our table and made the apology."

"Rachel says he's repeated the remarks since that time."

Dewey groaned. "The way things are going the Truxton-Ploughboy rematch in April could be a bloodbath."

II

CHARLES and Mattie stepped down from their carriage into a vast mob of people at the Clover Bottom racecourse.

Andy Jackson, animated and smiling broadly, greeted them. "This is the largest concourse of people I ever saw assembled," he commented, "unless in an army."

Dewey looked up at the low, dark clouds. "It may rain on the entire assemblage."

"It'll make no difference to Truxton. Dry or wet, he's going to win."

"The story is, Andy, that Truxton is injured, that he may have to forfeit."

Jackson seemed unconcerned. "It's true that he wrenched a muscle in his thigh two days ago, but—"

"I gather that you're not recommending a wager on Ploughboy." Charles laughed.

"In no way! Truxton is tough, like his owner."

Charles had heard, though, that the injury was serious. He got that from Sam Pryor, who had been retained by Jackson to prepare the horse for the special race. And he knew that Pryor had recommended twenty-four hours earlier that Andy pay the half forfeit on the three thousand dollar purse.

As a breeder, however, Dewey recognized the importance of this race. A win by either of the stallions would immediately increase the horse's worth at stud immeasurably.

The latest issue of the *Impartial Review* had made that clear. The fact that it was published by one of Rachel Jackson's nephews probably accounted for the Truxton bias:

> On Thursday the 3rd of April next, 1806, will be run the greatest and most important race ever run in the Western country, between Gen. Jackson's horse, Truxton, 6 years old carrying 124 pounds, and Capt. Joseph Erwin's horse, Ploughboy, 8 years old carrying 130 pounds, for the sum of 3,000 dollars.
>
> The present engagement with Ploughboy is such that he cannot be put to mares any sooner than the above stated time. . . . Gentlemen who wish to breed fine horses would do well not to put their mares to horses until after the race, as at that time it will be seen (barring accidents) whether or not he be the true bred racer.

Bon Marché had no horses running that day. Dewey wanted to be free to savor the excitement of the event. As he and Mattie strolled about the course, they came upon a temporary fenced-in corral, in which numerous blacks were milling about, chuckling, seeming to be thoroughly enjoying themselves.

"What's that?" Mattie asked.

Those are slaves who have been offered as wagers."

"Charles! No!"

"Yes, I'm afraid it's true," he answered sadly. He pointed to another corral nearby. "And those are horses being offered as bets. I'm never going to be able to get used to the fact that some people equate their blacks with beasts of burden." He thought that Funston Lee would be right at home here.

A finely dressed gentleman came up to them, bowing deeply.

"Major," Dewey said, acknowledging the bow with a slight one of his own. "May I present my wife, Matilda? Dear, this grinning oaf is Major William Terrell Lewis, who is, if I'm not mistaken, about to offer me some money on Ploughboy."

"Ma'am," Lewis said to Mattie. "It's true about the money. Captain Erwin has authorized me to accept two thousand dollars more on Ploughboy. You can have it all, Dewey, or any portion of it."

"Your largess wouldn't have anything to do with the rumors about Truxton's injury, would it?"

"They are not rumors, sir. We expect that Jackson will forfeit."

"Then why the rush for more bets?"

Major Lewis laughed. "Andy Jackson has been known to make foolish decisions on horse races. If he does so on this one, we are determined to capitalize on it."

"I'll pass for the moment, Major."

"Understandable." He started to move off.

"Excuse me, Major, one moment more. I'd like you to satisfy my curiosity about Charles Dickinson. Is he on the grounds?"

"No, he's in New Orleans on business." A wide grin. "His money's here, however."

"I can imagine it is."

Another bow to Mattie, and Lewis was gone.

"Is Truxton badly hurt, Charles?" Mattie wanted to know.

"Let's find out."

At the stall where Truxton was quartered, an anxious group was gathered around the thoroughbred stallion. Jackson, of course, was there. And John Coffee, and trainer Sam Pryor, and the former owner of Truxton, Virginian John Verell.

"Andy," Verell was saying, "I think we ought to pay the forfeit."

Jackson looked around the circle of advisers. Coffee nodded his agreement with Verell, as did Pryor.

Charles pressed forward to get a closer look at the bay horse. A large swollen knot was immediately evident on his left thigh. He moved around the stall with obvious difficulty.

Jackson clucked to the stallion, and the horse came to him. He massaged the swelling for a brief moment, then stood back to take in the whole animal with a glance. He stroked Truxton's nose, whispering something to him that the others couldn't hear.

Finally, Andy turned to his friends. "Gentlemen," he said, "Truxton will run."

News of the decision swept across the racecourse like wildfire, setting off another flurry of wagering, although with less enthusiasm in the Truxton camp. Nevertheless, thousands more were bet.

Jackson, himself, saddled the horse when it came time for the race and boosted the Negro jockey aboard.

There was tension in the air as the horses came to the start line, Jackson's big bay horse limping on his injured hind leg.

The drum tapped.

They were off, to a mighty roar from the crowd.

The roar turned to a collective gasp as Truxton, against all expectations and with little effort, quickly gained the lead. He held it during the first mile or two and, in the second time around, even increased it, winning going away.

Charles winced when he saw the condition of the horse as he crossed the finish line. The right front leg had gone lame, as well, and the plate on the left front had been sprung and was lying across the foot.

"Will he be able to start again?" Mattie asked.

"Not likely." He thought for a moment. "Of course, I'm not Andy Jackson."

It started to rain—hard, beating rain—adding another disadvantage to Truxton. Ploughboy, although beaten, came out of the first heat in good condition.

There was another mad rush of betting on Ploughboy. Certainly he would win the second heat. And the third? How could Truxton ever be expected to run a third heat?

A blacksmith did his repair job on Truxton's plates, although it was difficult under the prevailing weather conditions.

Rain poured down, soaking everyone, as the drum tapped for the second two miles. Immediately, the long, bony body of Truxton showed in front, even though Ploughboy's rider was whipping and driving.

"I can't believe what I'm seeing!" Charles said to Mattie.

Without using either the whip or the spur, Truxton's jockey urged him forward. Every stride took him farther ahead of Ploughboy. At the finish line, Truxton was the winner by sixty full yards!

A horseman standing by Charles held up his watch, staring at it in amazement. "Three minutes and fifty-seven!" he shouted to all around him. He repeated it in disbelief. Like a wave, word of the astounding time swept across the crowd.

Charles wiped the rain from his face.

"Mrs. Dewey," he said, in the manner of a pronouncement, "you have just seen a miracle. Your Cousin Andy is either a genius with a horse or the luckiest damned racing fool I've ever seen!"

III

"DID you notice the flurry of activity over at the newspaper office when you rode in?" James Jackson asked of his son-in-law as Charles walked into the store.

"No, nothing special that I could see."

"Well, a lot more folks than usual have been coming and going there today."

"For what reason, do you suppose?"

"It might be," James suggested, "because Charles Dickinson's back in town."

"Oh, God! And he's probably read all that inflammatory stuff from Andy in the paper."

"More than likely."

Charles shook his head. "Well, I can't worry about that. I have other matters of more concern to me."

Dewey had come to Nashville for a meeting with a fellow horse breeder named Joseph Coleman. In recent months, every visit to the town brought surprises for him. Nashville was growing rapidly; there was talk that it would soon be incorporated as a city. But it was in Jackson's store that the increasing sophistication of the frontier community was most noticeable.

James now offered shell combs, cotton pantaloons, ostrich feathers, shawls of silk and damask, long silk gloves, for the ladies, cashmere and satin, hosiery, hats, and even some recently published books from Philadelphia and Boston side by side with the staples he had always carried: blankets, saddles, nails, firearms, farm tools, and spirits.

Civilization was coming to the West. Swiftly. It was too bad, Charles thought, that Sarah Jackson couldn't have waited for it.

He walked to the Nashville Inn for his meeting.

"Dewey, there's a good chance," Coleman told him, "that we can get the English sire, Royalist, here in Nashville. He was bred by the Prince of Wales, you know."

Charles nodded. He knew of Royalist from the English studbook.

"I've been informed by agents in New York that he could be brought here in time for next year's stud service."

"I'm interested, of course. For how much?"

"The asking price is twenty-five hundred."

The master of Bon Marché thought about it. "We could use some English blood here. I'm in for a thousand."

Coleman smiled. "I was hoping you would be. Two other breeders, besides myself, want a share of him. We could move him around from farm to farm."

Charles brushed aside the details. "Do it in the way you think best, Joseph. I'm content to have him stand at your place—my stud barn is full at the moment. Just as long as I can get my mares to him."

When their luncheon was ended, and Charles was walking back to the hitching post in front of Jackson's store to get his horse, he spotted a knot of people in front of the newspaper office, talking excitedly.

As he came up to them, one of the men said, "It's settled, Mr. Dewey. There's to be a duel between Andy Jackson and Charles Dickinson!"

Without comment, Charles pushed his way through the cluster of Nashvillians into the office.

"Mr. Eastin," he asked of Rachel Jackson's nephew, "is it true? Is there to be a duel."

"Yes. I'm about to start printing tomorrow's issue. It's all in there."

"May I see it?"

The editor handed him a smudged stone proof of the first page. Dewey scanned it quickly.

Printed there was a letter from Dickinson in which he characterized Andrew Jackson as "a worthless scoundrel, a poltroon and a coward."

There followed a paragraph in which Eastin reported that Jackson had issued a formal challenge on May 23 and that Dickinson had replied in kind on the same day.

Charles looked up at the editor. "The twenty-third? That's today."

"It all came to a head this morning."

Dewey was angry. "Doesn't it bother you, Mr. Eastin, that you may have precipitated this by printing those scurrilous letters?"

"I print the news. I don't decide whether or not it's scurrilous."

"I would think that you would have more concern for the feelings of your Aunt Rachel."

The young editor gave him no answer.

"You're a damned fool, Eastin, and a dangerous one!"

Back at Bon Marché, Mattie already had the news. "Rachel sent a slave over with the information. She asks that you come to see her."

"For what purpose?"

"To ask you to accompany Andy to wherever the duel is to be fought."

Dewey shook his head vigorously. "No! Andy has that coterie of cronies to see him through it."

"I don't imagine she trusts any of them. She trusts *you*."

"And what am I to do, save his life?" His anger came from the realization that there was no way he *could* save the man's life if it was ordained that he was to die in the duel.

"You might, in some way, if you were there."

"No!"

"I want you to do this, Charles." She said it quietly, but he recognized the determination in her words.

"Mattie, you're asking too much. I want no more talk of this."

IV

A heavy fist knocked on the door. "Mr. Dewey! Five o'clock!"

"Thank you, General."

The knock hadn't wakened Charles Dewey. For one thing, the extremely uncomfortable bed at Miller's Tavern, just over the Kentucky-Tennessee border near a place called Harrison's Mills, would have kept a dead man awake. For another, his concern about what would happen in the morning had built a tension in him that made sleep impossible.

He didn't want to be there. Just before the knock he had been thinking of mounting his horse and riding back to Nashville. Yet, there he was. Mattie's unyielding pleas had made him a member of the four-man contingent accompanying Andrew Jackson to his duel with Charles Dickinson.

On the forty-mile ride from Nashville, Charles had consciously stayed by himself. He watched and listened to the others, impressed with the easy manner in which Jackson approached what could be his death. The talk as they rode was about everything but the duel. Indeed, there had been a virtual political monologue by Andy. And, for Dewey, it set in stone his image of Jackson: a man who reveled in violence, who saw nothing more glorious in life than deadly combat. Charles tried to understand it, but could not. To him, life was a precious thing. He had struggled too hard on the streets of Paris sustaining life to risk it in something as mercurial as a duel. Indeed, the thought of losing life on a battlefield was just as abhorrent to him. Andy, though, seemed to have a destiny in risking life.

On the ride he had made that clear, speaking bitterly of the current difficulties with the English.

"How long," Andy had intoned, "can we be expected to allow the impressment of our seaman and the intrusions on our commerce on the high seas? We *must* fight England again! In the last war I wasn't old enough to be of any real account. I pray that the next will come before I get too old to fight."

Now Dewey rose from the bed and pulled on his boots. He had tried to sleep in his clothes.

The Jackson party rode in virtual silence to a nearby grove of poplar trees on the banks of the Red River. A delicate mist was rising from the water in the early morning, putting a ghastly pall over the scene.

Thomas Overton, a brigadier general in the Tennessee militia, was Andy's second. Dr. Hanson Catlett was Dickinson's. The seconds met in the center of the grove and tossed a coin. Catlett won the choice of position. To Overton, then, fell the task of giving the command.

The night before, General Overton had let Charles see the written rules for the duel: "Distance, twenty-four feet; the parties to stand facing each other, with their pistols down perpendicularly. When they are READY, the single word FIRE! to be given; at which they are to fire as soon as they please. Should either fire before the word is given, the seconds pledge themselves to shoot him down instantly."

A contract for murder, Charles thought.

He stood now and watched as Jackson's dueling pistols, with barrels nine inches in length, were loaded with one-ounce balls of seventy caliber. Dr. Catlett paced off the twenty-four feet; the protagonists took their places.

Dewey noticed that Andy had put on an ill-fitting frock coat, reaching below his knees. He wondered why. Certainly the morning wasn't cool enough to warrant a coat.

Both men stood with their pistols down.

General Overton took a deep breath.

"Fire!"

Dickinson, a noted snapshooter, fired immediately.

A puff of dust came up from Jackson's big coat. It seemed to Dewey that Andy staggered slightly, but he couldn't be sure. He knew only that the duelist's left hand went to his chest.

Birds scattered from the tall poplars. The smoke from the black powder of Dickinson's shot drifted away on the mist.

"My God!" Dickinson cried in disbelief. "Have I missed him?" Involuntarily, he moved backward.

"Back to the mark, sir!" General Overton commanded, pointing his own pistol at the disconsolate younger man.

Dickinson took one step forward to the mark, but his head was turned away from Jackson, his eyes averted. He folded his arms. Dewey saw it as a gesture of resignation.

Jackson drew himself up as tall as he could, his left hand still on his chest. He raised his gun. Aimed. Pulled the trigger.

There was a sharp click as the hammer stopped at half-cock. The noise of it seemed deafening, although it was actually a small sound.

Dewey wanted to shout with delight. *It was over!* Providence had somehow intervened and stopped the fatal shot. "Honor" had been served.

But, no! His delight turned to horror as Jackson lowered the gun, calmly examined it, and then returned it to the firing position.

Once more he drew back the hammer.

Once more he aimed.

Once more his finger squeezed the trigger.

Once more the explosion of a pistol shot panicked the birds from the poplars.

Jackson didn't miss.

Dickinson's falling body was caught by his friends. Blood soaked his shirt before he could be gently lowered to the ground, flowing freely from a hole in his belly, just below the ribs. There was no doubt in anyone's mind that he was mortally wounded.

With as little concern for his adversary as he had shown when he recocked the pistol, Jackson strode to his horse.

General Overton noticed blood running into Andy's boot. "My God, you've been hit!"

Jackson smiled. "Oh, I believe that he pinked me. But I don't want those people to know." He nodded toward the Dickinson party.

The smile left his face, turning it hard. "I should have hit him," he said coldly, "even if he had shot me through the brain."

V

MATTIE had never seen her husband so angry. Or so unable to keep a rein on his emotions. Alternately shouting and weeping, he recounted for her what had happened in the Kentucky riverside grove.

"All that goddamn nonsense about a field of honor! It wasn't honor that I saw, but out-and-out murder!"

His wife let him rave on. She knew it was useless to try to reason with him. In fact, she didn't want to. She wanted him to cleanse himself of his ire.

"And trickery!" Charles shouted. "He wore a big, loose coat so that he could twist his skinny body around under it, making the narrowest possible target. Dickinson, on the other hand, faced him squarely, as had been agreed."

Mattie looked at him compassionately. He was hurting so.

"Can you believe it? His hammer stopped at half-cock. *That* was his shot. *That* should have ended it. But Andy—may he burn in hell!—took what amounted to a second shot!"

Charles put his head in his hands, crying again, in anger as much as in the pain of the memory. Words came with difficulty.

"And then . . . he . . . he had the effrontery to send that dying man a bottle of wine as a token of his esteem for a brave fellow! My God, how much evil is there in that so-called gentleman?"

There was a long silence.

Mattie spoke finally. "Was Andy seriously wounded?"

"Dickinson's shot nicked his breastbone, apparently. 'Pinked' him, as the heroic Andy put it." Charles spoke with bitter sarcasm. "The doctor says he has several broken ribs and also lost a good deal of blood. But he'll live—a fate he ill deserves! Damn him! *Damn him!*"

"Charles! You don't want him dead."

"Don't I?"

"No, you *don't!*" She wasn't sure, however. The reservoir of emotion that made Charles Dewey such an exciting lover could also make him hate with the same intensity.

"And that's not all, Mattie. When we got him home to Rachel—Lord, how that woman suffers with him!—she was not only concerned with Andy but with the Dickinsons as well. It was heartrending. She fell on her knees weeping. 'Oh, God have pity on the poor wife,' she said. 'Pity the baby in her womb.'"

His wife gasped. "Mrs. Dickinson's pregnant?"

"Yes! And if Rachel, whom Andy tells nothing, knew of it, then certainly Andy did, too, when he recocked that pistol and pulled the trigger for the second time!" He struggled to restrain his temper. "He *meant* to make an orphan of that unborn child!"

"Oh, Charles . . ." Tears came to Mattie's eyes.

"I'm finished with Andrew Jackson," Dewey said flatly. "This *whole family* is finished with Andrew Jackson!"

His intense hazel eyes bored into her, fixing the prohibition as something irreversible. For a lifetime.

Mattie didn't know how long she'd be able to obey.

27

WRITING to Andrew MacCallum was a catharsis for Charles.

Having forbidden the name of Andrew Jackson to be spoken at Bon Marché, he needed to relieve his venom somehow. He wrote swiftly, impelled by the hate he felt.

> Treachery seethes hereabouts under the guidance of Aaron Burr, abetted—God help us!—by my wife's cousin. A week ago (Jan. 3), when the depth of the Burr plot to separate the West from the Union became known, that "gentleman" who had earlier accepted the courtesy and honors of the Nashville citizens, was burned in effigy in the courthouse square. Rightly so! Although I admit to you, Andrew, that mob anger is not something I relish.
>
> What is so galling, so reprehensible, is Andrew Jackson's role in all this. It has become common knowledge here that Burr paid him thirty-five hundred dollars to build five riverboats at the Clover Bottom boatyard for Burr's treasonous expedition. Indeed, it is the belief of many prominent men in this area—and not my contention alone—that Jackson saw himself as a military leader of this terrible plot.

A sip of sherry before he continued.

> Naturally, now that Jefferson has warned 'all faithful citizens' to withdraw from Burr's unlawful enterprise, Andy has been trumpeting his innocence, claiming that he himself warned the national administration of Burr's treachery. He does not fool me, however! Are those two not broken from the same mold? Murdering duelists, both of them!
>
> There's word now that Jackson is calling for two brigades of volunteers to be put under arms for the purpose of capturing Burr. With Andy as the commander, of course. What a sham!

He stopped writing to re-read the paragraphs. A frown. Perhaps he was being too bitter.

Maybe I ought to have opened this letter with the standard wish for a happy and prosperous 1807. Indeed, it may well be that now that Burr is unmasked.

The children, Andrew, are becoming adults. So much so that I report to you that Franklin is formally courting a young lady. . . .

II

GRINNING sheepishly, Franklin paused in his grooming of a yearling colt. He glanced over to his younger brother who was forking straw into a stall.

"George . . . uh . . . I could use some advice."

"About what?"

A hesitation. "Women."

George laughed loudly. "Franklin! You?"

"It does seem unlikely, doesn't it?" He joined in his brother's laughter. "But I've met this young lady—"

"Who?"

"Malcolm Bolling's daughter, Amantha."

"Oh." George knew the girl and thought her a dullard. Certainly she wasn't much to look at, dumpy and plain, painfully shy.

Recognizing the doubt demonstrated by George, Franklin became sober again. "You don't approve."

"Of course I approve," George tried to assure him. "Amantha is a . . . a pleasant girl."

"Pleasant? You make it sound like a disease."

"Not so! I like Amantha."

"She is a bit shy, it seems."

"Hmmm."

"And not your type, probably."

George laughed again. "My type, brother, is any woman alive and breathing. But you mentioned advice . . ."

"Yes." Franklin swallowed hard. "I don't know how to make a beginning with her."

"What are her interests?"

"I don't know."

"Horses, maybe?"

"Yes, I guess. Her father has horses."

"*All* farmers have horses. I mean racehorses. Is she interested in racing?"

"I have no idea."

George shook his head in dismay. "Franklin, you're hopeless!"

Frowning sullenly, his brother went back to his grooming chores.

George felt sorry for him. "Franklin, you've just got to screw up your courage and *do* something."

"What?"

"A picnic, perhaps. Let it be known to her that you'd like to go on a picnic with her. Then take the carriage—the open two-seater—and drive out somewhere. Alone, of course."

Franklin nodded.

"And when you get to the picnic site . . . well, you let nature take its course."

"What does that mean?"

"What does that—?" Another hearty laugh. "Let me spell it out for you. You spread a blanket in a shady glen somewhere, you start a conversation . . . oh, about what she dreams, for example . . . and as she's telling you, you nonchalantly reach over and take her hand."

Franklin was listening intently.

"Once you have her hand, you move closer to her, and you kiss her."

"Kiss her!" The prospect seemed to shock him.

"Of course! If she won't let you kiss her, it's a sure sign that you ought to look for someone else."

"You mean she'd *let* me kiss her?"

"If she likes you."

Franklin thought for a moment. "Then what?"

His brother sighed. "Good Lord, Franklin, don't be so damned naive. Then you . . . well, you try to go further. You touch her. And, that allowed, you fondle her."

"Fondle her! I couldn't!"

George groaned. "Forget it! Just resign yourself to being a bachelor."

Franklin was defensive. "Since you seem to think I'm such a hopeless clod, perhaps that's what I'll be—a bachelor."

"Oh, for Christ's sake, Franklin, just take her on a picnic and see what happens."

III

CHARLES Dewey was trying to complete his letter to MacCallum. He realized, when he reviewed what he had written, that he hadn't spoken of what concerned him most.

> I worry, Andrew, what all these revelations about Jackson are doing to poor Mattie and, indeed, to our marriage. There are strains here at Bon Marché that concern me deeply. This is yet another demonstration of my need for your wisdom, dear friend. As unrealistic as this might seem to you at first reading, please consider this: I offer you the position of general manager of Bon Marché. You need only to set the price; I will pay it.

He was just finishing when there was a knock on the door of the drawing room.

"Come!"

Horace, the butler, entered. " 'Scuse me, Mistah Charles, but kin Ah talk to ya?"

"Certainly."

" 'Bout Marshall?"

"Is something wrong?"

"Oh, no, suh! It jest thet Marshall . . . well, he ten now."

Dewey smiled. "Time is so swift."

"Yas, suh. An' Ah bin wonderin', Mistah Charles, if mebbe Marshall could git wit' th' jockeys."

"At ten?"

"He a strong boy, Mistah Charles, an' Ah bin tryin' t' teach 'im some things. But, wit' this—" He held up the arm with the stump at the wrist.

"Isn't Marshall helping his mother here in the house?"

"Yas, suh. But he a boy! He gotta learn to be a man."

"Hmmm." Dewey shook his head. "I'm not sure, Horace, how Marshall's assignment to the jockey ranks will be viewed by the other blacks. Since he's your son, they might see it as favoritism."

"Yas, suh." Horace was crestfallen.

"I'd prefer, Horace, if Marshall stayed on the household staff."

"Yas, suh."

The black man started to leave the room. At the door, he turned back to his master. *"Please,* Mistah Charles!"

Dewey sighed. "Very well, Horace, we'll give it a try. Marshall is to report to Franklin."

The butler was perplexed. "But, suh—ya trains them jockeys."

"In this case," Charles answered sharply, "Franklin will be in charge. Is that clear?"

"Uh . . . yas, suh. Thank ya, suh."

Dewey rose from his desk, strode to the window, and stared out as Horace left the room. *If I hear one damned word around the track about Marshall's parentage!*

He pounded a fist into his palm.

IV

"MAYBE we're moving too fast, Mattie."

"There's no such thing, Charles," his wife replied, slightly annoyed by his uncharacteristic caution.

They were discussing the prospective purchase of three more parcels of land encompassing some nine hundred additional acres. And they were doing it in what Charles often called "the office"—in bed.

"The speculators are beginning to move in," Mattie went on, "and land values are going up. If anything is moving too fast, it's the price of land. We have an opportunity to acquire this property for a reasonable price—seven dollars an acre. Next month, it may be eight or nine, if indeed someone hasn't grabbed it by then."

Charles admired Mattie's keen business sense, but sixty-three hundred dollars seemed too much to pay at that time. "Our cash reserves," he said churlishly, "are too low."

She showed anger. "Am I the Bon Marché land agent or am I not?"

"You are, of course."

"Then I want to do this." She snuggled close to him, her voice going girlish. "Anyway, darling, I've already agreed to buy."

"Damn it, Mattie!" He stopped suddenly; he didn't want another argument. "I'm sorry." There was a pause. "It's just that we have little cash."

"How many yearlings do we have, Charles?"

"Thirty-four."

"And how many foals with mares right now?"

"Forty-one . . . no, forty-two."

She nodded. She already knew that. "And you're planning to keep *all* of them to racing age?"

He frowned, wondering where she was going with this discussion. "Most of them—yes. Racing is our primary business."

"Is it?"

"Of course it is!"

"Suppose, Charles," Mattie said carefully, "that we were to regard the horses as a crop? I mean, the way cotton is a crop, and wheat. We don't keep all of the beef cattle we breed. We cut some of them for steers and sell them like a crop, don't we?"

"Yes, but—"

"The future of Bon Marché will fully depend on crops—tobacco, cotton, wheat, oats, beef, fruit. . . . Why, we ought to plant fruit trees on three hundred of those new acres . . . and hay. Several hundred of the new acres can go into sweet hay as well. Darling, we could be the first plantation in this region to market the finest hay in New Orleans!"

Her plans astounded him. "What you're suggesting in expansion would require much more labor than we have."

"I'm aware of that. John Cotton tells me he can quickly supply us with half a hundred more blacks."

"Absolutely not!"

"But—"

"Cotton is associated with Andrew Jackson! I'll not deal with him!"

"But John controls the local market in slaves."

"No!"

She pouted. "I guess I misjudged your ambition."

"What's the meaning of that remark?"

"On the night we met," Mattie said softly, "you told me that you meant to have the finest plantation in Tennessee."

He smiled for the first time. "I did, didn't I?"

"Yes, you did. And if we acquire this additional land, we'll have some thirty-five hundred acres."

"Hmmm."

"And if you regard the horses as a crop, as I'm suggesting, next year you'd have . . . let's see . . . seventy-six young animals for sale. Why, think what an event that would be if we conducted an auction. Seventy-six of the finest young thoroughbreds in Tennessee! Buyers would come from the Carolinas and Kentucky and Virginia and Louisiana and Ohio . . ."

He raised a hand to try to halt her rush of words.

"And they'd all know of Bon Marché and its greatness!"

Now he laughed. "You're an expert in plumbing my ego, aren't you?"

"I like to think so." She kissed him. There was no mistaking the meaning of the kiss.

"Before we get to *that,*" he grinned, "may I be allowed one question?"

"Just one."

"If I market all of my horses, what the hell do I do for racing animals?"

"I'm confident, dear, that you'll be able to solve that problem."

"You are, eh?"

"Uh-huh."

"And are you also confident that you can have the master of Bon Marché— Lord, what a farce that title is!—make love to you any time you wish?"

She slowly pulled her nightdress over her head. "I'd give odds on that."

V

By the time Andrew MacCallum replied to Dewey's angry letter about Aaron Burr's plot and Andrew Jackson's possible role in it, Burr had been arrested and charged with treason. He was to be tried in Richmond, Virginia, before Chief Justice John Marshall.

MacCallum wrote back to Charles:

I respectfully suggest to you that subsequent events have revealed the Burr episode for what it truly is: downright comedic in its ineffectiveness. That he may have charmed any number of people enough to consider throwing in with him seems clear enough. But never, from everything I have learned, did Burr stand a single chance of being successful.

He's a sad, broken man now. He can never again be an effective force in this country, whether or not he is found guilty of treason. And there are learned men here at Princeton who seriously question whether a charge of treason can be made to stick against him.

Charles gritted his teeth as he read on, angered by the thought that Burr might escape punishment for his misdeeds.

As to you, Charles, what Burr has done and what Jackson may have done are not worth the unhappiness apparent in your letter to me. For God's sake, my good friend, don't ruin your marriage over such silliness!

Dewey found himself offended by MacCallum's word. "Silliness, is it?" he said aloud.

You asked for my advice, and I give it to you: Keep clear of Andrew Jackson, if you wish, but don't allow your opinion of him to endanger your relationship with Mattie or the rest of your family. You mention that the children are adults now. Allow them to be so, making their own decisions on whether or not they wish to be associated with Jackson in the future. I can't see that that will harm you in any way.

Remember when we studied the Greek philosophers? I commend to you now what Plutarch said: "A man should not allow himself to hate even his enemies, because if you indulge this passion on some occasions, it will rise of itself in others: if you hate your enemies, you will contact such a vicious habit of mind, as by degrees will break out upon those who are your friends."

Hate will debilitate you, Charles. It may well bring alienation from your fine family. Do not allow it to happen!

Dewey re-read the last paragraph again. He knew that Andrew was correct.

Finally, I appreciate your fine offer to join you in Tennessee. As before, I must decline, Charles, my friend, I am a hidebound academician, content here in Princeton. No matter how small "my price," as you put it, I would not be worth it. I send my love to your wife—perhaps someday I will meet her—and to the children. And, of course, my greatest affection to you.

Charles Dewey held the letter in his hand, staring at it. Did anyone ever have a wiser friend? For the first time in many months he thought of his guardian spirit and how it must have conspired to bring him together with Andrew MacCallum.

"Thank you," he said softly.

28

MORE than three hundred had been invited.

On May 28, 1808, Bon Marché overflowed with guests, summoned to celebrate the twenty-first birthday anniversary of Franklin Dewey, firstborn son of a one-time deserter from the French navy.

In a sense, the party also celebrated the majority of Charles Dewey's entire life. It symbolized the success he had achieved in his adopted country: at forty-three he had everything he had ever dreamed of, everything his guardian spirit had ever promised him.

Mattie Dewey, although she was in the role of a stepmother, had cheerfully undertaken the task of making the party the most lavish social event on the western frontier to that date. Huge tables had been set up in the oak grove on the broad front lawn of Bon Marché and spread with gleaming linen that her father had imported from Ireland. More than fifty of the blacks, carefully chosen for their skill as waiters and waitresses, were dressed in white linen, each wearing a wide silk sash of royal purple—the racing colors of Bon Marché.

Four Bon Marché beeves were turning on spits over fragrant hickory-wood fires. Dozens of large hams from Bon Marché's own smokehouse were distributed among the tables. Giant crystal bowls were filled to overflowing with fruits from the Bon Marché orchards: apples, peaches, pears, nuts of a half-dozen varieties. There was bourbon from the Bon Marché distillery. And hard apple cider. And pastries from the Bon Marché bakery.

Sweet-smelling bales of hay were scattered across the lawn, covered with more white linen, so that the guests would have a place to sit when they pleased. But the visitors, many of them seeing Bon Marché for the first time, preferred to stroll about, astounded by what Charles and Mattie Dewey had accomplished there: the well-built barns for the horses, the grain mill, the blacksmith shop, the tannery, the tobacco sheds, the training track, the smokehouse, the bakery, the summer kitchen (busier on this day than it had ever been), the miles of stone fences, the greenhouse for exotic flowers (each table featured a bouquet of flowers many of the guests didn't recognize), the fine brick carriage house, and the magnificent mansion.

There was curiosity, too, about the crude double-cabin on the edge of the grove, kept there by Mattie and Charles as a reminder of what Bon Marché had been at the beginning.

As the notes of an orchestra hired for the occasion drifted across the lawn, husband and wife found themselves together for a rare moment.

Charles took Mattie's hands. "Thank you," he said quietly. "It's just wonderful. I was thinking a moment or two ago of how proud Martha would have been, seeing her first child reach twenty-one." A pause. "For Martha, then, another thank-you, Mattie."

She smiled. "I gratefully accept the thanks of *both* of you."

"Lord, how fortunate we are! Not just for Franklin, you know, but for all the children." His eyes swept the lawn, seeking them out. "Corrine—a beautiful woman at eighteen. And the twins? Can you believe it: sixteen on their next birthday? And the Princess . . ."

They watched as little Alma May, already eight years old, skipped across the lawn, charming everyone, stopping to curtsy now and then.

"And Thomas," Charles went on. "He's such a shy one. I wonder where he's hiding out now?" He grinned. "And can we forget George?" His second son stood fifteen yards removed from them, surrounded by a small crowd of gaily chattering girls.

Dewey bent to kiss his petite wife on the lips.

She laughed. "I was thinking," she said, "about how we've enriched the merchants of Nashville by having this party. I believe that every dress, every hat, every coat, every piece of satin, silk, and lace, every fragrance must have been cleaned out of the stores."

He guffawed. "And every dollar out of the purses of a lot of gentlemen." A grimace. "Including this one."

"Don't complain, dear. You know you're enjoying this as much as Franklin is."

"More, I think. Oh . . . have you met the Bolling girl?"

"Amantha? She's a plain young lady, isn't she?"

"Hmmm. Mr. Shakespeare said that 'beauty is but a vain and doubtful good.' I suspect that Franklin must believe that. He seems smitten by her."

"Completely," Mattie agreed. "Now I think we've indulged ourselves enough with this *tête-à-tête*. Back to our guests."

The governor of Tennessee was there, and the mayor of Nashville, and most of the prominent families of western Tennessee, including the cream of the horse-racing fraternity. But *not* Andrew Jackson. He and Rachel had been invited—Mattie had insisted on that—but Andy had sent a brief, though proper, note of apology, saying that Rachel was not feeling well enough to "face the rigors of a social engagement at this time." Dewey didn't believe the excuse for a moment, but he welcomed it.

The party had started at noon; it was due to continue through dinner. At about five o'clock, as long shadows began to fall across the lawn, Charles stood on a hay bale in the center of the melee, and called for attention.

"Friends," he shouted, so that all might hear him, "Mrs. Dewey and I are pleased that you could all find time to do us the honor of being here. And to do our son, Franklin, the honor of celebrating the important twenty-first anniversary of his birth. Now, if the guest of honor would come forward . . ."

Franklin moved to where his father was perched on the hay bale, somewhat shyly holding the hand of Amantha Bolling.

"Franklin," his father said, "we—meaning the entire family—sought the perfect gift to mark this occasion. And we believe we have. George!"

Smiling broadly, George Washington Dewey led a well-muscled chestnut colt to the center of the lawn. He had to keep a strong hold on the animal, because it pranced about nervously, upset by being in the middle of so much humanity.

"Franklin, my son," Charles continued, "this is a yearling colt by the great Diomed, winner of the inaugural Epsom Derby in England."

Horsemen on the grounds applauded appreciatively, sending the yearling off on another dance.

"Diomed is the son of Florizel, out of Sister of Juno, by Spectator. And this colt is out of Mr. John Tayloe's mare, Castianira, also imported from England. Fine breeding for a fine young man!"

More applause.

"And we have already named this handsome young fellow, Franklin. We have called him Majority, so that he will always remind you of this happy occasion!"

George led the yearling to his brother and handed him the rope. Franklin beamed, running a hand over the smooth red coat of the colt, clucking to him. Still holding the lead rope, he climbed up on the bay bale to stand by his father.

"Thank you, sir," he said. Then, louder: "Thank you, all the members of my family, for this superb gift. I promise you that I will train him to live up to his royal blood."

Franklin turned to Dewey. "May I say more, Father?"

"It's your day, lad."

"I would also like to take advantage of this moment to make an announcement." He paused to hand the horse back to George. "I am proud to tell you all that Mr. Malcolm Bolling has given his permission for me to take his daughter in marriage."

The applause was universal.

Franklin reached down to pull Amantha up beside him. "Oh, yes, I almost forgot . . . her name is Amantha."

Laughter.

"We plan to be married on January first next, 1809." He turned to Charles. "That is, if you approve, sir."

Charles took an embarrassed Amantha in his arms, kissing her on the cheek. She blushed red. "I approve, son, most heartily. Now," he shouted, "a toast! To Franklin and Amantha—to their long happiness!"

The toast was drunk.

The young girls in the crowd quickly gathered around Amantha, giggling and chattering.

George, who had instructed one of the Negroes to take the yearling back to the barn, drew his brother aside.

"Franklin, you sly dog! I had no idea it had gone this far."

"Yes, well . . ." The older brother seemed embarrassed.

"The picnic ploy must have worked, eh?"

"I guess it did."

"You *guess* it did? What the hell does that mean?"

"Well," Franklin started hesitantly, "I *did* take your advice . . . but, it wasn't at all the way you described it."

"No?"

"No . . . You see, George, you must be more self-assured than I am. We . . . uh . . . well, we kissed, of course."

"Of course." His brother grinned wickedly.

"But . . . I don't know about nature taking its course."

"You mean, that's it?! Nothing else happened?"

"No."

George was incredulous. "You're still a virgin?"

Franklin nodded sadly. "You see, George . . . uh . . . Amantha wants to wait until the wedding night, and I—"

George cut him off with a raucous laugh. "Well, I'll be damned! I didn't know such things still happened in the enlightened nineteenth century!"

II

CHARLES yawned.

"I plan to start Matilda in the Gallatin Purse on Sunday."

"Finally!" Mattie teased him. "And I must say that you're not giving me this news with any great enthusiasm. How dare you, Charles Dewey, yawn when you speak of my namesake?"

He grinned at her. "In truth, she hasn't shown me much in training. No speed, certainly. Frankly, I'm disappointed with New York's produce. I guess it's the Messenger blood, but all of them are small, you know."

Another yawn. "God, I'm tired," he said. "I think I'll lay up the racing string after the Gallatin meeting. Or just let Franklin and George carry on with it."

Mattie showed some concern. "You have been working hard all summer. Maybe too hard, dear."

"Hmm, maybe. But it's been the best season we've ever had. Twenty-two . . . or is it twenty-three—"

"Twenty-three, dear."

"Yes, of course. Twenty-three wins for the Bon Marché purple. And some mighty handsome side wagers besides."

"Are you happy?"

"Uh-huh." He leaned over in the bed to kiss her lightly. "I could only be happier if I could change the name of that filly and use your name on something more promising. I don't want you to be embarrassed by what happens on Sunday."

"Is she so umpromising?"

He thought for a moment. Then he laughed. "She's a lot like you really: small and tough."

"Then she'll be a winner!"

"That's female logic," he said derisively.

"And that's not all bad," Mattie insisted. "It was my female logic that caused me to throw in with you . . . and Bon Marché."

"Then how can she lose?" He took her in his arms, kissing her eyes closed. They were content in each other.

"Charles?" It was a whisper.

"What?"

"I heard that you had an argument with Franklin over the use of Marshall at Gallatin."

Dewey frowned. "From Angelica, I'll bet."

"Yes. But I understand that Marshall has become quite a good young jockey."

"He shows promise."

She opened her eyes. "But you're not going to allow him to ride at Gallatin."

Her husband sighed. "As a matter of fact, Mrs. Dewey, he's going to be up on Matilda. It's a weight-for-age race, and he's the only one of the boys who can make ninety-eight pounds right now."

"I'm glad Marshall is going to ride, Charles."

He didn't reply.

"Aren't you?"

Dewey was annoyed. "If Franklin thinks he's ready, that's enough for me." Mattie decided that she had said enough.

III

FIVE horses went postward for the featured Gallatin Purse, the best of three four-mile heats. Matilda would be matched with another four-year-old filly named Lady's Choice, both carrying ninety-eight pounds, the low weight. A good five-year-old mare, Harpy, was assigned one hundred eight pounds. And two four-year-old colts, Blue Ridge and Rambler—the favorite in the event— were to carry an even hundred pounds.

Charles didn't make a bet with the public pool, as he usually did when a Bon Marché horse was running. Even though he had trained the filly, he turned the saddling and the handling of the jockey over to Franklin, and he acted only as a spectator—and one with seemingly little interest.

"This filly doesn't have a lot of speed," Franklin said to Marshall, who had never ridden Matilda before. "So just keep her as close to the pace as you can, in case something collapses in front of her."

Marshall nodded his understanding.

Franklin stole a glance at Charles, then moved close to the light-skinned boy in the saddle and whispered to him. "I want to win this race more than any I can think of. Don't run her legs off, brother."

Again Marshall nodded to his half brother.

Mattie, who had been seeking a wager, came up to Charles. "Can you believe my luck?" she said enthusiastically. "The gentleman who owns Blue Ridge has given me six-to-one odds."

"For how much?"

"His wife hesitated. "A thousand dollars."

"*What?* Good God, woman, are you stupid?" He stalked away from her angrily. He was thinking of seeking out Raymond Cross, the owner of Blue Ridge, and thrashing him for taking advantage of his wife.

Just before the runners were called to the post, Mattie had patted Marshall on the leg.

"Win this one for me," she said.

The boy smiled at her.

"And for your father."

Marshall's face went sober. "Yes, ma'am, I'll try."

When the drum tapped for the start, the two colts—as everyone had expected—went immediately to the lead. They traded the lead, back and forth, throughout most of the four miles. In the last fifty yards they surged toward the finish line as a team and crossed it that way.

The placing judges took a long time in discussion before it was announced: "A dead heat is declared, ladies and gentlemen, between Blue Ridge and Rambler!"

The crowd roared its approval.

The other four-year-old filly, Lady's Choice, had been third, ten lengths off the pace. Matilda, with Marshall riding easily, was two lengths farther back, in fourth. Surprisingly, the five-year-old mare, Harpy, was a poor last.

Marshall slid out of the saddle. "I did what you said," he told Franklin. "I didn't run her legs off. I could have passed Lady's Choice, but I didn't see any reason to do that."

"You did absolutely the right thing, Marshall. Let's get her ready for the second heat."

Mattie hadn't seen Charles since she had told him of her big wager. But it didn't matter; she wanted no more of his anger.

The field was called for the second heat.

"Same instructions," Franklin said to the jockey. "Just handle her easily. Don't use her up."

The second heat was almost an exact copy of the first. Blue Ridge and Rambler went quickly to the front and stayed there. The race ended the same way—astoundingly! The two colts were declared, once more, to have run a dead heat!

This time, however, it was Matilda who trailed them to the finish line, only six lengths off the winning pace. The mare, Harpy, was also closer up in fourth. And Lady's Choice, having run all of her race in the first heat, was distanced and was declared out of the third heat.

Charles had watched the first two heats from the refreshment pavilion along the home stretch, drinking bourbon all the while. After the second heat, he spoke to a stranger standing next to him.

"Are you a betting man, sir?"

"Sure thing."

"Would you consider taking some money on that filly, Matilda?"

"Anything you name, mister."

Charles emptied his glass. "For the whole race, sir, five hundred dollars!"

"Are you sober, mister?"

"No, but I'm not so drunk that I don't see what's been happening out there."

"You're a fool," the stranger said, "but you have a bet."

"Will you give me three to one?"

The man shrugged confidently. "Sure, why not?"

"Agreed," said Dewey, pumping the stranger's hand vigorously. He ordered another whiskey.

At the judges' stand on the course, a bitter verbal battle was being waged. Rambler had come out of the second heat with his hind legs bleeding, and his owner, one Wade Masters, was loudly complaining to the officials that his runner had been fouled—that he had been "jumped on" by Blue Ridge.

"They bumped, Mr. Masters. That was obvious," the steward was saying. "But we are convinced that it was accidental."

"Accidental be damned!" Masters screamed. "It was a deliberate foul and I want Blue Ridge disqualified."

The steward shook his head. "No, sir, it was accidental. It's a dead heat!"

"Then you'll run the rest of it without my horse," the owner yelled. "Rambler is drawn!"

"That's your choice, of course, Mr. Masters."

When the announcement was made to the crowd, a mad flurry of additional betting went on for the remaining colt, Blue Ridge.

Thus, only three horses were called to the start line for the third heat.

"Don't try to run with that colt," Franklin instructed Marshall. "Just be content to finish."

"I will."

The completion of the four miles was just as Franklin had wanted it. Blue Ridge shot to the front with early speed, and only in the last mile did the mare, Harpy, challenge him, falling short by a length at the end. Matilda was last.

Everyone on the course now seemed convinced that Blue Ridge would finally end the marathon race with another first in the fourth heat. Everyone but Franklin.

And Charles Dewey.

In the refreshment pavilion, Dewey was accepting all the bets on the outcome of the race.

"I have money for Matilda," he roared, quite drunk. "Either on the heat or the entire race."

He took any bet offered, at whatever odds, and some of it for even money. He seemed to have just enough sobriety to mark down the wagers in his small notebook. His risk exceeded three thousand dollars.

As he boosted Marshall aboard for the fourth heat, Franklin was very specific about his orders. "First, stay within striking distance of the colt. Don't worry about the mare, just keep the colt in sight. Two, no more than three, lengths off the pace."

Marshall listened to him intently. Soberly.

"Then, at the beginning of the fourth mile, make your move. But not suddenly. Increase the pressure slowly, but be sure, when you have a hundred yards to go, that you're abreast of him. That's the time to go to the whip."

Franklin smiled. "I don't think the colt will have enough left to hold you off."

The drum tapped for the fourth time. The crowd, having seen some of the finest racing in Tennessee, now seemed emotionally spent. They watched the early part of the heat in comparative silence.

Marshall did precisely what he had been told. In the last mile of four, he began urging Matilda forward. Gaining, gaining, ever gaining.

With one hundred yards still to go, and looking the Blue Ridge jockey squarely in the eye, Marshall cracked Matilda hard with the whip. She shot ahead, as a roar like thunder bounced off the surrounding hills. Blue Ridge bobbled momentarily—and was beaten a length. The mare, Harpy, finished four lengths back.

Raymond Cross, after inspecting his exhausted colt, approached the course officials: "Gentlemen, Blue Ridge is drawn. I have no desire to kill him." He sought out Mattie. "Ma'am, it seems I may owe you six thousand."

The mistress of Bon Marché was very calm, outwardly. "You think, then, that Matilda can win two heats?"

"I think so—yes." He laughed. "But you'll excuse me, I'm sure, if I cheer for the mare."

"Of course."

"If the mare wins, you know," Cross continued, "my horse and your horse will each have won once, but the bet is null and void without two wins."

"I understand the rules, sir."

Cross bowed clumsily. "I'm still enough of a gentleman, in my defeat, to wish you well, ma'am."

Franklin Dewey was speaking to his jockey: "She's tired, Marshall, but I think she has enough left to put away the mare. We had to go eight and thirty-seven to win the fourth heat. I'm certain that we'll not have to go nearly as fast to win this time."

"All right."

"Don't concern yourself at all with time. If the boy on Harpy wants the lead, let him have it. But stay close. Not more than a length out of it, please. If the mare walks, you walk. Save it all again for that last hundred yards. If you do, Marshall, we will have won the most amazing race ever run in Tennessee."

"Just as you say," Marshall assured him.

Franklin clapped him on the back and helped him into the saddle for the fifth time.

When Franklin turned around, his father was standing there. Weaving.

"I don't imagine," he said, the words slurred, "that you need my advice."

"No, sir."

"Good, good." He hung his head contritely. "May I speak to your jockey before he goes off?"

Franklin hesitated.

"Please . . ."

"Very well."

Charles staggered to the side of the filly and laid a hand on Marshall's thigh.

"I know I have acted the fool, Marshall, and I hope you'll be able to forgive me someday." He drew a deep breath, fighting the nausea he felt. "No matter how this turns out, I want you to know that I'm proud of you"—a long pause—"son."

"Thank you, sir."

"To the post!" the steward shouted.

The two remaining runners walked to the start line.

A tap of the drum.

Before the race had gone a half-mile, everyone at the track was aware of what the outcome would be. Harpy took the lead, setting a slow pace, flagging her tail. Matilda, under restraint, was just behind her.

They went that way, two tired horses on a dead-slow pace, for three and a half miles. On the final half mile, Marshall, hand-riding only, came abreast of Harpy. At the hundred-yard mark, he just clucked to his filly, and she took off, winning by four lengths.

Mattie's delighted scream could be heard all over the course.

Charles stood back and watched her collect the six thousand dollars from Raymond Cross.

George ran up to him, throwing his arms around his father, whirling him about. "Wasn't it grand, Father? Just grand!"

"Marvelous," Charles grunted, hoping he wouldn't throw up.

"Do you realize," George said, "that that wonderful filly has run *twenty miles* to win today?"

Dewey could barely stand straight. He handed his wagering book to George. "If you can decipher this mess, I wish you'd collect my bets."

George studied the book, his eyes opening wide. "My God, Father, you've won more than ten thousand dollars!"

Charles just stood there, weaving, his eyes hooded in drunkenness. "I'd give it all, George, to have back some angry words I said to your mother earlier."

"She'll forgive you, Father."

"I don't deserve forgiveness."

"Nonsense."

Dewey sank slowly to the ground, unable to stay on his feet any longer. "Damned fool, that's what I am!"

"Drunken fool, too," a voice said, "but I love you."

Charles looked up into Mattie's glowing face.

"Oh, Charles, Matilda did it!"

"Yes," he mumbled. "Just like you . . . small and tough."

He passed out.

IV

WITHIN the week a lawyer appeared at the Davidson County Court House in Nashville to file two petitions on behalf of his client, Squire Charles Dewey of the Bon Marche plantation.

The first asked that the court look favorably on a desire of Mr. Dewey to have one of his slaves, a lad called Marshall, given the legal name of Marshall Dewey. Attached to the petition was an affidavit declaring that the young man's parents were the aforementioned Charles Dewey and a slave woman, Angelica.

Another document was a manumission appeal, in which Dewey asked that one of his slaves, Marshall Dewey, a minor, be declared "now and forever" a free man.

At Bon Marché the family crowded around Matilda's stall, offering her carrots and fresh alfalfa hay.

"What's next for her, Charles?" Mattie asked.

"Next?" He laughed. "Can you imagine that she could ever be greater, in any other races, that she was last Sunday? I can't. And, since she could never top herself, I think she's earned retirement. To stud, of course."

"Just like a man!" his wife said, pretending to be annoyed. "Considering motherhood a retirement."

"I think she ought to go to the court of Predator." Charles looked to Franklin for confirmation of his choice.

"I think you're right, Father. His foals could use some stamina."

Dewey held out a leaf of hay to the filly. "What think you of that, Matilda? Could you add some guts to the babies of Predator?"

Drawing back her upper lip, exposing her teeth, the filly nickered loudly.

They all laughed.

29

CHARLES was weeping unashamedly.

He stood at the head of the long lane leading to the Bon Marché mansion, waving wildly at two riders coming toward him. They were only pygmies in the distance, unrecognizable by any normal eye, but Charles knew who they were. He had been waiting for days and now, in mid-December of 1808, the day had arrived.

As they drew closer, the familiar face of the lead rider came clear to him.

"Andrew!" Charles shouted.

The horse was spurred and Andrew MacCallum raced to Dewey's side. "Charles, my friend!"

Dismounting, the former tutor groaned. "Oh, God, the old legs are protesting mightily."

The two men embraced, holding each other for a long time in a kind of desperation. Abner Lower, who had made the trip to New Jersey to guide MacCallum to Bon Marché, sat on his horse and smiled.

Finally, Dewey held Andrew at arm's length, studying him. "Andrew, dear Andrew! How long has it been?"

"Twelve years."

"You've grown gray, Andrew."

"I *am* in my fifties, Charles. And a bit paunchy, too." He patted an ample stomach.

"Fifties, gray, paunchy—it doesn't make any difference. You're *here*—that's all that matters."

Dewey looked up at Lower.

"A difficult trip, Abner?"

"A lucky one," the guide reported. "The weather held for us. I was afraid we were goin' to have snow in the mountains coming out of Virginia, but I reckon we stayed in front of it all the while."

Charles wiped a hand over his teary face. "I'm grateful to you, Abner."

Lower nodded.

Taking MacCallum by the arm Charles propelled him toward Bon Marché. "It's only a short walk, Andrew. Or would you rather ride in?"

"If I never have to get up on that nag again, it'll satisfy me."

"You know, Andrew, if I had realized that it would take Franklin's wedding to get you here, I would have had him marry at sixteen."

MacCallum laughed. "I really believe you would have."

II

ANDREW had thought a great deal about what he would find in Tennessee. It would give him an opportunity, he had decided, to study the family unit on the frontier. He didn't mean to be totally academic about it; the visit to his dearest friend was paramount, of course. But he had spent all of his life in study, and he couldn't change now.

As Dewey proudly showed him around Bon Marché, Andrew made mental comparisons with plantations he had seen in Virginia. The way of life on those plantations was more leisurely, but few had the full range of facilities he found at Bon Marché—and the fair-minded management he could deduce almost immediately. Bon Marché, he concluded, was a happier place than any plantation he had ever seen that was based on a slave economy. There was less of the depressing master-slave attitude.

Dinner that night was in MacCallum's honor. Many toasts were drunk, many old stories revived. And the dinner hour went late. Finally, when Franklin asked his father to check on a sick foal with him, Andrew was left alone with Mattie. It was a welcome respite for him. She led him to the drawing room.

"A sherry, Andrew?"

"No, I think not. As always when I'm with Charles, I'm inclined to drink too much."

Mattie grinned. "He's spoken of nothing else for weeks but your arrival."

"Yes, we have a rare relationship. I find it difficult to put it into words."

"You have a good effect on Charles."

Andrew laughed, getting up to stand with his back to the fireplace. "I was about to say the same thing regarding you. Quite honestly, the Charles I knew in Virginia is different from the Tennessee Charles."

"In what way?" She was intrigued.

"Oh, he always had the same self-assurance, but he was . . . well, existing alone. It was Charles Dewey against the world, so to speak. Here I see him as a man who is guided and molded and nurtured. By you, Mattie."

She blushed at the compliment, but she was pleased. "You give me too much credit."

"I think not."

"His first wife—wasn't she supportive?"

He ran his hand through his hair, using the brief moment to organize his thoughts. "Supportive yes, but she didn't challenge him. Martha Dewey was a lovely woman—a beauty, I can tell you—and she loved him deeply. But

Charles had to be the impetus in everything. You've challenged him; you've made him more than he might have been."

She smiled wanly. "Nagged him, you mean."

"No, no, nothing like that at all," MacCallum protested. "You're strong. He needs that strength to complement his own." A chuckle. "Indeed, Mattie, you are the woman I've searched for and never found. I take vicarious pleasure in knowing that my dearest friend has found you."

Charles entered the room. "If that foal doesn't improve by the morning," he said sadly, "we may have to destroy it. I'm perplexed; I don't know what's wrong with it. But I do know that it's simply wasting away."

"Franklin must be distressed," Mattie commented.

"He is. I wish he wouldn't take every failure with a horse as his own guilt." He clapped his hands together to mark an end to that subject. "Well, what have you two been talking about?"

"Secrets," Mattie said, smiling.

"Indeed?"

"That's right," MacCallum confirmed.

"And I'm not to be taken into your confidence?"

"Never." His friend laughed.

Charles waited for more. It didn't come. He shrugged. "Well, I know when I've been shut out. A sherry, Andrew?"

"No, thank you. I've already had that kind offer from your wife, but your toasts at dinner were quite enough for me." He sighed. "Truthfully, Charles, I am rather tired."

"Of course, you must be. Let me show you to your room."

As the two friends climbed the stairway to the second floor, MacCallum said, "Mattie's a very special woman, Charles."

"Yes."

"I told you once that you were the luckiest man I knew, and I have to repeat it again."

"I give thanks every night for my good fortune."

They entered a large bedroom. Horace had already unpacked Andrew's clothes and put them away.

MacCallum began to undress. "I stopped at Elkwood on the way through Virginia."

"Oh?"

"Katherine is a very unhappy lady."

"That doesn't surprise me."

Andrew frowned. "You don't forgive easily, do you?"

"It isn't a case of forgiving or not forgiving, Andrew. Elkwood is part of my past. A long-gone part. I have nothing that ties me there anymore."

"Lee has become a drunken sot," the visitor went on. "And his affairs are common gossip throughout central Virginia."

"Why doesn't she leave him?"

"She can't. Statler's will, you'll recall, gave them Elkwood jointly. If she tries to get out, he'll tie her up in unending litigation."

"Hmmm."

"She'd like to hear from you, Charles."

"No, I can't do that."

"The children are her nieces and nephews," Andrew reminded him.

"Their recollection of her is minimal."

MacCallum groaned. "For God's sake, Charles, give her *something!* She's a woman alone."

"I'll give it some thought." He changed the subject.

III

THE days leading up to Christmas, and the wedding, were crowded with activities. Charles tried to fill every minute of Andrew's time until his friend, genuinely annoyed, asked him to desist.

"Charles, I'm not a child," he said as gently as he could. "I don't need to be led around."

"I've been smothering you," Dewey said gravely.

"Yes."

Charles shrugged. "I apologize for that, old friend. You have the free run of Bon Marché."

MacCallum, intent on his study now, sought out Corrine. "You may not know it," he said to the girl, "but you are your mother from head to toe. The same hair, the same eyes, the same . . . uh . . . womanliness, the same beauty."

Corrine flushed. "Thank you, Uncle Andrew. You embarrass me. But I don't remember much about my mother. She's more of a shadow than a reality."

"Your father doesn't speak of her?"

"Rarely."

"Hmmm. They were married, you know, when your mother was several years younger than you are now. Let's see, you're—"

"Eighteen." She said it with pride—perhaps even defiance.

"Is there a young man?"

"Oh, yes!" She became animated. "His name is William Holder. He's a lawyer." The happy animation turned suddenly to sadness. "Father doesn't care for him."

"Oh?"

"Billy, you see, doesn't hold any brief for horse racing and gambling. He considers such things . . . well, corruptive."

MacCallum laughed. "I can see where Charles might not see eye to eye with him."

"Billy's not awed by Father, as most people are." The words reflected her pride. "I'm afraid they've exchanged some heated words. Billy says gamblers are wastrels . . ."

"My, my."

". . . and horse race people are ne'er-do-wells."

"You seem to have a real problem, young lady."

"Oh, no," she replied, the defiance returning. "Billy and I *will* be married, just as soon as his career allows us to have a home of our own. He refuses to rely on Bon Marché money."

"Good for you. And him."

"You approve?" She seemed surprised that her father's close friend would side with her.

"Of course. I'm in favor of adults making their own way in life. You must do what you think is best for you, not what might be thought best for your father."

She kissed him on the cheek. Spontaneously. "I wish you were my father."

"No, you don't. Your father is a fine man; he'll come around. I said earlier that you had your mother's good looks. Now I know that you also have your father's grit. That's a fine combination."

Corrine gasped. "You think I'm like *him!*"

"Very much so."

The young girl shook her head. "I never thought of it that way before. But, I think you may be right. I *am* a Dewey, aren't I?"

IV

Louise Dewey, MacCallum learned quickly, wasn't at all like her older sister. At sixteen, she was willowy, pretty if not beautiful, and somewhat of a tomboy. Not a woman; not yet. But, there was a certain iciness in her that suggested she would mature into a woman of style. Of class. To Andrew, such an inevitability seemed preordained.

Andrew spent a morning at the training track, watching Louise handle spirited two-year-old thoroughbreds, riding them with an expertise of a jockey.

"You seem to be at ease on a horse," he said to her while she was unsaddling one of the young animals.

"It would be strange if I wasn't, don't you think?"

"Yes and no. Your sister, Corrine, doesn't seem to be interested in equines."

"Corry is a pill!"

"Oh, is she?"

"Yes, and a damned prude, too! Uncle Andrew, I get sick to my stomach sometimes with her. It's always Billy this and Billy that, as though Billy Holder had hung the moon."

"You don't like Holder?"

"He's all right, I guess. It's just that he's so certain about everything." She paused. "And I don't like the way he argues with Father. He doesn't show him any respect."

"And you think your father merits respect?"

"Of course I think he merits respect!" She grinned at him. "Uncle Andrew, you're baiting me."

"Guilty," MacCallum laughed.

"Why?"

"To get to know you better. To understand the younger generation of Deweys. To make up for all those years that I was away from you—from all of Charles's children."

Louise studied his face. "That makes sense, I guess. But I'm not special. I'm just me. I hope that doesn't disappoint you."

"Not at all. What do you want in life, Louise?"

"I never thought of it," she answered flippantly.

"I don't believe you."

She laughed. "You're wise, aren't you? Like Father."

"At times," he admitted.

"I know what I *don't* want. I don't want a Billy Holder. *If* I ever get married, I want a *man!* Someone mature."

"Like Charles Dewey?"

"Maybe. Maybe not. But a man who knows where he's going. Who isn't just a complainer, like Billy. A man who . . . well, Father says that everyone ought to shake the world a little bit. I guess I'm going to look for a shaker."

"You're the one, young lady, who's wise."

"Me? No. I told you, I'm just me." She grinned at him. "Would you wait for me, Uncle Andrew? Maybe, after I'm a few years older, Father would agree to my marrying *you.*"

"You're a terrible tease, Louise."

She sobered. "I don't think so." There was a moment of silence. "When I find my shaker, Uncle Andrew, there will be no teasing. I'll know!"

V

GEORGE Washington Dewey was a delight to MacCallum. Extroverted, jolly, candid, self-assured—in love with life. All of it.

"Louise claims," George said, "that you're studying us, Uncle Andrew. Are you?"

"Yes, in a sense."

"I never thought of the Deweys being worth study. Except, maybe, for Father." An extra thought: "And Mother."

"You like your stepmother." It was a statement, not a question.

"Better than that. I love her. She's tops! She makes Father very happy. They're great lovers, you know."

MacCallum smiled. "How old are you, George?"

"Nineteen."

"And you know about lovers?"

The young man chortled, dropping his voice into an intimate whisper. "Uncle Andrew, I know a little bit about horses, a little bit about gambling, a little bit about good food—and a great deal about love!"

"You do, eh?"

"Absolutely. I'm the best lover at Bon Marché. Except for Father, maybe."

"And what has made you such an expert?"

"Careful study. Like you, Uncle Andrew, I study people. Especially women."

"What have you learned?"

"Enough. For example, did you know that you can tell if a woman is going to be . . . uh . . . cooperative by the way she walks?"

"I'm afraid such a thing has been beyond *my* study." He was thoroughly amused by the conversation.

"Well, you can. Now, a woman who just minces along, with her legs held tightly together"—he demonstrated such a walk—"is not a good choice. But a woman who walks freely, unconcerned about the comparative positions of her legs"—he demonstrated another walk—"is a good candidate for . . ." He shrugged. "Well, you understand what I mean."

"That's an infallible test, is it?"

"Nine out of ten times," George assured him. "Not bad odds, eh?"

"Not bad at all."

"Of course, not all women who walk freely are candidates. Some are married and find themselves unavailable. Not all of them, you understand, but marriage is sometimes a barrier."

"I see. Have you any more of this wisdom for an old bachelor?"

"Eyes are important, but you have to study them carefully. It's subtle. Eyes tell you little things. If you hint at some . . . uh . . . indiscretion, and the eyes show no reaction, just forget it. But if the eyes moist over—just a tiny bit—the lady may be willing. Most often."

"Fascinating."

"The first thing I learned, Uncle Andrew, is *not* to listen to words from a woman. Words don't count at all. Some of the most outspoken women can be cold. On the other hand, some of the most shy girls—those who find it difficult to respond verbally—can be cold, as well. So you have to discount everything a woman says, unless it's 'yes' at the proper moment. Even then, the words aren't important. Few girls who are willing actually say 'yes.' They just go ahead and do it. Without words."

"I seem to be in the company of a connoisseur."

George shook his head doubtfully. "I don't know that any man can be a complete connoisseur of women. But I try."

"Do other things keep your interest?"

"Oh, sure. Dancing, gambling, books—and horses, of course."

"Of course."

"I'm not a serious student of horses, as Franklin is. Franklin is a superb horseman—better than Father in some ways. Women are more fun than horses, though."

"I gather from this conversation that you're not seriously thinking of marriage."

"Marriage? Certainly—someday, when it suits my purpose."

"What kind of woman will hold you?"

"I haven't worked it all out yet. She'd have to be strong, like Mattie. And loving, like Mattie."

Was every man seeking a Mattie Dewey? MacCallum wondered.

"And I believe I'd like it more if she were wealthy," George went on. "I mean, I'm going to be wealthy, aren't I? Assuming that Father doesn't cut me off." He laughed at such a foreign thought. "So that money wouldn't become a decisive factor in our relationship, she ought to have her own wealth. Right?"

"Far be it from me to disagree with your evaluation of what a woman ought to be."

"How is it that you haven't married, Uncle Andrew?"

"I haven't found the right woman."

"You've looked?"

"Not with your dedication, perhaps, but—"

"Have you ever been to bed with a woman?"

MacCallum told himself that he ought to be offended by the audacity of the question. But he wasn't. "Yes," he said, "I have."

"More than one?"

"More than one."

George clapped Andrew on the back. The gesture was man-to-man, not younger man to older man.

"Then there's hope for you yet," George Dewey assured him.

VI

LEE Dewey was difficult to talk to. He wasn't sullen or impolite or without words, but MacCallum had trouble getting through to the lad's inner thoughts.

They chatted amiably one day in the foaling barn, when Lee's chore was to keep watch on a foal that was having difficulty nursing because the mare had tender teats and was forever kicking the youngster away. They covered a lot of subjects: books, music, mathematics—Charles had bragged to Andrew about Lee's proficiency in mathematics—horses. But the sixteen-year-old—Louise's twin—seemed reticent about opening up, about taking the older man into his confidence.

Andrew persisted, looking for the key to unlock him.

"It seems to me that you have a unique opportunity here, Lee, with the horses. Few young men have the ready availability of such a superb training ground."

Lee just nodded.

"Perhaps you don't see horses in your future?"

There was no immediate answer, but MacCallum waited patiently.

"I guess I do," the boy said finally. "You can hardly be at Bon Marché without realizing that."

"But it's not what you want."

Another delay. "No."

"Would you care to tell me what you *do* want? What you dream of?"

Lee sighed. "Oh, it's not important. At least, Father would think it's not important."

"Why do you say that?"

"Father has made it clear that we are *all* to be fascinated by the horse business." For the first time some bitterness showed.

"I'm sure he hasn't precluded another outlet for his children."

"He hasn't said so, no."

"But you think he has."

"Yes. If I went to Father with any other thought but horses, he'd . . ." He didn't finish the sentence.

"He'd what?"

"He'd be disappointed." It seemed a weak answer.

"And you don't want to disappoint him."

"I guess not."

"Lee, let me say something, which I hope you'll believe. Charles Dewey is my dearest friend. But that doesn't mean I go carrying tales to him about everything I learn. Don't you want to tell me what you dream? In confidence?"

There was no answer.

"Lee, I'm *your* friend, too."

Another deep sigh. "I want to be an artist. A painter."

"That's marvelous!"

The boy shrugged.

"Do you believe you have talent for that?" MacCallum prodded.

"I hope so."

"You've done some things?"

"A few ink drawings."

"May I see them?"

Still the suspicion was there, the doubt. After another silent moment, Lee climbed quickly to the hayloft above the horse stalls. When he came down again, he handed a sheaf of drawing papers to Andrew.

MacCallum examined them slowly: a foal frolicking in the pasture, a reproduction of the Bon Marché mansion, the grain mill by the Richland Creek, an eerie grove of willow trees, portraits of his brothers and sisters, uncanny in their accuracy.

"Lee, these are wonderful. Truly wonderful! You should show them to your father and mother."

"Could you . . . ?"

"No," Andrew replied firmly. "This is something you have to do. You have to assert yourself. It seems to me you owe that to your talent."

Lee took back the drawings. "I will. Someday."

"Don't delay too long."

"You really think they're good?"

"I do."

"Thank you."

The boy climbed the ladder to the hayloft again, and Andrew heard him hiding the drawings once more.

Lee was hiding his future, MacCallum realized. It made him very sad.

VII

ON Christmas morning, Andrew accompanied Franklin Dewey on his rounds of the horse barns, observing his efficient dispatch of orders to the blacks assigned to the horses. He would soon be twenty-two, but MacCallum thought he seemed much older, much more mature, than that.

"Your father seems to have given you a lot of responsibility," the visitor commented.

"He has."

"That must make you proud."

Franklin looked at him soberly. "It frightens me, Uncle Andrew."

"For God's sake, why?"

"Because Father has told me that, in a few years, I'm to be put in charge of the entire horse operation. And I don't believe I can measure up to him."

"Do you think he expects that of you?"

"It's not Father I'm concerned about. It's myself. I *want* to be like him, and I don't think I can be."

"That's an artificial challenge, Franklin, and you ought not to impose it on yourself."

"Maybe not, but I can't help it." His brow furrowed in a frown. "I have many shortcomings, Uncle Andrew."

"Nonsense!"

"I do," Franklin insisted. "What would you say if I told you that George had to instruct me on how to court Amantha?"

MacCallum laughed. "I'd say that you had the good sense to go to the world's leading authority."

"I wish it were that humorous."

"Franklin, listen to me," Andrew said, putting his arm about the young man's shoulders. "All of us have doubts about ourselves. I myself have doubts. When I get back to New Jersey I have reason to believe that I'll be offered the post of dean of the college."

"That's great!"

"And I have doubts I can handle it. But you know what? I will. To the best of my ability. I can't do more than that."

The eldest Dewey son grimaced. "You don't have to compete with a legend."

Now MacCallum laughed so much that his sides ached. "Legend? Charles Dewey?!"

"Of course."

Andrew realized that the young man was dead serious.

"Your father," he said, "is not infallible. Thank God, no one is. This would be an impossible world in which to live if some of us were infallible. And you *won't* be. Live with that, Franklin. It's a universal truth."

Christmas Day moved swiftly: the exchange of gifts, the huge dinner, the entertainment at night, highlighted by little Alma May's recitation of the Christmas story according to St. Luke. Warm, comfortable, loving.

At the end of the day, Charles and Andrew, bundled against the cold of the night, strolled across the lawn in front of the mansion.

"Have you completed your study of the Dewey family?" Charles asked in a disinterested manner.

"The children spoke to you?"

"Several of them did. They are convinced that you will immortalize the Deweys in some way."

MacCallum didn't pick up his friend's bantering tone. "Do you realize that Franklin considers you a legend?"

"Oh, my God, he doesn't!"

"Yes. And he wonders how he can live up to it."

"That's serious, isn't it?"

"Very. And one more thing, if I may presume on our friendship: Lee is so frightened of your damned image that he won't tell you that he wants no part of the horse business; that he wants to be an artist!"

"An artist?"

"Yes, and from what I've seen of a few of his drawings, he has a unique talent."

Dewey moaned. "You must think me a terrible father. You've been here— what? ten days?—and already you know more about my family than I do."

"I don't think you terrible, Charles. It's just that you have a . . . well, putting a candid face on it . . . you have a profoundly self-centered outlook. You don't listen to others. No, let me put that another way: you don't *hear* others."

They strolled along for several minutes before Charles spoke again: "You've always been my alter ego, Andrew. What you have just told me is proof, once again, that I need your guidance. Won't you accept my offer and stay?"

"No. Even if I stayed, though, you'd still have to do what I'm advising now—*hear* them, Charles."

The master of Bon Marché sighed. "You're right, of course." He chuckled. "I have accepted your advice on one thing: I found a few minutes today to write a letter to Katherine, telling her of the progress of the children. And wishing her a happy New Year. I'm afraid, though, that I couldn't force myself to extend those greetings to Funston."

"It's a start, old friend, it's a start."

30

EVEN if he had not been told that Andrew Jackson would be a guest at the wedding of Franklin Dewey and Amantha Bolling, Andrew MacCallum would have known who he was. Jackson's appearance in the living room at Bon Marché, where the ceremony was to be held, started a buzz of comment.

MacCallum guessed that everyone in the room already knew Jackson; yet there was a special quality about the man that stirred an excitement in them in spite of their familiarity with him. A step behind him was a subdued woman, handsome enough, but made plain, Andrew thought, by her pained shyness. That had to be Aunt Rachel, Jackson's wife.

As Andrew watched them, Mattie walked up to the Jacksons, smiling sweetly and proudly, kissing them both on the cheek. Charles Dewey was not in evidence.

MacCallum waited until several of the other women drew Rachel into conversation, and Jackson stood alone for a moment.

"Excuse me, sir," Andrew said as he went quickly to Jackson's side. "My name is Andrew MacCallum. I'm a friend of Mr. Dewey. We knew each other in Virginia."

Andy pumped his hand amiably. "Of course. Charles has spoken of you. His tutor, weren't you?"

"Yes." He was surprised that Jackson knew even that much about him.

Jackson swept a hand to indicate all of Bon Marché. "Dewey has done a marvelous job here."

"Yes, he has." Although MacCallum had thought about what he wanted to say to him, the presence of the man kept him silent for a moment.

"I was wondering, General," Andrew started hesitantly, "what are your views on the election of James Madison?"

"I would have preferred Monroe," Jackson replied sternly. "Madison is . . . well, too much Jefferson's altar boy for my tastes."

MacCallum just nodded, hoping that Jackson would go on.

"Mr. Madison's election merely continues the policy of allowing the English to do as they damned please on the high seas—harassing our ships, impressing our seamen!" Jackson's ire had been quickly raised.

Again, MacCallum merely nodded, as though agreeing.

"Why, Madison has had the gall to interfere in the matter of denying General Wilkinson his rank," Andy raced on. "Here we are, on the eve of war, and that traitor is still at the head of the army!"

"You're convinced that Wilkinson is a traitor?"

"Could any intelligent man think otherwise?"

"But his co-conspirator, Mr. Burr, has been acquitted."

Jackson shook his head sadly. "Burr was a fool, but I'm not certain he intended treason." He shrugged. "It's of little consequence now; Burr has left the country. He doesn't matter any longer. What must continue to concern us, Mr. MacCallum, is that Madison will do nothing to restrain the English. Nothing! Our national honor is at stake, and Madison will be an image of Jefferson: too cowardly to resent a foreign outrage on our Republic!"

"What would you have Madison do?"

"I'd have him fight, sir!" Jackson permitted a slight smile to cross his angular face. "I pray that I will be given the opportunity to prove that real men, real patriots, can still fight!"

An eavesdropper next to them applauded spontaneously. Jackson whirled to silence him with a glare.

Turning back to MacCallum, embarrassment on his face, Jackson said, "Perhaps this isn't the occasion for the discussion of such a heated subject."

Andrew laughed. "You're right, of course, General. My apologies for precipitating it."

Jackson waved aside the apology, glancing about the room. "Perhaps I should seek out young Franklin. I have some advice I might give him about the sanctity of the marriage vows."

He strode off without another word. Only then did MacCallum notice that he wore a small formal sword. He wondered whether Andy also carried a pistol in his coat.

II

THE wedding ceremony was simple and dignified, conducted by the minister from the Presbyterian church in Nashville.

When it was ended and the orchestra was playing, the guests were treated to a lavish buffet, with more than adequate liquid refreshments, including champagne.

MacCallum strolled about, chatting with the Nashvillians he had already met, introducing himself to those he had not, impressed by the universal friendliness of the people. He came upon Charles.

"You made a handsome best man," Andrew said.

"I thought so, too," his friend laughed. "You know, I'm really happy for Franklin. Amantha is not the girl I would have chosen, but I believe she's right for him."

"Mattie tells me they will honeymoon in New Orleans."

"Yes. Can you believe they plan a month there?" He sighed. "I can't help but think about the quick honeymoon Mattie and I had—four days in the wilderness." He grinned mischievously. "I'll wager that Franklin and his bride won't know the same passion—"

"You're an evil man."

"True." Dewey tapped MacCallum's arm. "See that lady over there?" He inclined his head toward a handsome woman chatting with Mattie.

"The buxom one?"

"You've noticed! You might have asked: 'The woman standing with Mattie?'" Charles playfully slapped him on the back. "That's Mercy Callison, a recent widow. Her late husband was a lawyer in Nashville."

Dewey propelled Andrew across the room.

"Mrs. Callison," he said, "I'd like to present my dear friend, Andrew MacCallum. You two should have a lot in common. Mr. MacCallum is a professor at the college in Princeton. And Mrs. Callison, Andrew, was a teacher somewhere in Pennsylvania . . ."

"In York," the woman prompted him.

MacCallum bowed awkwardly, taking in the woman's pleasant face, flawless complexion, and intense dark eyes.

"Mattie was just mentioning you, Mr. MacCallum," she said easily. "As a matter of fact, she was about to escort me across the room to meet you."

"A pleasure," Andrew muttered, wondering why he felt so ill-at-ease.

Mattie spoke: "You'll both excuse us, I'm sure. We have other guests to greet." She tugged at Charles's arm, leading him away.

Mrs. Callison was amused. "It seems we have been thrown together to see what might happen."

Her candor was refreshing, but Andrew wasn't quite sure what he ought to say.

The dark eyes studied him. "If I may be bold, may I suggest that we not stand on formality. I'm Mercy. And you? Andy, perhaps?"

"No, please. I was never cursed with a nickname. Andrew will be just fine." He coughed nervously. "Charles tells me you're a widow."

"And Mattie tells me you're a bachelor."

Andrew relaxed a bit. "May I get you a drink, Mercy? Sherry? Champagne, perhaps?"

She wrinkled up her nose. Delightfully. "I'd much prefer a whiskey."

"Ah, a woman after my own heart."

Mercy Callison's tinkling laugh turned heads their way. "I believe, Andrew, that that's exactly what our friends had in mind."

III

IMMENSE gray clouds, roiling and churning in a stiff wind, approximating wads of filthy cotton, hung over the Nashville Inn. The dark early evening was suddenly turned into midday by a jagged slash of lightning, followed by a roaring boom of thunder that seemed to shake the hostelry.

MacCallum raised his eyebrows. "A thunderstorm in January?"

"Out here," Mercy explained, "there are no seasons to the weather. As a matter of fact, our weather is fairly consistent. Most of it bad."

They were seated in the dining room of the inn. It was the last Saturday in January and, for the third time since Franklin's wedding, MacCallum was entertaining the attractive widow. They always dined at the Nashville Inn; the town offered few such accommodations for a lady and gentleman to dine.

Andrew had learned a great deal about Mercy Callison in the few weeks he had known her. For one thing, she had been a mathematics instructor at a girls' academy in York, Pennsylvania—somewhat of a rarity among women teachers. For another, she had married a promising young lawyer, Calvin Callison, in York, where his father was a judge.

"The Callisons were an important family in York," Mercy had told him. "And Calvin was quite handsome—the catch of the season, I think, is the proper phrase. At the risk of sounding overly romantic, Cal swept me off my feet. We were married a month to the day after we met. That was considered somewhat scandalous.

"But we had a good life: a socially prominent young attorney and his pretty . . ." She giggled at that. ". . . wife. Cal, though, was restless. He wanted to go west, to seek new opportunities. And I, as a dutiful wife, came with him. Truthfully, I would have preferred to stay in Pennsylvania, but wives don't have the luxury, I'm afraid, of making such independent decisions."

She frowned at the memory. "Let's just say it didn't go well. We were in Knoxville for a time. Then in Kentucky, at Lexington. Then in some god-awful outpost in the Northwest that didn't even have a name—somewhere near Lake Michigan—where Cal hoped to make his own fortune. Then back to Lexington. And finally, here to Nashville. Cal died last February of pleurisy. He was just forty-two."

Mercy had told him that much. A biographical outline only, with no details and no emotion. It was plain that Calvin Callison had been a failure, but Andrew didn't know why. He had asked about children, a question that turned her bitter for the first time.

"Cal," she had said, "didn't have time for that."

Now, as they sat at dinner in the Nashville Inn, huge drops of rain began to splatter against the windows. The lightning and thunder continued unabated for nearly a half-hour. When it did abate, the rain continued—hard sheets of rain, driven horizontally by the high winds.

Andrew and Mercy decided to wait out the storm, ordering another whiskey after finishing their meal. The winds finally ended, but the rain persisted. Harder than before, it seemed.

"I fear it's going to continue all night," Mercy said.

"I believe you're right." Andrew got to his feet. "Come, I'll show you home, and then I'll get a room here at the inn. I certainly don't want to ride back to Bon Marché in that mess."

Mrs. Callison lived on the opposite side of the town from the inn, and they had gone only a hundred yards before their clothing was soaked through. At first it was uncomfortable, then disagreeable, and then it didn't matter. The dirt street had been turned into a river of sticky red mud, making the going hazardous. But before they had gone halfway, they were laughing together like happy children. Getting to her home became a game.

And when they reached the Callison home, Mercy found the door locked.

"Stupid, damned—" she muttered under her breath, pounding on the door. "Delilah, open this door immediately!"

A black servant girl opened the door, filling the frame with her ample body. "Ah sorry, Miss Mercy, but Morgan he done git fightin' drunk agin an' Ah lock so—"

Mercy sighed disgustedly. "Delilah, just step aside and let us come in, please." To Andrew: "Morgan is my Delilah's paramour from the livery stable." She started to laugh again at the absurdity of it all, with Andrew joining her.

Mercy entered the one-story brick house. MacCallum entered, too, but stood dripping just inside the sill.

"I'll say good night here," he announced. "I don't want to track all of this mud into your house."

She stared at him for a moment, water running down her face from her rain-soaked hair. "Andrew, my dear," she said with a note of annoyance, "don't be so damned prudish. We're both like drowned cats, and I'll not see you tramp back through the mud and the rain to the inn. You'll be ill by the time you get there."

Still he hesitated.

Mercy closed the door firmly and set the bolt. "Delilah," she ordered, "take Mr. MacCallum's hat, and his coats, and his boots, and put them into the pantry to dry. And then stir up that fire."

"Yas, ma'am."

"Now, that's settled," the widow said. "Try to make yourself comfortable by the fire, Andrew. I'll be right back."

Mercy disappeared into a room that Andrew guessed was a bedroom, and he heard her humming a silly little song. He stood with his back to the fireplace, but he knew he'd never get dry that way. Water dripped from his trousers and sizzled on the hearth.

He stepped aside for a moment as Delilah stirred the glowing embers and added more wood. The fire roared up quickly.

It was only a few minutes before Mercy, wearing a light robe and toweling her long black hair, returned. Andrew eyed her appreciatively; the robe showed off her good figure.

"Your turn now," she said gaily. "Go in there and get out of those wet clothes. I've laid out Cal's old robe—it's quite warm—and a towel." She grinned. "And a set of underclothes."

"Oh, I don't think—"

Mercy groaned. "Andrew, please. You can't stay in those wet clothes. Just go in there and do what I told you."

MacCallum entered the bedroom, closing the door behind him.

"When Mr. MacCallum is finished in there," Mrs. Callison said to the servant, "gather up all those wet clothes and hang them somewhere to dry."

"Yas, ma'am."

"And, Delilah—"

"Ma'am?"

"When you're finished, I don't want to see you again tonight."

"Yas, ma'am. Ah be in mah room, Miss Mercy, jest as quiet as—"

"With the door closed," her mistress interrupted.

"Oh, yas, ma'am!"

"Help me with this." Mercy started to push a small settee from its position against the wall so that it faced the flames of the fire.

"Miss Mercy?"

"Yes."

"It nice to see a man in th' house agin."

The widow laughed. "You're a romantic devil, Delilah."

"Yas, ma'am."

When the settee was in place, Mercy sat down, arranging the wrapper tightly around her legs.

Andrew came out of the bedroom, enfolded in the heavy robe. "Mr. Callison must have been a big man," he commented. "This robe could go around me twice."

"In stature he was big," she said lightly. "Join me here, Andrew, and get warm again."

He sat down on the settee, extending his bare feet toward the fire. "That does feel good."

Delilah scurried out of the bedroom, carrying the wet clothes.

"Fetch a bottle, Delilah," Mercy ordered.

"Yas, ma'am."

In what seemed to be only seconds, the black woman was back with a bottle of bourbon and two glasses. Mercy took the bottle in one hand, the glasses in the other, and pulled the cork out with her teeth.

"A little trick I learned from my husband," she said, after she had poured a liberal portion of the amber liquid into each glass. "Calvin was adept with a whiskey bottle."

Andrew didn't think it necessary to respond.

"You must have wondered why we moved around so much."

"I did, yes."

She took a deep breath, exhaling it slowly. "Cal was a drunkard. There's no way to put a good face on it. It was very sad. He was a man of ability—a fine lawyer. But he drank away every opportunity he ever had." She paused. "I told you that he died of pleurisy. Well, that's what I asked the doctor to say. In truth, the whiskey killed him."

"That *is* sad."

Mercy was pensive. "At least Cal taught me how to drink whiskey. But I guess that isn't much to get out of a marriage, is it?"

MacCallum patted her hand sympathetically. He couldn't remember when he had been more at ease with a woman and less sure about how he should act. That it was an intimate moment there was no doubt. He left his hand on hers as they sat silently that way, the crackling of the fire and the tick of the large clock in the corner and the steady beating of the rain on the roof the only sounds.

"Andrew?" she said softly.

"Yes?"

"I have a confession."

He chuckled. "Alexander Pope once suggested that a confession meant that one was wiser today than yesterday."

"Oh, I don't think it's that serious a confession. Certainly it has nothing to do with being wise."

"May I hear it?"

"When we were hurrying from the inn," she started hesitantly, "it ran through my mind that getting soaked by the rain, as we certainly did, would give me the opportunity to . . . well, keep you here. To set up an intimate situation with you, just as it has happened."

"But now you have second thoughts?" he suggested.

"In a sense. Sitting here so quietly and comfortably, it has occurred to me that you might not want an intimate situation. That you would think me . . . unladylike. Even brazen."

"No such thought crossed my mind."

"What has, then?"

"That I enjoy being with you. That I want to know more about you, the little things that may not seem significant to others. That I want us to be close friends."

"No more than that?"

His answer didn't come immediately.

"You didn't think of making love to me?" Her question bordered on petulance.

"Yes, I've thought of that."

"And?"

"I didn't want to offend you by making an overture. You've become too dear to me to risk offense."

Mercy laughed ever so slightly. "You really are a gentle man—that's meant to be two words—aren't you?"

"Perhaps a fool."

"No, not at all." She leaned toward him, brushing her lips against his. "I wouldn't be offended, Andrew."

He reached for her, taking her into his arms, kissing her with passion, feeling her body against him through the thin robe. And feeling good about it. Her eyes, he noticed, were misted over, just a bit. The laugh started inside him, and he tried to keep it there. He could not.

It clearly annoyed her. "Andrew . . . what—?"

"I'm so sorry," he tried to apologize. But he was still laughing. "It's just that young George Dewey, who imagines himself the world's premier roué, confided in me recently that a sure sign of a woman's desire could be found in the misting over of a woman's eyes."

"And mine have?" she interrupted.

"Yes."

"It seems that George's theory has some merit." She grew bolder. "I want you very much, Andrew."

"He also said that you could never believe a woman's *words* in matters of intimacy."

Mercy feigned anger. "What would anyone so young know about it?"

She got to her feet, Andrew's hand firmly in her grasp. Tugging at him. "I think we've done entirely too much talking about this subject, don't you?"

"I do."

The widow Callison guided him into the bedroom.

IV

CHARLES entered the dining room at Bon Marché, having completed his early-morning inspection of the horses, to find Mattie the only one at the breakfast table.

"Andrew's not down yet?" he asked.

"Horace tells me he's not in his room. Hasn't been all night, as a matter of fact."

"We did have a bad storm last night. He probably stayed at the inn."

"Sometimes, Charles Dewey, I can't believe how naive you are!"

"Naive?" His eyebrows shot up. "Oh, of course . . . Mercy Callison."

"Exactly."

Dewey grinned. "You really think so, huh?"

"Would you like to make a wager on it?"

"I'm a gambler, not a fool. Well, well . . . staid and proper Andrew."

"He's a man," Mattie said. "And Mercy is certainly a desirable woman."

"I admit that I'd like to see something develop there. For Andrew, of course, but also for purely selfish reasons. It would keep him here."

V

THERE was a knock on the bedroom door. "Good mornin', Miss Mercy," Delilah called out. "Ah has breakfas'."

"That woman is an incurable romantic," Mercy whispered to Andrew. She pulled the covers up to hide their nakedness. "Come!"

The black woman tiptoed into the room. "Oh, Mistah MacCallum, suh, Ah didn't knows ya was here!"

Mercy shook her head in disbelief. "Then why have you brought two chocolates and two toasts?"

Delilah dissolved into giggles.

"Thank you, Delilah," Andrew said.

The servant placed the tray on a table by the bed, but remained standing there.

"That will be all," her mistress said.

"Ya sure Ah caint git ya anythin' else, Miss Mercy?" She looked at Andrew. "Mistah MacCallum?"

"That will be all, Delilah," Mrs. Callison said firmly.

"Yas, ma'am." She bowed her way to the door. "Ah sure do hopes ya enjoys th' breakfas'."

"Delilah, *please.*"

"Yas, ma'am." She left the room, but the door stood ajar.

"Delilah!" Mercy shouted.

The servant's head appeared in the room again. "Ma'am?"

"The door!"

"Oh, yas, ma'am. 'Scuse me, ma'am." She closed the door gently.

They could hear her continuing giggles as she retreated to the pantry.

Mercy sighed. "Lord—"

"I think she's very refreshing." Andrew chuckled.

They ate the simple breakfast in comparative silence.

When they were finished, Andrew kissed her. "I suppose I ought to get back to Bon Marché."

"Must you?" Andrew could hear the disappointment in her voice.

"Not immediately, of course."

Mercy got out of the bed and went to the window. Andrew watched her appreciatively, thinking again what a sensuous body she had. She peeked out through the curtains.

"It's a nice day," she reported. "Sunny. Maybe we could go for a ride."

"Hmmm."

"After the noon meal, I was thinking. I'm sure Delilah is busy preparing it now."

"I certainly wouldn't want to disappoint Delilah."

"A brisk ride in the country," Mercy continued, "up along the Kentucky road. I know it's January, and all that, but maybe you'd enjoy seeing that area."

"I imagine I would."

"We might take a picnic meal along . . . for dinner, you know."

"Uh-huh."

She turned away from the window. "Do you have to go back at all today?"

He reached for her. "You know what we're doing again?"

"Talking too much?"

"Right."

Mercy went to him, snuggling down beside him. Slowly and comfortably they made love again. And they fell asleep again.

When MacCallum awoke, he kissed her closed eyes. She opened one. "Well, if it isn't Mr. Andrew MacCallum."

"An interloper."

"No you're not, Andrew, dear. You belong here—with me."

"I was thinking. Perhaps Delilah could take a note to Morgan, to deliver to Bon Marché."

"And what would you say in it?"

"That I'm going to be delayed, that they're not to concern themselves about me, that I've been detained in Nashville—"

"On business?" She laughed heartily.

"No, no. That I'm delayed in Nashville on a social engagement."

"For how long?"

"I could tell them not to expect me for . . ." He looked at her questioningly.

"How long can you put up with me?" she asked.

"If that were the criterion, I'd never return to Bon Marché."

She dropped her bantering tone. "That sounds for all the world like a proposal of some sort, Andrew."

"It is."

Soberly, she studied his face. "It *is,* isn't it?"

"Yes."

"May I suggest, Mr. MacCallum, that you write that damned note before you change your mind." Mercy called out: "Delilah!"

"Yas, ma'am," the voice answered from the pantry.

"Go find Morgan! He's to deliver a message to Bon Marché!"

"Yas, ma'am. Righ' 'way, ma'am!"

Her happy giggles filled the small house.

V

On Wednesday afternoon—four days after the rainy-night dinner at the Nashville Inn—Andrew MacCallum rode up the lane toward the Bon Marché mansion. Riding beside him, daringly astride, not using a lady's saddle, was Mercy Callison.

Charles, who was lunging a horse in a paddock adjacent to the lane, waved at them excitedly. Turning the horse over to a black, he ran to greet them.

"Where in the devil have you been, you old dog?"

"Didn't you get my note on Sunday?" Andrew asked.

"Sunday? Are you sure?" Dewey seemed mystified.

"Yes, of course. It was Sunday."

"Well, about noon on Monday a boy from the livery stable . . . uh? . . ."

"Morgan," MacCallum prompted.

"Yes—Morgan. He came riding in here—considerably drunk, according to Horace—with your message. He didn't say anything. He just gave the note to Horace and left."

Mercy smoldered. "Damn him!"

"We hadn't heard anything from you Saturday night," Charles went on, "and again on Sunday. By Monday, then, we were somewhat concerned. You'll have to admit, Andrew, that the note you sent was hardly filled with detail." He chuckled. "At least, we knew you were alive . . ." A knowing glance at Mercy. ". . . and well."

"I'm sorry if you were worried," his friend said.

"Would you like to volunteer some more information?" Dewey's curiosity was gnawing at him.

"There isn't much to report," MacCallum replied with studied nonchalance. "Unless, of course, you would be interested in the fact that we've been married."

Charles was stunned, his mouth gaping open. He sputtered. "Married! But when? Where?"

Andrew gestured to Mercy, deferring to her.

"Yesterday," she said. "At the Court House. Judge Overton performed the ceremony." She laughed. "We decided that we weren't very good at living in sin."

"Dear, *I* thought we were *reasonably* good at it," he corrected her, smirking devilishly. To Charles: "It's just that we believed our friends would be more satisfied if we took the proper legal steps."

"Come! Mattie must hear this!"

Charles raced ahead of them to the mansion, calling for his wife.

"He seems more delighted than we are," Mercy commented.

"He *couldn't* be more delighted than I am." He reached over to squeeze her hand.

In the mansion, as Charles poured toasts for the couple, Mattie excitedly drew the whole story from them.

"Isn't it wonderful, Charles?"

"Marvelous! Just marvelous!" He pumped Andrew's hand for perhaps the fourth time. "Just think—Dewey and MacCallum together at Bon Marché!"

"Oh . . ." Andrew showed doubt.

"What?"

"We haven't decided yet what we are going to do. For the moment, though, we'll live at Mercy's house in Nashville. We rode out here so that I could collect my clothes."

Mattie added: "Surely you'll stay now, Andrew?"

"It's one of the possibilities we'll consider, obviously." The answer implied no commitment.

"Whatever you need, Andrew," Dewey said, "you shall have. I told you once just to name your price. That offer still stands."

MacCallum smiled, trying to put aside the pressure from the Deweys. "I hope you'll allow us time for a honeymoon."

"Of course! Of course! We'll discuss it later."

"Yes—later."

31

"GENTLEMEN, we are about to start," George Dewey shouted. "The terms of the sale will be for cash only. And since you have been afforded ample opportunity to inspect the animals, each will be sold as is. From what I remember of my Latin, I believe the proper phrase is *caveat emptor,* gentlemen—let the buyer beware."

He looked around, smiling broadly, enjoying himself.

"When you have a winning bid, please go promptly to that table . . ." He pointed to where Mercy Callison MacCallum presided over a ledger. "Pay that handsome young woman. I caution you, sirs, that she is newly married!"

There was general laughter, joined by Mercy.

The late July day was cool and without the summer sultriness that usually plagued the Nashville area. Charles called the ideal weather "Bon Marché luck."

Several hundred people, most of them horsemen, were milling about in the oak grove on the front lawn of the plantation, brought together by the auctioning of sixty-eight of Bon Marché's untried racehorses: yearlings and two-year-olds.

As Mattie had predicted more than a year earlier when she first proposed the sale, buyers had come not only from Tennessee, but from Kentucky and the Carolinas and Virginia. There were even two from New York.

It had been a total family operation in the planning. Charles and Franklin had selected the horses to be offered; they had also researched the pedigrees. Lee had designed the catalog—it had been his idea to print up the list of the horses—and had devised the numbering of the thoroughbreds, painting the numbers on their hips with calsomine. The younger children, Alma May and Thomas, distributed the booklets to those attending. Corrine, Louise, and Amantha were the hostesses—moving about the lawn, making certain that Bon Marché bourbon was readily available to all.

Andrew MacCallum had volunteered to join overseer Abner Lower in showing the animals prior to the start of the sale. Mercy, in light of her mathematics background, was keeping the financial records. And Charles and Mattie strolled among the prospective buyers, greeting them, jollying them, talking up the merits of the Bon Marché breeding program.

George, glib and extroverted, was the natural choice to be the auctioneer.

"Gentlemen, let's begin!" he bellowed again. "If you will refer to your catalogs: number one will be a yearling filly by Premier Etoile, out of a good racing mare by Medley. For those of you unfamiliar with the stallion, Premier Etoile is a winning son of Skullduggery, unraced because of an accident at birth, but himself a son of the great Yorick. May I hear the first bid, please?"

"Fifty dollars," a voice cried.

George feigned distress, then laughed. "Well, it's a beginning anyway . . ."

The bidding quickly went to a hundred dollars, then two hundred, then three, then four. It halted for a moment and George, thoroughly enjoying himself, coaxed the bidding to five hundred fifty dollars.

"I have five hundred fifty dollars for this fine filly. Am I offered more?" He glanced about. "Very well, the filly is sold for five hundred fifty to that gentleman down there with the fine straw hat. May we know who you are, sir?"

"The name is Flanders," the man answered.

"And you are from—"

"Lexington, Kentucky."

"There you are!" George said, clapping his hands together enthusiastically. "Those Kentucky horsemen have a good eye for thoroughbreds. I recommend to the rest of you that you follow Mr. Flanders's lead."

Charles, frowning, whispered to Mattie: "I hope they don't follow that fellow's lead. That filly should have brought more."

"Patience. It has only started, dear."

George, also realizing that the filly had been sold cheaply, suggested an opening bid on the next offering. "Number two, gentlemen: a well-muscled yearling colt by Predator, a tough, competitive son of Shark, out of a highly qualified Virginia mare with eleven wins to her credit. Let's start the bidding at a reasonable four hundred. Do I hear five, five?"

The colt brought twenty-one hundred dollars. Dewey smiled. "That's more like it," he said to Mattie.

After that, the selling went quickly. Astonishingly so, in that there had never been a sale like it before in Tennessee, and no one—the sellers or the buyers—knew quite what to expect. It was fast-paced, and no other yearling of the thirty-five offered sold for as little as the initial filly.

There was money in the crowd; no doubt of that. When the first of thirty-three two-year-olds was offered—a handsome, gleaming colt by Cranium—the bidding rapidly reached five thousand dollars.

Prior to the sale, Charles and Franklin had tried to estimate what each horse would bring. They had agreed that number forty-seven, a two-year-old son of Arrangement, by Medley, should garner the top dollar. Disappointingly, it sold for forty-three hundred.

It was a smallish two-year-old colt by New York, a son of Messenger, that drew the most attention. Dewey had never liked the Messenger blood and was amazed when the bids swiftly exceeded five thousand dollars. Then six thousand.

"That's wrong, that's wrong," he muttered, making for the tree stump from which George was operating.

By the time he got there, his son had sold the thoroughbred for seven thousand!

"I want to say something, son," Charles said. George relinquished the stump to him.

"I'm sorry, gentlemen, to interrupt." He looked out at the faces below him. "I didn't see who made that winning bid."

A hand went up. "I did, Squire Dewey," a German-accented voice said. "August Schimmel."

"Oh, of course. Our winning bidder," he announced to the others, "is the gentleman who printed our catalogs. A recent arrival in Nashville, and we're most pleased to have him. Uh . . . I believe, quite honestly, that the bid of seven thousand dollars is excessive—too much for any untried thoroughbred."

A murmur of surprise ran through the grove.

"Perhaps the seller of horses shouldn't make such an admission, but I've always prided myself on being an honest man. I don't see how we can undo this sale and start over, so perhaps, Mr. Schimmel, you'll allow me to halve your risk by taking back fifty percent of the colt. That is, if you wouldn't mind being a partner with me."

"I'd be honored, sir."

"Good! We'll work out the details when this is over." Dewey jumped down from the stump, George going back to work, concluding the sale.

At the end, Mercy MacCallum totaled her ledger and held it up for Charles to read the sum: $181,500.

The figure stunned Charles for a moment. He made a quick mental calculation. Sixty-eight animals—an average of more than twenty-six hundred dollars apiece. That was fully eight hundred dollars over the average Dewey had anticipated.

He turned to Mattie, kissing her hard. "Mrs. Dewey," he said soberly, "you were born of genius."

She laughed merrily. "It has taken you a long time to realize it."

II

It was late—nearly midnight—when the successful day finally came to a close. Charles and Andrew sat alone in the drawing room, sipping sherry.

"Like old times, eh?" Charles suggested.

"Yes, it is." MacCallum gestured with his wineglass. "There seems to be something ritualistic about this, doesn't it?"

"Uh-huh. You know, Andrew, I don't know when I've been more proud than I am now. Of Mattie. Of all the children. Of Bon Marché. I think of it in that context because this plantation has become a flesh and blood thing to me."

"That's understandable."

A brief lull.

"Did you notice George," Dewey asked, "making off in his carriage with that blond young lady just after the sale?"

"That's what I love about George—the model of consistency."

"I hope her father isn't too worried about her whereabouts. He's one of those men who came in from South Carolina, I believe."

"If I were her father," Andrew chuckled, "I'd be showing some concern. Of course, he's probably not fully cognizant of our George's reputation." The chuckle turned to a full-throated laugh. "Maybe, though, her eyes won't mist over."

"What?"

MacCallum waved the question away. "Just a bit of expertise that George and I have shared."

"I see—another secret kept from your old friend."

"Men of the world, Charles, must maintain some secrets."

Dewey shrugged. "It seems to me that all that needs to be done now, Andrew, is to reach agreement on an arrangement for you at Bon Marché. It certainly was evident today that you—and Mercy—could have a significant role here."

"Yes, well . . ." A hesitation. "As a matter of fact, Mercy and I had decided that we'd take advantage of this occasion to discuss it with you. We thought that tomorrow we'd sit down and—"

"That's wonderful!" Charles interrupted. "Simply wonderful!"

Shock showed on MacCallum's face. "Oh, Lord!"

"What's the matter?"

"I don't suppose I can delay this until tomorrow." He sighed weakly. "The decision we have made, my dear friend, is that we can't stay. We'll be returning to Princeton within the month."

Dewey stared at him. Wordlessly. Disbelieving.

"The college has been after me, Charles, to return. I'm to be the dean. And Mercy . . . well, she'd rather return to the East as well. Perhaps to teach again."

Wearily, Charles pushed himself to his feet, moving to the fireplace, staring down into it, although there was no fire there to see. Without warning, he raised his arm and hurled the sherry glass into it. It shattered noisily, causing Andrew to flinch.

"Damn! Damn!" Dewey whirled around. "You can't do this, Andrew! It's wrong! Worse—it's stupid!"

His friend had thought there would be disappointment; the bitter anger was not something he had anticipated.

"You can't do this to me!" Charles raved. "No, sir, you can't!"

"To *you?*"

"Yes—to *me!* There's no damned rhyme or reason to what you're doing. Your place is *here.* If you value our friendship—as I certainly do—you'll stay!"

"You can't put our friendship on that basis. It has to be a sharing thing."

"Damn it! Don't you see that that's what I want to do! I want to *share* Bon Marché with you. What more could any man ask?"

Andrew struggled with a rising anger; one unreasonable temper was enough. "I ask for nothing, Charles."

"Is that what our friendship means to you? Nothing?"

MacCallum came to his feet, his hands outstretched in supplication. "Please, Charles, don't play childish word games with me."

"Childish, am I?"

"Sit down!"

After a defiant moment, Charles obeyed.

MacCallum knew that his rejection of Dewey's kind offer had hurt him deeply; that he needed to explain his own position calmly.

"I told you once, Charles, that you were self-centered."

"Another holier-than-thou lecture?"

"That you were self-centered and that you had to learn to *hear*. Not just listen, but hear."

"All right, I'm *hearing*." Charles set his face into a sullen mask.

Andrew spoke softly so that Charles would have to concentrate to make out the words.

"I want you to know that I am most appreciative of your offer, understanding, as I do, that it comes from the depth of your affection for me." He sighed. "But Princeton wants me to be its dean. I've worked my whole life with a goal of that kind in mind. Now it has been offered to me. I would be dishonest with myself if I didn't take it."

"Take it, then!"

"I mean to."

"Take it now!" Dewey was on his feet again, striding about the room, stirring up his anger once more. "Take it right this damned minute!"

He came to where Andrew was sitting, putting his face down close to him.

"Do you *hear* me! Right this damned minute!"

"Charles, I simply don't understand—"

"I want you to understand only one thing: get out! Now! You and that damned widow you married!"

Andrew's hand lashed out—an angry reflex—catching Charles high on the cheek. Instantly regretting it, Andrew sprang to his feet, attempting to take his friend in his arms.

Dewey backed off slightly. Then he drove a fist deep into Andrew's solar plexus. Gasping, the older man went to his knees before he collapsed into a heap on the floor.

Charles stood over him for a moment, looking at him with disgust. "Get out!"

He marched out of the room, out of the house.

Mattie and Mercy, drawn by the angry shouting, ran into the room.

"Oh, my God!" Mattie screamed. "Andrew, what happened?"

Both of the women knelt by the stricken man, Mercy, near tears, stroking his brow.

Taking deep breaths and feeling the recurring pain with each one, Mac-Callum was finally able to speak. "We had a disagreement." He forced a smile, trying to make light of it. "Charles was the better pugilist."

"A disagreement?" Mattie cried. "Why would Charles do anything like this?"

Andrew knew that he owed her the truth; still, he tried to soften it. "I told him that I couldn't accept his offer to stay at Bon Marché, that I had been offered the dean's post at Princeton . . . and the situation became . . . quite heated."

"You mean Charles did *this* because you told him you couldn't stay?"

"I'm afraid that I struck the first blow and—"

"Andrew, don't lie to me, please."

He sighed. "Very well, no more equivocation. Charles became enraged when I declined his offer. And he'd listen to no explanation about Princeton. When he said something I found offensive, I slapped him. He retaliated—with a good deal more vigor than I was ready for."

"Oh, my God, what are we going to do?" Mattie began to weep.

"I'm not sure. I think, though, that I ought to do what he demanded: I ought to get out." To Mercy: "Dear, would you pack, please? We'll leave immediately."

"No!" Mattie insisted vehemently. "You leave now and it'll never be the same again."

"Whether we stay or go," Andrew said with deep melancholy, "it can never be the same again. That became a reality in that terrible instant when we struck each other."

"We'll work it out."

"I don't think that's possible, Mattie, as much as I would wish for it, as much as I would like to turn back the clock half an hour."

Again Andrew spoke to Mercy: "Would you pack, dear?"

"Will you be able to ride?" Worry showed on his wife's pleasant face.

"Certainly. I'll be fine." He touched his abdomen. "I'm just a little tender, that's all."

Mercy hurried away.

MacCallum sat up with a slight groan.

Still kneeling beside him, Mattie Dewey let her control slip away. Her weeping became tearing sobs, making it difficult for her to catch her breath. Andrew offered his arms and she fell into them.

He patted her. "It's going to be all right," he tried to assure her. "In time, Mattie, in time."

Andrew MacCallum knew it would never be all right again. *There's a hint of madness there.* He ordered his mind to reject such a terrible thought.

Mercy had packed quickly. Horace had been sent to have their horses saddled. With reassurances to Mattie—words, empty words!—and promises that they would keep in touch, the MacCallums rode away.

Dewey, slumped in the darkness against a tree beside the lane, saw them go. He opened his mouth to call out to them, but no words came.

Sounds of the hooves on the hard-packed surface faded away into the night.

Rolling over, he retched into the grass.

III

"DAMN you, Marshall, I told you not to gallop that mare! I don't want her to leave her race on the training track!"

Dewey, livid with anger, was pounding his riding crop against his boot.

"I'm sorry," the jockey said, "she got away from me. She's full of it this morning. But she's gonna have plenty for the race."

"Are you presuming to tell me how to train a race horse?!"

"Oh, no, sir. I'm sorry if you thought so."

"Cool her out carefully," Charles ordered, "if you're not too stupid for that, too."

Marshall, the hurt frozen on his face, turned the mare quickly, trotting away toward the barn.

Franklin, who had witnessed the unhappy scene, came up to his father. "Don't you think you were a little hard on him?"

"Must I have arrogance from you, too?"

His son swallowed hard. He had rehearsed a little speech after nearly a week of outbursts of Dewey's sudden, irrational temper. In the house, at the barns, on the training track. No one escaped them, not even Mattie.

"Not arrogance, Father, but the truth. Ever since Uncle Andrew left here—"

"That man is *not* your uncle!"

"Ever since he left here so suddenly, you've been impossible. I don't know what happened between you two, and I'm not asking that you tell me. But I want you to know that what you're doing now is destroying this farm. No one can work properly under the goad of your uncontrollable anger. If I acted like that, you'd take a whip to me, and with good reason."

"That's enough!" Dewey started to walk away.

"No, you'll hear me, Father!"

The words stopped Charles in his tracks: Franklin had said, You'll *hear* me, not you'll *listen* to me. Andrew had said Charles would have to *hear* his children.

He turned back to Franklin. "Very well—go on."

"I can't watch you anymore, day after day, tearing yourself apart like this. If it's so painful for you, why don't you go into Nashville and have out whatever it is with Andrew? Finish it, for God's sake!"

"They've left for the East," he answered sullenly.

"Not yet. Not until Saturday."

"Oh? How do you know that?"

"I checked."

"You talked with Andrew?"

"Yes. He won't talk about what happened, but he seems rational, at least."

Charles stared at Franklin. "Is there more you want to say?"

"Yes. I think you ought to apologize to Marshall."

"Perhaps you're right."

They walked together to the training barn, where another black, not Marshall, was cooling out the mare.

"Where's Marshall?" Dewey demanded.

"Ah don' know, Mistah Charles. He jest come back from th' track, saddle up thet ole geldin' o' his, an' lit off down th' road. He never did say nothin' 'cept Ah was t' cool out this here mare."

"Tell Marshall I want to see him when he returns."

"Yah, suh. Jest as quick as he git back."

IV

Marshall Dewey was punishing the gray gelding with both whip and spur, racing him at breakneck speed toward Nashville. Tears of hurt and anger ran down his light brown face.

He didn't slow the lathered animal until he saw the town ahead of him. Then he stopped for a moment, wiping the tears away with his sleeves, squaring his shoulders, preparing for what he planned to do next. He kicked the gelding into a slow trot and headed him in the direction of Mercy Callison's house.

There he knocked lightly on the door. Delilah opened it.

"Is Mister Andrew here?"

The black woman looked at him suspiciously. "Who want him?"

"Tell him Marshall . . . Marshall Dewey."

Delilah went away, closing the door on him. In just a few seconds, Mac-Callum opened the door again.

"Marshall? Is something wrong?"

The boy struggled to keep from crying again. "I want to go with you when you leave."

"I think you'd better come in." He led the boy into the living room, where Mercy and Delilah were packing a large trunk.

"We have a guest, dear. I think he might like a cup of chocolate."

Mercy nodded to Delilah, who hustled away.

"Sit down, Marshall," Andrew said calmly.

The boy perched uneasily on the edge of the settee.

"Now, tell us why you want to go with us?"

"I want to be a jockey in New York," Marshall said defiantly.

"I see. Does Charles know?"

"He won't care."

"The two of you had an argument?"

The lad nodded.

Andrew sighed. "How old are you, Marshall?"

"I'll be twelve."

"Don't you think that's a bit young to go traipsing off to New York?"

"I'm free," Marshall answered quickly. "Horace says that means I can do whatever I want to."

"Yes, but . . ." MacCallum wanted to choose his words carefully. "It means, you must understand, that you can do anything you want when you're *grown*. When you're older, when you're a man, you can make your own decisions. Now, though, you're still bound to listen to your father."

Delilah brought the chocolate. For the first time, Marshall smiled. "Thank you." He took a sip. "It's good," he added politely.

"Marshall, I want you to listen to me carefully," Andrew went on. "Your father loves you."

"That's not true!"

"Oh, I think it is. I know things must look bad to you now. Maybe you won't fully understand all of these things, but your father . . . well, he has risked a lot for you. For one thing, he recognized you as his son, and that wasn't easy for him. And as you said, he made sure you were free. He made sure, too, that you had schooling with his other children. All of those things, Marshall, grew out of his love for you. He had no other reason to do them. And he'd be very unhappy if you went away now."

Marshall finished the chocolate, carefully setting the cup down on a small table by the settee. He seemed to be thinking about what he wanted to say next. Andrew waited for him.

"If you don't take me with you," he said slowly, "I'll go with somebody else. Or by myself. I won't go back to Bon Marché!"

Mercy entered the conversation. "Perhaps, dear," she said to her husband, "we could send a note to Bon Marché, telling Charles that Marshall is here and that he wants to go with us. If Charles approves, then that solves it, doesn't it?"

"We can't take a young boy with—"

"Of course we can!"

MacCallum's continuing doubts showed on his face.

"Is there any other way to handle this intelligently, dear?" Mercy added.

Andrew shrugged. "No, I guess not. But let's not have Morgan carry the message, eh?"

She smiled at him. "Write the note, Andrew, and I'll ask Mr. Parker at the inn to have one of his boys take it out there immediately."

V

"AND then he says," Charles Dewey was saying, " 'If you disapprove, I shall make certain that Marshall is brought back to Bon Marché at once. If you approve, we will assure you that we will do for Marshall as if he were our own son, continuing his education, caring for his health and well-being, making every effort to help him grow into a fine young man who will be a credit to you and to your family.' "

Charles looked up at the sober faces of the other members of the family. With some bitterness: "And he signs it 'With affection.' "

Angelica, who stood with Horace behind Dewey's chair at the dinner table, wept softly.

"All right," the master of Bon Marché continued, "since I seem to be the villain of the piece, perhaps some of you would like to share your wisdom with me on this matter."

Franklin's reply was immediate. "I think you ought to let him go, Father."

Franklin's wife nodded agreement.

"I concur," George added. "But I think you should provide money for his support."

Dewey looked at his daughters. "Well?"

"He's too young to go to New York," Corrine said firmly.

Louise shook her head. "I just don't know, Father."

"Lee?"

"I agree with Corrine."

Charles turned to his wife. "Mattie? You seem to have had a lot to say in the past week or so about my lack of feeling in the matter of *Professor* Andrew MacCallum. I imagine you also have an opinion on this."

Mattie flushed. "I'd appreciate your asking my opinion a good deal more if you'd keep the sarcasm out of this discussion."

He forced a smile. "I'm sorry, dear. It's difficult."

"You might make a greater effort."

Franklin interceded. "What *do* you think, Mother?"

"Were I Marshall's mother, I'd want to be consulted," she replied.

"You're right, of course." Charles turned around, looking up into Angelica's teary face. "Angelica, what would you have me do?"

"Will they be good to 'im?"

A slight pause. "I feel certain they will be."

"Will he be happy?"

"How can I answer that?"

Angelica dabbed a handkerchief at her eyes. "Well, he *unhappy* now. Mebbe if he goes . . ." She couldn't finish the thought.

Dewey buried his head in his hands. Only the sounds of breathing could be heard. For a minute. For two. His head came up, and his eyes searched every face.

"I have been . . . responsible . . . for what has happened . . . with Marshall." The words were spoken slowly. Painfully. "I ask all . . . of you to forgive me for that. His . . . mother is right. The lad is unhappy now. No one can guarantee another person's happiness. But if letting him go might contribute to it, I'm willing to have him go with the MacCallums."

"I think that's wise, dear," Mattie said quietly.

"Speak to them," Charles told her, "and see what financial arrangements need to be made. Do what you think is best."

"I will."

He got to his feet, leaning forward on the table with his hands. He seemed desperately tired.

"This matter is closed now. I want everyone to understand that it will not be a fit subject for further conversation in this house."

32

"HAVE you heard about Patton Anderson?" August Schimmel asked.

"What mischief has he been into now?"

"The ultimate, you might say. He's been killed in a duel."

"Oh, Lord! More of that!"

"Yes. And Jackson is making noises about his determination to bring the killer to justice. A man named David Magness, and Jackson would see him hang."

"If Andy ran this world, we'd be at each other's throats at every turn. What was the argument about?"

"Does it matter?"

"No, I guess not." Charles shook his head sadly. "Anderson was the man who introduced me to this area. He was a likeable sort, but thoroughly the scoundrel."

Schimmel, the owner-editor of the *Nashville Monitor,* had come to Bon Marché to discuss with Dewey the progress of their jointly owned racehorse: the colt by New York for which Schimmel had bid seven thousand dollars at Bon Marché's first auction.

A four-year-old now, Monitor—the horse had been named for the newspaper—was being prepared for his debut in the 1811 race meetings. They stood at the rail of the training track, watching as one of the black jockeys brought the untried thoroughbred out of the final turn and set him down for a two-furlong breeze through the straightaway.

"He has a bit of speed, August."

"He looks fine to me."

"I just wish he had more size. I'm concerned about his stamina. But we'll know soon enough how good he is."

"He's ready to start?"

"Yes, but just a dash, you know."

Dewey and Schimmel had been brought together by the horse, and they had found early on that they were compatible. Schimmel, whose German accent got heavier when he became excited, was a man of universal interests. A natural newspaperman, apparently, he had come to the United States with a fortune inherited from his father, a pottery manufacturer in Karlsruhe. He might have settled in one of the larger cities along the East Coast, and prospered there. Instead, he took the gamble of moving to the frontier of his new country, coming eventually to Nashville.

He was a tall, blond, square-cut man with a sober demeanor that complemented the moody sobriety Dewey had acquired after the departure of Andrew MacCallum. Mattie liked the German because he seemed to fill a gap in her husband's life.

As they walked away from the training track, Charles asked: "A Bon Marché whiskey, August?"

"That's always welcome."

"What are your views on developments in Washington?"

"The young warhawks?"

"Yes."

Schimmel scratched his chin contemplatively. "They seem to be in firm control of Congress, don't they? Henry Clay's election as Speaker proves that."

"Will they get war?"

"I believe they will."

"Lord!"

"But we must recognize that England is provoking a confrontation, with its continual harassment of our shipping." He reached into his pocket and pulled out several sheets of paper. "Just this morning I received a letter from our Representative."

"Ah, yes, the Jackson handmaiden, Felix Grundy."

"He may be that," the editor admitted, "but he points out, quite legitimately, I think, that the English are arming the Indians here in the West. Grundy feels strongly about that; he's had three brothers killed by Indians.

"He says"—Schimmel glanced at the letter—"that the English are urging 'the ruthless savages to tomahawk our women and children.' Several incidents of that type have been reported, you know. And Grundy adds: 'War is not to commence by sea or land, it is already begun, and some of the richest blood of our country has been shed.'"

Schimmel folded the letter, returning it to his pocket.

Charles groaned. "Well, be that as it may, I hope that *my* sons don't get drawn into war." He changed the subject. "You'll stay for dinner, of course."

"I'm afraid not, Charles. You see . . . uh . . . I have an engagement to take your daughter to dinner in Nashville."

"Louise?"

"Yes."

Dewey slapped him on the back. "Why, you sly devil! 'I want to see the horse,' you say. And all along you and Louise were—"

"Oh, it's nothing like that," Schimmel protested, embarrassed by Charles's roguish innuendo. "It's just that this new establishment is opening up, and it seems that there's something new in Nashville every week—and . . . well, Miss Louise has consented to accompany me."

"Louise is a very pretty girl," Charles said proudly.

"Yes, she is."

An elbow dug into the German's ribs. "I'm going to have to keep an eye on you, August." He was laughing.

The editor was not. "Charles, I assure you that I have nothing but the most honorable of intentions."

Dewey laughed even harder. "I recall using that line myself, Herr Schimmel. And finding myself married shortly thereafter."

II

CHARLES had changed. Not metamorphically—not from worm to butterfly, nor lamb to beast either. Nor in ways that were evident to casual observers of Bon Marché. But MacCallum's leaving—and Marshall's—had changed him.

Mattie found him less ebullient now; more sober, more restrained in his enthusiasms. He continued to work long hours with the horses; he gambled just as much. But success seemed to be of less consequence to him; failure less devastating.

At times, his new even-tempered approach to just about everything was irritating to Mattie. More than once she wished for the old Charles; the new one was so monotonously predictable. So lackluster.

Except for two things, totally unrelated.

One was his decision, announced without any other preliminary, that he was setting aside four hundred acres of the plantation for what he called a deer park.

"That outlying piece of land," he told Mattie, "on the other side of the number two wheat field, is still pretty much virgin territory. Why disturb it? We ought to preserve something of the wilderness for our grandchildren and their children and all of the generations to come. Keep it safe for the future."

"Yes, dear."

"I'm going to stock it with native animals—deer, buffalo, antelope—before they are all killed off." He clapped his hands together for emphasis. "As a matter of fact, I think I'll have the blacks start building a secure fence around that area."

"What blacks?" Mattie interrupted. "They're all fully employed now."

Dewey shrugged. "Well, get some more."

The reply was so uncharacteristic of her husband that Mattie gasped. She found the entire conversation a bit strange.

"In the past, Charles, you've always resisted my suggestions that we get more help."

"This, though," he said with determination, "is *important.*"

"Are you implying that other things were not—" She stopped, changing her mind. "Very well. How many hands will you need?"

"Oh, a dozen. Fifteen might be better."

"That will be rather costly."

He smiled at her tolerantly. "You must understand that this is an investment in the future. We ought to serve the future while struggling through the morass of the present. Don't you agree?"

The next day she had an agent acquire twelve more slaves for Bon Marché.

The second thing that stirred enthusiasm in the "new Charles" was Mattie herself. Their physical relationship had always been important to them, but now Charles seemed to believe it the top priority in their life together.

He made love to her with renewed intensity, never seeming to be content with what had been pleasurable the night before. He experimented, finding new ways to satisfy her. But always gently; stroking her and cooing to her and assuring her again and again of his love for her.

Mattie bloomed under the new attention, looking forward to her nighttime hours with him. Yet she was disquieted. She thought he was being driven to prove something to her, when that had never been necessary between them before. She wanted to talk to him about it, but could never find the opening words.

"I was reading the Bible this morning," he told her one night in bed.

She couldn't have been more surprised. "Really?"

"Oh, yes," Charles said soberly. "It's been said that the Bible is the repository of all wisdom, and I've come to believe that."

Mattie kept silent. She feared that whatever she said at that moment would be wrong.

"And, you know, one of the first orders that God gave—recorded in the first chapter of Genesis—was 'be fruitful and multiply.'"

She tried for a light tone. "Darling, I have the distinct feeling that you're leading up to something."

"I am." Still soberly. "I want to have another child."

"Charles!"

"I don't shock you, I hope."

"But you *do,* dear."

"Oh . . . why?"

"Charles Dewey, you're forty-six years old."

"That's not decrepit."

"And I'm past thirty now."

"Thirty-two, to be exact. Biologically a very good age to be a mother."

"And we're about to be grandparents, now that Amantha has made her announcement."

"I'll be the grandparent." He smiled for the first time in the conversation. "You're too young for that."

"Well, anyway, I really think we've done our bit in the fruitful-and-multiply business."

"Hmmm. I *really* want another baby from you. Perhaps more than one more."

"More than one!"

Dewey let out a long sigh. "I have realized, Mattie, that I've been a failure as a father. That I've been so preoccupied with other things that I haven't once turned my total attention to a child. I owe that kind of dedication to at least one of my children."

"Don't be silly! You've been a wonderful father. You *are* a wonderful father. And you have plenty of time yet to turn your greater attention to Alma May and to little Tom. My God, Alma's only ten, and Tom just nine."

Another sigh. "What I've been thinking of is *total* involvement from the moment the child leaves the womb."

"Charles, that's—"

"Crazy?"

"Don't put words in my mouth! I was going to say that such a thing is just not practical."

He laughed now. "You're right, of course. It's just that I love you so, and when I'm with you I have these . . . well, fantasies."

She kissed him.

"I love you for your fantasies, Mr. Dewey."

III

"TAKE him out easy and let him run freely."

Charles was giving instructions to one of the Bon Marché jockeys, a young fellow named Billy, for the handling of Monitor's debut. The Schimmel-Dewey horse had been entered in one of the dashes on the Clover Bottom fall card—a single heat at two miles.

"If he's in it as you start the last half-mile," the orders continued, "go to the whip and let's see what he has. If you're out of it, though, save him."

"Yas, suh."

"Billy, I just want to see how he fares in competition. We have a long way to go with him yet, so don't punish him."

Monitor was to be the only Bon Marché horse to be saddled by Charles during the meeting. The other horses carrying the purple silks of the plantation—twenty in all—would be under the guidance of his sons, Franklin and George.

Charles had other duties at the meeting; he was one of its stewards. Andy Jackson and his associates— it had been rumored that Jackson was desperately short of cash—had sold the Clover Bottom track to the new Nashville Jockey Club, financed largely by Dewey, Schimmel, and Joseph Coleman, the former mayor of Nashville and the horseman who had arranged for the importation of the English stallion, Royalist.

August Schimmel stood with Charles as he saddled their colt. "Are you betting on him?" the newspaper editor wanted to know.

"I wager on every Bon Marché runner."

"Not equally, though."

"No, that's true. I haven't decided yet how I feel about Monitor's chances. There will be eight maidens going to the post for this one, and I imagine he has as good a chance as the others."

"The public pool is offering three-to-one odds on him," Schimmel reported, "and I've been thinking of betting a thousand dollars on him."

Dewey's eyebrows rose, but he made no comment.

"Too much, do you think?"

"August, I've made it somewhat of a rule not to tout horses to my friends—even their own horses, as in this case. I can tell you only that he has a chance."

The editor seemed disappointed. "But not much of one?"

"If a thousand dollars isn't important to you . . ."

"I can afford it."

"Then follow your belief."

"How much are you going to bet?"

Charles thought for a moment. "A hundred, I think."

Schimmel scowled. "I'm going to stick with a thousand."

"Good for you." Dewey laughed, clapping him on the back. "I like a man who's willing to risk money on his convictions."

When it came time for the race and the starting drum tapped, Monitor was left in the shuffle at the start and was sixth coming away from the line, getting turf thrown in his face. He didn't improve his position, and Billy, following instructions, just permitted the horse to finish as he would in the last half-mile. Monitor was seventh at the end.

Schimmel tried to hide his disappointment with a shrug. "Well, that was an expensive lesson, wasn't it?"

"Yes, but we did get a lesson," Charles replied. "You can put it down to paying for experience. We learned a great deal in that race."

"We did?"

"Uh-huh."

Billy brought Monitor to where Charles and August were standing. "He don't laik dirt in his face, Mistah Charles."

"That's what we learned," Dewey said to his partner. "The next time out we'll race him into the lead and try to keep him there. August, we have a natural frontrunner."

"Is that good?"

"The one big secret of training, my friend, is to learn what the horse wants to do—what he's most comfortable with—and then you run him that way. Every time. Monitor stops when he gets dirt in his face, so we run him on the front."

"Can he win on the front?"

"I think he might. He didn't get used up too much today, so we'll try him again before the week is out."

IV

GEORGE Dewey rushed up excitedly.

"Father, I think you'd better come at once! Cousin Andy has—"

Charles ran after his son to the starting line, where Andrew Jackson, two pistols drawn and cocked, his legs spread wide apart, was preventing the start of the fourth race. Five horses were positioned along the line, their nervous jockeys trying to hold them in check. The starter's hand, grasping the stick, was frozen above the drum.

"General Jackson," Dewey bellowed, "put up your weapons!"

"Those damned scoundrels have fixed this race! And I'll not have a crooked race at my track!"

Charles looked around for his fellow stewards, seeing them coming on the dead run. He walked to Jackson's side.

"Sir, this is not your track any longer. It's the property of the Nashville Jockey Club, and the stewards of the club will decide what is to be done. Not you!"

Andy kept his pistols leveled at the field of horses.

"Then I suggest, sir," he snarled, "that you do your job! This is a fixed race."

"So you say." The two other stewards joined Dewey now. "Put up your pistols, sir!"

Jackson held his position.

Charles turned and shouted to all within earshot: "This race is suspended, pending an investigation by the stewards of the Nashville Jockey Club!"

The jockeys began to withdraw their horses. A relieved starter laid down his drum.

"The guns, General," Dewey demanded.

Jackson uncocked them carefully, jamming them into his waistband.

"There was no excuse for that, Jackson."

"There was all the excuse in the world!" Andy screamed at him. "I learned that One For All was to be the certain winner. The owners conspired to make him the winner at better than fifteen to one!"

By that time, the owners had gathered around Andy and the stewards, all shouting loudly, all denying Jackson's accusations.

One of them said: "I'll not stand for this insult! Jackson, you'd better be prepared to back up your charges or so help me, I'll demand satisfaction!"

Andy's hand went quickly to one of his pistols, but Dewey got his wrist in a viselike grip. "Damn you, Andy! There'll be no gunplay on this racecourse!"

Jackson shook his arm free. "Then you'd better get to the bottom of this!"

"And that's exactly what the stewards will do."

Everyone was shouting again.

Charles tried to restore order. "Everyone will be heard—but one at a time." He ordered that the nearby tavern be cleared out and that Jackson and the owners adjourn to that location for a hearing.

To the general crowd: "The fourth race is fully suspended! We'll make ready now for the fifth event. Post time for that will be in half an hour."

The fifth race went off without the stewards. For more than an hour they heard the testimony on the fourth race—first from Andrew Jackson, and then from the five owners in turn.

It was Dewey's view that there may have been some merit in what Jackson charged, but solid proof was lacking.

In the end, the three stewards huddled privately, discussing the best way to handle the volatile situation. Their decision was a compromise: the fourth race would not be run, then or ever, and the owners would be suspended from competition at Clover Bottom for two days.

Jackson wasn't satisfied. "Damn you, Dewey, you've let those scoundrels get away with their dastardly plotting! Were it me, I would have—"

"Shot them down?"

"Yes, damm it, if necessary!"

"Let me tell you something, Andy." Charles was forcing the angry words through his teeth. "If you ever again draw a weapon on this racecourse, I'll see that you're suspended from racing for life!"

"No man, sir, has that power!"

"I suggest, *General"*—he used the military title sarcastically—"that you don't test me."

Within forty-eight hours, four of the five owners involved had left Clover Bottom. The fifth remained—he lived in Nashville—but withdrew his horses from competition. Rumors had it that they had been frightened off by threats from Andy Jackson, or from someone using his name.

There was no proof, but Charles Dewey didn't doubt it. Not for a minute.

V

"I can't look at that filly," Dewey admitted, "and not feel some covetousness."

"She *is* a nice filly."

"Nice? She's more than that, Jesse, and you ought to know that better than anyone."

Captain Jesse Haynie laughed. "I guess I do. It's just that I'm not much on bragging. As a matter of fact, Maria makes it unnecessary to brag."

The two horsemen were standing by a stall at the Clover Bottom track, looking in at a chestnut filly of fine conformation.

"You got her in Virginia, didn't you?"

"Yes. She's by Diomed, out of a mare by Tayloe's Bellair."

Charles groaned. "When I raced in Virginia, Squire Tayloe's horses certainly gave me the fits. And now, here in Tennessee, it seems that the Tayloe ghost is going to prevail again. When I first saw that filly at Hartsville in the spring, Captain, I swear to you that I thought: 'There's nothing in the West that's going to beat her.'"

"What of Jackson's Truxton colt, Decatur?"

"He'll be no match for your Maria."

"The General has offered me five thousand a side."

"Really?"

"Yes. You seem surprised."

Dewey hesitated. "It's just that I didn't know that Andy could raise five thousand these days. He's put so much of his own money into that volunteer army of his."

"Well, that was the offer."

"Take it," the master of Bon Marché recommended. "We'll put on the match on the closing day of the meeting: the best of three two-mile heats. As a matter of fact, if you want to make it fifty thousand, I'll take whatever percentage you want to part with."

Haynie studied his face. "You're serious."

"Oh, yes, Captain! Deadly serious. I like to think I know a great racehorse when I see one—filly or colt."

Dewey, in his role as one of the managers of the Nashville Jockey Club, had invited Captain Haynie to bring his filly from Sumner County to the Clover Bottom fall meeting. However, word of the reputation of Haynie's Maria (that was her full name, in that Maria seemed to be a common name for fillies) had preceded her. There had been no challengers . . . until now.

Haynie was not the trainer of the filly. He had a good stable of runners under the firm hand of Green Berry Williams, who had built a name for himself as the best trainer in the West. Completing the team was a hunchback, four-foot-six Negro jockey called "Monkey" Simon, a young man not only talented aboard a race horse but a gifted musician as well. Dewey was going to have a party at Bon Marché at the end of the meeting, and he had made arrangements with Captain Haynie to have "Monkey" entertain.

There was a widely disseminated story that "Monkey" Simon had been a prince in his native Africa, but Charles had his doubts. He remembered a similar story from back in Virginia, where George Milton had claimed princely qualities for his Albert. Somehow that kind of tale seemed to make a few slaveowners proud. Charles, though, thought the stories sad—even if true.

The match between Jackson's Decatur and Haynie's Maria was made, drawing the largest crowd to Clover Bottom since the infamous Truxton-Ploughboy match. Dewey wagered heavily, booking nearly ten thousand dollars in bets on the filly. August Schimmel followed his lead. Decatur money was to be had rather easily, in spite of Maria's record of being unbeaten in six starts. Many backing Decatur believed that a good colt could always beat a good filly. Others remembered the exploits of Decatur's sire, Truxton. And still others bet on Decatur simply because he was Andrew Jackson's horse. Andy's popularity was that great in the community, a fact that astounded and even appalled Dewey.

The coffers of Bon Marché were greatly enriched that day. Haynie's Maria not only beat Decatur in two straight dash heats, but humbled him, winning easily.

Jackson, while reasonably gracious in defeat, let it be known that he'd try again against Haynie's Maria.

It was reported to Dewey that Andy was going to put out the word to Virginia breeders to find him the best four-mile horse in the state, "without regard to price."

Charles hoped that he would. He looked forward to letting Haynie's Maria, although he did not own her, make him wealthier. Especially at Andrew Jackson's expense.

VI

"Bon Marché has had its most successful year ever," Mattie wrote, "and we can now look forward to 1812 with real joy."

She was writing to the MacCallums in New Jersey, as she did with regularity. Her husband knew she did, because Mattie insisted on reading their replies at the dinner table. Charles didn't like it, but he permitted it. Mattie believed he wanted to hear news of his old friend. Yet there was no other sign that the breach could ever be healed.

"For one thing," she continued, "the new year will be special because we will have the opportunity to see our first grandchild grow. Little Carrie is so dear, and Amantha seems a natural mother. Charles is almost beside himself with happiness. Can you believe that on Christmas Day, when Carrie was only two weeks old, Charles actually carried that baby aboard a horse? He takes her everywhere with him—everywhere, that is, that Franklin and Amantha will permit."

Mattie paused. She was making light of her husband's preoccupation with the baby in the letter, but it concerned her deeply. She was remembering what he had called his fantasy of total involvement with a new baby. She thought of his words then: "from the moment the child leaves the womb."

She forced herself to concentrate once more on the letter: "But 1812 will also be special for Bon Marché because we are to have three—that's correct, *three*—weddings! George is to marry a young lady named Mary Harrison in February. I guess you might call her an heiress. Her father, a tobacco broker, is extremely wealthy. The ceremony is to be at their estate on Stones River. There's talk that they'll move to England, but I hope it's not true. Mary, however, keeps talking of the 'proper society' of London. George, who has more than sown his wild oats, as you know, is totally smitten with her and will do anything she asks. She's several years his senior and absolutely dominates him.

"In June, both of the older daughters will be married. Corrine will finally exchange the vows with her Billy. It's to be a simple ceremony in the Presbyterian church in Nashville, not at Bon Marché. Young Holder, you may recall, is a stuffy man who doesn't want to be 'corrupted' by Bon Marché. He expresses that sentiment over and over again ad nauseam. I'm amazed at how well Charles tolerates him."

She reread that paragraph and added a sentence: "In truth, I can't imagine what Corrine sees in him.

"Louise is going to marry August Schimmel, the owner of the newspaper, on the last day in June," Mattie continued. "He's ten years older than she, but a perfect gentleman. And rich enough to be involved with Charles in the ownership of several horses, the Clover Bottom track, and other enterprises that require considerable money. Charles admires him very much, as do I, and we will have a big, social wedding here. Charles and I have offered them quarters here at Bon Marché, possibly adding a wing, and we are hoping they will accept."

Mattie sighed to herself. Several times she had thought about asking Charles to append just a few lines to one of the letters. She thought about it again now, but once more she pushed the idea aside, not willing to risk a bitter scene.

"All are well here," she added, "and all send their love."

"All, that is," she said aloud, "except Charles Dewey."

33

LEE Dewey approached the subject gingerly. "Father, have you seen the announcement in the *Monitor* from Andy?" he asked of Charles at the dinner table.

"No, but I can tell you what it's about: another proclamation of impending war with England."

"Yes, it is," his son admitted, speaking slowly. "But this is a bit more than that."

Dewey looked up from his plate. "I suggest, Lee, that Jackson's warlike pronouncements are not a fit subject for discussion at this table."

"But, Father—"

"Certainly you can find something more pleasant to talk about!"

The young man was silenced.

"Charles?" Mattie pleaded.

"Oh, very well," her husband said, "what is it, Lee, that you find so fascinating?"

Lee picked up the newspaper. "It's dated the Hermitage, March 7, 1812, and he says: 'VOLUNTEERS TO ARMS!' That's in bold type. 'Citizens! Your government has yielded to the impulse of the nation. War is on the point of breaking out between the United States and Great Britain! and the martial hosts are summoned to the Tented Fields!'"

Charles snorted derisively.

"'A simple invitation is given for fifty thousand volunteers. Shall we, who have clamored for war, now skulk in the corner? Are we the titled Slaves of George the third? the military conscripts of Napoleon? or the frozen peasants of the Russian Czar? No—we are the free-born sons of the only Republic now existing in the world.'"

Lee stopped reading.

"Is that all?"

"No, sir, there's more."

"All in the same purple prose, I assume?"

His son smiled slightly. "Yes, sir, it is." He glanced again at the newspaper. "He says: 'The period of youth is the season for martial exploits.'"

"Enough!" Charles raised a hand. "Spare us, please Lee, further details of General Jackson's rabble-rousing."

"Yes, sir." He laid the newspaper aside. "Uh, sir?"

"Yes."

"I want to volunteer."

"No!" A fist smashed down on the table. Dishes and silverware jumped noisily. "Absolutely not!"

"But, Father—"

"Damn it! Enough! I said no and no it shall be!" He was screaming, his face livid.

"Charles, control your temper!" Mattie said sharply.

Dewey sighed. His voice calmed. "You're right, dear. I apologize." To Lee: "I didn't mean to shout at you, son. But let's look at this thing for the facts in it."

Lee nodded, disappointment on his young face.

"In the first place," Charles started, "the call for fifty thousand volunteers is for *all* of the country, not for Tennessee alone, as Jackson implies. Right?"

"Yes, sir."

"Secondly, does Jackson say there"—he stabbed a finger toward the newspaper—"that he has a commission from the United States government to raise an army?"

"No, sir."

"Of course he doesn't. The government in Washington, in its great wisdom, I think, has been reluctant to give a command to Andrew Jackson, distrusting—as do I—his ability to command in concert with a coordinated military plan that would be necessary were we at war.

"And that brings me to my third point: War has not been declared, has it?"

"No, sir."

"Hmmm. And finally, Lee, a most important point. You're needed here at Bon Marché. George has now gone off to England with his bride—we don't know when he might return, if ever—and Franklin and I need you here now more than ever. You can appreciate that, can't you?"

"Yes, sir." Lee was now thoroughly cowed by Dewey's arguments. He hung his head, staring at his plate.

"Very well. I said I had made my final point, but I do have one more." He looked around the table, setting his gaze on Mattie. "If the time comes when the country *needs* my sons in its defense, I will be the first to agree to their going."

He slapped a hand on the table, making the dishes dance again. "But never—I repeat, NEVER!—will I allow them to bear arms under the command of Major General Andrew Jackson!"

There was dead silence at the table.

Dewey's eyes stayed fixed on Mattie's. "Is that understood?" he asked quietly.

"Yes, dear," she answered.

II

THE baby giggled with delight, gaily waving her arms and legs, cooing at the mare chewing hay next to her.

Charles had placed little Carrie in the hayrack while he ministered to a sick foal in the stall.

"I think if we dose him tonight," he was saying to a black groom, "and again in the morning, he's going to come around."

"Yas, suh, Ah hopes so."

"So do I, Ephraim, so do I. I'd hate to lose another foal to whatever this is that's going around."

A scream rent the air!

Amantha rushed into the stall and snatched Carrie from the hayrack, cradling her protectively against her breast. "My baby, oh, my baby!"

She whirled on Charles, anger sparking from her eyes. "Are you crazy?" she shouted at him. "That horse could have—could have—"

Dewey tried to calm her. "That mare wouldn't hurt a fly. Carrie was in no danger." He laughed. "She was rather enjoying it, as a matter of fact."

"You damned old fool!" His son's wife stalked out of the stall, clutching her child tightly.

Chuckling, Charles watched her go. "There's no more vicious animal than a mother who believes her baby is threatened."

"Yas, suh." The slave was chuckling as well.

Later, though, at the Bon Marché mansion, Charles found no such amiable agreement.

"Damn you, Charles Dewey," Mattie shrieked at him, "have you lost all your senses?"

"If you're talking about the baby—"

"Of course I'm talking about the baby! Amantha came back here in absolute hysterics. And I can't say that I blame her!"

"The woman was overreacting. There was no danger at all."

"So you say! Well, there are new rules now, Charles. Hereafter, if you want to take little Carrie anywhere, you ask Amantha first. No more of this just snatching her away and taking her wherever you want!"

Charles sank wearily into a chair. "Mattie, listen to—"

"Carrie is not your child!"

He ran a hand across his eyes. "Mattie, do you believe that I would, for one single moment, place that baby in jeopardy?"

"No, of course not."

"And I didn't this time."

His wife sat down opposite him, calmer now. "Charles, you simply have to recognize that you can't continue to dominate that baby's life. Carrie is Amantha's child, and Franklin's. I appreciate how much you love her, but—"

"You're right. Once more." He sighed.

After a moment of silence: "I was going to tell you this at what I thought was a more appropriate moment. But maybe this *is* the appropriate moment. I'm pregnant, Charles."

His eyes opened wide in astonishment and delight. "Mattie, dear Mattie!" He rushed to her, pulling her to her feet, crushing her in his arms. "Oh, God, this is wonderful!"

"I have to tell you," she said softly, "that I would prefer that it weren't true."

"Why?"

"Because I've watched you with Carrie. And your . . . your possessiveness . . . well, it frightens me, Charles."

He held her at arm's length, staring at her. "Frightens you? How can you be frightened by love?"

"Ask yourself this: Is the way you've been behaving with Carrie rational?"

He looked into her eyes, then kissed her. "Perhaps I have been too possessive, as you suggest. I'll apologize to Amantha. And I promise you, dear, I'll be rational when our . . . when's it to be?"

"I think it's been two months. Or nearly so."

Dewey thought for a moment. "October, maybe. During the fall meeting at Clover Bottom."

Mattie's laughter echoed through the big house. "Charles, I believe even your funeral is going to be related to the dates of a racing meeting."

"I couldn't wish for anything more."

III

CHARLES lounged in an armed wooden chair in the print shop, his feet propped on a railing, scanning a freshly produced copy of the *Nashville Monitor.*

"Well, those young hotheads have their declaration of war now," he complained. "And I wonder what good it's going to do them? My God, a militia army and a navy of only twenty ships with a mere five hundred guns!"

Editor August Schimmel smiled wryly. "I've suggested in my editorial that the English may not even recognize that act of our Congress. That they're too busy with France to care what the United States does."

"When Andy Jackson reads that, he's going to come storming in here with another one of his rousing perorations."

"Probably. But it seems clear now that Madison isn't going to give him a commission for a command."

"Thank the Lord for that!"

Schimmel shrugged. "For the life of me I can't get stirred up over this war news. Do you realize that it will be only a week before I'll be married?"

"Uh-huh. And that's the reason I've come to Nashville—to pick up my new wedding suit at Jackson's store."

"I'll admit to you, Charles, that I'm a bit nervous about all this."

"A perfectly natural reaction." Dewey grinned at him.

"No, it's not just the thought of being married that makes me somewhat uneasy: it's the . . . well, the imposition we'll be placing on you and Mattie by moving into Bon Marche."

"Nonsense! We *want* you there. Work has already started on the new wing."

"And that's another thing. I'll not have you paying for the whole construction!"

"I'm so delighted to have you as my son-in-law, August," Charles said easily, "that I'll even agree with you on that. You'll pay for half. Is that satisfactory?"

"I'd feel much better about that kind of arrangement."

"Then that's the way it shall be."

Charles turned to watch Schimmel's assistants operating the small flatbed press, turning out copies of the *Monitor.*

"That's fascinating," he said idly, "the constant repetition of words being turned out there, to be read by God knows how many thousands of people. People you don't even know, August, and yet your words will influence them in some manner."

Schimmel nodded soberly. "It's a grave responsibility."

"Not all newspaper owners feel as you do. Some of them are nothing but scoundrels, using the printing press for their own narrow interests."

"Unhappily, that's true. But they don't last. The *Monitor* is . . . what? . . . the third newspaper to start in this community."

"Yes."

The editor set his square jaw firmly. "I intend to last, Charles, not only here but in other cities, too. There *is* a kind of power inherent in a newspaper, and I mean to use it for good. The country is growing, and my business is going to grow with it."

"A large ambition, August."

"So? Didn't I come to this country because such ambition could be realized? Didn't you?"

"I did, yes." He got to his feet. "I must get back."

"Could you spare me another moment?"

"Of course."

"Uh . . . Louise and I have talked about this a great deal, and she's going to take an active role in the newspaper."

"There are those who are going to be critical of you for bringing a woman into a man's world."

Schimmel showed some slight annoyance. "Isn't your wife a partner, so to speak, in Bon Marché?"

"Certainly. It's not me who's being critical. Louise will be a great asset to you."

"Good!" The editor pounded a fist into his palm. "Then it's settled."

Charles seemed surprised. "You don't need my approval, August."

"I thought perhaps you might object to your daughter in such a . . . well, such a public enterprise."

"The Dewey family, August, *is* a public enterprise!" Charles didn't laugh when he said it.

He rode easily back to Bon Marché, thinking of the happy time of the wedding—and then of being a father again. His merry whistle was echoed by the birds.

The butler, Horace, hurried out of the mansion when Dewey was still a hundred yards away.

"Mistah Charles," he cried, "come right 'way! It Miss Mattie!"

Dewey raced to the house, following the hustling black man up the stairs to the bedroom, where he found Angelica bending over the bed, ministering to her mistress.

"What's happened!"

Mattie opened her eyes. Weakly, she said, "I'm sorry, darling. But the baby—"

Terror came into his eyes as he turned to the slave woman. "Oh, my God, Angelica, not again!" He was thinking of Martha so many years earlier.

"She fine, Mistah Charles. Jest a bit weak, mebbe."

Charles went down on his knees by the bed, holding Mattie's hand. "Mattie, dear Mattie," he whispered.

She was asleep.

"Are you sure, Angelica?"

"Hones', she jest fine. A strong lady, Mistah Charles."

"She's got to be," he mumbled softly, "to put up with my damned foolishness."

IV

"So much is changing so fast," Charles said to Mattie one night in mid-December, "and now Christmas is coming around again, and I feel a bit sad about it."

"Oh? Why?"

"For one thing, George won't be here for the first time. And Corrine. Oh, I guess that pompous ass, Billy Holder, will allow Corrine to be here for an hour or two . . ." He sighed. "And I had thought that maybe we'd have . . . Oh, I'm just being somber, that's all."

"You were going to say that you looked forward to having a new baby at Christmas."

"No, of course not."

"Charles," Mattie said softly, "we can talk about it. I just think that maybe God had other plans for us."

"God certainly is saddled with a lot of heartaches, isn't he?"

"We ought to be happy for what we have, dear. Louise and August living here now; Franklin and Amantha looking forward to another child; Lee seeming to be content with his role here."

"You're right, of course. I admit to you, though, that I'm worried about George. I mean, this war has become a lot more serious than I had imagined it might be. And I wonder how an American is being accepted in London these days."

"With civility, I imagine. Could anyone be uncivil to George?"

Dewey laughed. "No, I guess not."

His wife opened a new subject. "I rode over to see Rachel this morning."

"How is she?"

"Terribly distressed. Andy is completely occupied with putting together his army, neglecting all else."

He smiled slightly. "I was willing to wager that he'd never have a command until the Cumberland froze over. Well, it *has* frozen over—and he has what he wanted. Still, it's not a commission from Madison, but from the governor, who had little choice but to give in to Andy's pressure."

"Rachel says this is the coldest winter she can remember here. And Andy is much distressed with the conditions of the volunteers in their tents. It's so bitter cold that they've used up all their firewood already—more than a thousand cords, I understand."

Charles grimaced. "Cold weather won't stop that devil Jackson! Nothing will stop him now."

"I guess it's supposed to be a secret," Mattie said, "but Rachel told me that they leave on January seventh: John Coffee with a regiment of cavalry down the Natchez Trace, and Andy with the infantry on the flatboats."

"God help those men!"

V

"GENERAL, sir!" The young officer saluted smartly.

"Well, Lieutenant Dewey," Major General Andrew Jackson said, smiling broadly. "I'm pleased to have you on my staff."

"Thank you, sir."

Jackson leaned close to the lieutenant, speaking quietly to him. "Lee, this is going to be a magnificent adventure. Your duty, you know, will be to document it—with your words and your pictures. You're going to be part of history being made."

"Yes, sir."

"In one sense, Lieutenant, I don't envy you."

"Sir?"

Jackson continued his intimate tone. "Well, there might be some grumbling among the staff about your late arrival, and you may hear some choice words about your being related to the commanding general . . . but, Lee, take that with good grace. You have an important mission with us. You need only be concerned with my orders."

"Yes, sir."

"Now, enough of this." His voice took on the stern tone of the commander. "Lieutenant Dewey, make ready to shove off!"

"Yes, sir!" Another salute.

Lee followed Jackson aboard the lead flatboat as broad backs pushed the heavy vessel into the ice-chocked river. A small crowd on the banks cheered, and Lee Dewey made a mental note to include that in his daily diary of the campaign.

VI

CHARLES was perplexed. Three times that morning he had asked the black grooms about the whereabouts of his son, Lee. Each time the answer was the same: "Ah ain't seed 'im, Mistah Charles."

The master of Bon Marché went looking for Franklin. "Have you seen Lee today?"

"No. I was just going to come to find you to ask the same question." Franklin frowned. "I've been doing nothing all morning but taking care of his duties."

Dewey shook his head. "That's not like Lee at all. Perhaps he's ill. But it's strange that I haven't been told anything."

He made for the mansion, where he found Mattie in the drawing room before the fireplace.

"Have you seen Lee this morning?"

She turned a tear-stained face to him. "He's gone, Charles."

"Gone? Gone where?"

Mattie reached out, handing him a crumpled note from Lee:

Dear Father and Mother, I don't expect that you will understand this, but I am joining General Jackson's expedition. I have been given a minor commission and am to act as the division's documentarian. Father, it hurt me to have to undertake this venture in this manner, but your intransigence in the matter of General Jackson left me no alternative. This is something I must do! Be assured that I will be in no personal danger; I will not be armed. Pray for the men who will be doing the fighting, and for the country they will be defending.

"Did you know of this beforehand?" Dewey roared, waving the note in Mattie's face.

"No!"

"When did you learn of it?"

"Just a few minutes ago when I found the note there on the mantel." She pointed.

"And you sit there like a ninny, doing nothing! Didn't you think I'd want to know!"

Mattie was silent for a moment. "I was afraid—Charles, your rage terrifies me."

"Can you assure me you had nothing to do with this?"

She didn't reply.

"Answer me!"

"I think I already have." She fought to keep her own temper in check.

He crumpled up the paper, hurling it into the fireplace. "Well, whether you knew or not is not important at this moment." He started for the door. "I'm going to get him back!"

"Charles!"

Her scream stopped him.

"If you go after him now, he'll hate you for it. Can't you for once bury your prejudice about Andy and see this for what it is? Lee needs to be his own man."

"Man! He's nothing but a boy!"

"You persist in seeing him that way, don't you? And that's exactly why he's gone!"

Dewey glared at her, the veins at his temples throbbing. "If I thought for a minute that you engineered this—"

Mattie sprang to her feet, rushing at her husband, putting her face close to him. Incensed. "Charles, you're an impossible bastard! As far as I'm concerned, you can go to hell!"

34

LIEUTENANT Lee Dewey blew on fingers numbed stiff by zero cold, trying once more to draw with a knife-sharpened charcoal. He had wanted to do some pen sketches of the first night encampment of General Jackson's infantry, but his ink had frozen solid.

He stood back now, away from the pitifully small campfires, studying the volunteers who had answered Tennessee's call to fight the British. More accurately, they had answered Jackson's call, coming from all corners of the state: farmers, mostly frontiersmen who had brought their rifles with them, knowing—as did their commander—that the smooth-bored muskets issued to the regular army simply didn't shoot straight. These were men who understood arms; who had counted on their rifles for life itself as they had carved out little pieces of the West for their own.

Tough men. Not professional soldiers, but men motivated to keep what they had suffered for. Ambitious men. Individualists who shared Andy's pride in the nation as they saw it: an "open" America, cleared of the English and Spanish and French, cleared of savage Indians, all of whom stood in the way of their personal free expansion, and the expansion that would certainly be needed for their children and grandchildren. Caring not at all for the proclamations of a central government back east somewhere. Fashioned on the same lathe as the general himself. Willing to fight now because he had asked them to fight.

Jackson's men.

Beholden to no other commander.

Uniforms, if the word could be used at all, were as diverse as the men: homespun cloth in nut brown and dark blue, buckskins, Indian blanketing, anything serviceable that might also keep them warm. A very few of the officers, young Dewey among them, affected a formal uniform of white breeches and waistcoats, signifying only that they had enough money to employ a tailor.

In the matter of uniforms Jackson saw the value of being little different than his men, of being indifferent to any formality of rank as expressed in mere clothing. The lanky leader made do with unpolished boots with floppy tops

that flapped against his bony knees, a simple short cloak made of blue homespun, a leather hat pulled down over his long hair, and broadcloth trousers into
the waistband of which he had jammed his dueling pistols.

But those who saw him never doubted for a minute that they were in the
presence of the commanding general!

Lieutenant Dewey, in spite of his cold fingers, tried to sketch the men,
seeking to preserve an accurate image of Andy Jackson's followers.

A corporal came up to him, saluting. "Sir, General Jackson requests that
you join him."

Dewey returned the salute, making his way to Andy's small tent. The general was there alone, seated at a field table, wrapped in blankets.

"Well, young Dewey, what are your impressions of the first day of our
adventure?"

Lee smiled. "I'm wondering, sir, whether I'll ever be warm again."

"Oh, you will be, once we get to our destination and engage the enemy."
He chuckled. "Warmly, I would hope."

"Yes, sir."

Jackson gestured to a second chair at the table. Lee sat down.

"I wanted to spend a few minutes with you," the general said, "to discuss,
for your documentation, the purpose of our being called to arms, and my
views on the situation."

Dewey nodded, settling himself for a monologue.

"We are called to reenforce General James Wilkinson"—at the mention of
the name, he grimaced—"at New Orleans. The original request from the War
Department was for fifteen hundred men. Twenty-five hundred of the finest
Tennessee has to offer quickly volunteered—and I can tell you that the rest of
the country is not so fortunate as to have such ready volunteers. When we
departed this morning we were two thousand seventy strong, infantry and
cavalry.

"The situation is such. Lieutenant Dewey, that I will be subordinate to
General Wilkinson." Once more his face was screwed up in disgust. "It's not
a role I would have chosen for myself."

"The same General Wilkinson who was associated with Burr?"

"Indeed. The War Department, in its wisdom, keeps him in command."
His ire was raised. "It's one of the numerous idiotic decisions being made in
Washington these days!"

Jackson paused to regain his composure. "Yet, I must accept this decision,
no matter how personally galling it may be. I ask nothing for myself, Dewey.
I'd have been content with the compensation of a sergeant. All I ever asked
was a chance to fight!"

"Yes, sir. What do you anticipate when we get to New Orleans?"

"I wish I knew. Right now my job is to push this army forward, to make as
much haste as possible, in spite of the ice on the rivers."

Lee had heard one report that, like the Cumberland, the Ohio was choked
with ice. They were moving north on the Cumberland into Kentucky, where
that river flowed into the Ohio, and then south again to reach the Mississippi.

A circuitous route to Natchez, Mississippi, their initial target. Coffee's cavalry, on the Natchez Trace, would ride nearly five hundred miles. The men in the boats would go twice that far to reach the same goal. And more.

"Let me tell you this," General Jackson was saying, "whatever challenge we find, we'll show them what Tennesseans are made of!"

II

IT was well after nightfall when Charles staggered into Bon Marché, nearly frozen, leading his limping horse. He had ridden off along the banks of the Cumberland in pursuit of his son, forcing the horse unmercifully, covering nearly twenty-five miles that way.

Then the horse had bowed a tendon in the right fore. His chase was ended.

He had no choice but to walk back home.

Four different times he had stopped to build a small fire to warm himself and the suffering animal. In his haste, he had brought no food, no provisions of any kind. He had to keep moving or freeze to death.

He led the horse into the barn, made warm by the heat of the accumulated equine bodies, and shouted to a black forking fresh straw into the stalls. "Take care of this horse. Rub him down well and take care of that leg as best you can. We'll work on it in the morning."

"Yas, suh." The slave stared at him, wanting to ask questions about where his master had been, but not daring to.

Dewey stalked out of the barn and half ran to the mansion. In the drawing room, where a welcome fire roared, he found Mattie at the desk, head bent over an account book.

"The damned horse bowed a leg," he announced angrily.

She didn't look up.

Going to the fireplace, he stretched out his hands to its glow. "Lord, I'm nearly frozen."

There was no comment.

He turned and glared at his wife. "It might be civil, at the very least, to offer me a hot meal."

Mattie ignored him.

"It's to be like that, is it?" he growled, moving to the door again, opening it, and bellowing down the hallway: "Horace!"

The butler came running.

"First, some coffee—as hot as you can make it. And then get me something to eat."

"Yas suh." He hurried away.

Charles picked up a crystal decanter from the sideboard and poured himself a full glass of whiskey, downing it in two swallows. That accomplished, he stood again in front of the fireplace, peeling off his outer clothing, one piece at a time, as his body warmed.

After several more silent minutes, Mattie rose from the desk, roughly shut the account book, and left the room, her eyes averted from her husband the entire time. She slammed the door of the drawing room behind her.

Dewey sighed. "As hot as you may be," he said aloud to the flames, "you could never be hotter than that woman is right now."

He didn't smile.

III

LEE Dewey never imagined that so many men could suffer so much without complaint. Though frostbitten fingers and toes were commonplace as the Jackson flotilla left the Cumberland and began drifting down the Ohio, no one complained. Perhaps the men knew that Andy wouldn't tolerate whiners. Certainly he had to be suffering with the rest of them, but he maintained an easy, jolly manner—encouraging, praising, demanding more of the men that they believed was in them. And getting it.

At least on this day the sun was shining brightly for the first time.

"If this good weather keeps up," the general said to Lieutenant Dewey, "we'll try to move ahead at night as well."

"Yes, sir."

Lee wondered how that was possible. The volunteers were exhausted by a day of constantly battling the icy floes on the river, moving them aside with heavy poles that were prone to snap under the exertion.

Now—suddenly, it seemed—the flotilla stopped. The ice had dammed up in front of them. Nothing could move.

Jackson took in the problem immediately.

"Over there!" he shouted to a captain. "Get some men to work on that pile of ice!" He was pointing to a seemingly solid wall of floes, slowly shifting and grinding together, becoming more impenetrable each minute.

Men from the first three boats leaped onto the ice and made their way to the jam. Sliding, falling, swearing, they attacked the icy dam with poles and axes and sledges, their work bringing sweat to their faces even though the temperature was barely above zero.

The artificial dam began to give way, with massive tearing sounds, and the men fled to their boats. But something worse had been unleashed. Giant blocks of ice behind the dam, weighing tons, were freed to race along on the strong current of the Ohio. One of the boats was struck on one side and then on the other by a small frozen mountain.

Planks of the heavy flatboat began to disintegrate under the pounding, tossing the men into the cruel waters. The thundering noise of the ice floes crashing together and the screams of the men became as one.

Young Dewey stared in horror as one of the soldiers was caught between two of the floes, crushed into a bloody nothing as the massive ice pieces rubbed together.

It took more than an hour for General Jackson and his officers to bring the flotilla ashore and to count the dead and injured. Two bodies were dragged from the water, both badly mangled. A roll call found yet another man missing and presumed drowned.

Broken arms and legs were common. Those who had been tossed into the river were stripped of their frozen clothing and warmed beside roaring fires, vigorously massaged by their companions in an effort to bring life back to limbs made immobile in the unequal battle against nature.

Jackson quickly appointed a party to move overland with the injured to seek medical care. The two bodies were to be carried along. The ground was too solidly frozen to bury them where they had died.

Lee sat with his drawing pad, attempting to re-create with his charcoal the death he had seen of that one man—to finish it before the protective mechanism of his brain would not let him see it any longer.

IV

IT was a month before Bon Marché heard from Lee. His letter, addressed to Mattie, was read by her at the dinner table.

> Bravery was just a word to me before this, but in the last several weeks I have seen more bravery than I could have imagined. The bitter cold and the ice on the rivers have made this a painful journey. It has been tolerable only because of the brave acts of countless anonymous men every day that we move forward toward the ultimate test—the war itself.
>
> My drawings are being made, as I had intended, but that, too, is difficult. I've had to forget about using ink because my supply has been ice since the day I left. Charcoal suffices for most of my work, but I've also done two oils. I'm pleased with them, partly because they were done under such extreme circumstances.
>
> I admit to you that, right now, I envy the warmth I know you have at Bon Marché. Yet I am glad that I came on this adventure.
>
> My fondest hope is that Father will find it in his heart to forgive me.

Mattie stopped reading for a moment. She looked up at her husband, believing that she saw tears in his eyes. But Charles sat glumly, silently.

> Two days ago there was a terrifying event—an earthquake that churned up the waters and swayed the giant trees along the banks. The earth literally rolled, I think, and General Jackson said the hand of God was upon us. This morning we found that the quake had been so severe, in one area ahead of us, that it changed the course of the Mississippi.

"That must have been the same one we felt here," Alma May said excitedly. "I imagine it was, dear."

Mattie went back to the reading:

> Our initial goal is Natchez, where General Jackson anticipates receiving orders that will take us into battle against the English . . .

V

LIEUTENANT Lee Dewey had known Andy Jackson ever since his family had come to Tennessee. He had seen his rages, his excesses of emotion, before. But nothing approached the anger he saw in the fighter at this moment.

Natchez had been reached against the greatest of odds; infantry and cavalry were there, reasonably intact. Now Jackson had received a communication from General James Wilkinson from his headquarters in New Orleans. As he read it, his face darkened, his teeth ground together, the veins in his neck expanded and throbbed.

Andy tossed the dispatch to young Dewey.

"It is my desire that you should halt in the vicinity of Natchez," Jackson's superior had written. "Several circumstances prevent my calling you lower down the river: the impracticability of providing for your horses, the health of the troops; the policy of holding your corps on the alert . . ."

Lee looked up. "What does he mean, sir, about holding the corps on the alert?"

"It means, damn it, that that traitorous ass Wilkinson wants to keep us immobile!" Jackson stamped about the confines of the tent. "Impotent, as he is! He means to keep me out of the fighting because he fears that I and my brave men will show him up for what he is: an incompetent, cowardly scoundrel!"

"Yes, sir." Lee wanted to say something that might cool Jackson's anger. "Perhaps, sir, this delay will be a blessing in disguise. A lot of the men are ill."

"The cure, Dewey, is for us to feel the heat of battle!"

"Yes, sir." Lee went back to reading the dispatch. Wilkinson had informed Jackson that a brigade inspector would be sent to muster the Tennessee troops into federal service, and that a paymaster would be on hand to pay them: "These officers," he had written, "will give every aid and facility, and if it is in my power to add to the comfort of the band of patriots under your orders, it is only necessary to point out the mode to me."

And so they waited. A week. Two weeks. During that time Dewey had heard—from another officer, not from Jackson himself—that Andy had requested the War Department to send him to Canada, where the American cause had floundered. He wanted to fight. Somewhere. Anywhere.

On the fifteenth day of inactivity at Natchez, General Jackson called his officers together. His face was pained.

"I have today," he told them, "received the following communication from the secretary of war, Mr. Armstrong." He shifted the paper in his hand so that he could read it better: " 'The causes for embodying the Corps under your command have ceased to exist.' "

Several of the officers gasped.

" 'You will on receipt of this consider it dismissed from public service.' "

"No! No!"

Jackson pressed on: " 'Deliver over to Major General Wilkinson all articles of public property. Accept for yourself and the Corps the thanks of the President of the United States.' "

Andy stopped reading. There was a stunned silence.

The lanky commander smiled wanly. "Gentlemen, we are going home as we came—proud, unbowed by adversity. General Wilkinson"—a cloud came over his face once again—"has had the temerity to suggest that I encourage my men to enlist in the Regular Army. But, by God, he shall not have them!"

Jackson was roaring now. "Every officer is to pass the word that any Regular recruiting officer is to be drummed out of camp! Tell all the men that this Corps will march home intact! It is my solemn responsibility to these brave men to return them to their loved ones. And I shall do it, with my own means!"

The next several days were crowded with activity. Lieutenant Dewey was given the task of counting the sick. There were many of them . . . too many of them. Lee witnessed a bitter scene between Jackson and Wilkinson's quartermaster, in which Andy demanded—and got—twenty days of rations. But wagons to carry the ill Tennesseans were not made available. Jackson had to hire eleven of them, paying out of his own pocket, with the horses necessary to draw them. Whatever else was needed for his men, and was not made available by the Regular Army, Andy bought on the strength of his signature scrawled on promissory notes.

It was mid-March when they left Natchez, facing an five-hundred-mile march.

General Andrew Jackson was afoot, striding out confidently in his mud-caked boots. The leader.

His own horses carried some of the ailing.

Lee Dewey followed along in Andy's footsteps, his drawings and his journal in a pack on his back. But his steps were stumbling, erratic.

He had a high fever.

VI

ABNER Lower approached Charles in the stud barn. The chief overseer at Bon Marché had a mission, but he wasn't certain how to carry it out.

"Charles," he said hesitantly, "I'd like to have a moment or two of your time."

"Certainly."

"I've been asked by Franklin and Louise to speak to you."

"Since when can't my children speak for themselves!"

"That's just it," the overseer said. "It seems that on the subject of Lee no one can speak to you these days, not even Mattie."

"So . . . the cabal against me is complete! They've even recruited you!"

"No, I would have recruited myself, Charles. This silence between you and Mattie is hurting everyone, me included. It's not natural, Charles."

"Mattie conspired with that damned Jackson to take Lee—"

Lower interrupted. "She *didn't*. Lee made his own decision, as a man."

Dewey grunted, leaning on a stall door. "Go on."

"Schimmel tells me that there's word that Jackson's Corps is on the way home. All of us want you to do the right thing with Mattie before Lee gets home. You don't want him to find this division when he returns."

"You seem to presume a great deal about what *I* want."

"I know how deeply you love your family, and that you must be just as miserable as everyone else is. Heal this thing," Abner pleaded. "Apologize to her."

"So it has to be *me* who does the apologizing!"

"Who else, Charles, but you?"

VII

"YOU should have seen him, Father! He was magnificent!"

Lee Dewey's enthusiasm belied the weak voice in which he spoke. He was ill, desperately so; the doctor reported that he had pneumonia. His face was ghostly white now as he lay in bed in his room at Bon Marché, the worried family members gathered about him.

"You don't have to tell us everything now," Charles said, holding his hand. "Save your strength. You'll have a whole lifetime to tell us of your adventures."

"No, I want to, Father. I would have died if it hadn't been for Andy. A lot of men would have died. Do you know that he walked nearly the entire eight hundred miles from Natchez? He gave his own horses to the men."

Charles patted his hand. "You must rest now, son," he said quietly.

"You've misjudged Andy," Lee insisted.

"It seems I may have." It was an admission that none gathered around the bed had ever expected to hear.

"You know what the men are calling him?"

"What?"

"Old Hickory. It's a fitting name for him, Father. He *is* as tough as hickory."

Dewey smiled at his son. "As are you. But tough or not, you need your rest. We're all going to get out of here now and let you sleep."

Charles leaned over and kissed Lee on the cheek. "God keep you, son."

The Deweys filed out of the room, Angelica remaining to minister to Lee.

"Have you seen his drawings, Father?" Louise asked.

"No."

They moved to the drawing room.

"You must look at them," Louise continued. "They're absolutely marvelous! They say more than Lee could ever tell us in words. August says they're the finest things he's ever seen. He says my twin has a great career ahead of him as a correspondent artist."

Louise spread the drawings out on the desk, turning them over slowly as Charles and Mattie, their hands clasped, studied them.

Brushing a tear from his cheek, the patriarch of the Dewey family said to his wife: "It seems, dear, that my son has a unique talent."

"*Our* son, Charles."

"Of course—our son." He held her in a tight embrace.

35

THE Deweys never would have known of it if Rachel Jackson hadn't confided in Mattie.

Charles, several weeks after Lee's return, rode to the Hermitage to thank Andrew Jackson for saving his son's life.

"Andy appreciated it so much," Rachel had said, "and I think that now, after all these years, they can find ways to be close friends."

Mattie understood that it was best if she said nothing to her husband about knowing of the visit to the Hermitage. It had been a private thing for Charles, and she tried to keep it that way for him.

August Schimmel had printed several pages of Lee's drawings, with some excerpts from his journal, in the *Nashville Monitor*. Also, he had sent one of the charcoal sketches to a New York publisher friend, and that sketch—showing the lanky Jackson marching defiantly along while, behind him, gravely ill men clung to the backs of his horses—was printed under the heading, "Old Hickory!"

Lee Dewey's talent had spread the fame of the frontier general to the East Coast.

II

CHARLES Dewey's newfound friendship with Andy Jackson was tenuous at best. What he had disliked about Jackson before still persisted: the quick temper, the resort to the pistol to settle any argument, the totally violent nature of the man. Charles recognized that his own angers were perhaps too close to the surface, and he made a determination to "like" Jackson, to excuse his excesses, to associate with him more and more.

He did that for Mattie.

And for Lee, whose admiration for General Jackson was a complete thing.

Charles reminded himself that Jackson was being badly used by the federal government. "A man of such obvious talent," he had said to August Schimmel, "ought to be allowed to fight."

The newspaper editor agreed with him, printing several editorials railing at the War Department for not employing Andy as a commander, especially since all else in the war seemed to be going so badly. Jackson, of course, agreed with the viewpoints expressed in the *Monitor,* and that, too, seemed to bring Charles and Andy closer together, in that Schimmel was perceived as being of Bon Marché.

Charles, then, kept silent when Jackson allowed himself to be dragged into yet another situation involving a duel. Dewey was appalled, because it obviously wasn't Jackson's fight at all.

Two officers of Andy's disbanded army—Major William Carroll and Ensign Lyttleton Johnston—became involved in a public dispute. Over what, Charles didn't care to know. But Johnston challenged Carroll to a duel, and Carroll replied that such a duel wasn't possible because Johnston wasn't a gentleman.

Enter Jesse Benton, the younger brother of Thomas Hart Benton, Jackson's close friend and a colonel on the ill-fated expedition to Natchez. Young Benton, who was to have been Ensign Johnston's second, found himself offended by Major Carroll's comments about his friend and himself challenged Carroll to a duel.

"Andy's been called in as a peacemaker," Dewey reported to editor Schimmel, "but I can't imagine he's going to be very comfortable in that role."

Charles was right. There was no peace.

The duel was set, with Jackson as the second for Major Carroll. It was a laughable thing. Jesse Benton was shot in the butt! The *Monitor* published the details of what had happened and all Nashville was amused.

But not Thomas Hart Benton. And, as it turned out, not Andy Jackson either. The dispute grew, the elder Benton writing to Jackson that the duel was seconded in a "savage, unequal, unfair, and base manner." Jackson replied: "It is the character of the man of honor, and particularly of a soldier, not to quarrel and brawl like fish women."

Dewey, worried, could confide only in Schimmel. "If the damned gossips would be quiet," he said, "this thing might die. But they keep after Andy, fueling his temper. He told me yesterday that he'd horsewhip Tom Benton the next time he saw him."

Schimmel shrugged. "Well, the Bentons are safely off in Franklin right now. Maybe a friend of Andy's can keep them apart until it cools off."

"Meaning me?"

"The others won't, will they?"

"No, I'm afraid not."

Six weeks went by without incident. Dewey was in a good mood as he rode into town to have a meal with Jackson at the Nashville Inn.

He stopped off at the newspaper office when he reached town.

"The Bentons are in town," his son-in-law said by way of greeting.

"Oh, good Lord! Where?"

"At the City Hotel."

Charles hurried toward the Nashville Inn. He met Andy and John Coffee strolling toward the post office. Dewey fell in step with them, trying to devise a plan in his mind to keep them from knowing that the Bentons were there.

His worst fears were realized!

The Benton brothers were standing on the wooden walk outside Talbot's Tavern, next to the City Hotel. They glared at Andy; Andy glared back. But no words were spoken.

At the post office Jackson picked up his mail, and the three of them started back toward the Nashville Inn. Opposite the City Hotel, they saw Jesse Benton disappearing inside the hotel. Charles breathed a sigh of relief.

It was premature.

Suddenly, Jackson whirled and made for the door of the hotel, cracking his riding crop against his boot.

"Andy, don't," Charles said, grasping his arm.

The general shook himself loose, striding like a man possessed into the hotel, Charles and Coffee in his wake.

In the hallway, just inside the hostelry, stood the massive form of Thomas Hart Benton.

His whip held menacingly, Jackson moved at the elder Benton. "Now defend yourself, you damned rascal!"

Benton's hand made a move toward his pistol, but Andy's was already drawn, pointed directly at Benton's face.

It became a stalking exercise, as Charles could only watch, fascinated by the drama. Jackson moved forward—one step, two, three. Benton retreated backward, keeping his eyes on the cocked pistol.

There was a shot!

Not from Jackson but from Jesse Benton, who had slipped through a doorway behind them and fired without warning. He had missed.

Two shots from Jackson at Tom Benton. Misses! It seemed impossible.

The elder Benton, pistols in both hands now, fired twice. One of the heavy balls smashed into Andy's shoulder, imbedding itself. He fell heavily.

Seconds only had passed.

As Dewey, on his knees, crawled to attend to Jackson, John Coffee rushed at Benton, firing at him and missing also. He continued his attack with the butt of his now spent pistol.

Sounds of the gunshots had brought Andy's other friends running from the nearby Nashville Inn.

Madness swirled around Charles as he tried to help the fallen Jackson.

Alexander Donelson, dagger in hand, joined Coffee in advancing on Tom Benton. The two men struck with their knives, wounding Benton several times. Benton continued to retreat. An unseen stairway, as he moved backward, became his undoing. He tumbled down the stairs, the walls bloodied from his wounds.

Another Jackson adherent, Stockley Hays, had cornered Jesse Benton, ramming a thin sword cane at his chest. It struck a large metal button on Jesse's coat and broke.

The young Benton had the advantage now. He put a pistol against Hays's heart and pulled the trigger. It misfired!

"For God's sake," Charles screamed to be heard above the melee, "come and help me with Andy! He's badly hurt!"

His cries seemed to end the insanity. Coffee, Hays, and Donelson rushed to Jackson's side and, with Dewey, lifted the skinny figure of Andrew Jackson and carried him to a room in the Nashville Inn.

Blood soaked through two mattresses as every doctor in Nashville was called to the inn to attend to the general.

Shouting could be heard in the square outside the hotel, and Charles went to the window. Both Bentons were standing out there, surrounded by their friends, shouting defiance at the wounded Jackson.

Tom held high a small sword that Andy had dropped during the fight. Symbolically, Benton broke it over his knee as a cheer went up from the Benton followers.

In disgust, Dewey turned away from the window to watch the doctors in their efforts to stem the profuse bleeding.

"I believe we may have to amputate the arm," one of them whispered.

Andy's eyes opened. His voice was weak.

"I'll keep my arm," he ordered.

III

It was difficult for Charles to be rational about what he had witnessed. Nevertheless, on his return to Bon Marché, he gave a deliberately unemotional report on the brawl, with as little detail as possible.

In bed that night, Mattie said quietly: "It was madness, wasn't it?"

"Yes."

"I'm deeply grateful that you weren't hurt."

Dewey was startled by her words. It was the first time he had thought about being in danger himself. He didn't comment.

She sighed. "We had a conversation like this once before—it seems to have been in another life—when you returned from that duel in Kentucky. You said then that this family would not involve itself with Andy Jackson again."

"I remember."

"But I persisted," Mattie went on. "I thought our association with Andy was important."

"Hmmm."

"Now I know that it isn't. Can you forgive me for putting the Jackson name above that of Dewey?"

"I never imagined that that was what you were doing."

His wife smiled. "I hate you, Charles, when you take that rational tone."

"Oh? I thought the rational, unemotional, levelheaded Charles Dewey was what you wanted."

"Stop that, Charles! You know perfectly well what I'm trying to say."

"Uh-huh."

"I'm trying to say that I love you, Charles Dewey, because you *are* Charles

Dewey—and not what I may try to make of you. And I certainly don't want you to be a handmaiden to Andy Jackson."

"Very well," he said flippantly, "I won't be."

"Or a handmaiden to anyone else, for that matter."

"Not even you?" he teased.

"Not even me."

BOOK THREE

A man is the creator of his own life. It's like
clay: you mold it and shape it, trying to make it
into something beautiful. And when it's
finished a man ought to fight like hell to
preserve his creation.
—Charles Dewey, 1845

36

LITTLE Carrie, nestled in her grandfather's lap, warmed by the fire in the drawing room and by Charles's love, clapped her hands in delight, giggling as he read from the book, acting out the story.

"And guess what happened next?"

"What? What?" the child demanded.

"Well, 'At midday they saw a beautiful snow-white bird sitting on a tree. It sang so beautifully that they stood still to listen to it. When it stopped, it fluttered its wings and flew around them.'" He pantomimed the flight of the bird with a hand. "'They followed it till they came to a little cottage, on the roof of which it settled itself. When they got quite near, they saw the little house was made of bread.' Imagine that! 'And it was roofed with cake.'"

"I love cake, Grandfather," Carrie said quite seriously.

He hugged the little girl, laughing. "So I've noticed. . . . 'The windows were of transparent sugar.' 'This will be something for us,' said Hänsel.' . . . Do you remember who Hänsel is?"

"He's the little boy."

"Right! And he's saying: 'We will have a good meal. I will have a piece of the roof, Gretel.'"

"That's the little girl," Carrie cried.

"It is, indeed. And Hänsel says to her, 'You can have a bit of the window, it will be nice and sweet.'"

"Can you really eat a window, Grandfather?"

"Of course you can, if it's made of sugar, as this one was. 'Hänsel stretched up and broke off a piece of the roof to try what it was like. Gretel went to the window and nibbled at that. And then—A gentle voice called out from within: "'Nibbling, nibbling like a mouse, Who's nibbling at my little house?'"

"I know, I know! It's Hänsel and Gretel!"

Dewey laughed at the enchantment of his granddaughter.

Mattie, who had been standing watching them for a few minutes, said, "While all that nibbling is going on seems a good place to end it for tonight. It's time for bed, young lady."

"Oh, Grandmother!"

"Your mother is never going to let you stay with us again if we don't see that you get your rest."

"Grandmother is right, Carrie. Off to bed!" He lifted her high, and Mattie took the child in her arms.

"You seem to be as delighted as the baby with those stories."

Charles laughed. "I guess I am. George couldn't have picked a better gift to send. He says that the tales by the Brothers Grimm are the sensation of the Continent."

"And of Bon Marché, too, it appears."

Dewey got to his feet, kissed his granddaughter good night, and watched, smiling, as Mattie carried her off toward their bedroom.

He poked the fire to a new flame, then went to the sideboard to pour himself a sherry. As he settled into the big chair again, he thought of what the passing years had brought to him. The big family Bible he had carried from Virginia and Mattie's meticulously kept farm journals documented the growth and successes of Bon Marché. Charles didn't have to refer to them to know what they contained.

October 1813 had seen a son born to Corrine, named William Holder, Junior. Dewey sighed, wishing Billy would let him see the baby more often. Only a few weeks later, little Carrie was presented with a baby brother, Richard, by Franklin and Amantha Dewey. And a second brother, Albert, the following year. Then, too, there were the twin daughters born to Louise and August Schimmel in 1814, christened Joy and Hope. Charles thought their names mirrored all that was Bon Marché.

Of course, it hadn't gone unnoticed on the plantation that Mattie's second cousin was called to war again. Given a Regular Army commission finally, Andrew Jackson was sent to avenge the massacre of four hundred Americans by the Creek Indians at Fort Mims, Alabama. Old Hickory, still nursing the shoulder wound given him in the brawl with the Bentons, destroyed the Creeks at Horseshoe Bend on Alabama's Tallapoosa River. Andy, on his own authority, then invaded Spanish Florida, routing a small British force at Pensacola, where the remnants of the Creek Indians and "maroons"—Negro slaves who had escaped from the United States—had been recruited to the English cause.

Ultimately, it was Jackson's destiny to go to New Orleans. There, early in January of 1815, he annihilated a numerically superior English army under the command of Major General Sir Edward Pakenham, inflicting more than two thousand casualties on the redcoats, while suffering only seventy-one himself.

Andy Jackson of Tennessee, frontier lawyer and duelist, plantation owner and slaveholder, gambler and horse racer, had become a national hero. It made little difference that the Battle of New Orleans was fought two weeks after a peace treaty had been signed in Europe. Jackson had restored America's pride.

At Bon Marché, Mattie Dewey quietly reflected that pride. But the talk of General Jackson was minimal. There was much more discussion of a plan to further extend the influence of the purple racing silks of the Dewey family.

Charles was to take a racing string to Charleston, still the most prestigious track in the South.

II

"Do you mean to tell me, Mr. Dewey," the handsome matron was saying, smiling sweetly, "that you've come all this way just to go racing?"

"I would have come the six hundred miles, and more, to know the charming hospitality I've received here in Charleston."

The matron cocked her head, studying him. "You'll pardon me, Mr. Dewey, but you're not at all the crude—I hope you'll excuse that word—frontiersman I would have expected to come from western Tennessee."

Annoyed, Charles smiled nevertheless. "It's true, ma'am, that some frontiersmen are crude. But I imagine the same percentages might apply in this area as well."

Her face darkened. "Not among the whites," she sniffed.

Dewey bowed to her. "My pardon, ma'am."

He was attending a reception in his honor at the magnificent Steepbrook, ancestral home of the Manigault family of Charleston, one of the "old families" of South Carolina, dating back to 1680 when the French Huguenots, denied the right to be Protestants in their native land, had come to the New World. It was a formal society of fine ladies and gentlemen, schooled in the arts, proper in their speech, both English and French, and confident of their wealth.

Nothing in Tennessee, not even Bon Marché, could match the vast Steepbrook estate. Or the Elms, the plantation of the influential Izard family, which he had also visited. These people were rice planters, owners of thousands of slaves. Charles was astonished by the number of house servants they used; the ladies, he deduced, were left with nothing to do but to be beautiful.

And on that night, as he looked around the ballroom of the Manigault mansion, he was impressed with the collective elegance of the women. Mrs. Julius Pringle (he hadn't learned what it was her husband did) particularly impressed him. Dark, wide eyes that looked at him coolly out of a flawless face, her lustrous black hair done up in flattering ringlet curls. And a somewhat shy Mrs. Henry Broughton Mazyck, always on her husband's arm, protectively it seemed, her young beauty so perfect as to defy adequate description, her brunette hair piled high on her head and fastened with a large Spanish comb studded with diamonds.

One of the women, Charles had to admit to himself, stirred erotic thoughts in him. She was the petite Mrs. Langdon Cheves, whose husband had just completed a term as Speaker of the House of Representatives. There was nothing reticent about her. She spoke and moved with a confidence that suggested she was comfortable in a male-dominated world. Unlike many of the women, she eschewed the popular ringlet coiffure and wore her auburn hair cut short, exposing all of the breath-catching beauty of her face. The decolletage of her gown displayed more soft shoulder and bosom than most of the other women; indeed, she had more worthy of display.

"I regret that my husband is away in Washington," Mrs. Cheves said to Charles. "He'd want to know all about your Andrew Jackson."

"Yes, General Jackson is a large figure in the nation now."

"Are you acquainted with him, Mr. Dewey?"

"Yes. He's my wife's cousin." He was uneasy with this woman; the desire that she aroused in him made him cautious.

"Well, then, do tell me about him."

Charles gave her a rather laudatory recital on the merits of Andy, omitting the things about the general that raised his own ire. He told her what he thought she'd want to hear.

"General Jackson seems a paragon."

He laughed. "Hardly. No man is, I'm afraid."

It came to him suddenly: *My God, she's just like Mattie!*

Dewey coughed nervously. "You'll pardon me, Mrs. Cheves, but you remind me so much of my wife. In many ways you're very similar: the confident manner, the auburn hair, the figure—" He stopped, realizing he had gone too far.

"Oh?" She laughed delightfully, her eyes opening wide. "Spoken, Mr. Dewey, like a man who has been away from home for too long a period."

"Please forgive me." His face reddened. "I meant nothing—"

"Of course you did, Mr. Dewey." She seemed to find delight in his discomfort. "I find your unique interest in me flattering."

He was left without words.

"Perhaps, Mr. Dewey," she went on, "if you find the time heavy on your hands, we might find it mutually beneficial to discuss further my astounding similarities with your wife. I'd be interested to know just how far they extend."

Her candor only reinforced the thought that she was like Mattie. Had she issued an invitation? No, Charles decided; she was toying with him. What an old fool he was!

Dewey was rescued, in a sense, by his host, Charles Izard Manigault, a grandson of the patriarch of the prolific family. After proper apologies to Mrs. Cheves, Manigault led him to a group of gentlemen anxious to discuss horse racing.

"We're very proud of our racing here," a man named Fenwick told him. "There was a Jockey Club in Charleston as early as 1734, even before the English thought of such a thing."

"I hope my horses will be up to your tradition," Dewey said.

"What have you brought with you, sir?"

Charles was eager to tell them. "Twelve young runners. I had special vans built to make the trip, four horses to a van." He smiled. "And to be perfectly honest, gentlemen, I hope to sell the horses here—to you. All are uncut males with breeding potential: sons of Royalist, a rather nice imported English sire; of New York, with Messenger bloodlines; of Predator, who is by Shark; of Arrangement, a solid racing son of Medley; and also two sons of a stallion I brought from Virginia when I first established headquarters in Nashville: Premier Etoile, who traces back to Yorick.''

"Impressive bloodlines, Mr. Dewey," another horseman commented, "but can they run?"

A laugh. "We'll just have to see, won't we? All are young—three to five— and their greatest racing potential is still in front of them.''

"A question, Mr. Dewey," Manigault said. "Why are they all for sale?"

"Because, sir, that's what we do at Bon Marche—breed to sell.''

He thought then of Mattie, who had devised that strategy for the plantation. And he thought, too, of Mrs. Cheves.

III

IT was a rare social engagement away from Bon Marché for the ladies—for Mattie; her stepdaughter, Louise; her daughter-in-law, Amantha; and her daughter, "Princess" Alma May. The occasion was the sixteenth birthday anniversary of Alma May.

The youngster had been disappointed that her father would be away from home at the Charleston races on that important date. She had told Mattie: "I don't think I want a party, Mother, if Father can't be here.''

But Louise had come home from the newspaper office with a report that a young showman from Philadelphia had rented a building on the public square in Nashville to convert into a temporary theater, the first such enterprise in the city. Mattie immediately made plans for them to attend the debut performance.

Making it a special time for the Princess was important to her mother. It was to be a full evening. They'd have dinner at Mr. Parker's Nashville Inn, then attend the play and stay the night at the inn. She bought a new dress for Alma May, and made sure that Horace, in full livery, would drive them to Nashville in the little-used formal coach.

Nashvillians turned out in impressive numbers for the introduction of the theater. The impresario, one Nathan Ludlum, was staging a comedy, *The Soldier's Daughter,* for the opening night and had proudly posted an SRO sign at the box office. He was surprised by the number of times he had to explain what the letters meant.

Mattie had bought seats in the first row, and she was delighted that Alma May was so excited about the event. They had gone through the entire dinner without the Princess mentioning the absence of her father.

Applause rolled through the little theater when the curtain parted for the first act. And the traveling players didn't disappoint the entertainment-starved Nashvillians. Ludlum—dark-haired, broad-shouldered, and slim—played the lead with professional aplomb.

Alma May leaned over to whisper to Mattie: "Isn't he handsome, Mother?"

"Hush, dear.''

"But isn't he?" she insisted.

"Yes, Princess, he's very handsome.''

It may have been that the actor could make out the whispered words, in that they were spoken so close to the stage, because Ludlum looked down at Alma May and smiled.

"Oh!"

Mattie looked over at her daughter, annoyed. "Do be quiet, Alma May."

"But he smiled at me, Mother!" The words were in more than a whisper now, turning other heads to them.

An elbow was dug into the young girl's ribs. Hard. It took that to silence the Princess.

When the play was ended and the cast had taken several curtain calls, Nathan Ludlum came to the apron of the stage.

"Thank you," he said exuberantly. "It is so nice to know that we are so warmly welcomed in Nashville. I hope we will continue to please you. And I hope, too, that I will be able to meet many of you"—he looked directly at the Princess—"at the door as you file out."

At the entrance, with Mattie and her party among the last to leave, Ludlum was particularly solicitous to Alma May.

"Ah, yes," he said, "the beautiful young lady in the front row." He took her hand.

Her mother spoke rather pointedly: "This was a present to her on her sixteenth birthday."

"Indeed." The actor smiled. "I'm most pleased to have shared it with you, Miss Dewey."

"Oh! You know my name?" The Princess was flustered.

"Of course. When someone so lovely graces my theater, I make an effort to find out who she is. Happy birthday, Miss Dewey." Ludlum bent to kiss her hand.

The young girl from Bon Marché danced back to the Nashville Inn.

As she and her mother undressed for bed in the room they shared, Alma May could speak of nothing but Nathan Ludlum.

"He's so handsome and so gallant, don't you think, Mother?"

"Yes, dear." She hid her frown from the Princess. The attention the actor had paid to her daughter worried her.

"And Louise says he's not married."

"That shouldn't be of concern to you."

"You might have thought twice, Mother," Alma May pouted, "about telling him that I was only sixteen."

"Yes, dear. Now, do go to sleep!"

In the tavern of the Nashville Inn at that hour, Ludlum sat with his fellow actors at a large table, drinking ale.

"Nat," one of them laughed, "I saw that little hand-kissing exhibition at the front door tonight. The bucolic type really isn't in keeping with your style, is it?"

"Bucolic?" Ludlum grinned wickedly. "You see, my friend, your comment is just another proof that you're never going to prosper in this world. Miss Dewey's father, you should know, is the richest man in western Tennessee!"

He raised his glass of ale in a toast.

"To money," he said.

IV

RACING at Charleston was elegantly social and all-pervasive; businesses and government offices closed for the races.

There were some surprises for Charles Dewey. He was astounded at the scale of wagering. Used to the flamboyant betting on the frontier, he knew what it was to see the backer of a horse risk property—real and human—on the outcome of a race. But never before had he seen so much cash money offered: hard money—gold and silver. Very little paper. Indeed, he had to amend his own wagering patterns, calling on the bank to exchange his paper money into large-denomination coins in order to keep pace with the Charlestonians. He did so willingly. And profitably.

Even more astonishing to Dewey was the quality of the horses. He had expected something much better in the way of competition. Starting six young horses in the first four days of racing, he saw five of them win convincingly; the sixth was beaten only a neck.

Thomas Pinckney, Junior, whose father and uncle had been stalwarts in the fight for American independence, was the first horseman to approach him with an offer for one of the Bon Marché runners.

"Your bloodlines, Mr. Dewey," Pinckney said, "seem to be devastating us."

"The luck of racing, sir."

"Not at all. That Predator colt that won today—the big bay—is he for sale?"

Charles grinned. This was what he had come for. But he began cautiously. "Any horse is for sale for the proper price."

"Ten thousand, sir."

The visitor struggled to keep the shock off his face. The price he had anticipated for the colt had been far exceeded by the offer.

"Perhaps, Mr. Pinckney, we should not rush into this."

"Oh? You have another offer?"

"Some interest has been expressed, yes." The white lie was just a part of horse-trading.

"Tell me what it is and I shall match it."

Charles needed time to think; there was a greater vein to be mined in Charleston than he had imagined. "I prefer that such offers be kept confidential."

"Of course."

"But when I do elect to sell him, you'll be given ample opportunity to compete for him."

"That seems fair to me, sir." Young Pinckney bowed slightly and retired.

Dewey needed a plan. It was clear to him now that he would have no difficulty selling the dozen colts he had brought with him. Pinckney's interest, he believed, only mirrored what was possible. He thought of Mattie and what ideas she might contribute; his wife, he admitted to himself, was a far shrewder bargainer than was he.

On the first Saturday of racing, his guardian spirit intervened. Mattie wasn't there, but Mrs. Langdon Cheves was.

"I'm disappointed in you, Mr. Dewey," she said to him, coming up on him suddenly when he was saddling a runner for the feature event.

"Ma'am?"

"I've waited a week to hear from you."

"Well, you see, the horses—"

"Now I've had to seek you out." She was playing the coquette. "I'm not accustomed, Mr. Dewey, to playing second fiddle to a bunch of horses."

Charles was uncomfortable. "I was . . . uh . . . concerned about the propriety of calling on a woman whose husband is absent—"

"I never knew," she interrupted, "that propriety was a concern of men. My experience has been that women have had to set the rules in such matters."

"Yes, well . . ." Once again her candor had cost him his words.

"Following that theory—to which I subscribe—you have an invitation for lunch tomorrow."

"If you wish."

"I wish, Mr. Dewey."

V

SEVERAL times in the hours between Saturday afternoon and Sunday noon Charles had decided that he would send a message to Mrs. Cheves declining her invitation.

He didn't.

He went because he wanted to be with her. Because, tossing sleeplessly in his bed that night, he could not erase the erotic thoughts he had about her. He even concluded, in one brief moment, that if she allowed him . . .

They had a delightful meal together, laughing and teasing. She captivated him. He found, as the meal ended and they strolled together on the vast lawn of the estate, that she became less and less like Mattie. The physical comparisons were still there, and the candor, but Mrs. Cheves had her own charm. She was more sophisticated than Mattie, more experienced in the world of "old society."

They sat on a low stone wall at the edge of the lawn, gazing out over the fields. Silently. She reached over and took his hand, holding it in her lap.

"Mr. Dewey," she began. "Oh, I can't keep calling you that, can I?"

"It's Charles."

"I'm Mary Elizabeth. I was a Dulles." She grinned. "But that doesn't mean anything to you, does it?"

"No," he admitted.

"Good! Because it's not important, really. What's important is that we be"—she hesitated—"friends."

"I agree."

"Friendship is what you seek in me?"

"Of course."

"No more than that?"

He looked into her eyes for a moment. "Mary Elizabeth, I'm not very good at this game. I'm not even sure that I appreciate it being played. It's childish, isn't it, to suggest any more than friendship?"

The lovely woman sighed. "I'm sorry. Teasing has become a defense with me. Langdon is away so much, and I do receive . . . well, proposals."

"So you talk your way out of them?"

"Exactly." A frown. "It's strange, Charles, but in this case I'd rather not have the defense."

"More teasing?"

"Truth."

He laughed at her. "Loneliness can be a great tempter."

Mary Elizabeth didn't comment. But she continued to cradle his hand in hers. When she spoke again, she changed the subject. "I hear everywhere, Charles, that your horses are the sensation of the race meeting."

"I've been very fortunate, that's true."

"Charles Manigault told me two nights ago that he covets one of your colts—one by Royalist, if I remember the conversation correctly. You'll have to excuse me, but I'm not much on racehorse pedigrees."

"Two of my colts are by Royalist."

"Anyway, Mr. Manigault seemed quite taken with one of them."

"I've had some offers on several of the horses, and while I hope to sell them all, I'm not quite sure how to proceed. Obviously, I want to get as much as I can. I also want to keep the friendship of these gentlemen."

"Let them bid on them," she suggested.

Charles shook his head. "I don't want to auction them. That takes too much preparation."

"Accept sealed bids, then."

He thought for a moment. "I believe that's the answer."

"May I help you with it?"

"Well . . ."

"Please! I want to! I'll let it be known—I do get around, you know—that you're accepting sealed bids, and then I'll gather them for you."

"I'm afraid that would be too much of in imposition."

"Nonsense! I'm going to do it." She laughed. "I'll be your horse agent. Is that the correct term?"

"It is indeed."

"Wonderful!" She was excited by the prospect. Impulsively, she leaned over and kissed him. And then her arms went around his neck and she kissed him again.

Charles responded, and they held each other, sitting on that stone wall, neither wanting to let go.

"This is rather public out here," she whispered.

"Hmmm."

She was on her feet, tugging at his hand. "Come."

He followed her into the entrance hall of the mansion, up the wide, curving stairway. She opened the door to the bedroom, beckoning that he enter.

"I think I've come far enough."

"Charles, this isn't teasing."

"I know."

"Don't you want me?"

"At this moment, more than anything I can imagine."

"But . . ."

" 'But love is blind, and lovers cannot see,' " he quoted, " 'the pretty follies that they themselves commit.' "

The spell was broken.

"Damn you!"

"What?"

"Spouting some stupid poetic morality at a time like this!" She was deeply annoyed.

"Shakespeare," he explained weakly.

"I don't care!"

There was an absurdity about the whole thing. When that came clear to Mary Elizabeth, she began to laugh. Charles laughed, too. They walked down the stairway, still clasping hands, as the laughter ran its course. At the door he kissed her cheek.

"Are you going to regret this?" she asked.

"No. We've done the right thing."

As he walked to his horse and heard the door closing behind him, he cursed under his breath.

Dewey didn't believe at all that they had done the right thing.

VI

MARY Elizabeth Cheves fulfilled her promise. She spread the word among her circle of wealthy Charlestonians about the sealed bids being accepted on the Bon Marché horses, and she gathered the bids for Charles.

In one happy afternoon together at her home, they opened the bids, culling out the highest ones. All twelve horses were sold, at an average price of over eight thousand dollars. Charles Manigault had bought the Royalist colt he coveted for twelve thousand five hundred—fully five thousand dollars over what was offered by another bidder.

Strangely, there was no bid at all from young Thomas Pinckney on the Predator colt for which he had earlier offered ten thousand dollars.

Charles wondered if he had offended Pinckney by not accepting that first offer. He shrugged. He thought the prices exorbitant, but he rationalized that the business of Bon Marché had to come first, not his rather old-fashioned ideas about the worth of a horse. There was money in Charleston; he would accept it.

Two more days were spent in the company of Mary Elizabeth Cheves, as the horses were delivered to the plantations in the vicinity of Charleston and payments accepted. His last morning in the fascinating city was spent at breakfast with Mrs. Cheves, a leisurely meal that neither one of them wanted to see end.

"I have in my saddlebag," he told her, "bank drafts for nearly one hundred thousand dollars. I've even sold the horse vans."

"You had a good agent."

"I did, indeed. Agents get fees for their work, you know. I figure that I owe you almost ten thousand dollars." He reached into his pocket for a bank draft he had drawn in her name.

She raised a hand to stop him. "You owe me nothing, Charles. Except your warm friendship."

"That you have—in full measure."

It was time to leave for Tennessee. He took her in his arms, kissing her tenderly.

Her head on his chest, she had the last word.

"Think sometime about what it might have been if it hadn't been for your damned 'pretty follies.'"

37

"YOU haven't had much opportunity," Mattie chuckled, "to tell us about Charleston, what with Alma May's constant babbling about that actor."

"The Princess does seem taken with him."

"Thank the Lord they've finished here now and have moved on to Kentucky. I don't know how I would have handled her if those actors had stayed."

"That young lady is in love with all of life. We'll see other such enthusiasms before she settles down."

Charles got into bed, gathering his wife into his arms for the first time in more than a month. "I thought about this moment a great deal."

"I guess neither one of us is very good at sleeping alone." She kissed him. "Now, tell me about Charleston."

Quickly, Dewey described the Charleston trip, the racing successes, the wagering coups, the unexpected windfall on the sale of the horses.

"You were very wise to sell the thoroughbreds with that sealed-bid device. It probably increased what you got for them. Quite substantially, it seems."

"No doubt about that."

He thought of Mary Elizabeth and was racked with guilt, hoping that his face didn't reveal it.

"And the people—were they hospitable?"

"Exceedingly so. Charles Manigault, a wealthy rice planter, had me as a guest one evening at the estate he calls Steepbrook—I want to tell you about that house later—and Henry Izard, of another old-line Charleston family, had me to The Elms, also quite magnificent. I was much impressed with all the horsemen."

"And the women?"

He saw another vision of Mrs. Cheves. Cool, lovely, desirable.

"Charles!"

"What?" He realized then that his thoughts of the lady from Charleston had prevented him from answering Mattie. "Oh, yes, the women . . ." He wondered what Mattie was thinking.

"The women," he went on, "seemed to me, for the most part, to be spoiled. They have so many house servants—seemingly three times what we employ—that I don't believe the ladies have anything at all to do. Except, perhaps, to be beautiful."

Why in the devil did I say that? Charles asked himself.

"Were they beautiful?"

"Well . . . attractive, let's say. They dress in fashion, of course, Charleston being much more sophisticated than Nashville."

"I see." Mattie frowned. "Do you want to tell me about her?"

Charles had a feeling of panic. "Who is that, dear?"

"The woman"—her tone was icy—"who seems to have captivated you."

"Mattie," he said, forcing a laugh, "you have a vivid imagination."

"Is that your answer?"

"Yes, dear, that's my answer. I suppose I should be flattered that you could be jealous—especially at my age—but, in truth, I can't recall that I was introduced to any unmarried women."

"She was married, then."

"Mattie, for God's sake!"

He ended the conversation by being more aggressive than usual in his love-making. But he wasn't convinced that Mattie would drop the subject.

She reads too damned well.

II

"DADDY! Daddy!" Alma May cried, rushing into the drawing room, waving a copy of the *Nashville Monitor*. "They're coming back! Just think of it, they're coming back!"

Her father grinned at her. "And who might that be, Princess?"

"Mr. Ludlum's acting company!" She placed the newspaper on the desk in front of him, jabbing a finger at an article. "They're going to settle here permanently, and there's to be an acting school in Nashville, Daddy!"

"That's very nice."

"Nice! It's the greatest thing ever to happen! I wonder why Louise didn't tell me about this."

"Maybe because she didn't see it with the same end-of-the-world enthusiasm that you seem to have."

"I'm going to enroll in the acting school!"

"Wait a minute, Princess. I think you ought to talk to your mother about this."

"She'll say yes if I can tell her that you said it was all right."

Charles laughed. "And that's exactly why the three of us will sit down calmly and discuss it together."

"Oh, Father!"

He was Father when Alma May was annoyed, Daddy at all other times.

"When does this marvelous happening take place?"

"In January, it says here."

"That's three months away, Princess. Do you think you'll be able to wait?" He was laughing at her again.

The young girl squeezed her way onto his lap and hugged him. "You'll like Nathan, Daddy. He's so—"

"Nathan? Do you know this young man well enough to call him by his first name?"

"Well, no," she confessed sheepishly. "But, Daddy, he's so handsome!"

"So I've been hearing. Now, Princess, take your unbounded enthusiasms elsewhere and let me finish my work."

Alma May sprang to her feet. "You *will* like him, Daddy! Just you wait and see!"

She skipped out of the room. Charles looked after her, smiling at the pleasant picture she made: her mother's auburn hair and fair skin, but taller, with slim, firm legs, her figure budding.

The Princess was a beautiful young woman. *Woman?* He had never seen his youngest daughter in that light before.

III

It was two days before Christmas 1816. Charles had gone out in the woods with a number of blacks to cut a yule log, continuing a tradition he had brought from Elkwood.

Mattie sat at her desk working on the ledgers when he returned.

"We found a spectacular yule log, dear," he reported.

"Oh? That's nice."

It was said with her old sarcasm, and he immediately recognized the danger signals. "Is something wrong?"

"I sent Horace into Nashville for the mail, since you haven't found time in the last few days to attend to that."

"Bad news in the mail?"

"No, I guess not. Not for you anyway." She held out a letter to him.

Charles took it. The envelope was addressed in a clearly feminine hand, carrying the postmark of Charleston, South Carolina. He didn't have to open it to know who had sent it.

He had no choice but to look at it right there. He did, scanning it quickly, trying to leave the impression that it was of little importance.

"Seasons greetings from Langdon Cheves and his wife." He swore inwardly when his voice wavered. "You may remember that Mr. Cheves has been the Speaker of the U.S. House of Representatives. I met them on my trip."

That last was a lie, and he wanted the words back as soon as he had said them. Dewey started to put the letter in his pocket.

"I'm not to be allowed to see it?"

"Of course, dear." He nonchalantly tossed the letter on the desk, going to the sidebar to pour himself a bourbon—to gird himself for what he knew was coming.

Mattie slowly unfolded the letter.

"Dearest Charles," it began. She raised her eyebrows. "It has been a disappointment to me that I haven't heard from you since that sad day when you rode away from Charleston. I know it's silly, but I feel a jealousy in knowing that you are in the bosom of your happy family while I am here, denied your fond companionship."

His wife glared up at Dewey, who had his back to her, idly studying a painting on the wall he had seen a thousand times.

"I write now to wish you the happiest of Christmases—with the sure knowledge that you return those wishes to me. It would make it easier, though, if I could hold a letter from you in my hands, knowing that you had touched the paper and that I might vicariously touch you again."

Mattie angrily brushed away a tear that was trying to make its way down her cheek.

"My days here have been lonely since you left. And I'm afraid, when Langdon returned, that I talked too much about you. Perhaps I was acting like a schoolgirl, but the memory of what we had together—and what we might have had—is too bright a one to dismiss lightly. That I cannot do."

Dewey's wife sobbed.

"Write to me, dear Charles, if only to assure me that you are well. And happy. Perhaps some day . . ."

It was signed, "With fondest love, Mary Elizabeth."

Mattie balled up the letter, hurling it toward the fireplace. It fell on the carpet, short of the flames.

"So, dearest Charles," she said quietly, but with a biting-edge tone, "Charleston wasn't all racehorses."

Dewey turned to her. "Mattie, believe me, nothing transpired between us. She was lonely, and she . . . perhaps suggested a possible—"

"Lonely because her husband wasn't there?"

"He was away in Washington."

"You told me you had met him!" Her anger was complete.

"Yes, I did." He sucked in a deep breath. "And that was a mistake."

"It certainly was!" She was weeping openly now.

"Mattie, please let me explain."

"The explanation, it seems to me, is abundantly clear in that." She pointed to the letter on the floor. " 'The memory of what we had together is too bright to dismiss.' "

Charles was at a disadvantage. He had merely glanced at the letter. But now his wife was quoting it back to him. He picked up the crumpled paper and smoothed it out. The incriminating words made him ill. How could Mary Elizabeth have been so indiscreet?

"Mattie, there's a perfectly logical explanation . . ." He looked pleadingly at her. "Mrs. Cheves was a friend, nothing more. She helped me with the sale of the horses, and we had some time to talk together."

Her sarcastic laugh stopped him. "Talk! Good Lord, Charles, you must think me stupid!"

"We talked together," he went on, "and became close friends. I admit, Mattie, that I was attracted to her. But the reason for that attraction was that she was so much like you in appearance and in personality."

"Oh, Charles," she sighed, "don't bother to go on with your lies."

"I speak the truth!" he shouted. "And, damn it, you'll listen to me!"

Mattie just shrugged. Getting to her feet, she went to the window, her back turned to him.

"I was attracted to her," he repeated, "and she to me. And we discussed that attraction." A pause. "There was an occasion, just before I left for home, that the opportunity for . . . uh . . . greater intimacy presented itself. But I stopped it there. I swear to you!"

She whirled on him. "And no embraces, no fondling, no kisses, I suppose!"

Dewey hung his head. "I kissed her, yes."

"Just to console a lonely wife?" That sarcasm again.

"No. I kissed her because I wanted to kiss her, because I wanted more from her. But at the end, I realized that I didn't want . . . well, damn it, I didn't want anyone but you!"

There was a long silence as she looked at him.

"And what now, Charles?"

"Nothing now. Whatever it was, and it was fleeting, is over."

"And I'm to accept your explanation?"

"Yes."

"And dismiss what's in that letter?"

"Yes."

"And go on loving you as before?"

"Yes."

Mattie shook her head in doubt. "You ask a great deal, Charles."

"I do, yes."

"And this Mary Elizabeth, what of her?"

"I'll remember her fondly."

"Charles Dewey, you are a lecherous old bastard!"

He grinned at her. "To that I'll confess."

His wife started for the door. Charles didn't try to stop her. With her hand on the doorknob, she turned to him. "You'll answer her letter, I imagine."

"No, I think not."

"Answer it, Charles, and get it out of your system." She thought for an instant. "Get it out of *our* system."

"Yes, dear."

"And stop being so damned agreeable!"

Mattie slammed the door behind her.

Dewey stood with the letter in his hand, reading it again. Slowly. Remembering.

Moving to the fireplace, he dropped the paper into the coals. The flames flared up and in them he saw the bright face of Mary Elizabeth. Warm and beautiful.

For a brief moment only.

It quickly turned to ashes.

IV

THE first week in 1817 brought good news to Bon Marché. George Dewey wrote from London that he and Mary were returning to the United States. "We have had enough of London," he said, "and are anxious to return home."

"Mary needs a new forum for her social bragging," Mattie suggested. "She has probably bored every Britisher to death by now."

"Now, dear," Charles said lightly, "let's be tolerant. Even Mary Harrison Dewey can get enough of high society."

"I doubt it."

"Father, I've made arrangements," the letter continued, "to acquire a fine English stallion, Boaster. He's to be transported on the ship with us." He gave the anticipated date of their arrival in New York. "Please make arrangements to have him brought to Bon Marché. I'm very high on him and he's to be my contribution to the 'cause.' I hope that you and Franklin will find a place for me there."

"Just think," Dewey said, "George is coming home. The place will be a lot brighter with him around."

"Maybe if you replied to him quickly," his wife sniggered, "you could persuade him to leave Mary behind."

"You are humorous at times."

"Who's being humorous?"

Their sardonic laughter filled the room.

"We do have a *real* problem, though, Charles. Alma May is being very insistent about joining Mr. Ludlum's acting class."

"I know. What do you think about it?"

"I have doubts, dear. But maybe if Louise is there to keep an eye on her—"

"The Princess tells me"—Charles grinned—"daily it seems, that the *finest people* in Nashville are enrolling in the acting program. Including young Sam Houston, I hear."

"And Louise says that it appears to be a legitimate enterprise."

Charles clapped his hands together. "Well, then, have we convinced each other?"

"I suspect we have. But I think we ought to send one of the maids with her each time. After all, we can't expect that Louise will be available to chaperone her at all times."

"A good point."

"Margaret might be a good choice."

"A bit young for that responsibility, isn't she?"

"She's very level-headed, and Angelica has trained her well. Someone nearer Alma May's age may be more palatable to her. I don't want to smother her, after all."

"Whatever you decide, dear."

"Margaret it will be, then." Mattie went to him, kissing him playfully. "Just as soon as you think you're ready for the Princess and her enthusiasm, let's tell her, shall we?"

A grimace. "Could you arrange to do that when I'm away somewhere?"

"Charles!"

"Just a thought."

V

MARY Dewey, as Mattie had feared, was holding forth at the dinner table at Bon Marché, inflicting a monologue of London society gossip on the entire Dewey family.

"The King is quite mad, you know, and no one sees him. And, for my tastes, the Prince Regent is little better. My dears, he's such a handsome devil, but the *scandals*! Women and gambling . . ."

George and Mary had returned to the plantation in mid-June, with Mary obviously pregnant. Of that, little was said; Mary seemed reluctant to talk about it. Mattie had to plan a large family dinner to welcome them, loathing the idea, knowing that it would serve as a platform for Mary's incessant, inane chatter, delivered now in an affected British accent.

"It's said, you know, that Prince George and Princess Caroline—she's such a light-headed snip!—don't really cohabitate. And that's not hard to believe, the Prince Regent can be an impossible bore. A scoundrel, really. Why I heard that—"

Mattie coughed, getting the attention of Louise, making signals with her eyes for her stepdaughter to move into the conversation.

"What you say is utterly fascinating," Louise interjected, entirely at ease with the falsehood. "Mary, I think you ought to consider writing several articles on your experiences for the *Monitor*. Then we might all read about your adventures at our leisure."

Her sister-in-law looked at her coldly. "I hardly imagine myself as a journalist, Louise. It seems such a . . . well, such a common calling."

George, who had been lounging back, his eyes half closed, squinting through the amber whiskey in his glass, jumped in quickly: "What Mary means, Louise, is that—"

Mary cut him off. "I'm perfectly capable of making my own explanations, Georgie."

Her husband shrugged.

But there was no further explanation to Louise, nor any hint of an apology. Mary was off on another story. "Paris is so much more gay than London."

Mattie had had enough. "When's the baby due, George?"

"Well, let's see . . ." He laughed. "I'd estimate the foaling in just less than two months."

"Georgie! Really! There are times when you can be so crude!" Mary looked around at the other Deweys. "It's talk like that that made me suggest"—she glared at her husband—"that we have the baby in Europe, where there's an appreciation of good taste and manners. Instead, Georgie insisted that we come back to Bon Marché—to this . . . well, this backward and uncouth region!"

A deep silence fell around the table.

After a few seocnds, Mary, smiling again, said, "I was speaking of Paris. It's so much more gay than London now that a Bourbon is back on the throne. Although I'll admit that this Louis—" She looked at George. "Oh, what is that number, Georgie? I can't ever seem to keep them straight."

"Louis the Eighteenth," he groaned.

"Yes, of course. It would be much easier if the French would consider different names for their kings, don't you think? Well, this Louis is rather old and quite obese." She smirked. "But the convenient French morals are still intact. Louis has a mistress, a Madame du Cayla, and it's said she *amuses* him. Isn't that droll?"

All eyes were glazed over.

"Say, I just realized," George interrupted once more, "that the Princess isn't here."

Mattie leaped at the new conversational bait with the eagerness of a hungry fish.

"She's rehearsing this evening at the Nashville theater. That's something new since you've been gone, George. The Princess is quite excited about it. She's to play Juliet."

Mary Dewey sniffed. "When one has lived in London for any length of time, one gets terribly sated on Shakespeare."

VI

ALMA May sat entranced as Nathan Ludlum began the famous soliloquy.

" 'But, soft! what light through yonder window breaks? It is the east, and Juliet is the sun! Arise, fair sun, and kill the envious moon, who is already sick and pale with grief, that thou her maid are far more fair than she.' "

Seated cross-legged on the stage, her eyes misty with emotion and locked on the handsome face of her Romeo, the Princess felt the desire in her. How dull those words had seemed when the tutor had intoned them at Bon Marché. And how alive now when spoken by a . . . lover!

" 'It is my lady; Oh, it is my love! Oh, that she knew she were! She speaks, yet she says nothing. What of that? Her eye discourses, I will answer it.' "

Alma May wondered how long she could go on this way—wanting him desperately and being denied what was so right.

" 'I am too bold, 'tis not to me she speaks: Two of the fairest stars in all the heaven, having some business, do intreat her eyes to twinkle in their spheres till they return. What if her eyes were there, they in her head? The brightness of her cheek would shame those stars, As daylight doth a lamp, her eyes in heaven would through the airy region stream so bright that birds would sing and think it were not night.' "

There was a silence. To Nathan Ludlum, perhaps, but not to Alma May. The noise of her heartbeat roared in her ears.

"Oh, God!" she moaned softly.

Slowly getting to her feet, she walked to where the actor stood in the center of the stage, his head bowed as if drained of emotion. She rose to her tiptoes, kissing him on the cheek.

Nathan reached for her, but she backed off a step.

"Wait," she whispered.

She turned to the chairs in front of the stage where the only audience was the black maid, Margaret.

"Maggie," Alma May called out, "go to the livery now and get the carriage. We'll be going home presently."

"But, Miss Alma, yer Momma sez Ah was to stay—"

"Maggie!"

Sullenly: "Yas, ma'am." Her training took over; a slave didn't contradict a white person. She started for the exit.

"And Maggie—"

"Ma'am?"

"There's no need to rush, you know."

"Yas, ma'am."

They watched her go. And when she had disappeared through the door, they fell into each other's arms hungrily, kissing and groping, the pent-up emotion unleashed.

Nathan led Alma May to the corner of the stage, where the curtain had been pulled back, and they slowly sank to the floor, hidden by the folds of cloth.

"Darling, I love you so," the Princess breathed. "How long can we go on like this?"

His hands answered her, roaming up under her skirt, searching. She didn't stop him. Not this time. It seemed only a moment. Perhaps a moment tinged with a kind of madness. Even a violent moment. But she didn't care. It was what she had wanted for so many weeks.

He spoke finally. "Princess, I *do* love you. You believe that, don't you?"

"Yes."

"Don't you think we ought to talk to your parents?"

The idea frightened her. "Oh, Nathan, how can we? Mother will—"

The actor kissed her tenderly. "Dearest, we have to be honest about it. This isn't the fiction of *Romeo and Juliet*. This is real! We love each other."

"Oh, yes, we do . . . we do!"

"Then let's tell them."

"When the time is right," she said.

"Soon?"

"Yes, dear, soon," she promised, kissing his face, feeling her passion stirring again.

They heard Margaret returning. Hurriedly rearranging his clothing, Nathan stepped out from behind the folds of the curtain to call out into the semi-darkness of the theater. "Margaret, Miss Alma is getting her hat and cape. She'll be with you shortly."

"Yas, suh."

The black woman didn't like that man. And she wasn't a fool. She knew she shouldn't have left them alone.

VII

"No! No!" Mattie screamed. "Absolutely not! I'll not permit it!"

Charles tried to be calm. "Your mother is right, Princess. Actors are a . . . well, an unstable lot. It's not the life for you, dear. Not at all."

"I love him!"

Alma May sat hunched on a straight-backed chair in the Bon Marché drawing room, her hands folded in her lap, her pretty face a somber stone carving.

"Love him!" Mattie shouted. "What do you know about love? You're seventeen years old . . . and I didn't raise you, educate you, and train you to be the wife of an itinerant ne'er-do-well actor!"

Her daughter stared at her defiantly. "You're the one who's always telling that story about how your mother wanted you to marry a rich merchant, and—"

"Your father was a substantial, mature man when I married him. But this actor—what is he?"

"Nathan is talented and ambitious. With a little help he could be the finest—"

"With the help of your father's money, I suppose!"

"Horses aren't the only thing worth spending money on!"

Dewey tried to mediate the argument. "Princess, we love you, and we don't want to see you make a mistake that will stay with you for the rest of your life. You *are* a bit young, you know, for such an important decision. Perhaps if you went away for a while? Maybe we should consider touring Europe for a few months."

"No!"

"I know that, right now, you find this man fascinating—"

"It's *more* than that."

"Maybe you think so at the moment, dear, but—"

"I'm going to have his baby."

Mattie gasped.

There was a frozen moment and then she advanced on her daughter, standing over her, shrieking at her. "You slut! You damned slut! How dare you?"

Charles was quickly between them. "Mattie," he said firmly, "please try to control yourself."

His wife pushed him aside, anger and hurt burning in her eyes. "Alma May, is this the truth?"

"Yes, Mother."

Mattie threw her hands in the air, beginning to stalk about the room. "Well, that ends it, doesn't it?! All my plans, all my dreams . . . you've destroyed them. You've destroyed them!"

Mattie Dewey began to weep. She had never wept like that before.

VIII

"Young man," Dewey said, his voice quavering, "you should understand that I am deeply distressed by what Alma May has told us."

"Sir?"

"Don't feign innocence with me, Ludlum!"

On the morning after the confrontation with Alma May, Charles had ridden into Nashville to see the actor. They stood now among the chairs in the empty theater. Opponents.

"Squire Dewey, I can only assume," Nathan said politely, "that the Princess has told you that we're in love."

The father felt his ire rise; he had promised himself that he'd be reasonable. He broke that promise.

"Damn you, Ludlum, you know what she told us! She's pregnant!"

Nathan stared at him in disbelief.

"You *did* know that . . ."

"No, sir, I didn't."

"Do you have any reason to doubt it?"

"If you mean did we—"

"That's exactly what I mean!"

Crestfallen: "Yes, sir, she could be pregnant." He wondered how much detail the Princess had revealed to her parents.

Dewey walked away from him. One step. Two. Three. Clenching and unclenching his fists. He turned slowly back to the actor.

"Ludlum, I'd like nothing better than to thrash you! But, unhappily, that would prove nothing. You intend to marry her, of course?"

"Naturally."

Nathan had been shocked by Charles's news, but now the whole thing was beginning to fall into place for him. Here, he knew, was the opportunity he had been seeking.

"Can you support Alma May with this?" Charles swept an arm to take in the makeshift theater.

"I make very little money."

"Just as I suspected." Dewey took a deep breath. "Listen to me, Ludlum, and listen to me well! Alma May's mother and I are not prepared to see her waste her youth in poverty, to put an honest face on it."

The actor held his breath.

"Therefore, we have decided to finance a proper theater for you and Alma here in Nashville. We'll make every effort to give your enterprise stability."

"That's very generous, sir."

"Shut up! But, so help me, if you bring that girl one moment of grief, I'll kill you! And, Ludlum, don't believe for a second that what I've just said is an idle threat!"

Nathan Ludlum just nodded soberly, not wanting to use the wrong words. Not now.

He wanted to cheer. He was to have a real theater!

38

THE Deweys put the best possible public face on it.

Alma May Dewey was to be married to thespian Nathan Ludlum, late of Philadelphia, in an elaborately staged outdoor ceremony at the plantation. She was seventeen; he, twenty-five.

Coincident with that revelation was the announcement in the *Nashville Monitor* of the plans of Squire and Mrs. Charles Dewey, of Bon Marché, to build a five-hundred-seat theater in the town square. Of brick and stone it was to be, modern in every respect, "designed to provide to Nashville and David-son County all manner of entertainments."

Mr. Ludlum, the impresario and general manager of the theater, was quoted: "In naming this important addition to the city the Dewey Theater, we are recognizing the continuing contributions of the Dewey family to the culture of our community."

That was not the way Nathan had wanted it. He had thought of it from the first moment he realized it was a possibility, as the Ludlum Theater. Charles had swiftly and vehemently dissuaded him of that idea.

"Don't imagine, Ludlum, that this building will be a gift to you. Or that it's being built as a monument to your ego. My wife and I will hold the deed on it. You—and the Princess, of course—will have the income from it, but *not* the ownership." Dewey had smiled. "Nor the name, either!"

The actor had learned rather quickly that he was dealing with western royalty. That Alma May's nickname of "The Princess" had validity.

In the hours immediately following his initial confrontation with Charles, Ludlum had sought out Alma May. He had ridden to Bon Marché, sending a message to her through one of the blacks. He needed answers.

She met him—in nightdress and robe—in the gelding shed, the barn farthest removed from the mansion. The hour was past midnight.

"Your father was quite angry," he told her. "It seems he knew something that I didn't—that you're pregnant."

"Oh? Did he tell you that?"

Her flippant tone surprised him. "Alma May, you *know* he did!"

"Yes." She giggled.

"Well—are you?"

She stuck out her chin. "No."

"But—"

"You wanted to marry me, didn't you?"

"Of course."

"And you thought that by marrying me you'd get your own theater."

"I wanted to marry you because I love you."

"But you wanted your own theater, too, didn't you?"

"Yes."

Alma May's lovely eyes opened wide. With innocence. "Well, now you have *both*."

"But, damn it, Princess, they'll find out soon enough that you lied about the baby!"

"Not if we do something about it right away." Her arms reached for him.

In a comfortable bed of sweet hay they tried to do something about it. Right away.

Ludlum couldn't object to her subterfuge; after all, as she had said, it had gotten him what he wanted. He recognized, too, that his own integrity was compromised. Although he had meant to use her, this young girl had undertaken to confound her parents and to involve him in her sophistry (as pleasant and as profitable as that might be), as if she had some *right* to do so—a right that shouldn't be challenged. In that sense, a *royal* right.

On the morning of his wedding, Ludlum again had the feeling that he was dealing with nobility. George Dewey came to see him in the bedroom at Bon Marché where Nathan was dressing for the ceremony. All smiles and outgoing, George, nevertheless, had come to issue a decree. At least that's the way Ludlum saw it.

"I understand you've already butted heads with Father."

Ludlum nodded, not sure of what he ought to say.

"And now here comes another Dewey." George laughed heartily. "Not to further chastise you, Nathan . . . uh, do they call you Nat?"

"Some do, yes."

"As I was saying, not to further chastise you, Nat, but to welcome you to the family!"

He offered his hand, and the bridegroom shook it gratefully.

"I'm really delighted with this marriage," George went on. "The Princess needs a good strong man."

He sat down, taking a cigar out of a leather case he carried in his coat, making a show of lighting it. He puffed out a wreath of smoke.

"I know one or two little things about you," the second son of Charles Dewey said. "For example, Alma May says that you don't smoke."

"That's true, I don't. I find that my voice becomes raspy when I do, and in the theater a clear voice is—"

George waved a hand imperiously. "Of course, of course." He hadn't come for a dialogue. "That's too bad, though. A fine cigar can be a great comfort."

Ludlum had no comment.

"I also know, Nat, old man, that there was in Pittsburgh, as it has been related to me, a young woman. What was her name?"

Silence from the actor.

"Ah, yes, I remember now: Rosalie McMurtry. And it's said that she had . . . uh . . . designs on you, that there even may have been a thought of an engagement, eh?"

"Mr. Dewey, I assure you—"

George smiled. "Of course, I understand those things. I had a dalliance or two myself before I married Mrs. Dewey. And I'm sure that such was the situation with Miss McMurtry."

"It was several years ago," Ludlum said weakly. "And I've not heard from her in—"

Another wave of the hand to silence him. "Obviously, Nat, I didn't come here to compare notes on our mutual . . . uh . . . indiscretions." He puffed on his cigar. "No, I just wanted to talk to you before the wedding to try to . . . well, to perhaps make it easier for you to get over the shoals, as it were, of being a member of the Dewey family.

"You're marrying into a *proud* family," George continued. "Our father literally created it from nothing. A street urchin in Paris, and now . . . What you see here at Bon Marché is only the physical manifestation of the family. The plantation and the horses and, yes, the wealth—is but a part of what it means to be a Dewey." He paused. "I'm boring you, Nat."

"Not at all."

"You see, Nat, being a Dewey means that you strive for excellence, not on a par with your contemporaries, but above that. You're an actor and, even though your name is Ludlum, you'll be a Dewey, too, in the public's perception. As such, you'll find it necessary to be the finest actor you can be."

Ludlum's discomfort was complete.

His brother-in-law-to-be blew a smoke ring and watched it circle lazily to the ceiling. "Oh, we don't always reach our goals, but the important thing is that we set them high."

"Of course. I understand."

"Good!" George rose from the chair. "I'm glad if I have been able to help you establish your priorities. Be assured, Nat, that if you ever need help, you'll find me readily available to you."

"Thank you. That's comforting." It wasn't, but he had to say something.

They shook hands again, and George moved to the door.

"Oh, by the way," he said, turning back to Ludlum, "you may be interested in knowing that Miss McMurtry—a sad young lady, apparently—had a daughter out of wedlock some time back. A few years ago, I think. But that must have been after you left Pittsburgh."

Nathan stared at him.

"Yes, indeed, a sad young lady." George sighed. "You know, Nat, women in those unhappy circumstances, left with a bastard child, sometimes do irrational things. I mean, just suppose that she somehow heard of your good fortune here in Nashville. Why, she might even be driven, in her desperation, to accuse you of being the father of her child."

The actor stood dumbly.

George waved a hand, dismissing such an alien thought. "But I guess not. Such things only happen in fiction or on the stage, right?"

Ludlum's stomach churned.

George smiled. "I sometimes think I should have been an actor myself. I'm often accused of overdramatizing certain situations. While Miss McMurtry *was* in somewhat dire straits, I understand that, just recently, some anonymous benefactor—" He stopped. "Well, that's of no consequence now, is it?"

He was through the door quickly.

Nathan was rooted there, staring at the closed door. Charles Dewey hadn't frightened him with his threats. But the son had.

Prince George, he thought, the Enforcer Knight.

II

CHARLES sat on a bale of hay, tears tracking down his cheeks. In front of him in the stall lay the massive body of Premier Etoile, dead at the advanced age of thirty-five.

"My God, Franklin," he said to his eldest son, "just think of what has transpired since that night when I saw Premier Etoile foaled and that kind man, Marshall Statler, allowed me to name him."

"Etoile served us well, Father."

A small smile. "Didn't he, though? He was a sturdy old gentleman, servicing mares right up to the end. I guess a male animal can't ask for more than that, eh?"

He got to his feet, going to the body, kneeling down and patting the stallion on the head. "Good ole fellow," he sighed. "Lord, Franklin, this makes me feel old. I've known this thoroughbred for two-thirds of my life. And I'm on the downhill side of it now."

"Nonsense."

"It's true, son. I'm fifty-two." He nodded toward the dead horse. "And he makes me remember all of the dreams I had when he was foal. I've been the most fortunate of men, Franklin. I believe I've realized them all."

Franklin cleared his throat. "Father, maybe this is the time to bring up something George and I have been discussing."

"About the old man, eh?"

"Not in that sense." His son smiled. "We did talk of you taking less responsibility . . ."

Charles nodded.

". . . but primarily, we've been discussing the age of our stallion band. We were going to suggest to you that Premier Etoile be retired."

"Go on."

"The truth, Father, is that the stallions are all on the oldish side. And we thought we ought to do something about that."

"What's your plan?"

"We believe that we ought to retire New York, Arrangement, Predator, and Cranium."

Dewey was astounded. "*All* of them!"

"Yes, sir. If you study the statistics, you'll realize, as we have, that they haven't been paying their way as stallions. Their books have dropped off drastically."

"Hmmm."

"Boaster, the stallion that George brought from England, is only nine, and he ought to head our new band. And the other imported stallion, Royalist, could be brought here permanently. He's fifteen, and he'd be our oldest."

"But Royalist is owned by a syndicate."

"Yes, sir, but I've talked with Joe Coleman. He and the others would be happy to sell out to us."

"And then what?" Charles was becoming annoyed that his sons had done so much without consulting him.

"We want to put Majority to stud."

"My God, son, he's still winning at the track!"

"That's true, but he's already ten, and we feel he'll make more money for us now as a stud horse. And, then, we'd also like to take Tough Guy off the track."

Charles had heard enough. "No! At seven he's just coming into his own as a racehorse."

"That's true, also, but he's so solid—being by Predator, out of Matilda—that there already have been queries about breeding to him."

"What else?"

"That's it for the moment. George and I believe that those four stallions will give us a new solid base."

"But only *four*, son?"

"Quality, not quantity, Father. Building on that base, then, we'd go into the open market for stallions. Maybe in Kentucky, Virginia, or even New York."

"What's available?"

"Not much, honestly. I wrote to William Amis in North Carolina asking whether Sir Archie is for sale—he's by Diomed, you know—and Amis has answered that he's not. But I believe Sir Archie is the best stallion in the country right now, and I want to send four mares, including Matilda, to him for the next breeding season. That mating—should she have a colt—would give us another potential stallion for the future."

Charles sank down on the bale of hay again. "The future? It belongs to you young men now, doesn't it?"

Franklin didn't try to answer the rhetorical question.

"What else is it that you see in the future for Bon Marché?"

His son replied hesitantly. "Sir . . . we thought that perhaps you'd welcome less responsibility."

"So you suggested earlier," Dewey growled.

"And we believe it would make good sense for the two of us to divide those responsibilities on an even basis: me in charge of breeding; George running the racing operation."

"And me?"

"You'd still be in overall charge, of course."

"But not much, eh?" He forced himself to laugh, but he felt hollow somehow, a shell of what he had been. Empty.

"We're only thinking of the growth of Bon Marché, Father."

That was the telling statement. Charles slapped his hands together in that way he had of punctuating decisions. "Well, let's not delay it needlessly. You're both correct, obviously. This will give me more time for my grandchildren—a pleasing prospect, I'll tell you."

He turned to leave the barn, his steps slow. "Have the blacks prepare a proper grave for that gallant animal." He nodded toward the body of Premier Etoile.

"It's already being done, Father."

"Yes . . . well"—he frowned—"of course it is."

III

"WHAT are you going to tell your parents?"

Nathan Ludlum was genuinely concerned. His young wife had just told him that their efforts to make her pregnant had failed again.

"It's going to become obvious, pretty quickly, that you're not going to have a baby."

The Princess sat in their bed, pouting. "Maybe I should have known, *before* we were married, whether you were capable or not."

The bitterness of her words shocked him. "Princess, don't talk like that." He tried to take her in his arms, but she edged away from him. "It's just that we haven't been fortunate, that's all."

Alma May began to cry. "I can't face Mother with this! I can't!"

"When the time comes, Princess, we'll face it together."

"Why *can't* you give me a baby?" she snapped at him.

"Dear, it's nothing like that at all."

"How can you be so damned sure?"

Nathan sighed. The proof of his manly abilities was somewhere in Pittsburgh. But he couldn't use it. He thought now of Charles Dewey and of George, and he was very uneasy.

"Princess, baby," he cooed to her. And he stroked her and fondled her and kissed her, using all the skills he had learned on the stage to win her as an audience again. Bringing her total attention to him.

When he had, they tried once more.

IV

MARY Harrison Dewey had a son, a strapping boy whose arrival buoyed Charles Dewey's flagging spirits.

"This is what life is all about," he said to George, as they stood by Mary's bed admiring the baby. "To see your blood reproduced over and over again. To realize that there is continuity in this insane world."

Charles bent and kissed Mary as she held the infant in her arms. "Thank you, Mary," he said softly.

"Well, George," he said brightly as he straightened up, "this is my seventh grandchild. A lucky number, some say. Have you decided on a name for this prodigy?"

"Yes, sir," his son answered quickly. "Charles Dewey the Second!"

"Oh, my!" He embraced George. "Oh, my!"

Mattie, watching the happy scene, brushed a tear from her cheek.

"Charles Dewey the Second," the grandfather said, addressing the baby, "may God favor you as he has the grateful man whose name you now carry."

He took Mattie's hand and they left the room.

"You might have consulted me about the name," Mary snapped angrily.

"Mary, there are times when the spontaneous decision is the only one to make." George smiled. "Couldn't you see how happy Father was?"

"Yes. But what of my father? He might be happy, too, if the baby were named for him."

"Mary, stop it! This should be a joyful moment."

His wife sighed. "Yes, Georgie. And it is. It's just that . . ."

George kissed her. "Mary, darling, I've never denied you anything, but this . . . well, it just had to be. And if we ever have a daughter, dear, she's going to be named Martha, for my mother."

Mary frowned.

"Do you remember what I told you when I asked you to marry me?"

"Georgie," Mary giggled, "you said so many naughty things."

He laughed. "I did, didn't I? But the most important thing I said was that the Dewey family would always come first."

V

It was stuffy in the small storage room, and dusty. Pieces of scenery were jammed in without any special order, making it difficult for them to move around. And there was no light.

Alma May kissed him. Desperately.

"Christ, I don't know about this, Alma!"

"You said you wanted me."

"I do," the young man said, "but if Nat—"

"Nathan's not going to know." She fondled him in the darkness, trying to arouse him. Trying to arouse herself.

His name was Gerald Parker, an actor in Ludlum's company. A pleasant enough fellow, but Alma May wouldn't have given him a second look in ordinary circumstances. The circumstances, however, were not ordinary for the Princess. She *needed* to be pregnant.

Groping with her hands, she found an open spot on the floor, pulling him down on top of her, loosening her clothing to make it easy for him. They came together, and he groaned slightly. Alma May put her fingers on his lips to silence him.

"Princess!" The shout came from the hallway outside the storage room.

"Oh, hell!"

"Don't stop." Even though she said it in a whisper, it was clearly an order.

"Princess!"

Alma May dug her fingers into his back. "For God's sake, Jerry, come! Come!"

The door of the storage room flew open, freezing them. It let in only a little light from the hallway, and the couple was hidden behind a piece of scenery.

"Is anyone in there?" Nathan shouted.

There was not even the sound of breathing.

"Damn it, where is she!" Nathan said aloud.

Without warning, the dust in the room made Parker sneeze.

"Who's in here?" Nathan called.

He stepped into the room, searching. And then he saw the dim outline of two figures on the floor. "Who in the hell is it?"

Nathan moved closer. The figures became recognizable. "You bastard!" Reaching down, he grabbed Parker by the collar, smashing a fist into his face, sending him sprawling into a piece of scenery that gave away under the impact, breaking and tearing.

Alma May cried out in fright.

Her husband, cursing, yanked her to her feet, propelling her out into the hallway, throwing her against the opposite wall. She collapsed in a terrified heap.

"Why?" he screamed at her. "Why?"

Parker, seeing his chance to escape, ran off down the hallway and out of the building.

"You bitch!"

"Nathan, please!" Alma May was weeping. "It's just that you weren't able—"

He kicked her. Viciously. In the stomach.

She shrieked in pain, gasping. "No, Nathan, no!" She tried to crawl away, and he kicked her again. She stopped moving and lost consciousness.

Nathan dropped to the floor, cradling her head in his lap. "Damn you," he said, "all this to cover a lie."

He thought then of her father and of his brother-in-law, and he shuddered.

VI

In truth, Nathan Ludlum was a consummate actor.

He had to be to carry off what had been decided after the incident in the theater storage room.

He carried the Princess to a doctor in Nashville, where it was discovered she had three broken ribs.

"If you had seen the height from which she fell off that ladder, Doctor,"

Nathan said, "I think you'd say that she was fortunate it's not more than a few broken ribs."

"How high would you say?"

"Twelve, maybe fourteen feet."

"Hmmm. She must have fallen on something to make such pronounced bruises on her abdomen." He pointed to the ugly purple marks made by Nathan's boot.

Alma May groaned as the doctor pulled the bandaging tight around her ribs.

"Well, the stage was littered with scenery," Nathan explained calmly. "She could have struck any number of objects."

He watched intently as the doctor finished his work.

"Sir," the actor began hesitantly, "my wife is pregnant."

The doctor frowned. "How long?"

"A month. No more than two, certainly."

"Well, this kind of trauma could cause her to miscarry, of course. But the fetus at that stage of development is very small. If she does abort now, it shouldn't be too dangerous for a healthy young woman. But you'll have to watch her, of course."

"I certainly will, Doctor." Nathan was showing the proper amount of loving concern.

"Now, I don't think you ought to try to get her back to Bon Marché in a carriage right now," the physician went on. "Perhaps you could make her comfortable for a couple of days at one of the inns."

"Of course. We'll go to Mr. Parker's establishment."

"Fine! I'll look in on her tomorrow morning."

At the Nashville Inn, Nathan made Alma May as comfortable as possible, then sat by the bed looking at her. She had said virtually nothing since the incident at the theater.

"May I ask, Princess," Nathan said quietly, "what is the next scene you plan for your little drama?"

"There's no need to be sarcastic."

Her husband shrugged. "I'm left with little else."

"You frightened me, Nathan," she said. "I thought you meant to kill me."

"I did."

"What stopped you, then?"

"What do you want me to say? Because I love you? Because I was concerned about our baby-to-be?"

"You're horrid!"

"What stopped me, Princess, was my own well-being. My selfishness, to put the correct face on it. I want that theater, Alma May. God help me, but I want it enough to put up with you."

"You never loved me!" Tears began.

"Don't play the tragedienne with me, Alma. Remember that I've seen the best in that role. We're stuck with each other. You because you're trapped with your silly little lie about being pregnant. And me because . . . well, because I haven't enough integrity to turn my back on the largess of the fine Deweys."

The Princess was quiet for a moment. "So what do we do?"

"We play this scene out to the end. It's terribly unfortunate, of course, but your *accident*, darling, is going to bring on a miscarriage. I suggest that it happen when you have your next period; with all that blood, who's to know the difference."

"The doctor will."

"It will be too late to call the doctor." A wry smile. "Nature will have taken over."

She looked at him as if seeing him for the first time. "You're really quite cold-blooded, aren't you?"

"Yes, when necessary," he admitted. "We're a matched pair, you know. It took a cold-blooded woman to carry off that assignation with Gerald. I only hope, after all this, that he hasn't impregnated you."

"He didn't."

Nathan Ludlum guffawed. "I was Nathan-to-the-rescue, then, intruding before the moment of ecstasy."

She tried not to at first, but she also laughed, seeing the black humor in their situation. "Yes, damn it, you did!"

"Poor Gerald! He's probably been ruined for life. He'll never be able to be with a woman again without remembering that door being opened."

The laugh died in his throat.

"And neither, Princess, will I."

39

EVERYWHERE the eye could see there were crowds along the banks of the Cumberland River. It was a chilly early March morning, a Thursday, in 1819.

For weeks the chief topic of conversation in Nashville had been the inauguration of steamboat service by the *General Jackson,* a luxury vessel built at the astounding cost of sixteen thousand dollars. And now the great day had arrived!

Several days before, Charles Dewey had staked out a vantage point near the principal dock at Nashville, at almost the exact spot where he had landed with his log rafts nearly twenty-one years earlier. He stood there, with five of his grandchildren, contemplating those years. Not dissatisfied, certainly, with what they had brought. But apprehensive.

His entire life had become his grandchildren, and while that pleased him, it left him feeling somehow unfulfilled. He had discussed that the night before with his son-in-law, August Schimmel.

"I have a feeling," he had said to the publisher, "that life is passing me by. I've been put out to pasture, and I don't like it."

Stoically German, Schimmel merely nodded. He had grown used to Dewey's monologues in their late-evening sessions in the drawing room. A ritual of sorts those meetings had become—an hour or two of conversation, always with sherry, or no conversation at all. Charles had laughingly dubbed the nightly chats "the Dewey-Schimmel confabs to solve the ills of the world."

"Franklin and George are doing things with the horse business," he had said with a complaining tone, "that I never dreamed possible. They like to maintain that I'm still in charge, but I'm not. And Lee? Well, he's off in the world, working for your newspaper, being a part of the history this country is making."

Charles tapped his copy of the *Nashville Monitor.* "This dispatch he wrote from Pittsburgh, for example." He started to read: "On the National Road in Pennsylvania these days a traveler is never out of sight of family groups, before and behind, in every imaginable conveyance, even some on bare feet, pressing toward the Ohio. The old America of the East seems to be breaking up and moving westward.' "

"Your son is a very perceptive observer," Schimmel commented.

"That's just it! He's out there, with a role to play, while I"—he shrugged—"I just sit here and vegetate."

"Nonsense. You're the mortar that holds this family together."

"Hmmm. Perhaps." Wryly: "There are days when the mortar shows a few cracks."

"Lee's drawing of the *General Jackson*," the publisher said, trying to make the conversation less somber, "has certainly excited the people of this community."

"It has. I suspect it was worth the money it cost you to send him to Pitts-burgh, where the vessel was being built."

"Absolutely. And I expect the trip to pay other dividends, too. Lee will be bringing with him on the steamboat information he gathered in Ohio on sev-eral newspaper properties that have become available. I hope we'll be able to acquire newspapers in Cincinnati, Columbia, and Marietta."

"That's rather ambitious, isn't it?"

"Yes, but I see it as only the beginning. Just as soon as I can, I'll send Lee to St. Louis to investigate the possibilities there. And I hope to visit Chicago for the same reason."

"A lot of money will be involved, August."

"Yes."

Dewey went to the sideboard to pour them another sherry.

"I've been thinking for some time that I ought to have another interest," he said. "Now, I know that you probably don't need my money, but . . . hell, August, you could halve your risk if you'd let me come in with you."

The publisher was surprised. "You'd really want to do that?"

"More than anything. Maybe slowly at first . . . Let me help you finance the St. Louis project, if there is to be one. Or Chicago."

"I can't think of anyone I'd rather have as a partner, Charles."

"Great!" He paused. "Until we get this thing under way it might be best to keep Mattie . . . uh . . . uninformed, shall we say? She seems to think that I gamble too much, anyway."

Schimmel smiled for the first time. "Whatever you wish, Charles."

"Well . . ." Charles clapped his hands together. "I think I ought to get to bed so that I can be up bright and early to take those youngsters to see the steamboat tomorrow."

From the distance came the full-throated bass call of the steamboat whistle, bringing Dewey's thoughts to the moment at hand. Everyone on the landing was cheering, although the *General Jackson* couldn't be seen as yet.

"Look down that way," Charles shouted over the noise to his grandchildren, pointing his finger. "It'll be coming around that bend, so keep your eyes glued there!"

Franklin's three children were with him: Carrie, Richard, and Albert. And the Schimmels' twin daughters, Joy and Hope. Charles held eight-year-old

Carrie and six-year-old Richard by the hand. The others, all close to five years old, were being shepherded by two of the Negro housemaids. Horace was there, too, with baskets of food and hot drinks.

Once again the steamboat whistle sounded, closer this time. A band on the dock struck up the popular tune, "The Eighth of January," commemorating Jackson's victory at New Orleans. Managers of the welcome celebration for Nashville's first steamboat had hoped that Old Hickory would be there personally to see the *General Jackson* arrive at Nashville, but the soldier was in Washington defending his unauthorized military invasion of Florida in pursuit of the Seminoles. A successful defense, as it turned out. Just two weeks earlier the public had learned that a treaty had been concluded with Spain, ceding the vast Florida Territory to the United States for a payment of five million dollars. Thus, Andy Jackson was an even bigger hero than had been anticipated when plans were made for the building of a steamboat in his honor.

"Grandfather, look!" little Carrie shrieked. "There it is! There it is!"

The splendid new boat came into view, the cord on its whistle held down so that its greeting was constant. It seemed that the band tried to play louder, and there was no question that the human roar increased in volume.

Carrie and Richard danced excitedly, tugging hard at Dewey's firm grasp. The five-year-olds, less impressed, were playing their own game of tag around the full skirts of the black housemaids.

"Look, Grandfather!" Richard shouted. "There's Uncle Lee! There's Uncle Lee!"

In his excitement he broke away from Dewey's grip and ran toward the edge of the bank, waving wildly to his uncle aboard the steamboat.

A foot caught on a rock. He was in the icy waters!

Charles pushed Carrie toward the housemaids, leaping into the water. One-armed Horace, after hesitating just an instant, followed him.

They couldn't find the boy! They couldn't find him!

Dewey plunged beneath the surface, but the sediment stirred up by the giant paddle wheels of the steamboat had made the waters opaque. He was as ineffective as a blind man!

He came up, gasping for air. So did Horace, thrashing wildly with one arm. Their eyes met, companions in terror.

Several other men were in the water now, joining the search. Charles dove again, sweeping his arms in wide circles, hoping that his hands would touch something. They didn't.

With his lungs seeming ready to burst, he surfaced again.

And Horace was there, his strong arm holding little Richard by the collar, the tiny head lolling to the side, the eyes open. Glassy.

Dewey grabbed the boy, thrusting him upward to waiting hands on the riverbank, then scrambling ashore himself.

Someone had already summoned a doctor, and he was working on the youngster, trying to force air into him. Feverishly. Trying. Trying.

The doctor sighed. His head was raised from his task and he shook it sadly.

"I'm sorry, Squire Dewey."

And on the dock the voices were raised in a cheer for the *General Jackson*. And the band played a gay tune.

II

ANNOYED, Charles adjusted his new spectacles.

"Damn!" *Those fellows had a lot to learn about making eyeglasses.*

He sat at his desk, the family Bible open in front of him, a pen in his hand. He stared at the names written there: a simple chronicle of the Dewey family. Inadequate, really, telling nothing of the joys. Or the heartaches.

The spectacles were jerked off; placed down roughly.

He ran a hand over his eyes. *Incompetent fools! The only thing those glasses did was make my eyes water!*

The pen was dipped into the inkwell. He wrote the new words carefully: "Daughter, Martha Dewey, to George and Mary (Harrison) Dewey, May 4, 1819."

Although he tried not to see it, the name of Richard Dewey was there. The Bible hadn't been opened since that day . . .

He'd have to do it sooner or later. Once more he wrote, next to Richard's name this time: "Gone to meet His Maker, March 11, 1819."

Charles studied that for a moment. He added one more word: "Drowned."

Mattie entered the drawing room. "Well, the doctor has just left."

"And what does he say?"

His wife shook her head. "Amantha's just not fighting. The pneumonia has gotten worse. I'm so afraid, Charles."

"And Franklin?"

"He's strong." A pause. "Like you."

He contemplated her words. "Like me? No, I don't think so, dear. He's much more level-headed. You know, I actually believe that he doesn't hate me, even though I killed his son."

"Charles, you've got to stop saying things like that!"

"Why? It's true, isn't it?"

"It's *not* true!" She was quivering with anger.

"Well . . ." He shrugged.

There was a long silence.

"Charles, you ought to go see Amantha," Mattie said.

"I can't face her."

"This false guilt is going to drive you mad. You've got to face the reality that it was an accident and nothing more!"

"If I had had a proper hold on his hand—"

"Damn you, Charles, stop it! You're going to drive me mad as well."

Dewey didn't comment. Instead, he picked up the spectacles and put them on again, squinting through them, going through a charade of seeming to test their effectiveness.

"You know, Mattie, I don't believe I need these things at all."

He opened the drawer of the desk, shoved the glasses into it, slamming it shut.

III

IT was just a small cemetery, set in a grove of tulip poplars some three hundred yards removed from the main house surrounded by a neat stone wall erected by the slaves. For all the careful planning that had gone into Bon Marché, no provision had been made for a burial place. Perhaps no one wanted to face the reality of that need.

When six-year-old Richard drowned, the need became paramount. It was Louise who suggested the quiet little grove for the final resting place of her nephew. And a tiny grave was dug there and a tiny oak coffin was lowered into the ground there.

Only then did the slaves begin the wall—strangely, without orders. Indeed, without even seeking permission. No one knew which of the blacks had initiated the project. It seemed to just begin one day, growing a few feet on every passage of the sun, when time could be taken from other duties.

They began to call it "Richie's Place."

It was to become more than that.

Quiet, introverted Amantha Dewey, the shock of the sudden death of her firstborn son not even allowing her to weep, became ill. "Pneumonia," the doctor had said. Maybe, medically, it was. But there are many mysteries that make up the human form. If it can be said that one has a will to live, the reverse can also be true. Amantha chose the latter.

She lingered into May, and that's all it had been: a lingering.

The Deweys stood now, heads bowed in grief, as the Presbyterian minister from town intoned the words of the commitment ritual. And they watched as Franklin stepped forward to sprinkle a handful of earth into his wife's grave, the noise of it striking the wooden box seeming to thunder through Richie's Place.

Charles turned away from it—from the scene and the sounds—and shuddered. He had not wanted to be there. Mattie had insisted that he come.

He was not the Charles Dewey they had known. His hair was in disarray, there was a stubble of whiskers on his face. He had drawn an old tattered shawl about him, as if it was cold but this May day was warm. This Charles Dewey was a wraith, not a real man. And not a sober one, either. A drunken specter.

It was over.

Charles hurried away, ahead of the others.

"Grandfather, wait for me!"

The child's voice stopped him. Carrie ran up to him, taking his hand.

"Will you read to me, Grandfather?"

"Oh, Carrie, some other time, perhaps."

Her sweet round face was troubled. "Don't you love me anymore, Grandfather?"

Dewey fell to his knees, gathering his granddaughter into his arms, hugging her tightly. "Of course I love you, Carrie." A sob. "More than life itself."

IV

"I TELL you, Franklin, it's not normal," George was saying to his brother. "Father spends every waking moment with Carrie. She's his *only* interest."

"You're overreacting."

"Am I? It seems to me that, as Carrie's father, you'd be more concerned than the rest of us."

"About what? Do you believe that Carrie's in any danger?"

"Of course not. But—"

"Are you worried about Father's sanity?"

"Well, it's—"

"Or would you rather have our Father the way he was at Amantha's funeral? Not caring about anything, sick with guilt about Richard's death, and drunk?"

"Of course I wouldn't!"

Franklin sighed. "Then leave it alone! I know this about it all: together they've saved each other. Little Carrie lost her brother and her mother in just a short period of time. Maybe she didn't understand it all, but I saw the grief in her. She turned to her grandfather, and he comforted her. On the other side of the coin, Father was convinced that he was responsible for Richard's drowning; he could find no reason to go on—with anything. Carrie gave him a reason.

"And have you seen what they've done together? I don't think I've ever seen a nine-year-old ride as well as Carrie does. And she reads better than most adults, and he has taught her skills in mathematics far above her age. She's interested in everything, because Father has made her interested: in trees and flowers and animals and the heavens and . . . my God, George, they've accomplished a miracle together!"

George wasn't fully convinced. "I don't know, Franklin. To me he seems to have withdrawn from the real world. I mean, President Monroe comes to Nashville, and he doesn't bother to accept the invitation to meet him. That's not Father, you know."

"George, George, be realistic. While the President was here, he was being fawned over by Andy Jackson." He laughed. "You know how Father would have reacted to that."

"Yes, but—"

"You went to the reception for Monroe, didn't you?"

"Yes."

"So Bon Marché was adequately represented, it seems to me. And what did you learn from meeting Monroe?"

"Well, he was most impressive, Franklin. And Mary was much taken with what he said when he visited the Nashville Female Academy. She tells me that the President expressed the view that women have the same claims on education and opportunities for gain as do the men."

Franklin laughed loudly. "Be careful, George. That sounds like dangerous talk to me. Mary may decide that she wants to wear trousers."

"Damn you!"

His brother continued to laugh. "No offense, George. But I don't really think Father missed anything by not meeting Monroe, do you?"

"Perhaps not," George admitted sullenly.

"And as for his . . . uh . . . preoccupation with Carrie, perhaps you ought to leave that to me, eh?" He quickly changed the subject. "That Sir Archie–Matilda colt—have you decided on a name for him?"

"Sir Matt, I believe. He's going to be a good one, Franklin. And I thought Mattie might be please with the name. I remember how delighted she was when Matilda . . ."

V

MATTIE was pleased with the colt's name, but not with what Charles had presented to her as a *fait accompli*.

"Charles! One hundred thousand dollars! And in an enterprise in which you have no experience!"

"I trust August," he replied.

"So do I! And I have no basic objection to investing in your children's— *our* children's —enterprises. But a hundred thousand dollars in a newspaper in St. Louis, and established as a trust for Carrie! I don't see the need for it. August has money of his own, and it seems to me that if there is to be a trust fund set up in any newspaper operations, August and Louise ought to do it for their own daughters."

"August was willing to let me in on this," Charles tried to explain.

"And you could think of nothing but to involve Carrie's future in what can be no more than a very risky venture?"

"Carrie's future is important to me."

"And to me, Charles. But I think you should realize that Carrie has a father! A perfectly capable father. You can't be everything to that child, Charles. Not grandfather, father, mother, and now *banker* to her. There has to be a limit!"

Charles had heard enough. "The commitment has been made," he said quietly, determinedly. "Carrie Dewey is now the half owner of a newspaper in St. Louis."

Mattie sighed. "I don't know why I try to talk to you anymore."

She went to the window of the drawing room, staring out at Bon Marché. Charles Dewey had built what she was looking at—with her help, of course. But it had been his vision, his determination, his wealth that had built it.

Turning, she went back to the chair opposite her husband. "There is one other thing I think we ought to talk about, Charles."

He nodded.

"It's the Princess," she frowned.

"Oh, I was under the impression that the theater was going quite well."

"The *theater* is fine, but—"

Dewey was suddenly angry. "If that bastard Ludlum has—"

"Charles, please! Can't you ever let me finish a thought?"

"I'm sorry. Please go on."

"It's not Ludlum, Charles, but Alma May. There have been entirely too many stories of her escapades in Nashville. She's been seen in the company of other men at numerous taverns, in circumstances that are less than discreet."

"Gossip?"

"Unfortunately, no. Two nights ago Louise saw her going into the City

Hotel, quite intoxicated, in the company of two men, also drunk. Louise followed her in and saw her disappear up the stairs to the rooms." Mattie screwed up her face in disgust. "Of course, Louise was in no position to follow her farther."

"The men? Did Louise recognize them?"

"No, it was quite late and dark."

"And Ludlum? What of him?"

"I don't know." She looked at him pleadingly. "I was hoping, Charles, that you could investigate this thing. If the Princess is in trouble—"

"Of course. I was thinking of taking Carrie to Nashville anyway for a little shopping tour. Maybe I'll stop at the theater. A surprise visit, you know."

Mattie struggled to restrain her temper. "This is not something in which you can involve that child, Charles."

"Hmmm. Perhaps not. If I can find time in the next week or so—"

"Tomorrow, Charles," she insisted, but keeping her voice under control.

"Carrie and I had planned a picnic for tomorrow."

Mattie screamed. No words, just a scream of frustration.

"What?" He seemed genuinely perplexed.

"George is right! Your preoccupation with Carrie has unhinged you! The Princess is in serious trouble and you prattle on like a madman about some damned picnic!"

His reply seemed calmly reasoned. "If tomorrow is what you wish, dear, tomorrow it will be."

40

It was ten o'clock when Dewey rode into Nashville.

The theater was locked tight. Securing his horse on the hitching rail in front, he walked around the back of the building and mounted the stairway to the comfortable living quarters that had been built above the auditorium.

He banged on the door. There was no answer. Again. Silence. A third knock.

A sleepy male voice called out: "Who's there?"

"Charles . . . Charles Dewey!"

There were shuffling noises from inside, and a key was turned. A disheveled Nathan Ludlum opened the door, his eyes squinting in the midmorning sunlight.

"I'm sorry if I've awakened you," Charles said easily.

"No, no . . . that's all right. It's just that we sleep late on those days when we have no performances."

"Hmmm."

Ludlum stood uneasily in the doorway.

"I just thought I'd come and pay you a little visit," Dewey explained. "It has been a long time since I've been here."

"Yes, it has. But . . . uh . . . we weren't expecting guests."

Charles laughed. "Guests? I'm family."

The actor stood aside, gesturing his father-in-law inside. The door opened into a small kitchen. It was badly disordered; soiled dishes were piled everywhere.

"As you can see," Ludlum apologized, "we really *weren't* expecting anyone."

"It seems that my knocking didn't wake the Princess."

"Well . . ." Nathan was decidedly uncomfortable. "No, sir, it didn't." He smiled. "Suppose, sir, you allow us time to get dressed and presentable, and then we can meet you, for a late breakfast perhaps, at the Nashville Inn. In a half-hour, shall we say?"

Charles was disquieted. "That won't be necessary, Nathan. We can just sit here and chat for a few minutes." He pulled a chair away from the table and sat down. "I have other things to do in Nashville before I return to Bon Marché. And I've already had breakfast."

"Yes, well . . ." Ludlum cleared his throat. "Alma May isn't here at this moment."

"Already at work, is she?"

His son-in-law sank down in a chair opposite him. "No, sir." The voice was hard. "She hasn't been here all night."

Dewey's eyebrows rose. "Oh?"

"As a matter of fact, she hasn't been here for two days."

"Two days!"

Ludlum nodded.

"For God's sake, man, let's stop this nonsense! Where in the hell is she?!"

"I can only guess."

"I want some explanations, and I want them right now!"

Nathan drew a deep breath. "Our marriage . . . hasn't been going too well lately. Alma May has found it necessary—oh, God, that's the wrong word—has found it more to her liking to seek the . . . companionship of other men."

"And you permit it?"

The actor shrugged.

"There's more to this than you're telling me. I want it all, Nathan!"

"Of course—you should know. Alma May was not pregnant when we were married. She said that only to overcome her mother's objections to the marriage. But we both thought that . . . well, that we could set it right by having her become pregnant immediately after we were married." He sighed. "It just didn't work out that way. The Princess, then, put the blame on me."

Charles was remembering the report George had gotten on Ludlum's fathering of an illegitimate child in Pittsburgh.

"She set out to prove that point," Nathan continued, "by attempting to become pregnant by . . . others. First there was an actor in the company . . ."

Nathan gave Dewey the details of having found his wife in the storage room with a colleague, of the violent confrontation, of the trumped-up story about a miscarriage.

Charles fought his growing anger. "And now—right at this moment—do you know where she is?"

"I have a pretty good idea."

"Find her," Dewey ordered, "and bring her back here. You have one hour!"

II

AUGUST Schimmel walked with Charles from the newspaper office to the Dewey Theater.

"I really appreciate this, August," Charles said. "I need your calming influence. I'm afraid of what my temper might do."

Schimmel patted him lightly on the arm, reassuringly.

The two men mounted the stairway to the theater living quarters, Charles opening the door without knocking. They found Alma May sitting disconsolately at the small table; her husband was leaning against the wall some four or five feet away from her.

Dewey just stared at his daughter for a moment, his arms stiff at his sides, the hands working angrily.

"Alma," he said coldly, "I don't give a damn what happens to you! I have only one concern right now: the well-being of your mother. If she knew how evil you are, what a tramp you've become—"

"Daddy, please, let me explain!"

"No explanation could possibly erase what I already know! And I don't want to know any more of your . . . *filth*. My purpose is to rectify this situation, to try to put a face on it so that it doesn't destroy Mattie."

The Princess sobbed.

"And spare me the tears! First, let me tell you something that *he* should have told you at the beginning." He gestured in the direction of his son-in-law. "He fathered a child in Pittsburgh more than two years ago!"

The young woman gasped.

"It doesn't matter any longer that he left the girl to fend for herself when she became pregnant. Nathan will just have to live with that. The important point, now, is that he's capable, and you can stop—you *will* stop—this insanity of trying to prove him inadequate. It's *you*, Alma May, who has the problem, not Nathan!"

"Oh, God! Oh, God!" She was weeping now.

"We are left with the reality of patching this up somehow. And it's going to be done this way. You and Nathan will make a public display of reconciliation. I don't give a damn what you do in your bedroom, but publicly you will be husband and wife once more.

"And if there is one more report, Alma, like those I've already heard, you will be totally cut off from the Deweys. You'll not get a penny more! You and your husband will have to find another way to live—and *not* in Nashville! Do you understand?"

"Yes, Daddy," the Princess sobbed.

"Furthermore, starting next week I will expect to see you at least once a week at Bon Marché for dinner. And you'll come there without your problems! Understood?"

"Yes, Daddy."

"Nathan?"

"Yes, sir."

Charles clapped his hands together. "One final word, Alma." He moved to her so that he stood over her. "Don't look to me for forgiveness. I'll play my role for the sake of Mattie. But you . . . you've acted like a whore, and so you will always be in my eyes!"

Charles whirled and was out the door quickly, Schimmel following him.

As they walked down the stairway, the publisher said quietly: "That last, Charles—it didn't have to be said."

"It was a moment for the truth," Dewey grunted.

III

THERE was an even greater truth in the inevitability of the passage of time. Charles felt it as a weight pressing down on him, as if time had a gravity of its own.

He was used to making his own opportunities; he liked to believe that he guided his own destiny. But the forces of time seemed to be taking that from him; forces at work in his family, and in the nation, perplexed him, even defied him.

The flood of immigrants into the western region of the country was changing the face of it. He read a dispatch in the *Nashville Monitor* that disquieted him. An English visitor had written: "The practical liberty of America is found in its great space and small population. Good land, dog-cheap everywhere, and for nothing, if you go for it, gives as much elbow room to every man as he chooses to take. Poor laborers, from every country in Europe, hear of this cheap land, are attracted to it, perhaps without any political opinions. They come, they toil, they prosper. This is the real liberty of America."

Twenty years earlier, Charles Dewey would have reveled in such a report. Now he wasn't so sure that what was happening was right. More and more, when he rode into Nashville, he found the streets crowded with men and women with unfamiliar faces. Strangers in *his* town. Strangers doing strange things.

Why there was that fellow, Ralph Earl, one of Andy Jackson's intimates, who was digging around in that Indian mound along the banks of the Cumberland, trying to uncover the secrets of the aborigines who had inhabited the area long before the white men had come. He's toying with sacred matters, Dewey thought, and he ought to leave the graves alone.

In a more mundane matter, there was talk of providing Nashville with a water system: a reservoir, with underground pipes running to every dwelling and business place. And at what cost? It seemed that everywhere money was being spent on grand schemes. In New York State there was begun something called the Erie Canal; it was stupidity to think that such a thing could be dug with pick and shovel, at whatever cost. And closer to home there was the federal government's vaunted Military Road—called the General Jackson Road, for God's sake!—connecting Nashville and New Orleans, just to reduce the distance between the two cities by two hundred miles. Money was literally being poured into the project.

Charles discussed all this one night with his publisher son-in-law.

"August, we're moving too fast," he insisted. "The country is being expanded beyond any hope of doing it with any intelligence. New states seem to be in place every time you turn around: Indiana, Mississippi, Illinois, Alabama, Missouri. Now we even have the Territory of Florida—and what the hell are we going to do with that?"

"Your attitude surprises me," Schimmel had said. "I seem to remember you talking enthusiastically at one time about the expansion of the nation to the Pacific Ocean."

"Yes, but with prudent speed. It's not unlike a horse race you know. Pace is all-important. Too much speed at the beginning will make it impossible to have anything left for the stretch run."

"A colorful analogy, but hardly applicable to the growth of a nation. What is happening now, it seems to me, is the American destiny. Our expansion is not only necessary, Charles, it is inevitable."

Dewey shook his head. "No, August, you've missed the undercurrent of what is happening. Regional animosities are coming to the surface. The New England states are suspicious of what is happening in the West and the South; they resent this growth, this apparent new wealth of an area that now has one-quarter of the nation's people."

"And that's as it should be," the publisher contended. "It won't be too many years before this area will elect a President."

Charles groaned. "Andy Jackson, I suppose!"

"Yes, and why not?"

"God help the country if Andy ever heads it!"

But that was only drawing-room talk between two friends. What bothered the master of Bon Marché even more was the loss of his last vestiges of control over the plantation.

It came clear to him one morning as he strolled among the horse barns, jollying the blacks, feeling good about being there. In his element. At the stallion barn, the good feeling evaporated as quickly as dew in the morning sunshine.

In one stall was a stallion he didn't recognize—a well-muscled dark bay giant with fire in his eyes.

"Who's this?" he asked of one of the grooms mucking out the stalls.

"Oh, dat's Eagle, suh."

"A new boarder, eh?"

"No, suh. Dat's a new stallion what Mistah Franklin done bring in from England."

"When?"

" 'Most a week ago, suh. He already been introduced to some ladies"—the slave chortled—"and he laik it, too."

Charles went looking for his son, his temper rising with each stride.

"I see we have a new stallion," he said to Franklin, making no effort to hide his annoyance.

"Yes. How do you like him?"

"Since I don't know anything about him at all, I can't very well make an appraisal, can I?"

Franklin calmly gave his father the details of Eagle's pedigree. "He's just the kind of new blood we need, Father."

"And you made that decision on your own?"

"Yes. Well, I did talk it over with George."

"And what of me?"

His son hesitated. "I was under the impression that I was in charge of the breeding."

"And I was under the impression," Charles snapped, "that I was still the owner of Bon Marché!"

"Of course. But you've been preoccupied—"

"Superseded, you mean!"

"Nothing like that at all, Father," Franklin answered, his own temper flaring. "You can't argue, sir, that you have shown little interest lately. It occurs to me that this is the first time in several weeks that I've seen you here at the barns."

Dewey struggled to maintain his composure. "And how much of *my* money was spent for this animal?"

"Seventy-five hundred plus the cost of bringing him here from England."

"And you believe you have the unquestioned authority to spend that kind of money without my approval?"

"I did get Mattie's permission," Franklin replied defensively.

Charles stared at him. "Mattie knew of this?"

"Naturally. She manages the Bon Marché finances, doesn't she?"

The bald truth of what his son had said came through to Dewey. He shrugged, walking away disconsolately.

Perhaps he had neglected to keep in touch, Charles admitted to himself, but what difference did it make? Franklin and George and Mattie were going to do exactly as they pleased, no matter what the head of the family said.

It was clear that he had been left with nothing to do but to chronicle the growth of the Deweys in the family Bible. George and Mary Dewey had added two more grandsons to the clan: Statler in 1820 and George, Jr., early in 1822. He guessed that the second generation of the Dewey family was in place.

And what did Charles know of them all? To him they were merely names in a Bible! Except for Carrie, of course.

Carrie—at least she was his. Everywhere Charles went, the youngster tagged after him like a shadow. They rode together, played together, and studied together. He bought her a new geography volume of the expanding country and they spent hours together going over it.

"Have you ever been to New York, Grandfather?"

"No."

"Philadelphia?"

"Yes," he said sadly, "I went there on my honeymoon with your grandmother."

"Grandmother Mattie?"

"No, darling, with your real grandmother. Your father's mother: Martha Statler Dewey. You remember that we've discussed her before."

"Oh, sure. Was Philadelphia grand, Grandfather?"

"Hmmm." He grinned at the child. "Yes, I suppose it was. It's been many years since—"

"I'd like to see those cities. Philadelphia and New York."

"Would you, now?" An idea was born. "Well, maybe . . ."

IV

"I'VE made a decision," Dewey said at dinner several nights later. He had thought of nothing else: the idea was set in stone. "I'm going to campaign a racing string of Bon Marché horses from Nashville to New York. And Carrie's going to go with me."

Mattie gasped. Franklin and George frowned.

"Yes," Charles went on determinedly, "I'll make a selection of . . . oh, let's say twenty horses. We'll take in the fall meeting at Charleston and then move on to Augusta and Virginia for the meetings at Petersburg and Richmond, and then Baltimore and finally, New York."

"But, Father," Franklin objected, "the cost of mounting such a trip would be—"

"Well within the capabilities of Bon Marché," Charles interrupted. He looked at his wife. "Unless you're going to tell me that we are suddenly impoverished."

"You know I'm not going to tell you that," Mattie answered heatedly, "but what you propose isn't practical, Charles. I mean, making such a long trip with a little girl—"

"We'll take one of the housemaids with us."

"And then there's your health to consider. After all, you're fifty-seven."

"And in good health! Also, I'm not ready to have myself thought of as a vegetable. If it's felt that the Bon Marché coffers can't, or won't, support this venture, then I'll just have to seek financing from other sources."

He winked at August Schimmel, who sat across the table from him.

"Damn you, Charles!" Mattie said angrily. "You suddenly come up with a scheme that defies common sense, and you expect us to agree to it without discussion. There would be so many things to plan."

"And I would plan them!" He got to his feet. "No, let me be more emphatic: I *will* do them!"

He clapped his hands together.

41

DEWEY got his way. Yet, he had doubts. Could he care properly for Carrie on such a long trip; maybe even one with some hazards? She was a bright child, and a self-sufficient one, but she was only eleven years old. He had once undertaken an arduous journey with small children and had vowed that he would never do that again. And now—?

Nevertheless, he went ahead with his planning, trying to convince himself that the adventure would be the best thing that could happen to a youngster at this time, trying to dismiss his doubts.

Help came from an unlikely source.

After one of the obligatory Bon Marché dinners attended by Alma May and Nathan Ludlum, the Princess sought him out. It was the first time she had talked directly to him since the bitter incident in the theater apartment.

"Could we walk, Father? Sometimes I think your drawing room has ears."

They strolled together, both of them uneasy, across the wide lawn.

"Father," Alma May said, "Nathan wants to leave Nashville."

"Oh, where will you be going?"

"Just Nathan, not me."

The sudden anger. "If that bastard Ludlum thinks he can—"

"Please, Father." She laid a hand on his arm. "Listen to me this time. Nathan and I are dreadfully unhappy. We don't have a marriage any longer, as you can imagine. It's my fault and it's his fault, too, I guess. We're going to get a divorce."

"Divorce! That's unheard of among the Deweys—"

"Always the Deweys, isn't it?" she said gravely. "Well, the Deweys can't live my life. Or poor Nathan's. If there is a hell on earth we've made it for each other. And we've finally decided that we've had enough of hell. And the Deweys be damned!"

Charles knew she was right.

"I wanted to tell you this tonight," the Princess went on, "because I have a proposal. I want to go with you on your trip. I can help you care for Carrie."

Her father shrugged. "And what of Mattie?"

"She'll probably be glad not to have me around for a while. I'd be an embarrassment to her during the divorce."

"One problem: what's to become of the theater?"

"Nathan will find a competent manger, and it should continue to show a profit for Bon Marché."

"You have it all planned out, I see."

"I'm my father's daughter," Alma May said softly.

II

MATTIE traced tiny patterns on her husband's bare chest with her fingertips. This man to whom she had been married for a quarter of a century, who often infuriated her—too often, who was going to leave now on a venture of which she didn't approve, was still her lover.

"Charles?"

"Hmmm?"

"Are you going to see *her* when you get to Charleston?" The question was asked in a whisper.

He laughed lightly. "You've said it yourself numerous times in the last month or two: I'm fifty-seven years old."

"If that's meant to reassure me, you haven't. I've just had proof of your abilities in bed."

He kissed her. Another laugh. "There are some things that just come naturally."

"And that's not reassuring, either. Answer me now: are you going to see Mrs. Cheves in Charleston?"

"Probably."

"And do you think she will be pleased to see you?"

"Probably not. I haven't communicated with her since I was last there."

"You never answered her letter?" Mattie hadn't known.

"No."

"Sometimes you surprise me."

And he did again. "Mattie, come with us."

"But you leave in the morning!"

"Just pack a few clothes. You can buy new ones in Charleston and Richmond. And in New York, too, if you wish."

"No, Charles, it's just not practical."

He chuckled. "It would give you an opportunity to meet Mary Elizabeth."

"Charles Dewey!"

They kissed, both of them laughing like young lovers for the sheer joy of being together.

"Charles," she whispered, "come back to me."

"Guaranteed," he said lightly.

III

FIFTY thousand dollars of the Bon Marché fortune had been committed to the racing journey to New York. Four new horse vans had been built—larger than the ones used on the earlier trip to Charleston, each designed to accommodate six horses, their tack, feed supplies, and gear. The heavy vans were to be drawn by teams of four draft horses.

As before, the purpose of the trip was to sell the products of Bon Marché breeding and to make the all-purple silks of the plantation known far beyond the boundaries of Tennessee. This time, however, prices had been set on the twenty-one thoroughbreds to be campaigned along the way. There would be no auctioning and no solicitation of sealed bids. Charles and his sons, Franklin and George, had carefully evaluated each horse and had established a minimum price for it.

"If you're fortunate enough, Father," Franklin had said, "to have no injuries that will make an animal unsalable, we ought to be able to double our investment."

It was a large entourage that trundled out of Bon Marché on an early August morning of 1822.

There were forty-three horses in all: the twenty-one runners, sixteen draft horses and six riding horses for Charles, Alma May, and little Carrie. And there were twenty slaves: four teamsters, a dozen grooms and handlers, three jockeys, and Alma May's housemaid, Margaret, who would also serve as a cook along the way when it wasn't possible to find accommodations at an inn.

Charles estimated, based on his past experience, that it would be many months before he saw Nashville again.

IV

THEY sat at dinner in a comfortable inn overlooking the prosperous waterfront neighborhood of Charleston, known as the East Battery. It had been a reasonably easy trip to South Carolina; they had experienced rain on only three of the twenty-nine days they had been on the road. But Charles, Alma May, and Carrie were all glad to be settled again, if only for the two weeks of the Charleston racing meeting.

"Did you really think you could sneak into town," a voice behind them said, "with that circus you've brought with you?"

Dewey didn't have to turn around to know who it was. But when he did, there was that same feeling he had known seven years earlier. He was excited by the beauty of Mary Elizabeth Cheves.

He came to his feet, taking her hands. "Mary Elizabeth—"

"Charles Dewey," she said quietly, "I ought to be very angry with you for not telling me you were coming." She went up on her toes and kissed his cheek. "But I'm not. It's enough that you're here now."

His face flushed, Charles said formally: "Mrs. Cheves, I'd like you to meet my youngest daughter, Alma May. Alma, this is Mrs. Langdon Cheves, wife of the former Speaker of the House of Representatives."

"Ah, yes, the Princess. My dear, you're going to have every swain in Charleston at your feet."

Alma May smiled, her eyes asking questions about who this woman was.

"And this is my first granddaughter, Carrie."

"My, my," Mary Elizabeth gushed, "aren't you a darling!"

Dewey realized that he was still holding her hands and he let go of them.

"Charles, this isn't a chance meeting," the woman said, dropping her voice into an intimate tone. "This is a small town, you know, and I heard about your arrival early this afternoon."

He laughed. "We didn't get here until noon."

"As I said, it's a small town. In any event, I talked Langdon into bringing me here tonight for dinner, in the hope of seeing you. I want you to meet him." To the daughter and granddaughter: "Excuse us, dears."

A firm hand on Dewey's arm, she guided him across the dining room.

An unsmiling Langdon Cheves rose as they approached his table.

"Darling," Mary Elizabeth said, "may I present Mr. Charles Dewey of Nashville."

Cheves nodded, offering his hand. "My wife has spoken of you often, Mr. Dewey. In horse racing, aren't you?"

"Breeding and racing, yes. I'm pleased to meet you, sir." He shook the hand.

"Won't you sit down, Mr. Dewey?" Cheves suggested politely.

"Well, my daughter and—"

"For just a moment, Charles." Mrs. Cheves had given an order.

Ill at ease, Dewey joined them at their table.

Cheves made conversation. "I appreciate a good race, Mr. Dewey, but I'm afraid I never had the time to indulge myself in the sport."

"The country should be grateful, sir, that your time was spent in the legislature."

"Yes, well . . ."

"Mr. Dewey is here with his daughter and granddaughter, dear," Mary Elizabeth said to her husband, "and I thought it might be possible to have a reception for them."

"Of course." Without enthusiasm.

"Oh, I wouldn't want you to go to any trouble—"

"Nonsense! We'd be honored." She cast a stern glance at Langdon Cheves.

"Honored," he echoed.

After a few more stiff moments, Charles was able to go back to his own table.

"That lady is pretty, Grandfather," Carrie chirped.

"Yes, she is."

Alma May made no comment at all, then.

When they had finished dinner, though, and had put little Carrie to bed, the Princess followed her father to his room. Charles retrieved a bottle of sherry from one of his traveling cases and poured for both of them.

"This Mrs. Cheves, Daddy," Alma May asked, "who is she?"

"An old friend."

"A friend who Mother knows about?"

Charles grinned. "Yes, Princess."

"Oh."

"And what is that supposed to mean?"

"It's just that Mrs. Cheves doesn't think of you as just an old friend."

"How did you arrive at that conclusion?" Dewey was amused.

"Her eyes," the Princess replied. "I could see it in her eyes. She'd go to bed with you if you gave her any encouragement."

"Young lady, I think this conversation has gone far enough!"

"I'm not a child anymore. Women see those things in other women."

He laughed loudly. "Well, Princess, I'll just have to take your word for that. And I'll say good night."

Alma May went to the door. "Daddy?"

"What now?"

"She *would*, you know. And I want you to know that if . . . well, Daddy, I can be discreet."

"Good night, Princess!"

Dewey shook his head disapprovingly as his daughter left the room . . . but he had never felt closer to her than he did at that moment.

V

RACING in Charleston had changed since Charles's last visit. Subtle changes, perhaps, but changes that made the racing more competitive. He started three horses on the first day of the meeting without a winner, either on the track or in the betting pool.

Shrugging off the losses—over the years he had learned to lose with grace—he decided that the long trip in the vans had taken a lot out of his animals. He immediately rented a fenced pasture and turned the thoroughbreds out into it to graze and unwind.

"There'll be time in the second week of the meeting," he told one of the jockeys, "to win our share of races."

And so, on the first Saturday night in Charleston, not the conqueror he had been seven years earlier, Dewey prepared himself for the reception at the Cheves mansion. He had sent Alma May on a shopping expedition, both for herself and for little Carrie. He wanted his women to be dressed in the highest style. The Princess chose for herself a gown that her father wouldn't have allowed her to wear in Nashville, with revealing décolletage and bare arms. She was gorgeous.

Charles, too, had made an effort to bring his wardrobe up to fashion. A Charleston tailor was pressed into hurried service to make him a suit with a velvet-collared coat, leg-hugging trousers, and a ruffled silk shirt featuring the high collars of the day.

"Father, you're handsome!" Alma May had exclaimed. "She's going to swoon!"

"That'll be enough of that, young lady." But he admitted to himself that he wanted to look just right for Mary Elizabeth.

Langdon Cheves and his wife had invited all of the first families of Charleston to the reception: the Izards, and the Manigaults, and the Mazycks, and the

Lowndeses, and the Pringles, and the Cogdells, and the Kinlochs, and the Pinckneys. The spacious parlors of the mansion were jammed.

Mary Elizabeth greeted them at the door. Effusively. She was even more beautiful than he had remembered, her auburn hair, longer now, piled high on her head, a silky white gown outlining her superb figure, scooped low in front, a single diamond on a delicate gold chain nestled just above the cleavage of her breasts.

She took his hand and led him, the Princess, and Carrie through the entrance hall. As they made their way through a crowd of people, Charles glanced up the long, winding stairway that led to the bedrooms above. She seemed to sense what he was thinking, squeezing his hand gently.

They crossed the main living room, Mary Elizabeth making quick introductions as they moved, but not stopping until they came to Langdon Cheves. He was standing, with an elbow on the mantel, in a circle of five or six other gentlemen.

"Darling," his wife said, "our guest of honor has arrived."

"Mr. Dewey," Cheves said, bowing slightly. "I believe you know some of these gentlemen from your last visit." He quickly ran over their names again, and handshakes were exchanged.

"The Royalist colt I purchased from you, Mr. Dewey," Charles Manigault interjected enthusiastically, "has done marvelously well. He earned himself out . . . oh, by seven or eight times. I have him at stud now."

"I'm delighted," Charles replied.

"Whiskey, Mr. Dewey?" Cheves wanted to know.

"Yes, please."

His host snapped his fingers, and a black waiter was instantly by his side with a silver tray loaded with crystal glasses filled with whiskey.

As Dewey took his drink he realized that Mary Elizabeth had left them. He could see her across the room, introducing the Princess to young men in the crowd.

"Are you here on another selling foray?" Manigault asked.

"In one sense only," Charles explained. "Actually, I'm on my way to New York to test the racing there. But I will sell along the way if sales develop."

"I understand, Mr. Dewey, that your first day of racing here wasn't too kind to you," Manigault said sympathetically.

"Not too kind," he admitted with a wry smile.

After a few more moments of racing talk, the conversation shifted to politics, with Langdon Cheves holding forth. Charles found himself bored, his eyes wandering about the room seeking out Mary Elizabeth. He caught only fleeting glances of her, but each time his heart pounded harder. *Old fool!* he thought.

"There's talk, Mr. Dewey," Cheves was saying, "that your General Jackson will be competing for the presidency in the next election. What think you of that?"

"Jackson is very popular."

"And is he popular with you, sir?"

Charles hadn't been paying enough close attention to gauge the sentiments of the men in the group. He answered cautiously. "Well, if there is to be a westerner in contention, I think I would prefer Henry Clay. But you must understand that I'm not too well versed on politics."

"Yes, of course," Cheves sniffed.

Only then did Charles remember that Clay and Cheves had been opponents for the post of Speaker of the House. He decided not to apologize for his preference of Clay for President.

The talk of politics continued without another effort by the host to draw Dewey into it. After another ten minutes of that, Charles excused himself quietly and left the group. No one seemed to notice his departure.

He found Mary Elizabeth chatting with a thin-faced, stern matron introduced to him as Mrs. Rawlins Lowndes.

Charles bowed to her. "Ma'am, an honor."

"We met the last time you were in Charleston," the woman said.

He didn't remember. "Of course," he lied. "It's just that there are so many beautiful women in Charleston that . . ." He let the sentence trail off with a shrug.

She smiled.

"Charles, have you run across that gentleman yet," Mrs. Cheves said pointedly, "who's interested in buying one of your horses? Oh, dear, which one was it, now?"

"Huger?" He picked a name of one of the Charleston horsemen he knew to be in the room.

"That's it—Mr. Huger. Have you seen him yet?"

"No."

"Well, I believe I saw him go out on the veranda a few moments ago." To the matron: "Would you excuse us, Mrs. Lowndes? Mr. Huger wanted very much to talk to Mr. Dewey."

A quick bow to the older woman and Charles and Mary Elizabeth were through the French doors onto the veranda. She pulled him behind a tall boxwood and threw her arms around his neck, kissing him wildly.

"Oh, God, it's been so long," she whispered.

He kissed her back, but was concerned. "This is dangerous business."

"Do you care?"

"Certainly I care. Your reputation—"

"To hell with it!"

"You don't mean that."

A wan smile. "No. Maybe you're just a fantasy, Charles Dewey, but I've missed you terribly." She frowned. "And I can't understand why you didn't write to me!"

"Because it wasn't the right—" He stopped. "Because my wife read your letter."

"Oh!"

"You might have been less . . . intimate, you know."

"Did I cause trouble for you?"

"For a time."

She laid her hand on his cheek. "What did you tell her about us?"

"That I would always remember you fondly."

"Will you?"

"Of course."

"Did you come back to Charleston to see me?"

"No," Charles said firmly. "I came back to race my horses—on my way to New York."

Mary Elizabeth pouted.

"I was convinced," he went on, "that you wouldn't speak to me again because I hadn't written to you."

"You were wrong."

Dewey sighed. "Yes. You know, my daughter said she saw in your eyes that you wanted to go bed with me."

"She's very perceptive."

"She said that women see those things in other women."

"That's true."

"And if she could see, then others can see it, too."

"Probably."

Her seeming lack of concern about the situation worried him. "I think we'd better go back inside."

"Very well." She laughed. "We really can't do much out here anyway."

They started toward the door.

"Your daughter, Charles, is very charming. I think she's going to like Charleston—and its young men."

VI

"My husband's name was Nat," the Princess said.

The tall, dark-haired young man was taken aback. "Your husband? But I was under the impression that you were an unmarried lady. Mrs. Cheves's introduction—"

Alma May chuckled. "Single, but not a maiden," she said, using the racetrack term. "I'm divorced."

"Really?" His eyes opened wide.

She had wondered what polite society would think of her divorce. And now she found herself amused by the reaction of this man she knew as Nathaniel Heyward II. Mrs. Cheves, in introducing him, had left no doubt about the importance of the Heyward family in Charleston.

They strolled along on the wide lawn in front of the Cheves mansion. The evening was warm, the sky clear, with only a few stars visible. He was smoking a long, thin cigar, puffing at it in a rather imperious manner.

"Does my divorce shock you?" she asked.

"No, no, certainly not!"

"Would you be interested to know that I don't believe you?"

"Really, Miss Dewey, I'm not a prude."

She was having fun with him. "Have you ever known a divorced woman before?"

"No, I can't say that I have."

"Tell me, then, what went through your mind when I told you that?"

He was flustered. "Oh, well, surprise, of course. I mean—"

"No thought that here might be a choice piece of fruit?"

She had silenced him. He puffed faster at the cigar.

"I'm sorry, Mr. Heyward," she said, laughing. "I didn't mean to make sport with you. And I apologize for having embarrassed you."

"You are a rather . . . gay person, aren't you?"

"I've had enough somber moments in my life."

"And your husband—your former husband—what did he do, Miss Dewey?"

"He was an actor."

Again the eyes opened wide. Again: "Really?"

Now the Princess laughed. She couldn't help it. The proper young man's reaction was farcical to her.

"Oh, my," she said, trying to stop laughing, "I really am being quite rude to you."

"I don't think that, Miss Dewey. It's just that I've never met anyone like you before."

"And you probably don't want to meet anyone like me again."

"Please don't say that, Miss Dewey!"

"My name is Alma May."

He nodded.

"Or Princess, if you prefer."

"Princess? That's perfect. It fits you admirably." He sobered. "You are quite beautiful, you know."

"Thank you, sir."

"I would like to have the opportunity to show you Charleston. It's quite a lovely place."

"I'd like that."

"Really?"

Another chuckle. "Yes, Nat, I *really* would. If you can stop being so surprised about everything I say."

"I am a boor, aren't I?"

"Not at all. I find you very charming."

He studied her face for a moment. Then he glanced at the ember of his shortening cigar, flipping it away into the grass.

He's going to kiss me, Alma May thought.

He didn't.

"Perhaps . . . uh, Princess"—he still was not comfortable with her nickname—"you would permit me to drive you to your lodgings tonight?"

"I'd like nothing better."

"Real—" He began to laugh. "I must get over that habit, mustn't I?"

"Yes, Nat, you must."

A small gong sounded from inside the house.

"The signal for supper," he explained. "Are you hungry, Miss . . . uh . . . Princess?"

"Uh-huh. But not for food."

He opened his mouth to reply, but closed it without having spoken.

Finally: "Princess, you *are* quite a tease, you know."

"I know."

He kissed her then.

Good Lord, finally!

42

"I'M not sure that I approve of your dalliance with this fellow Heyward." Dewey was angry with his daughter.

" 'This fellow Heyward,' " Alma May said, "is of one of the finest families in Charleston."

"All the more reason to—"

"And it's not a dalliance. Lord, Father, where do you get those old-fashioned words?"

Charles sighed. "Old-fashioned or not, you know what I'm talking about! You've been seeing this man every day since the reception. It's unseemly."

"No, Father, it's not. I enjoy his company; he enjoys mine. It's as simple as that."

"And as *innocent* as that?"

"At least he's not married."

"What is that supposed to mean?"

The Princess grinned at him. "Daddy, when Nathaniel and I were walking on the lawn the other night, I saw you with Mrs. Cheves hiding behind the boxwood."

"We weren't hiding."

"Maybe you should have been."

"Alma May, you're still my daughter, and I'll not stand for this insolence!"

"It's not insolence, Father; it's just a statement of fact."

"And this Heyward fellow," Charles groaned, "I suppose he saw us, too."

"No. I was distracting him, you might say. Shocking him with my candor, if you want the whole truth. Your secret is safe with me."

"What you saw," Charles tried to explain, "was an innocent kiss. One kiss, nothing more—and nothing more implied."

"Yes, Daddy." She was grinning again.

"Damn you! It *was* innocent!"

"I'll accept your protestations of innocence if you'll accept mine."

"That smacks of blackmail, young lady."

"Uh-huh. Or . . . let's just say we've reached an understanding."

Dewey sank down on the edge of his bed. "Princess, what am I going to do with you?"

"Accept me for what I am."

"And what is that?"

"Your daughter. Who loves you. And who knows how much you love Mother. And who knows, too, that you're a handsome, virile man—"

"I think I've heard enough."

"—who also loves another woman."

"No, you're wrong about that."

"Maybe."

"You *are*, Princess."

"Poor Daddy." She came to him and kissed him on the cheek. "Don't feel so guilty about loving Mary Elizabeth. You can no more stop that than you can stop the tides."

A smile came to his face. "You think yourself wise about these things, don't you?"

"I am, Daddy. I really am."

II

THE racing at Charleston went better for the Bon Marché entourage in the second week of the meeting. His horses properly rested after being turned out in the pasture, Dewey picked his spots carefully, relying on his experience. Nine horses carrying the purple silks were started. Seven were winners.

With only two racing days remaining, Charles was approached by Thomas Pinckney, Junior.

"The chestnut colt that won yesterday," Pinckney said. "The one you call Pour de Bon. Is he for sale?"

"Yes."

"You're not going to use that sealed-bid method again, are you? I'd much prefer to deal directly with you."

"No sealed bids this time, Mr. Pinckney. Pour de Bon's price is six thousand—take it or leave it."

"I'll take it."

"Fine. I'll prepare the pedigree papers for you."

"And you'll have my bank draft in the morning." Young Pinckney hesitated. "The name, sir? I'm not much on languages, but am I correct in assuming that Pour de Bon means 'in earnest'?"

"Yes, or 'for good and all,' to be more literal in the translation."

"Hmmm. Would you be disturbed if I changed the colt's name?"

"Once you've bought him, that's your prerogative."

"Good." Pinckney smiled. "I want to name him Cooper River. Not so elegant as your name, probably, but it'll let everyone know where he comes from now."

"Cooper River it is. I'll make that note on the pedigree papers."

The sale of the chestnut to Pinckney was the only one Dewey made in Charleston this time around. Several were interested in other animals, but the prices that had been set back at Bon Marché were not to their liking. Charles didn't mind; he had a long way to go yet. A long way, indeed.

He began to make plans to move the Bon Marché caravan on to Georgia.

III

UNCHARACTERISTICALLY, Dewey was having trouble getting to sleep. He had gone to bed early in preparation for the final day of racing at Charleston and for the work that then would have to be done to get under way again.

Alma May had gone with Nathaniel Heyward II to a soiree at the Elms, the Izard family plantation. He didn't expect that he would see her before dawn. And that disturbed his sleep, as well.

He stretched and sighed. Then he got out of bed and walked, naked, to the traveling case where his sherry was stored.

"Perhaps a sip of sherry," he said aloud to himself. The big clock in the corner of the room told him it was only nine o'clock. That's what was wrong, he decided. He had gone to bed too early.

There was a knock on the door.

Not loud. At first he thought that he was hearing a knock on a door farther along the hallway of the inn.

But it was repeated.

"Who is it?"

"Mary Elizabeth."

He had a feeling of panic. Hurriedly, he slipped on a robe and opened the door. She looked up and down the hallway before she came in.

"Isn't this foolishness?" he asked.

"It could be." She slipped off the cape that covered her dress. "Langdon has gone to Columbia on some political business."

They stood there in the middle of the room for a long time, it seemed to Dewey.

"I was just going to have a sherry," he said. "Would you join me?"

"Of course."

He poured the wine, gesturing her to the lone chair in the room. Instead, she sat on the edge of the bed. He handed her the glass, but remained standing.

Mary Elizabeth took a sip. "Are you just going to stand there?"

Charles went to the chair and sat down.

Her annoyance was obvious. "I guess I've made a mistake."

"Hmmm."

"Is that grunt an answer?"

"To what?"

"Oh, for God's sake, Charles! Do you imagine I came to your room—that I risked having someone see me in a public inn—to parry with you?"

"No."

Not a single smile had been exchanged between them. And now a silence fell. It went on interminably.

She drained the glass, made a show of setting it carefully on the small table by the bed, and got to her feet. Pulling her cape around her again, she said, with deep sarcasm: "Thank you for the sherry, Mr. Dewey."

Mary Elizabeth made for the door.

"No, wait!"

She stopped, not turning to him.

"Stay," he said. He went to her, turning her gently to face him, gathering her in his arms, holding her close. "If you knew the times I wished for this."

"I'm here now, Charles."

The cape slipped to the floor.

Slowly he undid the combs in her hair, the auburn locks falling to her shoulders, framing her flawless face.

"My God, woman," he breathed, "you are so beautiful."

Mary Elizabeth stretched to kiss him and, as they continued the kiss, he guided her to the bed. He undressed her, savoring the sight of every inch of smooth pink skin he exposed, and kissing her on each newly revealed area.

When he finished, he took off his robe, pulling the covers over them, gathering her in his arms, feeling her tingling warmth against him.

Nothing was said.

They made love, slowly at first. Then with growing ardor. Then with fury. And they slept. When they awoke again, Charles looked at the clock. In the dim light of the room he could make out that it was eleven o'clock. They hadn't said a word to each other in nearly two hours.

"When must you go?" he asked.

"Never."

"No—be serious."

She sighed. "Not until the morning."

"Maybe, just this once, the morning could be delayed."

He forced himself to think of nothing but Mary Elizabeth. And in the fantasies that accompanied their lovemaking there was nothing else in his life but this one woman.

It was about four o'clock when they heard whispered voices and light laughter in the hallway.

"The Princess and young Heyward," Charles said.

"Hmmm."

"Wouldn't it be wonderful if we were as young and as unencumbered as those two?"

"No, Charles. I don't envy them at all. There have never been two other people in the world—nor will there be—who have what we have right now."

"I suppose we must believe that." He suddenly felt very sad. And he wanted to weep in that sadness.

There was no delaying the morning.

He watched silently from the bed as she dressed, as she piled the auburn hair on top of her head again, as she made the transition from Miss Dulles to Mrs. Cheves.

When she was finished, she turned to him. "Will I ever see you again, Charles Dewey?"

"Probably not."

"Remember me," she said. She slipped through the door without looking back at him.

IV

ON the final afternoon of the Charleston race meeting, Dewey gleefully watched two more Bon Marché horses cross the finish line as winners.

He was preparing the vans for the departure when Alma May came up to him, Nathaniel Heyward II in tow.

"Have you two had a good day at the races?" Dewey asked.

"Your daughter is uncanny with her choices, sir. My problem is that I haven't followed her advice often enough."

Charles laughed. "Well, if you want one final piece of advice, young man, may I suggest that you back Mr. Pinckney's colt in the last event? A horse named Cooper River."

"You know this horse, sir?"

"Hmmm. Just a bit. I bred him."

"Well, maybe I can get even for the day." He pecked Alma May on the cheek. "Stay here for a moment, dear, while I get a wager down." He rushed off.

"I was awake during the night," Dewey said to the Princess, "and I heard you two in the hallway. Rather late wasn't it?"

"It must have been someone else, Daddy."

He made an idle gesture. "I'm not going to chastise you for your late hours—"

"No, it really must have been someone else," she insisted, grinning broadly. "You see, I stayed in Nathaniel's quarters last night."

"Oh?"

"Are you shocked, Daddy?"

"You want me to be shocked, don't you? Well, you're a grown woman—"

She kissed him gaily. "Daddy, you're so sweet! He's asked me to marry him."

"Now, that *does* shock me. And what have you answered?"

"I said no. The poor dear has taken the rejection pretty well, too."

Alma May looked around. "I haven't seen Mrs. Cheves here today."

"No."

"I thought surely she would come to bid you good-bye."

"Well, she hasn't."

She shook her head, perplexed. "I was so sure about what I saw in her eyes."

"Perhaps your father isn't the exciting, virile fellow you imagined him to be."

And Charles laughed. Oh, how he laughed.

43

It was an odyssey of sorts—a wandering journey to spread the fame of Bon Marché. A quest, too, by Charles Dewey for some peace of mind.

As they left the Atlantic coast, traveling north and a bit west some one hundred fifty miles to Augusta, Georgia, Charles was tempted several times to turn his horse south once more to go back to Charleston—to hold her again, to feel her smooth skin against him again. But that was a temptation to which he could not succumb.

He wished that he could be given the youth of Alma May; that he could view his passions with the same devil-may-care attitude that sustained the Princess in her determined efforts to throw off the memories of her unhappy marriage. But he couldn't do that. His maturity, his sense of right and wrong, even his perception of "sin" got in the way.

He was haunted by images. Of Mary Elizabeth risking her reputation for a few hours together in a hired bed. Of Mattie in a wilderness bower on their honeymoon asking, "How long will this last?" Of a guileless Martha poised naked on the bank of the James, walking into the water, her arms extended to him. Women he loved. Women he had used. His thoughts rewarded him with guilt.

And melancholy. *I'm too old for real love,* he thought. *Too old!*

The images and the guilt and the melancholy were part of Dewey's baggage as they moved from Charleston to Augusta and then into Virginia, to Petersburg and Richmond.

By the time the Bon Marché caravan got to Richmond to compete in the last few days of fall racing there, Charles had sold a dozen of his thoroughbred runners. For Alma May there had been at least as many conquests. Several times he had determined that he would speak to her about her indiscretions, but each time his own guilt intruded. He kept silent. The Princess, after all, was her own woman.

Little Carrie, then, became the beneficiary of Dewey's reluctance to deal with his daughter's imprudent ways. More and more he turned to the innocence of his granddaughter for his own well-being. They spent long hours together, reading to each other, discussing animals and birds and flowers and trees. They made numerous side trips so that Charles could show Carrie historical landmarks and tell her of the dramatic events that had occurred in those places.

It was an education for her, he told himself. There was a greater truth, however. Carrie Dewey, age eleven, represented his new purpose in life. Even his sanity.

It was because of Carrie that, when the racing was done at Richmond, Charles decided to return to Elkwood.

II

THEY stood there—the three of them: Charles, Alma May and Carrie—within the circle of giant boxwoods, looking down at the stone marking the grave of Marshall Statler.

"Your great-grandfather," Dewey said quietly to the little girl, "was the kindest man I have ever known. If I've accomplished anything at all in this life, it's because of the guidance of Marshall Statler. I only wish I could have been more like him."

His eyes came up, and he looked around the Elkwood of 1822. "How he loved this place! His wife—your great-grandmother, Carrie—had died when he was still a young man. And the love he had for her was channeled into this." He swept an arm to encompass the plantation.

But this wasn't the Elkwood of Marshall Statler. The plantation had become seedy and unkempt. The mansion needed paint, many of the pastures had reverted to weeds and thistles, some sections of fence were down, the slaves were ill-dressed and sullen-faced.

And Katherine? She was an old woman, her face lined and sallow, her body bent in a defeated attitude. If she had ever been beautiful—and Dewey tried to remember the beauty of spirit she once had—she was no longer. She was now, in sum, spiritless.

Katherine sat with them at tea in what had been Statler's stylish drawing room. The room, like the woman, was no longer beautiful. Charles remembered every piece of furniture in that room. It was all still there, worn and neglected.

"You know," Katherine was saying to Carrie, "I remember your father so well. Good Lord! Can it be more than a quarter of a century since I've seen Franklin? He was only"—she looked to Charles for confirmation—"nine when he left here."

"Yes—nine."

"Hmmm. Well, Carrie, I recall that your father was a sober lad. The most serious youngster I think I've ever seen. Is he still?"

Dewey laughed. "Franklin is still sober, yes. The steady rock, really, on which Bon Marché rests today. I'm very proud of him."

Katherine's voice took on a scolding tone. "Your few letters, Charles, didn't contain much news."

"Well, I—"

"And Lee? How is he?"

"Quite well. He has a fine career as a newspaper correspondent and artist. You'd like him."

The woman sighed deeply. "I remember so vividly the circumstances of his christening and how dear Martha tried to—" She stopped, wiping a hand across her eyes.

"How *is* Funston?" Charles asked.

"Here seldom," Katherine answered bitterly. "His father died, you know—"

"I didn't know."

"Funston now spends more time at Marsh Run than he does here." She smiled wanly. "And at other places. Certainly you've noticed how things have become run down around here."

Charles nodded.

"I don't seem to have the strength to contend with the management of it. There's so much to do," she continued wearily, "what with Elkwood and Fortunata—"

"Fortunata!" Dewey's eyebrows shot up.

"Of course—you didn't know. Six . . . or was it seven? . . . years ago, the main house burned."

"Damn!"

"Mr. Monkton was quite discouraged. Funston made him an offer and he accepted."

Charles sat silently, seething with anger that Funston Lee had, after all, acquired the Fortunata property. He had planned to show it to Carrie, but now he didn't want to set foot on it.

All that he wanted to do was to leave. They did—within the quarter-hour. It had been a mistake to return. A sad mistake.

III

"WE have rented an attractive, small house here in Baltimore," Charles wrote to Mattie, "so that we might have a proper place to stay during the winter."

Alma May came into the room, twirling around to show off a new dress.

"And where to tonight, Princess?"

"A soiree at the Grundys'."

"With whom, may I ask?"

"With David . . . uh . . ." She thought for a moment. "Oh, Daddy, I've only just met him."

Dewey frowned.

"When he calls for me, I'll introduce him to you, if I can remember his name." Alma May giggled. "You know, I'm not sure that I ever want to leave here. It's so much more gay than Nashville."

Charles forced a laugh. "There's still New York to conquer, Princess."

"I'm not so sure about that," she replied soberly. "New York isn't the South. How can a southern girl—"

"Admirably," her father interrupted. "If my observations of your activities since we left home are any indication."

"Do I detect a note of disapproval, Daddy?"

"It's a bit late for that, isn't it?" He sighed.

"Daddy, dear Daddy." She kissed him on the cheek. "Have I given you cause for worry?"

"At times."

Another kiss. "Don't concern yourself for me, Daddy. Just know that I've promised myself that I would live by a very simple philosophy: face every day as if it were the last."

"I'm not so sure I approve of that kind of fatalism. It seems so devoid of purpose."

"Oh, I have purpose, Daddy: to have a good time."

"That's not making much of a contribution with your life, is it?"

The Princess pondered his question, then shrugged. "I guess I'm just not a contributor, Daddy. I'm more of a taker." She laughed gaily. "But that just balances things out. If we didn't have takers, the contributors wouldn't have anyone to contribute to. And speaking of that . . ."

Charles groaned. "How much this time?"

"Just a hundred. There's this dress I haven't paid for yet."

He counted out the bills for her. "Perhaps if I stopped indulging your every whim, you'd understand what I'm trying to say to you."

Alma May threw her arms around him, squeezing hard. "Daddy, you're such a dear! But don't you understand that if I didn't get money from you, there are other men who would—"

"I don't want to hear things like that!" He tried to control his sudden anger. "Now, get out of here and let me write to your mother."

"And to Mary Elizabeth?" she asked.

"No, *not* to Mary Elizabeth."

"Have you written to her since we left Charleston?"

"No."

"I pity that poor woman. She's so much in love with you, and—"

The Negro maid, Margaret, entered the room. " 'Scuse me, Miss Alma. There's a Mister Abernathy askin' fer ya."

"Abernathy! Of course! Shall I bring him in for an introduction, Daddy?"

"Don't bother. I'll probably not see him again after tonight anyway."

Again she kissed him. "You're so understanding, Daddy. Thank you for the money."

He waved away the thanks. "Have a good time, Princess."

Alma May grinned wickedly. "Oh, I intend to." She was gone.

Charles turned back to the letter: "Tell Franklin that we'll be running several horses in Washington in November. The word is that we're going to get a look at that good New York champion, American Eclipse . . ."

IV

THERE was the contention that American Eclipse, at eight, was the greatest American-bred racehorse of all time. By Duroc, out of Miller's Damsel, by Messenger, the New York horse had been brought to the 1822 Washington meeting carrying an undefeated record. And his owner, Cornelius Van Ranst, was not shy in proclaiming the superiority of his runner.

Charles stood watching the big chestnut stallion being jogged in front of a huge crowd at the Washington track, the bloom on his gleaming red coat attesting to his good health.

"He certainly is a marvelous animal," Dewey said to a companion.

"Maybe, and maybe not. 'Marvelous' covers a lot of ground."

Charles's companion was a cocky little Irishman named William Ransom Johnson, a new generation of Virginia breeder whom Charles had met at the Petersburg meeting. Johnson was being called the Napoleon of the Turf, largely because, in the 1807–1808 season, he had started horses in sixty-three races and had won sixty. His ego allowed him to accept the title.

Charles had visited Johnson's fine stud farm, Oaklands, near the Petersburg track, and had admired a sign that stood at the entrance to the place: There Is Nothing So Good for the Inside of a Man as the Outside of a Horse.

"Were I you, Dewey," Johnson said to him now, "I'd place a substantial wager on Mr. Harrison's Sir Charles. It seems the name alone would put you in his corner."

Dewey laughed. "I've long since learned not to bet on a hunch."

"Well, sir, this is no hunch. Sir Charles is one of the best I've ever seen, and today's match against that New York animal"—the sarcasm was heavy—"will be proof of that."

As it turned out, the match race between American Eclipse and Sir Charles—four-mile heats at five thousand dollars a side—was never run. The Virginia horse rapped a tendon in the warm-up and James Harrison, his owner, withdrew the horse, paying a forfeit to Van Ranst.

Johnson was incensed. He railed at Harrison: "The honor of Virginia is at stake, sir!"

"But the horse—"

"Is better on three legs than that Eclipse is on four!"

Dewey was shocked when a substitute match was quickly arranged: a single four-mile heat at fifteen hundred dollars a side. But he wasn't shocked enough to refuse to place a wager. He bet a thousand dollars in the public pool. On American Eclipse.

He watched, without concern, as Sir Charles stayed with the New York thoroughbred for three of the four miles. Then, as Dewey had expected, the injured tendon gave way. American Eclipse just cantered to the finish line.

Johnson was not satisfied, nor were a lot of other proud Virginia breeders. Van Ranst was surrounded by southerners, with the Napoleon of the Turf as their spokesman.

"Sir," Johnson said pompously, "all Virginia challenges you. We offer you a match, over the Union Course on Long Island. At twenty thousand a side!"

Van Ranst smiled tolerantly. "With what horse?"

"With whatever Virginia horse is fit." Johnson goaded him. "If your Eclipse is as good as you say, does it matter which horse we bring?"

"No."

"Then it's done, sir! Will the last Tuesday of May be convenient?"

"Suit yourself."

"And the forfeit? Would three thousand be fair?"

"Agreed."

Charles Dewey thought they were all mad, but he was glad that he was going to be in New York for the confrontation.

V

"WE leave Baltimore in the morning," Charles reported to Mattie, "after having made our final start at the Baltimore spring meeting a successful one. Please inform Franklin and George that we have done well for the purple silks of Bon Marché and that our entourage is down to a single van, with only five runners remaining for the New York competition.

"Expect to be on Long Island by the end of the first week in May, having made arrangements to stay at the establishment of a Mr. William Niblo, and not knowing what really to expect there."

He paused a moment in his writing.

"We all miss everyone at Bon Marché. I especially miss you. It will be a happy moment when we return."

Charles sealed the letter. He sat in thought for a moment or two, then took another sheet of paper.

"Dearest Mary Elizabeth," he began. "It has been an eternity since . . ."

He stared at the words. A sigh. Then Dewey balled up the paper and hurled it into the fireplace.

44

THOUGH he was used to the excitement generated by races, Charles wasn't prepared for the frenzy over the great North-South match featuring the undefeated American Eclipse in New York.

Thousands were pouring into the city from the South; he read one report in a New York newspaper that estimated the number of visitors to be as many as twenty thousand. The New York newspapers, notably the *Evening Post*, owned by one Michael Burnham, devoted many columns every day to the impending race, having sent correspondents to Virginia to follow the training of the potential Virginia challengers.

Burnham, as it turned out, was a member of the syndicate that had posted the side purse of twenty thousand dollars for the New York champion. So, too, was William Niblo, at whose establishment Charles, Alma May, and Carrie were staying. It wasn't so much an inn as a large tavern frequented by the sporting crowd. However, Niblo had a few rooms available and had rented two of them to Dewey.

It was from Niblo that Charles got his understanding of the fervor with which the New Yorkers approached the match race.

"It seems strange to me," Dewey said to the tavern keeper at dinner on the night of his arrival, "that the North would put up only American Eclipse and allow the Johnson group to select any horse it wants, right up to the call to the post."

Niblo shrugged. "Not strange, Mr. Dewey. Eclipse can beat anything thrown against him. Anything!"

"Perhaps. But it seems to me that you've given the Virginians a great advantage. In the *Evening Post* tonight I see that Johnson still has three solid competitors in training: Betsey Richards and Childers, which I know to be highly experienced four-milers, and the four-year-old Henry, a very good son of Sir Archie."

The New Yorker seemed unconcerned. "Whatever the South has to offer, Eclipse will whip decisively."

"If Johnson decides to start Henry, your horse will have to give away considerable weight—one hundred eight to one twenty-six. From what I know of horses, I'd have to give Henry the nod with an eighteen-pound pull in the weights."

Niblo laughed. "Don't waste your money that way, sir. American Eclipse can carry any weight over any distance against any competitor. This country has never seen a horse like Eclipse."

"So I've been hearing." Dewey smiled at him. "But I'll decide my wagering strategy when it comes to race day. There's more I want to know before I bet."

"After you've studied it, Mr. Dewey, you'll still bet on Eclipse." He got to his feet. "You'll excuse me, sir. I have duties. Enjoy your dinner."

Charles was at dinner with Carrie. The Princess had gone off with a gentleman she had met shortly after their arrival at Niblo's place. Grandfather and granddaughter chatted about the things they wanted to see before leaving New York.

A voice interrupted them. "Sir?"

Dewey looked up to find a light-skinned Negro boy standing stiffly by the table. He squinted at him, sensing a familiarity. "Yes?"

"I'm Marshall," the young man said quietly. "Marshall Dewey."

"Good Lord!" Charles was stunned. Springing to his feet, he pumped the boy's hand enthusiastically. "How you've grown!"

"Yes, sir."

"Sit down, sit down." He gestured to his granddaughter. "This is Carrie, Franklin's oldest child."

The boy smiled for the first time. "Hello."

Carrie just stared. The young man was a stranger, one not identified in any way by her grandfather.

"How did you know we were here?" Charles asked.

"Mercy . . . uh . . . Mrs. MacCallum wrote to Bon Marché and got a reply saying you'd be here."

"I see." Charles was ill at ease, pleased to see Marshall, but not sure what to say to him.

"I have some bad news, sir."

"Oh?"

"Mr. MacCallum died."

Dewey's mouth fell open in shock. Tears filled his eyes.

"Nearly three weeks ago," Marshall went on. "The doctor said it was a brain stroke."

"Did he suffer?"

"No. It was quick."

"I see." Charles put his head in his hands and wept quietly. "We were the greatest of friends once."

"Yes, sir."

"But I was a terrible fool."

Marshall said nothing.

Taking a handkerchief from his pocket, Charles mopped his eyes. "Dear Andrew, dear Andrew."

"Uh . . . you are invited," the young man began hesitantly, "to visit the house in Princeton before you return home."

"I will. Yes, of course, I will."

Marshall stood. "Well, now that I've delivered the message—"

"No! Stay!" Charles put his hand on his son's arm. "Please stay. Tell us what you've been doing."

With seeming reluctance, the boy sat down again. "I've been riding here in New York, as you probably know, but I'm having trouble with weight. And now I'm assisting in the training of the horses of Mr. Henry Lynch."

"I've heard of him. He has a big stable, doesn't he?"

"Yes, sir."

"And you're happy there?"

"Yes, sir."

The wooden conversation soon turned into a silence.

"Marshall . . . have you ever thought of returning to Bon Marché?"

"No." The answer was firm.

"You know, Franklin and George and I have been talking about maintaining a racing string here in New York. Perhaps you could handle our horses for us."

"I'm not really a trainer yet."

"But I'm sure you'll be fine at it. Wouldn't you like to have a Bon Marché stable here?"

"I'm not sure, sir." He was demonstrating no enthusiasm for the idea.

"Well, suppose I have Franklin write to you about it? He's really running Bon Marché now."

"I'd be happy to hear from Franklin again."

"Good! You can deal with Franklin, then."

Once more Marshall stood. "I must go, sir."

"Of course." Dewey shook his hand again. "Will we see you at the Union Course?"

"I'll be there with several of the Lynch horses."

"We'll look for you."

The young man left hurriedly.

"Who is he, Grandfather?" Carrie asked.

"That was Marshall Dewey. He's my son." Charles didn't want to lie to her.

"But, he's—"

"Yes," Charles said softly, "he's half black. His mother is Angelica."

"Oh!"

He smiled at his granddaughter. "It was a long time ago, Carrie. A very long time ago. Long before you were born." Dewey summoned the waiter and paid for the dinner. "There will be time enough to tell you about it later."

II

THE *Evening Post* reported that Daniel Tompkins, the Vice President of the United States, would attend the North-South match race, and so would Aaron

Burr. Charles wondered how that was possible; he hadn't heard that Burr was back in the country. Andrew Jackson of Tennessee, the newly appointed governor of the Florida Territory, was also going to be on hand.

"It's all right if you want to pay your respects to your Cousin Andy," Dewey had said to Alma May, "but please don't involve me in it."

"Daddy, you can't go on hating him for the rest of your life."

"*Hate* is too strong a word, Princess," Charles insisted. "It's just that I prefer not to associate with him."

"Bobby says that Andy is offering large wagers on the southern horse."

"Bobby?"

Alma May smiled. "You haven't met him yet. Robert Stevens. His uncle has something to do with the Eclipse syndicate."

"Is that a fact?" Charles grinned. "So a southern girl *is* welcome in New York, then?"

"Yes," She wrinkled her nose. "I still prefer the southern men. These northerners are too brash for my taste. They give you the impression that they're doing you a favor when they ask you out."

"So I don't have to worry that you'll make a permanent arrangement with one of them." He was teasing her.

"No, Daddy. Or with any man for that matter. I've done all the marrying I intend to do."

"You're too young to make that kind of declaration."

"I mean it. I don't need the grief."

Charles just shook his head. But there was no time to discuss it further. The hour had arrived for them to leave for the racecourse in a carriage he had rented for the occasion.

The Long Island roads leading to the Union Course were jammed with carriages, all manner of carts, individual riders, and thousands of pedestrians. All the predictions in the newspapers as to the size of the crowd seemed to be borne out. One of the mounted men, Dewey knew, was a horseman employed by William Niblo, assigned to carry the results of the race to Niblo's tavern. If the news he carried was of an Eclipse victory, a white flag would be raised over the tavern; if the southern horse won, the flag would be black.

It took them more than an hour to traverse a distance that shouldn't have consumed more than thirty minutes. As soon as they arrived, the Princess skipped off to join Bobby Stevens. Charles, with Carrie by the hand, leisurely looked over both rivals. American Eclipse had the same healthy bloom that Charles had observed in him earlier in Washington. Henry—for he had been announced as the southern choice for the match—was more slight than Eclipse, but well muscled and on his toes.

The public betting pool was doing big business. But Charles got the impression that the side bets being made all around the track were of greater volume than the money being dumped into the pool. As for himself, he was having a difficult time making up his mind, until a chance meeting on the course with a New Yorker he had met earlier at Niblo's, a man named Oscar Farrington. A "sport"—one who called himself a professional gambler.

"Who do you like, Mr. Farrington?"

"Henry is being held the favorite—based on his low weight assignment and the fact that he's been carefully trained up to this start, while Eclipse hasn't campaigned since last November in Washington."

"But which horse do *you* like, Farrington?"

The gambler grinned. "One heat at a time, sir. That's the way I'm going to bet it." He leaned closer to Charles and dropped his voice to a whisper. "Rumor has it that the southerners have set up a betting coup. Henry is to be sacrificed in the first heat—fully extended to win that heat and the devil with the rest of the race."

"That's very hard to believe."

"Not if you consider that the southerners are making a great deal of noise about the first heat. They're offering any kind of wager. But very little is being said about the best of three heats. It's my understanding that vast sums of southern money are being bet on Eclipse to win the best of three. Not openly, of course. They're using agents to spread that money around. But everything I can learn tells me that there might be as much as a hundred thousand wagered on Eclipse to win the whole thing. And much of it from the South."

"Hmmm. Of course, what you say isn't impossible, but . . ."

Farrington shrugged. "Ask around yourself, Mr. Dewey. You'll see that I'm correct."

Charles did ask. And the volume of money being wagered on Henry to win the first heat did seem exorbitant to him, even allowing for the large number of southerners in the crowd. In the public pool, the odds on Henry to win the first heat had gone to even money, and Dewey quickly bet ten thousand dollars on him before the odds went lower. Maybe Farrington was right about the betting coup.

As the hour of the first heat approached, Charles and Carrie tried to find a vantage point from which to see it all. They finally crowded onto the top of a small knoll, and the grandfather hoisted the girl to his shoulders.

"How's that, dear?"

"Great, grandfather! I can see whole track."

Dewey laughed. "You may have to be my eyes."

A bugle sounded the call to the post, and a great roar went up from the crowd. Charles noticed that a third horseman, dressed in riding clothes, was positioning himself next to the two runners.

"Who's that?" he asked a man next to him.

"That," the other spectator said with a chuckle, "is the one and only Cadwallader Colden, the writer for the *American Turf Register*. He gallops along with the horses in the front stretch so that he can get a close-up view of the race."

"Each time around?" Charles asked in astonishment.

"Yep, he sure does. I've seen some races here when it would have been best to bet on Caldwallader's nag." He laughed heartily.

Off in the distance a voice was announcing the names of the jockeys. Dewey couldn't make out the words, but he already knew that William Crafts, a slender lad weighing only one hundred pounds, was up on American Eclipse and that an experienced Virginia rider, John Walden, had drawn the assignment on Henry.

The announcement ended, a hush fell on the crowd, the starter's drum tapped, and the hush turned to a massive scream. Charles had never heard anything louder.

Henry was away fast. Too fast, Dewey thought. Then he lost sight of them. "Where are they?" he called to Carrie.

"Henry's three lengths up, Grandfather. Under a tight hold."

Dewey smiled to himself. The youngster had learned well.

At the end of the first mile, with the newspaperman running the stretch alongside the competitors, young Crafts was whipping and driving American Eclipse, trying without success to close the gap. Charles would read later that Cadwallader Colden, from his unique mounted vantage point, thought that Henry's pace was "a killing one."

Henry was never fronted by the older horse. He won safely, crossing the finish line after four miles a solid length in front.

Charles went to look at the two horses. Henry seemed not used up at all. But then the time was announced: 7:37½—the fastest four miles ever run in America! The rumor of the betting coup may have had some merit. That kind of speed could not be duplicated in a second heat. Yet there was something strange. While the Virginia horse did not seem distressed, American Eclipse was heavily lathered, and there were cuts on his flank from the almost constant whipping.

A jockey change on the New York horse was made known to the crowd by a bull-voiced steward. An important one, Charles thought. The top jockey in America, thirty-eight-year-old Sam Purdy, would ride American Eclipse. He was closer to the weight assigned to the horse, making it unnecessary for Eclipse to carry the dead weight of lead slabs in his saddlecloth. That kind of change could have a salutary effect on Eclipse.

Dewey went to collect his even-money bet on Henry at the public pool. And while the twenty thousand dollars was being counted out to him, he asked about the prevailing odds on American Eclipse to win it all.

"Even money only, sir."

Charles frowned. So a lot of money had been bet on Eclipse. But why? he wondered. Henry ought to have been favored now. By damned, perhaps there had been a betting coup!

"Another bet, sir?" the pool clerk asked.

"Huh. Oh, no, not right now, thank you." Charles jammed the wad of money into his pocket and, with Carrie, began to stroll about the course. His horse sense told him that Henry, even though it was not evident to the eye, had a lot taken out of him by the swift first heat. And it told him, too, that Eclipse had never been beaten in a best-of-three match. Therefore, he ought to wager on American Eclipse, but he was no longer willing to risk a large bet for even money.

A piping, high voice stopped him in his tracks. It was saying: "I'll bet a year's crop of slaves on Henry!" He recognized the voice as that of Virginia Congressman John Randolph of Roanoke, whom he had known as a young man. A flamboyant horseman, Randolph was still betting heavily on Henry. If there had been a Virginia betting coup, wouldn't Randolph have known of it?

Charles sought out the congressman and found him in a knot of happy, celebrating Virginians, still exuberant about Henry's first-heat victory.

"Excuse me, sir," Dewey said, pushing through to Randolph. "I'm Charles Dewey. We met many years ago."

Randolph looked at him without recognition.

"I was with Marshall Statler."

"Of course, of course." The Virginia gentleman stuck out his hand. "I remember Mr. Statler quite well."

"I couldn't help overhearing your offer to bet a year's crop of slaves on Henry." Dewey grinned. "I'm not in the market for that kind of wager, but are you also offering hard money?"

"Absolutely! My friends and I have been offering six to four on Henry"— he gestured around the circle of gentlemen—"with no takers, I might add."

"I'll take it, sir." Charles felt the money in his pocket. "For fifteen thousand?"

"My God," Randolph piped, "a stranger in the wilderness! Shall we accommodate him, gentlemen?"

Quickly, the fifteen thousand dollars was apportioned among the Virginians, and Dewey had the wager he had been seeking. He had already won ten thousand on Henry's record-setting heat, and now, he was convinced he was going to win even more when Eclipse won the next two heats. He was as sure of that as he was certain his name was Charles Dewey.

He laughed to himself. *But your name isn't Charles Dewey, you fool—it's Charles Dupree!*

He and Carrie found a spot from which to view the second heat, closer this time. He watched Sam Purdy striding about nervously, smacking his whip—a thin, cruel-looking cattail affair—against his boot. A measure of arrogance showed in Purdy's face, and Charles liked that.

As the second heat was called, and Purdy brought American Eclipse to the line, Congressman Randolph could be heard screaming: "You can't do it, Mr. Purdy! You can't do it!"

He was wrong. Purdy's superior horsemanship became apparent early. He pressed the pace, keeping Henry within striking distance. On the last of the four miles, Purdy urged Eclipse abreast of Henry, cut in on the rail on the first turn to save ground, and on the backstretch began to pull away. American Eclipse won the second heat by two comfortable lengths.

For the third heat, there was a jockey change on the southern side. Trainer Arthur Taylor, who had been a noted jockey some years earlier, was pressed into service astride Henry. It made no difference. American Eclipse and Sam Purdy won by three easy lengths.

Had there been a betting coup? Had Henry been sacrificed in the first heat? Charles thought not, but he really didn't care. He—and Bon Marché—were now thirty-two thousand five hundred dollars richer! And he could turn his attention again to his own horses.

III

"OUR New York stay has seen nothing but profit," Charles wrote home. "We have taken our silks into seven races, winning four. And everything has been sold, including the last of the vans. The packet for New Orleans sails on April 20."

But Dewey had another chore to perform before he could leave New York. Putting Carrie in the charge of Alma May, he rode to Princeton, New Jersey, to see Mercy Callison MacCallum. He dreaded facing Andrew's widow; the guilt he felt about having destroyed the friendship so petulantly, so insanely, rode with him.

It was well past noon when he got to the MacCallum house on the college campus. The distance had been greater than he had anticipated. Mercy was heavier than Charles had remembered her. Her hair had grayed. And when she saw him at the door, she wept.

"Oh, Charles, it's so good to see you."

He embraced her. "The visit is too late, I'm afraid."

Mercy took his hand and led him into the house. The black servant, Delilah, who was still with her, served them tea in the small living room.

"There are times, Mercy, when words don't mean anything at all." Charles found it difficult to look directly at her. "And I won't bore you with platitudes. Andrew was once my dearest friend. I killed that friendship. I'll carry the blame for that to my grave. I just want you to know that if there is anything you need, you need only to make it known to me."

"I know," she replied softly. "But I'm content here. I do some tutoring, and that makes me feel of some use." She sighed. "We had nearly thirteen years together, Charles. It was a lifetime of love. I couldn't have asked for more."

Dewey was silent.

"We spoke of you just about a week before—" Mercy fought back the tears. "And Andrew said that when his time came . . . he wanted you to have something of his." She rose and went to a small desk in the corner and picked up a large book. "Andrew said that this was the most meaningful thing he could leave for you."

It was the large and very old English dictionary that MacCallum had used in the early years, when he was tutoring Dewey.

He took the book from her, hefting it. And he smiled slightly. "It wasn't the size of this book that gave me an education, it was the loving heart of the man who used it."

Dewey stayed for dinner at Mercy's insistence. And she plied him with questions about Bon Marché and its people. He gave her a rundown on all of the children and grandchildren. After several sherrys at the end of the meal, Charles came to his feet and bade her farewell.

"You can't make that long ride tonight," she protested. "You're welcome to stay here."

"No, I must get back to New York. We sail in just two days, and I have some business to attend to before I leave."

"But, Charles, it's nearly ten!"

He frowned. "The night holds no terror for me. Night or day, it seems, the specters of my mistakes haunt me. God, Mercy, I wish I could have talked to him just one more time."

"Please believe that that silly episode at Bon Marché didn't mean a damned thing to Andrew. He remembered you with great affection."

"As I did him."

They embraced again. He mounted his horse and rode away. It was almost dawn when he got back to the city. In the hours that had separated Princeton and New York he had devised a plan he saw as a final tribute to Andrew MacCallum.

IV

CHARLES Dewey had left Bon Marché with twenty slaves. Now, the horses and vans dispersed, their duties were ended. On the morning before his departure from New York, he called them all together. In his mind, Andrew stood there with him.

"I want you to know," he told the blacks, "that I appreciate how well you all worked on this trip. It's time now for Miss Alma May, Miss Carrie, and myself to return to Bon Marché. But you"—he spread his arms—"you are now free! Each one of you will have the proper papers to tell everyone that you are freemen. And one hundred dollars each to start a new life here in New York or wherever you choose to go."

The slaves stared at him unbelieving, saying nothing.

Charles drew the manumission documents from his coat pocket. "If you'll come to me, one by one, I'll give you your papers, and your money."

One of the older men, called Hezekiah, finally spoke. "Mistah Charles, Ah wants to go back to Bon Marché. Ah don' wanna stay here an'—"

He seemed genuinely frightened by the prospect of being a freeman. And that shocked Charles. He couldn't believe that such a thing was possible.

Hezekiah's bold words loosened the tongues of the others. And in just a few moments, Dewey's well-meaning plan was destroyed. Only four of the men chose freedom. All the others wanted to go home.

"Well, of course . . . I'll do what you want," Charles stammered. "We'll get horses so that you can go back to Bon Marché overland, and I'll give you some money for food and—" He stopped, still not believing what was happening.

Margaret, the housemaid, came forward then.

"Mistah Charles," she asked quietly, "kin Ah stay, too?"

That was another shock. He hadn't really wanted to set this woman free. She was Carrie's maid.

"Maggie, I'd appreciate it if you would come home with us. Miss Carrie counts on you."

"Yas, suh." Her jaw was set defiantly. "But Ah wants to be free!"

Disconcerted, Charles signed a paper for her and counted out a hundred dollars. Margaret took them, turned quickly, and hurried away.

But a majority—fifteen of the blacks—would be returning to Bon Marché. To slavery.

Dewey understood none of it.

45

In its more than a quarter of a century of existence, the name of Bon Marché had not been thought of by its neighbors as French. Dewey's accent had long since disappeared, softened first by the drawl of Virginia and then further by the flat twang of the frontier. *Bon* was alway pronounced "bun" by the Tennesseans, and *Marche* was made to sound like the month or was pronounced "mark." Indeed, the passage of time had virtually obliterated the stories of Charles's French beginnings as more and more new residents, unconcerned with the past history of the leading citizens, poured into the area.

Dewey, too, had stopped making references to his French heritage. As he had stopped nearly everything else since his return from New York. He seemed content, after his grand fling on the race circuits of the country, to turn full control of Bon Marché over to his two eldest sons and to his wife, Mattie. Carrie, his first grandchild, consumed all of his time, and what he once had been seemed of no importance to him.

But suddenly, early in 1825, Charles Dewey became French again. Nashville was enraptured by the news that Marie Joseph Paul Yves Roch Gilbert du Motier, the Marquis de Lafayette, was going to visit the city. It had been in excess of forty years since Lafayette had almost single-handedly brought the French into the American Revolution against the British, and had been rewarded with a commission of major general in George Washington's beleaguered army. And now he was back, at the age of sixty-seven, for what would be a farewell tour of his second country. He was to be lavishly feted in New York, in Boston, and in Washington, where a grateful Congress had voted him a cash gift—to replace the fortune he had lost during the revolutionary war—of two hundred thousand dollars plus a township of land in Florida. The entire nation insisted on honoring him, and it was, without question, the influence of Andrew Jackson that was bringing him to Nashville.

"Certainly Andy can't presume to speak for all of Tennessee on this matter of honoring Lafayette," Charles said one night in March during a late-hours discussion with his son-in-law, August Schimmel.

"I'm sure he doesn't intend to do that," Schimmel replied. He took a sip of sherry. "The word is that Jackson will rely on a committee of prominent citizens to help him plan the welcome. And it seems clear to me that you'll be included, Charles."

Dewey frowned. "You fail to understand Andy. I opposed him in last year's election, you'll recall, coming out publicly for Clay. He'll not forget that."

"Nonsense! Your lack of public support was, if you'll pardon me, of little consequence in the final analysis. It was the Congress that denied him the Presidency and gave it to Adams."

"Andy Jackson lives by one guiding principle," Charles interrupted. "You're either his friend or his enemy. There's no gray area with him. And if he perceives you as the enemy, as he does me, well . . . enemies are not to be rewarded in any way."

Dewey got to his feet and walked to the fireplace to stare into the dying embers. "I dearly want to be on that committee, August," he said quietly. "Not for any personal honor, but because it was Lafayette's example that gave me the courage, so many years ago when I was just a boy, to become an American."

"I'm certain you'll be asked to help plan the Lafayette celebration," Schimmel assured him.

The editor was wrong. Less than a week later a representative of General Jackson came to see him at the newspaper office.

"Mr. Schimmel," the emissary said, "I am charged by General Jackson to secure your help in the planning of the welcome for the Marquis de Lafayette."

"That's a distinct honor. May I ask who else is on the committee?"

The man ticked off the names of the others.

"And Charles Dewey? What of him?"

"No, he's not included."

"But surely you know that Dewey is a native of France, and fought on the French side during the American Revolution?"

"Hmmm."

"I can't think of anyone more qualified to be on this committee to honor General Lafayette."

The words were repeated. "He's not included."

"May I suggest that you point out to General Jackson Squire Dewey's availability?"

"That would be futile." The man shrugged. "You know as well as I do that Dewey declared himself against Andy in the presidential election."

"But that has nothing to do—"

"It has everything to do with it. Andy doesn't want him. As far as I'm concerned, that's the final word."

Schimmel grimaced. "Then I won't serve either."

Another shrug. "That's a foolish decision. You risk offending General Jackson."

"It's a risk I'll just have to take."

II

By Wednesday, May 4, the day that Lafayette was due to arrive in Nashville, Dewey's anger at having been shunted aside by Andy Jackson had run its course. Even the embarrassment he had felt in having to ask Mattie to intercede with her cousin to make certain they'd be invited to the dinner in Lafayette's honor at the Nashville Inn had passed.

He stood now on the edge of a massive crowd at the public square—Schimmel would write that the crowd exceeded twenty thousand—granddaughter Carrie beside him, and cheered with everyone else as a grand carriage drawn by four white horses brought Lafayette from the docks to a special stand built in the square.

As the French nobleman mounted the stand, the cheers grew even louder.

"You're looking at a truly great man," Charles told Carrie. "A man of unyielding principle and integrity, who risked position, wealth, and even life itself to fight for something he believed in: the independence of what was to become the United States of America."

"Who's that younger man with him?" the girl sked.

"His son, George Washington Lafayette, named for the general, as is your uncle George."

"Will you speak to General Lafayette, Grandfather?"

"I hope so—perhaps at the dinner tonight."

Once again Charles Dewey was frustrated. He and Mattie were assigned seats at the dinner as far away from the honored guest as was possible. When the meal ended and Charles tried to edge through the crowd, Lafayette was whisked out through a rear door and was off in the carriage to spend the night at The Hermitage.

There was almost no conversation as the Deweys drove back to Bon Marché in an open buggy.

"Are you angry, Charles?" Mattie asked.

"Yes."

"I hope your anger isn't going to cause you to do anything foolish."

Charles laughed. "No, no, Mattie. You can be at ease. I wouldn't give your vaunted *cousin* the satisfaction of knowing he has offended me. I can't believe that this nation thought him worthy to be its President! Thank God the Congress has frustrated him and Quincy Adams is now in the White House."

"There's another election in three years," Mattie reminded him.

"Yes, and isn't it obvious," Dewey groaned, "that Andy's running already . . . on the coattails of the honored Lafayette."

There was a long silence.

"You know," Dewey said eventually, "I was just thinking about that morning in that grove of trees in Kentucky—my God, it was way back in 1806— when Charles Dickinson might have rid us of Andy Jackson had he been more deliberate with his shot."

"Charles! That's dreadful!"

"Maybe. It's strange how history can turn on what seems at the time a minor event. If Dickinson had killed him in that duel we might now have a man of competence like Henry Clay in the presidency, instead of the prospect that Andy—"

"That's enough! I won't hear any more!"

Charles sighed. "My apologies, dear." He reached over and patted her hand. And then he grinned at her. "I promise, no more such maudlin talk. Now . . . you have your new gown for the ball tomorrow night?"

"Yes. It's lovely."

"And I'm sure you'll be the most beautiful woman there."

Mattie leaned over and kissed him on the cheek."

III

MARQUIS de Lafayette's age showed in his face. There were lines in it that told of his hard imprisonment in Prussian and Austrian jails after leading a French army against the Austrians. And there were lines, too, that mirrored his fight against the excesses of the French Revolution and, later, his political battle against Napoleon. His hair had thinned, the strands being combed forward on his forehead in an attempt to hide the loss.

But the old patriot stood ramrod straight in the receiving line at the ball in Nashville's new Masonic Hall. And smiles wreathed his face as he charmed each and every Tennessean presented to him.

Charles and Mattie, with Carrie in tow, arrived early for the ball. Dewey was determined to find the opportunity to talk to Lafayette. That came in mid-evening when, after a round of dances with some of the Nashville ladies, Lafayette was suddenly alone for a moment on the edge of the dance floor.

Dewey went up to him quickly. "General," he said, bowing deeply. "My name is Charles Dewey. Actually, Charles Dupree, a native of France."

Lafayette returned the bow.

"But now a citizen of America," Charles continued, "thanks to you."

"To me?"

"Yes, sir. You see I was in the crew of the *Ville de Paris* when you came aboard during the siege of Yorktown—"

"Ah! So we were comrades in arms?"

"That's putting too grand a face on it, sir. I was merely the cabin boy to Admiral de Grasse—"

Lafayette interrupted again. "Poor de Grasse. He's long been gone from us."

"I know. In any event, it was your shining example, your enthusiasm for this country, that made me determined to be an American.

"Well, I'm pleased to have influenced you in that manner. And what do you do as an American?"

"I run a horse farm, General. Here at Nashville. It's called Bon Marché."

The French nobleman grinned. "And is it a 'good bargain,' Mr. Dewey?"

"Indeed it is."

Lafayette took him by the arm and drew him away to a quiet corner. "As a fellow Frenchman, Mr. Dewey, may I presume to ask you a question about your farm?"

"Of course."

"Do you use slaves to run it?"

"Yes."

"Many?"

"Nearly two hundred, sir."

"And are you . . . content with that?"

Charles frowned. "No, General, I'm not."

"In the course of my tour of America, I have been . . . well, constantly distressed by the spectacle of slavery. It seems to me that it is so deeply engrained in the South that . . ." He shrugged.

"I, too, am distressed by it."

"Yet you engage in it."

"Yes." Dewey hung his head.

"Why?"

"The intensive labor needed to run a big plantation—"

Lafayette stopped him with a raised hand. "That's an argument I have heard before, Mr. Dewey. I mean no offense to you, sir, but it seems a poor defense for slavery. And worse: I see this issue dividing your nation. Don't you?"

"I do, yes."

"In that case, why continue with it?"

"Years ago, in Virginia, my father-in-law told me that men of greater minds than his—and he was an intelligent man—had struggled with the problem and had failed to find a solution. That problem still prevails, I'm afraid."

The Frenchman shook his head sadly. "I certainly hope someone comes forward with a solution before it is too late."

Dewey could only nod agreement. He changed the subject. "General, might I presume on you to present my granddaughter? She has been wanting to meet you."

"I'd be delighted."

Charles signaled to Carrie, who stood a few paces away, and she came to them.

"Your Grace, may I present my first granddaughter, Carrie Dewey?"

Carrie curtsied.

"Ah! Another American beauty!" Lafayette smiled at her. "May I ask, *mademoiselle*, how old you are?"

"Fourteen, sir."

"Then old enough, wouldn't you say, for a dance?"

He offered his arm, and they whirled onto the floor.

Hours later, when Charles and Mattie were in bed, Dewey asked: "Was the marquis a good dancer?"

"Extremely so. My God, what charm that man has! I think he danced with every woman present."

"Carrie was captivated by him."

Mattie sighed deeply.

"What?" Charles sensed disapproval in her.

"You have other grandchildren, you know. It seems to me that you ought to consider them at times. Joy and Hope might like to have danced with General Lafayette, too, you know."

"Louise and August could have taken them to the ball if they had wished," Dewey said defensively. "I give some special attention to Carrie because she is without a mother. I see nothing wrong in that."

His wife stayed quiet for a moment. "Are you going to the races Saturday?"

"No, I think not."

"But George has Sir Matt ready for his debut."

"I know, but I promised Carrie that we'd take a ride in the woods as part of her botany studies."

Mattie sighed again, then turned away from him, seeking sleep.

IV

SIR Matt was a strapping bay son of the noted Virginia-standing stallion, Sir Archie, by the great Diomed. The dam of the new Bon Marché competitor was the tough Matilda, who had carried Mattie's name in the unique five-heat, twenty-mile race back in 1808. As a brood mare she had been disappointing until mated with Sir Archie, but now George Dewey was convinced that he had a champion on his hands in the five-year-old Sir Matt.

His maiden race was to be at Gallatin, the scene of Matilda's triumph. George had kept the training of Sir Matt under wraps; he meant to make a killing with him in his first time out. Indeed, George did everything he could to keep the ability of his runner a secret.

When invited by the managers of the Gallatin track to enter a horse in the Gallatin Cup event he delayed his decision until the last moment. Then, seemingly reluctantly, he dropped Sir Matt's name into the entry box, with apologies.

"Gentlemen," he said, "I'm entering this nag only because you have been so fair to Bon Marché in the past."

He also undertook two other ploys. He instructed the Negro grooms not to work on Sir Matt. "I want him to look a little shaggy," he said. George also kept his best jockey off the horse, putting up an apprentice named Harry, a ninety-seven-pound lad riding his first race.

To the members of the Dewey family who had traveled to Gallatin for the event, George said: "I don't want to see any Bon Marché money wagered on the first heat. No money at all, do you understand? I'll tell you when the time is right."

Mattie was suspicious of his tactics. "George, is what you're doing . . . ethical?"

"Ethical?" Her son laughed. "All's fair in love, war, and horse racing. Haven't you ever heard that cliché?"

"George, I don't think I like this."

He hugged her. "Mother, indulge me a bit, will you? What can you really know about a maiden? I don't want us to waste our money, that's all."

When the bugle called the field to the post for the Gallatin Cup—the best of three heats at three miles each—George took the young jockey aside.

"Now, listen carefully to me, boy! I don't want you to do anything out there but keep from falling off. No whip, no spurs. Your only job is to keep him from being distanced. Do you understand?"

"Yas, suh."

"Our race is not in this first heat, Harry."

"Yas, suh."

George clapped him on the back and boosted him into the saddle. Harry trotted the horse to the starting line to join the eight other runners. The public pool, seeing very little money bet on Sir Matt had his odds at twenty-five to one.

When the drum tapped and the field sped away from the line, Harry, following his instructions to the letter, was nearly left at the post. Only through vigorous hand-riding in the course of the three miles did he keep the Bon Marché horse in contention at all. A Kentucky horse named Ridgerunner was the clear winner by three lengths over a Nashville mare called First in War, named, it was understood, to honor Andy Jackson.

Sir Matt was barely drawing a deep breath after his first heat, in which he finished sixth. George was grinning broadly.

The second heat was called. "Harry," George said sternly, "it's going to be a little more difficult this time. I want you to win this time, but right at the wire. The way I see it, you have only two horses to beat: First in War and that Kentucky animal, Ridgerunner."

The jockey nodded.

"But I don't want to see you in contention until the last half mile. Keep those two in sight and come on late."

"But—" The lad was perplexed.

"Don't worry about it, Harry. Sir Matt is clearly the best of them. He could beat them any day of the week and twice on Sunday." He laughed. "Just as long as you don't do it too soon."

"Yas, suh."

On his performance in the first heat, and because of the lack of Bon Marché money on him, Sir Matt went off in the second at forty to one.

Harry did his job once more, keeping Sir Matt within a few lengths of the leaders as Ridgerunner and First in War dueled for the lead. In the last three hundred yards the Bon Marché jockey, whipping and driving, first disposed of First in War and then caught Ridgerunner at the wire, winning by only a nose.

It was exactly what George Dewey wanted.

It was going to be a match race between Sir Matt and Ridgerunner in the third and final heat.

"Now," George announced to the family members, "bet the jewels."

The sudden large rush of Bon Marché money—George himself wagered ten thousand dollars—drove the odds down considerably for the third heat. Ridgerunner was held as the even-money favorite, but Sir Matt, getting little respect from the other bettors in the crowd, was allowed to go off at nine to one.

The drum tapped again, sending the two heat winners off the line. Sir Matt immediately went into the lead and lengthened his advantage with each stride. In the last mile, Harry just sat there, holding the reins loosely, as Sir Matt easily held off the rush of Ridgerunner and won by six lengths.

One of the managers of the track, after presenting George with the Gallatin Cup, drew him aside.

"We are not happy, Mr. Dewey," he said, "with what happened here today. There is the suspicion that you carried off a betting coup."

George's open face was all innocence. "The horse was a maiden before today—a true maiden. He had never competed at all. He simply found his legs in the last two heats, that's all."

The manager frowned. "There's no way we can prove otherwise, of course, but if we knew for certain that you did have a coup in mind, we'd start action to have you ruled off!"

"Would I risk the Bon Marché reputation for a mere few dollars?"

"Hmmm." The manager looked into his clear blue eyes. "Perhaps not."

"Just the luck of racing, sir," George said breezily. "The luck of racing!"

The "mere few dollars" that George had mentioned added up to nearly one hundred fifty thousand.

Mattie, deeply distressed, took the story to Charles that night.

"Well," he sighed, "it's not my concern any longer. George and Franklin are in charge now."

"Charles Dewey! Do you condone his actions?"

"If he engaged in a betting coup, of course not. But maiden horses are notoriously unpredictable runners, you know."

His wife was angry. "Charles, don't close your eyes to this! It's so obvious!"

"Obvious to whom?"

"To me!"

"Yes. Very well, I'll speak to George. But I'm sure the win was due to the idiosyncracies of an untried horse."

George agreed with that evaluation by his father.

V

CHARLES Dewey's interest in the fortunes of Bon Marché waned with each passing day. His life fell into an easy routine. His days were given over totally to Carrie: to her education, to her development as a young adult. He spent the late hours each evening in the drawing room with August Schimmel. He and the editor discussed what was happening in the world. Those two things contented Charles, even when the subjects talked about in the drawing room raised his ire.

"Where are we headed?" he asked sadly one night in mid-July 1826. "I mean, it seems that we're losing all of the old, stable leaders. What irony that John Adams and Thomas Jefferson should die on the same day—and on July Fourth, too. In some ways it seems, August, that the hope for the nation died on that day, as well."

"You're too melancholy, Charles."

"Am I? Doesn't the growth of sectionalism bother you? And this . . . polarization of political thought. Washington warned of that, you know. But now we see the establishment of two distinct political factions. On one side we have the Adams-Clay group, calling themselves the National Republicans. On the other side we have Andy and Calhoun and their sycophants trumpeting their cause as the Democrats. It's all factionalism and sectionalism, and we're going down the path to national destruction, I tell you!"

"I find the national debate stimulating," Schimmel countered, taking his usual position as the devil's advocate. "There are pains in growth. We cannot ignore them. They should be aired so that the intelligent decision can be made."

"Is there any intelligence left?" Charles said sarcastically. "When Lafayette was here, he asked me why we had placed our reliance in slavery. And I couldn't answer him. Does no one have the intelligence to deal with this problem?"

"Men of goodwill shall find the answer."

Dewey laughed. "Men of goodwill? Do you consider me a man of goodwill?"

"Of course."

"And yet I hold slaves. And will continue holding slaves because I can't figure out how to maintain Bon Marché without them. Isn't that insanity of a sort?"

And so the discussions continued night after night. When, finally, the national elections of 1828 came about, the two close friends found themselves on opposite sides—polarized, as the nation as a whole was polarized.

Editor Schimmel supported Andrew Jackson. Dewey opposed Jackson, even though he felt that John Quincy Adams had been a weak President. He would always oppose Jackson, but while he could discuss his opinions with Schimmel, Charles never spoke of them to Mattie. In truth, he talked to Mattie less and less. Their relationship had become "polite"—a terrible, debilitating word for two people who had once been so much in love.

In November, when the results of the presidential election were clear, Dewey said to Schimmel: "Well, now you have him, August. The great hero of New Orleans will be in the White House—the beneficiary of a spontaneous outpouring of public support. May God have mercy on the United States of America!"

VI

EARLY one morning a few days before Christmas, Mattie awakened Charles with the news.

"A rider just came in from The Hermitage," she said. "Rachel is dying. I think I ought to be there."

"Of course."

"I want you to go with me."

"Oh . . . do you think that's wise?"

"Charles, please."

Andy was disconsolate when they got there.

"The doctors say there's no hope." he reported. "Good God, what have I done? My ambition has killed her."

"Don't believe that for a minute, Cousin," Mattie said gently.

"No, it's true. Earlier this month she was in Nashville and happened upon one of those . . . those scurrilous pieces of campaign literature in which she— that dear, sweet, innocent woman—was slandered so . . . viciously about her marriage to me—" He stopped to brush away a tear. "An adultress, they called her. And worse! She broke down, weeping hysterically over the awful things that were written about her. And then her wounded heart gave way."

Andy slammed a fist into his palm.

"I swear to you, Cousin Mattie, the day of retribution must come!"

Rachel lingered throughout the day and into the night. Near midnight she breathed her last, cradled in her husband's arms. Andy cried inconsolably. It was less than three days to Christmas.

Charles Dewey actually felt sorry for the man.

She was buried in the garden of the home Jackson had built for her. It was a simple, short ceremony, disturbed only by the sound of the President-elect's weeping.

As Mattie and Charles walked away from the grave Andy fell in step with them.

"I have only my penance to look forward to now, Cousin," he said to Mattie, "to be served in that damned house in Washington!"

They didn't know what to say to him.

"It would be of some comfort to me, Mattie, if you would consent to be a member of my party at the inauguration. Rachel always loved you dearly."

"Of course, if that's what you want."

Jackson, his shoulders sagging, walked away from them and into the lonely Hermitage.

Mattie looked at Charles. "You won't mind if I go to Washington?"

"No. I'd be disappointed if you didn't go."

Mattie kissed him.

Before Andrew Jackson would go to Washington, a gravestone would be put at Rachel's resting place. And on it would be carved "a being so gentle and so virtuous, slander might wound, but could not dishonor."

46

MATTIE wrote to her family at Bon Marché:

I can hardly find the words to adequately describe what I feel now. All along the way from Nashville to Pittsburgh, when the riverboat put in for stops, great crowds came out to see Cousin Andy. But there was no political whooping-it-up, in the accepted sense of that phrase. They applauded him, of course, but with great dignity, it seemed to me. The people recognized that Andy is in mourning, and they respected that.

The carriage ride overland from Pittsburgh was very tiring, and as the miles dragged on, Cousin Andy said less and less. I fear for him. He has a great task ahead of him and, right now, little stomach for it.

At his request there was no great welcome in Washington for him, and no parties of any kind are planned. It's to be a simple, dignified inauguration. But I'm glad to be here, because I'm to see history being made, and also because that my presence is of some comfort to Andy. No one, though, can plumb the depth of his grief.

I have a room, comfortable enough, at the National Hotel, and you may write to me here . . .

II

CHARLES was disturbed. He was waiting for Carrie at the gelding barn, holding the reins of two saddled riding mares, but she was late. Very late. He had hoped to ride to Franklin and back that day, but the days were still short and unless they got started soon, darkness would overtake them before they could return.

"Here, boy!" he shouted to one of the Negro grooms. "Go see if you can stir up Miss Carrie. Tell her I'm waiting."

"Yas, suh." The black hurried away in the direction of the big house.

Dewey fumed as the minutes dragged on without the arrival of Carrie or any word from the black. Finally, the slave came running up.

"Ah sorry, Mistah Charles, but Miss Carrie she weren't at the house. An' I hadda look 'round fer her. She comin' now, though."

"Well, where in the hell—"

Carrie rushed onto the scene. Breathlessly, she kissed him on the cheek apologetically.

"I'm sorry, Grandfather, I got held up."

"What was so damned important?"

She laughed in the delightful way that always melted his anger. "I was talking to Alvin and I lost track of time."

"Who in the devil is Alvin?"

"Oh, you know Alvin, Grandfather. Alvin Mussmer, the son of the the field hands' overseer."

"Oh, yes," Charles growled, "Elmer's son. I'm not so sure that I approve of you consorting with—"

"We weren't consorting, Grandfather, just talking."

They mounted the mares.

"And what do you find to talk about with the likes of that Alvin fellow?"

"Lots of things. He's very sweet."

"Carrie, you have to remember your position here at Bon Marché."

"Oh, Grandfather," she said, annoyed now, "you're so stuffy sometimes."

"My only concern, young lady, is your well-being. If you won't look out for it, I must."

"Grandfather, I'm nearly eighteen."

"All the more reason to conduct yourself properly."

They rode off toward Franklin, the grandfather studying the young girl. She was very much like her grandmother, and Charles was remembering that he made love to Martha when she was only sixteen. That thought didn't reassure him in the slightest.

III

CHARLES was reading another letter from Mattie at the dinner table:

> Cousin Andy walked from the hotel to the Capitol for his inauguration, surprising a lot of people and pleasing them, too. They fell in behind him as he walked, and by the time he got to the Capitol there were thousands at his heels. A most impressive outpouring of devotion.
>
> It was somewhat overcast early in the day, but just as Andy walked out onto the platform where he was to take the oath, the sun burst through the clouds most brightly! It was like an omen, I thought.
>
> I wasn't on the stand and therefore couldn't hear his short speech, but I'm sure you'll all be reading about it in August's newspaper. (In answer to the query in your last letter, tell August that it's all right if he wants to reprint my letters, if he eliminates the purely personal matters.)

Charles looked up at his son-in-law. "There! You have your own correspondent in Washington."

"Good, good," Schimmel commented.

Charles turned his attention back to the letter.

After the speech and the oath-taking and the hand-shaking, Cousin Andy mounted a white horse and rode off toward the White House, again followed by the mob. As I told you earlier, there were no parties of celebration planned because of the period of mourning, but there had been a public announcement that the White House would be open to all who wanted to come.

Never have I seen anything like it, and I don't imagine I will ever again see such a demonstration. Food had been laid out on long tables in what I am told is the East Room, and it soon disappeared under the onslaught of hundreds. Andy was in the room (will I ever get accustomed to calling him the President?) and found himself shoved up against the wall by the press of bodies. How he got out I don't know; I didn't see his departure. I only know that somehow he was removed from the madness—and that's what it was: madness! I saw fights breaking out, more than one bloody nose, drapery torn down, cut glass and china smashed (worth how much, I wonder?), children passed out through windows so that they wouldn't be crushed, people standing with muddy boots on damask-covered furniture. I myself had difficulty getting out of the White House; my dress was ripped in three different places. But that was a small price to pay, I felt, for my safety.

As I was leaving the grounds, I saw White House servants opening casks of whiskey on the lawn. The intent, I imagine, was to lure the rabble out of the building. I hope it worked.

I'll be leaving here in two days. Just this morning I decided to go to Boston for a few days to see some old friends from my school days. I'll sail to New Orleans from there and duplicate the water trip you made, Charles, when you returned from your racing foray (is that the word I really want?).

I contemplated, for just a few hours, visiting Philadelphia to try to see Mother, but I've abandoned that idea. Indeed, I don't even know whether she is still alive. Isn't that sad?

"She sends her love to all of us," Charles said. "I imagine it may be at least two more months before we see her again."

Dewey went to his drawing room to work on the farm records and finances, a chore he had assumed again in Mattie's absence. After some time, Carrie entered the room.

"Am I disturbing you, Grandfather?"

"No, dear, I'm just finishing. Would you like a small sherry?"

"No." She shook her head. "Thank you." Sighing deeply, she dropped into a chair facing his desk. "For several days now I've been wanting to talk to you. I've rehearsed this so many times—"

"A problem?"

Carrie stared at him soberly. "I'm in love."

"Oh?" Dewey's eyebrows shot up.

"Yes, Grandfather. With Alvin, and I want to marry him."

"You're pulling my leg, of course." He grinned at her. Sometimes her sense of humor was a little . . . mischievous.

"No." She dropped her head, not looking at him any longer.

Charles was stunned. "You can't be serious, Carrie! Alvin Mussmer? A common . . . farm worker! What happened to all of our plans for college and for your future as a botanist, and—"

"I could still do those things."

"No!" Charles came to his feet. "No, damn it!" He pounded a fist on his desk. "Alvin Mussmer is simply not worthy of you! I will not permit it!"

Carrie raised her head again, meeting his eyes. "Grandfather . . . dear Grandfather, I know this is going to hurt you, but"—she sobbed—"I'm carrying his child."

"You're . . . you're *what?*"

Dewey sank slowly into his chair, dropping his head into his hands. "Does your father know of this?"

"No. I thought I owed it to you to come to you first."

He laughed sarcastically. "You thought you *owed* it to me! What you owed to me"—he was stammering—"was . . . was . . . Oh, God, how could you, Carrie?" He began to cry.

"Please, Grandfather, try to understand. I love him. He's a dear, sweet boy."

There was a long pause. A deep silence, broken only by the old man's weeping and Carrie's soft sobbing.

Suddenly, he slammed his fist on the desk again, then leaped to his feet and hurried toward the door.

"Grandfather, what are you going to do?"

"That son of a bitch!" Charles muttered. "That filthy son of a bitch!"

He was gone.

"Grandfather! Grandfather!" Carrie shouted after him. She began to run.

Dewey, his anger in control of him, rushed along the path toward that area of the farm where the four overseers' modest homes stood side by side. It was nearly a half-mile from the main house, and when he got here, he was breathing deeply. He pounded on the door of the Mussmer house.

Elmer Mussmer opened the door. "Squire Dewey, what—"

"Where's your son?!"

"In the feed mill right now, but—"

Charles took off at a dead run. Behind him he could hear Carrie screaming: "Grandfather! Wait! Wait!"

He burst through the door of the mill, where the boy was sacking grain.

"Mussmer, you dirty—" Dewey swung a fist, smashing it into Alvin's face, sending him sprawling, blood flowing from his nose.

Madly, he looked around for a weapon. He picked up a broken ax handle and swung it again and again at the huddled figure of young Mussmer. Alvin tried to crawl away from the attack, tried to regain his feet, but Charles kicked him viciously in the stomach. Once, twice, three times.

Then he fell on the boy and pummeled him with his fists, shouting, "I'll kill you, you bastard! I'll kill you!"

Dewey continued the beating even after Alvin was unconscious.

"Grandfather! Stop! Oh, please stop!" Carrie burst into the mill, followed by Elmer Mussmer, who grappled with the angry older man, pulling him off the boy.

"Squire Dewey, stop it! For God's sake, stop it!"

Charles lashed out wildly at the elder Mussmer, also knocking him to the floor. Only when Carrie threw herself at him, pounding her fists on his chest, did Dewey desist. He stood, then, with his legs spread wide, sucking in deep breaths, muttering oaths.

Carrie went to Alvin and cradled his bloody head in her lap, rocking him, weeping. "Oh, Alvin . . . dear Alvin."

Elmer pushed himself to his feet, edging away from Charles before he spoke. "Squire, what is happening?"

"I want that bastard off this farm!" He was screaming, pointing at the unconscious boy. "And you, Mussmer, and your wife, are to go with him!"

His edict given, Dewey turned and strode out of the mill.

IV

"I DON'T give a damn what you say, Franklin, Alvin Mussmer will *not* marry Carrie!"

"But she's pregnant by him!"

The two men, father and son, stood in the middle of the Bon Marché drawing room, shouting at each other. It was less than a half-hour since the beating.

"And you think her pregnancy is going to make the marriage *right?*" Charles yelled.

"No! But, damn it, Father, she *is* pregnant. And we must recognize that reality!"

"The only reality I recognize is that that boy is not fit to marry Carrie!"

Franklin groaned, walking to the wide windows, gazing out, trying to control his temper. To bring reason to the moment.

"Fit or not," the son said slowly, "we must make the best of this situation." He went to Charles and laid a consoling hand on his arm. "Father, neither of us likes this, but Carrie . . . well, Carrie has taken the decision out of our hands."

"Not out of my hands! That bastard leaves here tonight! I want all the Mussmers off this property!"

"No, Father, that's not the answer."

Dewey roughly shrugged his son's hand off his arm. "That *is* the answer! If you don't like it, you can leave Bon Marché, too!"

Franklin stared at him. "*That*, Father, I will not do!" He started for the door, stopped, and turned once more to Charles. "I made a terrible mistake in allowing you to dominate the life of my daughter—"

"She's my granddaughter!"

"—*My daughter,*" Franklin continued with determination. "Your preoccupation with Carrie was convenient for me, I'll admit that. She had no mother and your concern for her filled that gap, in a sense. But now that she needs me, I'm going to fight for her. She tells me she loves young Mussmer—"

"Love!" Charles scoffed.

"—and I'm going to arrange for them to be married at once."

"I forbid it!"

Franklin sighed deeply. "I don't know why I didn't see what you were up to before now."

"What I was up to?"

"You have indulged Carrie and ignored your own children."

Charles stared at him, trying not to comprehend what his eldest son was saying.

"When have you really cared about Thomas, for example?"

"I see Thomas every day," Dewey insisted.

"And what do you say to him in the course of any one day? 'Good morning, Thomas.' Do you call that caring about him?"

"He's a taciturn young man. Difficult to communicate with."

"Have you ever tried?"

Charles just looked at him sullenly, not answering.

"And poor Marshall? You've totally abandoned him."

"I offered to send him a racing string in New York, and he refused it."

"Oh, Father." Franklin was exasperated. "He was concerned that he wasn't ready for the opportunity. And in the nearly six years since then, have you ever again attempted to be a father to Marshall?"

Again, no reply.

His son shrugged. "Well, one bastard in the family is enough."

"Take care, Franklin!" Dewey interrupted angrily.

"What are you going to do—thrash me, too? I tell you now, Father, that Carrie and Alvin *will* be married!"

"Damn you, listen to me! *I forbid it!*"

"Not this time, old man, not this time." Franklin left his father standing alone in the drawing room.

V

MATTIE faced a crisis when she returned to Bon Marché in June.

Somehow the plantation still ran under the management of Franklin and George, but barely. Charles had instituted a series of petulant moves that had seriously disrupted the smooth operation of Bon Marché. For one thing, he had stopped keeping the financial records up to date, ignoring bills that had to be paid. Mattie found a pile of unopened angry letters from creditors scattered on the desk.

Charles had also announced that he was going to take over the training of the Bon Marché horses once more. When his sons challenged him on that decision, he circumvented their objections by giving firm, direct orders to the Negro grooms and handlers—and the slaves obeyed him. "Mistah Charles," after all, was still the master of Bon Marché in their eyes. Finally, Franklin and George gave in to him, fearing that the horses would suffer otherwise.

Except for the blacks with whom Dewey had to deal in the training regimen, he had become reclusive, no longer taking his meals with the rest of the family, but ordering the servants that he was to have his food in his bedroom suite. And that suite Mattie found in incredible disorder. Clothes scattered everywhere, the bed unmade for weeks, plates of half-eaten food allowed to mold where he had abandoned them—on dresser tops, on chairs, even on the floor. Tearful housemaids told Mattie: "Mistah Charles says we ain't to go in there no more."

And the mistress of Bon Marché found Carrie and Alvin Mussmer married and living in Franklin's house. The marriage didn't please her, but she put on a brave face about it, joking with Carrie about the prospect of becoming a great-grandmother.

"I'm much too young for that, you know," Mattie said, laughing.

Carrie simply nodded.

"Are you well, dear?"

"Yes." A pause. "But Grandfather hates me now."

"No, he doesn't. He may be a bit disappointed, but—"

"I *love* Alvin, Grandmother."

"Yes, I'm sure you do." She embraced the young girl. "And we all love you."

But those words did little to reassure Carrie. She saw before her the daily harassment of her husband by Charles: bitter denunciations of Alvin for everything he did, orders to the blacks not to work with the young man, constant cursing by her grandfather whenever he was within earshot of Mussmer. Alvin tried to stay away from him, but his efforts were useless. It was clear that Dewey meant to destroy him.

All that Mattie found. And more. A strange fruit of Charles's aberrant behavior was his sudden concern for Thomas Jefferson Dewey, his youngest son. As if to show Franklin wrong about how he had treated Thomas, Charles now took Thomas under his wing, drawing him into the racehorse training, tutoring him on the fine points. Indeed, Thomas became the only member of the family with whom Dewey communicated with any regularity. The others were likely to be met with mere grunts or terse curses.

Thomas obeyed his father, but he was uncomfortable with his new role. "I just feel that I want to get away from all this," he told his half brother, Franklin.

"No, don't. Stick with it. With all of his idiosyncracies, Father is a superb horseman. You'll learn much from him. God knows, he owes you at least that."

It was in her initial talk with Franklin and George that Mattie Dewey learned of the depth of the damage Charles had done.

"I'm going mad, Mother," Franklin said. "Creditors have been coming to my door at all hours, and I can tell them only that Father is just . . . well, just a little behind in the paperwork. But the truth is that he has ignored the bills. Several of our suppliers—Moses Till, for example, from whom we buy oats—won't deliver here anymore."

George was just as distraught. "Our saddler, too, has written us off—refusing to do any more business with Bon Marché. When I offered to help Father with the recordkeeping, he shouted at me, telling me to mind my own business. And he forbade Franklin and me to enter the drawing room when we offered to try to make sense of the papers."

"I'll pay the bills immediately," Mattie told them.

George shrugged. "That's only part of it, Mother. Now that Father is training the horses, I'm left with nothing to do here. Nothing at all. Mary is very discontented, and honestly, so am I. We've been discussing the possibility of moving on—"

"No, no!" Mattie pleaded. "I need you now more than ever. Give me a chance to set things right."

But setting things right wasn't easy. Even the matter of simply cleaning up the bedroom suite became a matter of contention between Mattie and Charles.

"Just leave things the way they are," Dewey said in an offhand manner. "Sometimes I think we place too much store in neatness."

"It isn't a question of just neatness, Charles. This place is *filthy*." She was trying to be calm. "I can't live in this kind of—"

"Then maybe you ought to find someplace else to live."

"Charles!"

He laughed at her. "Or perhaps I should!"

The next morning he moved out, taking a room at the Nashville Inn, riding to Bon Marché every day to continue with the training of the horses.

Mattie was distraught, but his action forced her to order her priorities.

First, Bon Marché.

Then the family.

And only then could she consider her continuing relationship with Charles Dewey.

47

A DAUGHTER was born to Alvin and Carrie Mussmer early in November of 1829. They named her Honey.

For the first time in months, Mattie and Charles were together as they waited in the living room of Franklin's home for news of the birth. Mattie had asked her husband to be there, and he had surprised her by agreeing, without the rancor he had always shown when matters involving Alvin Mussmer were raised.

"I told Carrie some time back," Mattie said, "that I'm much too young to be a great-grandmother."

"And so you are." Charles smiled, patting her affectionately on the arm. He sighed deeply. "Charles Dewey, though, is easily old enough to be a great-grandfather. And he can look down the road to his final days."

"That's nonsense, Charles."

"No, Mattie, it's not. It's reality. And there are nights when I think I might welcome the final day, seeing the havoc my dotage has brought."

"Charles, please stop that! You frighten me with such talk."

Once more he patted her arm. "I'm sorry, dear."

When they received the report of Honey's birth, and after they had both viewed the tiny pink child held in Carrie's arms, they walked together toward the mansion.

"Doesn't this merit a sherry?" Mattie asked.

"Yes, I suppose it does."

Alone in the drawing room, the sherry poured, they sat like strangers, uneasy, not talking.

Finally, Mattie said: "Isn't there an entry to be made in the Bible, Charles?"

"You do it. My writing has become too shaky."

She didn't want to argue with him. Taking the big Bible down from a shelf, she laid it open on the desk and entered the notation of the birth. It was the first time that anyone but Charles Dewey had written in the book.

That accomplished, she was determined to go further. "I wish you'd move back here, Charles."

"Why?"

"Because this is your home."

"No," he said quietly, "it's where I do my work as a horse trainer. It's not—"

"Charles, don't talk like that!"

"See? I've angered you again."

"You haven't. It's just that I want you back here."

"You do?" He seemed surprised.

"Of course."

He hesitated.

"Please, Charles. We *all* need you."

Dewey laughed then. "You were never a very convincing liar, Mattie. But I am tiring of the Nashville Inn."

"All the more reason to come home. It'll be like old times again."

They both knew that wasn't true.

II

NEW Orleans seemed to be what Mary Harrison Dewey had been seeking ever since she left London. The gay, cosmopolitan city on the crescent-shaped bend of the Mississippi fascinated her. "Society" here was a compelling mixture of French and Spanish cultures, seasoned with Acadian refugees, Dalmatian oystermen, gorgeous mulatto women—and the naughty gossip associated with them—*gens de couleur*, a rapidly growing population of *les Americains*, and even a smattering of the rough descendants of pirates.

Everything about the city excited her: the numerous *bal masques*, the quaint restaurants offering foods that mirrored the international complexity of the port, the busy cockpits, the gamblers, the riverboat captains, the stolid Choctaw squaws selling homeopathic roots and herbs in the French market, the Italian fruit peddlers, the turbaned mulatto women offering *gris-gris* and love potions, the *Theatre d'Orleans*, the saloons, and—although she was properly critical of them—the ubiquitous bordellos boasting *filles de joie* of every color and nationality.

To Mary, the major city in Louisiana—indeed, the fourth largest city in the nation—was alive and vivid in hue, while Nashville was perceived as being dull and uninspiring.

And then there was the racing in New Orleans.

George Washington Dewey and his wife had made the trip to take in the racing at the Eclipse course in the spring of 1831. But that had been just an excuse, really. George had felt that he had to get away from Bon Marché. It had become a dead end for him. When his stepmother had persuaded his father to return to the plantation, Charles had come back with a firm determination to retain his right to train the Bon Marché horses, thus making George little more than an assistant whose aid was never sought. On the rare occasions when he volunteered advice, the master of Bon Marché chose to ignore it.

If only for a month or two, New Orleans was an escape for him, an effort, perhaps his final effort—he was forty-two—to revive his self-esteem. He was pleased to find that he was warmly welcomed in the racetrack circles of the city, and to learn that he *did* have a reputation as a fine horse trainer, something he had been almost ready to forfeit at Bon Marché.

Mary reveled in the opulence of the Eclipse Course, loving the way ladies were catered to there. And George greatly admired the racing surface; it was like none he had ever seen before.

"This is the fastest track in the country," builder Yelverton Oliver told him. "We've made it so by hauling in tons of sand to mix with the natural soil, forming a cushion of sorts on which to run. The horses seem to take to it admirably."

"And with fewer sore legs, I'd imagine."

"Oh, definitely!" Oliver grinned at him. "I'm a bit disappointed, Mr. Dewey, that you haven't brought some of those Bon Marché horses we've been hearing about to compete here."

"I, too," George admitted. "Perhaps at a later meeting." But he knew that if he recommended it to his father it would never happen.

Oliver introduced George and Mary to a horseman named Pierre Pujol, and Pujol, in turn, insisted that they have dinner at his table in the dining room, which featured cut-crystal chandeliers, fine imported table linen, and a menu to match the quality of the furnishings. There was a constant flow of visitors to Pujol's table with names like Oubre, Capdeville, Lapeyrouse, Sabatier, and even a few of *les Americains* not unlike themselves: Barrow and Garrison and Adams and Wells and Chinn.

As the dessert was being served by stiffly formal black waiters who spoke proper French, Pujol got to his feet and gestured to George. "Come Dewey, let's take a look at the next field of runners."

Once out of earshot of the table, Pujol said, "I had a reason, Monsieur Dewey, for dragging you away from the others. Some of my friends become annoyed with me at times because I insist on exhibiting my sixth sense—my voodoo, no? But I sense things in people, sometimes more accurately than other times. And in you, Monsieur, I sense a feeling of frustration, of having reached a turn in the road—how do you say it?—a crossroads. I am right, yes?"

George was sober-faced. "Yes."

"Ah, I am pleased that I haven't lost my powers." He clapped George on the back. "Don't fear, Monsieur, I'm not a mind reader. Now that I've come this far, I have to admit to you that I don't know what frustrates you. But, if I am permitted a guess, it has to do with horses." He smiled. "That's not too perceptive, I imagine, in that you are a noted trainer."

The son of Charles Dewey also smiled. "You, sir, are disarming."

"And I find that a great tool."

They had reached the walking ring where they studied the horses being paraded for the bettors.

Without really knowing why, George decided to confide in this virtual stranger. "What you perceive, Mr. Pujol, is correct. I came to New Orleans to determine whether I might have a future here. For reasons I don't care to discuss right now, I've been thinking of making a change in my life . . ."

"Ah!"

". . . because I find that I have gone as far as I can in Tennessee."

"Will you establish a racing stable here, Monsieur?"

"I was thinking more along the lines of trying to associate myself with an already established stable."

Pujol raised his eyes to the heavens, as if giving thanks. "Wonderful! Wonderful! It just so happens, Monsieur Dewey, that I, too, have been thinking of making a change. Something of a convenient miracle, no? I have a string of forty horses stabled here at Eclipse—and a Cajun trainer who is an idiot! If only I could obtain the services of a trainer of your reputation . . ."

George Dewey pondered the Frenchman's words. "You're serious, aren't you?"

"*Absolument!*" Pujol launched into a detailed offer of employment, with liberal terms that astounded the visitor.

At the end of the day of racing, and alone in their hotel room, the Deweys talked of the idea of moving to New Orleans and training the racing string of Pierre Pujol.

"Oh, Georgie, could we?" Mary asked enthusiastically.

"Father will probably cut off my inheritance if we make this move."

"We're not exactly destitute, Georgie. And there's my money—"

Ordinarily, George would have been offended by such a remark. Now he wasn't. But he continued to be the devil's advocate. "And how will the children react?"

"They'll love it, Georgie! They're at an age now where they need new experiences. And Charles Two—imagine how he's going to prosper in this atmosphere. He's only fourteen, I know, but he's ready to blossom. New Orleans will make a gentleman of him."

George nodded agreement.

"God, I love the excitement here!" Mary rambled on. "Even the absurdities of the place. When you and Monsieur Pujol were away from our table, that young Mandeville—what a scoundrel he is!—well, he had us all sick with laughter. That young lady with him—" She stopped and raised her eyebrows. "Was she a lady, George?"

"If I had to swear to it," George grinned, "I'd probably have to say no."

"Anyway, that young lady dropped a coin that rolled under the table. And do you know what he did? He set fire to a five dollar bill so as to have enough light to find the coin and retrieve it." She was laughing. "Isn't that gauche?"

Her husband had to agree that it was.

George and Mary decided to accept Pujol's offer. They booked passage on the next steamboat heading north on the Mississippi, to return to Bon Marché for the last time.

III

MATTIE had a feeling that Bon Marché was closing in around her. Retrenching. Even stultifying. George's departure with his family affected her more than it seemed to concern Charles.

"He's a grown man," her husband had said, "and he's free to make his own decisions." Beyond that he wouldn't discuss it.

It was true, of course, that Franklin remained at Bon Marché, nominally in charge of the breeding, and Thomas Jefferson Dewey had been named assistant trainer. To outsiders it might have seemed that the Dewey family was still a cooperative venture in one of the largest thoroughbred operations in the state. But it wasn't so.

Franklin merely went through the motions, following his father's orders without question. Young Thomas was clearly unhappy with his job. Training horses was not what he wanted to do; unhappily, he wasn't certain what he did want to do. He was struggling, at the age of thirty, to find an identity for himself. To Mattie such juvenile vacillation was inexcusable.

And Charles Dewey himself had become preoccupied with the question of slavery. More and more the subject crept into his conversation. More and more he argued—in his late-night sessions with August Schimmel—that slavery would someday destroy the nation.

"Look what has just happened in Virginia," Charles said on a late-August evening in 1831, "in that insurrection led by that fellow Nat Turner. Sixty whites, some of them just babies in their cribs, hacked to death with axes and swords and God knows what else! And if we are to believe the reports in your newspaper, August, more than a hundred and twenty blacks killed in revenge. Does all of that not suggest to you that we're sitting on a powder keg?"

"It suggests to me," Schimmel said calmly, "that it's an isolated incident in a remote Virginia county, and nothing more."

"Lord, how mistaken you are, August!"

"But the authorities are in control again."

"And for how long? What would happen here, for example, if our blacks—more than two hundred fifty of them—would come under the influence of an angry slave who contended that the Messiah was leading him, as Turner did? Just like that"—he snapped his fingers—"revolt could break out here. And would we be able to turn them back? Of course not. We'd be murdered in our beds. And the so-called authorities would be left to react *after* the fact, killing the blacks and making matters worse. Slavery is the evil that causes that."

Schimmel challenged him. "If you feel so strongly about it, Charles, why don't you simply free your blacks?"

"Because my individual act would solve nothing. Hundreds of thousands would still be in bondage, still an explosive charge awaiting only a lighted fuse. No, the *nation* must act. The President"—he grimaced at the thought of Andy Jackson—"and the national legislature must act to end slavery while there is still a Union!"

"What you want, Charles, would require a whole re-education of white attitudes. And how do we accomplish that?"

"God knows. But accomplish it we must!"

Mattie heard the same tirade from her husband. While she felt that he might have some merit in his argument, what concerned her most was that both racing and breeding revenues were down at Bon Marché. That Charles's tight-fisted control, accompanied by Franklin's lethargy and Thomas's incompetence, was slowly but certainly having a debilitating effect. Threatening to destroy Bon Marché.

The plantation's mistress reasoned that new blood was needed. She turned to Asheville, North Carolina, for help.

IV

BROTHERS True and Able Jackson, young lawyers from Asheville, and first cousins of Mattie, came to Bon Marché to join the family for the Christmas holidays. True, the stolid elder brother at twenty-three, was already a portly young man with a receding hairline. Able, two years his brother's junior, was the handsome one of the pair, an extrovert with fine blond hair and startling blue eyes.

Together they had built a fine reputation in court circles in Asheville. And together they owned a modest racehorse stable.

To others in the Dewey family, the Jackson brothers were merely guests for the holidays. Mattie, though, had other plans. She made Christmas of 1831 a memorable one on the plantation, capped by a ball on Christmas Eve that rivaled anything that had been held at Bon Marché before.

On that evening, watching the dancers, she said to her stepdaughter, Louise Schimmel: "Joy and Hope seem taken with my cousins."

Louise laughed. "Mattie, you're an unconscionable matchmaker."

"Is there anything wrong with that?"

"No, I suppose not. But August and I have more immediate plans for the twins. They're only seventeen, you know, and we're thinking of sending them back east to college."

"Hmmm. Perhaps you're right."

Mattie planned another lavish ball for New Year's Eve, and after that, the Jackson brothers several times delayed their return to North Carolina. True took great interest in Charles's and Thomas's training methods with the racehorses; Able spent long hours with Franklin discussing thoroughbred breeding.

January lengthened into February and February into March. As April began, True and Able went to the Schimmel wing of the mansion for a discussion with August and Louise.

"You must be aware," True said, taking over the chores as spokesman for both Jacksons, "that my brother and I have become more than enamored with your daughters."

Louise registered surprise. "Honestly, I'm not aware of that."

"But certainly you know that we've been . . . uh . . . squiring your daughters."

"I know that you've danced with them at the balls here at Bon Marché," Louise interrupted. "And there have been several dinners with them in Nashville, but I had no idea that you were considering courting them!"

"That is our intention, ma'am."

August coughed nervously. "Under other circumstances, perhaps, we might welcome the attention of young men of your caliber. But we believe that the girls are too young to marry and that they ought to be first educated."

Able spoke for the first time. "Hope and Joy have given us reason to believe that they would welcome our suit, or *suits*, if I am to be grammatically correct."

"I take it, then," August said, showing a slight anger, "that you've discussed the prospect of marriage with our daughters."

"Yes, we have." That was True once more.

"Discreetly, of course," Able added.

"I'm opposed to any marriage for the twins at this time," Louise said firmly.

"If you'll pardon me, ma'am," True said, "I'd like to point out that on our father's death some two years ago we were left with a considerable fortune— perhaps not rivaling the economics of Bon Marché—but enough to make us both wealthy and competent to care for wives and families."

"I'm afraid you're not hearing us," the father said. "We wish that our daughters will attend college before they consider marriage."

"Yes, sir, and I appreciate that," True responded. "But we thought, perhaps, there might be a more compelling reason for agreeing to our suit . . ." He looked at his brother. ". . . or suits. We believe that we could, with Joy and Hope by our sides, make a salutary difference here at Bon Marché. At the risk of seeming egotistical, the plantation could use our . . . well, our management."

"You've discussed this with your Cousin Mattie, then?" Louise asked.

"We have."

Louise sighed. "What bothers me about all of this is that it sounds all the world like a business arrangement. Neither one of you has mentioned love!"

Able spoke. "Oh, that goes without saying, Mrs. Schimmel."

"Yesterday you were calling me Louise," she said sarcastically.

"Of course. And I apologize for that seeming formality. But if you are to be my mother-in-law—"

"Young man, you presume a great deal!"

August gently touched his wife's hand, silencing her. "Able . . . True . . ." He nodded to each young man in turn. "I'm sure you must realize that we must now discuss this within the family."

"Of course." True sprang to his feet, Able aping him. "We appreciate the opportunity to have met with you. And we hope for an affirmative answer."

The Jackson brothers quickly left the Schimmel wing.

"The arrogance of those two!" Louise sputtered. "And Mattie—damn her! This is her doing! She means to control Bon Marché through that pair. And what happens to Father?"

"Louise, calm yourself. What happens to Charles Dewey is not the primary consideration here, is it? It's what's best for our daughters that matters most."

"Yes, it is."

"And if Joy and Hope love the Jackson boys . . ."

V

IT was the first Saturday in June of 1832 that Joy Schimmel married True Jackson, and Hope Schimmel was wed to Able Jackson in a lavish outdoor double-wedding ceremony at Bon Marché.

Their mother had accepted the inevitability of the matches, but on the evening prior to the event, Louise said to August: "Now maybe we ought to consider what all this will do to Father."

"In all honesty, he seems pleased by it. He told me that he thinks the twins have made wise choices."

"He's finished at Bon Marché, you know," Louise said coldly. "Mattie has seen to that. And what of Franklin? He's the eldest son of Charles Dewey. Shouldn't he be given some consideration before the Jacksons trample over him?"

"I think you're overreacting, dear."

"I hope so."

He tried to jolly her. "Admit it now, Louise, you like True and Able."

"Yes." She thought for a moment. "But, damn it, I'm a Dewey! And I want the Dewey name always to be associated with Bon Marché."

"It will be," August assured her. "Nothing will ever be able to change that."

At the reception following the ceremony the next afternoon, Alma May came up to her mother, a new man in tow.

"Mother, I want you to meet Allen Carstairs. He's a . . . uh . . . what is it you do, Allen?"

"I'm a liquor salesman."

"Of course, how could I forget that?" the Princess giggled drunkenly, holding high a glass of champagne. "Allen, I want you to meet my mother, the formidable Mattie Dewey. Or should I say Mattie *Jackson* Dewey?"

Mattie shook the man's hand. "Alma May, you'll learn, Mr. Carstairs, has trouble holding her liquor. Or have you learned that already?"

"See! What did I tell you, Allen? My darling mother is an absolute genius at launching darts straight to the heart of the matter." She laughed loudly, turning heads their way. "Straight to the heart! That's Mattie Jackson!"

"Please, Princess," Mattie said quietly, "this is hardly the place for—"

"It's a *perfect* place to speak the truth!" she shouted. "On this day, the Jacksons shall eclipse the Deweys at Bon Marché. A bloodless victory, and I salute you for it, Mother!" She gestured wildly with her hands, spilling the contents of her glass on her companion.

"Alma May, be quiet!"

"Not anymore, Mother, darling. I just want you to know one thing. I'm gonna change my name back to Dewey! I'm gonna drop all that nonsense about having been Mrs. . . . oh, what the hell was that man's name? . . . oh, yes, about having been Mrs. Nathan Ludlum . . . and I'm gonna be Alma May Dewey again! PRINCESS ALMA MAY DEWEY!"

Now everyone was looking at them. Mattie started to walk away.

"AND MOTHER, THEN IT'S GOING TO BE THE DEWEYS AGAINST THE JACKSONS!" She was shouting now. "THE DEWEYS AGAINST THE JACKSONS! IN A FAIR FIGHT!"

She began to sink slowly to the grass.

"Or an *unfair* fight, if that's what you want, Mother." The Princess passed out.

VI

Two weeks after the double wedding, True Jackson made plans to import an Arabian stallion, Bagdad, to Bon Marché. The price was eight thousand dollars.

Franklin Dewey, the breeding manager, was not consulted.

Nor was the master of Bon Marché.

48

IT could not be said that Mattie Dewey had erred in putting the Jackson brothers in charge of Bon Marché.

The addition of Bagdad to the breeding shed was only one indication of the management that would be employed by True and Able. In just a few months, racing revenues increased; other breeders were being enticed back to Bon Marché stallions.

If there was a loss, it was a human one.

And, strangely, not involving Charles Dewey. He welcomed the brothers; he understood that the plantation had been stagnating, and he liked what he saw being done by the confident young men. There may have been moments when he wished that *he* had been able to effect the changes being made, but he didn't allow his own ego to intrude in what was being done for Bon Marché. After all, even though he was being consulted rarely, it was still *his* Bon Marché, and it was benefiting.

Alma May chided him for his complacency. "Daddy, those damned Jacksons are determined to wipe out any traces of Deweys at Bon Marché!"

He laughed at her. "Princess, you make it sound like a vendetta."

"That's exactly what it is!"

"No. It's change, dear. It's the inexorable movement of time. It's a lot of us getting older. It's reality facing us."

"Don't you care about the Dewey name anymore?"

"More than ever, I think. Perhaps if Mattie hadn't made her moves the Dewey name would have eventually been associated with failure. I wouldn't have liked that."

The Princess looked in his eyes. "Do you still love her, Daddy?"

"Yes."

"I mean like before—with the passion and all?"

"You may be thirty-three years old, Princess, but you're not old enough to ask me that question." But he was smiling when he said it.

"Do you still think of Mary Elizabeth Cheves?"

"Occasionally."

"Would you still be passionate with her if you met again?"

He sighed. "Alma May, someday you will know that passion doesn't rule us forever. That we can make our way in life without passionate love. Believe me, you'll discover that."

"God, I hope not!"

There was a small silence.

"But you know you've answered me, don't you?"

"What?"

"About Mother and passion and—"

His cheery laughter cut her off. "Princess, don't you have something better to do?"

"She's a damn fool, you know!"

II

ALMA May wasn't alone in her discontent with the Jackson regime at Bon Marché. Alvin Mussmer also resented it. He didn't like the way Able Jackson shunted his father-in-law aside in breeding decisions, not so much for Franklin's feelings, but because he saw his own future at Bon Marché in jeopardy.

He brought it up one evening at Franklin's dinner table. "Must you always do everything that Able tells you?"

"Able is a competent horseman," Franklin replied quietly.

"But can't you see that he walks all over you! I mean, you're the eldest son—don't you have some rights around here?"

"Whatever rights I might have, Alvin," Franklin said angrily, "I'll protect myself. I don't see where you have to concern yourself about it."

"I'm the husband of your daughter. I'd think that I'd be able to express an opinion."

"Your opinion is noted. I would like you to show more concern for your own welfare—and do a little work around here occasionally."

"What the hell does that mean?"

"It means that I'm aware of your taking advantage of being my son-in-law by sloughing off any task given you."

"I'll bet that bastard Jackson has been—"

Franklin brought his fist down hard on the table. "There'll be no more talk like that at this table! Do you understand, Alvin?"

Sullenly. "Yeah."

Later, alone in their bedroom, Carrie upbraided her husband. "What's the matter with you, Alvin? Insulting my father and then cursing at the table—"

"Shut up!"

"I won't shut up! You owe my father an apology, and I want you to do it tonight!"

"Apologize to a Dewey?" he replied sarcastically. "You don't apologize to Deweys around here anymore. You shit on them! If your name is Jackson, you can shit on Thomas Dewey, and you can shit on Franklin Dewey, and you can even shit on that old fool grandfather of yours!"

Screaming, Carrie attacked him, raking his face with her fingernails, drawing blood.

Alvin slapped her hard across the cheek, but she advanced on him again, her anger out of control.

Her husband smashed a fist into her cheek, slashing it with his knuckles. Blood ran down her smooth skin. She started to fall, but he hit her again, the fist catching her full in the mouth. Carrie felt teeth break.

Alvin stood over her, gasping for breath. "Well, let me tell you, Carrie Almightydewey, they're not going to shit on me!"

He stalked out of the room.

It was only later that it was learned that young Mussmer had raced to the gelding barn, saddled a horse—not his own—and rode away, making quick stops at the various pastures to open the gates and leave them open.

Several hours went by before the horses that had escaped could be rounded up by the slaves.

Overseer Elmer Mussmer presented himself to True Jackson.

"Mister Jackson, I don't know how to explain my son's actions, but I'll pay for the horse he took." An afterthought: "And maybe you'd be more comfortable if me and my wife left now, too."

True solemnly studied the distraught man, showing no emotion. "I don't want your money for the horse. The authorities have their own way of dealing with horse thieves."

"No! I don't want them to—"

"As for the second part of your offer," he continued coldly, "I believe I *will* accept that. It might be best all around if you didn't stay."

III

CHARLES had just written the date—April 9, 1834—in the family Bible. He sat, pen poised over the big volume, contemplating what he had to write next.

"I don't see why," he growled to Mattie, "they have to name the baby 'Andrew.'"

"Because they want him to carry the name of the President," Mattie explained. She didn't want to argue with him, but her husband's continuing complaints about her Cousin Andy annoyed her more than usual. "Just as you named one of your sons for George Washington and we named our son Thomas Jefferson."

"Yes, well . . ." He wrote, "Andrew Jackson, son of True and Joy (Schimmel) Jackson." "At least," he muttered, "we've got that name out of the way now."

Carrie entered the drawing room, four-year-old Honey Mussmer toddling in her wake, chattering gaily. The little girl rushed to her great-grandfather and Charles swept her up into his lap.

"Pop-pop, read me a story," Honey demanded.

"You, young lady," Charles chuckled, "are a demanding little wench."

Carrie sank into a chair, her face in a frown.

"Trouble, dear?" Mattie asked.

"No, not really. It's just that Able has told me that the divorce has now been approved and—"

"Well, now that that's settled," her grandmother said, "perhaps you can go about putting your life in order again."

"Yes." Carrie sighed. "When Able gave me the news, I wondered about Alvin again. I mean, what is he doing now? Is he well? I *did* love him once."

"There's no point mooning your life away over that bastard!" Dewey exclaimed.

"Charles! The baby!"

"Oh, yeah, I'm sorry." He picked up a book of fairy tales, searching it for a story he would read for Honey.

"Have you any plans, Carrie?" Mattie wanted to know.

The young woman just shrugged.

"You're only twenty-three. Your life hasn't exactly come to an end."

"Some days it seems so."

Charles spoke up. "You might take up your duties as a newspaper publisher."

"What?"

"A newspaper publisher. You are the half owner of the *St. Louis Challenger*, you know."

"What are you talking about, Grandfather?"

"The *St. Louis Challenger* is owned fifty percent by one Carrie Dewey. It was back when you were . . . nine, wasn't it Mattie?"

His wife nodded.

"Yes, nine. A trust fund was set up in your behalf and invested in a new newspaper August was starting in St. Louis. One hundred thousand dollars of the trust fund monies bought you half interest in it."

Carrie was astounded. "You mean I'm *really* the half owner of a newspaper?"

"And a very prosperous one."

"But . . . I never heard of this before."

"Well, it was a long time ago," Dewey said lightly, "and the whole thing just sort of . . . slipped through the cracks, you might say."

Carrie laughed gaily. "That's a lot of money to slip through the cracks!"

"Just a figure of speech."

"I don't know what to say. Tell me again—what's the name of the newspaper?"

"The *St. Louis Challenger.*"

"Do you think I could work there?"

"That's for August to say, of course. But if you're interested, I'm sure he'll make arrangements for you in St. Louis."

Carrie sobered. "Oh . . . but I can't possibly do it. I mean, Honey and all . . ."

"If you want to give it a try, dear, I'm sure your grandmother and I could arrange to have Honey as a guest for a while. Couldn't we, Mattie?"

"Ah, yes . . ." She wished Charles hadn't made such a snap decision. "Yes . . . yes . . . of course."

"That's settled, then." He flipped open the book. "Now, young Miss Honey, how about the story of a gentleman named Rumpelstiltskin? That's one we haven't read yet."

The child clapped her hands in delight.

IV

MATTIE was worried. She saw it happening all over again: Charles's preoccupation with little Honey, a delightful blonde-haired child, was a mirror repeat of the love and attention he had lavished on Honey's mother. Everything was the same—the riding lessons, the special tutoring to teach her to read, the walks in the woods to study the wonders of nature.

At first, Mattie believed that Carrie would quickly tire of the newspaper chores in St. Louis, but those hopes were quickly dashed.

In her first letter home, Carrie wrote: "What an exciting time this is! And St. Louis is such a vital town. Mr. Bonsal says I have some natural talent for the newspaper business, and in my ego I'm beginning to believe him."

Several weeks later, August Schimmel confirmed Carrie's quick adaptation to newspapering at the crowded family dinner table at Bon Marché.

"I had a letter from Wilson Bonsal today," he reported. "He's much pleased with Carrie's work. He says she'll soon be completing the apprenticeship he set up for her and will be assigned to a regular staff position."

"This Mr. Bonsal," Mattie asked, "what sort of man is he?"

"A veteran newspaperman. From Boston. I was very lucky to lure him to St. Louis."

"Young man? Old man? Married? Single?"

Schimmel laughed. "Mattie, you sound like a worried mother, but don't be. Will Bonsal is a man of fifty or fifty-one. And while single, he's married to the newspaper. I imagine that Carrie sees him as a father figure."

August was wrong. Very wrong. Early in December, Charles and Mattie received another letter from their granddaughter.

> I have marvelous news! Wilson Bonsal and I were married on Thanksgiving Day, and I can't remember when I've ever been happier. He's a bit older than I am, but a young man, really, in spirit. And we work together—really work together! And that, too, is part of the magic, I guess.
>
> I suppose I should say that I miss Bon Marché, but that would be a lie. I do miss Honey, of course, but I know you're spoiling her outrageously, and that she doesn't miss me. I want her here eventually, but for now, while Will and I are so busy together, I think it's wiser for her to stay at Bon Marché. I hope, Grandfather and Grandmother, that I'm not imposing too much on you if I ask you to care for Honey just a little longer.
>
> I know I have your love and best wishes in my new and wonderful and exciting life.

"Well," Charles said with a little laugh, "who could have anticipated this when I agreed to finance half of August's newspaper in St. Louis?"

"I don't like it," Mattie snapped.

"Oh . . . why not?"

"That man is twice her age. It won't work, Charles."

"I believe she needs a mature man."

"That's nonsense, and you know it! And now we're responsible for Honey, and—"

"We're responsible for all of the members of the Dewey family."

Mattie was angry now. "You know exactly what I'm talking about, Charles. I don't want a repeat of what happened with you and Carrie."

"Honey has Dewey blood in her veins, and I'm only doing what I know is best for her."

Mattie just sighed.

V

THOMAS Jefferson Dewey rode slowly, heading south and east, content in leaving Bon Marché behind. His destination was the Cherokee Indian lands of northern Georgia, and he feared he might be too late. Indeed, he had vacillated for several years in making his decision.

Young Dewey was convinced that he wasn't much of a man—a melancholy attitude brought on by being virtually ignored by his father for so many years, and reinforced by his seeming failure when Charles finally recognized him and made him assistant trainer of the Bon Marché horses. Yet, he might have had some modest success in that job if the Jacksons hadn't taken control of Bon Marché and set him back where he had been before: tolerated because he was Charles Dewey's son, but ignored.

Thomas had been thinking about leaving Bon Marché before his mother brought True and Able Jackson to the plantation. The first such stirrings came in 1828 when gold was discovered in the Cherokee country. But he hesitated, hesitated, hesitated . . .

And he listened at the family dinner table to his father's tirades about President Jackson's "damnable policies on the Indians. He means to wipe them all out. All of them! This Indian Removal Act"—that was in 1830—"is only Andy's first step in destroying every Indian east of the Mississippi. It's an evil act, I tell you!"

Characteristically, Thomas made no comment at the dinner table. But he'd devoured every story in the newspapers about the Indian situation: the forced emigration of the Choctaws in the dead of the bitter winter of 1831, driven into the icy Great Arkansas Swamp barefoot and nearly naked, decimated by disease. And he'd learned how the Creeks had been separated from their crops, their homes, and their lands in 1832, reduced to what one newspaper report said was destitution: "the incessant cry of the emaciated creatures being bread! bread! is beyond description distressing." Thomas had also heard the tales of the Black Hawk War in the spring of 1832, in which the Sauk and Fox followers of Chief Black Hawk were pursued by the Illinois militia into the Wisconsin wilderness and massacred—men, women and children.

What came through those stories to Thomas Dewey was not the same horror his father felt, but the realization that some men—*many men*— were making fortunes at the expense of the Indians. In land and property and, in Georgia, gold.

It was a latent need—perhaps not fully understood—to make his own fortune that motivated the young man. In northwest Georgia might be that opportunity. In the troubled lands of the once mighty nation of the Cherokees. And so he rode, in the spring of 1835, having convinced himself that he might *be somebody* there, that he might be able to shake off the mantle of failure he had worn at Bon Marché.

Why, he might even find some gold!

For a week he rode. And two. Crossing the Tennessee River into Cherokee country. His baggage was a modest provision of food, a loaded two-shot pistol, and the same indecisiveness that had plagued him at Bon Marché.

Darkness was just overtaking him when he trotted his gelding into a tiny settlement cut in the heavy forest. There was really only one substantial building—a small log hut and three or four tents. A fire was burning in the center of the clearing, and five men were huddled around it.

When he rode into the circle of light, he realized that three rifles were trained on him.

"Good evening," he called cheerily, wanting to make it clear that he was friendly. "What place is this?"

"Ain't got a name," one of the men growled.

Thomas started to dismount, but the spokesman shouted: "Hold it right there!"

Two of them got to their feet and, their guns still pointed at him menacingly, they came up to his horse. "Who are ya?"

"My name is Thomas Dewey."

"From where?"

"Tennessee. Nashville, Tennessee."

"Whatta ya doin' here?"

It was a simple question, if hostile. Young Dewey realized that he didn't have an immediate, convenient answer.

"Ah said, whatta ya doin' here?"

"Well, I'm . . . uh . . . looking for Cherokee territory."

"Why?"

"I understand a man might find gold—"

"Git down!"

Thomas dismounted, to be herded to the fire at rifle point.

"This gentleman," the spokesman said to the others, making an epithet of the word *gentleman*, "is Mr. Dewey. He comes from Tennessee to find gold."

Everyone laughed raucously.

"Coffee, *Mister* Dewey?"

"That would be welcome." Thomas squatted down by the fire, accepting a tin cup of steaming brew. He sipped at it, finding it extremely bitter. He wanted to spit it out, but thought better of it.

"Now, *Mister* Dewey," the spokesman said, "tell us 'bout this lookin' fer gold."

"All reports are that gold has been found in this area, on the Cherokee lands, and it seemed logical to follow up on those reports."

The obvious leader of the rough group of men studied him suspiciously. "Ya one of them Indian lovers?"

"What?"

"Well, ya don't look like no gold prospector to me . . ." The others nodded agreement. ". . . an' if ya ain't a gold prospector, mebbe yer one of them eastern bastards what's bleedin' their hearts out over the poor Cherokees."

"No. I'm who I said I was: Thomas Dewey of Nashville."

"Seen any Indians ridin' in here?"

"No."

"Ya wanna see an Indian?"

"Yes, I imagine so." The answer was tentative.

"See thet bastard right there?" the spokesman asked, pointing his rifle barrel toward one of his companions. "He's Indian, or half so. Show him, Morgan!"

The man took off his hat, turning a grinning face to the traveler. Thomas saw the high cheekbones that suggested Indian blood.

"That's an Indian, *Mister* Dewey. Ya like 'im?"

"He seems pleasant enough."

"He ain't!" the leader snarled. "He's a lyin', thievin', whorin' sonofabitch what'd cut his mother's heart out without battin' an eye. Now, how do ya like 'im?"

"Well, I—"

There was general derisive laughter again.

The leader's attitude seemed to change suddenly. "We're jest funnin' ya, Dewey. Don't git much chance to fun a gentleman."

Thomas smiled, relieved.

"Now . . . let's git serious. There is some gold hereabouts, but it takes a lot of work to git it out." He glanced at Dewey's horse. ". . . An' Ah don't see no tools to do thet with."

"Oh, I planned to buy equipment when I got here."

The spokesman shook his head sadly. "The nearest place where ya can git shovels an' such is 'most eighty miles away." He scratched his grizzled chin for a moment. " 'Course, we might be willin' to let ya have—"

He gestured to the half-breed, who tossed a shovel into the circle of light.

"Like this here shovel. We kin let ya have thet fer fifty dollars."

Thomas's eyes opened wide in surprise. "Fifty dollars!"

"What? Ain't ya got fifty dollars, *Mister* Dewey?"

"Of course. But fifty dollars is a ridiculous price for a shovel."

"Mebbe. But thet's what it is out here." He swept his arm to indicate the wilderness surrounding them.

Thomas coughed nervously. "I appreciate your help, of course, but I think I'll wait to get my equipment."

The leader sighed. "Now, thet's too bad, *Mister* Dewey. Too bad. Ah guess ya might say that I'm a bit offended—"

"Oh, please, I didn't mean to offend."

"Yessir, offended by yer refusal of our kind offer . . ."

Once more there was a universal nod of agreement.

". . . an Ah'm real sorry, *Mister* Dewey, to tell ya thet we jest can't let ya leave here with all thet money yer carryin'."

He squeezed the trigger of the rifle. Only a few feet away from young Dewey, he couldn't miss. The lead ball tore a terrible hole in his forehead.

Thomas Jefferson Dewey, age thirty-four, was dead instantly eighteen days after he had left Bon Marché.

It was nearly the end of May before the news reached the plantation in a letter from one Captain Morrison of the Georgia State Guard. The body had been found, he reported, on a routine patrol through the dangerous Cherokee region:

> Your son obviously stumbled on to a band of cutthroats, and was gunned down and robbed. His money was taken, and his boots, and we found no horse in the vicinity, so we must assume that it was stolen, as well.
>
> Fortunately, his papers were left on him, enabling me to perform this sad duty. You have my profound sympathy. It seems I am called on more and more to write letters of this type in these troubled times.

Charles grieved, but did not weep.

Nor did he tell his distraught wife that he blamed the death of their son on the brutal Indian policies of the administration of President Andrew Jackson.

49

"CHARLES, you can't keep filling that child's head with this nonsense!"

Mattie waved a copy of the *Liberator*, William Lloyd Garrison's uncompromising abolitionist newspaper, in front of his face.

"My Lord, I can't even understand how this is allowed to be sent through the mails." She dropped the paper on Dewey's desk. "But it's a lot worse, I think, to use it as a study tool for Honey. There's something . . . uh . . . uh . . . *sinful* about that."

Charles grinned, trying to dampen his wife's vehemence. "Mattie, dear, I try only to expose Honey to the views that are shaping her world—the world in which she'll have to live."

"And you honestly think the views of the rabble-rouser Garrison will *shape*, as you put it, Honey's world?"

"Yes, I do. Immeasurably, I would think."

Mattie grunted in exasperation. "I think I liked you better, Charles, when I was second in your priorities to the horses."

"That was never true!"

". . . And I resent it, I really resent it, when your preoccupations with the slavery issue allows you no time at all for me, or the rest of the family."

"That's another of your famous generalizations, dear."

She glared at him.

"Permit me to try to explain something," Charles went on. "Mr. Garrison, while he may be unorthodox in his methods, believes, as do I, that slavery is a moral issue—that it is, in the final analysis, immoral. And if it is immoral, then it ought to be done away with; the central government ought to take the lead in acting against that immorality. Garrison says only that. I agree with him."

"And you expect all others to agree with you!"

Another grin. "I can only *hope* that others will agree. I know that I can't *expect* them to."

"Damn you and your semantics! I started out this conversation by saying that you shouldn't expose an innocent six-year-old to the garbage of William

Lloyd Garrison, and you've twisted it around once more to a lecture on the morality of slavery."

"The *im*morality," he chided her.

"You try, it's clear to me, to make others who don't agree with you . . . well, to make them out as evil. I resent that. I'm not evil. There are generations and generations of people who have been slaveholders who weren't evil. Do you consider yourself evil?"

"Perhaps."

"That's not an answer, Charles! Do you or do you not consider yourself personally evil because you own slaves?"

"I'd prefer if it were not so."

"But it *is* so. And does that make you evil?"

"No."

"Well, then—"

"Mattie, I admit to you that I don't have an answer. If I did, I'd have used it years ago. But that doesn't stop me from being certain that slavery is immoral. Nor does it stop my belief that if some political solution is not found for the slavery issue it's going to tear this country apart."

"But—"

He held up a hand to stop her. ". . . And because I know that we are headed for disaster, I think it valid for little Honey to understand that."

"And that brings us full circle." She sighed.

"Still without an answer."

"Yes—still without an answer."

They sat silently for a moment or two.

"May I bring up another point of agitation?" Mattie asked.

Charles laughed. "Why not?"

Her voice was low, calm. "Don't allow yourself to be hurt by Honey as you were by Carrie."

He pondered that. "I risk that, don't I?"

"Yes."

"I suppose it's a risk I have to take."

She saw the sadness in that basically good man. "Very well, Charles, I promise that I've said my last word on the subject."

II

IT wasn't just Honey's education that took Charles and the young girl to Nashville on the day after Christmas 1835 to stand on Market Street and watch the desperate, ragged line of Cherokee Indians, cowed by their guard of Regular Army guns, shuffling along toward their new home across the Mississippi. What motivated the elder Dewey was a belief—maybe a hope—that he was somehow honoring Thomas Jefferson Dewey, who had died on Cherokee lands. He knew that his son's death had been ignoble, that he had been killed by common cutthroats. But he wanted to associate that death with a defense of the Indians in their hour of trial. That way Thomas's loss would have some meaning. And Charles allowed himself that private lie.

"Where are they going, Pop-Pop?"

"To somewhere in the Oklahoma Territory."

"Why?"

"Because greedy men want their lands, because promises made to them have been broken, because a lot of people everywhere don't think of Indians as being worth much."

"Oh." A pause. "They look very cold, Pop-Pop."

"Yes." He watched the unhappy parade, the marchers inadequately clothed, some of them barefoot. And he looked into the faces of the men, women, and children and saw no hope there. A few tears started down his cheek.

Honey looked up at him, sober-faced, squeezing his hand.

When the column had passed them, headed for an overnight encampment on the edge of Nashville, Charles and Honey made their way to the Methodist church where a Pastor Robison, one of a band of ministers who were accompanying the Cherokees, was to speak. The church was packed. The impact of what they had seen that day had affected many Nashvillians.

"Brothers and sisters," the pastor said, "I don't have to tell you, because you've seen it with your own eyes, of the horrors that have been afflicted on these people that some call savages. Yet, those of us of faith, or belief, in Jesus Christ our Lord, He who died on the cross for *all* men—not just white American citizens, but *all* men!—are as much responsible for this as is our government.

"I don't tell you this just to make you feel guilty. But you *are* guilty. I am guilty. We are *all guilty!* This didn't happen overnight. There is not one single political administration in Washington on which to fix blame. The removal of the Cherokees from their ancestral lands is the result of long, detailed planning, well known to everyone for years. And yet, we Americans who profess Christianity, who loudly proclaim that we are our brother's keeper, remained silent.

"We remained silent when the Choctaws were moved west. We remained silent when the Chickasaws were driven out of their homes. We remained silent when the Creeks were herded across the Mississippi. Our lips spoke no words of protest when the Seminoles were made to leave Florida. Our guilt has been our silence!"

Pastor Robison sighed deeply. There was not another sound in the crowded church. He dropped his voice.

"This is not the first time, of course, that men of goodwill have remained silent on a moral issue and have therefore become moral cowards. Unhappily, history is replete with such incidents. And, it seems clear, it is too late now to stop what has been put into being for the Cherokees. What we must promise ourselves now . . . what we must promise our God now—once and for all—is that we will never again allow silence to be our guilt. Our sin.

"What you have seen here today, in your streets, is only a small part of what is happening. There are other such columns, taking different routes to their new homes. I submit to you that the phrase 'new homes' is the worst of misnomers. They are being driven like dumb cattle to lands they have never seen before. To a place without shelter. Without food. Without work. And, tragically, without hope.

"When the Cherokee migration was begun in October, from Georgia and east Tennessee, there were thirteen thousand Cherokees rounded up for the move west. Today, as best we can determine, that number has shrunk to eleven thousand."

There were gasps in the audience.

"How many more must die before this trek is ended?"

Another heavy sigh. "I have seen so much in the nearly three months of this forced march that my heart is heavy with it. My mind won't let me remember all of the horrors. If it did I would certainly go mad. But just two days ago, as we approached Nashville, there was a Cherokee girl of not more than sixteen. She was called Flower of the Sun, and was as beautiful as that name would imply. And she was pregnant to nearly the end of her term. Her husband—the son of a chief, I learned—had been killed by white men. Where and under what circumstances I do not know. The time came for her to deliver her child. I stopped with her by the side of the road, as the soldiers prodded the rest of the column forward, in the hope that I might be able to assist her. No army doctor was made available. It was a breech birth, and—God help me—I was not competent."

His voice broke. "That young mother and that unborn child both died, an incompetent white man their only companion."

Many in the congregation were also crying.

The pastor slammed a hand down on the pulpit, the sound ricocheting into the consciences of the listeners.

"Those two—that young woman who shouldn't have had an enemy in the world and that innocent babe—were murdered by governmental indifference!" His eyes swept the audience. "And they were murdered by our silence!"

The speaker dropped his head and let several seconds go by before he started again.

"Several weeks ago, a colleague watching this sad march, said to me, 'Those people are walking the trail of tears.' *The trail of tears?* How profound that is. How true.

"And what can you do now? Well, in realistic terms, you must do what the government cannot or will not do. You must feed these people. You must provide shelter for them when they get to where the soldiers are driving them. You must give them the tools with which to carve out a new and meaningful life—plows, hoes, shovels, harrows. For if they are to survive at all, they must certainly be able to till the soil.

"There is an informal group from the Christian ministry—pastors like myself—who are soliciting funds in every community we cross. I ask you now, as humbly and as sincerely as I can, to help these troubled people.

"Help them! HELP THEM! So that they might find hope at the end of their trail of tears. May God bless you in your charity."

Pastor Robison left the pulpit.

Collection plates were quickly passed. Quickly filled. Charles emptied his pockets of money. He didn't stop to count it, but he knew there must have been more than three hundred dollars.

On their ride back to Bon Marché, Charles and Honey were silent for a long time.

Finally, Honey spoke: "The pastor said that something like this shouldn't happen again. Do you think he was talking about the slaves?"

Dewey looked over at her, surprised and pleased by the perceptiveness of the nine-year-old youngster.

"Yes, I imagine he was," Charles answered.

"I'll remember, Pop-Pop."

III

"WHAT do you think, Charles?" Able Jackson asked.

Dewey studied the firmly built bay stallion, circling him, breaking down the components of the animal in his mind, bringing the years of his experience into the answer.

"Outstanding!" he said.

The thoroughbred they had before them in the stallion barn at Bon Marché was Priam, the winner of the 1830 English Derby.

"I can't tell you how pleased I am by your approval," Able said. "I had a few doubts, I'll tell you, about paying the asking price. But the London agent assured me that Priam was in top condition and—"

"How much?"

"I'm almost embarrassed to tell you—ten thousand. Plus the cost of bringing him over, and that seems to get more expensive all the time."

"Seems fair enough," Charles commented. He turned to Franklin, who stood with them. "What do you think, son?"

"Good. Yes—good." He seemed almost uninterested.

Dewey laughed loudly. "Come on now, Franklin, it's not you who's getting married tomorrow. It is just your son."

Franklin nodded. "I guess I have been preoccupied with the plans for the wedding." He patted the stallion's neck. "I'm really glad to see a horse like Priam here. He might be the finest import ever brought to this area."

"That was the intent," Able said confidently. "There's no reason that we can't make Bon Marché the center of quality breeding."

"I always thought it was," Charles said.

"Oh, of course, it *has* been," the younger Jackson brother replied quickly, fearing he had offended the founder. "It's just that I get carried away with the opportunities available here."

"I think this is perhaps a good time to tell you something I've been meaning to say." Charles was sober-faced. "We—Franklin and I, as survivors of the beginning, you might say—are most appreciative of the energy you and True are putting into Bon Marché. It gives us old war-horses time to indulge other pursuits."

"That's a most welcome comment, sir."

"Yes, indeed. Time to indulge other pursuits. I've just accepted the presidency of the Davidson County Agricultural Society, and Franklin, I know . . ." He patted his son on the back. " . . . is busy with the organization of his new hunt. How goes that, son?"

"Fine, fine. And you're right, Father, I never had the time before for things of that nature."

Franklin didn't want to tell his father that he had organized the hunt only because he had nothing else to do—because the Jacksons continued to ignore his advice on breeding matters.

IV

HE was twenty-six and handsome in his lieutenant's uniform. A graduate of the military academy at West Point, Albert Dewey, youngest child of Franklin and the late Amantha Dewey, was back at Bon Marché for his marriage to Virginia Stoker, a beauty from the most prominent banking family in Nashville.

His best man was to be his cousin, Charles Dewey II, who had come all the way from New Orleans for the wedding. He had brought with him a letter to Mattie from his mother.

> Charles Two will have to represent all of us from this branch of the family at Albert's wedding. Statler, I hasten to tell you, is himself going to be married before June is out to a girl named Harriet Walston, of one of "the" families of New Orleans, and I have so many duties.

Mattie groaned aloud as she read that news. She could just hear Mary gushing.

> We all just love New Orleans. Just love it! Georgie's duties with Monsieur Pujol's racing stable have been going marvelously well, to the point where Monsieur Pujol has offered him a partnership. Perhaps he heard that Georgie was planning to start his own stable after finishing the latest Metairie Course meeting as the leading trainer.
>
> I must run now—have a tea this afternoon for the ladies of the drama society. Make certain that Charles Two behaves himself. Georgie said just the other day that Two reminds him of himself at an earlier age. We all send our love to dear Albert and his bride.

Charles roared when he read the letter. "Listen, Mattie, if my namesake is anything like his father, we ought to send out letters of warning to the parents of maiden young ladies in this county."

One of those letters might well have gone to Brian Stoker, the stuffy father of the bride. He and his equally snobbish wife, Maybelle, were deeply concerned about Virginia's marriage to Lieutenant Dewey. While they appreciated the wealth of the Deweys, and indeed they felt a certain pride in the community gossip that spoke of the merger of two great fortunes. But the Stokers were not happy about being associated with the horse racing gentry, nor were they delighted with the prospect of having their daughter traveling across the country to be with her soldier husband at unknown, and probably unworthy, military installations.

Maybe it was their preoccupation with their concern for Virginia that caused them to take lightly the extroverted, self-assured Charles Dewey II, who *was*, in truth, the mirror of his father's youth. He played the role assiduously. And the stage was set for him when he met the younger sister of the bride-to-be.

Elizabeth Stoker was a stunning brunette with sensuous violet eyes, clear, white skin, and a figure that rivaled her sister's and, as Charles saw it, even excelled Virginia's in certain key points. He was drawn to her like a bee to a fragrant flower.

Young Charles didn't wait for a formal introduction. At a pre-wedding dinner for the two families, the visitor from New Orleans went to Elizabeth immediately, bowed to her formally, and grinned impishly.

"Hello," he said. "I wish to tell you that you are the most beautiful woman in the room."

He was pleased when she didn't giggle or make coy objections to his compliment.

"I'm Charles Dewey the Second, a cousin of the bridegroom and the best man. And you are the sister of the bride. Elizabeth, isn't it?"

"Yes, Mr. Dewey."

His grin grew larger. "There are a lot of Mr. Deweys around here, but I'm not one of them. My name is Charles. Family and friends call me Two."

"Two?" She laughed.

"Yes. My mother's invention. She has a . . . well, a *cute* sense of humor. It was confusing to call me Charles when I was growing up, because when anyone referred to 'Charles' they meant my grandfather. So, Two was convenient."

"I like it."

"And you? What do they call you? Liz? Beth? Betty? What?"

"Beth."

"Very well. That takes care of the introductions. Now, let me show you around Bon Marché, Beth." He took her arm and began to guide her out of the room.

She held back. "Isn't dinner about to be served?"

"We have plenty of time. My grandfather likes to have everyone well fortified with spirits before a family dinner. It makes his stories more palatable."

Beth laughed again, and they left the mansion. Charles had already decided to show her the mares and foals first. Women always loved the foals.

As they walked, he gave her a brief autobiography. "I live in New Orleans," he said. "I'm twenty-three years old and unmarried. My father is a very good horse trainer. My mother, bless her, is a social climber. My grandfather, who started Bon Marché, is a legend. And my stepgrandmother runs the legend. There! Now you know all about me and we're done with those boring matters."

"What do *you* do . . . uh . . . Two?" She seemed uncomfortable with the nickname.

"Me?" He laughed. "I live, Beth."

"Is that all?"

"Ah, that's everything! Don't you realize that most people don't live; they just exist. I, on the other hand, live to the fullest. I'm a connoisseur of living. I appreciate and savor the finest aspects of living: excellent wines, succulent food, beautiful paintings, good music"—he smiled—"and fascinating women."

She seemed perplexed. "But how do you support yourself?"

"My father has money. My mother, too. And my grandfather is one of the wealthiest men in Tennessee. I use their money. They permit that graciously. Perhaps that's because I don't use their money in any *mean* way."

Beth shook her head disapprovingly. "That seems so . . . uh . . ."

"Profligate?"

"Yes."

Charles shrugged. "It's not. Living is an art, Beth. And I practice the art better than anyone I know."

They had reached the pasture, and he boosted Elizabeth up onto the fence, then perched beside her.

"You see before you," he said, "the results of years of careful breeding of one strain of equines—the thoroughbred. An animal bred, in this case, for its speed and stamina. Bred as a competitor. There are perhaps fifty mares in that field, with their most recent progeny. Cash value? Oh . . . who knows? Maybe a million dollars. Maybe more. But it's an example of how man can manipulate an animal. It proves that man is very adept at manipulation, because man has a brain to think. Am I boring you?"

"Not at all." She was sincere.

"For example, most of those mares are already back in foal, carrying the babies they will drop next year. A mare, you see, is a life-giving machine under our manipulation. She comes into heat somewhere around nine days after she has given birth, and if everything is physically correct, she is bred then. She doesn't have to think about it at all. A man leads a stallion to her, who is aroused by her menstrual odors, the stallion mounts her, and, in one swift ejaculation, she is bred once more. Efficient. Natural. And rewarding to the man, because that foal, which may have been conceived in those few seconds, may grow up to be the winner of many races, and much money."

Beth grimaced. "You make it sound so cold."

"In a sense, it is," he admitted. "You must understand that man is the only animal capable of love and hate. These horses—and, indeed, cattle and sheep and dogs and other animals—breed for only one reason—to reproduce themselves. And they do it with their kind, regardless of beauty or age or, at times, without regard for what we call inbreeding. On the other side of the coin, the fox kills a rabbit for only one reason—to obtain food. He doesn't hate the rabbit. He feels no emotion for his victim, one way or another.

"And that's the basic difference between man and the lower animals. Man mates for love, desire, or pleasure. Man kills for hate, wantonly, cruelly. But that's the way life is.''

"I really hadn't thought about it," Beth sighed. "Somehow it's all a bit sad, isn't it?"

"I never believed that the realities of life were sad. It's a pattern, a mosaic, preordained by nature. Or God, if you wish." He put his arm around her, drew her to him, and kissed her on the lips. "You see, that was a kiss. An act of love known only to the animal man. A pleasurable act. Some animals may seem to kiss, but they don't. Only man knows what a kiss is and how nice it can be."

She laughed. "It seems to me that you've used a long explanation to steal a kiss."

"Oh, I didn't steal it. You wanted to be kissed by me."

"You are the most egotistical—"

He kissed her once more. And Beth responded.

"Egotism has nothing to do with it," he said. "It's simply knowing when to kiss, and when it might be the most satisfying."

"I think it's time for dinner, don't you?"

"Probably."

He helped her down from the fence. As they strolled back to the mansion, they entwined their hands.

"You know," Beth said, "you made a point of saying that animals breed only to reproduce themselves. But doesn't man do that, too? I mean, take Albert and Virginia. Isn't their intent, to be married, to reproduce themselves?"

"I don't know Albert's intent. I haven't talked to him about it."

"And I haven't talked to Virginia about it, either. But I'd imagine that they want to have children."

"They could have them without being married."

"Charles!"

"Biologically, that's true, isn't it?"

"Yes."

"So . . . what does marriage add to that? Marriage is a convenience, a convention of our society. But . . . well, how old are you?"

"Sixteen." She seemed shy for the first time.

He stopped, staring at her. "Sixteen? I can hardly believe that. You're so much of a woman."

Beth blushed.

"Anyway," he went on, "even at the young age of sixteen, you could bear a child, couldn't you?"

"Yes, I guess."

"But to do so, you believe you have to be married?"

"Certainly."

"Not true. Because man is capable of love, the most pure, loving thing would be for two people to produce a child in that love. Just because their love was strong enough and meaningful enough to want to have a manifestation of it in the form of a child. And a child, it seems to me, would be more loved because convention was defied in producing it.''

"I'm not sure I want to hear this." She pulled her hand away.

"I'm sorry," young Charles said apologetically. "Perhaps I've gone too far."

Beth was silent.

"Have I?"

"I'm not sure. It's just that no one ever talked to me about all this before."

They were mounting the front steps of the mansion when they heard the dinner chimes sounding inside the house.

"You see," Charles laughed, "we didn't miss a damned thing."

V

THREE days later, at noon on a bright June Saturday, Lieutenant Albert Dewey and Miss Virginia Stoker were wed. For Mrs. Stoker, and for Mattie Dewey as well, it was a social triumph.

By two o'clock, the last champagne toast having been drunk, the new-lyweds drove away from the plantation on the first leg of their honeymoon trip, planned as a long, leisurely journey to Albert's new station with the U.S. Army cavalry in Illinois.

Charles Dewey II made his way to Mr. and Mrs. Stoker, presenting himself with a proper bow.

"Sir . . . ma'am, I wonder whether I might have your permission to go riding with Miss Elizabeth?" He smiled at them. "Everything has been so busy around here that I haven't had the opportunity to show your daughter all of Bon Marché, as I've promised her I would. And since I, too, must leave soon, to go back to New Orleans, this might be the last opportunity to do so."

Brian Stoker looked at his wife. "Well, I imagine that might be all right, Mr. Dewey. What do you think, dear?"

Charles cut in. "I'll make certain that Miss Elizabeth is delivered home at any hour you say, ma'am."

"Well, I suppose . . . yes, very well. We want her home, of course, before nightfall."

"Of course." Another bow. "You do me great honor."

The young man ran to where he knew, by prearrangement, Beth would be waiting for him.

"What did they say, Two?"

"They said yes."

She laughed happily.

"And you owe me five dollars. It was a wager of honor, young lady."

"You're amazing, Two. I would have been willing to bet you much more that they'd say no."

"I know."

She struck out at him. Playfully. "You're too damned confident."

They hurried to the gelding barn where Charles ordered a black to saddle two riding horses.

"Where are we going?" Beth asked as the slave held the gate open for them.

"To a special place."

They rode for nearly an hour, their chatter mostly inanities, until they finally came into a large, cool grove of red cedars.

"This is it," he said, stopping his horse and sliding to the ground. "My grandfather showed me this place years ago. It's where he and Mattie spent their honeymoon."

"Right here? Out in the open?"

"Uh-huh. I haven't been here since I was a small boy, but it's still as beautiful as I remember it."

He helped her dismount.

"It is lovely." She gazed about. "And I can see why they chose it for a honeymoon."

Charles tethered the horses to a sapling, walking to her, taking her hands and finding a spot for them to sit down. He sank to the ground, patting the earth next to him.

Beth joined him, drawing up her knees, wrapping her arms around them. "You know, I can almost feel them here. There's an aura about this place—an aura of lovers."

"I thought I was supposed to be the romantic."

She didn't comment directly. "I wonder if Virginia and Albert have such a lovely place for their first night together?"

He chuckled. "Hardly. The Nashville Inn isn't my idea of a romantic spot."

"That's where they stopped? Virginia didn't confide in me."

"She probably thought you were too young for such things. But I know for certain that that's where Albert planned to stop."

"Isn't that sad? Why didn't you tell Albert about this place?"

"Do you think Virginia would have come here?"

"No." She giggled. "Not Virginia!"

There was a silence.

"Two?"

"Hmmm?"

"Why did you bring me here?"

"Because it's beautiful. And because I wanted you to see it."

"Only that?"

"Uh-huh. No—that's a lie. I brought you here because I wanted to be alone with you. Because I want to make love to you."

"That's what I thought."

"You're disarming me, Beth."

She leaned over against him. "I didn't think I could ever do that, Two. You seem so sure of everything. Maybe I shouldn't have come, because I'm *not* so sure of everything. But the day . . . I don't know . . . the day just . . . Well, Virginia looked so happy. Did you see the way she looked at Albert when they exchanged their vows?"

"Yes."

"It was like I was seeing Virginia for the first time."

He let her talk.

"And I thought, will I ever . . . ever be that much in love? Then I thought of what we had planned . . . I mean, riding off together . . . and I was suddenly caught up with—"

"Desire?"

"I don't know. I just wanted to be with you. Alone. With no one else within miles of us. To see if I could feel what Virginia's eyes told me she felt."

"Hmmm."

"Does that make sense?"

"Yes."

"And now that I *am* alone with you"—she gazed about—"in this lovely place, I don't know what I feel. Part of me is happy. But part of me is frightened, too."

Charles took her in his arms. "I certainly don't want you to be frightened."

"I've never been alone with a man before." She laughed lightly. "As a matter of fact, no man except my father had ever kissed me before you kissed me on the night of the dinner."

"I find that hard to believe."

"No, it's true. I've been very defensive with boys, until now."

"And now?"

Beth shrugged. "I'm here, Two."

50

CHARLES Dewey II three times postponed his return to New Orleans and was finding it difficult to make believable excuses to his mother about why he didn't want to leave Nashville.

The Deweys of Bon Marché knew why, of course. He was constantly in the company of Elizabeth Stoker. It became a favorite topic of discussion between Mattie and the elder Charles.

"Do you think Two wants to marry that girl?" Mattie asked one evening.

"I suppose I can confide in you—"

"Charles! Sometimes you're insulting!"

"He told me a week ago that he had gone to Brian Stoker and that insufferable wife of his and asked for permission to marry Beth. They turned him down flat."

"Why?"

"The age of the girl."

"That's a *most* valid point, of course."

"Two doesn't think so."

"Do you think he's being genuine, Charles? Does he love her?"

Dewey grinned. "If I haven't forgotten what young love is all about, I'd say that he does. And she him, of course. She dotes on him."

A week later, Charles II came to see his grandfather.

"Sir, is it possible that you could find me a position here at Bon Marché?"

Charles's eyes opened wide. "You want to *work*, Two?"

The Deweys laughed together.

"That doesn't seem to be in keeping with my reputation, does it, Grandfather? But the truth is that Mother has stopped sending me an allowance. She wants me back in New Orleans. I suspect that she's found a proper French girl for me—a *socially* proper French girl, that is—and I'm ruining her plans by staying here."

"I'm certain that we can employ you in some way," the elder Dewey said. "I'll speak to True and Able today and have them find something for you."

"Uh . . . sir . . . I wonder whether I might impose on your generosity and ask for some kind of advance?"

"Of course. I can understand that a young gentleman needs a few dollars—"

"Not just a few, Grandfather. I need enough to buy a house in Nashville."

"Buy a house? But why?"

"So that Beth and I can move into it."

The older man brightened. "Then the Stokers have finally given their approval?"

"No, sir."

"But . . . I don't understand."

Two sighed. "Grandfather, Beth is going to have a baby. In seven months. And we want our own place before it becomes obvious—"

"Do the Stokers know of this?"

"Not yet."

"You'll marry without their approval."

"No. We don't need to be married."

"Of course you *need* to be married. The girl's pregnant!"

"Marriage is just an artificial convention, Grandfather. We don't need it to prove our love for each other."

"That's hogwash!"

"I didn't expect that you'd understand." Two got to his feet, prepared to leave. "But I did think, sir, that I could count on you."

Dewey thought for a moment. "How much do you need?"

"Nineteen hundred. You know that small brick house at the end of Market, the one that stands alone?"

"Yes." The young man was talking of the house in which Andrew Mac-Callum had lived with his bride, Mercy Callison. "Yes," he repeated sadly, "I know it very well."

"It's available again and it seems ideal for us."

Charles went to his strongbox and counted out twenty-five hundred dollars. "No one is to know about this."

"Thank you, Grandfather. You're a real friend."

"A romantic old fool would be a more accurate description."

II

In February of 1841 a son was born to Charles Dewey II and Elizabeth Stoker in the little brick house that carried so many memories for the great-grand-father of the baby. And it was only the old man who went to visit them, offering his blessings.

"I wish, Mattie," he said a day or two later, "that you'd go see them. They need someone. The Stokers have cut them off, and Mary Dewey has written them a most bitter letter. Those young people are in love and—"

"I see enough of Two here," Mattie snapped. "And I certainly don't intend to make it appear that I approve of this . . . this . . . what? I think what they're doing is sinful!"

"Oh?"

"Don't you?"

"Sin, like beauty, must be in the eye of the beholder. I see them only as young people who may be making a mistake. But what good does it do to condemn them? As a matter of fact, I'm rather pleased with the way that Two has turned around his life. He's working very hard with the Bon Marché cattle herd. Both Able and True are pleased with his work as well."

"So I understand," Mattie said grudgingly.

"Go see them."

"No, I can't." She paused. "Have they named the child yet?"

"Yes," Her husband grinned sheepishly, "they're calling him Charles Dewey the Third."

"Charles! They haven't!"

"But they have."

"That's the worst kind of insult to you! Isn't it bad enough that Two, behaving so irresponsibly with this girl, already carries your name? But now . . . to name a bastard—"

He patted her arm. "Mattie, dear Mattie, what possible difference does it make in my life? I've concluded, after seventy-six years of living, that I shouldn't waste energy on matters I can't change. There are so many things so desperately wrong in this world that a simple thing like naming a baby for me seems so insignificant."

"But, Charles, a bastard!"

Dewey smiled wryly. "It's not the first, is it?"

III

TRUE Jackson's appearance belied his intelligence and his skills. Portly— some might have called him dumpy—with only a few strands of hair running in irregular patterns over his skull, True was not in any way handsome. And his sober demeanor—he was a man who never really laughed at a witticism— at times gave him the look of a dullard. And, while he may not have been witty or glib, he was the possessor of an extraordinary mind, one that led to innovation.

"I'm afraid I've overstepped myself this time, Charles," he said soberly. "I've let my enthusiasm for an idea make me ignore reality."

"The futurity, eh?"

"Yes." The elder Jackson brother groaned. "I honestly thought that the prospect of a purse of a hundred and fifty thousand dollars would attract every horseman in the state."

"I was of the same opinion. Every comment I heard on the idea of a futurity was one of great enthusiasm. I'd even say that your announcement caused a sensation."

"Until the money came due," True replied sarcastically.

The two men sat in the Bon Marché drawing room. It wasn't often that True came to Charles. As the nominal general manager of the plantation he had enough confidence to do his job without the need for frequent consultations. Thus, it had been without any participation by Dewey that Jackson had announced the establishment of a Tennessee Futurity—a race in 1843 for the yet unborn foals of 1839. Those foals nominated, for five thousand dollars each, would run as four-year-olds for the "guaranteed" large purse, the first six finishers sharing in the monies.

It hadn't worked out well at all. By the end of 1838, when the nominations were closed, only thirty horsemen had been sufficiently intrigued by the prospects of a futurity to pay nominating fees. Indeed, there were fewer than thirty individual horsemen—Bon Marché had nominated ten of its foals-to-be.

"Some of those who have nominated," Jackson reported, "have now reneged on their payments. The way it looks now, we won't have enough horses left to have a decent field answer to the starter."

"Two horses make a race."

Another groan. "I'm afraid it will be only a little bit better than that."

"It doesn't matter," Charles assured him.

"What *does* matter, though," True said firmly, "is that I was injudicious enough to guarantee the purse—"

"Hmmm."

"—and not nearly enough money has come in to pay it."

Dewey seemed unconcerned. "Then we must make it up, mustn't we, when the time comes?"

"Oh, that's not the reason I came to see you," True interjected hurriedly. "I've already decided to make up the monies with my own funds. I simply came to you now to assure you that the good name of Bon Marché will not be harmed by my reckless and stupid act."

"You proposed the futurity in the name of Bon Marché, didn't you?"

"Yes, but—"

"Then Bon Marché will stand whatever loss there is."

"Charles, I can't let you do that! You'd be paying for my error."

The older man grinned at him. "When Mattie was busy talking up the attributes of the brothers Jackson—before you joined us—she never mentioned infallibility. If you only knew the mistakes I've made over the years—"

"No, I can't allow it!"

"The matter is closed," Dewey growled. "Now, is there anything else you wish to discuss?"

True hesitated. "Yes, there is. Uh . . . it's Franklin. I'm worried about him. Since Albert married and left to take up his military duties, and with Carrie also married and preoccupied with the newspaper in St. Louis, Franklin is totally alone. I've asked Able to involve him in the breeding decisions, but Franklin seems not to care—about that or anything else."

"Franklin has his interests in the hunt club."

"That's a time killer only, Charles."

"And now you wish to assume the guilt for Franklin's loneliness, too?"

"No, but—"

"True, hear me out. Mattie, in her wisdom, saw fit to bring you and Able here to run Bon Marché. You've done it admirably. But in doing this job, you're not expected to assume any responsibilities for the idiosyncrasies of the

Deweys. You young men are the future of Bon Marché—you and several of my grandchildren, I hope. Franklin is a part of the past. So, too, is this old relic." He sighed. "Care for the future, Squire Jackson, and leave the past to the dying."

"Charles, don't say things like—"

"Enough! Get the hell out of here!"

IV

CHARLES and Honey sat in a small carriage on a knoll at the edge of a cluster of trees, well bundled against the chill of early October. The sun, just rising over the horizon, was an unappealing dull orange—it looked dirty, some-how—and it cast almost no heat on the partially overcast day. The grasses were browning and the spent leaves on the trees, while still offering some color, were ready to fall to the next stiff breeze. Only the green pines stayed constant.

"I think this is an ideal place," Charles was saying, "to see the most excit-ing part of the hunt. I would think that the hounds will drive the fox across that pasture down below us"—he pointed—"and straight up the rise to that brush growing over the stone wall. He'll want to use that brush for cover, but the hounds will be too close on his tail for him to stay there. So he'll race across that small clearing just opposite us there and try to lose the dogs in the woods, weaving in and out among the trees, trying to confuse the pursuers."

"But he won't succeed, will he, Pop-Pop?" Honey said sadly.

"No, he won't. Oh, some of the pack will be confused for a moment or two, veering off in odd directions. But the best of the dogs will stay hard on his trail."

Dewey stood up in the carriage to continue his narrative. "He'll be driven out of those woods and down the grade across that small pasture bordered by the creek. At the water, the fox will hesitate. Deciding what his chances are if he plunges in and tries to swim across. Those few moments of indecision will cost him. The hounds will bring him to ground there—and the hunt will be over."

"Must it be that way?"

"I could be wrong about *this* fox, of course," her great-grandfather said. "He may not be concerned about the water, plunging right in and maintaining his advantage. If he does cross the stream, then his chances are very good. There are thick woods on the other side, with all manner of wild animals—deer and turkey among them—and the droppings from them will confuse the dogs. The fox will be able to find a hole in which to hide, and the hounds will have lost the day."

"I hope this fox likes the water," the young girl said. "I don't want to see it killed."

Charles studied Honey's sober face. It was a beautiful one at fifteen. And behind it was a mind that he had come to greatly admire. He took pride in the fact that he had helped mold that mind. This girl, when she became a woman, would be a factor in the world, he believed. She was not only intelligent;

Honey Mussmer—or Honey Dewey, as he liked to think of her—had a heart big enough to accommodate everyone she met, and every creature, even the fox, whose very minutes were now numbered.

"I'll join you in your concern for the fox," the old man said. "Now, the most exciting part of a hunt, of course, is supposed to be the horsemanship. If the horses are sound, and the leadership of the hunt intelligent—and we must assume he is, with Franklin as the master—the riders will be hard on the heels of the hounds when they break out into that pasture below us.

"They'll slow a bit coming up the hill, of course, and the horsemen will have to edge to their left when the fox and the hounds take on that brush-covered stone wall. The mounts will have lost their momentum and won't be able to clear the wall. Instead, they'll have to be content to jump the nearby rail fence. But they'll make up the lost ground going down the hill, and will be close at hand when the decision time for the fox is reached at the creek."

Charles shivered.

"Are you cold, Pop-Pop?"

"It is a bit more chilly than I had figured."

Honey reached behind her in the carriage, picking up a blanket, unfolding it, and draping it over his shoulders.

"Thank you, dear, that's much better."

Off in the distance they heard the shrill, clear sound of the hunting horn. And then the counterpoint of the deep baying of the hounds, swiftly coming closer.

"Watch now!" Charles said. "At the edge of the pasture down there. We ought to be seeing the fox any moment now!"

There was a quick flash of red.

"There he is, Pop-Pop!"

"Yes!"

"Run! Run!" Honey screamed, jumping up and down in her excitement, causing the carriage to rock and making the horse nervous. "Oh, dear God, run!"

The hounds came on to the pasture, perhaps thirty yards behind the streaking fox. And just behind them, no more than fifteen yards back, the scarlet of the riders' coats. Now there was a cacophony: the voices of the hounds, now that they were closer, were no longer alike—some were bass, some soprano; the hooves of the horses beat the rhythm on the cold, hard pasture; and a discordant accompaniment to it all was Honey's constant shout: "Run, damn you, run!"

The fox reached the stone fence, diving into the snarl of brush that nearly covered it. The heavier dogs, trying to leap the fence, entangled themselves momentarily in the brush before scrambling to the ground on the other side. At that obstacle the fox had gained ground, maybe as much as five yards.

"He's going to get away, Pop-Pop!"

"He's certainly giving them a run for it."

Dewey's attention turned to the riders nearing the top of the rise. Franklin, bent over the neck of his big gray thoroughbred gelding, was whipping and driving. Madly, it seemed. Charles held his breath. His son seemed to be heading straight for the half-hidden stone wall.

Leaping to his feet, Charles waved his arms wildly. "No! No!" he shouted. "Not there! The rails, Franklin, the rails!"

He was unseen. And unheard.

Franklin asked the gelding to jump. As he did, his front hooves cut into the brush and clipped the top stone. The horse tumbled crazily over the wall, hurling Franklin over his head, smashing him to the ground. Instinctively, the animal came to his feet, but the right foreleg hung crookedly, a jagged bone having torn through the skin. A few hobbling steps and the horse was down again, thrashing his legs in panicked pain, his great sides heaving.

Charles whipped his horse in action, careening the carriage across the uneven surface of the pasture. Honey held on tightly, sobbing.

No more than half a minute had gone by until Dewey halted the carriage by Franklin's still form. He leaped out, shoving away two of the riders who were trying to help the fallen master of the hunt. Franklin's unseeing eyes stared up at his father.

"Oh, God," the old man wept. "Oh, dear God!"

He tried to gather his son in his arms. The head lolled. His neck had been broken.

"I tried to warn you, son," Charles said softly.

There was a pistol shot. The injured horse was being dispatched.

Charles didn't look up. He rocked the body of his eldest son in his arms. Slowly. Tenderly. As he had done years earlier at Fortunata when Franklin was such a sober youngster.

All was confusion around them. Riders and horses milling about. And panting, winded dogs, recalled from the chase by the master of the hounds.

In the center of it was Honey, fighting back her tears, knowing that this was a moment that called for her strength. The dead rider was her grandfather. The grief-stricken man was her beloved great-grandfather. They needed her now.

She turned to several of the men standing next to her. "Help me get them into the carriage." It was an order.

Several of the huntsmen guided Charles back to the carriage, helping him into it. Others carried the body of Franklin, putting it next to the elder Dewey so that his arms could cradle it. Honey gently put the blanket around them. And she picked up the reins.

"Let me drive, miss," one of the men offered.

"No," she replied sternly, "I'll do it."

She whacked the reins hard on the back of the horse, turning the carriage toward Bon Marché.

"We're going home now, Pop-Pop."

A strange thought crossed her mind. She struggled with it, trying to dismiss it. She knew it was wrong under these tragic circumstances, but it made her want to smile.

The fox had escaped.

51

"CHARLES, you're doing too much," Mattie warned. But quietly, not wanting to nag. "Those nature walks, and the almost daily trips to the capital—"

"Now that Nashville is the state capital," her husband said defensively, "there's a great opportunity for Honey to learn the workings of our government. She may play a role in it someday."

"Charles, be realistic. She's a woman. What role could she play?"

"Who can tell? This country is heading toward a great upheaval. It may need her someday."

"Yes, Charles." Mattie sighed. She wanted to object—again—to his preoccupation with the young girl, but didn't dare. Honey was all he had left in life. Franklin and Thomas were dead, George was in New Orleans, Corrine's marriage to Billy Holder had almost completely alienated her from her father, Louise was constantly busy with the newspaper, Lee always seemed to be away on his correspondent duties, and Alma May . . . well, the Princess had her own way of life. That life appalled Mattie, but she couldn't do anything about it. She felt that Alma May's scandalous social activities with numerous Nashville "gentlemen" were best left alone. Her mother didn't want to know the details.

Even Bon Marché was no longer a concern of Charles Dewey. Nor was she, Mattie admitted sadly. They still slept in the same room, but what they once had together had evaporated. There were times when she wondered whether they were even friends any longer.

In sum, Charles had his great-granddaughter. And Mattie didn't want to do anything that would take Honey from him.

"I'll want to send Honey to the Nashville Female Academy next year," Dewey said.

"Yes, dear."

"She's very special, you know. And I need to give her all the help I can."

"Of course. But I *am* worried about your health."

"Nonsense." He smiled. "I have the stamina of a thoroughbred."

Charles clapped his hands together. The subject was closed.

II

JANUARY 31 was always observed at Bon Marché as Dewey's birthday. He had no idea when his birthday really was, but back in Virginia he and Martha had selected that date as a convenient one to celebrate. January 31 was before the foaling season, and there were no race meetings to intrude.

Now, as that date approached in 1845, Honey Mussmer scurried around planning the party for her great-grandfather's eightieth birthday anniversary. Mattie, because she wanted it to be a special day as well, gave the young girl her head. It was agreed, after numerous discussions with others in the family, that there would be only one gift for Charles, to be presented following a special family dinner.

After the last toast had been drunk, Honey brought Charles's warm outer clothing to him at the table.

"Put these on, Pop-Pop," she said, smiling sweetly, "because we have to go outside for what happens next."

"If we're going out in the cold," Dewey chortled, "perhaps I ought to have another bourbon." He held out his empty glass, to have it filled by his son-in-law, August Schimmel. He drank it down. "Now, young lady, I'm well fortified, so let's proceed."

With Honey proudly leading the way into the night, followed by a large entourage of Deweys and Jacksons, laughing and chattering, they left the house to proceed to the exercise ring nearest the mansion.

After the family had positioned itself along the fence, Honey called out: "We're ready to start!"

On that signal, a dozen slaves, carrying large torches, filed into the ring, lighting it. Following them came the sober True Jackson, leading a muscular bay horse outfitted with a distinctive white halter.

"Pop-Pop, this is for you," Honey announced loudly. "The first foal by Priam, out of a Bagdad mare. He's four years old, and he'll be ready to race this spring."

"Oh, my—" Dewey's eyes filled with tears.

"But that's not all, Pop-Pop," the young girl continued. "He's been named in your honor. From all of us, Pop-Pop, this is *Charles Dewey!*"

Applause broke out, and the horse tugged excitedly at the lead rope.

Honey took her great-grandfather's hand and led him through the gate and into the ring, where True turned the lead rope over to him. Charles marched around the ring, proudly showing off his birthday present, the tears streaming down his face.

"There's one other thing," said True Jackson. "As the trainer of his magnificent animal, Miss Honey has allowed me to announce that Charles Dewey has been nominated for a special race at Clover Bottom's spring meeting in April—the first running of the Bon Marché Cup!"

More applause.

"And as the trainer, I have acquired the services of an outstanding jockey from New York. His name is Marshall Dewey!"

The old man's mouth gaped open. There were no words. He groped to hand the lead rope to True and then he sank to his knees, overcome with emotion. Honey knelt beside him, putting her arms around him, rocking him.

"We love you, Pop-Pop. We love you very much."

III

IT was cool and rainy on the last Saturday in April of 1845 when the Bon Marché Cup was to be contested. True Jackson, as a steward of the Nashville Jockey Club, had used his influence to put together an outstanding field of runners for the premier event. He understood that Charles Dewey the man would not have tolerated seeing Charles Dewey the thoroughbred matched against inferior opponents.

In the days between the birthday celebration and April 26, the old master of Bon Marché was present at every workout of the horse, giving advice to True and, at times, turning the advice into orders. He seemed to have been given a new life, and Honey tagged after him everywhere he went, caring for his smallest needs.

Three weeks before the race, Marshall arrived from New York, looking trim and fit. Charles embraced him and said what he had rehearsed over and over in his mind: "Son, there is too little time for prolonged apologies. I just want you to know that I'm sorry for what I've done to you, more sorry than you can imagine. I'm pleased that you think enough of me to come back here." A nervous cough. "And now let's see how you and the equine Charles Dewey get along."

It was a fact that Marshall hadn't ridden in a race in some years; he was now a trainer in New York, not a rider any longer. But when True Jackson had written to him, and Marshall had agreed to ride in the Bon Marché Cup, he went into a strenuous dieting regimen. He weighed one hundred ten pounds when he arrived in Tennessee.

In spite of the inclement weather, there was a large crowd at the Clover Bottom course. Umbrellas grew like mushrooms; under one of them stood the guest of honor.

Betting was brisk for the four-mile three-heat event, with a Nashville Jockey Club added purse of twenty-five thousand dollars. While Charles Dewey was the sentimental favorite in the public pool, the true favorite probably should have been a Kentucky horse, Invader, the undefeated winner of his first four starts.

Dewey's horse was bet down to even money, annoying the old man.

"Damn it," he complained to Honey, "those are artificial odds. Charles Dewey doesn't rate even money. I appreciate the compliment, of course, but not as a bettor. I'd love to take those odds on Invader." He leaned down to Honey and said to her sotto voce, "I don't suppose I could sneak a bet on Invader?"

"Pop-Pop!"

Charles roared with laughter. "No, I suppose not."

He made a great show of wagering five thousand dollars in the public pool on his own horse, causing others at the track to follow his example. He felt bad about that, but he was trapped by circumstances.

True had him officiate at the saddling of Charles Dewey, and stood aside as Charles instructed the jockey. "Don't kill him, son," he said softly so that others couldn't hear. "I suspect that you're in over your head. Try to keep Invader in sight. He's your competition."

Twelve horses answered the starter's call, and when the drum tapped, Invader sprang to the lead. He kept it for the entire four miles, winning under restraint over another Nashville horse, Cumberland, an easy five lengths to the good. Charles Dewey was third, beaten by nine lengths.

The old man wasn't surprised.

Rain was coming down harder when the second heat was called. "Now you'll find out," he said to Marshall, "whether this horse can run in the soft going."

Invader was the wire-to-wire winner of the second heat in the slow time of 8:08¾. Marshall had done better with Charles Dewey, bringing him second with a vigorous ride, but still four lengths off the Kentucky horse. The perpetual Bon Marché Cup would spend its first year in the neighboring state.

Marshall was full of apologies. "I'm sorry, Father. I know how much this day meant to you."

Dewey grinned. "I know how to lose, son. I've had a lot of experience in that. And experience, really, is what counted in that race. Invader was simply the better horse, that's all."

True Jackson was also apologetic. "I had such hopes, Charles, that I could—"

Dewey cut him off with a clap on the back. "Charles Dewey will carry my name across the finish line in front a lot of times before he's done." He grinned broadly. "Come! There's a victory celebration going on at the tavern."

At eighty, Charles Dewey got quite drunk before the day was ended.

IV

CHARLES was late in rising the next morning, and when he came into the dining room he found only Mattie and Honey still at the breakfast table.

"Perhaps I should finally admit," he said cheerily, "that I'm really eighty. I don't seem to be able to drink as well as I used to."

Mattie looked with concern at his flushed face. "Are you well, dear?"

"Well? Certainly. It's just that my recuperative powers are slower these days."

Honey went to him, putting a small hand on his forehead. "Pop-Pop, you're hot! You have a fever."

"Hmmm, maybe a little one."

"After you've eaten, Charles," Mattie ordered, "I want you back in bed. You were wet yesterday, and you have to admit that you were quite intoxicated."

"Maybe you're right. I think I could use some more sleep."

He toyed with his food, then returned to bed, falling asleep almost immediately. But he dozed fitfully. Honey, who stayed with him, worried that his fever was growing.

At lunchtime, she reported her fears to Mattie. "I think we ought to call a doctor." A slave was dispatched to Nashville to fetch Dr. Martin Almond, who had come from Maryland to the West.

The doctor was frank after his examination. "It's pneumonia, I fear. And I don't have to tell you how serious that may be in a gentleman of Mr. Dewey's advanced age."

Mattie and Honey were solemn.

"I've given him a purgative, and I want you to watch him closely. If his fever gets higher, please send someone for me immediately. Otherwise I'll come in the morning again."

Honey wanted to stay in the room all night. Mattie vetoed that. "I'll be there, dear," she said kindly. "You can take over during the day."

April lengthened into May with Charles Dewey still bedridden. Dr. Almond's periodic use of the lancet to drain away the old man's bad blood seemed to do little good. Honey assisted in those operations, but had to turn her ahead away so that she wouldn't see her great-grandfather's blood dripping from the tiny incision into a crockery bowl. And the good doctor dosed his patient frequently, trying to purge the sickness, first with something he identified as "Ipecac," which caused Charles to vomit profusely, and then with a chloride of mercury compound—Almond told Honey it was "calomel"—which caused saliva to pour from Charles's mouth.

"The heavy discharge of saliva," the doctor explained, "is cleansing the system."

But each day found Charles Dewey growing weaker. There were periods when he was only semiconscious, when he mumbled unintelligible words.

Only in mid-May, when the doctor turned to giving him tea made from Indian herbs, did Charles seem to improve, even gaining enough strength to ask for food, then hungrily wolfing down the beef broth prepared by the black cooks. After a day or two, he could even sit up. He seemed to want to talk.

"There's someone I have to say something to," he said to Honey one afternoon. "Could you fetch Alma May for me, please."

Honey raced away on her errand, returning with Dewey's youngest daughter.

He stretched out his hands to her, and Alma May took them, falling to her knees beside the bed. "Father, you look so much better!"

"You've been here before?" He was perplexed.

"Daily, Father. It's just that you couldn't talk to me."

A deep sigh. "I'm being so much trouble for you all." He looked up at Honey. "Dear, could you leave us alone for a moment or two?"

Hurt showed on the young face, but she left the bedroom.

"Princess, you must do something for me."

"Of course."

"Tell Mary Elizabeth—"

"Shall I ask her to come here?"

"No, no." He smiled weakly. "There won't be time for that."

"Father!"

"No, it's true, Princess. But I do want Mary Elizabeth to know . . . well, what has happened to me." He frowned. "That is, if she's still living herself."

"I'll make sure I get in touch with her."

"Good, good." He patted her hand. "Maybe it's best, Princess, if this remains our little secret."

"It will, Father."

He groaned.

"Are you in pain?"

"No, Princess . . . just thinking of what an old fool I am, to believe that Mary Elizabeth would really care what has happened to me."

"She loved you once, Father."

"Hmmm."

There was a quiet moment between them.

"Do me one other thing—?"

"What?"

"Stay with Bon Marché. It needs your peculiar strength, Alma May. And care for Honey, please."

The Princess fought back the tears. "I'll do as you ask, Father."

She kissed him and left the room. Honey returned hurriedly.

"I made you unhappy with my little *tête-à-tête* with Alma May?"

"No." The reply was sullen.

"I had to talk to her about something that happened a long, long time ago, before you were born. I admit to you, Honey, that it's a secret. Everyone is due a secret or two in their lives."

"I don't have any secrets from you, Pop-Pop."

He smiled. "No, I don't believe you do. And I appreciate that. I appreciate, too, how you've worked with me over the years. I've tried to teach you, dear, to be self-sufficient, so that you can go on without me when I'm—"

"Stop that, Pop-Pop!"

"Oh, I'm not giving up without a fight, Honey. That's not my nature." He struggled to prop himself up on the pillows, and Honey moved quickly to help him.

"Let me tell you something: A man is the creator of his own life. It's like clay; you mold it and shape it, trying to make it into something beautiful. And when it's finished, a man ought to fight like hell to preserve his creation."

Honey nodded agreement.

"And I'm fighting like hell, dear. I promise you that." He drew a deep breath. "All of this talk has left me a bit weary. I think I could sleep now."

Honey lowered him and straightened the covers around him, holding his hand as he slept.

V

HE improved not at all after that. Perhaps the Indian herbs had reached the zenith of their magic. The fever returned.

Dr. Almond went to Mattie. "Mrs. Dewey, there is a new drug called quinine. It is distilled, as I understand it, from the dried bark of a Peruvian tree, the cinchona. One of the properties of quinine is that it is supposed to reduce fever. I've obtained some, and I'd like to try it, although it is frightfully expensive."

"Money is not a problem, Doctor."

"Nevertheless, I do consider eight dollars an ounce an exorbitant price."

Mattie wanted to laugh. Just a few weeks earlier she had seen her husband throw away five thousand dollars on a wager he knew was only a token gesture. On a thoroughbred racehorse named Charles Dewey.

With a straight face, she said, "Please use the quinine, Doctor, if you think it might help."

Almond dosed Dewey liberally with the new drug. The fever came down dramatically. Another large dose of quinine was administered. And the next day yet another. Charles slept a lot.

But he didn't seem to really improve.

May 1845 ended on a Saturday. That evening, Dr. Almond felt that his patient was slipping away from him. It was time, he believed, to resort again to what he had been taught in medical school. To forget about Indian herbs and new drugs. He reached into his medical bag for his lancet and the crockery bowl. Once more Honey held the bowl.

The doctor made an incision in the vein in Dewey's wrist. No blood came; or only a drop or two. But no easy flow. He frowned, knitting his brows in thought. He recalled the words of one of his professors: "recourse to the jugular."

Almond followed that advice, making another incision. When the bowl was half full, he stemmed the flow of blood with a bandage and took the bowl from Honey.

There was a ring of satisfaction in his voice. "We certainly have drawn off the bad blood this time, young lady."

The doctor left the comatose Dewey in the care of Mattie and Honey, and for the first time, Mattie allowed the girl to stay in the room overnight. There seemed good reason to do so.

They took turns sitting awake by the side of his bed, listening to the labored breathing, watching for any telltale flutter of the eyelids that would let them know he was awakening.

At dawn on Sunday—June had arrived—his eyes did open. Dimly, Charles could see two figures leaning over the bed.

"Mattie?" His voice was very weak.

"Yes, dear. Honey is here, too."

He tried to smile, but he seemed not to have the strength to move the necessary muscles.

"I've . . . been thinking . . . a great deal . . . Mattie." He was laboring with the words.

"Don't talk, Charles. Save your strength."

"I have . . . nothing more to save it for. There's something I must do before . . . I die. I must make sure that all the slaves are freed."

Mattie gasped.

"It's a moral . . . necessity, Mattie."

"We'll talk about this when you're well, dear."

"No, no." He tried to rise, but couldn't summon the strength. "I have no . . . time anymore. I want the slaves . . . freed. Do you hear me, Mattie?"

"I hear you, Charles." She bent down and kissed him on the lips.

"Thank . . . you."

The eyes stared. The labored breathing stopped.

Honey screamed in her pain.

Mattie gathered the girl in her arms, and they wept together. Two women Charles Dewey had loved.

VI

SOMEHOW lunch was served and eaten that day.

The housemaids had cleaned up the bedroom, had washed the corpse under Mattie's direction, and had dressed Charles Dewey, as he had often requested, in his riding clothes. Laid out on his bed, he received the grief-stricken members of his large family for the last time.

Dusk came. Mattie and Honey sat alone in the drawing room as the widow made the inevitable entry into the massive family Bible.

"When are you going to free the slaves?" Honey wanted to know.

"What?" The question shocked Mattie.

"The slaves? When are you going to free them? During the funeral ceremonies would be a good time to do it."

"Oh, my darling, Mattie said sadly. "I *can't* free them."

"But Pop-Pop wanted that!"

"I know. But, Honey . . . well, it's so very complicated. You'll learn as you grow up that wanting something and having it for certain are often two different things."

Honey was on her feet, shouting at her great-grandmother. "With his dying breath he asked you to promise that the slaves would be freed. With his *dying* breath! And you promised!"

"No, dear, I didn't."

"You did! You did! I heard you!"

Mattie came toward her, holding out her arms to the distraught girl. "Honey, you must understand that Pop-Pop wasn't . . . well, wasn't in command of all his senses at the end—"

"You lie!"

"—and he might not have known what he was asking me to do."

"He knew!" Honey screamed. "He told me so many times that the day would come when the slaves would have to be freed."

"I know. But he didn't mean now—this way."

"He did! He said so with his dying breath!"

Mattie moved to her again, beseeching her. "Please, Honey, let's sit down and talk about this calmly."

"So you can lie to me?"

"Of course not."

"We don't have to talk about it." The girl was backing toward the door. "I know what I heard. He asked you to free the slaves, and you *promised!*"

"No, Honey, believe me—that wasn't the way it was at all."

"You bitch! I hope you rot in hell."

Honey rushed from the room, crying hysterically. Mattie looked after her, debating on whether to follow. Finally, she returned to the desk, sinking disconsolately into the chair in front of the Bible. Her mind made a sum of what was written there: Charles Dewey (Charles Dupree)—two wives, seven children, eleven grandchildren, twenty-three great-grandchildren. A family. She stared at the names. For how long, she didn't know.

A housemaid burst into the room. "Miss Mattie, come quick! It Miss Honey!"

Mattie raced after her, out of the house and across the twenty or so yards to the carriage barn. True and Able were already there, along with a few slaves, gathered around the still form of Honey Mussmer, a rope twisted about her neck.

"Ah tried to save her, Miss Mattie!" one of the black men wailed. "Ah cut her down jest soon as—"

True handed Mattie a crumpled piece of paper. "I found this on the floor."

Mattie took it, reading the scrawled words: "I want to be with Pop-Pop."

VII

HUNDREDS attended the funeral services for Charles Dewey, and for his greatgranddaughter, two days later. They crowded the small tulip poplar grove encompassing the family cemetery. Many of them didn't know they were in Richie's Place.

There were eulogies, maybe a dozen of them from prominent citizens of the community. And the proper words were read from Scripture. Mattie heard none of them. She stood dumbly, responding only to the guiding hands of her daughter, Alma May. It was over in an hour or so, but time meant nothing to the mistress of Bon Marché. She had used up her reservoir of emotion. She was totally spent.

A week later, stonecutters erected a granite slab over the grave where Charles Dewey's body was buried. It said:

CHARLES DUPREE DE GRASSE DEWEY
1765–1845
Aide-toi, le ciel t'aidera.

That was exactly the way Charles had designated it should be in his will. It may have raised some questions, but his widow was determined that the answers would stay with Dewey.

Next to his stone was a smaller one:

HONEY MUSSMER DEWEY
1829–1845
She Loved!

Pop-Pop, Mattie reasoned, would like that.

And he would have liked, too, what happened the next morning. Charles Dewey II came to see Mattie. He seemed tentative and ill at ease.

"I know that you don't approve of me, Grandmother, but I did want you to know that on the day before Grandfather's funeral, Elizabeth and I were married at the courthouse. We did that to honor his memory."

Mattie embraced him. "If only Charles could have known."

"He'll know, Grandmother, he'll know."

EPILOGUE

ALMA May Dewey walked slowly into the Masonic Hall in Nashville to attend the annual meeting of the Davidson County Agricultural Society. In any other venue she would not have been nervous, displaying her usual self-confidence. But not tonight, not here. Tonight, four months after her father's death, she was to represent *him,* to speak *his* words.

Her nervousness was enhanced by the knowledge that she was the first woman ever to appear at a meeting of the agricultural society. Again, she was used to dealing with all-male circumstances. But not tonight, not here.

The chairman of the meeting was waiting for her. He escorted her to the front of the hall where he deposited her in a seat next to the rostrum, facing the audience. The hall was nearly full when she arrived, and she had to wait only a few minutes before the meeting began.

"We meet tonight," the chairman said, "under sad circumstances. All too recently the Davidson County Agricultural Society lost two of its distinguished founders. On April first Squire Charles Dewey of Bon Marché was called to his God. And, ironically, just a week later this society, this city, this state, this nation, was deprived of the wisdom and the heroism of a former president of the United States, the honorable General Andrew Jackson. I ask now that all of the members stand for a moment of silent prayer in memory of those two great men."

There was a shuffling of feet and a squeaking of chairs as the members came to their feet. Finally, though, the noise stopped and there was a silence, with heads bowed reverently.

"Thank you," the chairman said eventually. "You may be seated again."

He coughed nervously as he began his introduction of Alma May. "It has been the custom of this organization that its president shall address the body at the beginning of the annual meetings. When Squire Dewey died, I contacted Bon Marché and asked whether it was known if the squire had already committed his speech to paper. Our guest tonight informed me that he had, and graciously offered to deliver it herself. Gentlemen, allow me to present a daughter of Charles Dewey, Miss Alma May Dewey."

There was a polite, unsure applause.

The Princess trembled as she went to the rostrum, unfolded several sheets of foolscap, and placed them in front of her.

She looked up at the sober faces. "I hope that I have not mispresented the notes that I found among my father's papers as a completed speech. He had obviously started working on the speech prior to the outset of his illness, but in all honesty, it was not a speech as such. I have made those notes into a speech, arranging them in some order that I believe intelligible. What I am about to read, though, are Charles Dewey's words, not mine. They reflect his views totally."

She dropped her eyes to the papers, and began to read:

" 'Among all the numerous varieties of domestic animals which a benevolent Providence has created for the use of man, the blood horse stands preeminent, without a compeer in the animal kingdom.' "

Alma May didn't know it, nor did anyone else in the hall, but the opening words had been spoken before, by a man named Marshall Statler to a young Frenchman newly arrived in America.

" 'In beauty he is without a rival—a coat as fine as the finest satin; his eye, in repose, as mild and gentle as a lamb; under excitement as bright as the eagle and as bold as the lion, denoting the energy of his nature; his skin as thin and elastic as the fawn; his form as perfect and well placed as beautifully defined muscles can make it.

" 'This is his exterior, or that which is visible to the human eye. But there is an interior, or invisible, structure which contributes more perhaps to his powers than even his perfect exterior formation. His large heart and capacious lungs give him the wind of a high-bred hound; his large blood vessels and soft, thin skin enable him to throw off the excess heat that must be generated by great and rapid exertion; his muscles firm and beautifully defined with bone of ivory texture—all combine to give him strength, endurance, action, and beauty far exceeding all of the equine race.' "

The members of the agricultural society were quiet. Attentive. They understood that they were hearing words from the grave.

" 'The uninstructed in horseology may ask, 'What do you mean by a blood horse, or thoroughbred? I mean the horse which traces back, with certainty, through a long line of distinguished ancestry to the beautiful and game little creatures which were imported into England from the deserts of Arabia about the middle of the sixteenth century. How they came there, or by what means they had been brought to the degree of perfection they possessed at that early period, I am not able to answer. From that time to the present the best talent of intelligent breeders has been zealously and energetically employed throughout the world, aided, too, by all the leading governments (except our own) to develop and improve this noble animal. They have not failed.

" 'By attention to his comfort, with a liberal supply of proper food from infancy to maturity, his size has been enlarged, consequently his strength and speed increased; though beautiful when brought from his native desert, he is now magnificent. He has been made so nearly perfect that breeders of the present period are puzzled to know what further improvement can be anticipated.' "

Alma May's mouth was dry. She wished for a sip of water. None being available, she swallowed hard and continued: " 'To form an idea of the wonderful power of the blood horse, we will suppose his weight to be nine hundred pounds, this being about the weight of the racehorse. By the strength of his muscle he carries this weight together with his rider, one hundred pounds more, making one thousand pounds, not on a downgrade, but on a horizontal line, a mile in one minute and forty-three seconds, almost equaling the power of what we know of steam. Of all animated nature the feathered tribe alone can equal his speed. If we imagine a feathered monster of equal weight, I doubt whether he could surpass him in his flight.

" 'The uninformed may see him only as a beautiful creature, imagining that he is bred for a race alone and being fit for nothing else, believing he has no other value than occasionally to contribute to the amusement of the public on the racecourse.

" 'This is an egregious error!' "

The Princess looked up. "My father had written an exclamation point there, and I probably didn't read it with the verve he intended."

There were a few chuckles.

" 'The racecourse is only the school to educate and prepare him to exhibit his wonderful powers in competition with the best of the royal family—a field the plebeian dare not enter, no scrub ever having won a prize with thoroughbred competitors. Ten drops of plebeian blood in one thousand would endanger his success.

" 'The racecourse is, therefore, a necessity, for through its instrumentality the blood horse has been brought to his present high degree of perfection. Human judgment is often in error, but on no subject more frequently than in the opinions we form on the relative power and value of the horse. It is as easy to judge the powers and qualities of man by the eye, and all will admit the fallibility of such judgment.

" 'No, my friends, we can only judge correctly the intellectual and moral worth of our great men when we view them on the world's stage in competition with distinguished competitors. Without a theater the world could never have known those distinguished delineators of human character whose names now fill many an honored page in human history. The same is true of the blooded horse. The racecourse is his stage, his theater.' "

She paused, knowing that the next words might offend some in the audience.

" 'I am aware of the prejudices existing against the racecourse by religionists, generally on account of its immoral tendency. That these prejudices are not altogether groundless, I admit; but that the immoralities of a well-regulated racecourse are greatly magnified by those who know the least of their operations, I am perfectly satisfied; that it may be still further improved, I earnestly desire.

" 'For more than sixty years I have been a breeder of the blood horse, and an active participator in his education and development, and can affirm that vice and immorality do not necessarily attach to racing and, as before remarked, the racecourse is a necessity, for without it the breeder could not know the superior horses and the best strains to propagate, and without this knowledge his improvement would cease and deterioration begin.' "

Alma May turned to the final page.

" 'Here the question arises whether we will permit this noble and most useful creature, which has been brought to his present degree of perfection by the efforts of breeders for near two hundred years—and by the expenditure of as many millions of dollars—to retrograde into the coarse and clumsy brute he represented previous to the introduction of the Arab, or go on to improve and develop still higher and more useful qualities. For one, I advocate his preservation, and at the same time call upon the moralist to unite with me in the effort to remove all objectionable features that may attach to the institution so necessary for his development.

" 'Beauty, speed, action, durability, and the many admirable qualities I claim for this magnificent animal do not constitute his chief—nay, nor his greatest—value. His mission is to improve his race. The pure and unadulterated blood which flows in his veins improves and gives additional value to ALL the horse family.' "

Alma May Dewey looked up, her misting eyes surveying the audience.

"Gentlemen, those are the words of a man who was in love with the thoroughbred horse—the late Charles Dewey, master of Bon Marché."